D1097144

THE STORIES OF
F. SCOTT FITZGERALD

THE STORIES OF
F. Scott Fitzgerald

A Selection of 28 Stories

With an Introduction by

MALCOLM COWLEY

CHARLES SCRIBNER'S SONS

NEW YORK

CONTENTS

IV. LAST ACT AND EPILOGUE

INTRODUCTION

THOSE who were lucky enough to be born a little before the end of the old century, in any of the years from 1895 to 1900, went through much of their lives with a feeling that the new century had been placed in their charge; it was like a business in financial straits that could now be rescued by a change of management. As Americans and optimists they believed that the business was fundamentally sound and would triumph over its predecessors. They identified themselves with the century; its teens were their teens, its world war was theirs to fight and its reckless twenties were their twenties. As they launched forward on their careers they looked about them for spokesmen and the first they found was F. Scott Fitzgerald.

At twenty-three, when he published his first novel, Fitzgerald had the sort of background that his generation regarded as representative. He was a Midwestern boy, born in St. Paul on September 24, 1896, to a family of Irish descent that had some social standing and a very small fortune inherited by the mother. The father was not a business success, so that the fortune kept decreasing year by year, and the Fitzgeralds, like all people in their situation, had to think a lot about money. It was help from a maiden aunt that enabled Scott to fulfill his early dream of going to an Eastern preparatory school and then going to Princeton.

He liked to imagine himself as the hero of romantic dramas and he worked hard to cut a figure among his classmates. At the Newman School, after an interval of being the most unpopular boy, he had redeemed himself by making the football team and winning first prize in the field day. At Princeton he was taken into what he regarded as the best of the eating clubs—the Cottage—after turning down bids to three others, and he wrote a large part of two musical comedies produced with success by the Triangle Club. The second of these was

The Evil Eye, with lyrics by Fitzgerald and libretto by Edmund Wilson. The *Daily Princetonian* reported that when it was performed in Chicago on January 7, 1916, "Three hundred young ladies occupied the front rows of the house and following the show, they stood up, gave the Princeton locomotive and tossed their bouquets at cast and chorus."

They were among the first of Fitzgerald's flappers and he would have loved them, all three hundred, but he didn't make the triumphal tour with the Triangle show. He had withdrawn from college at the end of November, largely because of illness, but also because his marks had fallen so low that there was every chance of his being suspended after the midyear examinations. He had to abandon his dream of being president of the Triangle Club and a big man in his class. "A year of terrible disappointments and the end of all college dreams," he wrote in the ledger that served as a bookkeeping record of his triumphs and defeats. "Everything bad in it was my own fault." The next year, 1916–17, was described in the ledger as "A pregnant year of endeavor. Outwardly a failure with moments of danger but the foundation of my literary life." He was back at Princeton and was paying more attention to his studies, besides writing furiously for the *Tiger* and the *Nassau Lit*. At this time he started a novel rightly called *The Romantic Egotist*.

In the fall of 1917, after passing a special examination, he received a provisional commission as second lieutenant in the Regular Army. He went off to training camp, where he finished most of the novel during week-ends, and then served in Alabama as aide-de-camp to Major General J. A. Ryan. It was at a dance in Montgomery that he fell in love with a judge's daughter, Zelda Sayre, whom he described to his friends as "the most beautiful girl in Alabama *and* Georgia"; one state wasn't big enough to encompass his admiration. "I didn't have the two top things: great animal magnetism or money," he wrote years afterward in his notebook. "I had the two second things, though: good looks and intelligence. So I always got the top girl."

He was engaged to the judge's daughter, but they couldn't marry until he was able to support her. After being discharged from the Army, Fitzgerald went to New York and looked for a job. *The Romantic Egotist* had been rejected by Scribner's, with letters from Maxwell Perkins that showed a real interest in Fitzgerald's future work. His stories were coming back from the magazines and at one time he had 122 rejection slips pinned in a frieze around his cheap bedroom on Morningside Heights. The job he found was with an advertising agency and his pay started at $90 a month, with not much chance of rapid advancement; the only praise he received was for a slogan written for a steam laundry in Muscatine, Iowa: "We Keep

You Clean in Muscatine." He was trying to save money, but the girl in Alabama saw that the effort was hopeless and broke off the engagement on the score of common sense. Fitzgerald borrowed from his classmates, stayed drunk for three weeks and then went home to St. Paul to rewrite his novel under a new title. This time Scribner's accepted it and the book was published at the end of March, 1920.

This Side of Paradise was a very young man's novel and memory book. The author put into it samples of everything he had written until that time: short stories, poems, essays, fragments of autobiography, sketches and dialogues. Some of the material had already been printed in the *Nassau Lit,* so that his friends described the book as the collected works of F. Scott Fitzgerald. It also had suggestions of being the collected works of Compton Mackenzie and H. G. Wells, with more than a hint of *Stover at Yale;* but for all its faults and borrowings it was held together by its energy, honesty, self-confidence and it spoke in the voice of a new generation. His contemporaries recognized the voice as their own and his elders listened.

Suddenly the magazines were eager to print Fitzgerald's stories and willing to pay high prices for them. The result shows in his big ledger: in 1919 he earned $879 by his writing; in 1920 he earned—and spent—$18,850. Early success had been added to everything else that made him stand out as a representative of his generation; and Fitzgerald himself was beginning to believe in his representative quality. He was learning that when he wrote truly about his dreams and misadventures and discoveries, other people recognized themselves in the picture.

The point has to be made that Fitzgerald was not "typical" of his own age or any other. He lived harder than most people have ever lived and acted out his dreams with an extraordinary intensity of emotion. The dreams themselves were not at all unusual; in the beginning they were dreams of becoming a football star and a big man in college, of being a hero on the battlefield, of winning through to financial success and of getting the top girl; they were the commonplace aspirations shared by almost all the young men of his time and social class. It was the emotion he put into them, and the honesty with which he expressed the emotion, that made them seem distinguished. By feeling intensely he made his readers believe in the unique value of the world in which they lived. Years afterward he would say, writing in the third person, that he continued to feel grateful to the Jazz Age because "It bore him up, flattered him and gave him more money than he had dreamed of, simply for telling people that he felt as they did."

At the beginning of April, 1920, Zelda came to New York and they were married in the rectory of St. Patrick's Cathedral—although

Zelda's family was Episcopalian and Scott had ceased to be a good Catholic. They set up housekeeping at the Biltmore. To their bewilderment they found themselves adopted, not as a Midwesterner and a Southerner respectively, not even as detached observers, but—Scott afterward wrote—"as the arch type of what New York wanted." Arthur Mizener, in his biography of Fitzgerald, has vividly re-created that year of the happy whirlwind. A new age was beginning and Scott and Zelda were venturing into it innocently, hand in hand. Zelda said, "It was always tea-time or late at night." Scott said, "We felt like small children in a great bright unexplored barn."

Scott also said, "America was going on the greatest, gaudiest spree in history and there was going to be plenty to tell about it." There is still plenty to tell about it, in the light of a new age that is curious about the 1920's and persistently misjudges them. The gaudiest spree in history was also a moral revolt and beneath the revolt there were social transformations. The 1920's were the age when Puritanism was under attack, with the Protestant churches losing their dominant position. They were the age when the country ceased to be English and Scottish and when the children of later immigrations moved forward to take their place in the national life. They were the age when American culture became urban instead of rural and when New York set the social and intellectual standards for the country—while its own standards were being set by transplanted Southerners and Midwesterners like the two Fitzgeralds.

More essentially the 1920's were the age when a *production* ethic—of saving and self-denial in order to accumulate capital for new enterprises—gave way to a *consumption* ethic that was needed to provide markets for the new commodities endlessly streaming from the production lines. Instead of being told to save, people were being instructed in a thousand ways to buy, enjoy, use once and throw away in order to buy a later and more expensive model. They followed the instructions, with the result that more goods were produced and consumed and money was easier to earn than ever before. "The Jazz Age now raced along under its own power," Fitzgerald said, "served by great filling stations full of money. . . . Even when you were broke you didn't worry about money, because it was in such profusion around you."

That explains the background of the 1920's and their sense of reckless freedom, but it does not explain the figures in the foreground. The members of Fitzgerald's generation were not interested at the time in underlying social movements, any more than they were interested in local or international politics. What they felt in their hearts was that they had made an absolute break with the standards of the older generation. There was not the sharp distinction between

highbrow and lowbrow (or liberal and conservative) that would later
divide American society; in those days the real gulf was between
the young and the old. The younger set paid few visits to their parents'
homes and some of them hardly exchanged a social word with men
or women over forty. The elders were discredited in their eyes by
the war, by prohibition, by the Red scare of 1919–20 and by scandals
like that of Teapot Dome. So much the better: the youngsters had a
free field in which to test their own standards of the good life.

Those standards were simple and almost savage. The spokesmen
for the new generation recognized the value of food, travel, love and
intoxication, the value of honest craftmanship—when they had time
for it—and the value of truth; absolutely anything seemed excusable
if one simply told the truth about it. They liked to say yes to every
proposal that promised excitement. Will you take a new job, throw
up the job, go to Paris and starve, travel round the world in a
freighter? Will you get married, leave your husband, spend a week-
end for two in Biarritz? Will you ride around New York on the roof
of a taxi and then take a bath in the Plaza fountain? "WYBMADIITY?"
read a sign on the mirror behind the bar of the Dizzy Club. Late at
night you asked the bartender what it meant and he answered, "Will
you buy me a drink if I tell you?" The answer was yes, always yes,
and the fictional heroine of the 1920's was Serena Blandish, the girl
who couldn't say no. Or the heroine was Joyce's Molly Bloom as she
dreamed about her first lover: ". . . and I thought well as well him
as another and then I asked him with my eyes to ask again yes and
then he asked me would I yes to say yes my mountain flower and
first I put my arms around him yes and drew him down to me so he
could feel my breasts all perfume yes and his heart was going like
mad and yes I said yes I will Yes."

The masculine ideal of the 1920's was what Fitzgerald calls "the
old dream of being an entire man in the Goethe-Byron-Shaw tradition, with an opulent American touch, a sort of combination of
J. P. Morgan, Topham Beauclerk and St. Francis of Assisi." The
entire man would be one who "did everything," good and bad, who
realized all the potentialities of his nature and thereby achieved
wisdom. The entire man, in the 1920's, was the one who followed the
Rule of the Thelemites as revealed to Pantagruel: *Fais ce que voul-
dras*, "Do what you will." But that rule implied a second imperative,
like an echo: "Will!" To be admired by the 1920's young men had
to will all sorts of actions and had to possess enough energy and
courage to carry out even their momentary wishes. They lived in the
moment with what they liked to call "an utter disregard of consequences." In spirit they all made their pilgrimage to the Abbey of
Thelema; they consulted the oracle of the Divine Bottle and, like

Pantagruel, they received for answer the one word *Trinch*. They obeyed the oracle and drank, in those days of the Volstead Act when drinking was a rite of comradeship and an act of rebellion. As Fitzgerald would say, they drank "cocktails before meals like Americans, wines and brandies like Frenchmen, beer like Germans, whiskey-and-soda like the English . . . this preposterous *mélange* that was like some gigantic cocktail in a nightmare." They drank and they also worked, with something of the same desperation; they worked to earn social rank, to sell, to advertise, to organize, to invent and to create enduring works of art. In ten years they gave a new tempo to American society.

The 1920's were a good age for works of art and in some ways they were a bad age for artists as persons. The works of art have come down to us and we are now finding again how honest and impressive they were in their often fragmentary fashion. Some of the artists have also survived while others have gone under; in general the age did not encourage them to develop steadily or to achieve unified careers. The age is now being blamed for the relative failures of Fitzgerald and others like him, but a great deal of this talk is sentimental. They did not fail as artists or we should not be rereading their works. If they failed in their personal lives it was not because they were victims of the historical environment; it was—among other reasons— because they acted on dangerous principles which happened to be those of the age, but which they also took into themselves and accepted as their own. In that sense they succumbed like the age itself, not so much to the pressure of exterior forces as by inner necessity.

Fitzgerald not only represented the age but came to suspect that he had helped to create it, by setting the patterns of conduct that were followed by persons a little younger than himself. "If I had anything to do with creating the manners of the contemporary American girl I certainly made a botch of the job," he said in a 1925 letter. In his notebook he observed that one of his relatives was still a flapper in the 1930's. "There is no doubt," he added, "that she originally patterned herself upon certain immature and unfortunate writings of mine, so that I have a special indulgence for —— as for one who has lost an arm or a leg in one's service." A drunken young man teetered up to his door and said, "I had to see you. I feel I owe you more than I can say. I feel that you formed my life." It was not the young man—later a successful novelist—but Fitzgerald himself who was the principal victim of his capacity for creating fictional types in life. "Sometimes," he told another visitor late at night, "I don't know whether Zelda and I are real or whether we are characters in one of my novels."

That was in the spring of 1933, a few weeks after the banks had closed all over the country. The Fitzgeralds were living at La Paix, a brown wooden late-Victorian lodge on a thirty-acre estate near Baltimore—"La Paix (my God!)" Scott wrote at the head of a letter. In the afternoon the house had been filled with little sounds of life— the colored cook and her relatives arguing in the kitchen, Zelda talking to her nurse or rustling about her studio as she painted furiously, Scott somewhere in a back room dictating to his secretary, then their daughter coming home from school and playing under the big oak trees on the lawn. Zelda wasn't well enough to come down to dinner, but the visitor was taken to see her afterward; her face was emaciated and twitched as she talked and her mouth twisted itself into unhappy shapes. After dinner the sounds of life died away from the house. Little Scottie was put to bed, the cook and her friends went home, Zelda had to rest and big Scott wandered from room to room with a glass in his hand, explaining that it was water; then, as he started another trip to refill the glass in the kitchen, he confessed that it was gin. There was not enough furniture, there were no carpets to absorb the inhuman noises of the night. Everything creaked and echoed. The visitor sat alone in the one big chair in the almost empty living room and thought that the house was the perfect setting for a ghost story, with Scott and Zelda as ghosts, the golden boy of 1920 and the belle of two states. Their generation had been defeated by life—so it seemed at the time—and yet in their own defeat they were still its representative figures.

2

In victory and defeat Fitzgerald retained a quality that very few writers are able to acquire: a sense of living in history. Manners and morals were changing all through his life and he set himself the task of recording the changes. They were revealed to him, not by statistics or news reports, but in terms of living characters, and the characters were revealed by gestures, each appropriate to a certain year. He wrote: "One day in 1926 we"—meaning the members of his generation—"looked down and found we had flabby arms and a fat pot and couldn't say boop-boop-a-doop to a Sicilian. . . . By 1927 a wide-spread neurosis began to be evident, faintly signaled, like a nervous beating of the feet, by the popularity of cross-word puzzles. . . . By this time"—also in 1927—"contemporaries of mine had begun to disappear into the dark maw of violence. . . . By 1928 Paris had grown suffocating. With each new shipment of Americans spewed up by the boom the quality fell off, until toward the end there was something sinister about the crazy boatloads."

He tried to find the visible act that revealed a moral quality in-

herent in a certain moment of time. He was haunted by time, as if
he wrote in a room full of clocks and calendars. He made lists by the
hundred, including lists of the popular songs, the football players,
the top debutantes (with the types of beauty they cultivated), the
hobbies and the slang expressions of a given year; he felt that all
these names and phrases belonged to the year and helped to reveal
its momentary color. "After all," he said in an otherwise undistin-
guished magazine story, "any given moment has its value; it can be
questioned in the light of after-events, but the moment remains. The
young prince in velvet gathered in lovely domesticity around the
queen amid the hush of rich draperies may presently grow up to be
Pedro the Cruel or Charles the Mad, but the moment of beauty was
there."

Fitzgerald lived in his great moments, and lived in them again
when he remembered their drama; but he also stood apart from them
and coldly reckoned their causes and consequences. That is his
doubleness or irony and it is one of his distinguishing marks as a
writer. He took part in the ritual orgies of his time, but he also kept
a secretly detached position, regarding himself as a pauper living
among millionaires, a Celt among Sassenachs and a sullen peasant
among the nobility; he said that his point of vantage "was the
dividing line between two generations," prewar and postwar. Always
he cultivated a double vision. In his novels and stories he was trying
to present the glitter of life in the Princeton eating clubs, on the
North Shore of Long Island, in Hollywood and on the French
Riviera; he surrounded his characters with a mist of admiration, and
at the same time he kept driving the mist away. He liked to know
"where the milk is watered and the sugar sanded, the rhinestone
passed for diamond and the stucco for stone." It was as if all his
stories described a big dance to which he had taken, as he once wrote,
the prettiest girl:

> "There was an orchestra—Bingo-Bango
> Playing for us to dance the tango
> And the people all clapped as we arose
> For her sweet face and my new clothes—"

and as if at the same time he stood outside the ballroom, a little Midwestern boy with his nose to the glass, wondering how much the
tickets cost and who paid for the music. But it was not a dance he
was watching so much as it was a drama of conflicting manners and
aspirations in which he was both the audience and the leading actor.
As audience he kept a cold eye on the actor's performance. He wrote
of himself when he was twenty, "I knew that at bottom I lacked the

essentials. At the last crisis, I knew I had no real courage, persever-
ance or self-respect." Sixteen years later he was just as critical, if in
a more discriminating fashion, and he said to the visitor at La Paix,
"I've got a very limited talent. I'm a workman of letters, a professional. I know when to write and when to stop writing." It was the
maximum of critical detachment, but it was combined with the maximum of immersion in the drama. He said in his notebook, and without the least exaggeration, "Taking things hard, from Ginevra to Joe
Mank—," mentioning the names of his first unhappy love and of a
Hollywood producer who, so he thought, had ruined one of his best
scripts: "That's the stamp that goes into my books so that people
can read it blind like Braille."

The drama he watched and in which he played—and overplayed—
a leading part was a moral drama leading to rewards and punishments. "Sometimes I wish I had gone along with that gang," he said
in a letter that discussed musical comedies and mentioned Cole
Porter and Rogers and Hart; "but I guess I am too much a moralist
at heart and want to preach at people in some acceptable form, rather
than to entertain them." The morality he wanted to preach was a
simple one, in the midst of the prevailing confusion. Its four cardinal
virtues were Industry, Discipline, Responsibility (in the sense of
being kind to people and meeting one's obligations) and Maturity
(in the sense of learning to regard failure as inevitable, and yet of
making one's best efforts always). The good people in his stories had
these virtues and the bad ones had the corresponding vices. "All I
believe in in life," he wrote to his daughter, "is the rewards for virtue
(according to your talents) and the *punishments* for not fulfilling
your duties, which are doubly costly."

The handle by which he took hold of his characters was their
dreams. These, as I said, might be commonplace or even cheap, but
almost always Fitzgerald managed to surround them with an atmosphere of the mysterious and illimitable or of the pitifully doomed.
His great scenes were, so to speak, played to music: sometimes the
music from a distant ballroom, sometimes that of a phonograph playing a German tango, sometimes the wind in the leaves, sometimes the
stark music of the heart. When there was no music at least there
were pounding rhythms: "The city's quick metropolitan rhythm of
love and birth and death that supplied dreams to the unimaginative";
"The rhythm of the week-end, with its birth, its planned gaieties and
its announced end"; "New York's flashing, dynamic good looks, its
tall man's quick-step." Fitzgerald's dream of his mature years, after
he had outgrown the notion of becoming a big man in college, was
also set to a sort of music, perhaps that of the *Unfinished Symphony*;
it was the dream of becoming a great writer, specifically a great

novelist who would do for American society in our time what Turgeniev, for example, had done for the old regime in Russia.

It was not his dream to be a poet, yet that was how he started and
in some ways he remained a poet primarily. He said of himself, "The
talent that matures early is usually of the poetic type, which mine
was in large part." His favorite author was Keats, not Turgeniev or
Flaubert. "I suppose I've read it a hundred times," he said about the
"Ode on a Grecian Urn." "About the tenth time I began to know
what it was about, and caught the chime in it and the exquisite inner
mechanics. Likewise with the 'Nightingale,' which I can never read
without tears in my eyes; likewise 'The Pot of Basil,' with its great
stanzas about the two brothers. . . . Knowing these things very
young and granted an ear, one could scarcely ever afterwards be
unable to distinguish between gold and dross in what one read."
When his daughter was learning to be a writer he advised her to read
Keats and Browning and try her hand at a sonnet in iambic pentam-
eter. He added, "The only thing that will help you is poetry, which
is the most concentrated form of style."

Fitzgerald himself was a poet who never learned some of the ele-
mentary rules for writing prose. His grammar was shaky and his
spelling definitely bad; for example he wrote "ect." more often than
"etc." and misspelled the name of his friend Monsignor Fay on the
dedication page of *This Side of Paradise*. In his letters he always
missspelled the given names of his first and last loves. He was not
a student, for all the books he read; not a theoretician and perhaps
one should flatly say, not a thinker. He counted on his friends to do
much of his thinking for him; at Princeton it was John Peale Bishop,
he said, who "made me see, in the course of a couple of months, the
difference between poetry and non-poetry." Twenty years later, at the
time of his crack-up, he was compelled to re-examine his scale of
values and found thinking incredibly difficult; he compared it to "the
moving about of great secret trunks." He was then forced to the conclusion "That I had done very little thinking, save within the
problems of my craft. For twenty years a certain man had been my
intellectual conscience. That man was Edmund Wilson." Another
contemporary, Ernest Hemingway, "had been an artistic conscience
to me. I had not imitated his infectious style, because my own style,
such as it is, was formed before he published anything, but there was
an awful pull toward him when I was on a spot."

Fitzgerald was making the confession in order to keep straight
with himself, not to forestall any revelation that might have been
made by his critics. The critics would have said that there was little
of Hemingway's influence in his work, and hardly more of Wilson's—
although he once wrote a story about two dogs, "Shaggy's Morning,"

that is a delicate and deliberate burlesque of the Hemingway manner. By listening hard one can overhear a few, a very few, suggestions of Hemingway in the dialogue of other stories, especially the later ones, but Fitzgerald was faithful to his own vision of the world and his own way of expressing it. His debt to Hemingway and Wilson is real, but hard to define. In spite of what he said, they didn't supply him with an artistic or intellectual conscience, since he had always possessed a lively conscience of his own; but they did serve as models of literary conduct by which he tested his moral attitude toward the problems of his craft.

To satisfy his conscience he kept trying to write, not merely as well as he could, like an honest literary craftsman, but somehow better than he was able. There was more than one occasion when he actually surpassed himself—that is, when he so immersed himself in a subject that it carried him beyond his usual or natural capacities as demonstrated in the past. The writing of *The Great Gatsby* was among the first of these occasions. There are scenes in the novel—like Nick's first conversation with Daisy, like the party at Gatsby's, like Nick's farewell to Gatsby and like his final meditations on the story—that are not only better than anything Fitzgerald had previously written but are not even foreshadowed in his earlier work. "I can never remember the times when I wrote anything," he said in his notebook—"*This Side of Paradise* time or *Beautiful and Damned* or *Gatsby* time, for instance. Lived in story." By living in the story he became wiser, so it seemed, than he was in ordinary life. He said that sometimes he went back and read his own books for advice on his problems: "How much I know sometimes—how little at others," he added.

By choice and fate he wrote what might be called the novel of centrality, that is, the novel dealing with representative young men and women in what seemed to be a central situation. The characters would not be hopeless people chained by their prejudices and at the mercy of social and economic forces—"creatures of their environment," in a favorite phrase of the naturalistic writers. Instead they would have talent and opportunities and at least an apparent freedom of movement, so that the decisions they made would have an effect not only on their own careers but on the lives of others, by giving examples to be shunned or followed: like himself his heroes would be exemplary. The story, of whatever length, would be concerned with how they prospered in the world, how they fell in love and how they made or failed to make an adjustment with life. It is the story that Stendhal told in *The Red and the Black* and Dickens told in *Great Expectations*: given a society with many false standards, how will a young man rise in it, by what advantages, what stratagems? Fitzgerald laid the story in his own time and his social observation was not much inferior to that of the masters.

I do not find it a serious flaw in his work that the heroes ended by resembling himself or that he gave most of them Irish names or at least (to Dick Diver, of *Tender Is the Night*) a faint Irish melody in the voice in order to make the identification stronger. Sometimes the heroes started as very different persons and were transformed imperceptibly, as he worked over them, into an image of the author. When his friend Bishop wrote him a critical letter about *The Great Gatsby* Fitzgerald answered, "Also you are right about Gatsby being blurred and patchy. I never at any one time saw him clear myself— for he started out as one man I knew and then changed into myself— the amalgam was never clear in my mind." Actually the book gains as well as loses by the blurredness of Gatsby; it gains in mystery what it loses in definition. Dick Diver also started out as one man Fitzgerald knew "and then changed into myself"—changed so completely that Dick's fate was a prophecy of what would happen to the author; but again the change adds a new quality to the novel. Fitzgerald's personal life, enlarged as it was by his sympathies and his gift for putting himself in others' places, was more interesting than other lives he might have invented or merely observed; he had every reason for writing disguised autobiographies, as authors have done from the beginning. "There never was a good biography of a good novelist," he said in his notebook. "There couldn't be. He is too many people, if he's any good." What he meant was that the heroes of his stories were never himself as he was in life, but himself as projected into different situations, such as might have been encountered by members of his spiritual family. "Books are like brothers," he said. "I am an only child. Gatsby my imaginary eldest brother, Amory"— in *This Side of Paradise*—"my younger, Anthony"—in *The Beautiful and Damned*—"my worry, Dick my comparatively good brother, but all of them far from home."

In life and art Fitzgerald set a high value on persistent effort. "After all, Max, I am a plodder," he said in one of his letters to Maxwell Perkins. "One time I had a talk with Ernest Hemingway, and I told him, against all logic that was then current, that I was the tortoise and he was the hare, and that's the truth of the matter, that everything I have ever attained has been through long and persistent struggle while it is Ernest who has a touch of genius which enables him to bring off extraordinary things with facility. I have no facility. I have a facility for being cheap, if I want to indulge that . . . but when I decided to be a serious man, I tried to struggle over every point until I have made myself into a slow-moving Behemoth." Moving slowly with *Tender Is the Night* he wrote a manuscript of

400,000 words and put aside three-fourths of it, including a number of scenes that were as good as any in the finished novel. After the book was published and was apparently forgotten he started revising it again, for a new edition that might or might not be printed. *The Last Tycoon* would have been a short novel of 50,000 words and it was only half-finished at his death, but his notes and drafts and synopses and character sketches are valuable in themselves. There are three drafts of the first chapter and the third draft is an extremely effective piece of writing that struck into new territory for Fitzgerald. But he wrote at the head of the chapter, "Rewrite from mood. Has become stilted with rewriting. Don't look [at previous draft]. Rewrite from mood." On the fourth and the tenth revision he still would have been unsatisfied, unless the chapter fitted exactly to the outlines of his dream.

He devoted less care to his stories than to his novels, since he regarded himself as a novelist primarily. "Stories are best written in either one jump or three, according to the length," he told his daughter. "The three-jump story should be done on three successive days, then a day or so for revise and off she goes. This of course is an ideal—" and in his later years Fitzgerald seldom achieved it. There were stories that he kept revising for months or even years, but he never regarded them as his best. Writing stories paid him better than any other literary work. In 1929, for example, he earned $27,000 by his stories and only $5,450 from all other sources, including $31.77 described as "royalty from book." Books were, however, his first interest and it was the novel, not the short story, that he described as "the strongest and supplest medium for conveying thought and emotion from one human being to another."

His publishers used to bring out a collection of Fitzgerald's stories one or two seasons after the appearance of each of his novels. It was a wise custom because, in a sense, the stories clustered around the novel that was written during the same period. Most of the early ones might have dealt with the further adventures of Amory and Isabelle and Rosalind, the three so-wicked youngsters in *This Side of Paradise*. His first long story, "May Day" (1920), was in some respects a preliminary sketch for his second novel, *The Beautiful and Damned*. Fitzgerald said that "Winter Dreams" (1922) was a first version of *The Great Gatsby*, and "Absolution" (1924) was originally intended as a prologue to *Gatsby*. During the next seven years he wrote many stories about Americans in Paris, on the Riviera and in Switzerland—the backgrounds he would use in *Tender Is the Night*—and among them is "One Trip Abroad" (1930), which, though it is one of the weaker stories in the group, would serve as a preview of the finished novel.

The stories contributed to the novels in still another fashion. On the magazine clip sheets of a very early one, "The Smilers," Fitzgerald wrote in a bold hand, "This story has been stripped of any phrases of interest and is positively not to be republished in any form." The "phrases of interest" were copied into his notebook, where they were classified alphabetically under various headings—A' for Anecdotes, B for Bright Clippings, C for Conversation and Things Overhead—and were thus kept in dead storage, but readily available, until the day when he might be able to incorporate them into a novel. The clip sheets were then consigned to a big folder marked "Junked and Dismantled Stories." Not only the failed stories but many that deserved better treatment were stripped of their useful parts like a worn-out automobile. He was willing to sacrifice a whole story, sometimes a good one, for the sake of a sentence or two that might strengthen a scene in *Tender Is the Night* or *The Last Tycoon*.

But that wasn't Fitzgerald's final judgment on the stories as a group. Like other serious American writers he had the old and usually unsatisfied ambition to leave behind him a definitive body of work. There would be, so he planned, a uniform edition of his writings and in it the stories would occupy almost as much space as the novels. The Collected Works of F. Scott Fitzgerald would fill seventeen volumes. There would be seven novels, including three still to be written, and one of these, *In the Darkest Hour*, would be in two volumes. Besides the novels there would be seven volumes of short stories, one volume of poetry and plays and a final volume of essays. Nor was this all: at the age of fifty-five or sixty Fitzgerald was to prepare a Revised Edition in twelve volumes—probably in dull, rich bindings like the New York Edition of Henry James—and once again the stories would be given their full place. He must have felt as we do today, that many of them are as good in their more impulsive fashion as the novels he rewrote so often. They are like the sketches of a gifted artist, sharp and immediate in their perceptions, so that they bring us face to face with the artist's world. Even the worst of the stories have sudden insights that are like flinging back curtains from windows hidden in what had seemed to be flimsily decorated walls, while the best stories are suffused with emotion and their insights are everywhere. "I have asked a lot of my emotions—one hundred and twenty stories," Fitzgerald said in a prose poem that he wrote two years before leaving for Hollywood. "The price was high, right up with Kipling, because there was one little drop of something —not blood, not a tear, not my seed, but me more intimately than these, in every story, it was the extra I had." And he added, because he was then in a state of physical illness and nervous exhaustion, "Now it has gone and I am just like you now."

3

During the years 1935 and 1936 he suffered from a complete physical and emotional breakdown. It was never a secret and Fitzgerald described it at the time, in "The Crack-Up" and two other articles printed by *Esquire* in the spring of 1936. The articles revealed the intimate worries of an author who had come to regard himself "as a cracked plate, the kind that one wonders whether it is worth preserving. . . . It can never again be warmed on the stove nor shuffled with the other plates in the dishpan; it will not be brought out for company, but it will do to hold crackers late at night or to go into the ice box under left-overs."

The causes of his breakdown are not mysterious and Arthur Mizener has described them with great understanding in *The Far Side of Paradise*. The symptoms were described by Fitzgerald himself and they were excruciatingly painful, but by no means unusual. We have been living through an age of emotional breakdowns. By now the case records of brilliant men, hundreds and thousands of them, who have gone to pieces are available to physicians and there is nothing suffered by Fitzgerald that has not been Greek-named and catalogued in the medical textbooks. There are, however, two features of his experience that make it something more than a commonplace case history. The first feature is the unusual candor with which he wrote about it. He was, it is true, a little less than completely honest about his alcoholism, but that is a symptom of the disease itself and one he tried hard to overcome. He revealed everything else, on condition that it did not hurt others but only himself.

I do not think it is fair to use the cant word "exhibitionism" in connection with the three articles he wrote for *Esquire*. They contain no hint that he was deriving a twisted pleasure from torturing himself in public. What they do suggest is a sense of duty. It is as if he was saying, "When I undertook to be a certain type of writer I also undertook to tell the essential truth about my world and myself. The task has been pleasant at moments in the past and now that it is supremely painful I still must tell the truth at the cost of losing my self-respect if I fail to do so." Without bravado and with fewer excuses than he might well have offered, he simply told his story. Writers have done that before, but usually they have waited until long afterward, when the story was no longer shameful and they could even boast of having found a path back to health. They have offered all sorts of self-degrading confessions, but on one point they have remained silent; they have admitted everything except the possibility of having lost their talent. Fitzgerald told the story in the

midst of his crack-up, with no cure for it in sight, and he truly
shocked his literary colleagues by suggesting that his talent might
have vanished with his emotional vitality.

In his memorial poem to Fitzgerald, John Peale Bishop set down
his memory of those tortured years:

> "I have lived with you the hour of your humiliation,
> I have seen you turn upon the others in the night
> And of sad self-loathing
> Concealing nothing
> Heard you cry: *I am lost. But you are lower!*
> And you had that right.
> The damned do not so own to their damnation."

Fitzgerald for all his tortures was still in purgatory and not in those
cold circles of hell where the heart congeals. Because he clung to his
honesty and his sense of values he suffered more than the truly
damned. "It was despair, despair, despair—despair day and night,"
said a nurse who cared for him in 1936. He spent his sleepless nights
brooding over what he had failed to accomplish. About three o'clock,
he said, the real horror "would develop over the roof-tops, and in the
strident horns of night-owl taxis and the shrill monody of revelers'
arrival over the way. Horror and waste—

"—Waste and horror—what I might have been and done that is
lost, spent, gone, dissipated, unrecapturable." "In a real dark night
of the soul it is always three o'clock in the morning, day after day."
At times like these a man keeps his sanity by force of will or loses it
by what amounts to a deliberate decision. Fitzgerald did not retreat
into dreams or delusions or any other substitutes for the maternal
womb. There was a hard core in his character—call it Midwestern
Puritanism if you will, or middle-class Irish Catholicism, or simple
obstinacy—and it kept him from denying his obligations to his
family and his creditors and his talent as an artist. He met the obligations, and that is the second truly remarkable feature of Fitzgerald's case: not his symptoms or his sufferings, but his sense of
duty and his will to survive.

He had suffered a permanent defeat and he did not try to hide its
consequences from himself or the world. "A man does not recover
from such jolts," Fitzgerald said in one of his articles for *Esquire*—
"he becomes a different person and, eventually, the new person finds
new things to care about." In the summer of 1937 the new person was
strong enough to make a trip to Hollywood. Fitzgerald had been
given a six months' contract by Metro-Goldwyn-Mayer, and when
the contract expired in January 1938 it was renewed for a year at an

increased salary. He was drinking very little and proved to be a
capable screen craftsman, although his best scenarios were not produced in the form in which he wrote them. During his first eighteen
months in Hollywood he earned $88,391, paid off his big debts and
put his insurance policies in order.

The story is not a simple one of moral redemption and success in a
new field. At the beginning of February 1939, a week after the M-G-M
contract ran out, he was sent East by Walter Wanger; with the help
of Budd Schulberg he was to write a film about the Dartmouth
Winter Carnival. He began drinking on the eastbound plane, got into
a violent disagreement with Wanger and continued drinking at Dartmouth and in New York; it was his biggest, saddest, most desperate
spree. But that wasn't his end, even though it was the end of the principal character in Schulberg's novel about the trip, *The Disenchanted*;
Fitzgerald's story went on.

He found a new studio job and quickly lost it; then Zelda was
well enough for a vacation from the sanitarium and he took her on a
trip to Havana, where he began drinking again. Back in Hollywood he couldn't find another job and suspected that the producers
had put his name on an informal blacklist. He took to his bed; for
three months he was under the care of day and night nurses. It was
a recurrence of tuberculosis, he told his friends (who suspected a
recurrence of alcoholism), and it was complicated by "a nervous
breakdown of such severity that for a long time it threatened to
paralyze both arms—or to quote the doctor: 'The Good Lord tapped
you on the shoulder.'" After a partial recovery in the summer he
faced another crisis, to which he referred obliquely in his letters; it
was "that personally and publicly dreary month of Sept. last [when]
about everything went to pieces all at once"—and still it wasn't the
end of the story.

In the past he had often exaggerated his physical troubles for
dramatic effect, but it seems that he wasn't exaggerating when he said
that all through the winter of 1939–40 he suffered from "the awful
lapses and sudden reverses and apparent cures and thorough poisoning effect of lung trouble. Suffice to say there were months with a
high of 99.8, months at 99.6 and then up and down and a stabilization
at 99.2 every afternoon when I could write in bed." His Hollywood
friends report that he was gray-faced and emaciated and seldom left
his room, but he was writing again—if only for a few hours each day
—and that was the important news. Although seven of his books were
still in print nobody was buying them, and his name was almost
forgotten; now he was setting out to regain his place in literature.

His record of production for the last year of his life would have
been remarkable for a man in perfect health. He began the year by

making plans for a novel and, simultaneously, by writing twenty stories for *Esquire,* including seventeen in the Pat Hobby series. Most of the Hobby stories weren't very good by his own standards, but they caught the Hollywood atmosphere and they also made fun of the author's weaknesses, thereby proving that Fitzgerald hadn't lost his ironic attitude toward himself or his gift of double vision. Suddenly he resumed his interrupted correspondence with his friends and he sent his daughter an extraordinary series of letters that continued all through the year; perhaps they were too urgent and too full of tired wisdom for a girl in college, but then Fitzgerald was writing them as a sort of personal and literary testament. In the spring he wrote—and twice rewrote from the beginning—a scenario based on his story, "Babylon Revisited"; it was the best of his scenarios and, according to the producer who ordered it, the best he ever read. Shirley Temple wasn't available for the part of Honoria and the story has never been filmed. Once more Fitzgerald began drinking; then he sobered up and went to work for a studio in September, earning enough, he thought, to carry him through the writing of *The Last Tycoon.* Work on it was delayed by a serious heart attack in November, but for most of the month he was writing steadily. He had said in a letter to his daughter, "I wish now I'd *never* relaxed or looked back—but said at the end of *The Great Gatsby:* 'I've found my line—from now on this comes first. This is my immediate duty—without this I am nothing.'" In the year 1940 he had found his line again, and had found something more than that, since he now possessed a deeper sense of the complexities of life than he had when writing *Gatsby.* He was doing his best work of the year in December and it was some of the best he ever did. He had been sober for a long time and seemed to be less worried about illness, when suddenly, four days before Christmas, there was a second coronary attack and he died—not like a strayed reveler but like a partner of the elder J. P. Morgan, working too hard until his heart gave out.

At the time of his death Fitzgerald had written about 160 stories in all; the exact number would be hard to determine because some of his work was on the borderline between fiction and the informal essay or "magazine piece." The forty-six stories that went into his four published collections include most of the best ones, but not all of them, because Fitzgerald was a shrewd but erratic judge of his own work. The last collection, *Taps at Reveille,* appeared in 1935 and the stories of the last years have never been reprinted.

That is the background of the present selection, in which I have tried to gather together the best stories written at all stages of Fitzgerald's career. If the selection has any virtues except those of the stories themselves, it owes them to the help I received from several friends and students of Fitzgerald—as notably from his daughter, Mrs. Samuel J. Lanahan, who made several useful suggestions; from Harold Ober, his literary agent, who supplied me with many items of information, including a list of Fitzgerald's published work; from Alexander Clark, curator of manuscripts at the Princeton University Library, who is presently in charge of Fitzgerald's notes and correspondence; from Charles Scribner's Sons, his publishers, who made the volume possible (and patiently waited for it); and from Arthur Mizener, who let me read his fine biography of Fitzgerald in manuscript and showed me his notes on the circumstances in which many of the stories were written. The faults of the selection are strictly mine.

I thought it best to devote the bulk of the volume to the work of the middle period, 1926–31, when Fitzgerald was giving most of his time to shorter fiction. His first two volumes, *Flappers and Philosophers* (1920) and *Tales of the Jazz Age* (1922), received full attention in their own age and from these I have taken only four stories in all (after hesitating a long time before including "May Day"). From *All the Sad Young Men* (1926) I have taken five, or a little more than half the book. From *Taps at Reveille* (1935), which was underestimated by the reviewers, I have taken nine and to these I have added three other stories written at the same period as those in *Taps* but omitted from the volume, I think mistakenly. The selection ends with seven of the shorter pieces that Fitzgerald wrote after his crack-up.

Taken together the twenty-eight stories compose an informal history of two decades in American life, or rather of one decade with its long aftermath. The history is more intimate than anything in the textbooks and it is in some ways more vivid than the picture of the time that we find in Fitzgerald's novels, where the material was composed and recomposed; the stories were written closer to the scene and retain the emotion of the moment. But they do more than merely speak for their time, since they also speak for the author; and taken together they form a sort of journal of his whole career. It was a different career from the one we had expected to find after reading his first books and hearing about his decline. What seems important in it now is not the early success and not the neglect and heartbreak of his later years, and not even the contrast between them that lends an easy point to other men's novels; it is above all the struggle against defeat and the sort of qualified triumph he earned by the struggle. Fitzgerald remains an exemplar and archetype, but not of the 1920's alone; in the end he represents the human spirit in one of its permanent forms.

MALCOLM COWLEY

I

Early Success

THE seven stories in this first group belong to the period of Fitzgerald's early success and have as background his first loves, his marriage to Zelda Sayre (after their engagement had been broken because of his poverty) and the glitter of their new life among the rich. The stories were written between the fall of 1919, when he was twenty-three and heard the great news that his novel had been accepted, and the spring of 1924, when the Fitzgeralds decided to live in Europe. Two of them were reprinted in *Flappers and Philosophers* (1920), two in *Tales of the Jazz Age* (1922) and the last three in *All the Sad Young Men* (1926).

The book opens with the best of Fitzgerald's fantasies, "The Diamond as Big as the Ritz." Although it was written in the winter of 1921–22, it is printed out of its chronological order because it clearly states a theme that would often recur in his work. A middle-class boy falls in love with the heiress to a great fortune and she returns his love, but the boy is murdered by her family or destroyed by her wealth. "The Diamond as Big as the Ritz" can have a happy ending —at least for the lovers—because it is a fantasy; but the plot would reappear in *The Great Gatsby* and there it would be carried to its tragic conclusion. Having fallen in love with the rich Mrs. Buchanan, Gatsby would be murdered as efficiently as were the visitors to Braddock Washington's diamond mountain.

The other six stories in the group are reprinted in the order of their magazine publication. "Bernice Bobs Her Hair" is the best of the flapper stories that made Fitzgerald's reputation as a popular writer. When it was published in the spring of 1920, bobbed hair was a national issue like the Volstead Act, and the young author received hundreds of letters from excited readers of the *Saturday Evening Post*. Many were shocked by the "line" that Marjorie invented to make her cousin popular. It was copied from life, or at least from the remarks that Fitzgerald himself had composed for his pretty young sister Annabel when she was going to her first big dances. . . . "The Ice Palace" (1920) grew out of his worries in the autumn before his marriage, when he was living at home in St. Paul and was making frantic visits to Zelda in Alabama. The contrast between North and South was one of his favorite themes; he would return to it in "The Last of the Belles" and in several uncollected pieces. . . . "May Day" (1920) is the longest and most ambitious of his early stories. It catches the spirit of the crazy spring when we were all coming back from the wars and when Fitzgerald, besides looking vainly for a job, was drinking too much with his classmates at the Knickerbocker bar; he projected his sense of failure into the character of Gordon Sterrett. More than that, he interwove two other plots into that of Sterrett's failure with greater skill than he had shown before and would usually show in the future; he never learned to be a good engineer of plots. Soon, however, he became a better judge of persons and situations than he was when writing "May Day."

There is more depth of feeling in the last three stories. "Winter Dreams" (1922) was suggested by an earlier episode in the author's life: at Princeton he had been in love with a debutante who was something like Judy Jones in the story (later she would reappear as the heroine of the Josephine series). In other respects "Winter Dreams" is not at all a copy of Fitzgerald's life, but it offers a revealing summary of his early feelings about love and money and social position. . . . "The Sensible Thing" (1924) is autobiographical in the strict sense; it is the story of his broken and renewed engagement to Zelda Sayre. . . . "Absolution" (1924) is rich in memories of his Catholic boyhood and his propensity for living in an imaginary world. At first it was intended as a prologue to *The Great Gatsby*; then Fitzgerald decided it was better to leave Gatsby's background wrapped in mist. But the story retains its connection with the novel, which was a turning point in his career. He was working on a deeper level of experience than he had attempted to reach in the past, and he continued to work on it in the best of the stories that followed.

THE DIAMOND AS BIG AS THE RITZ

JOHN T. UNGER came from a family that had been well known in Hades—a small town on the Mississippi River—for several generations. John's father had held the amateur golf championship through many a heated contest; Mrs. Unger was known "from hot-box to hot-bed," as the local phrase went, for her political addresses; and young John T. Unger, who had just turned sixteen, had danced all the latest dances from New York before he put on long trousers. And now, for a certain time, he was to be away from home. That respect for a New England education which is the bane of all provincial places, which drains them yearly of their most promising young men, had seized upon his parents. Nothing would suit them but that he should go to St. Midas' School near Boston—Hades was too small to hold their darling and gifted son.

Now in Hades—as you know if you ever have been there—the names of the more fashionable preparatory schools and colleges mean very little. The inhabitants have been so long out of the world that, though they make a show of keeping up to date in dress and manners and literature, they depend to a great extent on hearsay, and a function that in Hades would be considered elaborate would doubtless be hailed by a Chicago beef-princess as "perhaps a little tacky."

John T. Unger was on the eve of departure. Mrs. Unger, with maternal fatuity, packed his trunks full of linen suits and electric fans, and Mr. Unger presented his son with an asbestos pocket-book stuffed with money.

"Remember, you are always welcome here," he said. "You can be sure, boy, that we'll keep the home fires burning."

"I know," answered John huskily.

"Don't forget who you are and where you come from," continued his father proudly, "and you can do nothing to harm you. You are an Unger—from Hades."

So the old man and the young shook hands and John walked away with tears streaming from his eyes. Ten minutes later he had passed outside the city limits, and he stopped to glance back for the last time. Over the gates the old-fashioned Victorian motto seemed strangely attractive to him. His father had tried time and time again to have it changed to something with a little more push and verve about it, such as "Hades—Your Opportunity," or else a plain "Welcome" sign set over a hearty handshake pricked out in electric lights. The old motto was a little depressing, Mr. Unger had thought—but now. . . .

So John took his look and then set his face resolutely toward his destination. And, as he turned away, the lights of Hades against the sky seemed full of a warm and passionate beauty.

St. Midas' School is half an hour from Boston in a Rolls-Pierce motor-car. The actual distance will never be known, for no one, except John T. Unger, had ever arrived there save in a Rolls-Pierce and probably no one ever will again. St. Midas' is the most expensive and the most exclusive boys' preparatory school in the world.

John's first two years there passed pleasantly. The fathers of all the boys were money-kings and John spent his summers visiting at fashionable resorts. While he was very fond of all the boys he visited, their fathers struck him as being much of a piece, and in his boyish way he often wondered at their exceeding sameness. When he told them where his home was they would ask jovially, "Pretty hot down there?" and John would muster a faint smile and answer, "It certainly is." His response would have been heartier had they not all made this joke—at best varying it with, "Is it hot enough for you down there?" which he hated just as much.

In the middle of his second year at school, a quiet, handsome boy named Percy Washington had been put in John's form. The newcomer was pleasant in his manner and exceedingly well dressed even for St. Midas', but for some reason he kept aloof from the other boys. The only person with whom he was intimate was John T. Unger, but even to John he was entirely uncommunicative concerning his home or his family. That he was wealthy went without saying, but beyond a few such deductions John knew little of his friend, so it promised rich confectionery for his curiosity when Percy invited him to spend the summer at his home "in the West." He accepted, without hesitation.

It was only when they were in the train that Percy became, for the first time, rather communicative. One day while they were eating lunch in the dining-car and discussing the imperfect characters of several of the boys at school, Percy suddenly changed his tone and made an abrupt remark.

"My father," he said, "is by far the richest man in the world."

"Oh," said John, politely. He could think of no answer to make to this confidence. He considered "That's very nice," but it sounded hollow and was on the point of saying, "Really?" but refrained since it would seem to question Percy's statement. And such an astounding statement could scarcely be questioned.

"By far the richest," repeated Percy.

"I was reading in the *World Almanac,*" began John, "that there was one man in America with an income of over five million a year and four men with incomes of over three million a year, and——"

"Oh, they're nothing," Percy's mouth was a half-moon of scorn. "Catch-penny capitalists, financial small-fry, petty merchants and money-lenders. My father could buy them out and not know he'd done it."

"But how does he——"

"Why haven't they put down *his* income tax? Because he doesn't pay any. At least he pays a little one—but he doesn't pay any on his *real* income."

"He must be very rich," said John simply. "I'm glad. I like very rich people.

"The richer a fella is, the better I like him." There was a look of passionate frankness upon his dark face. "I visited the Schnlitzer-Murphys last Easter. Vivian Schnlitzer-Murphy had rubies as big as hen's eggs, and sapphires that were like globes with lights inside them——"

"I love jewels," agreed Percy enthusiastically. "Of course I wouldn't want any one at school to know about it, but I've got quite a collection myself. I used to collect them instead of stamps."

"And diamonds," continued John eagerly. "The Schnlitzer-Murphys had diamonds as big as walnuts——"

"That's nothing." Percy had leaned forward and dropped his voice to a low whisper. "That's nothing at all. My father has a diamond bigger than the Ritz-Carlton Hotel."

II

The Montana sunset lay between two mountains like a gigantic bruise from which dark arteries spread themselves over a poisoned sky. An immense distance under the sky crouched the village of Fish, minute, dismal, and forgotten. There were twelve men, so it was said, in the village of Fish, twelve sombre and inexplicable souls who sucked a lean milk from the almost literally bare rock upon which a mysterious populatory force had begotten them. They had become a race apart, these twelve men of Fish, like some species developed by an early whim of nature, which on second thought had abandoned them to struggle and extermination.

Out of the blue-black bruise in the distance crept a long line of moving lights upon the desolation of the land, and the twelve men of Fish gathered like ghosts at the shanty depot to watch the passing of the seven o'clock train, the Transcontinental Express from Chicago. Six times or so a year the Transcontinental Express, through some inconceivable jurisdiction, stopped at the village of Fish, and when this occurred a figure or so would disembark, mount into a buggy that always appeared from out of the dusk, and drive off toward the bruised sunset. The observation of this pointless and preposterous phenomenon had become a sort of cult among the men of Fish. To observe, that was all; there remained in them none of the vital quality of illusion which would make them wonder or speculate, else a religion might have grown up around these mysterious visitations. But the men of Fish were beyond all religion—the barest and most savage tenets of even Christianity could gain no foothold on that barren rock—so there was no altar, no priest, no sacrifice; only each night at seven the silent concourse by the shanty depot, a congregation who lifted up a prayer of dim, anæmic wonder.

On this June night, the Great Brakeman, whom, had they deified any one, they might well have chosen as their celestial protagonist, had ordained that the seven o'clock train should leave its human (or inhuman) deposit at Fish. At two minutes after seven Percy Washington and John T. Unger disembarked, hurried past the spellbound, the agape, the fearsome eyes of the twelve men of Fish, mounted into a buggy which had obviously appeared from nowhere, and drove away.

After half an hour, when the twilight had coagulated into dark, the silent negro who was driving the buggy hailed an opaque body somewhere ahead of them in the gloom. In response to his cry, it turned upon them a luminous disk which regarded them like a malignant eye out of the unfathomable night. As they came closer, John saw that it was the tail-light of an immense automobile, larger and more magnificent than any he had ever seen. Its body was of gleaming metal richer than nickel and lighter than silver, and the hubs of the wheels were studded with iridescent geometric figures of green and yellow—John did not dare to guess whether they were glass or jewel.

Two negroes, dressed in glittering livery such as one sees in pictures of royal processions in London, were standing at attention beside the car and as the two young men dismounted from the buggy they were greeted in some language which the guest could not understand, but which seemed to be an extreme form of the Southern negro's dialect.

"Get in," said Percy to his friend, as their trunks were tossed to the ebony roof of the limousine. "Sorry we had to bring you this far in that buggy, but of course it wouldn't do for the people on the train or those Godforsaken fellas in Fish to see this automobile."

"Gosh! What a car!" This ejaculation was provoked by its interior. John saw that the upholstery consisted of a thousand minute and exquisite tapestries of silk, woven with jewels and embroideries, and set upon a background of cloth of gold. The two armchair seats in which the boys luxuriated were covered with stuff that resembled duvetyn, but seemed woven in numberless colors of the ends of ostrich feathers.

"What a car!" cried John again, in amazement.

"This thing?" Percy laughed. "Why, it's just an old junk we use for a station wagon."

By this time they were gliding along through the darkness toward the break between the two mountains.

"We'll be there in an hour and a half," said Percy, looking at the clock. "I may as well tell you it's not going to be like anything you ever saw before."

If the car was any indication of what John would see, he was prepared to be astonished indeed. The simple piety prevalent in Hades has the earnest worship of and respect for riches as the first article of its creed—had John felt otherwise than radiantly humble before them, his parents would have turned away in horror at the blasphemy.

They had now reached and were entering the break between the two mountains and almost immediately the way became much rougher.

"If the moon shone down here, you'd see that we're in a big gulch," said Percy, trying to peer out of the window. He spoke a few words into the mouthpiece and immediately the footman turned on a search-light and swept the hillsides with an immense beam.

"Rocky, you see. An ordinary car would be knocked to pieces in half an hour. In fact, it'd take a tank to navigate it unless you knew the way. You notice we're going uphill now."

They were obviously ascending, and within a few minutes the car was crossing a high rise, where they caught a glimpse of a pale moon newly risen in the distance. The car stopped suddenly and several figures took shape out of the dark beside it—these were negroes also. Again the two young men were saluted in the same dimly recogniz- able dialect; then the negroes set to work and four immense cables dangling from overhead were attached with hooks to the hubs of the great jeweled wheels. At a resounding "Hey-yah!" John felt the car being lifted slowly from the ground—up and up—clear of the tallest rocks on both sides—then higher, until he could see a wavy, moonlit valley stretched out before him in sharp contrast to the quagmire of rocks that they had just left. Only on one side was there still rock—

and then suddenly there was no rock beside them or anywhere around.

It was apparent that they had surmounted some immense knife-blade of stone, projecting perpendicularly into the air. In a moment they were going down again, and finally with a soft bump they were landed upon the smooth earth.

"The worst is over," said Percy, squinting out the window. "It's only five miles from here, and our own road—tapestry brick—all the way. This belongs to us. This is where the United States ends, father says."

"Are we in Canada?"

"We are not. We're in the middle of the Montana Rockies. But you are now on the only five square miles of land in the country that's never been surveyed."

"Why hasn't it? Did they forget it?"

"No," said Percy, grinning, "they tried to do it three times. The first time my grandfather corrupted a whole department of the State survey; the second time he had the official maps of the United States tinkered with—that held them for fifteen years. The last time was harder. My father fixed it so that their compasses were in the strongest magnetic field ever artificially set up. He had a whole set of surveying instruments made with a slight defection that would allow for this territory not to appear, and he substituted them for the ones that were to be used. Then he had a river deflected and he had what looked like a village built up on its banks—so that they'd see it, and think it was a town ten miles farther up the valley. There's only one thing my father's afraid of," he concluded, "only one thing in the world that could be used to find us out."

"What's that?"

Percy sank his voice to a whisper.

"Aeroplanes,' he breathed. "We've got half a dozen anti-aircraft guns and we've arranged it so far—but there've been a few deaths and a great many prisoners. Not that we mind *that*, you know, father and I, but it upsets mother and the girls, and there's always the chance that some time we won't be able to arrange it."

Shreds and tatters of chinchilla, courtesy clouds in the green moon's heaven, were passing the green moon like precious Eastern stuffs paraded for the inspection of some Tartar Khan. It seemed to John that it was day, and that he was looking at some lads sailing above him in the air, showering down tracts and patent medicine circulars, with their messages of hope for despairing, rockbound hamlets. It seemed to him that he could see them look down out of the clouds and stare—and stare at whatever there was to stare at in this place whither he was bound— What then? Were they induced to land by some insidious device there to be immured far from patent

medicines and from tracts until the judgment day—or, should they
fail to fall into the trap, did a quick puff of smoke and the sharp
round of a splitting shell bring them drooping to earth—and "upset"
Percy's mother and sisters. John shook his head and the wraith of a
hollow laugh issued silently from his parted lips. What desperate
transaction lay hidden here? What a moral expedient of a bizarre
Crœsus? What terrible and golden mystery? . . .

The chinchilla clouds had drifted past now and outside the Montana night was bright as day. The tapestry brick of the road was
smooth to the tread of the great tires as they rounded a still, moonlit
lake; they passed into darkness for a moment, a pine grove, pungent
and cool, then they came out into a broad avenue of lawn and John's
exclamation of pleasure was simultaneous with Percy's taciturn
"We're home."

Full in the light of the stars, an exquisite château rose from the
borders of the lake, climbed in marble radiance half the height of an
adjoining mountain, then melted in grace, in perfect symmetry, in
translucent feminine languor, into the massed darkness of a forest of
pine. The many towers, the slender tracery of the sloping parapets,
the chiselled wonder of a thousand yellow windows with their oblongs
and hectagons and triangles of golden light, the shattered softness of
the intersecting planes of star-shine and blue shade, all trembled on
John's spirit like a chord of music. On one of the towers, the tallest,
the blackest at its base, an arrangement of exterior lights at the top
made a sort of floating fairyland—and as John gazed up in warm en-
chantment the faint acciaccare sound of violins drifted down in a
rococo harmony that was like nothing he had ever heard before.
Then in a moment the car stopped before wide, high marble steps
around which the night air was fragrant with a host of flowers. At
the top of the steps two great doors swung silently open and amber
light flooded out upon the darkness, silhouetting the figure of an
exquisite lady with black, high-piled hair, who held out her arms
toward them.

"Mother," Percy was saying, "this is my friend, John Unger, from
Hades."

Afterward John remembered that first night as a daze of many
colors, of quick sensory impressions, of music soft as a voice in love,
and of the beauty of things, lights and shadows, and motions and
faces. There was a white-haired man who stood drinking a many-
hued cordial from a crystal thimble set on a golden stem. There was
a girl with a flowery face, dressed like Titania with braided sapphires
in her hair. There was a room where the solid, soft gold of the walls
yielded to the pressure of his hand, and a room that was like a
platonic conception of the ultimate prison—ceiling, floor, and all, it

was lined with an unbroken mass of diamonds, diamonds of every size and shape, until, lit with tall violet lamps in the corners, it dazzled the eyes with a whiteness that could be compared only with itself, beyond human wish or dream.

Through a maze of these rooms the two boys wandered. Sometimes the floor under their feet would flame in brilliant patterns from lighting below, patterns of barbaric clashing colors, of pastel delicacy, of sheer whiteness, or of subtle and intricate mosaic, surely from some mosque on the Adriatic Sea. Sometimes beneath layers of thick crystal he would see blue or green water swirling, inhabited by vivid fish and growths of rainbow foliage. Then they would be treading on furs of every texture and color or along corridors of palest ivory, unbroken as though carved complete from the gigantic tusks of dinosaurs extinct before the age of man. . . .

Then a hazily remembered transition, and they were at dinner—where each plate was of two almost imperceptible layers of solid diamond between which was curiously worked a filigree of emerald design, a shaving sliced from green air. Music, plangent and unobtrusive, drifted down through far corridors—his chair, feathered and curved insidiously to his back, seemed to engulf and overpower him as he drank his first glass of port. He tried drowsily to answer a question that had been asked him, but the honeyed luxury that clasped his body added to the illusion of sleep—jewels, fabrics, wines, and metals blurred before his eyes into a sweet mist. . . .

"Yes," he replied with a polite effort, "it certainly is hot enough for me down there."

He managed to add a ghostly laugh; then, without movement, without resistance, he seemed to float off and away, leaving an iced dessert that was pink as a dream. . . . He fell asleep.

When he awoke he knew that several hours had passed. He was in a great quiet room with ebony walls and a dull illumination that was too faint, too subtle, to be called a light. His young host was standing over him.

"You fell asleep at dinner," Percy was saying. "I nearly did, too—it was such a treat to be comfortable again after this year of school. Servants undressed and bathed you while you were sleeping."

"Is this a bed or a cloud?" sighed John. "Percy, Percy—before you go, I want to apologize."

"For what?"

"For doubting you when you said you had a diamond as big as the Ritz-Carlton Hotel."

Percy smiled.

"I thought you didn't believe me. It's that mountain, you know."

"What mountain?"

"The mountain the château rests on. It's not very big. for a mountain. But except about fifty feet of sod and gravel on top it's solid diamond. *One* diamond, one cubic mile without a flaw. Aren't you listening? Say——"

But John T. Unger had again fallen asleep.

III

Morning. As he awoke he perceived drowsily that the room had at the same moment become dense with sunlight. The ebony panels of one wall had slid aside on a sort of track, leaving his chamber half open to the day. A large negro in a white uniform stood beside his bed.

"Good-evening," muttered John, summoning his brains from the wild places.

"Good-morning, sir. Are you ready for your bath, sir? Oh, don't get up—I'll put you in, if you'll just unbutton your pajamas—there. Thank you, sir."

John lay quietly as his pajamas were removed—he was amused and delighted; he expected to be lifted like a child by this black Gargantua who was tending him, but nothing of the sort happened; instead he felt the bed tilt up slowly on its side—he began to roll, startled at first, in the direction of the wall, but when he reached the wall its drapery gave way, and sliding two yards farther down a fleecy incline he plumped gently into water the same temperature as his body.

He looked about him. The runway or rollway on which he had arrived had folded gently back into place. He had been projected into another chamber and was sitting in a sunken bath with his head just above the level of the floor. All about him, lining the walls of the room and the sides and bottom of the bath itself, was a blue aquarium, and gazing through the crystal surface on which he sat, he could see fish swimming among amber lights and even gliding without curiosity past his outstretched toes, which were separated from them only by the thickness of the crystal. From overhead, sunlight came down through sea-green glass.

"I suppose, sir, that you'd like hot rosewater and soapsuds this morning, sir—and perhaps cold salt water to finish."

The negro was standing beside him.

"Yes," agreed John, smiling inanely, "as you please." Any idea of ordering this bath according to his own meagre standards of living would have been priggish and not a little wicked.

The negro pressed a button and a warm rain began to fall, apparently from overhead, but really, so John discovered after a moment, from a fountain arrangement near by. The water turned to a pale rose color and jets of liquid soap spurted into it from four miniature walrus heads at the corners of the bath. In a moment a dozen little paddle-wheels, fixed to the sides, had churned the mixture into a radiant rainbow of pink foam which enveloped him softly with its delicious lightness, and burst in shining, rosy bubbles here and there about him.

"Shall I turn on the moving-picture machine, sir?" suggested the negro deferentially. "There's a good one-reel comedy in this machine to-day, or I can put in a serious piece in a moment, if you prefer it."

"No, thanks," answered John, politely but firmly. He was enjoying his bath too much to desire any distraction. But distraction came. In a moment he was listening intently to the sound of flutes from just outside, flutes dripping a melody that was like a waterfall, cool and green as the room itself, accompanying a frothy piccolo, in play more fragile than the lace of suds that covered and charmed him.

After a cold salt-water bracer and a cold fresh finish, he stepped out and into a fleecy robe, and upon a couch covered with the same material he was rubbed with oil, alcohol, and spice. Later he sat in a voluptuous chair while he was shaved and his hair was trimmed.

"Mr. Percy is waiting in your sitting-room," said the negro, when these operations were finished. "My name is Gygsum, Mr. Unger, sir. I am to see to Mr. Unger every morning."

John walked out into the brisk sunshine of his living-room, where he found breakfast waiting for him and Percy, gorgeous in white kid knickerbockers, smoking in an easy chair.

IV

This is a story of the Washington family as Percy sketched it for John during breakfast.

The father of the present Mr. Washington had been a Virginian, a direct descendant of George Washington, and Lord Baltimore. At the close of the Civil War he was a twenty-five-year-old Colonel with a played-out plantation and about a thousand dollars in gold.

Fitz-Norman Culpepper Washington, for that was the young Colonel's name, decided to present the Virginia estate to his younger brother and go West. He selected two dozen of the most faithful blacks, who, of course, worshipped him, and bought twenty-five tickets to the West, where he intended to take out land in their names and start a sheep and cattle ranch.

When he had been in Montana for less than a month and things were going very poorly indeed, he stumbled on his great discovery. He had lost his way when riding in the hills, and after a day without food he began to grow hungry. As he was without his rifle, he was forced to pursue a squirrel, and in the course of the pursuit he noticed that it was carrying something shiny in its mouth. Just before it vanished into its hole—for Providence did not intend that this squirrel should alleviate his hunger—it dropped its burden. Sitting down to consider the situation Fitz-Norman's eye was caught by a gleam in the grass beside him. In ten seconds he had completely lost his appetite and gained one hundred thousand dollars. The squirrel, which had refused with annoying persistence to become food, had made him a present of a large and perfect diamond.

Late that night he found his way to camp and twelve hours later all the males among his darkies were back by the squirrel hole digging furiously at the side of the mountain. He told them he had discovered a rhinestone mine, and, as only one or two of them had ever seen even a small diamond before, they believed him, without question. When the magnitude of his discovery became apparent to him, he found himself in a quandary. The mountain was *a* diamond—it was literally nothing else but solid diamond. He filled four saddle bags full of glittering samples and started on horseback for St. Paul. There he managed to dispose of half a dozen small stones—when he tried a larger one a storekeeper fainted and Fitz-Norman was arrested as a public disturber. He escaped from jail and caught the train for New York, where he sold a few medium-sized diamonds and received in exchange about two hundred thousand dollars in gold. But he did not dare to produce any exceptional gems—in fact, he left New York just in time. Tremendous excitement had been created in jewelry circles, not so much by the size of his diamonds as by their appearance in the city from mysterious sources. Wild rumors became current that a diamond mine had been discovered in the Catskills, on the Jersey coast, on Long Island, beneath Washington Square. Excursion trains, packed with men carrying picks and shovels began to leave New York hourly, bound for various neighboring El Dorados. But by that time young Fitz-Norman was on his way back to Montana.

By the end of a fortnight he had estimated that the diamond in the mountain was approximately equal in quantity to all the rest of the diamonds known to exist in the world. There was no valuing it by any regular computation, however, for it was *one solid diamond*—and if it were offered for sale not only would the bottom fall out of the market, but also, if the value should vary with its size in the usual arithmetical progression, there would not be enough gold in the world to buy a tenth part of it. And what could any one do with a diamond that size?

It was an amazing predicament. He was, in one sense, the richest

man that ever lived—and yet was he worth anything at all? If his
secret should transpire there was no telling to what measures the
Government might resort in order to prevent a panic, in gold as well
as in jewels. They might take over the claim immediately and institute a monopoly.

There was no alternative—he must market his mountain in secret.
He sent South for his younger brother and put him in charge of his
colored following—darkies who had never realized that slavery was
abolished. To make sure of this, he read them a proclamation that
he had composed, which announced that General Forrest had reor-
ganized the shattered Southern armies and defeated the North in
one pitched battle. The negroes believed him implicitly. They passed
a vote declaring it a good thing and held revival services immediately.

Fitz-Norman himself set out for foreign parts with one hundred
thousand dollars and two trunks filled with rough diamonds of all
sizes. He sailed for Russia in a Chinese junk and six months after
his departure from Montana he was in St. Petersburg. He took obscure lodgings and called immediately upon the court jeweller, announcing that he had a diamond for the Czar. He remained in St.
Petersburg for two weeks, in constant danger of being murdered,
living from lodging to lodging, and afraid to visit his trunks more
than three or four times during the whole fortnight.

On his promise to return in a year with larger and finer stones, he
was allowed to leave for India. Before he left, however, the Court
Treasurers had deposited to his credit, in American banks, the sum
of fifteen million dollars—under four different aliases.

He returned to America in 1868, having been gone a little over
two years. He had visited the capitals of twenty-two countries and
talked with five emperors, eleven kings, three princes, a shah, a khan,
and a sultan. At that time Fitz-Norman estimated his own wealth
at one billion dollars. One fact worked consistently against the dis-
closure of his secret. No one of his larger diamonds remained in the
public eye for a week before being invested with a history of enough
fatalities, amours, revolutions, and wars to have occupied it from the
days of the first Babylonian Empire.

From 1870 until his death in 1900, the history of Fitz-Norman
Washington was a long epic in gold. There were side issues, of course
—he evaded the surveys, he married a Virginia lady, by whom he
had a single son, and he was compelled, due to a series of unfortunate
complications, to murder his brother, whose unfortunate habit of
drinking himself into an indiscreet stupor had several times endan-
gered their safety. But very few other murders stained these happy
years of progress and expansion.

Just before he died he changed his policy, and with all but a few million dollars of his outside wealth bought up rare minerals in bulk, which he deposited in the safety vaults of banks all over the world, marked as bric-à-brac. His son, Braddock Tarleton Washington, followed this policy on an even more tensive scale. The minerals were converted into the rarest of all elements—radium—so that the equivalent of a billion dollars in gold could be placed in a receptacle no bigger than a cigar box.

When Fitz-Norman had been dead three years his son, Braddock, decided that the business had gone far enough. The amount of wealth that he and his father had taken out of the mountain was beyond all exact computation. He kept a note-book in cipher in which he set down the approximate quantity of radium in each of the thousand banks he patronized, and recorded the alias under which it was held. Then he did a very simple thing—he sealed up the mine.

He sealed up the mine. What had been taken out of it would support all the Washingtons yet to be born in unparalleled luxury for generations. His one care must be the protection of his secret, lest in the possible panic attendant on its discovery he should be reduced with all the property-holders in the world to utter poverty.

This was the family among whom John T. Unger was staying. This was the story he heard in his silver-walled living-room the morning after his arrival.

V

After breakfast, John found his way out the great marble entrance, and looked curiously at the scene before him. The whole valley, from the diamond mountain to the steep granite cliff five miles away, still gave off a breath of golden haze which hovered idly above the fine sweep of lawns and lakes and gardens. Here and there clusters of elms made delicate groves of shade, contrasting strangely with the tough masses of pine forest that held the hills in a grip of dark-blue green. Even as John looked he saw three fawns in single file patter out from one clump about a half mile away and disappear with awkward gayety into the black-ribbed half-light of another. John would not have been surprised to see a goat-foot piping his way among the trees or to catch a glimpse of pink nymph-skin and flying yellow hair between the greenest of the green leaves.

In some such cool hope he descended the marble steps, disturbing faintly the sleep of two silky Russian wolfhounds at the bottom, and set off along a walk of white and blue brick that seemed to lead in no particular direction.

He was enjoying himself as much as he was able. It is youth's felicity as well as its insufficiency that it can never live in the present, but must always be measuring up the day against its own radiantly imagined future—flowers and gold, girls and stars, they are only pre-figurations and prophecies of that incomparable, unattainable young dream.

John rounded a soft corner where the massed rosebushes filled the air with heavy scent, and struck off across a park toward a patch of moss under some trees. He had never lain upon moss, and he wanted to see whether it was really soft enough to justify the use of its name as an adjective. Then he saw a girl coming toward him over the grass. She was the most beautiful person he had ever seen.

She was dressed in a white little gown that came just below her knees, and a wreath of mignonettes clasped with blue slices of sapphire bound up her hair. Her pink bare feet scattered the dew before them as she came. She was younger than John—not more than sixteen.

"Hello," she cried softly, "I'm Kismine."

She was much more than that to John already. He advanced toward her, scarcely moving as he drew near lest he should tread on her bare toes.

"You haven't met me," said her soft voice. Her blue eyes added, "Oh, but you've missed a great deal!" . . . "You met my sister, Jasmine, last night. I was sick with lettuce poisoning," went on her soft voice, and her eyes continued, "and when I'm sick I'm sweet—and when I'm well."

"You have made an enormous impression on me," said John's eyes, "and I'm not so slow myself"—"How do you do?" said his voice. "I hope you're better this morning."—"You darling," added his eyes tremulously.

John observed that they had been walking along the path. On her suggestion they sat down together upon the moss, the softness of which he failed to determine.

He was critical about women. A single defect—a thick ankle, a hoarse voice, a glass eye—was enough to make him utterly indifferent. And here for the first time in his life he was beside a girl who seemed to him the incarnation of physical perfection.

"Are you from the East?" asked Kismine with charming interest.

"No," answered John simply. "I'm from Hades."

Either she had never heard of Hades, or she could think of no pleasant comment to make upon it, for she did not discuss it further.

"I'm going East to school this fall," she said. "D'you think I'll like it? I'm going to New York to Miss Bulge's. It's very strict, but you see over the weekends I'm going to live at home with the family in our New York house, because father heard that the girls had to go walking two by two."

"Your father wants you to be proud," observed John.

"We are," she answered, her eyes shining with dignity. "None of us has ever been punished. Father said we never should be. Once when my sister Jasmine was a little girl she pushed him down-stairs and he just got up and limped away.

"Mother was—well, a little startled," continued Kismine, "when she heard that you were from—from where you *are* from, you know. She said that when she was a young girl—but then, you see, she's a Spaniard and old-fashioned."

"Do you spend much time out here?" asked John, to conceal the fact that he was somewhat hurt by this remark. It seemed an unkind allusion to his provincialism.

"Percy and Jasmine and I are here every summer, but next summer Jasmine is going to Newport. She's coming out in London a year from this fall. She'll be presented at court."

"Do you know," began John hesitantly, "you're much more sophisticated than I thought you were when I first saw you?"

"Oh, no, I'm not," she exclaimed hurriedly. "Oh, I wouldn't think of being. I think that sophisticated young people are *terribly* common, don't you? I'm not at all, really. If you say I am, I'm going to cry."

She was so distressed that her lip was trembling. John was impelled to protest:

"I didn't mean that; I only said it to tease you."

"Because I wouldn't mind if I *were*," she persisted "but I'm *not*. I'm very innocent and girlish. I never smoke, or drink, or read anything except poetry. I know scarcely any mathematics or chemistry. I dress *very* simply—in fact, I scarcely dress at all. I think sophisticated is the last thing you can say about me. I believe that girls ought to enjoy their youths in a wholesome way."

"I do too," said John heartily.

Kismine was cheerful again. She smiled at him, and a still-born tear dripped from the corner of one blue eye.

"I like you," she whispered, intimately. "Are you going to spend all your time with Percy while you're here, or will you be nice to me? Just think—I'm absolutely fresh ground. I've never had a boy in love with me in all my life. I've never been allowed even to *see* boys alone—except Percy. I came all the way out here into this grove hoping to run into you, where the family wouldn't be around."

Deeply flattered, John bowed from the hips as he had been taught at dancing school in Hades.

"We'd better go now," said Kismine sweetly. "I have to be with mother at eleven. You haven't asked me to kiss you once. I thought boys always did that nowadays."

John drew himself up proudly.

"Some of them do," he answered, "but not me. Girls don't do that sort of thing—in Hades."

Side by side they walked back toward the house.

VI

John stood facing Mr. Braddock Washington in the full sunlight. The elder man was about forty with a proud, vacuous face, intelligent eyes, and a robust figure. In the mornings he smelt of horses— the best horses. He carried a plain walking-stick of gray birch with a single large opal for a grip. He and Percy were showing John around.

"The slaves' quarters are there." His walking-stick indicated a cloister of marble on their left that ran in graceful Gothic along the side of the mountain. "In my youth I was distracted for a while from the business of life by a period of absurd idealism. During that time they lived in luxury. For instance, I equipped every one of their rooms with a tile bath."

"I suppose," ventured John, with an ingratiating laugh, "that they used the bathtubs to keep coal in. Mr. Schnlitzer-Murphy told me that once he——"

"The opinions of Mr. Schnlitzer-Murphy are of little importance, I should imagine," interrupted Braddock Washington, coldly. "My slaves did not keep coal in their bathtubs. They had orders to bathe every day, and they did. If they hadn't I might have ordered a sulphuric acid shampoo. I discontinued the baths for quite another reason. Several of them caught cold and died. Water is not good for certain races—except as a beverage."

John laughed, and then decided to nod his head in sober agreement. Braddock Washington made him uncomfortable.

"All these negroes are descendants of the ones my father brought North with him. There are about two hundred and fifty now. You notice that they've lived so long apart from the world that their original dialect has become an almost indistinguishable patois. We bring a few of them up to speak English—my secretary and two or three of the house servants.

"This is the golf course," he continued, as they strolled along the velvet winter grass. "It's all a green, you see—no fairway, no rough, no hazards."

He smiled pleasantly at John.

"Many men in the cage, father?" asked Percy suddenly.

Braddock Washington stumbled, and let forth an involuntary curse.

"One less than there should be," he ejaculated darkly—and then added after a moment, "We've had difficulties."

"Mother was telling me," exclaimed Percy, "that Italian teacher——"

"A ghastly error," said Braddock Washington angrily. "But of course there's a good chance that we may have got him. Perhaps he fell somewhere in the woods or stumbled over a cliff. And then there's always the probability that if he did get away his story wouldn't be believed. Nevertheless, I've had two dozen men looking for him in different towns around here."

"And no luck?"

"Some. Fourteen of them reported to my agent that they'd each killed a man answering to that description, but of course it was probably only the reward they were after——"

He broke off. They had come to a large cavity in the earth about the circumference of a merry-go-round and covered by a strong iron grating. Braddock Washington beckoned to John, and pointed his cane down through the grating. John stepped to the edge and gazed. Immediately his ears were assailed by a wild clamor from below.

"Come on down to Hell!"

"Hello, kiddo, how's the air up there?"

"Hey! Throw us a rope!"

"Got an old doughnut, Buddy, or a couple of second-hand sandwiches?"

"Say, fella, if you'll push down that guy you're with, we'll show you a quick disappearance scene."

"Paste him one for me, will you?"

It was too dark to see clearly into the pit below, but John could tell from the coarse optimism and rugged vitality of the remarks and voices that they proceeded from middle-class Americans of the more spirited type. Then Mr. Washington put out his cane and touched a button in the grass, and the scene below sprang into light.

"These are some adventurous mariners who had the misfortune to discover El Dorado," he remarked.

Below them there had appeared a large hollow in the earth shaped like the interior of a bowl. The sides were steep and apparently of polished glass, and on its slightly concave surface stood about two dozen men clad in the half costume, half uniform, of aviators. Their upturned faces, lit with wrath, with malice, with despair, with cynical humor, were covered by long growths of beard, but with the exception of a few who had pined perceptibly away, they seemed to be a well-fed, healthy lot.

Braddock Washington drew a garden chair to the edge of the pit and sat down.

"Well, how are you, boys?" he inquired genially.

A chorus of execration in which all joined except a few too dispirited to cry out, rose up into the sunny air, but Braddock Washington heard it with unruffled composure. When its last echo had died away he spoke again.

"Have you thought up a way out of your difficulty?"

From here and there among them a remark floated up.

"We decided to stay here for love!"

"Bring us up there and we'll find us a way!"

Braddock Washington waited until they were again quiet. Then he said:

"I've told you the situation. I don't want you here. I wish to heaven I'd never seen you. Your own curiosity got you here, and any time that you can think of a way out which protects me and my interests I'll be glad to consider it. But so long as you confine your efforts to digging tunnels—yes, I know about the new one you've started—you won't get very far. This isn't as hard on you as you make it out, with all your howling for the loved ones at home. If you were the type who worried much about the loved ones at home, you'd never have taken up aviation."

A tall man moved apart from the others, and held up his hand to call his captor's attention to what he was about to say.

"Let me ask you a few questions!" he cried. "You pretend to be a fair-minded man."

"How absurd. How could a man of *my* position be fair-minded toward *you*? You might as well speak of a Spaniard being fair-minded toward a piece of steak."

At this harsh observation the faces of the two dozen steaks fell, but the tall man continued:

"All right!" he cried. "We've argued this out before. You're not a humanitarian and you're not fair-minded, but you're human—at least you say you are—and you ought to be able to put yourself in our place for long enough to think how—how—how——"

"How what?" demanded Washington, coldly.

"—how unnecessary——"

"Not to me."

"Well,—how cruel——"

"We've covered that. Cruelty doesn't exist where self-preservation is involved. You've been soldiers: you know that. Try another."

"Well, then, how stupid."

"There," admitted Washington, "I grant you that. But try to think of an alternative. I've offered to have all or any of you painlessly executed if you wish. I've offered to have your wives, sweethearts, children, and mothers kidnapped and brought out here. I'll enlarge your place down there and feed and clothe you the rest of your lives. If there was some method of producing permanent amnesia I'd have all of you operated on and released immediately, somewhere outside of my preserves. But that's as far as my ideas go."

"How about trusting us not to peach on you?" cried some one.

"You don't proffer that suggestion seriously," said Washington, with an expression of scorn. "I did take out one man to teach my daughter Italian. Last week he got away."

A wild yell of jubilation went up suddenly from two dozen throats and a pandemonium of joy ensued. The prisoners clog-danced and cheered and yodled and wrestled with one another in a sudden up-rush of animal spirits. They even ran up the glass sides of the bowl as far as they could, and slid back to the bottom upon the natural cushions of their bodies. The tall man started a song in which they all joined——

> *"Oh, we'll hang the kaiser*
> *On a sour apple tree——"*

Braddock Washington sat in inscrutable silence until the song was over.

"You see," he remarked, when he could gain a modicum of atten-tion. "I bear you no ill-will. I like to see you enjoying yourselves. That's why I didn't tell you the whole story at once. The man—what was his name? Critchtichiello?—was shot by some of my agents in fourteen different places."

Not guessing that the places referred to were cities, the tumult of rejoicing subsided immediately.

"Nevertheless," cried Washington with a touch of anger, "he tried to run away. Do you expect me to take chances with any of you after an experience like that?"

Again a series of ejaculations went up.

"Sure!"

"Would your daughter like to learn Chinese?"

"Hey, I can speak Italian! My mother was a wop."

"Maybe she'd like t'learna speak N'Yawk!"

"If she's the little one with the big blue eyes I can teach her a lot of things better than Italian."

"I know some Irish songs—and I could hammer brass once't."

Mr. Washington reached forward suddenly with his cane and pushed the button in the grass so that the picture below went out instantly, and there remained only that great dark mouth covered dismally with the black teeth of the grating.

"Hey!" called a single voice from below, "you ain't goin' away without givin' us your blessing?"

But Mr. Washington, followed by the two boys, was already strolling on toward the ninth hole of the golf course, as though the pit and its contents were no more than a hazard over which his facile iron had triumphed with ease.

VII

July under the lee of the diamond mountain was a month of blanket nights and of warm, glowing days. John and Kismine were in love. He did not know that the little gold football (inscribed with the legend *Pro deo et patria et St. Mida*) which he had given her rested on a platinum chain next to her bosom. But it did. And she for her part was not aware that a large sapphire which had dropped one day from her simple coiffure was stowed away tenderly in John's jewel box.

Late one afternoon when the ruby and ermine music room was quiet, they spent an hour there together. He held her hand and she gave him such a look that he whispered her name aloud. She bent toward him—then hesitated.

"Did you say 'Kismine'?" she asked softly, "or——"

She had wanted to be sure. She thought she might have misunderstood.

Neither of them had ever kissed before, but in the course of an hour it seemed to make little difference.

The afternoon drifted away. That night when a last breath of music drifted down from the highest tower, they each lay awake, happily dreaming over the separate minutes of the day. They had decided to be married as soon as possible.

VIII

Every day Mr. Washington and the two young men went hunting or fishing in the deep forests or played golf around the somnolent course—games which John diplomatically allowed his host to win—or swam in the mountain coolness of the lake. John found Mr. Washington a somewhat exacting personality—utterly uninterested in any ideas or opinions except his own. Mrs. Washington was aloof and reserved at all times. She was apparently indifferent to her two daughters, and entirely absorbed in her son Percy, with whom she held interminable conversations in rapid Spanish at dinner.

Jasmine, the elder daughter, resembled Kismine in appearance—except that she was somewhat bow-legged, and terminated in large hands and feet—but was utterly unlike her in temperament. Her favorite books had to do with poor girls who kept house for widowed fathers. John learned from Kismine that Jasmine had never recovered from the shock and disappointment caused her by the termination of the World War, just as she was about to start for Europe as a canteen expert. She had even pined away for a time, and Braddock Washington had taken steps to promote a new war in the Balkans—but she had seen a photograph of some wounded Serbian soldiers and lost interest in the whole proceedings. But Percy and Kismine seemed to have inherited the arrogant attitude in all its harsh magnificence from their father. A chaste and consistent selfishness ran like a pattern through their every idea.

John was enchanted by the wonders of the château and the valley. Braddock Washington, so Percy told him, had caused to be kidnapped a landscape gardener, an architect, a designer of stage settings, and a French decadent poet left over from the last century. He had put his entire force of negroes at their disposal, guaranteed to supply them with any materials that the world could offer, and left them to work out some ideas of their own. But one by one they had shown their uselessness. The decadent poet had at once begun bewailing his separation from the boulevards in spring—he made some vague remarks about spices, apes, and ivories, but said nothing that was of any practical value. The stage designer on his part wanted to make the whole valley a series of tricks and sensational effects—a state of things that the Washingtons would soon have grown tired of. And as for the architect and the landscape gardener, they thought only in terms of convention. They must make this like this and that like that.

But they had, at least, solved the problem of what was to be done with them—they all went mad early one morning after spending the night in a single room trying to agree upon the location of a fountain, and were now confined comfortably in an insane asylum at Westport, Connecticut.

"But," inquired John curiously, "who did plan all your wonderful reception rooms and halls, and approaches and bathrooms——?"

"Well," answered Percy, "I blush to tell you, but it was a moving-picture fella. He was the only man we found who was used to playing with an unlimited amount of money, though he did tuck his napkin in his collar and couldn't read or write."

As August drew to a close John began to regret that he must soon go back to school. He and Kismine had decided to elope the following June.

"It would be nicer to be married here," Kismine confessed, "but of course I could never get father's permission to marry you at all. Next to that I'd rather elope. It's terrible for wealthy people to be married in America at present—they always have to send out bulletins to the press saying that they're going to be married in remnants, when what they mean is just a peck of old second-hand pearls and some used lace worn once by the Empress Eugénie."

"I know," agreed John fervently. "When I was visiting the Schnlitzer-Murphys, the eldest daughter, Gwendolyn, married a man whose father owns half of West Virginia. She wrote home saying what a tough struggle she was carrying on on his salary as a bank clerk—and then she ended up by saying that 'Thank God, I have four good maids anyhow, and that helps a little.' "

"It's absurd," commented Kismine. "Think of the millions and millions of people in the world, laborers and all, who get along with only two maids."

One afternoon late in August a chance remark of Kismine's changed the face of the entire situation, and threw John into a state of terror.

They were in their favorite grove, and between kisses John was indulging in some romantic forebodings which he fancied added poignancy to their relations.

"Sometimes I think we'll never marry," he said sadly. "You're too wealthy, too magnificent. No one as rich as you are can be like other girls. I should marry the daughter of some well-to-do wholesale hardware man from Omaha or Sioux City, and be content with her half-million."

"I knew the daughter of a wholesale hardware man once," remarked Kismine. "I don't think you'd have been contented with her. She was a friend of my sister's. She visited here."

"Oh, then you've had other guests?" exclaimed John in surprise.

Kismine seemed to regret her words.

"Oh, yes," she said hurriedly, "we've had a few."

"But aren't you—wasn't your father afraid they'd talk outside?"

"Oh, to some extent, to some extent," she answered. "Let's talk about something pleasanter."

But John's curiosity was aroused.

"Something pleasanter!" he demanded. "What's unpleasant about that? Weren't they nice girls?"

To his great surprise Kismine began to weep.

"Yes—th—that's the—the whole t-trouble. I grew qu-quite attached to some of them. So did Jasmine, but she kept inv-viting them anyway. I couldn't under*stand* it."

A dark suspicion was born in John's heart.

"Do you mean that they *told*, and your father had them—removed?"

"Worse than that," she muttered brokenly. "Father took no chances—and Jasmine kept writing them to come, and they had *such* a good time!"

She was overcome by a paroxysm of grief.

Stunned with the horror of this revelation, John sat there open-mouthed, feeling the nerves of his body twitter like so many sparrows perched upon his spinal column.

"Now, I've told you, and I shouldn't have," she said, calming suddenly and drying her dark blue eyes.

"Do you mean to say that your father had them *murdered* before they left?"

She nodded.

"In August usually—or early in September. It's only natural for us to get all the pleasure out of them that we can first."

"How abominable! How—why, I must be going crazy! Did you really admit that——"

"I did," interrupted Kismine, shrugging her shoulders. "We can't very well imprison them like those aviators, where they'd be a continual reproach to us every day. And it's always been made easier for Jasmine and me, because father had it done sooner than we expected. In that way we avoided any farewell scene——"

"So you murdered them! Uh!" cried John.

"It was done very nicely. They were drugged while they were asleep—and their families were always told that they died of scarlet fever in Butte."

"But—I fail to understand why you kept on inviting them!"

"I didn't," burst out Kismine. "I never invited one. Jasmine did. And they always had a very good time. She'd give them the nicest presents toward the last. I shall probably have visitors too—I'll harden up to it. We can't let such an inevitable thing as death stand in the way of enjoying life while we have it. Think how lonesome it'd be out here if we never had *any* one. Why, father and mother have sacrificed some of their best friends just as we have."

"And so," cried John accusingly, "and so you were letting me make love to you and pretending to return it, and talking about marriage, all the time knowing perfectly well that I'd never get out of here alive——"

"No," she protested passionately. "Not any more. I did at first. You were here. I couldn't help that, and I thought your last days might as well be pleasant for both of us. But then I fell in love with you, and—and I'm honestly sorry you're going to—going to be put away—though I'd rather you'd be put away than ever kiss another girl."

"Oh, you would, would you?" cried John ferociously.

"Much rather. Besides, I've always heard that a girl can have more fun with a man whom she knows she can never marry. Oh, why did I tell you? I've probably spoiled your whole good time now, and we were really enjoying things when you didn't know it. I knew it would make things sort of depressing for you."

"Oh, you did, did you?" John's voice trembled with anger. "I've heard about enough of this. If you haven't any more pride and decency than to have an affair with a fellow that you know isn't much better than a corpse, I don't want to have any more to do with you!"

"You're not a corpse!" she protested in horror. "You're not a corpse! I won't have you saying that I kissed a corpse!"

"I said nothing of the sort!"

"You did! You said I kissed a corpse!"

"I didn't!"

Their voices had risen, but upon a sudden interruption they both subsided into immediate silence. Footsteps were coming along the path in their direction, and a moment later the rose bushes were parted displaying Braddock Washington, whose intelligent eyes set in his good-looking vacuous face were peering in at them.

"Who kissed a corpse?" he demanded in obvious disapproval.

"Nobody," answered Kismine quickly. "We were just joking."

"What are you two doing here, anyhow?" he demanded gruffly. "Kismine, you ought to be—to be reading or playing golf with your sister. Go read! Go play golf! Don't let me find you here when I come back!"

Then he bowed at John and went up the path.

"See?" said Kismine crossly, when he was out of hearing. "You've spoiled it all. We can never meet any more. He won't let me meet you. He'd have you poisoned if he thought we were in love."

"We're not, any more!" cried John fiercely, "so he can set his mind at rest upon that. Moreover, don't fool yourself that I'm going to stay around here. Inside of six hours I'll be over those mountains, if I have to gnaw a passage through them, and on my way East."

They had both got to their feet, and at this remark Kismine came close and put her arm through his.

"I'm going, too."

"You must be crazy——"

"Of course I'm going," she interrupted impatiently.

"You most certainly are not. You——"

"Very well," she said quietly, "we'll catch up with father now and talk it over with him."

Defeated, John mustered a sickly smile.

"Very well, dearest," he agreed, with pale and unconvincing affection, "we'll go together."

His love for her returned and settled placidly on his heart. She was his—she would go with him to share his dangers. He put his arms about her and kissed her fervently. After all she loved him; she had saved him, in fact.

Discussing the matter, they walked slowly back toward the château. They decided that since Braddock Washington had seen them together they had best depart the next night. Nevertheless, John's lips were unusually dry at dinner, and he nervously emptied a great spoonful of peacock soup into his left lung. He had to be carried into the turquoise and sable card-room and pounded on the back by one of the under-butlers, which Percy considered a great joke.

IX

Long after midnight John's body gave a nervous jerk, and he sat suddenly upright, staring into the veils of somnolence that draped the room. Through the squares of blue darkness that were his open windows, he had heard a faint far-away sound that died upon a bed of wind before identifying itself on his memory, clouded with uneasy dreams. But the sharp noise that had succeeded it was nearer, was just outside the room—the click of a turned knob, a footstep, a whisper, he could not tell; a hard lump gathered in the pit of his stomach, and his whole body ached in the moment that he strained agonizingly to hear. Then one of the veils seemed to dissolve, and he saw a vague figure standing by the door, a figure only faintly limned and blocked in upon the darkness, mingled so with the folds of the drapery as to seem distorted, like a reflection seen in a dirty pane of glass.

With a sudden movement of fright or resolution John pressed the button by his bedside, and the next moment he was sitting in the green sunken bath of the adjoining room, waked into alertness by the shock of the cold water which half filled it.

He sprang out, and, his wet pajamas scattering a heavy trickle of water behind him, ran for the aquamarine door which he knew led out onto the ivory landing of the second floor. The door opened noiselessly. A single crimson lamp burning in a great dome above lit the magnificent sweep of the carved stairways with a poignant beauty. For a moment John hesitated, appalled by the silent splendor massed about him, seeming to envelop in its gigantic folds and contours the solitary drenched little figure shivering upon the ivory landing. Then simultaneously two things happened. The door of his own sitting-

room swung open, precipitating three naked negroes into the hall—
and, as John swayed in wild terror toward the stairway, another
door slid back in the wall on the other side of the corridor, and John
saw Braddock Washington standing in the lighted lift, wearing a fur
coat and a pair of riding boots which reached to his knees and displayed, above, the glow of his rose-colored pajamas.

On the instant the three negroes—John had never seen any of them
before, and it flashed through his mind that they must be the professional executioners—paused in their movement toward John, and
turned expectantly to the man in the lift, who burst out with an im-
perious command:

"Get in here! All three of you! Quick as hell!"

Then, within the instant, the three negroes darted into the cage,
the oblong of light was blotted out as the lift door slid shut, and
John was again alone in the hall. He slumped weakly down against
an ivory stair.

It was apparent that something portentous had occurred, something which, for the moment at least, had postponed his own petty
disaster. What was it? Had the negroes risen in revolt? Had the
aviators forced aside the iron bars of the grating? Or had the men of
Fish stumbled blindly through the hills and gazed with bleak, joyless
eyes upon the gaudy valley? John did not know. He heard a faint
whir of air as the lift whizzed up again, and then, a moment later,
as it descended. It was probable that Percy was hurrying to his
father's assistance, and it occurred to John that this was his opportunity to join Kismine and plan an immediate escape. He waited
until the lift had been silent for several minutes; shivering a little
with the night cool that whipped in through his wet pajamas, he returned to his room and dressed himself quickly. Then he mounted a
long flight of stairs and turned down the corridor carpeted with Russian sable which led to Kismine's suite.

The door of her sitting-room was open and the lamps were lighted.
Kismine, in an angora kimono, stood near the window of the room in
a listening attitude, and as John entered noiselessly, she turned
toward him.

"Oh, it's you!" she whispered, crossing the room to him. "Did you
hear them?"

"I heard your father's slaves in my——"

"No," she interrupted excitedly. "Aeroplanes!"

"Aeroplanes? Perhaps that was the sound that woke me."

"There're at least a dozen. I saw one a few moments ago dead
against the moon. The guard back by the cliff fired his rifle and that's
what roused father. We're going to open on them right away."

"Are they here on purpose?"

"Yes—it's that Italian who got away——"

Simultaneously with her last word, a succession of sharp cracks tumbled in through the open window. Kismine uttered a little cry, took a penny with fumbling fingers from a box on her dresser, and ran to one of the electric lights. In an instant the entire château was in darkness—she had blown out the fuse.

"Come on!" she cried to him. "We'll go up to the roof garden, and watch it from there!"

Drawing a cape about her, she took his hand, and they found their way out the door. It was only a step to the tower lift, and as she pressed the button that shot them upward he put his arms around her in the darkness and kissed her mouth. Romance had come to John Unger at last. A minute later they had stepped out upon the star-white platform. Above, under the misty moon, sliding in and out of the patches of cloud that eddied below it, floated a dozen dark-winged bodies in a constant circling course. From here and there in the valley flashes of fire leaped toward them, followed by sharp detonations. Kismine clapped her hands with pleasure, which a moment later, turned to dismay as the aeroplanes at some pre-arranged signal, began to release their bombs and the whole of the valley became a panorama of deep reverberate sound and lurid light.

Before long the aim of the attackers became concentrated upon the points where the anti-aircraft guns were situated, and one of them was almost immediately reduced to a giant cinder to lie smouldering in a park of rose bushes.

"Kismine," begged John, "you'll be glad when I tell you that this attack came on the eve of my murder. If I hadn't heard that guard shoot off his gun back by the pass I should now be stone dead——"

"I can't hear you!" cried Kismine, intent on the scene before her. "You'll have to talk louder!"

"I simply said," shouted John, "that we'd better get out before they begin to shell the Château!"

Suddenly the whole portico of the negro quarters cracked asunder, a geyser of flame shot up from under the colonnades, and great fragments of jagged marble were hurled as far as the borders of the lake.

"There go fifty thousand dollars' worth of slaves," cried Kismine, "at prewar prices. So few Americans have any respect for property."

John renewed his efforts to compel her to leave. The aim of the aeroplanes was becoming more precise minute by minute, and only two of the anti-aircraft guns were still retaliating. It was obvious that the garrison, encircled with fire, could not hold out much longer.

"Come on!" cried John, pulling Kismine's arm, "we've got to

go. Do you realize that those aviators will kill you without question if they find you?"

She consented reluctantly.

"We'll have to wake Jasmine!" she said, as they hurried toward the lift. Then she added in a sort of childish delight: "We'll be poor, won't we? Like people in books. And I'll be an orphan and utterly free. Free and poor! What fun!" She stopped and raised her lips to him in a delighted kiss.

"It's impossible to be both together," said John grimly. "People have found that out. And I should choose to be free as preferable of the two. As an extra caution you'd better dump the contents of your jewel box into your pockets."

Ten minutes later the two girls met John in the dark corridor and they descended to the main floor of the château. Passing for the last time through the magnificence of the splendid halls, they stood for a moment out on the terrace, watching the burning negro quarters and the flaming embers of two planes which had fallen on the other side of the lake. A solitary gun was still keeping up a sturdy popping, and the attackers seemed timorous about descending lower, but sent their thunderous fireworks in a circle around it, until any chance shot might annihilate its Ethiopian crew.

John and the two sisters passed down the marble steps, turned sharply to the left, and began to ascend a narrow path that wound like a garter about the diamond mountain. Kismine knew a heavily wooded spot half-way up where they could lie concealed and yet be able to observe the wild night in the valley—finally to make an escape, when it should be necessary, along a secret path laid in a rocky gully.

X

It was three o'clock when they attained their destination. The obliging and phlegmatic Jasmine fell off to sleep immediately, leaning against the trunk of a large tree, while John and Kismine sat, his arm around her, and watched the desperate ebb and flow of the dying battle among the ruins of a vista that had been a garden spot that morning. Shortly after four o'clock the last remaining gun gave out a clanging sound and went out of action in a swift tongue of red smoke. Though the moon was down, they saw that the flying bodies were circling closer to the earth. When the planes had made certain that the beleaguered possessed no further resources, they would land and the dark and glittering reign of the Washingtons would be over.

With the cessation of the firing the valley grew quiet. The embers of the two aeroplanes glowed like the eyes of some monster crouching in the grass. The château stood dark and silent, beautiful without light as it had been beautiful in the sun, while the woody rattles of Nemesis filled the air above with a growing and receding complaint. Then John perceived that Kismine, like her sister, had fallen sound asleep.

It was long after four when he became aware of footsteps along the path they had lately followed, and he waited in breathless silence until the persons to whom they belonged had passed the vantage-point he occupied. There was a faint stir in the air now that was not of human origin, and the dew was cold; he knew that the dawn would break soon. John waited until the steps had gone a safe distance up the mountain and were inaudible. Then he followed. About half-way to the steep summit the trees fell away and a hard saddle of rock spread itself over the diamond beneath. Just before he reached this point he slowed down his pace, warned by an animal sense that there was life just ahead of him. Coming to a high boulder, he lifted his head gradually above its edge. His curiosity was rewarded; this is what he saw:

Braddock Washington was standing there motionless, silhouetted against the gray sky without sound or sign of life. As the dawn came up out of the east, lending a cold green color to the earth, it brought the solitary figure into insignificant contrast with the new day.

While John watched, his host remained for a few moments absorbed in some inscrutable contemplation; then he signalled to the two negroes who crouched at his feet to lift the burden which lay between them. As they struggled upright, the first yellow beam of the sun struck through the innumerable prisms of an immense and exquisitely chiselled diamond—and a white radiance was kindled that glowed upon the air like a fragment of the morning star. The bearers staggered beneath its weight for a moment—then their rippling muscles caught and hardened under the wet shine of the skins and the three figures were again motionless in their defiant impotency before the heavens.

After a while the white man lifted his head and slowly raised his arms in a gesture of attention, as one who would call a great crowd to hear—but there was no crowd, only the vast silence of the mountain and the sky, broken by faint bird voices down among the trees. The figure on the saddle of rock began to speak ponderously and with an inextinguishable pride.

"You out there—" he cried in a trembling voice. "You—there—!" He paused, his arms still uplifted, his head held attentively as though he were expecting an answer. John strained his eyes to see whether there might be men coming down the mountain, but the mountain was bare of human life. There was only sky and a mocking flute of wind along the tree-tops. Could Washington be praying? For a moment John wondered. Then the illusion passed—there was something in the man's whole attitude antithetical to prayer.

"Oh, you above there!"

The voice was become strong and confident. This was no forlorn supplication. If anything, there was in it a quality of monstrous condescension.

"You there——"

Words, too quickly uttered to be understood, flowing one into the other. . . . John listened breathlessly, catching a phrase here and there, while the voice broke off, resumed, broke off again—now strong and argumentative, now colored with a slow, puzzled impatience. Then a conviction commenced to dawn on the single listener, and as realization crept over him a spray of quick blood rushed through his arteries. Braddock Washington was offering a bribe to God!

That was it—there was no doubt. The diamond in the arms of his slaves was some advance sample, a promise of more to follow.

That, John perceived after a time, was the thread running through his sentences. Prometheus Enriched was calling to witness forgotten sacrifices, forgotten rituals, prayers obsolete before the birth of Christ. For a while his discourse took the form of reminding God of this gift or that which Divinity had deigned to accept from men— great churches if he would rescue cities from the plague, gifts of myrrh and gold, of human lives and beautiful women and captive armies, of children and queens, of beasts of the forest and field, sheep and goats, harvests and cities, whole conquered lands that had been offered up in lust or blood for His appeasal, buying a meed's worth of alleviation from the Divine wrath—and now he, Braddock Washington, Emperor of Diamonds, king and priest of the age of gold, arbiter of splendor and luxury, would offer up a treasure such as princes before him had never dreamed of, offer it up not in suppliance, but in pride.

He would give to God, he continued, getting down to specifications, the greatest diamond in the world. This diamond would be cut with many more thousand facets than there were leaves on a tree, and yet the whole diamond would be shaped with the perfection of a stone no bigger than a fly. Many men would work upon it for many years. It would be set in a great dome of beaten gold, wonderfully carved and equipped with gates of opal and crusted sapphire. In the middle would be hollowed out a chapel presided over by an altar of iridescent, decomposing, ever-changing radium which would burn out the eyes of any worshipper who lifted up his head from prayer—and on this altar there would be slain for the amusement of the Divine

Benefactor any victim He should choose, even though it should be the greatest and most powerful man alive.

In return he asked only a simple thing, a thing that for God would be absurdly easy—only that matters should be as they were yesterday at this hour and that they should so remain. So very simple! Let but the heavens open, swallowing these men and their aeroplanes—and then close again. Let him have his slaves once more, restored to life and well.

There was no one else with whom he had ever needed to treat or bargain.

He doubted only whether he had made his bribe big enough. God had His price, of course. God was made in man's image, so it had been said: He must have His price. And the price would be rare—no cathedral whose building consumed many years, no pyramid constructed by ten thousand workmen, would be like this cathedral, this pyramid.

He paused here. That was his proposition. Everything would be up to specifications and there was nothing vulgar in his assertion that it would be cheap at the price. He implied that Providence could take it or leave it.

As he approached the end his sentences became broken, became short and uncertain, and his body seemed tense, seemed strained to catch the slightest pressure or whisper of life in the spaces around him. His hair had turned gradually white as he talked, and now he lifted his head high to the heavens like a prophet of old—magnificently mad.

Then, as John stared in giddy fascination, it seemed to him that a curious phenomenon took place somewhere around him. It was as though the sky had darkened for an instant, as though there had been a sudden murmur in a gust of wind, a sound of far-away trumpets, a sighing like the rustle of a great silken robe—for a time the whole of nature round about partook of this darkness: the birds' song ceased; the trees were still, and far over the mountain there was a mutter of dull, menacing thunder.

That was all. The wind died along the tall grasses of the valley. The dawn and the day resumed their place in a time, and the risen sun sent hot waves of yellow mist that made its path bright before it. The leaves laughed in the sun, and their laughter shook the trees until each bough was like a girl's school in fairyland. God had refused to accept the bribe.

For another moment John watched the triumph of the day. Then, turning, he saw a flutter of brown down by the lake, then another flutter, then another, like the dance of golden angels alighting from the clouds. The aeroplanes had come to earth.

John slid off the boulder and ran down the side of the mountain to the clump of trees, where the two girls were awake and waiting for him. Kismine sprang to her feet, the jewels in her pockets jingling, a question on her parted lips, but instinct told John that there was no time for words. They must get off the mountain without losing a moment. He seized a hand of each, and in silence they threaded the tree-trunks, washed with light now and with the rising mist. Behind them from the valley came no sound at all, except the complaint of the peacocks far away and the pleasant undertone of morning.

When they had gone about half a mile, they avoided the park land and entered a narrow path that led over the next rise of ground. At the highest point of this they paused and turned around. Their eyes rested upon the mountainside they had just left—oppressed by some dark sense of tragic impendency.

Clear against the sky a broken, white-haired man was slowly descending the steep slope, followed by two gigantic and emotionless negroes, who carried a burden between them which still flashed and glittered in the sun. Half-way down two other figures joined them— John could see that they were Mrs. Washington and her son, upon whose arm she leaned. The aviators had clambered from their machines to the sweeping lawn in front of the château, and with rifles in hand were starting up the diamond mountain in skirmishing formation.

But the little group of five which had formed farther up and was engrossing all the watchers' attention had stopped upon a ledge of rock. The negroes stooped and pulled up what appeared to be a trap-door in the side of the mountain. Into this they all disappeared, the white-haired man first, then his wife and son, finally the two negroes, the glittering tips of whose jeweled head-dresses caught the sun for a moment before the trap-door descended and engulfed them all.

Kismine clutched John's arm.

"Oh," she cried wildly, "where are they going? What are they going to do?"

"It must be some underground way of escape——"

A little scream from the two girls interrupted his sentence.

"Don't you see?" sobbed Kismine hysterically. "The mountain is wired!"

Even as she spoke John put up his hands to shield his sight. Before their eyes the whole surface of the mountain had changed suddenly to a dazzling burning yellow, which showed up through the jacket of turf as light shows through a human hand. For a moment the intolerable glow continued, and then like an extinguished filament it disappeared, revealing a black waste from which blue smoke arose slowly, carrying off with it what remained of vegetation and of human flesh. Of the aviators there was left neither blood nor bone—they were consumed as completely as the five souls who had gone inside.

Simultaneously, and with an immense concussion, the château literally threw itself into the air, bursting into flaming fragments as it rose, and then tumbling back upon itself in a smoking pile that lay projecting half into the water of the lake. There was no fire—what smoke there was drifted off mingling with the sunshine, and for a few minutes longer a powdery dust of marble drifted from the great featureless pile that had once been the house of jewels. There was no more sound and the three people were alone in the valley.

XI

At sunset John and his two companions reached the high cliff which had marked the boundaries of the Washingtons' dominion, and looking back found the valley tranquil and lovely in the dusk. They sat down to finish the food which Jasmine had brought with her in a basket.

"There!" she said, as she spread the table-cloth and put the sandwiches in a neat pile upon it. "Don't they look tempting? I always think that food tastes better outdoors."

"With that remark," remarked Kismine, "Jasmine enters the middle class."

"Now," said John eagerly, "turn out your pocket and let's see what jewels you brought along. If you made a good selection we three ought to live comfortably all the rest of our lives."

Obediently Kismine put her hand in her pocket and tossed two handfuls of glittering stones before him.

"Not so bad," cried John, enthusiastically. "They aren't very big, but—Hello!" His expression changed as he held one of them up to the declining sun. "Why, these aren't diamonds! There's something the matter!"

"By golly!" exclaimed Kismine, with a startled look. "What an idiot I am!"

"Why, these are rhinestones!" cried John.

"I know." She broke into a laugh. "I opened the wrong drawer. They belonged on the dress of a girl who visited Jasmine. I got her to give them to me in exchange for diamonds. I'd never seen anything but precious stones before."

"And this is what you brought?"

"I'm afraid so." She fingered the brilliants wistfully. "I think I like these better. I'm a little tired of diamonds."

"Very well," said John gloomily. "We'll have to live in Hades. And you will grow old telling incredulous women that you got the wrong

drawer. Unfortunately your father's bank-books were consumed with
him."

"Well, what's the matter with Hades?"

"If I come home with a wife at my age my father is just as liable
as not to cut me off with a hot coal, as they say down there."

Jasmine spoke up.

"I love washing," she said quietly. "I have always washed my own
handkerchiefs. I'll take in laundry and support you both."

"Do they have washwomen in Hades?" asked Kismine innocently.

"Of course," answered John. "It's just like anywhere else."

"I thought—perhaps it was too hot to wear any clothes."

John laughed.

"Just try it!" he suggested. "They'll run you out before you're
half started."

"Will father be there?" she asked.

John turned to her in astonishment.

"Your father is dead," he replied somberly. "Why should he go to
Hades? You have it confused with another place that was abolished
long ago."

After supper they folded up the table-cloth and spread their
blankets for the night.

"What a dream it was," Kismine sighed, gazing up at the stars.
"How strange it seems to be here with one dress and a penniless
fiancé!"

"Under the stars," she repeated. "I never noticed the stars before.
I always thought of them as great big diamonds that belonged to
some one. Now they frighten me. They make me feel that it was all
a dream, all my youth."

"It *was* a dream," said John quietly. "Everybody's youth is a
dream, a form of chemical madness."

"How pleasant then to be insane!"

"So I'm told," said John gloomily. "I don't know any longer. At
any rate, let us love for a while, for a year or so, you and me. That's
a form of divine drunkenness that we can all try. There are only
diamonds in the whole world, diamonds and perhaps the shabby gift
of disillusion. Well, I have that last and I will make the usual nothing
of it." He shivered. "Turn up your coat collar, little girl, the night's
full of chill and you'll get pneumonia. His was a great sin who first
invented consciousness. Let us lose it for a few hours."

So wrapping himself in his blanket he fell off to sleep.

BERNICE BOBS HER HAIR

AFTER DARK on Saturday night one could stand on the first tee of the golf-course and see the country-club windows as a yellow expanse over a very black and wavy ocean. The waves of this ocean, so to speak, were the heads of many curious caddies, a few of the more ingenious chauffeurs, the golf professional's deaf sister—and there were usually several stray, diffident waves who might have rolled inside had they so desired. This was the gallery.

The balcony was inside. It consisted of the circle of wicker chairs that lined the wall of the combination clubroom and ballroom. At these Saturday-night dances it was largely feminine; a great babel of middle-aged ladies with sharp eyes and icy hearts behind lorgnettes and large bosoms. The main function of the balcony was critical. It occasionally showed grudging admiration, but never approval, for it is well known among ladies over thirty-five that when the younger set dance in the summer-time it is with the very worst intentions in the world, and if they are not bombarded with stony eyes stray couples will dance weird barbaric interludes in the corners, and the more popular, more dangerous, girls will sometimes be kissed in the parked limousines of unsuspecting dowagers.

But, after all, this critical circle is not close enough to the stage to see the actors' faces and catch the subtler byplay. It can only frown and lean, ask questions and make satisfactory deductions from its set of postulates, such as the one which states that every young man with a large income leads the life of a hunted partridge. It never really appreciates the drama of the shifting, semicruel world of adolescence. No; boxes, orchestra-circle, principals, and chorus are represented by the medley of faces and voices that sway to the plaintive African rhythm of Dyer's dance orchestra.

From sixteen-year-old Otis Ormonde, who has two more years at Hill School, to G. Reece Stoddard, over whose bureau at home hangs a Harvard law diploma; from little Madeleine Hogue, whose hair still feels strange and uncomfortable on top of her head, to Bessie MacRae, who has been the life of the party a little too long—more than ten years—the medley is not only the centre of the stage but contains the only people capable of getting an unobstructed view of it.

With a flourish and a bang the music stops. The couples exchange artificial, effortless smiles, facetiously repeat *"la*-de-*da-da* dum-*dum,"* and then the clatter of young feminine voices soars over the burst of clapping.

A few disappointed stags caught in midfloor as they had been about to cut in subsided listlessly back to the walls, because this was not like the riotous Christmas dances—these summer hops were considered just pleasantly warm and exciting, where even the younger marrieds rose and performed ancient waltzes and terrifying fox trots to the tolerant amusement of their younger brothers and sisters.

Warren McIntyre, who casually attended Yale, being one of the unfortunate stags, felt in his dinner-coat pocket for a cigarette and strolled out onto the wide, semidark veranda, where couples were scattered at tables, filling the lantern-hung night with vague words and hazy laughter. He nodded here and there at the less absorbed and as he passed each couple some half-forgotten fragment of a story played in his mind, for it was not a large city and every one was Who's Who to every one else's past. There, for example, were Jim Strain and Ethel Demorest, who had been privately engaged for three years. Every one knew that as soon as Jim managed to hold a job for more than two months she would marry him. Yet how bored they both looked, and how wearily Ethel regarded Jim sometimes, as if she wondered why she had trained the vines of her affection on such a wind-shaken poplar.

Warren was nineteen and rather pitying with those of his friends who hadn't gone East to college. But, like most boys, he bragged tremendously about the girls of his city when he was away from it. There was Genevieve Ormonde, who regularly made the rounds of dances, house-parties, and football games at Princeton, Yale, Williams, and Cornell; there was black-eyed Roberta Dillon, who was quite as famous to her own generation as Hiram Johnson or Ty Cobb; and, of course, there was Marjorie Harvey, who besides having a fairylike face and a dazzling, bewildering tongue was already justly celebrated for having turned five cart-wheels in succession during the past pump-and-slipper dance at New Haven.

Warren, who had grown up across the street from Marjorie, had long been "crazy about her." Sometimes she seemed to reciprocate his feeling with a faint gratitude, but she had tried him by her infallible test and informed him gravely that she did not love him. Her test was that when she was away from him she forgot him and had affairs with other boys. Warren found this discouraging, especially as Marjorie had been making little trips all summer, and for the first two or three days after each arrival home he saw great heaps of mail on the Harveys' hall table addressed to her in various masculine handwritings. To make matters worse, all during the month of August she had been visited by her cousin Bernice from Eau Claire, and it seemed impossible to see her alone. It was always necessary to hunt round and find some one to take care of Bernice. As August waned this was becoming more and more difficult.

Much as Warren worshipped Marjorie, he had to admit that Cousin Bernice was sorta dopeless. She was pretty, with dark hair and high color, but she was no fun on a party. Every Saturday night he danced a long arduous duty dance with her to please Marjorie, but he had never been anything but bored in her company.

"Warren"—a soft voice at his elbow broke in upon his thoughts, and he turned to see Marjorie, flushed and radiant as usual. She laid a hand on his shoulder and a glow settled almost imperceptibly over him.

"Warren," she whispered, "do something for me—dance with Bernice. She's been stuck with little Otis Ormonde for almost an hour."

Warren's glow faded.

"Why—sure," he answered half-heartedly.

"You don't mind, do you? I'll see that you don't get stuck."

" 'Sall right."

Marjorie smiled—that smile that was thanks enough.

"You're an angel, and I'm obliged loads."

With a sigh the angel glanced round the veranda, but Bernice and Otis were not in sight. He wandered back inside, and there in front of the women's dressing-room he found Otis in the centre of a group of young men who were convulsed with laughter. Otis was brandishing a piece of timber he had picked up, and discoursing volubly.

"She's gone in to fix her hair," he announced wildly. "I'm waiting to dance another hour with her."

Their laughter was renewed.

"Why don't some of you cut in?" cried Otis resentfully. "She likes more variety."

"Why, Otis," suggested a friend, "you've just barely got used to her."

"Why the two-by-four, Otis?" inquired Warren, smiling.

"The two-by-four? Oh, this? This is a club. When she comes out I'll hit her on the head and knock her in again."

Warren collapsed on a settee and howled with glee.

"Never mind, Otis," he articulated finally. "I'm relieving you this time."

Otis simulated a sudden fainting attack and handed the stick to Warren.

"If you need it, old man," he said hoarsely.

No matter how beautiful or brilliant a girl may be, the reputation of not being frequently cut in on makes her position at a dance unfortunate. Perhaps boys prefer her company to that of the butterflies with whom they dance a dozen times an evening, but youth in this jazz-nourished generation is temperamentally restless, and the idea of fox-trotting more than one full fox trot with the same girl is distasteful, not to say odious. When it comes to several dances and the intermissions between she can be quite sure that a young man, once relieved, will never tread on her wayward toes again.

Warren danced the next full dance with Bernice, and finally, thankful for the intermission, he led her to a table on the veranda. There was a moment's silence while she did unimpressive things with her fan.

"It's hotter here than in Eau Claire," she said.

Warren stifled a sigh and nodded. It might be for all he knew or cared. He wondered idly whether she was a poor conversationalist because she got no attention or got no attention because she was a poor conversationalist.

"You going to be here much longer?" he asked, and then turned rather red. She might suspect his reasons for asking.

"Another week," she answered, and stared at him as if to lunge at his next remark when it left his lips.

Warren fidgeted. Then with a sudden charitable impulse he decided to try part of his line on her. He turned and looked at her eyes.

"You've got an awfully kissable mouth," he began quietly.

This was a remark that he sometimes made to girls at college proms when they were talking in just such half dark as this. Bernice distinctly jumped. She turned an ungraceful red and became clumsy with her fan. No one had ever made such a remark to her before.

"Fresh!"—the word had slipped out before she realized it, and she bit her lip. Too late she decided to be amused, and offered him a flustered smile.

Warren was annoyed. Though not accustomed to have that remark taken seriously, still it usually provoked a laugh or a paragraph of sentimental banter. And he hated to be called fresh, except in a joking way. His charitable impulse died and he switched the topic.

"Jim Strain and Ethel Demorest sitting out as usual," he commented.

This was more in Bernice's line, but a faint regret mingled with her relief as the subject changed. Men did not talk to her about kissable mouths, but she knew that they talked in some such way to other girls.

"Oh, yes," she said, and laughed. "I hear they've been mooning round for years without a red penny. Isn't it silly?"

Warren's disgust increased. Jim Strain was a close friend of his brother's, and anyway he considered it bad form to sneer at people for not having money. But Bernice had had no intention of sneering. She was merely nervous.

II

When Marjorie and Bernice reached home at half after midnight they said good night at the top of the stairs. Though cousins, they were not intimates. As a matter of fact Marjorie had no female intimates—she considered girls stupid. Bernice on the contrary all through this parent-arranged visit had rather longed to exchange those confidences flavored with giggles and tears that she considered an indispensable factor in all feminine intercourse. But in this respect she found Marjorie rather cold; felt somehow the same difficulty in talking to her that she had in talking to men. Marjorie never giggled, was never frightened, seldom embarrassed, and in fact had very few of the qualities which Bernice considered appropriately and blessedly feminine.

As Bernice busied herself with tooth-brush and paste this night she wondered for the hundredth time why she never had any attention when she was away from home. That her family were the wealthiest in Eau Claire; that her mother entertained tremendously, gave little dinners for her daughter before all dances and bought her a car of her own to drive round in, never occurred to her as factors in her home-town social success. Like most girls she had been brought up on the warm milk prepared by Annie Fellows Johnston and on novels in which the female was beloved because of certain mysterious womanly qualities, always mentioned but never displayed.

Bernice felt a vague pain that she was not at present engaged in being popular. She did not know that had it not been for Marjorie's campaigning she would have danced the entire evening with one man; but she knew that even in Eau Claire other girls with less position and less pulchritude were given a much bigger rush. She attributed this to something subtly unscrupulous in those girls. It had never worried her, and if it had her mother would have assured her that the other girls cheapened themselves and that men really respected girls like Bernice.

She turned out the light in her bathroom, and on an impulse decided to go in and chat for a moment with her aunt Josephine, whose light was still on. Her soft slippers bore her noiselessly down the carpeted hall, but hearing voices inside she stopped near the partly opened door. Then she caught her own name, and without any definite intention of eavesdropping lingered—and the thread of the conversation going on inside pierced her consciousness sharply as if it had been drawn through with a needle.

"She's absolutely hopeless!" It was Marjorie's voice. "Oh, I know what you're going to say! So many people have told you how pretty and sweet she is, and how she can cook! What of it? She has a bum time. Men don't like her."

"What's a little cheap popularity?"

Mrs. Harvey sounded annoyed.

"It's everything when you're eighteen," said Marjorie emphatically. "I've done my best. I've been polite and I've made men dance with her, but they just won't stand being bored. When I think of that goregous coloring wasted on such a ninny, and think what Martha Carey could do with it—oh!"

"There's no courtesy these days."

Mrs. Harvey's voice implied that modern situations were too much for her. When she was a girl all young ladies who belonged to nice families had glorious times.

"Well," said Marjorie, "no girl can permanently bolster up a lame-duck visitor, because these days it's every girl for herself. I've even tried to drop her hints about clothes and things, and she's been furious—given me the funniest looks. She's sensitive enough to know she's not getting away with much, but I'll bet she consoles herself by thinking that she's very virtuous and that I'm too gay and fickle and will come to a bad end. All unpopular girls think that way. Sour grapes! Sarah Hopkins refers to Genevieve and Roberta and me as gardenia girls! I'll bet she'd give ten years of her life and her European education to be a gardenia girl and have three or four men in love with her and be cut in on every few feet at dances."

"It seems to me," interrupted Mrs. Harvey rather wearily, "that you ought to be able to do something for Bernice. I know she's not very vivacious."

Marjorie groaned.

"Vivacious! Good grief! I've never heard her say anything to a boy except that it's hot or the floor's crowded or that she's going to school in New York next year. Sometimes she asks them what kind of car they have and tells them the kind she has. Thrilling!"

There was a short silence, and then Mrs. Harvey took up her refrain:

"All I know is that other girls not half so sweet and attractive get partners. Martha Carey, for instance, is stout and loud, and her mother is distinctly common. Roberta Dillon is so thin this year that she looks as though Arizona were the place for her. She's dancing herself to death."

"But, mother," objected Marjorie impatiently, "Martha is cheerful and awfully witty and an awfully slick girl, and Roberta's a marvellous dancer. She's been popular for ages!"

Mrs. Harvey yawned.

"I think it's that crazy Indian blood in Bernice," continued Marjorie. "Maybe she's a reversion to type. Indian women all just sat round and never said anything."

"Go to bed, you silly child," laughed Mrs. Harvey. "I wouldn't have told you that if I'd thought you were going to remember it. And I think most of your ideas are perfectly idiotic," she finished sleepily.

There was another silence, while Marjorie considered whether or not convincing her mother was worth the trouble. People over forty can seldom be permanently convinced of anything. At eighteen our convictions are ills from which we look; at forty-five they are caves in which we hide.

Having decided this, Marjorie said good night. When she came out into the hall it was quite empty.

III

While Marjorie was breakfasting late next day Bernice came into the room with a rather formal good morning, sat down opposite, stared intently over and slightly moistened her lips.

"What's on your mind?" inquired Marjorie, rather puzzled.

Bernice paused before she threw her hand-grenade.

"I heard what you said about me to your mother last night."

Marjorie was startled, but she showed only a faintly heightened color and her voice was quite even when she spoke.

"Where were you?"

"In the hall. I didn't mean to listen—at first."

After an involuntary look of contempt Marjorie dropped her eyes and became very interested in balancing a stray corn-flake on her finger.

"I guess I'd better go back to Eau Claire—if I'm such a nuisance." Bernice's lower lip was trembling violently and she continued on a wavering note: "I've tried to be nice, and—and I've been first neglected and then insulted. No one ever visited me and got such treatment."

Marjorie was silent.

"But I'm in the way, I see. I'm a drag on you. Your friends don't like me." She paused, and then remembered another one of her grievances. "Of course I was furious last week when you tried to hint to me that that dress was unbecoming. Don't you think I know how to dress myself?"

"No," murmured Marjorie less than half-aloud.

"What?"

"I didn't hint anything," said Marjorie succinctly. "I said, as I remember, that it was better to wear a becoming dress three times straight than to alternate it with two frights."

"Do you think that was a very nice thing to say?"

"I wasn't trying to be nice." Then after a pause: "When do you want to go?"

Bernice drew in her breath sharply.

"Oh!" It was a little half-cry.

Marjorie looked up in surprise.

"Didn't you say you were going?"

"Yes, but——"

"Oh, you were only bluffing!"

They stared at each other across the breakfast-table for a moment. Misty waves were passing before Bernice's eyes, while Marjorie's face wore that rather hard expression that she used when slightly intoxicated undergraduates were making love to her.

"So you were bluffing," she repeated as if it were what she might have expected.

Bernice admitted it by bursting into tears. Marjorie's eyes showed boredom.

"You're my cousin," sobbed Bernice. "I'm v-v-visiting you. I was to stay a month, and if I go home my mother will know and she'll wah-wonder——"

Marjorie waited until the shower of broken words collapsed into little sniffles.

"I'll give you my month's allowance," she said coldly, "and you can spend this last week anywhere you want. There's a very nice hotel——"

Bernice's sobs rose to a flute note, and rising of a sudden she fled from the room.

An hour later, while Marjorie was in the library absorbed in composing one of those non-committal, marvellously elusive letters that only a young girl can write, Bernice reappeared, very red-eyed and consciously calm. She cast no glance at Marjorie but took a book at random from the shelf and sat down as if to read. Marjorie seemed absorbed in her letter and continued writing. When the clock showed noon Bernice closed her book with a snap.

"I suppose I'd better get my railroad ticket."

This was not the beginning of the speech she had rehearsed upstairs, but as Marjorie was not getting her cues—wasn't urging her to be reasonable; it's all a mistake—it was the best opening she could muster.

"Just wait till I finish this letter," said Marjorie without looking round. "I want to get it off in the next mail."

After another minute, during which her pen scratched busily, she turned round and relaxed with an air of "at your service." Again Bernice had to speak.

"Do you want me to go home?"

"Well," said Marjorie, considering, "I suppose if you're not having a good time you'd better go. No use being miserable."

"Don't you think common kindness——"

"Oh, please don't quote 'Little Women'!" cried Marjorie impatiently. "That's out of style."

"You think so?"

"Heavens, yes! What modern girl could live like those inane females?"

"They were the models for our mothers."

Marjorie laughed.

"Yes, they were—not! Besides, our mothers were all very well in their way, but they know very little about their daughters' problems."

Bernice drew herself up.

"Please don't talk about my mother."

Marjorie laughed.

"I don't think I mentioned her."

Bernice felt that she was being led away from her subject.

"Do you think you've treated me very well?"

"I've done my best. You're rather hard material to work with."

The lids of Bernice's eyes reddened.

"I think you're hard and selfish, and you haven't a feminine quality in you."

"Oh, my Lord!" cried Marjorie in desperation. "You little nut! Girls like you are responsible for all the tiresome colorless marriages; all those ghastly inefficiencies that pass as feminine qualities. What a blow it must be when a man with imagination marries the beautiful bundle of clothes that he's been building ideals round, and finds that she's just a weak, whining, cowardly mass of affectations!"

Bernice's mouth had slipped half open.

"The womanly woman!" continued Marjorie. "Her whole early life is occupied in whining criticisms of girls like me who really do have a good time."

Bernice's jaw descended farther as Marjorie's voice rose.

"There's some excuse for an ugly girl whining. If I'd been irretrievably ugly I'd never have forgiven my parents for bringing me into the world. But you're starting life without any handicap—" Marjorie's little fist clinched. "If you expect me to weep with you you'll be disappointed. Go or stay, just as you like." And picking up her letters she left the room.

Bernice claimed a headache and failed to appear at luncheon. They had a matinée date for the afternoon, but the headache persisting, Marjorie made explanations to a not very downcast boy. But when she returned late in the afternoon she found Bernice with a strangely set face waiting for her in her bedroom.

"I've decided," began Bernice without preliminaries, "that maybe you're right about things—possibly not. But if you'll tell me why your friends aren't—aren't interested in me I'll see if I can do what you want me to."

Marjorie was at the mirror shaking down her hair.

"Do you mean it?"

"Yes."

"Without reservations? Will you do exactly what I say?"

"Well, I——"

"Well nothing! Will you do exactly as I say?"

"If they're sensible things."

"They're not! You're no case for sensible things."

"Are you going to make—to recommend——"

"Yes, everything. If I tell you to take boxing lessons you'll have to do it. Write home and tell your mother you're going to stay another two weeks."

"If you'll tell me——"

"All right—I'll just give you a few examples now. First, you have no ease of manner. Why? Because you're never sure about your personal appearance. When a girl feels that she's perfectly groomed and dressed she can forget that part of her. That's charm. The more parts of yourself you can afford to forget the more charm you have."

"Don't I look all right?"

"No; for instance, you never take care of your eyebrows. They're black and lustrous, but by leaving them straggly they're a blemish. They'd be beautiful if you'd take care of them in one-tenth the time you take doing nothing. You're going to brush them so that they'll grow straight."

Bernice raised the brows in question.

"Do you mean to say that men notice eyebrows?"

"Yes—subconsciously. And when you go home you ought to have your teeth straightened a little. It's almost imperceptible, still——"

"But I thought," interrupted Bernice in bewilderment, "that you despised little dainty feminine things like that."

"I hate dainty minds," answered Marjorie. "But a girl has to be dainty in person. If she looks like a million dollars she can talk about Russia, ping-pong, or the League of Nations and get away with it."

"What else?"

"Oh, I'm just beginning! There's your dancing."

"Don't I dance all right?"

"No, you don't—you lean on a man; yes, you do—ever so slightly. I noticed it when we were dancing together yesterday. And you dance standing up straight instead of bending over a little. Probably some old lady on the side-line once told you that you looked so dignified that way. But except with a very small girl it's much harder on the man, and he's the one that counts."

"Go on." Bernice's brain was reeling.

"Well, you've got to learn to be nice to men who are sad birds. You look as if you'd been insulted whenever you're thrown with any except the most popular boys. Why, Bernice, I'm cut in on every few feet—and who does most of it? Why, those very sad birds. No girl can afford to neglect them. They're the big part of any crowd. Young boys too shy to talk are the very best conversational practice. Clumsy boys are the best dancing practice. If you can follow them and yet look graceful you can follow a baby tank across a barb-wire sky-scraper."

Bernice sighed profoundly, but Marjorie was not through.

"If you go to a dance and really amuse, say, three sad birds that dance with you; if you talk so well to them that they forget they're stuck with you, you've done something. They'll come back next time, and gradually so many sad birds will dance with you that the attractive boys will see there's no danger of being stuck—then they'll dance with you."

"Yes," agreed Bernice faintly. "I think I begin to see."

"And finally," concluded Marjorie, "poise and charm will just come. You'll wake up some morning knowing you've attained it, and men will know it too."

Bernice rose.

"It's been awfully kind of you—but nobody's ever talked to me like this before, and I feel sort of startled."

Marjorie made no answer but gazed pensively at her own image in the mirror.

"You're a peach to help me," continued Bernice.

Still Marjorie did not answer, and Bernice thought she had seemed too grateful.

"I know you don't like sentiment," she said timidly.

Marjorie turned to her quickly.

"Oh, I wasn't thinking about that. I was considering whether we hadn't better bob your hair."

Bernice collapsed backward upon the bed.

IV

On the following Wednesday evening there was a dinner-dance at the country club. When the guests strolled in Bernice found her place-card with a slight feeling of irritation. Though at her right sat G. Reece Stoddard, a most desirable and distinguished young bachelor, the all-important left held only Charley Paulson. Charley lacked height, beauty, and social shrewdness, and in her new enlightenment Bernice decided that his only qualification to be her partner was that he had never been stuck with her. But this feeling of irritation left with the last of the soup-plates, and Marjorie's specific instruction came to her. Swallowing her pride she turned to Charley Paulson and plunged.

"Do you think I ought to bob my hair, Mr. Charley Paulson?"

Charley looked up in surprise.

"Why?"

"Because I'm considering it. It's such a sure and easy way of attracting attention."

Charley smiled pleasantly. He could not know this had been rehearsed. He replied that he didn't know much about bobbed hair. But Bernice was there to tell him.

"I want to be a society vampire, you see," she announced coolly, and went on to inform him that bobbed hair was the necessary prelude. She added that she wanted to ask his advice, because she had heard he was so critical about girls.

Charley, who knew as much about the psychology of women as he did of the mental states of Buddhist contemplatives, felt vaguely flattered.

"So I've decided," she continued, her voice rising slightly, "that early next week I'm going down to the Sevier Hotel barber-shop, sit in the first chair, and get my hair bobbed." She faltered, noticing that the people near her had paused in their conversation and were listening; but after a confused second Marjorie's coaching told, and she finished her paragraph to the vicinity at large. "Of course I'm charging admission, but if you'll all come down and encourage me I'll issue passes for the inside seats."

There was a ripple of appreciative laughter, and under cover of it G. Reece Stoddard leaned over quickly and said close to her ear: "I'll take a box right now."

She met his eyes and smiled as if he had said something surpassingly brilliant.

"Do you believe in bobbed hair?" asked G. Reece in the same undertone.

"I think it's unmoral," affirmed Bernice gravely. "But, of course, you've either got to amuse people or feed 'em or shock 'em." Marjorie had culled this from Oscar Wilde. It was greeted with a ripple of laughter from the men and a series of quick, intent looks from the girls. And then as though she had said nothing of wit or moment Bernice turned again to Charley and spoke confidentially in his ear.

"I want to ask you your opinion of several people. I imagine you're a wonderful judge of character."

Charley thrilled faintly—paid her a subtle compliment by overturning her water.

Two hours later, while Warren McIntyre was standing passively in the stag line abstractedly watching the dancers and wondering whither and with whom Marjorie had disappeared, an unrelated perception began to creep slowly upon him—a perception that Bernice, cousin to Marjorie, had been cut in on several times in the past five minutes. He closed his eyes, opened them and looked again. Several minutes back she had been dancing with a visiting boy, a matter easily accounted for; a visiting boy would know no better. But now she was dancing with some one else, and there was Charley Paulson headed for her with enthusiastic determination in his eye. Funny—Charley seldom danced with more than three girls an evening.

Warren was distinctly surprised when—the exchange having been effected—the man relieved proved to be none other than G. Reece Stoddard himself. And G. Reece seemed not at all jubilant at being relieved. Next time Bernice danced near, Warren regarded her intently. Yes, she was pretty, distinctly pretty; and to-night her face seemed really vivacious. She had that look that no woman, however histrionically proficient, can successfully counterfeit—she looked as if she were having a good time. He liked the way she had her hair arranged, wondered if it was brilliantine that made it glisten so. And that dress was becoming—a dark red that set off her shadowy eyes and high coloring. He remembered that he had thought her pretty when she first came to town, before he had realized that she was dull. Too bad she was dull—dull girls unbearable—certainly pretty though.

His thoughts zigzagged back to Marjorie. This disappearance would be like other disappearances. When she reappeared he would demand where she had been—would be told emphatically that it was none of his business. What a pity she was so sure of him! She basked in the knowledge that no other girl in town interested him; she defied him to fall in love with Genevieve or Roberta.

Warren sighed. The way to Marjorie's affections was a labyrinth indeed. He looked up. Bernice was again dancing with the visiting boy. Half unconsciously he took a step out from the stag line in her direction, and hesitated. Then he said to himself that it was charity. He walked toward her—collided suddenly with G. Reece Stoddard.

"Pardon me," said Warren.

But G. Reece had not stopped to apologize. He had again cut in on Bernice.

That night at one o'clock Marjorie, with one hand on the electric-light switch in the hall, turned to take a last look at Bernice's sparkling eyes.

"So it worked?"

"Oh, Marjorie, yes!" cried Bernice.

"I saw you were having a gay time."

"I did! The only trouble was that about midnight I ran short of talk. I had to repeat myself—with different men of course. I hope they won't compare notes."

"Men don't," said Marjorie, yawning, "and it wouldn't matter if they did—they'd think you were even trickier."

She snapped out the light, and as they started up the stairs Bernice grasped the banister thankfully. For the first time in her life she had been danced tired.

"You see," said Marjorie at the top of the stairs, "one man sees another man cut in and he thinks there must be something there. Well, we'll fix up some new stuff to-morrow. Good night."

"Good night."

As Bernice took down her hair she passed the evening before her in review. She had followed instructions exactly. Even when Charley Paulson cut in for the eighth time she had simulated delight and had apparently been both interested and flattered. She had not talked about the weather or Eau Claire or automobiles or her school, but had confined her conversation to me, you, and us.

But a few minutes before she fell asleep a rebellious thought was churning drowsily in her brain—after all, it was she who had done it. Marjorie, to be sure, had given her her conversation, but then Marjorie got much of her conversation out of things she read. Bernice had bought the red dress, though she had never valued it highly before Marjorie dug it out of her trunk—and her own voice had said the words, her own lips had smiled, her own feet had danced. Marjorie nice girl—vain, though—nice evening—nice boys—like Warren—Warren—Warren—what's-his-name—Warren——

She fell asleep.

V

To Bernice the next week was a revelation. With the feeling that people really enjoyed looking at her and listening to her came the foundation of self-confidence. Of course there were numerous mistakes at first. She did not know, for instance, that Draycott Deyo was studying for the ministry; she was unaware that he had cut in on her because he thought she was a quiet, reserved girl. Had she known these things she would not have treated him to the line which began "Hello, Shell Shock!" and continued with the bathtub story— "It takes a frightful lot of energy to fix my hair in the summer— there's so much of it—so I always fix it first and powder my face and put on my hat; then I get into the bathtub, and dress afterward. Don't you think that's the best plan?"

Though Draycott Deyo was in the throes of difficulties concerning baptism by immersion and might possibly have seen a connection, it must be admitted that he did not. He considered feminine bathing an immoral subject, and gave her some of his ideas on the depravity of modern society.

But to offset that unfortunate occurrence Bernice had several signal successes to her credit. Little Otis Ormonde pleaded off from a trip East and elected instead to follow her with a puppylike devotion, to the amusement of his crowd and to the irritation of G. Reece Stoddard, several of whose afternoon calls Otis completely ruined by the disgusting tenderness of the glances he bent on Bernice. He even told her the story of the two-by-four and the dressing-room to show her how frightfully mistaken he and every one else had been in their first judgment of her. Bernice laughed off that incident with a slight sinking sensation.

Of all Bernice's conversation perhaps the best known and most universally approved was the line about the bobbing of her hair.

"Oh, Bernice, when you goin' to get the hair bobbed?"

"Day after to-morrow maybe," she would reply, laughing. "Will you come and see me? Because I'm counting on you, you know."

"Will we? You know! But you better hurry up."

Bernice, whose tonsorial intentions were strictly dishonorable, would laugh again.

"Pretty soon now. You'd be surprised."

But perhaps the most significant symbol of her success was the gray car of the hypercritical Warren McIntyre, parked daily in front of the Harvey house. At first the parlor-maid was distinctly startled when he asked for Bernice instead of Marjorie; after a week of it she told the cook that Miss Bernice had gotta holda Miss Marjorie's best fella.

And Miss Bernice had. Perhaps it began with Warren's desire to rouse jealousy in Marjorie; perhaps it was the familiar though unrecognized strain of Marjorie in Bernice's conversation; perhaps it was both of these and something of sincere attraction besides. But somehow the collective mind of the younger set knew within a week that Marjorie's most reliable beau had made an amazing face-about and was giving an indisputable rush to Marjorie's guest. The question of the moment was how Marjorie would take it. Warren called Bernice on the 'phone twice a day, sent her notes, and they were frequently seen together in his roadster, obviously engrossed in one of those tense, significant conversations as to whether or not he was sincere.

Marjorie on being twitted only laughed. She said she was mighty glad that Warren had at last found some one who appreciated him. So the younger set laughed, too, and guessed that Marjorie didn't care and let it go at that.

One afternoon when there were only three days left of her visit Bernice was waiting in the hall for Warren, with whom she was going to a bridge party. She was in rather a blissful mood, and when Marjorie—also bound for the party—appeared beside her and began casually to adjust her hat in the mirror, Bernice was utterly unprepared for anything in the nature of a clash. Marjorie did her work very coldly and succinctly in three sentences.

"You may as well get Warren out of your head," she said coldly.

"What?" Bernice was utterly astounded.

"You may as well stop making a fool of yourself over Warren McIntyre. He doesn't care a snap of his fingers about you."

For a tense moment they regarded each other—Marjorie scornful, aloof; Bernice astounded, half-angry, half-afraid. Then two cars drove up in front of the house and there was a riotous honking. Both of them gasped faintly, turned, and side by side hurried out.

All through the bridge party Bernice strove in vain to master a rising uneasiness. She had offended Marjorie, the sphinx of sphinxes. With the most wholesome and innocent intentions in the world she had stolen Marjorie's property. She felt suddenly and horribly guilty.

After the bridge game, when they sat in an informal circle and the conversation became general, the storm gradually broke. Little Otis Ormonde inadvertently precipitated it.

"When you going back to kindergarten, Otis?" some one had asked.

"Me? Day Bernice gets her hair bobbed."

"Then your education's over," said Marjorie quickly. "That's only a bluff of hers. I should think you'd have realized."

"That a fact?" demanded Otis, giving Bernice a reproachful glance.

Bernice's ears burned as she tried to think up an effectual comeback. In the face of this direct attack her imagination was paralyzed.

"There's a lot of bluffs in the world," continued Marjorie quite pleasantly. "I should think you'd be young enough to know that, Otis."

"Well," said Otis, "maybe so. But gee! With a line like Bernice's——"

"Really?" yawned Marjorie. "What's her latest bon mot?"

No one seemed to know. In fact, Bernice, having trifled with her muse's beau, had said nothing memorable of late.

"Was that really all a line?" asked Roberta curiously.

Bernice hesitated. She felt that wit in some form was demanded of her, but under her cousin's suddenly frigid eyes she was completely incapacitated.

"I don't know," she stalled.

"Splush!" said Marjorie. "Admit it!"

Bernice saw that Warren's eyes had left a ukulele he had been tinkering with and were fixed on her questioningly.

"Oh, I don't know!" she repeated steadily. Her cheeks were glowing.

"Splush!" remarked Marjorie again.

"Come through, Bernice," urged Otis. "Tell her where to get off."

Bernice looked round again—she seemed unable to get away from Warren's eyes.

"I like bobbed hair," she said hurriedly, as if he had asked her a question, "and I intend to bob mine."

"When?" demanded Marjorie.

"Any time."

"No time like the present," suggested Roberta.

Otis jumped to his feet.

"Good stuff!" he cried. "We'll have a summer bobbing party. Sevier Hotel barber-shop, I think you said."

In an instant all were on their feet. Bernice's heart throbbed violently.

"What?" she gasped.

Out of the group came Marjorie's voice, very clear and contemptuous.

"Don't worry—she'll back out!"

"Come on, Bernice!" cried Otis, starting toward the door.

Four eyes—Warren's and Marjorie's—stared at her, challenged
her, defied her. For another second she wavered wildly.

"All right," she said swiftly, "I don't care if I do."

An eternity of minutes later, riding down-town through the late
afternoon beside Warren, the others following in Roberta's car close
behind, Bernice had all the sensations of Marie Antoinette bound
for the guillotine in a tumbrel. Vaguely she wondered why she did
not cry out that it was all a mistake. It was all she could do to keep
from clutching her hair with both hands to protect it from the suddenly hostile world. Yet she did neither. Even the thought of her
mother was no deterrent now. This was the test supreme of her
sportsmanship; her right to walk unchallenged in the starry heaven
of popular girls.

Warren was moodily silent, and when they came to the hotel he
drew up at the curb and nodded to Bernice to precede him out.
Roberta's car emptied a laughing crowd into the shop, which presented two bold plate-glass windows to the street.

Bernice stood on the curb and looked at the sign, Sevier Barber-
Shop. It was a guillotine indeed, and the hangman was the first barber, who, attired in a white coat and smoking a cigarette, leaned
nonchalantly against the first chair. He must have heard of her; he
must have been waiting all week, smoking eternal cigarettes beside
that portentous, too-often-mentioned first chair. Would they blind-
fold her? No, but they would tie a white cloth round her neck lest
any of her blood—nonsense—hair—should get on her clothes.

"All right, Bernice," said Warren quickly.

With her chin in the air she crossed the sidewalk, pushed open
the swinging screen-door, and giving not a glance to the uproarious,
riotous row that occupied the waiting bench, went up to the first
barber.

"I want you to bob my hair."

The first barber's mouth slid somewhat open. His cigarette dropped
to the floor.

"Huh?"

"My hair—bob it!"

Refusing further preliminaries, Bernice took her seat on high. A
man in the chair next to her turned on his side and gave her a glance,
half lather, half amazement. One barber started and spoiled little
Willy Schuneman's monthly haircut. Mr. O'Reilly in the last chair
grunted and swore musically in ancient Gaelic as a razor bit into his

cheek. Two bootblacks became wide-eyed and rushed for her feet. No, Bernice didn't care for a shine.

Outside a passer-by stopped and stared; a couple joined him; half a dozen small boys' noses sprang into life, flattened against the glass; and snatches of conversation borne on the summer breeze drifted in through the screen-door.

"Lookada long hair on a kid!"

"Where'd yuh get 'at stuff? 'At's a bearded lady he just finished shavin'."

But Bernice saw nothing, heard nothing. Her only living sense told her that this man in the white coat had removed one tortoise-shell comb and then another; that his fingers were fumbling clumsily with unfamiliar hairpins; that this hair, this wonderful hair of hers, was going—she would never again feel its long voluptuous pull as it hung in a dark-brown glory down her back. For a second she was near breaking down, and then the picture before her swam mechanically into her vision—Marjorie's mouth curling in a faint ironic smile as if to say:

"Give up and get down! You tried to buck me and I called your bluff. You see you haven't got a prayer."

And some last energy rose up in Bernice, for she clinched her hands under the white cloth, and there was a curious narrowing of her eyes that Marjorie remarked on to some one long afterward.

Twenty minutes later the barber swung her round to face the mirror, and she flinched at the full extent of the damage that had been wrought. Her hair was not curly, and now it lay in lank lifeless blocks on both sides of her suddenly pale face. It was ugly as sin—she had known it would be ugly as sin. Her face's chief charm had been a Madonna-like simplicity. Now that was gone and she was—well, frightfully mediocre—not stagy; only ridiculous, like a Greenwich Villager who had left her spectacles at home.

As she climbed down from the chair she tried to smile—failed miserably. She saw two of the girls exchange glances; noticed Marjorie's mouth curved in attenuated mockery—and that Warren's eyes were suddenly very cold.

"You see"—her words fell into an awkward pause—"I've done it."

"Yes, you've—done it," admitted Warren.

"Do you like it?"

There was a half-hearted "Sure" from two or three voices, another awkward pause, and then Marjorie turned swiftly and with serpent-like intensity to Warren.

"Would you mind running me down to the cleaners?" she asked. "I've simply got to get a dress there before supper. Roberta's driving right home and she can take the others."

Warren stared abstractedly at some infinite speck out the window. Then for an instant his eyes rested coldly on Bernice before they turned to Marjorie.

"Be glad to," he said slowly.

VI

Bernice did not fully realize the outrageous trap that had been set for her until she met her aunt's amazed glance just before dinner.

"Why, Bernice!"

"I've bobbed it, Aunt Josephine."

"Why, child!"

"Do you like it?"

"Why, Ber-nice!"

"I suppose I've shocked you."

"No, but what'll Mrs. Deyo think to-morrow night? Bernice, you should have waited until after the Deyos' dance—you should have waited if you wanted to do that."

"It was sudden, Aunt Josephine. Anyway, why does it matter to Mrs. Deyo particularly?"

"Why, child," cried Mrs. Harvey, "in her paper on 'The Foibles of the Younger Generation' that she read at the last meeting of the Thursday Club she devoted fifteen minutes to bobbed hair. It's her pet abomination. And the dance is for you and Marjorie!"

"I'm sorry."

"Oh, Bernice, what'll your mother say? She'll think I let you do it."

"I'm sorry."

Dinner was an agony. She had made a hasty attempt with a curling-iron, and burned her finger and much hair. She could see that her aunt was both worried and grieved, and her uncle kept saying, "Well, I'll be darned!" over and over in a hurt and faintly hostile tone. And Marjorie sat very quietly, intrenched behind a faint smile, a faintly mocking smile.

Somehow she got through the evening. Three boys called; Marjorie disappeared with one of them, and Bernice made a listless unsuccessful attempt to entertain the two others—sighed thankfully as she climbed the stairs to her room at half past ten. What a day!

When she had undressed for the night the door opened and Marjorie came in.

"Bernice," she said, "I'm awfully sorry about the Deyo dance. I'll give you my word of honor I'd forgotten all about it."

" 'Sall right," said Bernice shortly. Standing before the mirror she passed her comb slowly through her short hair.

"I'll take you down-town to-morrow," continued Marjorie, "and the hairdresser'll fix it so you'll look slick. I didn't imagine you'd go through with it. I'm really mighty sorry."

"Oh, 'sall right!"

"Still it's your last night, so I suppose it won't matter much."

Then Bernice winced as Marjorie tossed her own hair over her shoulders and began to twist it slowly into two long blond braids until in her cream-colored negligée she looked like a delicate painting of some Saxon princess. Fascinated, Bernice watched the braids grow. Heavy and luxurious they were, moving under the supple fingers like restive snakes—and to Bernice remained this relic and the curling-iron and a to-morrow full of eyes. She could see G. Reece Stoddard, who liked her, assuming his Harvard manner and telling his dinner partner that Bernice shouldn't have been allowed to go to the movies so much; she could see Draycott Deyo exchanging glances with his mother and then being conscientiously charitable to her. But then perhaps by to-morrow Mrs. Deyo would have heard the news; would send round an icy little note requesting that she fail to appear—and behind her back they would all laugh and know that Marjorie had made a fool of her; that her chance at beauty had been sacrificed to the jealous whim of a selfish girl. She sat down suddenly before the mirror, biting the inside of her cheek.

"I like it," she said with an effort. "I think it'll be becoming."

Marjorie smiled.

"It looks all right. For heaven's sake, don't let it worry you!"

"I won't."

"Good night, Bernice."

But as the door closed something snapped within Bernice. She sprang dynamically to her feet, clinching her hands, then swiftly and noiselessly crossed over to her bed and from underneath it dragged out her suitcase. Into it she tossed toilet articles and a change of clothing. Then she turned to her trunk and quickly dumped in two drawerfuls of lingerie and summer dresses. She moved quietly, but with deadly efficiency, and in three-quarters of an hour her trunk was locked and strapped and she was fully dressed in a becoming new travelling suit that Marjorie had helped her pick out.

Sitting down at her desk she wrote a short note to Mrs. Harvey, in which she briefly outlined her reasons for going. She sealed it, addressed it, and laid it on her pillow. She glanced at her watch. The train left at one, and she knew that if she walked down to the Marborough Hotel two blocks away she could easily get a taxicab.

Suddenly she drew in her breath sharply and an expression flashed into her eyes that a practised character reader might have connected vaguely with the set look she had worn in the barber's chair—

somehow a development of it. It was quite a new look for Bernice—
and it carried consequences.

She went stealthily to the bureau, picked up an article that lay
there, and turning out all the lights stood quietly until her eyes became accustomed to the darkness. Softly she pushed open the door
to Marjorie's room. She heard the quiet, even breathing of an un-
troubled conscience asleep.

She was by the bedside now, very deliberate and calm. She acted
swiftly. Bending over she found one of the braids of Marjorie's hair,
followed it up with her hand to the point nearest the head, and then
holding it a little slack so that the sleeper would feel no pull, she
reached down with the shears and severed it. With the pigtail in
her hand she held her breath. Marjorie had muttered something in
her sleep. Bernice deftly amputated the other braid, paused for an
instant, and then flitted swiftly and silently back to her own room.

Down-stairs she opened the big front door, closed it carefully behind her, and feeling oddly happy and exuberant stepped off the
porch into the moonlight, swinging her heavy grip like a shopping-
bag. After a minute's brisk walk she discovered that her left hand
still held the two blond braids. She laughed unexpectedly—had to
shut her mouth hard to keep from emitting an absolute peal. She was
passing Warren's house now, and on the impulse she set down her
baggage, and swinging the braids like pieces of rope flung them at
the wooden porch, where they landed with a slight thud. She laughed
again, no longer restraining herself.

"Huh!" she giggled wildly. "Scalp the selfish thing!"

Then picking up her suitcase she set off at a half-run down the
moonlit street.

1920   *Flappers and Philosophers*

THE ICE PALACE

THE SUNLIGHT dripped over the house like golden paint over an art jar, and the freckling shadows here and there only intensified the rigor of the bath of light. The Butterworth and Larkin houses flanking were intrenched behind great stodgy trees; only the Happer house took the full sun, and all day long faced the dusty road-street with a tolerant kindly patience. This was the city of Tarleton in southernmost Georgia, September afternoon.

Up in her bedroom window Sally Carrol Happer rested her nineteen-year-old chin on a fifty-two-year-old sill and watched Clark Darrow's ancient Ford turn the corner. The car was hot—being partly metallic it retained all the heat it absorbed or evolved—and Clark Darrow sitting bolt upright at the wheel wore a pained, strained expression as though he considered himself a spare part, and rather likely to break. He laboriously crossed two dust ruts, the wheels squeaking indignantly at the encounter, and then with a terrifying expression he gave the steering-gear a final wrench and deposited self and car approximately in front of the Happer steps. There was a plaintive heaving sound, a death-rattle, followed by a short silence; and then the air was rent by a startling whistle.

Sally Carrol gazed down sleepily. She started to yawn, but finding this quite impossible unless she raised her chin from the window-sill, changed her mind and continued silently to regard the car, whose owner sat brilliantly if perfunctorily at attention as he waited for an answer to his signal. After a moment the whistle once more split the dusty air.

"Good mawnin'."

With difficulty Clark twisted his tall body round and bent a distorted glance on the window.

" 'Tain't mawnin', Sally Carrol."

"Isn't it, sure enough?"

"What you doin'?"

"Eatin' 'n apple."

"Come on go swimmin'—want to?"

"Reckon so."

"How 'bout hurryin' up?"

"Sure enough."

Sally Carrol sighed voluminously and raised herself with profound inertia from the floor, where she had been occupied in alternately destroying parts of a green apple and painting paper dolls for her younger sister. She approached a mirror, regarded her expression with a pleased and pleasant languor, dabbed two spots of rouge on her lips and a grain of powder on her nose, and covered her bobbed corn-colored hair with a rose-littered sunbonnet. Then she kicked over the painting water, said, "Oh, damn!"—but let it lay—and left the room.

"How you, Clark?" she inquired a minute later as she slipped nimbly over the side of the car.

"Mighty fine, Sally Carrol."

"Where we go swimmin'?"

"Out to Walley's Pool. Told Marylyn we'd call by an' get her an' Joe Ewing."

Clark was dark and lean, and when on foot was rather inclined to stoop. His eyes were ominous and his expression somewhat petulant except when startlingly illuminated by one of his frequent smiles. Clark had "a income"—just enough to keep himself in ease and his car in gasoline—and he had spent the two years since he graduated from Georgia Tech in dozing round the lazy streets of his home town, discussing how he could best invest his capital for an immediate fortune.

Hanging round he found not at all difficult; a crowd of little girls had grown up beautifully, the amazing Sally Carroll foremost among them; and they enjoyed being swum with and danced with and made love to in the flower-filled summery evenings—and they all liked Clark immensely. When feminine company palled there were half a dozen other youths who were always just about to do something, and meanwhile were quite willing to join him in a few holes of golf, or a game of billiards, or the consumption of a quart of "hard yella licker." Every once in a while one of these contemporaries made a farewell round of calls before going up to New York or Philadelphia or Pittsburgh to go into business, but mostly they just stayed round in this languid paradise of dreamy skies and firefly evenings and noisy niggery street fairs—and especially of gracious, soft-voiced girls, who were brought up on memories instead of money.

The Ford having been excited into a sort of restless resentful life Clark and Sally Carrol rolled and rattled down Valley Avenue into Jefferson Street, where the dust road became a pavement; along opiate Millicent Place, where there were half a dozen prosperous, substantial mansions; and on into the down-town section. Driving was perilous here, for it was shopping time; the population idled casually across the streets and a drove of low-moaning oxen were being urged along in front of a placid street-car; even the shops seemed only yawning their doors and blinking their windows in the sunshine before retiring into a state of utter and finite coma.

"Sally Carrol," said Clark suddenly, "it a fact that you're engaged?"

She looked at him quickly.

"Where'd you hear that?"

"Sure enough, you engaged?"

" 'At's a nice question!"

"Girl told me you were engaged to a Yankee you met up in Asheville last summer."

Sally Carrol sighed.

"Never saw such an old town for rumors."

"Don't marry a Yankee, Sally Carrol. We need you round here."

Sally Carrol was silent a moment.

"Clark," she demanded suddenly, "who on earth shall I marry?"

"I offer my services."

"Honey, you couldn't support a wife," she answered cheerfully. "Anyway, I know you too well to fall in love with you."

" 'At doesn't mean you ought to marry a Yankee," he persisted.

"S'pose I love him?"

He shook his head.

"You couldn't. He'd be a lot different from us, every way."

He broke off as he halted the car in front of a rambling, dilapidated house. Marylyn Wade and Joe Ewing appeared in the doorway.

" 'Lo, Sally Carrol."

"Hi!"

"How you-all?"

"Sally Carrol," demanded Marylyn as they started off again, "you engaged?"

"Lawdy, where'd all this start? Can't I look at a man 'thout everybody in town engagin' me to him?"

Clark stared straight in front of him at a bolt on the clattering wind-shield.

"Sally Carrol," he said with a curious intensity, "don't you like us?"

"What?"

"Us down here?"

"Why, Clark, you know I do. I adore all you boys."

"Then why you gettin' engaged to a Yankee?"

"Clark, I don't know. I'm not sure what I'll do, but—well, I want to go places and see people. I want my mind to grow. I want to live where things happen on a big scale."

"What you mean?"

"Oh, Clark, I love you, and I love Joe here, and Ben Arrot, and you-all, but you'll—you'll——"

"We'll all be failures?"

"Yes. I don't mean only money failures, but just sort of—of ineffectual and sad, and—oh, how can I tell you?"

"You mean because we stay here in Tarleton?"

"Yes, Clark; and because you like it and never want to change things or think or go ahead."

He nodded and she reached over and pressed his hand.

"Clark," she said softly, "I wouldn't change you for the world. You're sweet the way you are. The things that'll make you fail I'll love always—the living in the past, the lazy days and nights you have, and all your carelessness and generosity."

"But you're goin' away?"

"Yes—because I couldn't ever marry you. You've a place in my heart no one else ever could have, but tied down here I'd get restless. I'd feel I was—wastin' myself. There's two sides to me, you see. There's the sleepy old side you love; an' there's a sort of energy—the feelin' that makes me do wild things. That's the part of me that may be useful somewhere, that'll last when I'm not beautiful any more."

She broke off with characteristic suddenness and sighed, "Oh, sweet cooky!" as her mood changed.

Half closing her eyes and tipping back her head till it rested on the seat-back she let the savory breeze fan her eyes and ripple the fluffy curls of her bobbed hair. They were in the country now, hurrying between tangled growths of bright-green coppice and grass and tall trees that sent sprays of foliage to hang a cool welcome over the road. Here and there they passed a battered Negro cabin, its oldest white-haired inhabitant smoking a corncob pipe beside the door, and half a dozen scantily clothed pickaninnies parading tattered dolls on the wild-grown grass in front. Farther out were lazy cotton-fields, where even the workers seemed intangible shadows lent by the sun to the earth, not for toil, but to while away some age-old tradition in the golden September fields. And round the drowsy picturesqueness, over the trees and shacks and muddy rivers, flowed the heat, never hostile, only comforting, like a great warm nourishing bosom for the infant earth.

"Sally Carrol, we're here!"

"Poor chile's soun' asleep."

"Honey, you dead at last outa sheer laziness?"

"Water, Sally Carrol! Cool water waitin' for you!"

Her eyes opened sleepily.

"Hi! she murmured, smiling.

II

In November Harry Bellamy, tall, broad, and brisk, came down from his Northern city to spend four days. His intention was to settle a matter that had been hanging fire since he and Sally Carrol had met in Asheville, North Carolina, in midsummer. The settlement took only a quiet afternoon and an evening in front of a glowing open fire, for Harry Bellamy had everything she wanted; and, besides, she loved him—loved him with that side of her she kept especially for loving. Sally Carrol had several rather clearly defined sides.

On his last afternoon they walked, and she found their steps tending half-unconsciously toward one of her favorite haunts, the cemetery. When it came in sight, gray-white and golden-green under the cheerful late sun, she paused, irresolute, by the iron gate.

"Are you mournful by nature, Harry?" she asked with a faint smile.

"Mournful? Not I."

"Then let's go in here. It depresses some folks, but I like it."

They passed through the gateway and followed a path that led through a wavy valley of graves—dusty-gray and mouldy for the fifties; quaintly carved with flowers and jars for the seventies; ornate and hideous for the nineties, with fat marble cherubs lying in sodden sleep on stone pillows, and great impossible growths of nameless granite flowers. Occasionally they saw a kneeling figure with tributary flowers, but over most of the graves lay silence and withered leaves with only the fragrance that their own shadowy memories could waken in living minds.

They reached the top of a hill where they were fronted by a tall, round head-stone, freckled with dark spots of damp and half grown over with vines.

"Margery Lee," she read; "1844–1873. Wasn't she nice? She died when she was twenty-nine. Dear Margery Lee," she added softly. "Can't you see her, Harry?"

"Yes, Sally Carrol."

He felt a little hand insert itself into his.

"She was dark, I think; and she always wore her hair with a ribbon in it, and gorgeous hoop-skirts of alice blue and old rose."

"Yes."

"Oh, she was sweet, Harry! And she was the sort of girl born to stand on a wide, pillared porch and welcome folks in. I think perhaps a lot of men went away to war meanin' to come back to her; but maybe none of 'em ever did."

He stooped down close to the stone, hunting for any record of marriage.

"There's nothing here to show."

"Of course not. How could there be anything there better than just 'Margery Lee,' and that eloquent date?"

She drew close to him and an unexpected lump came into his throat as her yellow hair brushed his cheek.

"You see how she was, don't you, Harry?"

"I see," he agreed gently. "I see through your precious eyes. You're beautiful now, so I know she must have been."

Silent and close they stood, and he could feel her shoulders trembling a little. An ambling breeze swept up the hill and stirred the brim of her floppidy hat.

"Let's go down there!"

She was pointing to a flat stretch on the other side of the hill where along the green turf were a thousand grayish-white crosses stretching in endless, ordered rows like the stacked arms of a battalion.

"Those are the Confederate dead," said Sally Carrol simply.

They walked along and read the inscriptions, always only a name and a date, sometimes quite indecipherable.

"The last row is the saddest—see, 'way over there. Every cross has just a date on it, and the word 'Unknown.' "

She looked at him and her eyes brimmed with tears.

"I can't tell you how real it is to me, darling—if you don't know."

"How you feel about it is beautiful to me."

"No, no, it's not me, it's them—that old time that I've tried to have live in me. These were just men, unimportant evidently or they wouldn't have been 'unknown'; but they died for the most beautiful thing in the world—the dead South. You see," she continued, her voice still husky, her eyes glistening with tears, "people have these dreams they fasten onto things, and I've always grown up with that dream. It was so easy because it was all dead and there weren't any disillusions comin' to me. I've tried in a way to live up to those past standards of noblesse oblige—there's just the last remnants of it, you know, like the roses of an old garden dying all round us—streaks of strange courtliness and chivalry in some of these boys an' stories I used to hear from a Confederate soldier who lived next door, and a few old darkies. Oh, Harry, there was something, there was some thing! I couldn't ever make you understand, but it was there."

"I understand," he assured her again quietly.

Sally Carrol smiled and dried her eyes on the tip of a handkerchief protruding from his breast pocket.

"You don't feel depressed, do you, lover? Even when I cry I'm happy here, and I get a sort of strength from it."

Hand in hand they turned and walked slowly away. Finding soft

grass she drew him down to a seat beside her with their backs against
the remnants of a low broken wall.

"Wish those three old women would clear out," he complained. "I
want to kiss you, Sally Carrol."

"Me, too."

They waited impatiently for the three bent figures to move off,
and then she kissed him until the sky seemed to fade out and all her
smiles and tears to vanish in an ecstasy of eternal seconds.

Afterward they walked slowly back together, while on the corners
twilight played at somnolent black-and-white checkers with the end
of day.

"You'll be up about mid-January," he said, "and you've got to stay
a month at least. It'll be slick. There's a winter carnival on, and if
you've never really seen snow it'll be like fairy-land to you. There'll
be skating and skiing and tobogganing and sleigh-riding, and all
sorts of torchlight parades on snow-shoes. They haven't had one for
years, so they're going to make it a knock-out."

"Will I be cold, Harry?" she asked suddenly.

"You certainly won't. You may freeze your nose, but you won't
be shivery cold. It's hard and dry, you know."

"I guess I'm a summer child. I don't like any cold I've ever seen."

She broke off and they were both silent for a minute.

"Sally Carrol," he said very slowly, "what do you say to—
March?"

"I say I love you."

"March?"

"March, Harry."

III

All night in the Pullman it was very cold. She rang for the porter
to ask for another blanket, and when he couldn't give her one she
tried vainly, by squeezing down into the bottom of her berth and
doubling back the bedclothes, to snatch a few hours' sleep. She
wanted to look her best in the morning.

She rose at six and sliding uncomfortably into her clothes stumbled
up to the diner for a cup of coffee. The snow had filtered into the
vestibules and covered the floor with a slippery coating. It was in-
triguing, this cold, it crept in everywhere. Her breath was quite visible
and she blew into the air with a naïve enjoyment. Seated in the
diner she stared out the window at white hills and valleys and
scattered pines whose every branch was a green platter for a cold
feast of snow. Sometimes a solitary farmhouse would fly by, ugly
and bleak and lone on the white waste; and with each one she had

an instant of chill compassion for the souls shut in there waiting
for spring.

As she left the diner and swayed back into the Pullman she experienced a surging rush of energy and wondered if she was feeling the
bracing air of which Harry had spoken. This was the North, the
North—her land now!

"Then blow, ye winds, heigho!
    A-roving I will go,"

she chanted exultantly to herself.

"What's 'at?" inquired the porter politely.

"I said: 'Brush me off.' "

The long wires of the telegraph-poles doubled; two tracks ran up
beside the train—three—four; came a succession of white-roofed
houses, a glimpse of a trolley-car with frosted windows, streets—
more streets—the city.

She stood for a dazed moment in the frosty station before she saw
three fur-bundled figures descending upon her.

"There she is!"

"Oh, Sally Carrol!"

Sally Carrol dropped her bag.

"Hi!"

A faintly familiar icy-cold face kissed her, and then she was in a
group of faces all apparently emitting great clouds of heavy smoke;
she was shaking hands. There were Gordon, a short, eager man of
thirty who looked like an amateur knocked-about model for Harry,
and his wife, Myra, a listless lady with flaxen hair under a fur automobile cap. Almost immediately Sally Carrol thought of her as
vaguely Scandinavian. A cheerful chauffeur adopted her bag, and
amid ricochets of half-phrases, exclamations, and perfunctory listless "my dears" from Myra, they swept each other from the
station.

Then they were in a sedan bound through a crooked succession of
snowy streets where dozens of little boys were hitching sleds behind
grocery wagons and automobiles.

"Oh," cried Sally Carrol, "I want to do that! Can we, Harry?"

"That's for kids. But we might——"

"It looks like such a circus!" she said regretfully.

Home was a rambling frame house set on a white lap of snow, and
there she met a big, gray-haired man of whom she approved, and a
lady who was like an egg, and who kissed her—these were Harry's
parents. There was a breathless indescribable hour crammed full of
half-sentences, hot water, bacon and eggs and confusion; and after

that she was alone with Harry in the library, asking him if she dared
smoke.

It was a large room with a Madonna over the fireplace and rows
upon rows of books in covers of light gold and dark gold and shiny
red. All the chairs had little lace squares where one's head should
rest, the couch was just comfortable, the books looked as if they
had been read—some—and Sally Carrol had an instantaneous vision
of the battered old library at home, with her father's huge medical
books, and the oil-paintings of her three great-uncles, and the old
couch that had been mended up for forty-five years and was still
luxurious to dream in. This room struck her as being neither attractive nor particularly otherwise. It was simply a room with a lot of
fairly expensive things in it that all looked about fifteen years old.

"What do you think of it up here?" demanded Harry eagerly.
"Does it surprise you? Is it what you expected, I mean?"

"You are, Harry," she said quietly, and reached out her arms to
him.

But after a brief kiss he seemed anxious to extort enthusiasm from
her.

"The town, I mean. Do you like it? Can you feel the pep in the
air?"

"Oh, Harry," she laughed, "you'll have to give me time. You can't
just fling questions at me."

She puffed at her cigarette with a sigh of contentment.

"One thing I want to ask you," he began rather apologetically;
"you Southerners put quite an emphasis on family, and all that—
not that it isn't quite all right, but you'll find it a little different
here. I mean—you'll notice a lot of things that'll seem to you sort of
vulgar display at first, Sally Carrol; but just remember that this is
a three-generation town. Everybody has a father, and about half
of us have grandfathers. Back of that we don't go."

"Of course," she murmured.

"Our grandfathers, you see, founded the place, and a lot of them
had to take some pretty queer jobs while they were doing the found-
ing. For instance, there's one woman who at present is about the
social model for the town; well, her father was the first public ash
man—things like that."

"Why," said Sally Carrol, puzzled, "did you s'pose I was goin' to
make remarks about people?"

"Not at all," interrupted Harry; "and I'm not apologizing for any
one either. It's just that—well, a Southern girl came up here last
summer and said some unfortunate things, and—oh, I just thought
I'd tell you."

Sally Carrol felt suddenly indignant—as though she had been unjustly spanked—but Harry evidently considered the subject closed, for he went on with a great surge of enthusiasm.

"It's carnival time, you know. First in ten years. And there's an ice palace they're building now that's the first they've had since eighty-five. Built out of blocks of the clearest ice they could find—on a tremendous scale."

She rose and walking to the window pushed aside the heavy Turkish portières and looked out.

"Oh!" she cried suddenly. "There's two little boys makin' a snow man! Harry, do you reckon I can go out an' help 'em?"

"You dream! Come here and kiss me."

She left the window rather reluctantly.

"I don't guess this is a very kissable climate, is it? I mean, it makes you so you don't want to sit round, doesn't it?"

"We're not going to. I've got a vacation for the first week you're here, and there's a dinner-dance to-night."

"Oh, Harry," she confessed, subsiding in a heap, half in his lap, half in the pillows, "I sure do feel confused. I haven't got an idea whether I'll like it or not, an' I don't know what people expect, or anythin'. You'll have to tell me, honey."

"I'll tell you," he said softly, "if you'll just tell me you're glad to be here."

"Glad—just awful glad!" she whispered, insinuating herself into his arms in her own peculiar way. "Where you are is home for me, Harry."

And as she said this she had the feeling for almost the first time in her life that she was acting a part.

That night, amid the gleaming candles of a dinner-party, where the men seemed to do most of the talking while the girls sat in a haughty and expensive aloofness, even Harry's presence on her left failed to make her feel at home.

"They're a good-looking crowd, don't you think?" he demanded. "Just look round. There's Spud Hubbard, tackle at Princeton last year, and Junie Morton—he and the red-haired fellow next to him were both Yale hockey captains; Junie was in my class. Why, the best athletes in the world come from these States round here. This is a man's country, I tell you. Look at John J. Fishburn!"

"Who's he?" asked Sally Carrol innocently.

"Don't you know?"

"I've heard the name."

"Greatest wheat man in the Northwest, and one of the greatest financiers in the country."

She turned suddenly to a voice on her right.

"I guess they forgot to introduce us. My name's Roger Patton."

"My name is Sally Carrol Happer," she said graciously.

"Yes, I know. Harry told me you were coming."

"You a relative?"

"No, I'm a professor."

"Oh," she laughed.

"At the university. You're from the South, aren't you?"

"Yes; Tarleton, Georgia."

She liked him immediately—a reddish-brown mustache under watery blue eyes that had something in them that these other eyes lacked, some quality of appreciation. They exchanged stray sentences through dinner, and she made up her mind to see him again.

After coffee she was introduced to numerous good-looking young men who danced with conscious precision and seemed to take it for granted that she wanted to talk about nothing except Harry.

"Heavens," she thought, "they talk as if my being engaged made me older than they are—as if I'd tell their mothers on them!"

In the South an engaged girl, even a young married woman, expected the same amount of half-affectionate badinage and flattery that would be accorded a débutante, but here all that seemed banned. One young man, after getting well started on the subject of Sally Carrol's eyes, and how they had allured him ever since she entered the room, went into a violent confusion when he found she was visiting the Bellamys—was Harry's fiancée. He seemed to feel as though he had made some risqué and inexcusable blunder, became immediately formal, and left her at the first opportunity.

She was rather glad when Roger Patton cut in on her and suggested that they sit out a while.

"Well," he inquired, blinking cheerily, "how's Carmen from the South?"

"Mighty fine. How's—how's Dangerous Dan McGrew? Sorry, but he's the only Northerner I know much about."

He seemed to enjoy that.

"Of course," he confessed, "as a professor of literature I'm not supposed to have read Dangerous Dan McGrew."

"Are you a native?"

"No, I'm a Philadelphian. Imported from Harvard to teach French. But I've been here ten years."

"Nine years, three hundred an' sixty-four days longer than me."

"Like it here?"

"Uh-huh. Sure do!"

"Really?"

"Well, why not? Don't I look as if I were havin' a good time?"

"I saw you look out the window a minute ago—and shiver."

"Just my imagination," laughed Sally Carrol. "I'm used to havin'

everythin' quiet outside, an' sometimes I look out an' see a flurry of
snow, an' it's just as if somethin' dead was movin'."

He nodded appreciatively.

"Ever been North before?"

"Spent two Julys in Asheville, North Carolina."

"Nice-looking crowd, aren't they?" suggested Patton, indicating
the swirling floor.

Sally Carrol started. This had been Harry's remark.

"Sure are! They're—canine."

"What?"

She flushed.

"I'm sorry; that sounded worse than I meant it. You see I always
think of people as feline or canine, irrespective of sex."

"Which are you?"

"I'm feline. So are you. So are most Southern men an' most of
these girls here."

"What's Harry?"

"Harry's canine distinctly. All the men I've met to-night seem to be
canine."

"What does 'canine' imply? A certain conscious masculinity as
opposed to subtlety?"

"Reckon so. I never analyzed it—only I just look at people an'
say 'canine' or 'feline' right off. It's right absurd, I guess."

"Not at all. I'm interested. I used to have a theory about these
people. I think they're freezing up."

"What?"

"I think they're growing like Swedes—Ibsenesque, you know. Very
gradually getting gloomy and melancholy. It's these long winters.
Ever read any Ibsen?"

She shook her head.

"Well, you find in his characters a certain brooding rigidity.
They're righteous, narrow, and cheerless, without infinite possibilities
for great sorrow or joy."

"Without smiles or tears?"

"Exactly. That's my theory. You see there are thousands of Swedes
up here. They come, I imagine, because the climate is very much like
their own, and there's been a gradual mingling. There're probably
not half a dozen here to-night, but—we've had four Swedish gover-
nors. Am I boring you?"

"I'm mighty interested."

"Your future sister-in-law is half Swedish. Personally I like her,
but my theory is that Swedes react rather badly on us as a whole.
Scandinavians, you know, have the largest suicide rate in the world."

"Why do you live here if it's so depressing?"

"Oh, it doesn't get me. I'm pretty well cloistered, and I suppose books mean more than people to me anyway."

"But writers all speak about the South being tragic. You know— Spanish señoritas, black hair and daggers an' haunting music."

He shook his head.

"No, the Northern races are the tragic races—they don't indulge in the cheering luxury of tears."

Sally Carrol thought of her graveyard. She supposed that that was vaguely what she had meant when she said it didn't depress her.

"The Italians are about the gayest people in the world—but it's a dull subject," he broke off. "Anyway, I want to tell you you're marrying a pretty fine man."

Sally Carrol was moved by an impulse of confidence.

"I know. I'm the sort of person who wants to be taken care of after a certain point, and I feel sure I will be."

"Shall we dance? You know," he continued as they rose, "it's encouraging to find a girl who knows what she's marrying for. Nine-tenths of them think of it as a sort of walking into a moving-picture sunset."

She laughed, and liked him immensely.

Two hours later on the way home she nestled near Harry in the back seat.

"Oh, Harry," she whispered, "it's so co-old!"

"But it's warm in here, darling girl."

"But outside it's cold; and oh, that howling wind!"

She buried her face deep in his fur coat and trembled involuntarily as his cold lips kissed the tip of her ear.

IV

The first week of her visit passed in a whirl. She had her promised toboggan-ride at the back of an automobile through a chill January twilight. Swathed in furs she put in a morning tobogganing on the country-club hill; even tried skiing, to sail through the air for a glorious moment and then land in a tangled laughing bundle on a soft snowdrift. She liked all the winter sports, except an afternoon spent snow-shoeing over a glaring plain under pale yellow sunshine, but she soon realized that these things were for children—that she was being humored and that the enjoyment round her was only a reflection of her own.

At first the Bellamy family puzzled her. The men were reliable and she liked them; to Mr. Bellamy especially, with his iron-gray hair and energetic dignity, she took an immediate fancy, once she found that he was born in Kentucky; this made of him a link between the old life and the new. But toward the women she felt a definite hostility. Myra, her future sister-in-law, seemed the essence of spiritless conventionality. Her conversation was so utterly devoid of personality that Sally Carrol, who came from a country where a certain amount of charm and assurance could be taken for granted in the women, was inclined to despise her.

"If those women aren't beautiful," she thought, "they're nothing. They just fade out when you look at them. They're glorified domestics. Men are the centre of every mixed group."

Lastly there was Mrs. Bellamy, whom Sally Carrol detested. The first day's impression of an egg had been confirmed—an egg with a cracked, veiny voice and such an ungracious dumpiness of carriage that Sally Carrol felt that if she once fell she would surely scramble. In addition, Mrs. Bellamy seemed to typify the town in being innately hostile to strangers. She called Sally Carrol "Sally," and could not be persuaded that the double name was anything more than a tedious ridiculous nickname. To Sally Carrol this shortening of her name was like presenting her to the public half clothed. She loved "Sally Carrol"; she loathed "Sally." She knew also that Harry's mother disapproved of her bobbed hair; and she had never dared smoke down-stairs after that first day when Mrs. Bellamy had come into the library sniffing violently.

Of all the men she met she preferred Roger Patton, who was a frequent visitor at the house. He never again alluded to the Ibsenesque tendency of the populace, but when he came in one day and found her curled upon the sofa bent over "Peer Gynt" he laughed and told her to forget what he'd said—that it was all rot.

And then one afternoon in her second week she and Harry hovered on the edge of a dangerously steep quarrel. She considered that he precipitated it entirely, though the Serbia in the case was an unknown man who had not had his trousers pressed.

They had been walking homeward between mounds of high-piled snow and under a sun which Sally Carrol scarcely recognized. They passed a little girl done up in gray wool until she resembled a small Teddy bear, and Sally Carrol could not resist a gasp of maternal appreciation.

"Look! Harry!"

"What?"

"That little girl—did you see her face?"

"Yes, why?"

"It was red as a little strawberry. Oh, she was cute!"

"Why, your own face is almost as red as that already! Everybody's healthy here. We're out in the cold as soon as we're old enough to walk. Wonderful climate!"

She looked at him and had to agree. He was mighty healthy-looking; so was his brother. And she had noticed the new red in her own cheeks that very morning.

Suddenly their glances were caught and held, and they stared for a moment at the street-corner ahead of them. A man was standing there, his knees bent, his eyes gazing upward with a tense expression as though he were about to make a leap toward the chilly sky. And then they both exploded into a shout of laughter, for coming closer they discovered it had been a ludicrous momentary illusion produced by the extreme bagginess of the man's trousers.

"Reckon that's one on us," she laughed.

"He must be a Southerner, judging by those trousers," suggested Harry mischievously.

"Why, Harry!"

Her surprised look must have irritated him.

"Those damn Southerners!"

Sally Carrol's eyes flashed.

"Don't call 'em that!"

"I'm sorry, dear," said Harry, malignantly apologetic, "but you know what I think of them. They're sort of—sort of degenerates—not at all like the old Southerners. They've lived so long down there with all the colored people that they've gotten lazy and shiftless."

"Hush your mouth, Harry!" she cried angrily. "They're not! They may be lazy—anybody would be in that climate—but they're my best friends, an' I don't want to hear 'em criticised in any such sweepin' way. Some of 'em are the finest men in the world."

"Oh, I know. They're all right when they come North to college, but of all the hangdog, ill-dressed, slovenly lot I ever saw, a bunch of small-town Southerners are the worst!"

Sally Carrol was clinching her gloved hands and biting her lip furiously.

"Why," continued Harry, "there was one in my class at New Haven, and we all thought that at last we'd found the true type of Southern aristocrat, but it turned out that he wasn't an aristocrat at all—just the son of a Northern carpetbagger, who owned about all the cotton round Mobile."

"A Southerner wouldn't talk the way you're talking now," she said evenly.

"They haven't the energy!"

"Or the somethin' else."

"I'm sorry, Sally Carrol, but I've heard you say yourself that you'd never marry——"

"That's quite different. I told you I wouldn't want to tie my life to any of the boys that are round Tarleton now, but I never made any sweepin' generalities."

They walked along in silence.

"I probably spread it on a bit thick, Sally Carrol. I'm sorry."

She nodded but made no answer. Five minutes later as they stood in the hallway she suddenly threw her arms round him.

"Oh, Harry," she cried, her eyes brimming with tears, "let's get married next week. I'm afraid of having fusses like that. I'm afraid, Harry. It wouldn't be that way if we were married."

But Harry, being in the wrong, was still irritated.

"That'd be idiotic. We decided on March."

The tears in Sally Carrol's eyes faded; her expression hardened slightly.

"Very well—I suppose I shouldn't have said that."

Harry melted.

"Dear little nut!" he cried. "Come and kiss me and let's forget."

That very night at the end of a vaudeville performance the orchestra played "Dixie" and Sally Carrol felt something stronger and more enduring than her tears and smiles of the day brim up inside her. She leaned forward gripping the arms of her chair until her face grew crimson.

"Sort of get you, dear?" whispered Harry.

But she did not hear him. To the spirited throb of the violins and the inspiring beat of the kettledrums her own old ghosts were marching by and on into the darkness, and as fifes whistled and sighed in the low encore they seemed so nearly out of sight that she could have waved good-by.

"Away, away,
Away down South in Dixie!
Away, away,
Away down South in Dixie!"

V

It was a particularly cold night. A sudden thaw had nearly cleared the streets the day before, but now they were traversed again with a powdery wraith of loose snow that travelled in wavy lines before the feet of the wind, and filled the lower air with a fine-particled mist. There was no sky—only a dark, ominous tent that draped in the tops of the streets and was in reality a vast approaching army of snowflakes—while over it all, chilling away the comfort from the brown-and-green glow of lighted windows and muffling the steady trot of the horse pulling their sleigh, interminably washed the north wind. It was a dismal town after all, she thought—dismal.

Sometimes at night it had seemed to her as though no one lived here—they had all gone long ago—leaving lighted houses to be covered in time by tombing heaps of sleet. Oh, if there should be snow on her grave! To be beneath great piles of it all winter long, where even her headstone would be a light shadow against light shadows. Her grave—a grave that should be flower-strewn and washed with sun and rain.

She thought again of those isolated country houses that her train had passed, and of the life there the long winter through—the ceaseless glare through the windows, the crust forming on the soft drifts of snow, finally the slow, cheerless melting, and the harsh spring of which Roger Patton had told her. Her spring—to lose it forever—with its lilacs and the lazy sweetness it stirred in her heart. She was laying away that spring—afterward she would lay away that sweetness.

With a gradual insistence the storm broke. Sally Carrol felt a film of flakes melt quickly on her eyelashes, and Harry reached over a furry arm and drew down her complicated flannel cap. Then the small flakes came in skirmish-line, and the horse bent his neck patiently as a transparency of white appeared momentarily on his coat.

"Oh, he's cold, Harry," she said quickly.

"Who? The horse? Oh, no, he isn't. He likes it!"

After another ten minutes they turned a corner and came in sight of their destination. On a tall hill outlined in vivid glaring green against the wintry sky stood the ice palace. It was three stories in the air, with battlements and embrasures and narrow icicled windows, and the innumerable electric lights inside made a gorgeous transparency of the great central hall. Sally Carrol clutched Harry's hand under the fur robe.

"It's beautiful!" he cried excitedly. "My golly, it's beautiful, isn't it! They haven't had one here since eighty-five!"

Somehow the notion of there not having been one since eighty-five oppressed her. Ice was a ghost, and this mansion of it was surely peopled by those shades of the eighties, with pale faces and blurred snow-filled hair.

"Come on, dear," said Harry.

She followed him out of the sleigh and waited while he hitched the horse. A party of four—Gordon, Myra, Roger Patton, and another girl—drew up beside them with a mighty jingle of bells. There were quite a crowd already, bundled in fur or sheepskin, shouting and calling to each other as they moved through the snow, which was now so thick that people could scarcely be distinguished a few yards away.

"It's a hundred and seventy feet tall," Harry was saying to a muffled figure beside him as they trudged toward the entrance; "covers six thousand square yards."

She caught snatches of conversation: "One main hall"—"walls twenty to forty inches thick"—"and the ice cave has almost a mile of—"—"this Canuck who built it——"

They found their way inside, and dazed by the magic of the great crystal walls Sally Carrol found herself repeating over and over two lines from "Kubla Khan":

> "It was a miracle of rare device,
> A sunny pleasure-dome with caves of ice!"

In the great glittering cavern with the dark shut out she took a seat on a wooden bench, and the evening's oppression lifted. Harry was right—it was beautiful; and her gaze travelled the smooth surface of the walls, the blocks for which had been selected for their purity and clearness to obtain this opalescent, translucent effect.

"Look! Here we go—oh, boy!" cried Harry.

A band in a far corner struck up "Hail, Hail, the Gang's All Here!" which echoed over to them in wild muddled acoustics, and then the lights suddenly went out; silence seemed to flow down the icy sides and sweep over them. Sally Carrol could still see her white breath in the darkness, and a dim row of pale faces over on the other side.

The music eased to a sighing complaint, and from outside drifted in the full-throated resonant chant of the marching clubs. It grew louder like some pæan of a viking tribe traversing an ancient wild; it swelled—they were coming nearer; then a row of torches appeared, and another and another, and keeping time with their moccasined feet a long column of gray-mackinawed figures swept in, snowshoes slung at their shoulders, torches soaring and flickering as their voices rose along the great walls.

The gray column ended and another followed, the light streaming luridly this time over red toboggan caps and flaming crimson mackinaws, and as they entered they took up the refrain; then came a long platoon of blue and white, of green, of white, of brown and yellow.

"Those white ones are the Wacouta Club," whispered Harry eagerly. "Those are the men you've met round at dances."

The volume of the voices grew; the great cavern was a phantasmagoria of torches waving in great banks of fire, of colors and the rhythm of soft-leather steps. The leading column turned and halted, platoon deployed in front of platoon until the whole procession made a solid flag of flame, and then from thousands of voices burst a mighty shout that filled the air like a crash of thunder, and sent the torches wavering. It was magnificent, it was tremendous! To Sally Carrol it was the North offering sacrifice on some mighty altar to the gray pagan God of Snow. As the shout died the band struck up again and there came more singing, and then long reverberating cheers by each club. She sat very quiet listening while the staccato cries rent the stillness; and then she started, for there was a volley of explosion, and great clouds of smoke went up here and there through the cavern—the flash-light photographers at work—and the council was over. With the band at their head the clubs formed in column once more, took up their chant, and began to march out.

"Come on!" shouted Harry. "We want to see the labyrinths downstairs before they turn the lights off!"

They all rose and started toward the chute—Harry and Sally Carrol in the lead, her little mitten buried in his big fur gantlet. At the bottom of the chute was a long empty room of ice, with the ceiling so low that they had to stoop—and their hands were parted. Before she realized what he intended Harry had darted down one of the half-dozen glittering passages that opened into the room and was only a vague receding blot against the green shimmer.

"Harry!" she called.

"Come on!" he cried back.

She looked round the empty chamber; the rest of the party had evidently decided to go home, were already outside somewhere in the blundering snow. She hesitated and then darted in after Harry.

"Harry!" she shouted.

She had reached a turning-point thirty feet down; she heard a faint muffled answer far to the left, and with a touch of panic fled toward it. She passed another turning, two more yawning alleys.

"Harry!"

No answer. She started to run straight forward, and then turned like lightning and sped back the way she had come, enveloped in a sudden icy terror.

She reached a turn—was it here?—took the left and came to what should have been the outlet into the long, low room, but it was only another glittering passage with darkness at the end. She called again but the walls gave back a flat, lifeless echo with no reverberations. Retracing her steps she turned another corner, this time following a wide passage. It was like the green lane between the parted waters of the Red Sea, like a damp vault connecting empty tombs.

She slipped a little now as she walked, for ice had formed on the bottom of her overshoes; she had to run her gloves along the half-slippery, half-sticky walls to keep her balance.

"Harry!"

Still no answer. The sound she made bounced mockingly down to the end of the passage.

Then on an instant the lights went out, and she was in complete darkness. She gave a small, frightened cry, and sank down into a cold little heap on the ice. She felt her left knee do something as she fell, but she scarcely noticed it as some deep terror far greater than any fear of being lost settled upon her. She was alone with this presence that came out of the North, the dreary loneliness that rose from ice-bound whalers in the Arctic seas, from smokeless, trackless wastes where were strewn the whitened bones of adventure. It was an icy breath of death; it was rolling down low across the land to clutch at her.

With a furious, despairing energy she rose again and started blindly down the darkness. She must get out. She might be lost in here for days, freeze to death and lie embedded in the ice like corpses she had read of, kept perfectly preserved until the melting of a glacier. Harry probably thought she had left with the others—he had gone by now; no one would know until late next day. She reached pitifully for the wall. Forty inches thick, they had said—forty inches thick!

"Oh!"

On both sides of her along the walls she felt things creeping, damp souls that haunted this palace, this town, this North.

"Oh, send somebody—send somebody!" she cried aloud.

Clark Darrow—he would understand; or Joe Ewing; she couldn't be left here to wander forever—to be frozen, heart, body, and soul. This her—this Sally Carrol! Why, she was a happy thing. She was a happy little girl. She liked warmth and summer and Dixie. These things were foreign—foreign.

"You're not crying," something said aloud. "You'll never cry any more. Your tears would just freeze; all tears freeze up here!"

She sprawled full length on the ice.

"Oh, God!" she faltered.

A long single file of minutes went by, and with a great weariness she felt her eyes closing. Then some one seemed to sit down near her and take her face in warm, soft hands. She looked up gratefully.

"Why, it's Margery Lee," she crooned softly to herself. "I knew you'd come." It really was Margery Lee, and she was just as Sally Carrol had known she would be, with a young, white brow, and wide, welcoming eyes, and a hoop-skirt of some soft material that was quite comforting to rest on.

"Margery Lee."

It was getting darker now and darker—all those tombstones ought to be repainted, sure enough, only that would spoil 'em, of course. Still, you ought to be able to see 'em.

Then after a succession of moments that went fast and then slow, but seemed to be ultimately resolving themselves into a multitude of blurred rays converging toward a pale-yellow sun, she heard a great cracking noise break her new-found stillness.

It was the sun, it was a light; a torch, and a torch beyond that, and another one, and voices; a face took flesh below the torch, heavy arms raised her, and she felt something on her cheek—it felt wet. Some one had seized her and was rubbing her face with snow. How ridiculous—with snow!

"Sally Carrol! Sally Carrol!"

It was Dangerous Dan McGrew; and two other faces she didn't know.

"Child, child! We've been looking for you two hours! Harry's half-crazy!"

Things came rushing back into place—the singing, the torches, the great shout of the marching clubs. She squirmed in Patton's arms and gave a long low cry.

"Oh, I want to get out of here! I'm going back home. Take me home"—her voice rose to a scream that sent a chill to Harry's heart as he came racing down the next passage—"to-morrow!" she cried with delirious, unrestrained passion—"To-morrow! To-morrow! To-morrow!"

VI

The wealth of golden sunlight poured a quite enervating yet oddly comforting heat over the house where day long it faced the dusty stretch of road. Two birds were making a great to-do in a cool spot found among the branches of a tree next door, and down the street a colored woman was announcing herself melodiously as a purveyor of strawberries. It was April afternoon.

Sally Carrol Happer, resting her chin on her arm, and her arm on an old window-seat gazed sleepily down over the spangled dust whence the heat waves were rising for the first time this spring. She was watching a very ancient Ford turn a perilous corner and rattle and groan to a jolting stop at the end of the walk. She made no sound, and in a minute a strident familiar whistle rent the air. Sally Carrol smiled and blinked.

"Good mawnin'."

A head appeared tortuously from under the car-top below.

"'Tain't mawnin', Sally Carrol."

"Sure enough!" she said in affected surprise. "I guess maybe not."

"What you doin'?"

"Eatin' green peach. 'Spect to die any minute."

Clark twisted himself a last impossible notch to get a view of her face.

"Water's warm as a kettla steam, Sally Carrol. Wanta go swimmin'?"

"Hate to move," sighed Sally Carrol lazily, "but I reckon so."

Decline of Gordon Sterrett, blackmailed by + forced to marry lower-class girl, who finally kills himself. Other aspects of complex plot: GS's failed affair in college / p(?)
friend Philip Dean's failed love w old girl Edith Bradin. Yale frat dance at (who won't lend him money) Delmonico's + morning after. Two soldiers in search of liquor who find work —

MAY DAY — *celebration of spring on May 1, 1919(?)*

wrecking office of socialist newspaper + break leg of Edith's elder brother.

prologue

THERE had been a war fought and won and the great city of the
conquering people was crossed with triumphal arches and vivid with
thrown flowers of white, red, and rose. All through the long spring
days the returning soldiers marched up the chief highway behind
the strump of drums and the joyous, resonant wind of the brasses,
while merchants and clerks left their bickerings and figurings and,
crowding to the windows, turned their white-bunched faces gravely
upon the passing battalions.

Never had there been such splendor in the great city, for the vic-
torious war had brought plenty in its train, and the merchants had
flocked thither from the South and West with their households to
taste of all the luscious feasts and witness the lavish entertainments
prepared—and to buy for their women furs against the next winter
and bags of golden mesh and varicolored slippers of silk and silver
and rose satin and cloth of gold.

So gaily and noisily were the peace and prosperity impending
hymned by the scribes and poets of the conquering people that more
and more spenders had gathered from the provinces to drink the
wine of excitement, and faster and faster did the merchants dispose
of their trinkets and slippers until they sent up a mighty cry for
more trinkets and more slippers in order that they might give in
barter what was demanded of them. Some even of them flung up their
hands helplessly, shouting:

"Alas! I have no more slippers! and alas! I have no more trinkets!
May Heaven help me, for I know not what I shall do!"

But no one listened to their great outcry, for the throngs were far
too busy—day by day, the foot-soldiers trod jauntily the highway
and all exulted because the young men returning were pure and
brave, sound of tooth and pink of cheek, and the young women of the
land were virgins and comely both of face and of figure.

So during all this time there were many adventures that happened
in the great city, and, of these, several—or perhaps one—are here
set down.

83

I

At nine o'clock on the morning of the first of May, 1919, a young man spoke to the room clerk at the Biltmore Hotel, asking if Mr. Philip Dean were registered there, and if so, could he be connected with Mr. Dean's rooms. The inquirer was dressed in a well-cut, shabby suit. He was small, slender, and darkly handsome; his eyes were framed above with unusually long eyelashes and below with the blue semicircle of ill health, this latter effect heightened by an unnatural glow which colored his face like a low, incessant fever.

Mr. Dean was staying there. The young man was directed to a telephone at the side.

After a second his connection was made; a sleepy voice hello'd from somewhere above.

"Mr. Dean?"—this very eagerly—"it's Gordon, Phil. It's Gordon Sterrett. I'm down-stairs. I heard you were in New York and I had a hunch you'd be here."

The sleepy voice became gradually enthusiastic. Well, how was Gordy, old boy! Well, he certainly was surprised and tickled! Would Gordy come right up, for Pete's sake!

A few minutes later Philip Dean, dressed in blue silk pajamas, opened his door and the two young men greeted each other with a half-embarrassed exuberance. They were both about twenty-four, Yale graduates of the year before the war; but there the resemblance stopped abruptly. Dean was blond, ruddy, and rugged under his thin pajamas. Everything about him radiated fitness and bodily comfort. He smiled frequently, showing large and prominent teeth.

"I was going to look you up," he cried enthusiastically. "I'm taking a couple of weeks off. If you'll sit down a sec I'll be right with you. Going to take a shower."

As he vanished into the bathroom his visitor's dark eyes roved nervously around the room, resting for a moment on a great English travelling bag in the corner and on a family of thick silk shirts littered on the chairs amid impressive neckties and soft woollen socks.

Gordon rose and, picking up one of the shirts, gave it a minute examination. It was of very heavy silk, yellow with a pale blue stripe—and there were nearly a dozen of them. He stared involuntarily at his own shirt-cuffs—they were ragged and linty at the edges and soiled to a faint gray. Dropping the silk shirt, he held his coat-sleeves down and worked the frayed shirt-cuffs up till they were out of sight. Then he went to the mirror and looked at himself with listless, unhappy interest. His tie, of former glory, was faded and thumb-creased—it served no longer to hide the jagged buttonholes of

his collar. He thought, quite without amusement, that only three
years before he had received a scattering vote in the senior elections
at college for being the best-dressed man in his class.

Dean emerged from the bathroom polishing his body.

"Saw an old friend of yours last night," he remarked.

"Passed her in the lobby and couldn't think of her name to save my
neck. That girl you brought up to New Haven senior year."

Gordon started.

"Edith Bradin? That whom you mean?"

" 'At's the one. Damn good looking. She's still sort of a pretty
doll—you know what I mean: as if you touched her she'd smear."

He surveyed his shining self complacently in the mirror, smiled
faintly, exposing a section of teeth.

"She must be twenty-three anyway," he continued.

"Twenty-two last month," said Gordon absently.

"What? Oh, last month. Well, I imagine she's down for the Gamma
Psi dance. Did you know we're having a Yale Gamma Psi dance
to-night at Delmonico's? You better come up, Gordy. Half of New
Haven'll probably be there. I can get you an invitation."

Draping himself reluctantly in fresh underwear, Dean lit a cigarette and sat down by the open window, inspecting his calves and
knees under the morning sunshine which poured into the room.

"Sit down, Gordy," he suggested, "and tell me all about what
you've been doing and what you're doing now and everything."

Gordon collapsed unexpectedly upon the bed; lay there inert and
spiritless. His mouth, which habitually dropped a little open when
his face was in repose, became suddenly helpless and pathetic.

"What's the matter?" asked Dean quickly.

"Oh, God!"

"What's the matter?"

"Every God damn thing in the world," he said miserably. "I've
absolutely gone to pieces, Phil. I'm all in."

"Huh?"

"I'm all in." His voice was shaking.

Dean scrutinized him more closely with appraising blue eyes.

"You certainly look all shot."

"I am. I've made a hell of mess of everything." He paused. "I'd
better start at the beginning—or will it bore you?"

"Not at all; go on." There was, however, a hesitant note in Dean's
voice. This trip East had been planned for a holiday—to find Gordon
Sterrett in trouble exasperated him a little.

"Go on," he repeated, and then added half under his breath, "Get
it over with."

"Well," began Gordon unsteadily, "I got back from France in

February, went home to Harrisburg for a month, and then came down to New York to get a job. I got one—with an export company. They fired me yesterday."

"Fired you?"

"I'm coming to that, Phil. I want to tell you frankly. You're about the only man I can turn to in a matter like this. You won't mind if I just tell you frankly, will you, Phil?"

Dean stiffened a bit more. The pats he was bestowing on his knees grew perfunctory. He felt vaguely that he was being unfairly saddled with responsibility; he was not even sure he wanted to be told. Though never surprised at finding Gordon Sterrett in mild difficulty, there was something in this present misery that repelled him and hardened him, even though it excited his curiosity.

"Go on."

"It's a girl."

"Hm." Dean resolved that nothing was going to spoil his trip. If Gordon was going to be depressing, then he'd have to see less of Gordon.

"Her name is Jewel Hudson," went on the distressed voice from the bed. "She used to be 'pure,' I guess, up to about a year ago. Lived here in New York—poor family. Her people are dead now and she lives with an old aunt. You see it was just about the time I met her that everybody began to come back from France in droves—and all I did was to welcome the newly arrived and go on parties with 'em. That's the way it started, Phil, just from being glad to see everybody and having them glad to see me."

"You ought to've had more sense."

"I know," Gordon paused, and then continued listlessly. "I'm on my own now, you know, and Phil, I can't stand being poor. Then came this darn girl. She sort of fell in love with me for a while and, though I never intended to get so involved, I'd always seem to run into her somewhere. You can imagine the sort of work I was doing for those exporting people—of course, I always intended to draw; do illustrating for magazines; there's a pile of money in it."

"Why didn't you? You've got to buckle down if you want to make good," suggested Dean with cold formalism.

"I tried, a little, but my stuff's crude. I've got talent, Phil; I can draw—but I just don't know how. I ought to go to art school and I can't afford it. Well, things came to a crisis about a week ago. Just as I was down to about my last dollar this girl began bothering me. She wants some money; claims she can make trouble for me if she doesn't get it."

"Can she?"

"I'm afraid she can. That's one reason I lost my job—she kept calling up the office all the time, and that was sort of the last straw down there. She's got a letter all written to send to my family. Oh, she's got me, all right. I've got to have some money for her."

There was an awkward pause. Gordon lay very still, his hands clenched by his side.

"I'm all in," he continued, his voice trembling. "I'm half crazy, Phil. If I hadn't known you were coming East, I think I'd have killed myself. I want you to lend me three hundred dollars."

Dean's hands, which had been patting his bare ankles, were suddenly quiet—and the curious uncertainty playing between the two became taut and strained.

After a second Gordon continued:

"I've bled the family until I'm ashamed to ask for another nickel."

Still Dean made no answer.

"Jewel says she's got to have two hundred dollars."

"Tell her where she can go."

"Yes, that sounds easy, but she's got a couple of drunken letters I wrote her. Unfortunately she's not at all the flabby sort of person you'd expect."

Dean made an expression of distaste.

"I can't stand that sort of woman. You ought to have kept away."

"I know," admitted Gordon wearily.

"You've got to look at things as they are. If you haven't got money you've got to work and stay away from women."

"That's easy for you to say," began Gordon, his eyes narrowing. "You've got all the money in the world."

"I most certainly have not. My family keep darn close tab on what I spend. Just because I have a little leeway I have to be extra careful not to abuse it."

He raised the blind and let in a further flood of sunshine.

"I'm no prig, Lord knows," he went on deliberately. "I like pleasure—and I like a lot of it on a vacation like this, but you're—you're in awful shape. I never heard you talk just this way before. You seem to be sort of bankrupt—morally as well as financially."] theme

"Don't they usually go together?"

Dean shook his head impatiently.

"There's a regular aura about you that I don't understand. It's a sort of evil."

"It's an air of worry and poverty and sleepless nights," said Gordon, rather defiantly.

"I don't know."

"Oh, I admit I'm depressing. I depress myself. But, my God, Phil, a week's rest and a new suit and some ready money and I'd be like—like I was. Phil, I can draw like a streak, and you know it. But half

the time I haven't had the money to buy decent drawing materials
—and I can't draw when I'm tired and discouraged and all in. With
a little ready money I can take a few weeks off and get started."

"How do I know you wouldn't use it on some other woman?"

"Why rub it in?" said Gordon quietly.

"I'm not rubbing it in. I hate to see you this way."

"Will you lend me the money, Phil?"

"I can't decide right off. That's a lot of money and it'll be darn
inconvenient for me."

"It'll be hell for me if you can't—I know I'm whining, and it's all
my own fault but—that doesn't change it."

"When could you pay it back?"

This was encouraging. Gordon considered. It was probably wisest
to be frank.

"Of course, I could promise to send it back next month, but—I'd
better say three months. Just as soon as I start to sell drawings."

"How do I know you'll sell any drawings?"

A new hardness in Dean's voice sent a faint chill of doubt over
Gordon. Was it possible that he wouldn't get the money?

"I supposed you had a little confidence in me."

"I did have—but when I see you like this I begin to wonder."

"Do you suppose if I wasn't at the end of my rope I'd come to
you like this? Do you think I'm enjoying it?" He broke off and bit
his lip, feeling that he had better subdue the rising anger in his voice.
After all, he was the suppliant.

"You seem to manage it pretty easily," said Dean angrily. "You
put me in the position where, if I don't lend it to you, I'm a sucker
—oh, yes, you do. And let me tell you it's no easy thing for me to get
hold of three hundred dollars. My income isn't so big but that a
slice like that won't play the deuce with it."

He left his chair and began to dress, choosing his clothes carefully. Gordon stretched out his arms and clenched the edges of the
bed, fighting back a desire to cry out. His head was splitting and
whirring, his mouth was dry and bitter and he could feel the fever
in his blood resolving itself into innumerable regular counts like a
slow dripping from a roof.

Dean tied his tie precisely, brushed his eyebrows, and removed a
piece of tobacco from his teeth with solemnity. Next he filled his
cigarette case, tossed the empty box thoughtfully into the waste
basket, and settled the case in his vest pocket.

"Had breakfast?" he demanded.

"No; I don't eat it any more."

"Well, we'll go out and have some. We'll decide about that money
later. I'm sick of the subject. I came East to have a good time.

"Let's go over to the Yale Club," he continued moodily, and then added with an implied reproof: "You've given up your job. You've got nothing else to do."

"I'd have a lot to do if I had a little money," said Gordon pointedly.

"Oh, for Heaven's sake drop the subject for a while! No point in glooming on my whole trip. Here, here's some money."

He took a five-dollar bill from his wallet and tossed it over to Gordon, who folded it carefully and put it in his pocket. There was an added spot of color in his cheeks, an added glow that was not fever. For an instant before they turned to go out their eyes met and in that instant each found something that made him lower his own glance quickly. For in that instant they quite suddenly and definitely hated each other.

II

Fifth Avenue and Forty-fourth Street swarmed with the noon crowd. The wealthy, happy sun glittered in transient gold through the thick windows of the smart shops, lighting upon mesh bags and purses and strings of pearls in gray velvet cases; upon gaudy feather fans of many colors; upon the laces and silks of expensive dresses; upon the bad paintings and the fine period furniture in the elaborate show rooms of interior decorators.

Working-girls, in pairs and groups and swarms, loitered by these windows, choosing their future boudoirs from some resplendent display which included even a man's silk pajamas laid domestically across the bed. They stood in front of the jewelry stores and picked out their engagement rings, and their wedding rings and their platinum wrist watches, and then drifted on to inspect the feather fans and opera cloaks; meanwhile digesting the sandwiches and sundaes they had eaten for lunch.

All through the crowd were men in uniform, sailors from the great fleet anchored in the Hudson, soldiers with divisional insignia from Massachusetts to California wanting fearfully to be noticed, and finding the great city thoroughly fed up with soldiers unless they were nicely massed into pretty formations and uncomfortable under the weight of a pack and rifle.

Through this medley Dean and Gordon wandered; the former interested, made alert by the display of humanity at its frothiest and gaudiest; the latter reminded of how often he had been one of the crowd, tired, casually fed, overworked, and dissipated. To Dean the struggle was significant, young, cheerful; to Gordon it was dismal, meaningless, endless.

In the Yale Club they met a group of their former classmates who greeted the visiting Dean vociferously. Sitting in a semicircle of lounges and great chairs, they had a highball all around.

Gordon found the conversation tiresome and interminable. They lunched together *en masse*, warmed with liquor as the afternoon began. They were all going to the Gamma Psi dance that night—it promised to be the best party since the war.

"Edith Bradin's coming," said some one to Gordon. "Didn't she used to be an old flame of yours? Aren't you both from Harrisburg?"

"Yes." He tried to change the subject. "I see her brother occasionally. He's sort of a socialistic nut. Runs a paper or something here in New York."

"Not like his gay sister, eh?" continued his eager informant. "Well, she's coming to-night with a junior named Peter Himmel."

Gordon was to meet Jewel Hudson at eight o'clock—he had promised to have some money for her. Several times he glanced nervously at his wrist watch. At four, to his relief, Dean rose and announced that he was going over to Rivers Brothers to buy some collars and ties. But as they left the Club another of the party joined them, to Gordon's great dismay. Dean was in a jovial mood now, happy, expectant of the evening's party, faintly hilarious. Over in Rivers' he chose a dozen neckties, selecting each one after long consultations with the other man. Did he think narrow ties were coming back? And wasn't it a shame that Rivers couldn't get any more Welsh Margotson collars? There never was a collar like the "Covington."

Gordon was in something of a panic. He wanted the money immediately. And he was now inspired also with a vague idea of attending the Gamma Psi dance. He wanted to see Edith—Edith whom he hadn't met since one romantic night at the Harrisburg Country Club just before he went to France. The affair had died, drowned in the turmoil of the war and quite forgotten in the arabesque of these three months, but a picture of her, poignant, debonnaire, immersed in her own inconsequential chatter, recurred to him unexpectedly and brought a hundred memories with it. It was Edith's face that he had cherished through college with a sort of detached yet affectionate admiration. He had loved to draw her—around his room had been a dozen sketches of her—playing golf, swimming—he could draw her pert, arresting profile with his eyes shut.

They left Rivers' at five-thirty and paused for a moment on the sidewalk.

"Well," said Dean genially, "I'm all set now. Think I'll go back to the hotel and get a shave, haircut, and massage."

"Good enough," said the other man, "I think I'll join you."

Gordon wondered if he was to be beaten after all. With difficulty he restrained himself from turning to the man and snarling out, "Go on away, damn you!" In despair he suspected that perhaps Dean had spoken to him, was keeping him along in order to avoid a dispute about the money.

They went into the Biltmore—a Biltmore alive with girls—mostly from the West and South, the stellar débutantes of many cities gathered for the dance of a famous fraternity of a famous university. But to Gordon they were faces in a dream. He gathered together his forces for a last appeal, was about to come out with he knew not what, when Dean suddenly excused himself to the other man and taking Gordon's arm led him aside.

"Gordy," he said quickly, "I've thought the whole thing over carefully and I've decided that I can't lend you that money. I'd like to oblige you, but I don't feel I ought to—it'd put a crimp in me for a month."

Gordon, watching him dully, wondered why he had never before noticed how much those upper teeth projected.

"—I'm mighty sorry, Gordon," continued Dean, "but that's the way it is."

He took out his wallet and deliberately counted out seventy-five dollars in bills.

"Here," he said, holding them out, "here's seventy-five; that makes eighty all together. That's all the actual cash I have with me, besides what I'll actually spend on the trip."

Gordon raised his clenched hand automatically, opened it as though it were a tongs he was holding, and clenched it again on the money.

"I'll see you at the dance," continued Dean. "I've got to get along to the barber shop."

"So-long," said Gordon in a strained and husky voice.

"So-long."

Dean began to smile, but seemed to change his mind. He nodded briskly and disappeared.

But Gordon stood there, his handsome face awry with distress, the roll of bills clenched tightly in his hand. Then, blinded by sudden tears, he stumbled clumsily down the Biltmore steps.

III

About nine o'clock of the same night two human beings came out of a cheap restaurant in Sixth Avenue. They were ugly, ill-nourished, devoid of all except the very lowest form of intelligence, and without even that animal exuberance that in itself brings color into life; they were lately vermin-ridden, cold, and hungry in a dirty town of

a strange land; they were poor, friendless; tossed as driftwood from
their births, they would be tossed as driftwood to their deaths. They
were dressed in the uniform of the United States Army, and on the
shoulder of each was the insignia of a drafted division from New
Jersey, landed three days before.

The taller of the two was named Carrol Key, a name hinting that
in his veins, however thinly diluted by generations of degeneration,
ran blood of some potentiality. But one could stare endlessly at the
long, chinless face, the dull, watery eyes, and high cheek-bones, without finding a suggestion of either ancestral worth or native resourcefulness.

His companion was swart and bandy-legged, with rat-eyes and a
much-broken hooked nose. His defiant air was obviously a pretense,
a weapon of protection borrowed from that world of snarl and snap,
of physical bluff and physical menace, in which he had always lived.
His name was Gus Rose.

Leaving the café they sauntered down Sixth Avenue, wielding
toothpicks with great gusto and complete detachment.

"Where to?" asked Rose, in a tone which implied that he would not
be surprised if Key suggested the South Sea Islands.

"What you say we see if we can getta holda some liquor?" Prohibition was not yet. The ginger in the suggestion was caused by the
law forbidding the selling of liquor to soldiers.

Rose agreed enthusiastically.

"I got an idea," continued Key, after a moment's thought, "I got a
brother somewhere."

"In New York?"

"Yeah. He's an old fella." He meant that he was an elder brother.
"He's a waiter in a hash joint."

"Maybe he can get us some."

"I'll say he can!"

"B'lieve me, I'm goin' to get this darn uniform off me to-morra.
Never get me in it again, neither. I'm goin' to get me some regular
clothes."

"Say, maybe I'm not."

As their combined finances were something less than five dollars,
this intention can be taken largely as a pleasant game of words, harm-
less and consoling. It seemed to please both of them, however, for
they reinforced it with chuckling and mention of personages high in
biblical circles, adding such further emphasis as "Oh, boy!" "You
know!" and "I'll say so!" repeated many times over.

The entire mental pabulum of these two men consisted of an
offended nasal comment extended through the years upon the institution—army, business, or poorhouse—which kept them alive, and

toward their immediate superior in that institution. Until that very morning the institution had been the "government" and the immediate superior had been the "Cap'n"—from these two they had glided out and were now in the vaguely uncomfortable state before they should adopt their next bondage. They were uncertain, resentful, and somewhat ill at ease. This they hid by pretending an elaborate relief at being out of the army, and by assuring each other that military discipline should never again rule their stubborn, liberty-loving wills. Yet, as a matter of fact, they would have felt more at home in a prison than in this new-found and unquestionable freedom.

Suddenly Key increased his gait. Rose, looking up and following his glance, discovered a crowd that was collecting fifty yards down the street. Key chuckled and began to run in the direction of the crowd; Rose thereupon also chuckled and his short bandy legs twinkled beside the long, awkward strides of his companion.

Reaching the outskirts of the crowd they immediately became an indistinguishable part of it. It was composed of ragged civilians somewhat the worse for liquor, and of soldiers representing many divisions and many stages of sobriety, all clustered around a gesticulating little Jew with long black whiskers, who was waving his arms and delivering an excited but succinct harangue. Key and Rose, having wedged themselves into the approximate parquet, scrutinized him with acute suspicion, as his words penetrated their common consciousness.

"—What have you got outa the war?" he was crying fiercely. "Look arounja, look arounja! Are you rich? Have you got a lot of money offered you?—no; you're lucky if you're alive and got both your legs; you're lucky if you came back an' find your wife ain't gone off with some other fella that had the money to buy himself out of the war! That's when you're lucky! Who got anything out of it except J. P. Morgan an' John D. Rockerfeller?"

At this point the little Jew's oration was interrupted by the hostile impact of a fist upon the point of his bearded chin and he toppled backward to a sprawl on the pavement.

"God damn Bolsheviki!" cried the big soldier-blacksmith who had delivered the blow. There was a rumble of approval, the crowd closed in nearer.

The Jew staggered to his feet, and immediately went down again before a half-dozen reaching-in fists. This time he stayed down, breathing heavily, blood oozing from his lip where it was cut within and without.

There was a riot of voices, and in a minute Rose and Key found themselves flowing with the jumbled crowd down Sixth Avenue under the leadership of a thin civilian in a slouch hat and the brawny soldier who had summarily ended the oration. The crowd had marvelously swollen to formidable proportions and a stream of more noncommittal citizens followed it along the sidewalks lending their moral support by intermittent huzzas.

"Where we goin'?" yelled Key to the man nearest him.

His neighbor pointed up to the leader in the slouch hat.

"That guy knows where there's a lot of 'em! We're goin' to show 'em!"

"We're goin' to show 'em!" whispered Key delightedly to Rose, who repeated the phrase rapturously to a man on the other side.

Down Sixth Avenue swept the procession, joined here and there by soldiers and marines, and now and then by civilians, who came up with the inevitable cry that they were just out of the army themselves, as if presenting it as a card of admission to a newly formed Sporting and Amusement Club.

Then the procession swerved down a cross street and headed for Fifth Avenue and the word filtered here and there that they were bound for a Red meeting at Tolliver Hall.

"Where is it?"

The question went up the line and a moment later the answer floated back. Tolliver Hall was down on Tenth Street. There was a bunch of other sojers who was goin' to break it up and was down there now!

But Tenth Street had a faraway sound and at the word a general groan went up and a score of the procession dropped out. Among these were Rose and Key, who slowed down to a saunter and let the more enthusiastic sweep on by.

"I'd rather get some liquor," said Key as they halted and made their way to the sidewalk amid cries of "Shell hole!" and "Quitters!"

"Does your brother work around here?" asked Rose, assuming the air of one passing from the superficial to the eternal.

"He oughta," replied Key. "I ain't seen him for a coupla years. I been out to Pennsylvania since. Maybe he don't work at night anyhow. It's right along here. He can get us some o'right if he ain't gone."

They found the place after a few minutes' patrol of the street—a shoddy tablecloth restaurant between Fifth Avenue and Broadway. Here Key went inside to inquire for his brother George, while Rose waited on the sidewalk.

"He ain't here no more," said Key emerging. "He's a waiter up to Delmonico's."

Rose nodded wisely, as if he'd expected as much. One should not be surprised at a capable man changing jobs occasionally. He knew a waiter once—there ensued a long conversation as they walked as

May Day

to whether waiters made more in actual wages than in tips—it was decided that it depended on the social tone of the joint wherein the waiter labored. After having given each other vivid pictures of millionaires dining at Delmonico's and throwing away fifty-dollar bills after their first quart of champagne, both men thought privately of becoming waiters. In fact, Key's narrow brow was secreting a resolution to ask his brother to get him a job.

"A waiter can drink up all the champagne those fellas leave in bottles," suggested Rose with some relish, and then added as an afterthought, "Oh, boy!"

By the time they reached Delmonico's it was half past ten, and they were surprised to see a stream of taxis driving up to the door one after the other and emitting marvelous, hatless young ladies, each one attended by a stiff young gentleman in evening clothes.

"It's a party," said Rose with some awe. "Maybe we better not go in. He'll be busy."

"No, he won't. He'll be o'right."

After some hesitation they entered what appeared to them to be the least elaborate door and, indecision falling upon them immediately, stationed themselves nervously in an inconspicuous corner of the small dining-room in which they found themselves. They took off their caps and held them in their hands. A cloud of gloom fell upon them and both started when a door at one end of the room crashed open, emitting a comet-like waiter who streaked across the floor and vanished through another door on the other side.

There had been three of these lightning passages before the seekers mustered the acumen to hail a waiter. He turned, looked at them suspiciously, and then approached with soft, catlike steps, as if prepared at any moment to turn and flee.

"Say," began Key, "say, do you know my brother? He's a waiter here."

"His name is Key," annotated Rose.

Yes, the waiter knew Key. He was up-stairs, he thought. There was a big dance going on in the main ballroom. He'd tell him.

Ten minutes later George Key appeared and greeted his brother with the utmost suspicion; his first and most natural thought being that he was going to be asked for money.

George was tall and weak chinned, but there his resemblance to his brother ceased. The waiter's eyes were not dull, they were alert and twinkling, and his manner was suave, in-door, and faintly superior. They exchanged formalities. George was married and had three children. He seemed fairly interested, but not impressed by the news that Carrol had been abroad in the army. This disappointed Carrol.

"George," said the younger brother, these amenities having been disposed of, "we want to get some booze, and they won't sell us none. Can you get us some?"

George considered.

"Sure. Maybe I can. It may be half an hour, though."

"All right," agreed Carrol, "we'll wait."

At this Rose started to sit down in a convenient chair, but was haled to his feet by the indignant George.

"Hey! Watch out, you! Can't sit down here! This room's all set for a twelve o'clock banquet."

"I ain't goin' to hurt it," said Rose resentfully. "I been through the delouser."

"Never mind," said George sternly, "if the head waiter seen me here talkin' he'd romp all over me."

"Oh."

The mention of the head waiter was full explanation to the other two; they fingered their overseas caps nervously and waited for a suggestion.

"I tell you," said George, after a pause, "I got a place you can wait; you just come here with me."

They followed him out the far door, through a deserted pantry and up a pair of dark winding stairs, emerging finally into a small room chiefly furnished by piles of pails and stacks of scrubbing brushes, and illuminated by a single dim electric light. There he left them, after soliciting two dollars and agreeing to return in half an hour with a quart of whiskey.

"George is makin' money, I bet," said Key gloomily as he seated himself on an inverted pail. "I bet he's making fifty dollars a week."

Rose nodded his head and spat.

"I bet he is, too."

"What'd he say the dance was of?"

"A lot of college fellas. Yale College."

They both nodded solemnly at each other.

"Wonder where that crowda sojers is now?"

"I don't know. I know that's too damn long to walk for me."

"Me too. You don't catch me walkin' that far."

Ten minutes later restlessness seized them.

"I'm goin' to see what's out here," said Rose, stepping cautiously toward the other door.

It was a swinging door of green baize and he pushed it open a cautious inch.

"See anything?"

For answer Rose drew in his breath sharply.

"Doggone! Here's some liquor I'll say!"

"Liquor?"

Key joined Rose at the door, and looked eagerly.

"I'll tell the world that's liquor," he said, after a moment of concentrated gazing.

It was a room about twice as large as the one they were in—and in it was prepared a radiant feast of spirits. There were long walls of alternating bottles set along two white covered tables; whiskey, gin, brandy, French and Italian vermouths, and orange juice, not to mention an array of syphons and two great empty punch bowls. The room was as yet uninhabited.

"It's for this dance they're just starting," whispered Key; "hear the violins playin'? Say, boy, I wouldn't mind havin' a dance."

They closed the door softly and exchanged a glance of mutual comprehension. There was no need of feeling each other out.

"I'd like to get my hands on a coupla those bottles," said Rose emphatically.

"Me too."

"Do you suppose we'd get seen?"

Key considered.

"Maybe we better wait till they start drinkin' 'em. They got 'em all laid out now, and they know how many of them there are."

They debated this point for several minutes. Rose was all for getting his hands on a bottle now and tucking it under his coat before any one came into the room. Key, however, advocated caution. He was afraid he might get his brother in trouble. If they waited till some of the bottles were opened it'd be all right to take one, and everybody'd think it was one of the college fellas.

While they were still engaged in argument George Key hurried through the room and, barely grunting at them, disappeared by way of the green baize door. A minute later they heard several corks pop, and then the sound of crackling ice and splashing liquid. George was mixing the punch.

The soldiers exchanged delighted grins.

"Oh, boy!" whispered Rose.

George reappeared.

"Just keep low, boys," he said quickly. "I'll have your stuff for you in five minutes."

He disappeared through the door by which he had come.

As soon as his footsteps receded down the stairs, Rose, after a cautious look, darted into the room of delights and reappeared with a bottle in his hand.

"Here's what I say," he said, as they sat radiantly digesting their first drink. "We'll wait till he comes up, and we'll ask him if we can't just stay here and drink what he brings us—see. We'll tell him

we haven't got any place to drink it—see. Then we can sneak in
there whenever there ain't nobody in that there room and tuck a
bottle under our coats. We'll have enough to last us a coupla days—
see?"

"Sure," agreed Rose enthusiastically. "Oh, boy! And if we want to
we can sell it to sojers any time we want to."

They were silent for a moment thinking rosily of this idea. Then
Key reached up and unhooked the collar of his O. D. coat.

"It's hot in here, ain't it?"

Rose agreed earnestly.

"Hot as hell."

IV

She was still quite angry when she came out of the dressing-room
and crossed the intervening parlor of politeness that opened onto the
hall—angry not so much at the actual happening which was, after
all, the merest commonplace of her social existence, but because it
had occurred on this particular night. She had no quarrel with herself. She had acted with that correct mixture of dignity and reticent
pity which she always employed. She had succinctly and deftly
snubbed him.

It had happened when their taxi was leaving the Biltmore—hadn't
gone half a block. He had lifted his right arm awkwardly—she was
on his right side—and attempted to settle it snugly around the crimson fur-trimmed opera cloak she wore. This in itself had been a mistake. It was inevitably more graceful for a young man attempting
to embrace a young lady of whose acquiescence he was not certain, to
first put his far arm around her. It avoided that awkward movement
of raising the near arm.

His second *faux pas* was unconscious. She had spent the afternoon
at the hairdresser's; the idea of any calamity overtaking her hair
was extremely repugnant—yet as Peter made his unfortunate attempt
the point of his elbow had just faintly brushed it. That was his
second *faux pas*. Two were quite enough.

He had begun to murmur. At the first murmur she had decided
that he was nothing but a college boy—Edith was twenty-two, and
anyhow, this dance, first of its kind since the war, was reminding
her, with the accelerating rhythm of its associations, of something
else—of another dance and another man, a man for whom her feelings had been little more than a sad-eyed, adolescent mooniness.
Edith Bradin was falling in love with her recollection of Gordon
Sterrett.

So she came out of the dressing-room at Delmonico's and stood for a second in the doorway looking over the shoulders of a black dress in front of her at the groups of Yale men who flitted like dignified black moths around the head of the stairs. From the room she had left drifted out the heavy fragrance left by the passage to and fro of many scented young beauties—rich perfumes and the fragile memory-laden dust of fragrant powders. This odor drifting out acquired the tang of cigarette smoke in the hall, and then settled sensuously down the stairs and permeated the ballroom where the Gamma Psi dance was to be held. It was an odor she knew well, exciting, stimulating, restlessly sweet—the odor of a fashionable dance.   *narcissism*

She thought of her own appearance. Her bare arms and shoulders ✓ were powdered to a creamy white. She knew they looked very soft and would gleam like milk against the black backs that were to silhouette them tonight. The hairdressing had been a success; her reddish mass of hair was piled and crushed and creased to an arrogant marvel of mobile curves. Her lips were finely made of deep carmine; the irises of her eyes were delicate, breakable blue, like china eyes. She was a complete, infinitely delicate, quite perfect thing of beauty, flowing in an even line from a complex coiffure to two small slim feet.

She thought of what she would say to-night at this revel, faintly presaged already by the sounds of high and low laughter and slippered footsteps, and movements of couples up and down the stairs. She would talk the language she had talked for many years—her line—made up of the current expressions, bits of journalese and college slang strung together into an intrinsic whole, careless, faintly provocative, delicately sentimental. She smiled faintly as she heard a girl sitting on the stairs near her say: "You don't know the half of it, dearie!"

And as she smiled her anger melted for a moment, and closing her eyes she drew in a deep breath of pleasure. She dropped her arms to her side until they were faintly touching the sleek sheath that covered and suggested her figure. She had never felt her own softness so much nor so enjoyed the whiteness of her own arms.

"I smell sweet," she said to herself simply, and then came another thought—"I'm made for love."

She liked the sound of this and thought it again; then in inevitable succession came her new-born riot of dreams about Gordon. The twist of her imagination which, two hours before, had disclosed to her her unguessed desire to see him again, seemed now to have been leading up to this dance, this hour.

For all her sleek beauty, Edith was a grave, slow-thinking girl. There was a streak in her of that same desire to ponder, of that adolescent idealism that had turned her brother socialist and pacifist.

Henry Bradin had left Cornell, where he had been an instructor in economics, and had come to New York to pour the latest cures for incurable evils into the columns of a radical weekly newspaper.

Edith, less fatuously, would have been content to cure Gordon Sterrett. There was a quality of weakness in Gordon that she wanted to take care of; there was a helplessness in him that she wanted to protect. And she wanted someone she had known a long while, someone who had loved her a long while. She was a little tired; she wanted to get married. Out of a pile of letters, half a dozen pictures and as many memories, and this weariness, she had decided that next time she saw Gordon their relations were going to be changed. She would say something that would change them. There was this evening. This was her evening. All evenings were her evenings.

Then her thoughts were interrupted by a solemn undergraduate with a hurt look and an air of strained formality who presented himself before her and bowed unusually low. It was the man she had come with, Peter Himmel. He was tall and humorous, with horned-rimmed glasses and an air of attractive whimsicality. She suddenly rather disliked him—probably because he had not succeeded in kissing her.

"Well," she began, "are you still furious at me?"

"Not at all."

She stepped forward and took his arm.

"I'm sorry," she said softly. "I don't know why I snapped out that way. I'm in a bum humor to-night for some strange reason. I'm sorry."

"S'all right," he mumbled, "don't mention it."

He felt disagreeably embarrassed. Was she rubbing in the fact of his late failure?

"It was a mistake," she continued, on the same consciously gentle key. "We'll both forget it." For this he hated her.

A few minutes later they drifted out on the floor while the dozen swaying, sighing members of the specially hired jazz orchestra informed the crowded ballroom that "if a saxophone and me are left alone why then two is com-pan-ee!"

A man with a mustache cut in.

"Hello," he began reprovingly. "You don't remember me."

"I can't just think of your name," she said lightly—"and I know you so well."

"I met you up at—" His voice trailed disconsolately off as a man with very fair hair cut in. Edith murmured a conventional "Thanks, loads—cut in later," to the *inconnu*.

The very fair man insisted on shaking hands enthusiastically. She placed him as one of the numerous Jims of her acquaintance—last name a mystery. She remembered even that he had a peculiar rhythm in dancing and found as they started that she was right.

"Going to be here long?" he breathed confidentially.

She leaned back and looked up at him.

"Couple of weeks."

"Where are you?"

"Biltmore. Call me up some day."

"I mean it," he assured her. "I will. We'll go to tea."

"So do I—Do."

A dark man cut in with intense formality.

"You don't remember me, do you?" he said gravely.

"I should say I do. Your name's Harlan."

"No-ope. Barlow."

"Well, I knew there were two syllables anyway. You're the boy that played the ukulele so well up at Howard Marshall's house party."

"I played—but not——"

A man with prominent teeth cut in. Edith inhaled a slight cloud of whiskey. She liked men to have had something to drink; they were so much more cheerful, and appreciative and complimentary—much easier to talk to.

"My name's Dean, Philip Dean," he said cheerfully. "You don't remember me, I know, but you used to come up to New Haven with a fellow I roomed with senior year, Gordon Sterrett."

Edith looked up quickly.

"Yes, I went up with him twice—to the Pump and Slipper and the Junior prom."

"You've seen him, of course," said Dean carelessly. "He's here to-night. I saw him just a minute ago."

Edith started. Yet she had felt quite sure he would be here.

"Why, no, I haven't——"

A fat man with red hair cut in.

"Hello, Edith," he began.

"Why—hello there——"

She slipped, stumbled lightly.

"I'm sorry, dear," she murmured mechanically.

She had seen Gordon—Gordon very white and listless, leaning against the side of a doorway, smoking and looking into the ball-room. Edith could see that his face was thin and wan—that the hand he raised to his lips with a cigarette was trembling. They were dancing quite close to him now.

"—They invite so darn many extra fellas that you—" the short man was saying.

"Hello, Gordon," called Edith over her partner's shoulder. Her heart was pounding wildly.

xl   His large dark eyes were fixed on her. He took a step in her direction. Her partner turned her away—she heard his voice bleating——

"—but half the stags get lit and leave before long, so——"

Then a low tone at her side.

"May I, please?"

She was dancing suddenly with Gordon; one of his arms was around her; she felt it tighten spasmodically; felt his hand on her back with the fingers spread. Her hand holding the little lace handkerchief was crushed in his.

"Why Gordon," she began breathlessly.

"Hello, Edith."

She slipped again—was tossed forward by her recovery until her face touched the black cloth of his dinner coat. She loved him—she knew she loved him—then for a minute there was silence while a strange feeling of uneasiness crept over her. Something was wrong.

Of a sudden her heart wrenched, and turned over as she realized what it was. He was pitiful and wretched, a little drunk, and miserably tired.

"Oh—" she cried involuntarily.

His eyes looked down at her. She saw suddenly that they were blood-streaked and rolling uncontrollably.

"Gordon," she murmured, "we'll sit down; I want to sit down."

They were nearly in mid-floor, but she had seen two men start toward her from opposite sides of the room, so she halted, seized Gordon's limp hand and led him bumping through the crowd, her mouth tight shut, her face a little pale under her rouge, her eyes trembling with tears.

She found a place high up on the soft-carpeted stairs, and he sat down heavily beside her.

"Well," he began, staring at her unsteadily, "I certainly am glad to see you, Edith."

She looked at him without answering. The effect of this on her was immeasurable. For years she had seen men in various stages of intoxication, from uncles all the way down to chauffeurs, and her feelings had varied from amusement to disgust, but here for the first time she was seized with a new feeling—an unutterable horror.

"Gordon," she said accusingly and almost crying, "you look like the devil."

He nodded. "I've had trouble, Edith."

"Trouble?"

"All sorts of trouble. Don't you say anything to the family, but I'm all gone to pieces. I'm a mess, Edith."

His lower lip was sagging. He seemed scarcely to see her.

"Can't you—can't you," she hesitated, "can't you tell me about it, Gordon? You know I'm always interested in you."

She bit her lip—she had intended to say something stronger, but found at the end that she couldn't bring it out.

Gordon shook his head dully. "I can't tell you. You're a good woman. I can't tell a good woman the story."

"Rot," she said, defiantly. "I think it's a perfect insult to call any one a good woman in that way. It's a slam. You've been drinking, Gordon."

"Thanks." He inclined his head gravely. "Thanks for the information."

"Why do you drink?"

"Because I'm so damn miserable."

"Do you think drinking's going to make it any better?"

"What you doing—trying to reform me?"

"No; I'm trying to help you, Gordon. Can't you tell me about it?"

"I'm in an awful mess. Best thing you can do is to pretend not to know me."

"Why, Gordon?"

"I'm sorry I cut in on you—it's unfair to you. You're pure woman—and all that sort of thing. Here, I'll get some one else to dance with you."

He rose clumsily to his feet, but she reached up and pulled him down beside her on the stairs.

"Here, Gordon. You're ridiculous. You're hurting me. You're acting like a—like a crazy man——"

"I admit it. I'm a little crazy. Something's wrong with me, Edith. There's something left me. It doesn't matter."

"It does, tell me."

"Just that. I was always queer—little bit different from other boys. All right in college, but now it's all wrong. Things have been snapping inside me for four months like little hooks on a dress, and it's about to come off when a few more hooks go. I'm very gradually going loony."

He turned his eyes full on her and began to laugh, and she shrank away from him.

"What *is* the matter?"

"Just me," he repeated. "I'm going loony. This whole place is like a dream to me—this Delmonico's——"

As he talked she saw he had changed utterly. He wasn't at all light and gay and careless—a great lethargy and discouragement had come over him. Revulsion seized her, followed by a faint, surprising boredom. His voice seemed to come out of a great void.

"Edith," he said, "I used to think I was clever, talented, an artist.

Now I know I'm nothing. Can't draw, Edith. Don't know why I'm telling you this."

She nodded absently.

"I can't draw, I can't do anything. I'm poor as a church mouse." He laughed, bitterly and rather too loud. "I've become a damn beggar, a leech on my friends. I'm a failure. I'm poor as hell."

Her distaste was growing. She barely nodded this time, waiting for her first possible cue to rise.

Suddenly Gordon's eyes filled with tears.

"Edith," he said, turning to her with what was evidently a strong effort at self-control, "I can't tell you what it means to me to know there's one person left who's interested in me."

He reached out and patted her hand, and involuntarily she drew it away.

"It's mighty fine of you," he repeated.

"Well," she said slowly, looking him in the eye, "any one's always glad to see an old friend—but I'm sorry to see you like this, Gordon."

There was a pause while they looked at each other, and the momentary eagerness in his eyes wavered. She rose and stood looking at him, her face quite expressionless.

"Shall we dance?" she suggested, coolly.

—Love is fragile—she was thinking—but perhaps the pieces are saved, the things that hovered on lips, that might have been said. The new love words, the tendernesses learned, are treasured up for the next lover.

V

Peter Himmel, escort to the lovely Edith, was unaccustomed to being snubbed; having been snubbed, he was hurt and embarrassed, and ashamed of himself. For a matter of two months he had been on special delivery terms with Edith Bradin and, knowing that the one excuse and explanation of the special delivery letter is its value in sentimental correspondence, he had believed himself quite sure of his ground. He searched in vain for any reason why she should have taken this attitude in the matter of a simple kiss.

Therefore when he was cut in on by the man with the mustache he went out into the hall and, making up a sentence, said it over to himself several times. Considerably deleted, this was it:

"Well, if any girl ever led a man on and then jolted him, she did— and she has no kick coming if I go out and get beautifully boiled."

So he walked through the supper room into a small room adjoining it, which he had located earlier in the evening. It was a room in which there were several large bowls of punch flanked by many bottles. He took a seat beside the table which held the bottles.

At the second highball, boredom, disgust, the monotony of time, the turbidity of events, sank into a vague background before which glittering cobwebs formed. Things became reconciled to themselves, things lay quietly on their shelves; the troubles of the day arranged themselves in trim formation and at his curt wish of dismissal, marched off and disappeared. And with the departure of worry came brilliant, permeating symbolism. Edith became a flighty, negligible girl, not to be worried over; rather to be laughed at. She fitted like a figure of his own dream into the surface world forming about him. He himself became in a measure symbolic, a type of the continent bacchanal, the brilliant dreamer at play.

Then the symbolic mood faded and as he sipped his third highball his imagination yielded to the warm glow and he lapsed into a state similar to floating on his back in pleasant water. It was at this point that he noticed that a green baize door near him was open about two inches, and that through the aperture a pair of eyes were watching him intently.

"Hm," murmured Peter calmly.

The green door closed—and then opened again—a bare half inch this time.

"Peek-a-boo," murmured Peter.

The door remained stationary and then he became aware of a series of tense intermittent whispers.

"One guy."

"What's he doin'?"

"He's sittin' lookin'."

"He better beat it off. We gotta get another li'l' bottle."

Peter listened while the words filtered into his consciousness.

"Now this," he thought, "is most remarkable."

He was excited. He was jubilant. He felt that he had stumbled upon a mystery. Affecting an elaborate carelessness he arose and walked around the table—then, turning quickly, pulled open the green door, precipitating Private Rose into the room.

Peter bowed.

"How do you do?" he said.

Private Rose set one foot slightly in front of the other, poised for fight, flight, or compromise.

"How do you do?" repeated Peter politely.

"I'm o'right."

"Can I offer you a drink?"

Private Rose looked at him searchingly, suspecting possible sarcasm.

"O'right," he said finally.

Peter indicated a chair.

"Sit down."

"I got a friend," said Rose, "I got a friend in there." He pointed to the green door.

"By all means let's have him in."

Peter crossed over, opened the door and welcomed in Private Key, very suspicious and uncertain and guilty. Chairs were found and the three took their seats around the punch bowl. Peter gave them each a highball and offered them a cigarette from his case. They accepted both with some diffidence.

"Now," continued Peter easily, "may I ask why you gentlemen prefer to lounge away your leisure hours in a room which is chiefly furnished, as far as I can see, with scrubbing brushes. And when the human race has progressed to the stage where seventeen thousand chairs are manufactured on every day except Sunday—" he paused. Rose and Key regarded him vacantly. "Will you tell me," went on Peter, "why you choose to rest yourselves on articles intended for the transportation of water from one place to another?"

At this point Rose contributed a grunt to the conversation.

"And lastly," finished Peter, "will you tell me why, when you are in a building beautifully hung with enormous candelabra, you prefer to spend these evening hours under one anemic electric light?"

Rose looked at Key; Key looked at Rose. They laughed; they laughed uproariously; they found it was impossible to look at each other without laughing. But they were not laughing with this man —they were laughing at him. To them a man who talked after this fashion was either raving drunk or raving crazy.

"You are Yale men, I presume," said Peter, finishing his highball and preparing another.

They laughed again.

"Na-ah."

"So? I thought perhaps you might be members of that lowly section of the university known as the Sheffield Scientific School."

"Na-ah."

"Hm. Well, that's too bad. No doubt you are Harvard men, anxious to preserve your incognito in this—this paradise of violet blue, as the newspapers say."

"Na-ah," said Key scornfully, "we was just waitin' for somebody."

"Ah," exclaimed Peter, rising and filling their glasses, "very interestin'. Had a date with a scrublady, eh?"

They both denied this indignantly.

"It's all right," Peter reassured them, "don't apologize. A scrublady's as good as any lady in the world. Kipling says 'Any lady and *are sisters*

Judy O'Grady/under the skin.' "

"Sure," said Key, winking broadly at Rose.

"My case, for instance," continued Peter, finishing his glass. "I got a girl up there that's spoiled. Spoildest darn girl I ever saw. Refused to kiss me; no reason whatsoever. Led me on deliberately to think sure I want to kiss you and then plunk! Threw me over! What's the younger generation comin' to?"

"Say tha's hard luck," said Key— "that's awful hard luck."

"Oh boy!" said Rose.

"Have another?" said Peter.

"We got in a sort of fight for a while," said Key after a pause, "but it was too far away."

"A fight?—tha's stuff!" said Peter, seating himself unsteadily. "Fight 'em all! I was in the army."

"This was with a Bolshevik fella."

"Tha's stuff!" exclaimed Peter, enthusiastic. "That's what I say! Kill the Bolshevik! Exterminate 'em!"

"We're Americuns," said Rose, implying a sturdy, defiant patriotism.

"Sure," said Peter. "Greatest race in the world! We're all Americuns! Have another."

They had another.

VI

At one o'clock a special orchestra, special even in a day of special orchestras, arrived at Delmonico's, and its members, seating themselves arrogantly around the piano, took up the burden of providing music for the Gamma Psi Fraternity. They were headed by a famous flute-player, distinguished throughout New York for his feat of standing on his head and shimmying with his shoulders while he played the latest jazz on his flute. During his performance the lights were extinguished except for the spotlight on the flute-player and another roving beam that threw flickering shadows and changing kaleidoscopic colors over the massed dancers.

Edith had danced herself into that tired, dreamy state habitual only with débutantes, a state equivalent to the glow of a noble soul after several long highballs. Her mind floated vaguely on the bosom of the music; her partners changed with the unreality of phantoms under the colorful shifting dusk, and to her present coma it seemed as if days had passed since the dance began. She had talked on many fragmentary subjects with many men. She had been kissed once and made love to six times. Earlier in the evening different undergraduates had danced with her, but now, like all the more popular girls

there, she had her own entourage—that is, half a dozen gallants had
singled her out or were alternating her charms with those of some
other chosen beauty; they cut in on her in regular, inevitable succession.

Several times she had seen Gordon—he had been sitting a long
time on the stairway with his palm to his head, his dull eyes fixed
at an infinite speck on the floor before him, very depressed, he looked,
and quite drunk—but Edith each time had averted her glance hurriedly. All that seemed long ago; her mind was passive now, her senses
were lulled to trance-like sleep; only her feet danced and her voice
talked on in hazy sentimental banter.

But Edith was not nearly so tired as to be incapable of moral indignation when Peter Himmel cut in on her, sublimely and happily
drunk. She gasped and looked up at him.

"Why, *Peter!*"

"I'm a li'l' stewed, Edith."

"Why, Peter, you're a *peach,* you are! Don't you think it's a bum
way of doing—when you're with me?"

Then she smiled unwillingly, for he was looking at her with owlish
sentimentality varied with a silly spasmodic smile.

"Darlin' Edith," he began earnestly, "you know I love you, don't
you?"

"You tell it well."

"I love you—and I merely wanted you to kiss me," he added sadly.

His embarrassment, his shame, were both gone. She was a mos'
beautiful girl in whole worl'. Mos' beautiful eyes, like stars above.
He wanted to 'pologize—firs', for presuming try to kiss her; second,
for drinking—but he'd been so discouraged 'cause he had thought
she was mad at him——

The red-fat man cut in, and looking up at Edith smiled radiantly.

"Did you bring any one?" she asked.

No. The red-fat man was a stag.

"Well, would you mind—would it be an awful bother for you to—
to take me home to-night?" (this extreme diffidence was a charming
affectation on Edith's part—she knew that the red-fat man would
immediately dissolve into a paroxysm of delight).

"Bother? Why, good Lord, I'd be darn glad to! You know I'd be
darn glad to."

"Thanks *loads!* You're awfully sweet."

She glanced at her wrist-watch. It was half-past one. And, as she
said "half-past one" to herself, it floated vaguely into her mind that
her brother had told her at luncheon that he worked in the office of
his newspaper until after one-thirty every evening.

Edith turned suddenly to her current partner.

"What street is Delmonico's on, anyway?"

"Street? Oh, why Fifth Avenue, of course."

"I mean, what cross street?"

"Why—let's see—it's on Forty-fourth Street."

This verified what she had thought. Henry's office must be across the street and just around the corner, and it occurred to her immediately that she might slip over for a moment and surprise him, float in on him, a shimmering marvel in her new crimson opera cloak and "cheer him up." It was exactly the sort of thing Edith revelled in doing—an unconventional, jaunty thing. The idea reached out and gripped at her imagination—after an instant's hesitation she had decided.

"My hair is just about to tumble entirely down," she said pleasantly to her partner; "would you mind if I go and fix it?"

"Not at all."

"You're a peach."

A few minutes later, wrapped in her crimson opera cloak, she flitted down a side-stairs, her cheeks glowing with excitement at her little adventure. She ran by a couple who stood at the door—a weak-chinned waiter and an over-rouged young lady, in hot dispute—and opening the outer door stepped into the warm May night.

VII

The over-rouged young lady followed her with a brief, bitter glance —then turned again to the weak-chinned waiter and took up her argument.

"You better go up and tell him I'm here," she said defiantly, "or I'll go up myself."

"No, you don't!" said George sternly.

The girl smiled sardonically.

"Oh, I don't, don't I? Well, let me tell you I know more college fellas and more of 'em know me, and are glad to take me out on a party, than you ever saw in your whole life."

"Maybe so——"

"Maybe so," she interrupted. "Oh, it's all right for any of 'em like that one that just ran out—God knows where *she* went—it's all right for them that are asked here to come or go as they like—but when I want to see a friend they have some cheap, ham-slinging, bring-me-a-doughnut waiter to stand here and keep me out."

"See here," said the elder Key indignantly, "I can't lose my job. Maybe this fella you're talkin' about doesn't want to see you."

"Oh, he wants to see me all right."

"Anyways, how could I find him in all that crowd?"

"Oh, he'll be there," she asserted confidently. "You just ask any-body for Gordon Sterrett and they'll point him out to you. They all know each other, those fellas."

She produced a mesh bag, and taking out a dollar bill handed it to George.

"Here," she said, "here's a bribe. You find him and give him my message. You tell him if he isn't here in five minutes I'm coming up."

George shook his head pessimistically, considered the question for a moment, wavered violently, and then withdrew.

In less than the allotted time Gordon came down-stairs. He was drunker than he had been earlier in the evening and in a different way. The liquor seemed to have hardened on him like a crust. He was heavy and lurching—almost incoherent when he talked.

" 'Lo, Jewel," he said thickly. "Came right away. Jewel, I couldn't get that money. Tried my best."

"Money nothing!" she snapped. "You haven't been near me for ten days. What's the matter?"

He shook his head slowly.

"Been very low, Jewel. Been sick."

"Why didn't you tell me if you were sick. I don't care about the money that bad. I didn't start bothering you about it at all until you began neglecting me."

Again he shook his head.

"Haven't been neglecting you. Not at all."

"Haven't! You haven't been near me for three weeks, unless you been so drunk you didn't know what you were doing."

"Been sick, Jewel," he repeated, turning his eyes upon her wearily.

"You're well enough to come and play with your society friends here all right. You told me you'd meet me for dinner, and you said you'd have some money for me. You didn't even bother to ring me up."

"I couldn't get any money."

"Haven't I just been saying that doesn't matter? I wanted to see you, Gordon, but you seem to prefer your somebody else."

He denied this bitterly.

"Then get your hat and come along," she suggested.

Gordon hesitated—and she came suddenly close to him and slipped her arms around his neck.

"Come on with me, Gordon," she said in a half whisper. "We'll go over to Devineries' and have a drink, and then we can go up to my apartment."

"I can't, Jewel,——"

"You can," she said intensely.

"I'm sick as a dog!"

"Well, then, you oughtn't to stay here and dance."

With a glance around him in which relief and despair were mingled, Gordon hesitated; then she suddenly pulled him to her and kissed him with soft, pulpy lips.

"All right," he said heavily. "I'll get my hat."

VIII

When Edith came out into the clear blue of the May night she found the Avenue deserted. The windows of the big shops were dark; over their doors were drawn great iron masks until they were only shadowy tombs of the late day's splendor. Glancing down toward Forty-second Street she saw a commingled blur of lights from the all-night restaurants. Over on Sixth Avenue the elevated, a flare of fire, roared across the street between the glimmering parallels of light at the station and streaked along into the crisp dark. But at Forty-fourth Street it was very quiet.

Pulling her cloak close about her Edith darted across the Avenue. She started nervously as a solitary man passed her and said in a hoarse whisper—"Where bound, kiddo?" She was reminded of a night in her childhood when she had walked around the block in her pajamas and a dog had howled at her from a mystery-big back yard.

In a minute she had reached her destination, a two-story, comparatively old building on Forty-fourth, in the upper windows of which she thankfully detected a wisp of light. It was bright enough outside for her to make out the sign beside the window—the *New York Trumpet*. She stepped inside a dark hall and after a second saw the stairs in the corner.

Then she was in a long, low room furnished with many desks and hung on all sides with file copies of newspapers. There were only two occupants. They were sitting at different ends of the room, each wearing a green eye-shade and writing by a solitary desk light.

For a moment she stood uncertainly in the doorway, and then both men turned around simultaneously and she recognized her brother.

"Why, Edith!" He rose quickly and approached her in surprise, removing his eye-shade. He was tall, lean, and dark, with black, piercing eyes under very thick glasses. They were far-away eyes that seemed always fixed just over the head of the person to whom he was talking.

He put his hands on her arms and kissed her cheek.

"What is it?" he repeated in some alarm.

"I was at a dance across at Delmonico's, Henry," she said excitedly, "and I couldn't resist tearing over to see you."

"I'm glad you did." His alertness gave way quickly to a habitual vagueness. "You oughtn't to be out alone at night though, ought you?"

The man at the other end of the room had been looking at them curiously, but at Henry's beckoning gesture he approached. He was loosely fat with little twinkling eyes, and, having removed his collar and tie, he gave the impression of a Middle-Western farmer on a Sunday afternoon.

"This is my sister," said Henry. "She dropped in to see me."

"How do you do?" said the fat man, smiling. "My name's Bartholomew, Miss Bradin. I know your brother has forgotten it long ago."

Edith laughed politely.

"Well," he continued, "not exactly gorgeous quarters we have here, are they?"

Edith looked around the room.

"They seem very nice," she replied. "Where do you keep the bombs?"

"The bombs?" repeated Bartholomew, laughing. "That's pretty good—the bombs. Did you hear her, Henry? She wants to know where we keep the bombs. Say, that's pretty good."

Edith swung herself around onto a vacant desk and sat dangling her feet over the edge. Her brother took a seat beside her.

"Well," he asked, absent-mindedly, "how do you like New York this trip?"

"Not bad. I'll be over at the Biltmore with the Hoyts until Sunday. Can't you come to luncheon to-morrow?"

He thought a moment.

"I'm especially busy," he objected, "and I hate women in groups."

"All right," she agreed, unruffled. "Let's you and me have luncheon together."

"Very well."

"I'll call for you at twelve."

Bartholomew was obviously anxious to return to his desk, but apparently considered that it would be rude to leave without some parting pleasantry.

"Well"—he began awkwardly.

They both turned to him.

"Well, we—we had an exciting time earlier in the evening."

The two men exchanged glances.

"You should have come earlier," continued Bartholomew, somewhat encouraged. "We had a regular vaudeville."

"Did you really?"

"A serenade," said Henry. "A lot of soldiers gathered down there in the street and began to yell at the sign."

"Why?" she demanded.

"Just a crowd," said Henry, abstractedly. "All crowds have to howl. They didn't have anybody with much initiative in the lead, or they'd probably have forced their way in here and smashed things up."

"Yes," said Bartholomew, turning again to Edith, "you should have been here."

He seemed to consider this a sufficient cue for withdrawal, for he turned abruptly and went back to his desk.

"Are the soldiers all set against the Socialists?" demanded Edith of her brother. "I mean do they attack you violently and all that?"

Henry replaced his eye-shade and yawned.

"The human race has come a long way," he said casually, "but most of us are throw-backs; the soldiers don't know what they want, or what they hate, or what they like. They're used to acting in large bodies, and they seem to have to make demonstrations. So it happens to be against us. There've been riots all over the city to-night. It's May Day, you see."

"Was the disturbance here pretty serious?"

"Not a bit," he said scornfully. "About twenty-five of them stopped in the street about nine o'clock, and began to bellow at the moon."

"Oh"— She changed the subject. "You're glad to see me, Henry?"

"Why, sure."

"You don't seem to be."

"I am."

"I suppose you think I'm a—a waster. Sort of the World's Worst Butterfly."

Henry laughed.

"Not at all. Have a good time while you're young. Why? Do I seem like the priggish and earnest youth?"

"No—" She paused, "—but somehow I began thinking how absolutely different the party I'm on is from—from all your purposes. It seems sort of—of incongruous, doesn't it?—me being at a party like that, and you over here working for a thing that'll make that sort of party impossible ever any more, if your ideas work."

"I don't think of it that way. You're young, and you're acting just as you were brought up to act. Go ahead—have a good time."

Her feet, which had been idly swinging, stopped and her voice dropped a note.

"I wish you'd—you'd come back to Harrisburg and have a good time. Do you feel sure that you're on the right track——"

"You're wearing beautiful stockings," he interrupted. "What on earth are they?"

"They're embroidered," she replied, glancing down. "Aren't they cunning?" She raised her skirts and uncovered slim, silk-sheathed calves. "Or do you disapprove of silk stockings?"

He seemed slightly exasperated, bent his dark eyes on her piercingly.

"Are you trying to make me out as criticizing you in any way, Edith?"

"Not at all——"

She paused. Bartholomew had uttered a grunt. She turned and saw that he had left his desk and was standing at the window.

"What is it?" demanded Henry.

"People," said Bartholomew, and then after an instant: "Whole jam of them. They're coming from Sixth Avenue."

"People."

The fat man pressed his nose to the pane.

"Soldiers, by God!" he said emphatically. "I had an idea they'd come back."

Edith jumped to her feet, and running over joined Bartholomew at the window.

"There's a lot of them!" she cried excitely. "Come here, Henry!"

Henry readjusted his shade, but kept his seat.

"Hadn't we better turn out the lights?" suggested Bartholomew.

"No. They'll go away in a minute."

"They're not," said Edith, peering from the window. "They're not even thinking of going away. There's more of them coming. Look—there's a whole crowd turning the corner of Sixth Avenue."

By the yellow glow and blue shadows of the street lamp she could see that the sidewalk was crowded with men. They were mostly in uniform, some sober, some enthusiastically drunk, and over the whole swept an incoherent clamor and shouting.

Henry rose, and going to the window exposed himself as a long silhouette against the office lights. Immediately the shouting became a steady yell, and a rattling fusillade of small missiles, corners of tobacco plugs, cigarette-boxes, and even pennies beat against the window. The sounds of the racket now began floating up the stairs as the folding doors revolved.

"They're coming up!" cried Bartholomew.

Edith turned anxiously to Henry.

"They're coming up, Henry."

From down-stairs in the lower hall their cries were now quite audible.

"—God damn Socialists!"

"Pro-Germans! Boche-lovers!"

"Second floor, front! Come on!"

"We'll get the sons——"

The next five minutes passed in a dream. Edith was conscious that the clamor burst suddenly upon the three of them like a cloud of rain, that there was a thunder of many feet on the stairs, that Henry had seized her arm and drawn her back toward the rear of the office. Then the door opened and an overflow of men were forced into the room—not the leaders, but simply those who happened to be in front.

"Hello, Bo!"

"Up late, ain't you?"

"You an' your girl. Damn *you!*"

She noticed that two very drunken soldiers had been forced to the front, where they wobbled fatuously—one of them was short and dark, the other was tall and weak of chin.

Henry stepped forward and raised his hand.

"Friends!" he said.

The clamor faded into a momentary stillness, punctuated with mutterings.

"Friends!" he repeated, his far-away eyes fixed over the heads of the crowd, "you're injuring no one but yourselves by breaking in here to-night. Do we look like rich men? Do we look like Germans? I ask you in all fairness——"

"Pipe down!"

"I'll say you do!"

"Say, who's your lady friend, buddy?"

A man in civilian clothes, who had been pawing over a table, suddenly held up a newspaper.

"Here it is!" he shouted. "They wanted the Germans to win the war!"

A new overflow from the stairs was shouldered in and of a sudden the room was full of men all closing around the pale little group at the back. Edith saw that the tall soldier with the weak chin was still in front. The short dark one had disappeared.

She edged slightly backward, stood close to the open window, through which came a clear breath of cool night air.

Then the room was a riot. She realized that the soldiers were surging forward, glimpsed the fat man swinging a chair over his head—instantly the lights went out, and she felt the push of warm bodies under rough cloth, and her ears were full of shouting and trampling and hard breathing.

A figure flashed by her out of nowhere, tottered, was edged sideways, and of a sudden disappeared helplessly out through the open window with a frightened, fragmentary cry that died staccato on the bosom of the clamor. By the faint light streaming from the building backing on the area Edith had a quick impression that it had been the tall soldier with the weak chin.

Anger rose astonishingly in her. She swung her arms wildly, edged blindly toward the thickest of the scuffling. She heard grunts, curses, the muffled impact of fists.

"Henry!" she called frantically, "Henry!"

Then, it was minutes later, she felt suddenly that there were other figures in the room. She heard a voice, deep, bullying, authoritative; she saw yellow rays of light sweeping here and there in the fracas. The cries became more scattered. The scuffling increased and then stopped.

Suddenly the lights were on and the room was full of policemen, clubbing left and right. The deep voice boomed out:

"Here now! Here now! Here now!"

And then:

"Quiet down and get out! Here now!"

The room seemed to empty like a wash-bowl. A policeman fast-grappled in the corner released his hold on his soldier antagonist and started him with a shove toward the door. The deep voice continued. Edith perceived now that it came from a bull-necked police captain standing near the door.

"Here now! This is no way! One of your own sojers got shoved out of the back window an' killed hisself!"

"Henry!" called Edith, "Henry!"

She beat wildly with her fists on the back of the man in front of her; she brushed between two others; fought, shrieked, and beat her way to a very pale figure sitting on the floor close to a desk.

"Henry," she cried passionately, "what's the matter? What's the matter? Did they hurt you?"

His eyes were shut. He groaned and then looking up said disgustedly——

"They broke my leg. My God, the fools!"

"Here now!" called the police captain. "Here now! Here now!"

IX

"Childs', Fifty-ninth Street," at eight o'clock of any morning differs from its sisters by less than the width of their marble tables or the degree of polish on the frying-pans. You will see there a crowd of poor people with sleep in the corners of their eyes, trying to look straight before them at their food so as not to see the other poor people. But Childs', Fifty-ninth, four hours earlier is quite unlike any Childs' restaurant from Portland, Oregon, to Portland, Maine. Within its pale but sanitary walls one finds a noisy medley of chorus girls, college boys, débutantes, rakes, *filles de joie*—a not unrepresentative mixture of the gayest of Broadway, and even of Fifth Avenue.

In the early morning of May the second it was unusually full. Over the marble-topped tables were bent the excited faces of flappers whose fathers owned individual villages. They were eating buckwheat cakes and scrambled eggs with relish and gusto, an accomplishment that it would have been utterly impossible for them to repeat in the same place four hours later.

Almost the entire crowd were from the Gamma Psi dance at Delmonico's except for several chorus girls from a midnight revue who sat at a side table and wished they'd taken off a little more make-up after the show. Here and there a drab, mouse-like figure, desperately out of place, watched the butterflies with a weary, puzzled curiosity. But the drab figure was the exception. This was the morning after May Day, and celebration was still in the air.

Gus Rose, sober but a little dazed, must be classed as one of the drab figures. How he had got himself from Forty-fourth Street to Fifty-ninth Street after the riot was only a hazy half-memory. He had seen the body of Carrol Key put in an ambulance and driven off, and then he had started up town with two or three soldiers. Somewhere between Forty-fourth Street and Fifty-ninth Street the other soldiers had met some women and disappeared. Rose had wandered to Columbus Circle and chosen the gleaming lights of Childs' to minister to his craving for coffee and doughnuts. He walked in and sat down.

All around him floated airy, inconsequential chatter and high-pitched laughter. At first he failed to understand, but after a puzzled five minutes he realized that this was the aftermath of some gay party. Here and there a restless, hilarious young man wandered fraternally and familiarly between the tables, shaking hands indiscriminately and pausing occasionally for a facetious chat, while excited waiters, bearing cakes and eggs aloft, swore at him silently, and bumped him out of the way. To Rose, seated at the most inconspicuous and least crowded table, the whole scene was a colorful circus of beauty and riotous pleasure.

He became gradually aware, after a few moments, that the couple seated diagonally across from him, with their backs to the crowd, were not the least interesting pair in the room. The man was drunk. He wore a dinner coat with a dishevelled tie and shirt swollen by spillings of water and wine. His eyes, dim and bloodshot, roved unnaturally from side to side. His breath came short between his lips.

"He's been on a spree!" thought Rose.

The woman was almost if not quite sober. She was pretty, with dark eyes and feverish high color, and she kept her active eyes fixed on her companion with the alertness of a hawk. From time to time she would lean and whisper intently to him, and he would answer by inclining his head heavily or by a particularly ghoulish and repellent wink.

Rose scrutinized them dumbly for some minutes, until the woman gave him a quick, resentful look; then he shifted his gaze to two of the most conspicuously hilarious of the promenaders who were on a protracted circuit of the tables. To his surprise he recognized in one of them the young man by whom he had been so ludicrously entertained at Delmonico's. This started him thinking of Key with a vague sentimentality, not unmixed with awe. Key was dead. He had fallen thirty-five feet and split his skull like a cracked cocoanut.

"He was a darn good guy," thought Rose mournfully. "He was a darn good guy, o'right. That was awful hard luck about him."

The two promenaders approached and started down between Rose's table and the next, addressing friends and strangers alike with jovial familiarity. Suddenly Rose saw the fair-haired one with the prominent teeth stop, look unsteadily at the man and girl opposite, and then begin to move his head disapprovingly from side to side.

The man with the blood-shot eyes looked up.

"Gordy," said the promenader with the prominent teeth, "Gordy."

"Hello," said the man with the stained shirt thickly.

Prominent Teeth shook his finger pessimistically at the pair, giving the woman a glance of aloof condemnation.

"What'd I tell you Gordy?"

Gordon stirred in his seat.

"Go to hell!" he said.

Dean continued to stand there shaking his finger. The woman began to get angry.

"You go away!" she cried fiercely. "You're drunk, that's what you are!"

"So's he," suggested Dean, staying the motion of his finger and pointing it at Gordon.

Peter Himmel ambled up, owlish now and oratorically inclined.

"Here now," he began as if called upon to deal with some petty dispute between children. "Wha's all trouble?"

"You take your friend away," said Jewel tartly. "He's bothering us."

"What's 'at?"

"You heard me!" she said shrilly. "I said to take your drunken friend away."

Her rising voice rang out above the clatter of the restaurant and a waiter came hurrying up.

"You gotta be more quiet!"

"That fella's drunk," she cried. "He's insulting us."

"Ah-ha, Gordy," persisted the accused. "What'd I tell you." He turned to the waiter. "Gordy an' I friends. Been tryin' help him, haven't I, Gordy?"

Gordy looked up.

"Help me? Hell, no!"

Jewel rose suddenly, and seizing Gordon's arm assisted him to his feet.

"Come on, Gordy!" she said, leaning toward him and speaking in a half whisper. "Let's us get out of here. This fella's got a mean drunk on."

Gordon allowed himself to be urged to his feet and started toward the door. Jewel turned for a second and addressed the provoker of their flight.

"I know all about *you!*" she said fiercely. "Nice friend, you are, I'll say. He told me about you."

Then she seized Gordon's arm, and together they made their way through the curious crowd, paid their check, and went out.

"You'll have to sit down," said the waiter to Peter after they had gone.

"What's 'at? Sit down?"

"Yes—or get out."

Peter turned to Dean.

"Come on," he suggested. "Let's beat up this waiter."

"All right."

They advanced toward him, their faces grown stern. The waiter retreated.

Peter suddenly reached over to a plate on the table beside him and picking up a handful of hash tossed it into the air. It descended as a languid parabola in snowflake effect on the heads of those near by.

"Hey! Ease up!"

"Put him out!"

"Sit down, Peter!"

"Cut out that stuff!"

Peter laughed and bowed.

"Thank you for your kind applause, ladies and gents. If some one will lend me some more hash and a tall hat we will go on with the act."

The bouncer hustled up.

"You've gotta get out!" he said to Peter.

"Hell, no!"

"He's my friend!" put in Dean indignantly.

A crowd of waiters were gathering. "Put him out!"

"Better go, Peter."

There was a short struggle and the two were edged and pushed toward the door.

"I got a hat and a coat here!" cried Peter.

"Well, go get 'em and be spry about it!"

The bouncer released his hold on Peter, who, adopting a ludicrous air of extreme cunning, rushed immediately around to the other table, where he burst into derisive laughter and thumbed his nose at the exasperated waiters.

"Think I just better wait a l'il' longer," he announced.

The chase began. Four waiters were sent around one way and four another. Dean caught hold of two of them by the coat, and another struggle took place before the pursuit of Peter could be resumed; he was finally pinioned after overturning a sugar-bowl and several cups of coffee. A fresh argument ensued at the cashier's desk, where Peter attempted to buy another dish of hash to take with him and throw at policemen.

But the commotion upon his exit proper was dwarfed by another phenomenon which drew admiring glances and a prolonged involuntary "Oh-h-h!" from every person in the restaurant.

The great plate-glass front had turned to a deep creamy blue, the color of a Maxfield Parrish moonlight—a blue that seemed to press close upon the pane as if to crowd its way into the restaurant. Dawn had come up in Columbus Circle, magical, breathless dawn, silhouetting the great statue of the immortal Christopher, and mingling in a curious and uncanny manner with the fading yellow electric light inside.

X

Mr. In and Mr. Out are not listed by the census-taker. You will search for them in vain through the social register or the births, marriages, and deaths, cr the grocer's credit list. Oblivion has swallowed them and the testimony that they ever existed at all is vague and shadowy, and inadmissible in a court of law. Yet I have it upon the best authority that for a brief space Mr. In and Mr. Out lived, breathed, answered to their names and radiated vivid personalities of their own.

During the brief span of their lives they walked in their native garments down the great highway of a great nation; were laughed at, sworn at, chased, and fled from. Then they passed and were heard of no more.

They were already taking form dimly, when a taxicab with the top open breezed down Broadway in the faintest glimmer of May dawn. In this car sat the souls of Mr. In and Mr. Out discussing with amazement the blue light that had so precipitately colored the sky behind the statue of Christopher Columbus, discussing with bewilderment the old, gray faces of the early risers which skimmed palely along the street like blown bits of paper on a gray lake. They were agreed on all things, from the absurdity of the bouncer in Childs' to the absurdity of the business of life. They were dizzy with the extreme maudlin happiness that the morning had awakened in their glowing souls. Indeed, so fresh and vigorous was their pleasure in living that they felt it should be expressed by loud cries.

"Ye-ow-ow!" hooted Peter, making a megaphone with his hands— and Dean joined in with a call that, though equally significant and symbolic, derived its resonance from its very inarticulateness.

"Yo-ho! Yea! Yoho! Yo-buba!"

Fifty-third Street was a bus with a dark, bobbed-hair beauty atop; Fifty-second was a street cleaner who dodged, escaped, and sent up a yell of, "Look where you're aimin'!" in a pained and grieved voice. At Fiftieth Street a group of men on a very white sidewalk in front of a very white building turned to stare after them, and shouted:

"Some party, boys!"

At Forty-ninth Street Peter turned to Dean. "Beautiful morning," he said gravely, squinting up his owlish eyes.

"Probably is."

"Go get some breakfast, hey?"

Dean agreed—with additions.

"Breakfast and liquor."

"Breakfast and liquor," repeated Peter, and they looked at each other, nodding. "That's logical."

Then they both burst into loud laughter.

"Breakfast and liquor! Oh, gosh!"

"No such thing," announced Peter.

"Don't serve it? Ne'mind. We force 'em serve it. Bring pressure bear."

"Bring logic bear."

The taxi cut suddenly off Broadway, sailed along a cross street, and stopped in front of a heavy tomb-like building in Fifth Avenue.

"What's idea?"

The taxi-driver informed them that this was Delmonico's.

This was somewhat puzzling. They were forced to devote several minutes to intense concentration, for if such an order had been given there must have been a reason for it.

"Somep'm 'bouta coat," suggested the taxi-man.

That was it. Peter's overcoat and hat. He had left them at Delmonico's. Having decided this, they disembarked from the taxi and strolled toward the entrance arm in arm.

"Hey!" said the taxi-driver.

"Huh?"

"You better pay me."

They shook their heads in shocked negation.

"Later, not now—we give orders, you wait."

The taxi-driver objected; he wanted his money now. With the scornful condescension of men exercising tremendous self-control they paid him.

Inside Peter groped in vain through a dim, deserted check-room in search of his coat and derby.

"Gone, I guess. Somebody stole it."

"Some Sheff student."

"All probability."

"Never mind," said Dean, nobly. "I'll leave mine here too—then we'll both be dressed the same."

He removed his overcoat and hat and was hanging them up when his roving glance was caught and held magnetically by two large squares of cardboard tacked to the two coat-room doors. The one on the left-hand door bore the word "In" in big black letters, and the one on the right-hand door flaunted the equally emphatic word "Out."

"Look!" he exclaimed happily——

Peter's eyes followed his pointing finger.

"What?"

"Look at the signs. Let's take 'em."

"Good idea."

"Probably pair very rare an' valuable signs. Probably come in handy."

Peter removed the left-hand sign from the door and endeavored to conceal it about his person. The sign being of considerable proportions, this was a matter of some difficulty. An idea flung itself at him, and with an air of dignified mystery he turned his back. After

an instant he wheeled dramatically around, and stretching out his
arms displayed himself to the admiring Dean. He had inserted the
sign in his vest, completely covering his shirt front. In effect, the
word "In" had been painted upon his shirt in large black letters.

"Yoho!" cheered Dean. "Mister In."

He inserted his own sign in like manner.

"Mister Out!" he announced triumphantly. "Mr. In meet Mr.
Out."

They advanced and shook hands. Again laughter overcame them
and they rocked in a shaken spasm of mirth.

"Yoho!"

"We probably get a flock of breakfast."

"We'll go—go to the Commodore."

Arm in arm they sallied out the door, and turning east in Forty-
fourth Street set out for the Commodore.

As they came out a short dark soldier, very pale and tired, who
had been wandering listlessly along the sidewalk, turned to look
at them.

He started over as though to address them, but as they immediately bent on him glances of withering unrecognition, he waited
until they had started unsteadily down the street, and then followed at about forty paces, chuckling to himself and saying, "Oh,
boy!" over and over under his breath, in delighted, anticipatory
tones.

Mr. In and Mr. Out were meanwhile exchanging pleasantries concerning their future plans.

"We want liquor; we want breakfast. Neither without the other.
One and indivisible."

"We want both 'em!"

"Both 'em!"

It was quite light now, and passers-by began to bend curious
eyes on the pair. Obviously they were engaged in a discussion, which
afforded each of them intense amusement, for occasionally a fit of
laughter would seize upon them so violently that, still with their
arms interlocked, they would bend nearly double.

Reaching the Commodore, they exchanged a few spicy epigrams
with the sleepy-eyed doorman, navigated the revolving door with
some difficulty, and then made their way through a thinly populated
but startled lobby to the dining-room, where a puzzled waiter
showed them an obscure table in a corner. They studied the bill of
fare helplessly, telling over the items to each other in puzzled
mumbles.

"Don't see any liquor here," said Peter reproachfully.

The waiter became audible but unintelligible.

"Repeat," continued Peter, with patient tolerance, "that there seems to be unexplained and quite distasteful lack of liquor upon bill of fare."

"Here!" said Dean confidently, "let me handle him." He turned to the waiter—"Bring us—bring us—" he scanned the bill of fare anxiously. "Bring us a quart of champagne and a—a—probably ham sandwich."

The waiter looked doubtful.

"Bring it!" roared Mr. In and Mr. Out in chorus.

The waiter coughed and disappeared. There was a short wait during which they were subjected without their knowledge to a careful scrutiny by the headwaiter. Then the champagne arrived, and at the sight of it Mr. In and Mr. Out became jubilant.

"Imagine their objecting to us having champagne for breakfast—jus' imagine."

They both concentrated upon the vision of such an awesome possibility, but the feat was too much for them. It was impossible for their joint imaginations to conjure up a world where any one might object to any one else having champagne for breakfast. The waiter drew the cork with an enormous *pop*—and their glasses immediately foamed with pale yellow froth.

"Here's health, Mr. In."

"Here's the same to you, Mr. Out."

The waiter withdrew; the minutes passed; the champagne became low in the bottle.

"It's—it's mortifying," said Dean suddenly.

"Wha's mortifying?"

"The idea their objecting us having champagne breakfast."

"Mortifying?" Peter considered. "Yes, tha's word—mortifying."

Again they collapsed into laughter, howled, swayed, rocked back and forth in their chairs, repeating the word "mortifying" over and over to each other—each repetition seeming to make it only more brilliantly absurd.

After a few more gorgeous minutes they decided on another quart. Their anxious waiter consulted his immediate superior, and this discreet person gave implicit instructions that no more champagne should be served. Their check was brought.

Five minutes later, arm in arm, they left the Commodore and made their way through a curious, staring crowd along Forty-second Street, and up Vanderbilt Avenue to the Biltmore. There, with sudden cunning, they rose to the occasion and traversed the lobby, walking fast and standing unnaturally erect.

Once in the dining-room they repeated their performance. They were torn between intermittent convulsive laughter and sudden spas-

modic discussions of politics, college, and the sunny state of their
dispositions. Their watches told them that it was now nine o'clock,
and a dim idea was born in them that they were on a memorable
party, something that they would remember always. They lingered
over the second bottle. Either of them had only to mention the word
"mortifying" to send them both into riotous gasps. The dining-room
was whirring and shifting now; a curious lightness permeated and
rarefied the heavy air.

They paid their check and walked out into the lobby.

It was at this moment that the exterior doors revolved for the
thousandth time that morning, and admitted into the lobby a very
pale young beauty with dark circles under her eyes, attired in a
much-rumpled evening dress. She was accompanied by a plain stout
man, obviously not an appropriate escort.

At the top of the stairs this couple encountered Mr. In and
Mr. Out.

"Edith," began Mr. In, stepping toward her hilariously and making a sweeping bow, "darling, good morning."

The stout man glanced questioningly at Edith, as if merely asking
her permission to throw this man summarily out of the way.

" 'Scuse familiarity," added Peter, as an afterthought. "Edith,
good-morning."

He seized Dean's elbow and impelled him into the foreground.

"Meet Mr. In, Edith, my bes' frien'. Inseparable. Mr. In and
Mr. Out."

Mr. Out advanced and bowed; in fact, he advanced so far and
bowed so low that he tipped slightly forward and only kept his balance by placing a hand lightly on Edith's shoulder.

"I'm Mr. Out, Edith," he mumbled pleasantly, "S'misterin Mister-
out."

" 'Smisterinanout," said Peter proudly.

But Edith stared straight by them, her eyes fixed on some infinite
speck in the gallery above her. She nodded slightly to the stout man,
who advanced bull-like and with a sturdy brisk gesture pushed
Mr. In and Mr. Out to either side. Through this alley he and Edith
walked.

But ten paces farther on Edith stopped again—stopped and
pointed to a short, dark soldier who was eyeing the crowd in general, and the tableau of Mr. In and Mr. Out in particular, with a
sort of puzzled, spell-bound awe.

"There," cried Edith. "See there!"

Her voice rose, became somewhat shrill. Her pointing finger shook
slightly.

"There's the soldier who broke my brother's leg."

There were a dozen exclamations; a man in a cutaway coat left his place near the desk and advanced alertly; the stout person made a sort of lightning-like spring toward the short, dark soldier, and then the lobby closed around the little group and blotted them from the sight of Mr. In and Mr. Out.

But to Mr. In and Mr. Out this event was merely a particolored iridescent segment of a whirring, spinning world.

They heard loud voices; they saw the stout man spring; the picture suddenly blurred.

Then they were in an elevator bound skyward.

"What floor, please?" said the elevator man.

"Any floor," said Mr. In.

"Top floor," said Mr. Out.

"This is the top floor," said the elevator man.

"Have another floor put on," said Mr. Out.

"Higher," said Mr. In.

"Heaven," said Mr. Out.

XI

In a bedroom of a small hotel just off Sixth Avenue Gordon Sterrett awoke with a pain in the back of his head and a sick throbbing in all his veins. He looked at the dusky gray shadows in the corners of the room and at a raw place on a large leather chair in the corner where it had long been in use. He saw clothes, dishevelled, rumpled clothes on the floor and he smelt stale cigarette smoke and stale liquor. The windows were tight shut. Outside the bright sunlight had thrown a dust-filled beam across the sill—a beam broken by the head of the wide wooden bed in which he had slept. He lay very quiet—comatose, drugged, his eyes wide, his mind clicking wildly like an unoiled machine.

It must have been thirty seconds after he perceived the sunbeam with the dust on it and the rip on the large leather chair that he had the sense of life close beside him, and it was another thirty seconds after that before he realized he was irrevocably married to Jewel Hudson.

He went out half an hour later and bought a revolver at a sporting goods store. Then he took a taxi to the room where he had been living on East Twenty-seventh Street, and, leaning across the table that held his drawing materials, fired a cartridge into his head just behind the temple.

1920   *Tales of the Jazz Age*

WINTER DREAMS

SOME of the caddies were poor as sin and lived in one-room houses with a neurasthenic cow in the front yard, but Dexter Green's father owned the second best grocery-store in Black Bear—the best one was "The Hub," patronized by the wealthy people from Sherry Island —and Dexter caddied only for pocket-money.

In the fall when the days became crisp and gray, and the long Minnesota winter shut down like the white lid of a box, Dexter's skis moved over the snow that hid the fairways of the golf course. At these times the country gave him a feeling of profound melancholy —it offended him that the links should lie in enforced fallowness, haunted by ragged sparrows for the long season. It was dreary, too, that on the tees where the gay colors fluttered in summer there were now only the desolate sand-boxes knee-deep in crusted ice. When he crossed the hills the wind blew cold as misery, and if the sun was out he tramped with his eyes squinted up against the hard dimensionless glare.

In April the winter ceased abruptly. The snow ran down into Black Bear Lake scarcely tarrying for the early golfers to brave the season with red and black balls. Without elation, without an interval of moist glory, the cold was gone.

Dexter knew that there was something dismal about this Northern spring, just as he knew there was something gorgeous about the fall. Fall made him clinch his hands and tremble and repeat idiotic sentences to himself, and make brisk abrupt gestures of command to imaginary audiences and armies. October filled him with hope which November raised to a sort of ecstatic triumph, and in this mood the fleeting brilliant impressions of the summer at Sherry Island were ready grist to his mill. He became a golf champion and defeated Mr. T. A. Hedrick in a marvellous match played a hundred times over the fairways of his imagination, a match each detail of which he changed about untiringly—sometimes he won with almost laughable ease, sometimes he came up magnificently from behind. Again, stepping from a Pierce-Arrow automobile, like Mr. Mortimer Jones, he strolled frigidly into the lounge of the Sherry Island Golf Club— or perhaps, surrounded by an admiring crowd, he gave an exhibition of fancy diving from the spring-board of the club raft. . . . Among those who watched him in open-mouthed wonder was Mr. Mortimer Jones.

And one day it came to pass that Mr. Jones—himself and not his ghost—came up to Dexter with tears in his eyes and said that Dexter was the — — best caddy in the club, and wouldn't he decide not to quit if Mr. Jones made it worth his while, because every other — — caddy in the club lost one ball a hole for him—regularly——

"No, sir," said Dexter decisively, "I don't want to caddy any more." Then, after a pause: "I'm too old."

"You're not more than fourteen. Why the devil did you decide just this morning that you wanted to quit? You promised that next week you'd go over to the State tournament with me."

"I decided I was too old."

Dexter handed in his "A Class" badge, collected what money was due him from the caddy master, and walked home to Black Bear Village.

"The best — — caddy I ever saw," shouted Mr. Mortimer Jones over a drink that afternoon. "Never lost a ball! Willing! Intelligent! Quiet! Honest! Grateful!"

The little girl who had done this was eleven—beautifully ugly as little girls are apt to be who are destined after a few years to be inexpressibly lovely and bring no end of misery to a great number of men. The spark, however, was perceptible. There was a general ungodliness in the way her lips twisted down at the corners when she smiled, and in the—Heaven help us!—in the almost passionate quality of her eyes. Vitality is born early in such women. It was utterly in evidence now, shining through her thin frame in a sort of glow.

She had come eagerly out on to the course at nine o'clock with a white linen nurse and five small new golf-clubs in a white canvas bag which the nurse was carrying. When Dexter first saw her she was standing by the caddy house, rather ill at ease and trying to conceal the fact by engaging her nurse in an obviously unnatural conversation graced by startling and irrelevant grimaces from herself.

"Well, it's certainly a nice day, Hilda," Dexter heard her say. She drew down the corners of her mouth, smiled, and glanced furtively around, her eyes in transit falling for an instant on Dexter.

Then to the nurse:

"Well, I guess there aren't very many people out here this morning, are there?"

The smile again—radiant, blatantly artificial—convincing.

"I don't know what we're supposed to do now," said the nurse looking nowhere in particular.

"Oh, that's all right. I'll fix it up."

Dexter stood perfectly still, his mouth slightly ajar. He knew that if he moved forward a step his stare would be in her line of vision—if he moved backward he would lose his full view of her face. For a moment he had not realized how young she was. Now he remembered having seen her several times the year before—in bloomers.

Suddenly, involuntarily, he laughed, a short abrupt laugh—then, startled by himself, he turned and began to walk quickly away.

"Boy!"

Dexter stopped.

"Boy——"

Beyond question he was addressed. Not only that, but he was treated to that absurd smile, that preposterous smile—the memory of which at least a dozen men were to carry into middle age.

"Boy, do you know where the golf teacher is?"

"He's giving a lesson."

"Well, do you know where the caddy-master is?"

"He isn't here yet this morning."

"Oh." For a moment this baffled her. She stood alternately on her right and left foot.

"We'd like to get a caddy," said the nurse. "Mrs. Mortimer Jones sent us out to play golf, and we don't know how without we get a caddy."

Here she was stopped by an ominous glance from Miss Jones, followed immediately by the smile.

"There aren't any caddies here except me," said Dexter to the nurse, "and I got to stay here in charge until the caddy-master gets here."

"Oh."

Miss Jones and her retinue now withdrew, and at a proper distance from Dexter became involved in a heated conversation, which was concluded by Miss Jones taking one of the clubs and hitting it on the ground with violence. For further emphasis she raised it again and was about to bring it down smartly upon the nurse's bosom, when the nurse seized the club and twisted it from her hands.

"You damn little mean old *thing!*" cried Miss Jones wildly.

Another argument ensued. Realizing that the elements of comedy were implied in the scene, Dexter several times began to laugh, but each time restrained the laugh before it reached audibility. He could not resist the monstrous conviction that the little girl was justified in beating the nurse.

The situation was resolved by the fortuitous appearance of the caddy-master, who was appealed to immediately by the nurse.

"Miss Jones is to have a little caddy, and this one says he can't go."

"Mr. McKenna said I was to wait here till you came," said Dexter quickly.

"Well, he's here now." Miss Jones smiled cheerfully at the caddy-master. Then she dropped her bag and set off at a haughty mince toward the first tee.

"Well?" The caddy-master turned to Dexter. "What you standing there like a dummy for? Go pick up the young lady's clubs."

"I don't think I'll go out to-day," said Dexter.

"You don't——"

"I think I'll quit."

The enormity of his decision frightened him. He was a favorite caddy, and the thirty dollars a month he earned through the summer were not to be made elsewhere around the lake. But he had received a strong emotional shock, and his perturbation required a violent and immediate outlet.

It is not so simple as that, either. As so frequently would be the case in the future, Dexter was unconsciously dictated to by his winter dreams.

II

Now, of course, the quality and the seasonability of these winter dreams varied, but the stuff of them remained. They persuaded Dexter several years later to pass up a business course at the State university—his father, prospering now, would have paid his way—for the precarious advantage of attending an older and more famous university in the East, where he was bothered by his scanty funds. But do not get the impression, because his winter dreams happened to be concerned at first with musings on the rich, that there was anything merely snobbish in the boy. He wanted not association with glittering things and glittering people—he wanted the glittering things themselves. Often he reached out for the best without knowing why he wanted it—and sometimes he ran up against the mysterious denials and prohibitions in which life indulges. It is with one of those denials and not with his career as a whole that this story deals.

He made money. It was rather amazing. After college he went to the city from which Black Bear Lake draws its wealthy patrons. When he was only twenty-three and had been there not quite two years, there were already people who liked to say: "Now *there's* a boy——" All about him rich men's sons were peddling bonds precariously, or investing patrimonies precariously, or plodding through the two dozen volumes of the "George Washington Commercial Course," but Dexter borrowed a thousand dollars on his college degree and his confident mouth, and bought a partnership in a laundry.

It was a small laundry when he went into it, but Dexter made a specialty of learning how the English washed fine woolen golf-stockings without shrinking them, and within a year he was catering to the trade that wore knickerbockers. Men were insisting that their Shetland hose and sweaters go to his laundry, just as they had in-sisted on a caddy who could find golf-balls. A little later he was doing their wives' lingerie as well—and running five branches in different parts of the city. Before he was twenty-seven he owned the largest string of laundries in his section of the country. It was then that he sold out and went to New York. But the part of his story that con-cerns us goes back to the days when he was making his first big success.

When he was twenty-three Mr. Hart—one of the gray-haired men who liked to say "Now there's a boy"—gave him a guest card to the Sherry Island Golf Club for a week-end. So he signed his name one day on the register, and that afternoon played golf in a foursome with Mr. Hart and Mr. Sandwood and Mr. T. A. Hedrick. He did not consider it necessary to remark that he had once carried Mr. Hart's bag over this same links, and that he knew every trap and gully with his eyes shut—but he found himself glancing at the four caddies who trailed them, trying to catch a gleam or gesture that would remind him of himself, that would lessen the gap which lay between his present and his past.

It was a curious day, slashed abruptly with fleeting, familiar im-pressions. One minute he had the sense of being a trespasser—in the next he was impressed by the tremendous superiority he felt toward Mr. T. A. Hedrick, who was a bore and not even a good golfer any more.

Then, because of a ball Mr. Hart lost near the fifteenth green, an enormous thing happened. While they were searching the stiff grasses of the rough there was a clear call of "Fore!" from behind a hill in their rear. And as they all turned abruptly from their search a bright new ball sliced abruptly over the hill and caught Mr. T. A. Hedrick in the abdomen.

"By Gad!" cried Mr. T. A. Hedrick, "they ought to put some of these crazy women off the course. It's getting to be outrageous."

A head and a voice came up together over the hill:

"Do you mind if we go through?"

"You hit me in the stomach!" declared Mr. Hedrick wildly.

"Did I?" The girl approached the group of men. "I'm sorry. I yelled 'Fore!'"

Her glance fell casually on each of the men—then scanned the fairway for her ball.

"Did I bounce into the rough?"

It was impossible to determine whether this question was ingenuous or malicious. In a moment, however, she left no doubt, for as her partner came up over the hill she called cheerfully:

"Here I am! I'd have gone on the green except that I hit something."

As she took her stance for a short mashie shot, Dexter looked at her closely. She wore a blue gingham dress, rimmed at throat and shoulders with a white edging that accentuated her tan. The quality of exaggeration, of thinness, which had made her passionate eyes and down-turning mouth absurd at eleven, was gone now. She was arrestingly beautiful. The color in her cheeks was centred like the color in a picture—it was not a "high" color, but a sort of fluctuating and feverish warmth, so shaded that it seemed at any moment it would recede and disappear. This color and the mobility of her mouth gave a continual impression of flux, of intense life, of passionate vitality—balanced only partially by the sad luxury of her eyes.

She swung her mashie impatiently and without interest, pitching the ball into a sand-pit on the other side of the green. With a quick, insincere smile and a careless "Thank you!" she went on after it.

"That Judy Jones!" remarked Mr. Hedrick on the next tee, as they waited—some moments—for her to play on ahead. "All she needs is to be turned up and spanked for six months and then to be married off to an old-fashioned cavalry captain."

"My God, she's good-looking!" said Mr. Sandwood, who was just over thirty.

"Good-looking!" cried Mr. Hedrick contemptuously, "she always looks as if she wanted to be kissed! Turning those big cow-eyes on every calf in town!"

It was doubtful if Mr. Hedrick intended a reference to the maternal instinct.

"She'd play pretty good golf if she'd try," said Mr. Sandwood.

"She has no form," said Mr. Hedrick solemnly.

"She has a nice figure," said Mr. Sandwood.

"Better thank the Lord she doesn't drive a swifter ball," said Mr. Hart, winking at Dexter.

Later in the afternoon the sun went down with a riotous swirl of gold and varying blues and scarlets, and left the dry, rustling night of Western summer. Dexter watched from the veranda of the Golf Club, watched the even overlap of the waters in the little wind, silver molasses under the harvest-moon. Then the moon held a finger to her lips and the lake became a clear pool, pale and quiet. Dexter put on his bathing-suit and swam out to the farthest raft, where he stretched dripping on the wet canvas of the springboard.

There was a fish jumping and a star shining and the lights around the lake were gleaming. Over on a dark peninsula a piano was playing the songs of last summer and of summers before that—songs from "Chin-Chin" and "The Count of Luxemburg" and "The Chocolate Soldier"—and because the sound of a piano over a stretch of water had always seemed beautiful to Dexter he lay perfectly quiet and listened.

The tune the piano was playing at that moment had been gay and new five years before when Dexter was a sophomore at college. They had played it at a prom once when he could not afford the luxury of proms, and he had stood outside the gymnasium and listened. The sound of the tune precipitated in him a sort of ecstasy and it was with that ecstasy he viewed what happened to him now. It was a mood of intense appreciation, a sense that, for once, he was magnificently attuned to life and that everything about him was radiating a brightness and a glamour he might never know again.

A low, pale oblong detached itself suddenly from the darkness of the Island, spitting forth the reverberated sound of a racing motorboat. Two white streamers of cleft water rolled themselves out behind it and almost immediately the boat was beside him, drowning out the hot tinkle of the piano in the drone of its spray. Dexter raising himself on his arms was aware of a figure standing at the wheel, of two dark eyes regarding him over the lengthening space of water— then the boat had gone by and was sweeping in an immense and purposeless circle of spray round and round in the middle of the lake. With equal eccentricity one of the circles flattened out and headed back toward the raft.

"Who's that?" she called, shutting off her motor. She was so near now that Dexter could see her bathing-suit, which consisted apparently of pink rompers.

The nose of the boat bumped the raft, and as the latter tilted rakishly he was precipitated toward her. With different degrees of interest they recognized each other.

"Aren't you one of those men we played through this afternoon?" she demanded.

He was.

"Well, do you know how to drive a motor-boat? Because if you do I wish you'd drive this one so I can ride on the surf-board behind. My name is Judy Jones"—she favored him with an absurd smirk— rather, what tried to be a smirk, for, twist her mouth as she might, it was not grotesque, it was merely beautiful—"and I live in a house over there on the Island, and in that house there is a man waiting for

me. When he drove up at the door I drove out of the dock because he
says I'm his ideal."

There was a fish jumping and a star shining and the lights around
the lake were gleaming. Dexter sat beside Judy Jones and she explained how her boat was driven. Then she was in the water, swimming to the floating surf-board with a sinuous crawl. Watching her
was without effort to the eye, watching a branch waving or a sea-gull
flying. Her arms, burned to butternut, moved sinuously among the
dull platinum ripples, elbow appearing first, casting the forearm back
with a cadence of falling water, then reaching out and down, stabbing
a path ahead.

They moved out into the lake; turning, Dexter saw that she was
kneeling on the low rear of the now uptilted surf-board.

"Go faster," she called, "fast as it'll go."

Obediently he jammed the lever forward and the white spray
mounted at the bow. When he looked around again the girl was
standing up on the rushing board, her arms spread wide, her eyes
lifted toward the moon.

"It's awful cold," she shouted. "What's your name?"

He told her.

"Well, why don't you come to dinner to-morrow night?"

His heart turned over like the fly-wheel of the boat, and, for the
second time, her casual whim gave a new direction to his life.

III

Next evening while he waited for her to come down-stairs, Dexter
peopled the soft deep summer room and the sun-porch that opened
from it with the men who had already loved Judy Jones. He knew
the sort of men they were—the men who when he first went to college
had entered from the great prep schools with graceful clothes and
the deep tan of healthy summers. He had seen that, in one sense, he
was better than these men. He was newer and stronger. Yet in ac-
knowledging to himself that he wished his children to be like them
he was admitting that he was but the rough, strong stuff from which
they eternally sprang.

When the time had come for him to wear good clothes, he had
known who were the best tailors in America, and the best tailors in
America had made him the suit he wore this evening. He had acquired that particular reserve peculiar to his university, that set it
off from other universities. He recognized the value to him of such
a mannerism and he had adopted it; he knew that to be careless in
dress and manner required more confidence than to be careful. But
carelessness was for his children. His mother's name had been Krim-

lich. She was a Bohemian of the peasant class and she had talked broken English to the end of her days. Her son must keep to the set patterns.

At a little after seven Judy Jones came down-stairs. She wore a blue silk afternoon dress, and he was disappointed at first that she had not put on something more elaborate. This feeling was accentuated when, after a brief greeting, she went to the door of a butler's pantry and pushing it open called: "You can serve dinner, Martha." He had rather expected that a butler would announce dinner, that there would be a cocktail. Then he put these thoughts behind him as they sat down side by side on a lounge and looked at each other.

"Father and mother won't be here," she said thoughtfully.

He remembered the last time he had seen her father, and he was glad the parents were not to be here to-night—they might wonder who he was. He had been born in Keeble, a Minnesota village fifty miles farther north, and he always gave Keeble as his home instead of Black Bear Village. Country towns were well enough to come from if they weren't inconveniently in sight and used as footstools by fashionable lakes.

They talked of his university, which she had visited frequently during the past two years, and of the near-by city which supplied Sherry Island with its patrons, and whither Dexter would return next day to his prospering laundries.

During dinner she slipped into a moody depression which gave Dexter a feeling of uneasiness. Whatever petulance she uttered in her throaty voice worried him. Whatever she smiled at—at him, at a chicken liver, at nothing—it disturbed him that her smile could have no root in mirth, or even in amusement. When the scarlet corners of her lips curved down, it was less a smile than an invitation to a kiss.

Then, after dinner, she led him out on the dark sun-porch and deliberately changed the atmosphere.

"Do you mind if I weep a little?" she said.

"I'm afraid I'm boring you," he responded quickly.

"You're not. I like you. But I've just had a terrible afternoon. There was a man I cared about, and this afternoon he told me out of a clear sky that he was poor as a church-mouse. He'd never even hinted it before. Does this sound horribly mundane?"

"Perhaps he was afraid to tell you."

"Suppose he was," she answered. "He didn't start right. You see, if I'd thought of him as poor—well, I've been mad about loads of poor men, and fully intended to marry them all. But in this case, I hadn't thought of him that way, and my interest in him wasn't strong enough to survive the shock. As if a girl calmly informed her fiancé that she was a widow. He might not object to widows, but——

"Let's start right," she interrupted herself suddenly. "Who are you, anyhow?"

For a moment Dexter hesitated. Then:

"I'm nobody," he announced. "My career is largely a matter of futures."

"Are you poor?"

"No," he said frankly, "I'm probably making more money than any man my age in the Northwest. I know that's an obnoxious remark, but you advised me to start right."

There was a pause. Then she smiled and the corners of her mouth drooped and an almost imperceptible sway brought her closer to him, looking up into his eyes. A lump rose in Dexter's throat, and he waited breathless for the experiment, facing the unpredictable compound that would form mysteriously from the elements of their lips. Then he saw—she communicated her excitement to him, lavishly, deeply, with kisses that were not a promise but a fulfilment. They aroused in him not hunger demanding renewal but surfeit that would demand more surfeit . . . kisses that were like charity, creating want by holding back nothing at all.

It did not take him many hours to decide that he had wanted Judy Jones ever since he was a proud, desirous little boy.

IV

It began like that—and continued, with varying shades of intensity, on such a note right up to the dénouement. Dexter surrendered a part of himself to the most direct and unprincipled personality with which he had ever come in contact. Whatever Judy wanted, she went after with the full pressure of her charm. There was no divergence of method, no jockeying for position or premeditation of effects—there was a very little mental side to any of her affairs. She simply made men conscious to the highest degree of her physical loveliness. Dexter had no desire to change her. Her deficiencies were knit up with a passionate energy that transcended and justified them.

When, as Judy's head lay against his shoulder that first night, she whispered, "I don't know what's the matter with me. Last night I thought I was in love with a man and to-night I think I'm in love with you——"—it seemed to him a beautiful and romantic thing to say. It was the exquisite excitability that for the moment he controlled and owned. But a week later he was compelled to view this same quality in a different light. She took him in her roadster to a picnic supper, and after supper she disappeared, likewise in her road-

ster, with another man. Dexter became enormously upset and was
scarcely able to be decently civil to the other people present. When
she assured him that she had not kissed the other man, he knew she
was lying—yet he was glad that she had taken the trouble to lie to
him.

He was, as he found before the summer ended, one of a varying
dozen who circulated about her. Each of them had at one time been
favored above all others—about half of them still basked in the solace
of occasional sentimental revivals. Whenever one showed signs of
dropping out through long neglect, she granted him a brief honeyed
hour, which encouraged him to tag along for a year or so longer.
Judy made these forays upon the helpless and defeated without
malice, indeed half unconscious that there was anything mischievous
in what she did.

When a new man came to town every one dropped out—dates
were automatically cancelled.

The helpless part of trying to do anything about it was that she
did it all herself. She was not a girl who could be "won" in the
kinetic sense—she was proof against cleverness, she was proof against
charm; if any of these assailed her too strongly she would immediately resolve the affair to a physical basis, and under the magic of
her physical splendor the strong as well as the brilliant played her
game and not their own. She was entertained only by the gratifica-
tion of her desires and by the direct exercise of her own charm. Perhaps from so much youthful love, so many youthful lovers, she had
come, in self-defense, to nourish herself wholly from within.

Succeeding Dexter's first exhilaration came restlessness and dissatisfaction. The helpless ecstasy of losing himself in her was opiate
rather than tonic. It was fortunate for his work during the winter
that those moments of ecstasy came infrequently. Early in their acquaintance it had seemed for a while that there was a deep and spon-
taneous mutual attraction—that first August, for example—three
days of long evenings on her dusky veranda, of strange wan kisses
through the late afternoon, in shadowy alcoves or behind the protecting trellises of the garden arbors, of mornings when she was fresh
as a dream and almost shy at meeting him in the clarity of the rising
day. There was all the ecstasy of an engagement about it, sharpened
by his realization that there was no engagement. It was during those
three days that, for the first time, he had asked her to marry him.
She said "maybe some day," she said "kiss me," she said "I'd like to
marry you," she said "I love you"—she said—nothing.

The three days were interrupted by the arrival of a New York
man who visited at her house for half September. To Dexter's agony,
rumor engaged them. The man was the son of the president of a

great trust company. But at the end of a month it was reported that Judy was yawning. At a dance one night she sat all evening in a motor-boat with a local beau, while the New Yorker searched the club for her frantically. She told the local beau that she was bored with her visitor, and two days later he left. She was seen with him at the station, and it was reported that he looked very mournful indeed.

On this note the summer ended. Dexter was twenty-four, and he found himself increasingly in a position to do as he wished. He joined two clubs in the city and lived at one of them. Though he was by no means an integral part of the stag-lines at these clubs, he managed to be on hand at dances where Judy Jones was likely to appear. He could have gone out socially as much as he liked—he was an eligible young man, now, and popular with down-town fathers. His confessed devotion to Judy Jones had rather solidified his position. But he had no social aspirations and rather despised the dancing men who were always on tap for the Thursday or Saturday parties and who filled in at dinners with the younger married set. Already he was playing with the idea of going East to New York. He wanted to take Judy Jones with him. No disillusion as to the world in which she had grown up could cure his illusion as to her desirability.

Remember that—for only in the light of it can what he did for her be understood.

Eighteen months after he first met Judy Jones he became engaged to another girl. Her name was Irene Scheerer, and her father was one of the men who had always believed in Dexter. Irene was light-haired and sweet and honorable, and a little stout, and she had two suitors whom she pleasantly relinquished when Dexter formally asked her to marry him.

Summer, fall, winter, spring, another summer, another fall—so much he had given of his active life to the incorrigible lips of Judy Jones. She had treated him with interest, with encouragement, with malice, with indifference, with contempt. She had inflicted on him the innumerable little slights and indignities possible in such a case— as if in revenge for having ever cared for him at all. She had beckoned him and yawned at him and beckoned him again and he had responded often with bitterness and narrowed eyes. She had brought him ecstatic happiness and intolerable agony of spirit. She had caused him untold inconvenience and not a little trouble. She had insulted him, and she had ridden over him, and she had played his interest in her against his interest in his work—for fun. She had done everything to him except to criticise him—this she had not done—it seemed to him only because it might have sullied the utter indifference she manifested and sincerely felt toward him.

When autumn had come and gone again it occurred to him that he

could not have Judy Jones. He had to beat this into his mind but he
convinced himself at last. He lay awake at night for a while and
argued it over. He told himself the trouble and the pain she had
caused him, he enumerated her glaring deficiencies as a wife. Then
he said to himself that he loved her, and after a while he fell asleep.
For a week, lest he imagined her husky voice over the telephone or
her eyes opposite him at lunch, he worked hard and late, and at night
he went to his office and plotted out his years.

At the end of a week he went to a dance and cut in on her once.
For almost the first time since they had met he did not ask her to sit
out with him or tell her that she was lovely. It hurt him that she did
not miss these things—that was all. He was not jealous when he saw
that there was a new man to-night. He had been hardened against
jealousy long before.

He stayed late at the dance. He sat for an hour with Irene Scheerer
and talked about books and about music. He knew very little about
either. But he was beginning to be master of his own time now, and
he had a rather priggish notion that he—the young and already
fabulously successful Dexter Green—should know more about such
things.

That was in October, when he was twenty-five. In January, Dexter
and Irene became engaged. It was to be announced in June, and they
were to be married three months later.

The Minnesota winter prolonged itself interminably, and it was
almost May when the winds came soft and the snow ran down into
Black Bear Lake at last. For the first time in over a year Dexter was
enjoying a certain tranquillity of spirit. Judy Jones had been in
Florida, and afterward in Hot Springs, and somewhere she had been
engaged, and somewhere she had broken it off. At first, when Dexter
had definitely given her up, it had made him sad that people still
linked them together and asked for news of her, but when he began
to be placed at dinner next to Irene Scheerer people didn't ask him
about her any more—they told him about her. He ceased to be an
authority on her.

May at last. Dexter walked the streets at night when the darkness
was damp as rain, wondering that so soon, with so little done, so
much of ecstasy had gone from him. May one year back had been
marked by Judy's poignant, unforgivable, yet forgiven turbulence—
it had been one of those rare times when he fancied she had grown
to care for him. That old penny's worth of happiness he had spent
for this bushel of content. He knew that Irene would be no more than
a curtain spread behind him, a hand moving among gleaming tea-
cups, a voice calling to children . . . fire and loveliness were gone,
the magic of nights and the wonder of the varying hours and seasons

. . . slender lips, down-turning, dropping to his lips and bearing him up into a heaven of eyes. . . .The thing was deep in him. He was too strong and alive for it to die lightly.

In the middle of May when the weather balanced for a few days on the thin bridge that led to deep summer he turned in one night at Irene's house. Their engagement was to be announced in a week now —no one would be surprised at it. And to-night they would sit together on the lounge at the University Club and look on for an hour at the dancers. It gave him a sense of solidity to go with her—she was so sturdily popular, so intensely "great."

He mounted the steps of the brownstone house and stepped inside.

"Irene," he called.

Mrs. Scheerer came out of the living-room to meet him.

"Dexter," she said, "Irene's gone up-stairs with a splitting headache. She wanted to go with you but I made her go to bed."

"Nothing serious, I——"

"Oh, no. She's going to play golf with you in the morning. You can spare her for just one night, can't you, Dexter?"

Her smile was kind. She and Dexter liked each other. In the living-room he talked for a moment before he said good-night.

Returning to the University Club, where he had rooms, he stood in the doorway for a moment and watched the dancers. He leaned against the door-post, nodded at a man or two—yawned.

"Hello, darling."

The familiar voice at his elbow startled him. Judy Jones had left a man and crossed the room to him—Judy Jones, a slender enamelled doll in cloth of gold: gold in a band at her head, gold in two slipper points at her dress's hem. The fragile glow of her face seemed to blossom as she smiled at him. A breeze of warmth and light blew through the room. His hands in the pockets of his dinner-jacket tightened spasmodically. He was filled with a sudden excitement.

"When did you get back?" he asked casually.

"Come here and I'll tell you about it."

She turned and he followed her. She had been away—he could have wept at the wonder of her return. She had passed through enchanted streets, doing things that were like provocative music. All mysterious happenings, all fresh and quickening hopes, had gone away with her, come back with her now.

She turned in the doorway.

"Have you a car here? If you haven't, I have."

"I have a coupé."

In then, with a rustle of golden cloth. He slammed the door. Into so many cars she had stepped—like this—like that—her back against the leather, so—her elbow resting on the door—waiting. She would have been soiled long since had there been anything to soil her—except herself—but this was her own self outpouring.

With an effort he forced himself to start the car and back into the street. This was nothing, he must remember. She had done this before, and he had put her behind him, as he would have crossed a bad account from his books.

He drove slowly down-town and, affecting abstraction, traversed the deserted streets of the business section, peopled here and there where a movie was giving out its crowd or where consumptive or pugilistic youth lounged in front of pool halls. The clink of glasses and the slap of hands on the bars issued from saloons, cloisters of glazed glass and dirty yellow light.

She was watching him closely and the silence was embarrassing, yet in this crisis he could find no casual word with which to profane the hour. At a convenient turning he began to zigzag back toward the University Club.

"Have you missed me?" she asked suddenly.

"Everybody missed you."

He wondered if she knew of Irene Scheerer. She had been back only a day—her absence had been almost contemporaneous with his engagement.

"What a remark!" Judy laughed sadly—without sadness. She looked at him searchingly. He became absorbed in the dashboard.

"You're handsomer than you used to be," she said thoughtfully. "Dexter, you have the most rememberable eyes."

He could have laughed at this, but he did not laugh. It was the sort of thing that was said to sophomores. Yet it stabbed at him.

"I'm awfully tired of everything, darling." She called every one darling, endowing the endearment with careless, individual comraderie. "I wish you'd marry me."

The directness of this confused him. He should have told her now that he was going to marry another girl, but he could not tell her. He could as easily have sworn that he had never loved her.

"I think we'd get along," she continued, on the same note, "unless probably you've forgotten me and fallen in love with another girl."

Her confidence was obviously enormous. She had said, in effect, that she found such a thing impossible to believe, that if it were true he had merely committed a childish indiscretion—and probably to show off. She would forgive him, because it was not a matter of any moment but rather something to be brushed aside lightly.

"Of course you could never love anybody but me," she continued, "I like the way you love me. Oh, Dexter, have you forgotten last year?"

"No, I haven't forgotten."

"Neither have I!"

Was she sincerely moved—or was she carried along by the wave of her own acting?

"I wish we could be like that again," she said, and he forced himself to answer:

"I don't think we can."

"I suppose not. . . . I hear you're giving Irene Scheerer a violent rush."

There was not the faintest emphasis on the name, yet Dexter was suddenly ashamed.

"Oh, take me home," cried Judy suddenly; "I don't want to go back to that idiotic dance—with those children."

Then, as he turned up the street that led to the residence district, Judy began to cry quietly to herself. He had never seen her cry before.

The dark street lightened, the dwellings of the rich loomed up around them, he stopped his coupé in front of the great white bulk of the Mortimer Joneses' house, somnolent, gorgeous, drenched with the splendor of the damp moonlight. Its solidity startled him. The strong walls, the steel of the girders, the breadth and beam and pomp of it were there only to bring out the contrast with the young beauty beside him. It was sturdy to accentuate her slightness—as if to show what a breeze could be generated by a butterfly's wing.

He sat perfectly quiet, his nerves in wild clamor, afraid that if he moved he would find her irresistibly in his arms. Two tears had rolled down her wet face and trembled on her upper lip.

"I'm more beautiful than anybody else," she said brokenly, "why can't I be happy?" Her moist eyes tore at his stability—her mouth turned slowly downward with an exquisite sadness: "I'd like to marry you if you'll have me, Dexter. I suppose you think I'm not worth having, but I'll be so beautiful for you, Dexter."

A million phrases of anger, pride, passion, hatred, tenderness fought on his lips. Then a perfect wave of emotion washed over him, carrying off with it a sediment of wisdom, of convention, of doubt, of honor. This was his girl who was speaking, his own, his beautiful, his pride.

"Won't you come in?" He heard her draw in her breath sharply. Waiting.

"All right," his voice was trembling, "I'll come in."

V

It was strange that neither when it was over nor a long time afterward did he regret that night. Looking at it from the perspective of ten years, the fact that Judy's flare for him endured just one month seemed of little importance. Nor did it matter that by his yielding he subjected himself to a deeper agony in the end and gave serious hurt to Irene Scheerer and to Irene's parents, who had befriended him. There was nothing sufficiently pictorial about Irene's grief to stamp itself on his mind.

Dexter was at bottom hard-minded. The attitude of the city on his action was of no importance to him, not because he was going to leave the city, but because any outside attitude on the situation seemed superficial. He was completely indifferent to popular opinion. Nor, when he had seen that it was no use, that he did not possess in himself the power to move fundamentally or to hold Judy Jones, did he bear any malice toward her. He loved her, and he would love her until the day he was too old for loving—but he could not have her. So he tasted the deep pain that is reserved only for the strong, just as he had tasted for a little while the deep happiness.

Even the ultimate falsity of the grounds upon which Judy terminated the engagement that she did not want to "take him away" from Irene—Judy, who had wanted nothing else—did not revolt him. He was beyond any revulsion or any amusement.

He went East in February with the intention of selling out his laundries and settling in New York—but the war came to America in March and changed his plans. He returned to the West, handed over the management of the business to his partner, and went into the first officers' training-camp in late April. He was one of those young thousands who greeted the war with a certain amount of relief, welcoming the liberation from webs of tangled emotion.

VI

This story is not his biography, remember, although things creep into it which have nothing to do with those dreams he had when he was young. We are almost done with them and with him now. There is only one more incident to be related here, and it happens seven years farther on.

It took place in New York, where he had done well—so well that there were no barriers too high for him. He was thirty-two years old, and, except for one flying trip immediately after the war, he had not been West in seven years. A man named Devlin from Detroit came into his office to see him in a business way, and then and there this incident occurred, and closed out, so to speak, this particular side of his life.

"So you're from the Middle West," said the man Devlin with careless curiosity. "That's funny—I thought men like you were probably

born and raised on Wall Street. You know—wife of one of my best
friends in Detroit came from your city. I was an usher at the wedding."

Dexter waited with no apprehension of what was coming.

"Judy Simms," said Devlin with no particular interest; "Judy
Jones she was once."

"Yes, I knew her." A dull impatience spread over him. He had
heard, of course, that she was married—perhaps deliberately he had
heard no more.

"Awfully nice girl," brooded Devlin meaninglessly, "I'm sort of
sorry for her."

"Why?" Something in Dexter was alert, receptive, at once.

"Oh, Lud Simms has gone to pieces in a way. I don't mean he ill-
uses her, but he drinks and runs around——"

"Doesn't she run around?"

"No. Stays at home with her kids."

"Oh."

"She's a little too old for him," said Devlin.

"Too old!" cried Dexter. "Why, man, she's only twenty-seven."

He was possessed with a wild notion of rushing out into the streets
and taking a train to Detroit. He rose to his feet spasmodically.

"I guess you're busy," Devlin apologized quickly. "I didn't
realize——"

"No, I'm not busy," said Dexter, steadying his voice. "I'm not busy
at all. Not busy at all. Did you say she was—twenty-seven? No, I
said she was twenty-seven."

"Yes, you did," agreed Devlin dryly.

"Go on, then. Go on."

"What do you mean?"

"About Judy Jones."

Devlin looked at him helplessly.

"Well, that's—I told you all there is to it. He treats her like the
devil. Oh, they're not going to get divorced or anything. When he's
particularly outrageous she forgives him. In fact, I'm inclined to
think she loves him. She was a pretty girl when she first came to
Detroit."

A pretty girl! The phrase struck Dexter as ludicrous.

"Isn't she—a pretty girl, any more?"

"Oh, she's all right."

"Look here," said Dexter, sitting down suddenly. "I don't understand. You say she was a 'pretty girl' and now you say she's 'all
right.' I don't understand what you mean—Judy Jones wasn't a
pretty girl, at all. She was a great beauty. Why, I knew her, I knew
her. She was——"

Devlin laughed pleasantly.

"I'm not trying to start a row," he said. "I think Judy's a nice girl and I like her. I can't understand how a man like Lud Simms could fall madly in love with her, but he did." Then he added: "Most of the women like her."

Dexter looked closely at Devlin, thinking wildly that there must be a reason for this, some insensitivity in the man or some private malice.

"Lots of women fade just like *that*," Devlin snapped his fingers. "You must have seen it happen. Perhaps I've forgotten how pretty she was at her wedding. I've seen her so much since then, you see. She has nice eyes."

A sort of dullness settled down upon Dexter. For the first time in his life he felt like getting very drunk. He knew that he was laughing loudly at something Devlin had said, but he did not know what it was or why it was funny. When, in a few minutes, Devlin went he lay down on his lounge and looked out the window at the New York sky-line into which the sun was sinking in dull lovely shades of pink and gold.

He had thought that having nothing else to lose he was invulnerable at last—but he knew that he had just lost something more, as surely as if he had married Judy Jones and seen her fade away before his eyes.

The dream was gone. Something had been taken from him. In a sort of panic he pushed the palms of his hands into his eyes and tried to bring up a picture of the waters lapping on Sherry Island and the moonlit veranda, and gingham on the golf-links and the dry sun and the gold color of her neck's soft down. And her mouth damp to his kisses and her eyes plaintive with melancholy and her freshness like new fine linen in the morning. Why, these things were no longer in the world! They had existed and they existed no longer.

For the first time in years the tears were streaming down his face. But they were for himself now. He did not care about mouth and eyes and moving hands. He wanted to care, and he could not care. For he had gone away and he could never go back any more. The gates were closed, the sun was gone down, and there was no beauty but the gray beauty of steel that withstands all time. Even the grief he could have borne was left behind in the country of illusion, of youth, of the richness of life, where his winter dreams had flourished.

"Long ago," he said, "long ago, there was something in me, but now that thing is gone. Now that thing is gone, that thing is gone. I cannot cry. I cannot care. That thing will come back no more."

"THE SENSIBLE THING"

AT THE Great American Lunch Hour young George O'Kelly straightened his desk deliberately and with an assumed air of interest. No one in the office must know that he was in a hurry, for success is a matter of atmosphere, and it is not well to advertise the fact that your mind is separated from your work by a distance of seven hundred miles.

But once out of the building he set his teeth and began to run, glancing now and then at the gay noon of early spring which filled Times Square and loitered less than twenty feet over the heads of the crowd. The crowd all looked slightly upward and took deep March breaths, and the sun dazzled their eyes so that scarcely any one saw any one else but only their own reflection on the sky.

George O'Kelly, whose mind was over seven hundred miles away, thought that all outdoors was horrible. He rushed into the subway, and for ninety-five blocks bent a frenzied glance on a car-card which showed vividly how he had only one chance in five of keeping his teeth for ten years. At 137th Street he broke off his study of commercial art, left the subway, and began to run again, a tireless, anxious run that brought him this time to his home—one room in a high, horrible apartment-house in the middle of nowhere.

There it was on the bureau, the letter—in sacred ink, on blessed paper—all over the city, people, if they listened, could hear the beating of George O'Kelly's heart. He read the commas, the blots, and the thumb-smudge on the margin—then he threw himself hopelessly upon his bed.

He was in a mess, one of those terrific messes which are ordinary incidents in the life of the poor, which follow poverty like birds of prey. The poor go under or go up or go wrong or even go on, somehow, in a way the poor have—but George O'Kelly was so new to poverty that had any one denied the uniqueness of his case he would have been astounded.

Less than two years ago he had been graduated with honors from The Massachusetts Institute of Technology and had taken a position with a firm of construction engineers in southern Tennessee. All his life he had thought in terms of tunnels and skyscrapers and great squat dams and tall, three-towered bridges, that were like dancers holding hands in a row, with heads as tall as cities and skirts of cable strand. It had seemed romantic to George O'Kelly to change the sweep of rivers and the shape of mountains so that life could flourish in the old bad lands of the world where it had never taken root before. He loved steel, and there was always steel near him in his dreams, liquid steel, steel in bars, and blocks and beams and formless plastic masses, waiting for him, as paint and canvas to his hand. Steel inexhaustible, to be made lovely and austere in his imaginative fire . . .

At present he was an insurance clerk at forty dollars a week with his dream slipping fast behind him. The dark little girl who had made this mess, this terrible and intolerable mess, was waiting to be sent for in a town in Tennessee.

In fifteen minutes the woman from whom he sublet his room knocked and asked him with maddening kindness if, since he was home, he would have some lunch. He shook his head, but the interruption aroused him, and getting up from the bed he wrote a telegram.

"Letter depressed me have you lost your nerve you are foolish and just upset to think of breaking off why not marry me immediately sure we can make it all right——"

He hesitated for a wild minute, and then added in a hand that could scarcely be recognized as his own: "In any case I will arrive to-morrow at six o'clock."

When he finished he ran out of the apartment and down to the telegraph office near the subway stop. He possessed in this world not quite one hundred dollars, but the letter showed that she was "nervous" and this left him no choice. He knew what "nervous" meant—that she was emotionally depressed, that the prospect of marrying into a life of poverty and struggle was putting too much strain upon her love.

George O'Kelly reached the insurance company at his usual run, the run that had become almost second nature to him, that seemed best to express the tension under which he lived. He went straight to the manager's office.

"I want to see you, Mr. Chambers," he announced breathlessly.

"Well?" Two eyes, eyes like winter windows, glared at him with ruthless impersonality.

"I want to get four days' vacation."

"Why, you had a vacation just two weeks ago!" said Mr. Chambers in surprise.

"That's true," admitted the distraught young man, "but now I've got to have another."

"Where'd you go last time? To your home?"

"No, I went to—a place in Tennessee."

"Well, where do you want to go this time?"

"Well, this time I want to go to—a place in Tennessee."

"You're consistent, anyhow," said the manager dryly. "But I didn't realize you were employed here as a travelling salesman."

"I'm not," cried George desperately, "but I've got to go."

"All right," agreed Mr. Chambers, "but you don't have to come back. So don't!"

"I won't." And to his own astonishment as well as Mr. Chambers' George's face grew pink with pleasure. He felt happy, exultant—for the first time in six months he was absolutely free. Tears of gratitude stood in his eyes, and he seized Mr. Chambers warmly by the hand.

"I want to thank you," he said with a rush of emotion, "I don't want to come back. I think I'd have gone crazy if you'd said that I could come back. Only I couldn't quit myself, you see, and I want to thank you for—for quitting for me."

He waved his hand magnanimously, shouted aloud, "You owe me three days' salary but you can keep it!" and rushed from the office. Mr. Chambers rang for his stenographer to ask if O'Kelly had seemed queer lately. He had fired many men in the course of his career, and they had taken it in many different ways, but none of them had thanked him—ever before.

II

Jonquil Cary was her name, and to George O'Kelly nothing had ever looked so fresh and pale as her face when she saw him and fled to him eagerly along the station platform. Her arms were raised to him, her mouth was half parted for his kiss, when she held him off suddenly and lightly and, with a touch of embarrassment, looked around. Two boys, somewhat younger than George, were standing in the background.

"This is Mr. Craddock and Mr. Holt," she announced cheerfully. "You met them when you were here before."

Disturbed by the transition of a kiss into an introduction and suspecting some hidden significance, George was more confused when he found that the automobile which was to carry them to Jonquil's house belonged to one of the two young men. It seemed to put him at a disadvantage. On the way Jonquil chattered between the front and back seats, and when he tried to slip his arm around her under cover of the twilight she compelled him with a quick movement to take her hand instead.

"Is this street on the way to your house?" he whispered. "I don't recognize it."

"It's the new boulevard. Jerry just got this car to-day, and he wants to show it to me before he takes us home."

When, after twenty minutes, they were deposited at Jonquil's house, George felt that the first happiness of the meeting, the joy he had recognized so surely in her eyes back in the station, had been dissipated by the intrusion of the ride. Something that he had looked forward to had been rather casually lost, and he was brooding on this as he said good night stiffly to the two young men. Then his ill-humor faded as Jonquil drew him into a familiar embrace under the dim light of the front hall and told him in a dozen ways, of which the best was without words, how she had missed him. Her emotion reassured him, promised his anxious heart that everything would be all right.

They sat together on the sofa, overcome by each other's presence, beyond all except fragmentary endearments. At the supper hour Jonquil's father and mother appeared and were glad to see George. They liked him, and had been interested in his engineering career when he had first come to Tennessee over a year before. They had been sorry when he had given it up and gone to New York to look for something more immediately profitable, but while they deplored the curtailment of his career they sympathized with him and were ready to recognize the engagement. During dinner they asked about his progress in New York.

"Everything's going fine," he told them with enthusiasm. "I've been promoted—better salary."

He was miserable as he said this—but they were all *so* glad.

"They must like you," said Mrs. Cary, "that's certain—or they wouldn't let you off twice in three weeks to come down here."

"I told them they had to," explained George hastily; "I told them if they didn't I wouldn't work for them any more."

"But you ought to save your money," Mrs. Cary reproached him gently. "Not spend it all on this expensive trip."

Dinner was over—he and Jonquil were alone and she came back into his arms.

"So glad you're here," she sighed. "Wish you never were going away again, darling."

"Do you miss me?"

"Oh, so much, so much."

"Do you—do other men come to see you often? Like those two kids?"

The question surprised her. The dark velvet eyes stared at him.

"Why, of course they do. All the time. Why—I've told you in let-ters that they did, dearest."

This was true—when he had first come to the city there had been already a dozen boys around her, responding to her picturesque fragility with adolescent worship, and a few of them perceiving that her beautiful eyes were also sane and kind.

"Do you expect me never to go anywhere"—Jonquil demanded, leaning back against the sofa-pillows until she seemed to look at him from many miles away—"and just fold my hands and sit still—for-ever?"

"What do you mean?" he blurted out in a panic. "Do you mean you think I'll never have enough money to marry you?"

"Oh, don't jump at conclusions so, George."

"I'm not jumping at conclusions. That's what you said."

George decided suddenly that he was on dangerous grounds. He had not intended to let anything spoil this night. He tried to take her again in his arms, but she resisted unexpectedly, saying:

"It's hot. I'm going to get the electric fan."

When the fan was adjusted they sat down again, but he was in a supersensitive mood and involuntarily he plunged into the specific world he had intended to avoid.

"When will you marry me?"

"Are you ready for me to marry you?"

All at once his nerves gave way, and he sprang to his feet.

"Let's shut off that damned fan," he cried, "it drives me wild. It's like a clock ticking away all the time I'll be with you. I came here to be happy and forget everything about New York and time——"

He sank down on the sofa as suddenly as he had risen. Jonquil turned off the fan, and drawing his head down into her lap began stroking his hair.

"Let's sit like this," she said softly, "just sit quiet like this, and I'll put you to sleep. You're all tired and nervous and your sweet-heart'll take care of you."

"But I don't want to sit like this," he complained, jerking up sud-denly, "I don't want to sit like this at all. I want you to kiss me. That's the only thing that makes me rest. And anyways I'm not nervous—it's you that's nervous. I'm not nervous at all."

To prove that he wasn't nervous he left the couch and plumped himself into a rocking-chair across the room.

"Just when I'm ready to marry you you write me the most nervous letters, as if you're going to back out, and I have to come rushing down here——"

"You don't have to come if you don't want to."

"But I *do* want to!" insisted George.

It seemed to him that he was being very cool and logical and that she was putting him deliberately in the wrong. With every word they were drawing farther and farther apart—and he was unable to stop himself or to keep worry and pain out of his voice.

But in a minute Jonquil began to cry sorrowfully and he came back to the sofa and put his arm around her. He was the comforter now, drawing her head close to his shoulder, murmuring old familiar things until she grew calmer and only trembled a little, spasmodically, in his arms. For over an hour they sat there, while the evening pianos thumped their last cadences into the street outside. George did not move, or think, or hope, lulled into numbness by the premonition of disaster. The clock would tick on, past eleven, past twelve, and then Mrs. Cary would call down gently over the banister —beyond that he saw only to-morrow and despair.

III

In the heat of the next day the breaking-point came. They had each guessed the truth about the other, but of the two she was the more ready to admit the situation.

"There's no use going on," she said miserably, "you know you hate the insurance business, and you'll never do well in it."

"That's not it," he insisted stubbornly; "I hate going on alone. If you'll marry me and come with me and take a chance with me, I can make good at anything, but not while I'm worrying about you down here."

She was silent a long time before she answered, not thinking— for she had seen the end—but only waiting, because she knew that every word would seem more cruel than the last. Finally she spoke:

"George, I love you with all my heart, and I don't see how I can ever love any one else but you. If you'd been ready for me two months ago I'd have married you—now I can't because it doesn't seem to be the sensible thing."

He made wild accusations—there was some one else—she was keeping something from him!

"No, there's no one else."

This was true. But reacting from the strain of this affair she had found relief in the company of young boys like Jerry Holt, who had the merit of meaning absolutely nothing in her life.

George didn't take the situation well, at all. He seized her in his arms and tried literally to kiss her into marrying him at once. When this failed, he broke into a long monologue of self-pity, and ceased only when he saw that he was making himself despicable in her sight. He threatened to leave when he had no intention of leaving, and refused to go when she told him that, after all, it was best that he should.

For a while she was sorry, then for another while she was merely kind.

"You'd better go now," she cried at last, so loud that Mrs. Cary came down-stairs in alarm.

"Is something the matter?"

"I'm going away, Mrs. Cary," said George brokenly. Jonquil had left the room.

"Don't feel so badly, George." Mrs. Cary blinked at him in helpless sympathy—sorry and, in the same breath, glad that the little tragedy was almost done. "If I were you I'd go home to your mother for a week or so. Perhaps after all this is the sensible thing——"

"Please don't talk," he cried. "Please don't say anything to me now!"

Jonquil came into the room again, her sorrow and her nervousness alike tucked under powder and rouge and hat.

"I've ordered a taxicab," she said impersonally. "We can drive around until your train leaves."

She walked out on the front porch. George put on his coat and hat and stood for a minute exhausted in the hall—he had eaten scarcely a bite since he had left New York. Mrs. Cary came over, drew his head down and kissed him on the cheek, and he felt very ridiculous and weak in his knowledge that the scene had been ridiculous and weak at the end. If he had only gone the night before—left her for the last time with a decent pride.

The taxi had come, and for an hour these two that had been lovers rode along the less-frequented streets. He held her hand and grew calmer in the sunshine, seeing too late that there had been nothing all along to do or say.

"I'll come back," he told her.

"I know you will," she answered, trying to put a cheery faith into her voice. "And we'll write each other—sometimes."

"No," he said, "we won't write. I couldn't stand that. Some day I'll come back."

"I'll never forget you, George."

They reached the station, and she went with him while he bought his ticket. . . .

"Why, George O'Kelly and Jonquil Cary!"

It was a man and a girl whom George had known when he had worked in town, and Jonquil seemed to greet their presence with relief. For an interminable five minutes they all stood there talking;

then the train roared into the station, and with ill-concealed agony in his face George held out his arms toward Jonquil. She took an uncertain step toward him, faltered, and then pressed his hand quickly as if she were taking leave of a chance friend.

"Good-by, George," she was saying, "I hope you have a pleasant trip."

"Good-by, George. Come back and see us all again."

Dumb, almost blind with pain, he seized his suitcase, and in some dazed way got himself aboard the train.

Past clanging street-crossings, gathering speed through wide suburban spaces toward the sunset. Perhaps she too would see the sunset and pause for a moment, turning, remembering, before he faded with her sleep into the past. This night's dusk would cover up forever the sun and the trees and the flowers and laughter of his young world.

IV

On a damp afternoon in September of the following year a young man with has face burned to a deep copper glow got off a train at a city in Tennessee. He looked around anxiously, and seemed relieved when he found that there was no one in the station to meet him. He taxied to the best hotel in the city where he registered with some satisfaction as George O'Kelly, Cuzco, Peru.

Up in his room he sat for a few minutes at the window looking down into the familiar street below. Then with his hand trembling faintly he took off the telephone receiver and called a number.

"Is Miss Jonquil in?"

"This is she."

"Oh—" His voice after overcoming a faint tendency to waver went on with friendly formality.

"This is George O'Kelly. Did you get my letter?"

"Yes. I thought you'd be in to-day."

Her voice, cool and unmoved, disturbed him, but not as he had expected. This was the voice of a stranger, unexcited, pleasantly glad to see him—that was all. He wanted to put down the telephone and catch his breath.

"I haven't seen you for—a long time." He succeeded in making this sound offhand. "Over a year."

He knew how long it had been—to the day.

"It'll be awfully nice to talk to you again."

"I'll be there in about an hour."

He hung up. For four long seasons every minute of his leisure had been crowded with anticipation of this hour, and now this hour was here. He had thought of finding her married, engaged, in love—he had not thought she would be unstirred at his return.

There would never again in his life, he felt, be another ten months like these he had just gone through. He had made an admittedly remarkable showing for a young engineer—stumbled into two unusual opportunities, one in Peru, whence he had just returned, and another, consequent upon it, in New York, whither he was bound. In this short time he had risen from poverty into a position of unlimited opportunity.

He looked at himself in the dressing-table mirror. He was almost black with tan, but it was a romantic black, and in the last week, since he had had time to think about it, it had given him consider-, able pleasure. The hardiness of his frame, too, he appraised with a sort of fascination. He had lost part of an eyebrow somewhere, and he still wore an elastic bandage on his knee, but he was too young not to realize that on the steamer many women had looked at him with unusual tributary interest.

His clothes, of course, were frightful. They had been made for him by a Greek tailor in Lima—in two days. He was young enough, too, to have explained this sartorial deficiency to Jonquil in his otherwise laconic note. The only further detail it contained was a request that he should *not* be met at the station.

George O'Kelly, of Cuzco, Peru, waited an hour and a half in the hotel, until, to be exact, the sun had reached a midway position in the sky. Then, freshly shaven and talcum-powdered toward a somewhat more Caucasian hue, for vanity at the last minute had overcome romance, he engaged a taxicab and set out for the house he knew so well.

He was breathing hard—he noticed this but he told himself that it was excitement, not emotion. He was here; she was not married— that was enough. He was not even sure what he had to say to her. But this was the moment of his life that he felt he could least easily have dispensed with. There was no triumph, after all, without a girl concerned, and if he did not lay his spoils at her feet he could at least hold them for a passing moment before her eyes.

The house loomed up suddenly beside him, and his first thought was that it had assumed a strange unreality. There was nothing changed—only everything was changed. It was smaller and it seemed shabbier than before—there was no cloud of magic hovering over its roof and issuing from the windows of the upper floor. He rang the door-bell and an unfamiliar colored maid appeared. Miss Jonquil would be down in a moment. He wet his lips nervously and walked into the sitting-room—and the feeling of unreality increased. After all, he saw, this was only a room, and not the enchanted chamber where he had passed those poignant hours. He sat in a chair, amazed to find it a chair, realizing that his imagination had distorted and colored all these simple familiar things.

Then the door opened and Jonquil came into the room—and it was as though everything in it suddenly blurred before his eyes. He had not remembered how beautiful she was, and he felt his face grow pale and his voice diminish to a poor sigh in his throat.

She was dressed in pale green, and a gold ribbon bound back her dark, straight hair like a crown. The familiar velvet eyes caught his as she came through the door, and a spasm of fright went through him at her beauty's power of inflicting pain.

He said "Hello," and they each took a few steps forward and shook hands. Then they sat in chairs quite far apart and gazed at each other across the room.

"You've come back," she said, and he answered just as tritely: "I wanted to stop in and see you as I came through."

He tried to neutralize the tremor in his voice by looking anywhere but at her face. The obligation to speak was on him, but, unless he immediately began to boast, it seemed that there was nothing to say. There had never been anything casual in their previous relations— it didn't seem possible that people in this position would talk about the weather.

"This is ridiculous," he broke out in sudden embarrassment. "I don't know exactly what to do. Does my being here bother you?"

"No." The answer was both reticent and impersonally sad. It depressed him.

"Are you engaged?" he demanded.

"No."

"Are you in love with some one?"

She shook her head.

"Oh." He leaned back in his chair. Another subject seemed exhausted—the interview was not taking the course he had intended.

"Jonquil," he began, this time on a softer key, "after all that's happened between us, I wanted to come back and see you. Whatever I do in the future I'll never love another girl as I've loved you."

This was one of the speeches he had rehearsed. On the steamer it had seemed to have just the right note—a reference to the tenderness he would always feel for her combined with a non-committal attitude toward his present state of mind. Here with the past around him, beside him, growing minute by minute more heavy on the air, it seemed theatrical and stale.

She made no comment, sat without moving, her eyes fixed on him with an expression that might have meant everything or nothing.

"You don't love me any more, do you?" he asked her in a level voice.

"No."

When Mrs. Cary came in a minute later, and spoke to him about his success—there had been a half-column about him in the local paper—he was a mixture of emotions. He knew now that he still wanted this girl, and he knew that the past sometimes comes back —that was all. For the rest he must be strong and watchful and he would see.

"And now," Mrs. Cary was saying, "I want you two to go and see the lady who has the chrysanthemums. She particularly told me she wanted to see you because she'd read about you in the paper."

They went to see the lady with the chrysanthemums. They walked along the street, and he recognized with a sort of excitement just how her shorter footsteps always fell in between his own. The lady turned out to be nice, and the chrysanthemums were enormous and extraordinarily beautiful. The lady's gardens were full of them, white and pink and yellow, so that to be among them was a trip back into the heart of summer. There were two gardens full, and a gate between them; when they strolled toward the second garden the lady went first through the gate.

And then a curious thing happened. George stepped aside to let Jonquil pass, but instead of going through she stood still and stared at him for a minute. It was not so much the look, which was not a smile, as it was the moment of silence. They saw each other's eyes, and both took a short, faintly accelerated breath, and then they went on into the second garden. That was all.

The afternoon waned. They thanked the lady and walked home slowly, thoughtfully, side by side. Through dinner, too, they were silent. George told Mr. Cary something of what had happened in South America, and managed to let it be known that everything would be plain sailing for him in the future.

Then dinner was over, and he and Jonquil were alone in the room which had seen the beginning of their love affair and the end. It seemed to him long ago and inexpressibly sad. On that sofa he had felt agony and grief such as he would never feel again. He would never be so weak or so tired and miserable and poor. Yet he knew that that boy of fifteen months before had had something, a trust, a warmth that was gone forever. The sensible thing—they had done the sensible thing. He had traded his first youth for strength and carved success out of despair. But with his youth, life had carried away the freshness of his love.

"You won't marry me, will you?" he said quietly.

Jonquil shook her dark head.

"I'm never going to marry," she answered.

He nodded.

"I'm going on to Washington in the morning," he said.

"Oh——"

"I have to go. I've got to be in New York by the first, and meanwhile I want to stop off in Washington."

"Business!"

"No-o," he said as if reluctantly. "There's some one there I must see who was very kind to me when I was so—down and out."

This was invented. There was no one in Washington for him to see —but he was watching Jonquil narrowly, and he was sure that she winced a little, that her eyes closed and then opened wide again.

"But before I go I want to tell you the things that happened to me since I saw you, and, as maybe we won't meet again, I wonder if—if just this once you'd sit in my lap like you used to. I wouldn't ask except since there's no one else—yet—perhaps it doesn't matter."

She nodded, and in a moment was sitting in his lap as she had sat so often in that vanished spring. The feel of her head against his shoulder, of her familiar body, sent a shock of emotion over him. His arms holding her had a tendency to tighten around her, so he leaned back and began to talk thoughtfully into the air.

He told her of a despairing two weeks in New York which had terminated with an attractive if not very profitable job in a construction plant in Jersey City. When the Peru business had first presented itself it had not seemed an extraordinary opportunity. He was to be third assistant engineer on the expedition, but only ten of the American party, including eight rodmen and surveyors, had ever reached Cuzco. Ten days later the chief of the expedition was dead of yellow fever. That had been his chance, a chance for anybody but a fool, a marvellous chance——

"A chance for anybody but a fool?" she interrupted innocently.

"Even for a fool," he continued. "It was wonderful. Well, I wired New York——"

"And so," she interrupted again, "they wired that you ought to take a chance?"

"Ought to!" he exclaimed, still leaning back. "That I *had* to. There was no time to lose——"

"Not a minute?"

"Not a minute."

"Not even time for—" she paused.

"For what?"

"Look."

He bent his head forward suddenly, and she drew herself to him in the same moment, her lips half open like a flower.

"Yes," he whispered into her lips. "There's all the time in the world. . . ."

All the time in the world—his life and hers. But for an instant as he kissed her he knew that though he search through eternity he could never recapture those lost April hours. He might press her close now till the muscles knotted on his arms—she was something desirable and rare that he had fought for and made his own—but never again an intangible whisper in the dusk, or on the breeze of night. . . .

Well, let it pass, he thought; April is over, April is over. There are all kinds of love in the world, but never the same love twice.

1924   *All the Sad Young Men*

ABSOLUTION

THERE was once a priest with cold, watery eyes, who, in the still of the night, wept cold tears. He wept because the afternoons were warm and long, and he was unable to attain a complete mystical union with our Lord. Sometimes, near four o'clock, there was a rustle of Swede girls along the path by his window, and in their shrill laughter he found a terrible dissonance that made him pray aloud for the twilight to come. At twilight the laughter and the voices were quieter, but several times he had walked past Romberg's Drug Store when it was dusk and the yellow lights shone inside and the nickel taps of the soda-fountain were gleaming, and he had found the scent of cheap toilet soap desperately sweet upon the air. He passed that way when he returned from hearing confessions on Saturday nights, and he grew careful to walk on the other side of the street so that the smell of the soap would float upward before it reached his nostrils as it drifted, rather like incense, toward the summer moon.

But there was no escape from the hot madness of four o'clock. From his window, as far as he could see, the Dakota wheat thronged the valley of the Red River. The wheat was terrible to look upon and the carpet pattern to which in agony he bent his eyes sent his thought brooding through grotesque labyrinths, open always to the unavoidable sun.

One afternoon when he had reached the point where the mind runs down like an old clock, his housekeeper brought into his study a beautiful, intense little boy of eleven named Rudolph Miller. The little boy sat down in a patch of sunshine, and the priest, at his walnut desk, pretended to be very busy. This was to conceal his relief that some one had come into his haunted room.

Presently he turned around and found himself staring into two enormous, staccato eyes, lit with gleaming points of cobalt light. For a moment their expression startled him—then he saw that his visitor was in a state of abject fear.

"Your mouth is trembling," said Father Schwartz, in a haggard voice.

The little boy covered his quivering mouth with his hand.

"Are you in trouble?" asked Father Schwartz, sharply. "Take your hand away from your mouth and tell me what's the matter."

The boy—Father Schwartz recognized him now as the son of a parishioner, Mr. Miller, the freight-agent—moved his hand reluctantly off his mouth and became articulate in a despairing whisper. "Father Schwartz—I've committed a terrible sin."

"A sin against purity?"

"No, Father . . . worse."

Father Schwartz's body jerked sharply.

"Have you killed somebody?"

"No—but I'm afraid—" the voice rose to a shrill whimper.

"Do you want to go to confession?"

The little boy shook his head miserably. Father Schwartz cleared his throat so that he could make his voice soft and say some quiet, kind thing. In this moment he should forget his own agony, and try to act like God. He repeated to himself a devotional phrase, hoping that in return God would help him to act correctly.

"Tell me what you've done," said his new soft voice.

The little boy looked at him through his tears, and was reassured by the impression of moral resiliency which the distraught priest had created. Abandoning as much of himself as he was able to this man, Rudolph Miller began to tell his story.

"On Saturday, three days ago, my father he said I had to go to confession, because I hadn't been for a month, and the family they go every week, and I hadn't been. So I just as leave go, I didn't care. So I put it off till after supper because I was playing with a bunch of kids and father asked me if I went, and I said 'no,' and he took me by the neck and he said 'You go now,' so I said 'All right,' so I went over to church. And he yelled after me: 'Don't come back till you go.' . . ."

II

"On Saturday, Three Days Ago."

The plush curtain of the confessional rearranged its dismal creases, leaving exposed only the bottom of an old man's old shoe. Behind the curtain an immortal soul was alone with God and the Reverend Adolphus Schwartz, priest of the parish. Sound began, a labored whispering, sibilant and discreet, broken at intervals by the voice of the priest in audible question.

Rudolph Miller knelt in the pew beside the confessional and waited, straining nervously to hear, and yet not to hear what was

being said within. The fact that the priest was audible alarmed him.
His own turn came next, and the three or four others who waited
might listen unscrupulously while he admitted his violations of the
Sixth and Ninth Commandments.

Rudolph had never committed adultery, nor even coveted his neighbor's wife—but it was the confession of the associate sins that was
particularly hard to contemplate. In comparison he relished the less
shameful fallings away—they formed a grayish background which
relieved the ebony mark of sexual offenses upon his soul.

He had been covering his ears with his hands, hoping that his refusal to hear would be noticed, and a like courtesy rendered to him
in turn, when a sharp movement of the penitent in the confessional
made him sink his face precipitately into the crook of his elbow. Fear
assumed solid form, and pressed out a lodging between his heart and
his lungs. He must try now with all his might to be sorry for his
sins—not because he was afraid, but because he had offended God.
He must convince God that he was sorry and to do so he must first
convince himself. After a tense emotional struggle he achieved a
tremulous self-pity, and decided that he was now ready. If, by
allowing no other thought to enter his head, he could preserve this
state of emotion unimpaired until he went into that large coffin set
on end, he would have survived another crisis in his religious life.

For some time, however, a demoniac notion had partially possessed
him. He could go home now, before his turn came, and tell his mother
that he had arrived too late, and found the priest gone. This, unfortunately, involved the risk of being caught in a lie. As an alternative
he could say that he *had* gone to confession, but this meant that he
must avoid communion next day, for communion taken upon an un-
cleansed soul would turn to poison in his mouth, and he would
crumple limp and damned from the altar-rail.

Again Father Schwartz's voice became audible.

"And for your——"

The words blurred to a husky mumble, and Rudolph got excitedly
to his feet. He felt that it was impossible for him to go to confession
this afternoon. He hesitated tensely. Then from the confessional came
a tap, a creak, and a sustained rustle. The slide had fallen and the
plush curtain trembled. Temptation had come to him too late. . . .

"Bless me, Father, for I have sinned. . . . I confess to Almighty
God and to you, Father, that I have sinned. . . . Since my last confession it has been one month and three days. . . . I accuse myself
of—taking the Name of the Lord in vain. . . ."

This was an easy sin. His curses had been but bravado—telling of
them was little less than a brag.

". . . of being mean to an old lady."

The wan shadow moved a little on the latticed slat.

"How, my child?"

"Old lady Swenson," Rudolph's murmur soared jubilantly. "She got our baseball that we knocked in her window, and she wouldn't give it back, so we yelled 'Twenty-three, Skidoo,' at her all afternoon. Then about five o'clock she had a fit, and they had to have the doctor."

"Go on, my child."

3. "Of—of not believing I was the son of my parents."

"What?" The interrogation was distinctly startled.

"Of not believing that I was the son of my parents."

"Why not?"

"Oh, just pride," answered the penitent airily.

F ["You mean you thought you were too good to be the son of your parents?"

"Yes, Father." On a less jubilant note.

"Go on."

4.-6. "Of being disobedient and calling my mother names. Of slandering people behind their back. Of smoking——"

Rudolph had now exhausted the minor offenses, and was approaching the sins it was agony to tell. He held his fingers against his face like bars as if to press out between them the shame in his heart.

7. "Of dirty words and immodest thoughts and desires," he whispered very low.

"How often?"

"I don't know."

"Once a week? Twice a week?"

"Twice a week."

"Did you yield to these desires?"

"No, Father."

"Were you alone when you had them?"

"No Father. I was with two boys and a girl."

"Don't you know, my child, that you should avoid the occasions of sin as well as the sin itself? Evil companionship leads to evil desires and evil desires to evil actions. Where were you when this happened?"

"In a barn in back of——"

"I don't want to hear any names," interrupted the priest sharply.

"Well, it was up in the loft of this barn and this girl and—a fella, they were saying things—saying immodest things, and I stayed."

"You should have gone—you should have told the girl to go."

He should have gone! He could not tell Father Schwartz how his pulse had bumped in his wrist, how a strange, romantic excitement had possessed him when those curious things had been said. Perhaps in the houses of delinquency among the dull and hard-eyed incorrigible girls can be found those for whom has burned the whitest fire.

"Have you anything else to tell me?"

"I don't think so, Father."

Rudolph felt a great relief. Perspiration had broken out under his tight-pressed fingers.

"Have you told any lies?"

The question startled him. Like all those who habitually and instinctively lie, he had an enormous respect and awe for the truth. Something almost exterior to himself dictated a quick, hurt answer. "Oh, no, Father, I never tell lies."

For a moment, like the commoner in the king's chair, he tasted the pride of the situation. Then as the priest began to murmur conventional admonitions he realized that in heroically denying he had told lies, he had committed a terrible sin—he had told a lie in confession.

In automatic response to Father Schwartz's "Make an act of contrition," he began to repeat aloud meaninglessly:

"Oh, my God, I am heartily sorry for having offended Thee. . . ."

He must fix this now—it was a bad mistake—but as his teeth shut on the last words of his prayer there was a sharp sound, and the slat was closed.

A minute later when he emerged into the twilight the relief in coming from the muggy church into an open world of wheat and sky postponed the full realization of what he had done. Instead of worrying he took a deep breath of the crisp air and began to say over and over to himself the words "Blatchford Sarnemington, Blatchford Sarnemington!"

Blatchford Sarnemington was himself, and these words were in effect a lyric. When he became Blatchford Sarnemington a suave nobility flowed from him. Blatchford Sarnemington lived in great sweeping triumphs. When Rudolph half closed his eyes it meant that Blatchford had established dominance over him and, as he went by, there were envious mutters in the air: "Blatchford Sarnemington! There goes Blatchford Sarnemington."

He was Blatchford now for a while as he strutted homeward along the staggering road, but when the road braced itself in macadam in order to become the main street of Ludwig, Rudolph's exhilaration faded out and his mind cooled, and he felt the horror of his lie. God, of course, already knew of it—but Rudolph reserved a corner of his mind where he was safe from God, where he prepared the subterfuges with which he often tricked God. Hiding now in this corner he considered how he could best avoid the consequences of his misstatement.

At all costs he must avoid communion next day. The risk of anger-

ing God to such an extent was too great. He would have to drink
water "by accident" in the morning, and thus, in accordance with a
church law, render himself unfit to receive communion that day. In
spite of its flimsiness this subterfuge was the most feasible that occurred to him. He accepted its risks and was concentrating on how
best to put it into effect, as he turned the corner by Romberg's Drug
Store and came in sight of his father's house.

III

Rudolph's father, the local freight-agent, had floated with the second wave of German and Irish stock to the Minnesota-Dakota
country. Theoretically, great opportunities lay ahead of a young man
of energy in that day and place, but Carl Miller had been incapable
of establishing either with his superiors or his subordinates the reputation for approximate immutability which is essential to success in
a hierarchic industry. Somewhat gross, he was, nevertheless, insuffi-
ciently hard-headed and unable to take fundamental relationships
for granted, and this inability made him suspicious, unrestful, and
continually dismayed.

His two bonds with the colorful life were his faith in the Roman
Catholic Church and his mystical worship of the Empire Builder,
James J. Hill. Hill was the apotheosis of that quality in which Miller
himself was deficient—the sense of things, the feel of things, the hint
of rain in the wind on the cheek. Miller's mind worked late on the
old decisions of other men, and he had never in his life felt the balance of any single thing in his hands. His weary, sprightly, under-
sized body was growing old in Hill's gigantic shadow. For twenty
years he had lived alone with Hill's name and God.

On Sunday morning Carl Miller awoke in the dustless quiet of six
o'clock. Kneeling by the side of the bed he bent his yellow-gray hair
and the full dapple bangs of his mustache into the pillow, and prayed
for several minutes. Then he drew off his night-shirt—like the rest
of his generation he had never been able to endure pajamas—and
clothed his thin, white, hairless body in woollen underwear.

He shaved. Silence in the other bedroom where his wife lay nervously asleep. Silence from the screened-off corner of the hall where
his son's cot stood, and his son slept among his Alger books, his collection of cigar-bands, his mothy pennants—"Cornell," "Hamlin,"
and "Greetings from Pueblo, New Mexico"—and the other possessions of his private life. From outside Miller could hear the shrill
birds and the whirring movement of the poultry, and, as an undertone, the low, swelling click-a-tick of the six-fifteen through-train
for Montana and the green coast beyond. Then as the cold water

dripped from the wash-rag in his hand he raised his head suddenly—
he had heard a furtive sound from the kitchen below.

He dried his razor hastily, slipped his dangling suspenders to his
shoulder, and listened. Some one was walking in the kitchen, and he
knew by the light footfall that it was not his wife. With his mouth
faintly ajar he ran quickly down the stairs and opened the kitchen
door.

Standing by the sink, with one hand on the still dripping faucet
and the other clutching a full glass of water, stood his son. The boy's
eyes, still heavy with sleep, met his father's with a frightened, reproachful beauty. He was barefooted, and his pajamas were rolled
up at the knees and sleeves.

For a moment they both remained motionless—Carl Miller's brow
went down and his son's went up, as though they were striking a
balance between the extremes of emotion which filled them. Then the
bangs of the parent's mustache descended portentously until they
obscured his mouth, and he gave a short glance around to see if anything had been disturbed.

The kitchen was garnished with sunlight which beat on the pans
and made the smooth boards of the floor and table yellow and clean
as wheat. It was the centre of the house where the fire burned and the
tins fitted into tins like toys, and the steam whistled all day on a
thin pastel note. Nothing was moved, nothing touched—except the
faucet where beads of water still formed and dripped with a white
flash into the sink below.

"What are you doing?"

"I got awful thirsty, so I thought I'd just come down and get——"

"I thought you were going to communion."

A look of vehement astonishment spread over his son's face.

"I forgot all about it."

"Have you drunk any water?"

"No——"

As the word left his mouth Rudolph knew it was the wrong answer,
but the faded indignant eyes facing him had signalled up the truth
before the boy's will could act. He realized, too, that he should never
have come down-stairs; some vague necessity for verisimilitude had
made him want to leave a wet glass as evidence by the sink; the
honesty of his imagination had betrayed him.

"Pour it out," commanded his father, "that water!"

Rudolph despairingly inverted the tumbler.

"What's the matter with you, anyways?" demanded Miller angrily

"Nothing."

"Did you go to confession yesterday?"

"Yes."

"Then why were you going to drink water?"

"I don't know—I forgot."

"Maybe you care more about being a little bit thirsty than you do about your religion."

"I forgot." Rudolph could feel the tears straining in his eyes.

"That's no answer."

"Well, I did."

"You better look out!" His father held to a high, persistent, inquisitory note: "If you're so forgetful that you can't remember your religion something better be done about it."

Rudolph filled a sharp pause with:

"I can remember it all right."

"First you begin to neglect your religion," cried his father, fanning his own fierceness, "the next thing you'll begin to lie and steal, and the *next* thing is the *reform* school!"

Not even this familiar threat could deepen the abyss that Rudolph saw before him. He must either tell all now, offering his body for what he knew would be a ferocious beating, or else tempt the thunderbolts by receiving the Body and Blood of Christ with sacrilege upon his soul. And of the two the former seemed more terrible—it was not so much the beating he dreaded as the savage ferocity, outlet of the ineffectual man, which would lie behind it.

"Put down that glass and go up-stairs and dress!" his father ordered, "and when we get to church, before you go to communion, you better kneel down and ask God to forgive you for your carelessness."

Some accidental emphasis in the phrasing of this command acted like a catalytic agent on the confusion and terror of Rudolph's mind. A wild, proud anger rose in him, and he dashed the tumbler passionately into the sink.

His father uttered a strained, husky sound, and sprang for him. Rudolph dodged to the side, tipped over a chair, and tried to get beyond the kitchen table. He cried out sharply when a hand grasped his pajama shoulder, then he felt the dull impact of a fist against the side of his head, and glancing blows on the upper part of his body. As he slipped here and there in his father's grasp, dragged or lifted when he clung instinctively to an arm, aware of sharp smarts and strains, he made no sound except that he laughed hysterically several times. Then in less than a minute the blows abruptly ceased. After a lull during which Rudolph was tightly held, and during which they both trembled violently and uttered strange, truncated words, Carl Miller half dragged, half threatened his son up-stairs.

"Put on your clothes!"

· Rudolph was now both hysterical and cold. His head hurt him, and there was a long, shallow scratch on his neck from his father's finger-nail, and he sobbed and trembled as he dressed. He was aware of his mother standing at the doorway in a wrapper, her wrinkled face compressing and squeezing and opening out into new series of wrinkles which floated and eddied from neck to brow. Despising her nervous ineffectuality and avoiding her rudely when she tried to touch his neck with witch-hazel, he made a hasty, choking toilet. Then he followed his father out of the house and along the road toward the Catholic church.

2nd confession during church by father, communion, dresses him

IV

They walked without speaking except when Carl Miller acknowledged automatically the existence of passers-by. Rudolph's uneven breathing alone ruffled the hot Sunday silence.

His father stopped decisively at the door of the church.

"I've decided you'd better go to confession again. Go in and tell Father Schwartz what you did and ask God's pardon."

"You lost your temper, too!" said Rudolph quickly.

Carl Miller took a step toward his son, who moved cautiously backward.

"All right, I'll go."

"Are you going to do what I say?" cried his father in a hoarse whisper.

"All right."

Rudolph walked into the church, and for the second time in two days entered the confessional and knelt down. The slat went up almost at once.

"I accuse myself of missing my morning prayers."

"Is that all?"

"That's all."

2nd confession — doesn't admit

A maudlin exultation filled him. Not easily ever again would he be able to put an abstraction before the necessities of his ease and pride. An invisible line had been crossed, and he had become aware of his isolation—aware that it applied not only to those moments when he was Blatchford Sarnemington but that it applied to all his inner life. Hitherto such phenomena as "crazy" ambitions and petty shames and fears had been but private reservations, unacknowledged before the throne of his official soul. Now he realized unconsciously that his private reservations were himself—and all the rest a garnished front and a conventional flag. The pressure of his environment had driven him into the lonely secret road of adolescence.

He knelt in the pew beside his father. Mass began. Rudolph knelt up—when he was alone he slumped his posterior back against the

seat—and tasted the consciousness of a sharp, subtle revenge. Beside
him his father prayed that God would forgive Rudolph, and asked
also that his own outbreak of temper would be pardoned. He glanced
sidewise at this son, and was relieved to see that the strained, wild
look had gone from his face and that he had ceased sobbing. The
Grace of God, inherent in the Sacrament, would do the rest, and perhaps after Mass everything would be better. He was proud of
Rudolph in his heart, and beginning to be truly as well as formally
sorry for what he had done.

Usually, the passing of the collection box was a significant point
for Rudolph in the services. If, as was often the case, he had no
money to drop in he would be furiously ashamed and bow his head
and pretend not to see the box, lest Jeanne Brady in the pew behind
should take notice and suspect an acute family poverty. But to-day
he glanced coldly into it as it skimmed under his eyes, noting with
casual interest the large number of pennies it contained.

When the bell rang for communion, however, he quivered. There
was no reason why God should not stop his heart. During the past
twelve hours he had committed a series of mortal sins increasing in
gravity, and he was now to crown them all with a blasphemous
sacrilege.

Matt 8.8 *Lord, I am not worthy that thou should come under my roof; but*

"*Domine, non sum dignus; ut intres sub tectum meum; sed*
tantum dic verbo, et sanabitur anima mea. . . ." *speak the word only;*
my soul [shall be healed]

There was a rustle in the pews, and the communicants worked
their ways into the aisle with downcast eyes and joined hands. Those
of larger piety pressed together their finger-tips to form steeples.
Among these latter was Carl Miller. Rudolph followed him toward
the altar-rail and knelt down, automatically taking up the napkin
under his chin. The bell rang sharply, and the priest turned from
the altar with the white Host held above the chalice:

"*Corpus Domini nostri Jesu Christi custodiat animam tuam in*
vitam æternam."

A cold sweat broke out on Rudolph's forehead as the communion
began. Along the line Father Schwartz moved, and with gathering
nausea Rudolph felt his heart-valves weakening at the will of God.
It seemed to him that the church was darker and that a great quiet
had fallen, broken only by the inarticulate mumble which announced
the approach of the Creator of Heaven and Earth. He dropped his
head down between his shoulders and waited for the blow.

Then he felt a sharp nudge in his side. His father was poking him
to sit up, not to slump against the rail; the priest was only two
places away.

"*Corpus Domini nostri Jesu Christi custodiat animam tuam in*
vitam æternam."

The body of our Lord Jesus Christ cares for your soul in eternal life.

Rudolph opened his mouth. He felt the sticky wax taste of the ✓
wafer on his tongue. He remained motionless for what seemed an interminable period of time, his head still raised, the wafer undissolved
in his mouth. Then again he started at the pressure of his father's
elbow, and saw that the people were falling away from the altar like
leaves and turning with blind downcast eyes to their pews, alone
with God.

Rudolph was alone with himself, drenched with perspiration and
deep in mortal sin. As he walked back to his pew the sharp taps of
his cloven hoofs were loud upon the floor, and he knew that it was a
dark poison he carried in his heart.

"Sagitta Volante in Dei"

The beautiful little boy with eyes like blue stones, and lashes that
sprayed open from them like flower-petals had finished telling his
sin to Father Schwartz—and the square of sunshine in which he sat
had moved forward half an hour into the room. Rudolph had become
less frightened now; once eased of the story a reaction had set in.
He knew that as long as he was in the room with this priest God
would not stop his heart, so he sighed and sat quietly, waiting for the
priest to speak.

Father Schwartz's cold watery eyes were fixed upon the carpet
pattern on which the sun had brought out the swastikas and the flat
bloomless vines and the pale echoes of flowers. The hall-clock ticked
insistently toward sunset, and from the ugly room and from the
afternoon outside the window arose a stiff monotony, shattered now
and then by the reverberate clapping of a far-away hammer on the
dry air. The priest's nerves were strung thin and the beads of his
rosary were crawling and squirming like snakes upon the green felt
of his table top. He could not remember now what it was he should
say.

Of all the things in this lost Swede town he was most aware of this
little boy's eyes—the beautiful eyes, with lashes that left them reluctantly and curved back as though to meet them once more.

For a moment longer the silence persisted while Rudolph waited,
and the priest struggled to remember something that was slipping
farther and farther away from him, and the clock ticked in the broken
house. Then Father Schwartz stared hard at the little boy and remarked in a peculiar voice:

"When a lot of people get together in the best places things go
glimmering."

Rudolph started and looked quickly at Father Schwartz's face.

"I said—" began the priest, and paused, listening. "Do you hear the hammer and the clock ticking and the bees? Well, that's no good. The thing is to have a lot of people in the centre of the world, wherever that happens to be. Then"—his watery eyes widened knowingly —"things go glimmering."

"Yes, Father," agreed Rudolph, feeling a little frightened.

"What are you going to be when you grow up?"

"Well, I was going to be a baseball-player for a while," answered Rudolph nervously, "but I don't think that's a very good ambition, so I think I'll be an actor or a Navy officer."

Again the priest stared at him.

"I see *exactly* what you mean," he said, with a fierce air.

Rudolph had not meant anything in particular, and at the implication that he had, he became more uneasy.

"This man is crazy," he thought, "and I'm scared of him. He wants me to help him out some way, and I don't want to."

"You look as if things went glimmering," cried Father Schwartz wildly. "Did you ever go to a party?"

"Yes, Father."

"And did you notice that everybody was properly dressed? That's what I mean. Just as you went into the party there was a moment when everybody was properly dressed. Maybe two little girls were standing by the door and some boys were leaning over the banisters, and there were bowls around full of flowers."

"I've been to a lot of parties," said Rudolph, rather relieved that the conversation had taken this turn.

"Of course," continued Father Schwartz triumphantly, "I knew you'd agree with me. But my theory is that when a whole lot of people get together in the best places things go glimmering all the time."

Rudolph found himself thinking of Blatchford Sarnemington.

"Please listen to me!" commanded the priest impatiently. "Stop worrying about last Saturday. Apostasy implies an absolute damnation only on the supposition of a previous perfect faith. Does that fix it?"

Rudolph had not the faintest idea what Father Schwartz was talking about, but he nodded and the priest nodded back at him and returned to his mysterious preoccupation.

"Why," he cried, "they have lights now as big as stars—do you realize that? I heard of one light they had in Paris or somewhere that was as big as a star. A lot of people had it—a lot of gay people. They have all sorts of things now that you never dreamed of."

"Look here—" He came nearer to Rudolph, but the boy drew

away, so Father Schwartz went back and sat down in his chair, his
eyes dried out and hot. "Did you ever see an amusement park?"
"No, Father."

"*Araby*"

"Well, go and see an amusement park." The priest waved his hand
vaguely. "It's a thing like a fair, only much more glittering. Go to
one at night and stand a little way off from it in a dark place—
under dark trees. You'll see a big wheel made of lights turning in the
air, and a long slide shooting boats down into the water. A band
playing somewhere, and a smell of peanuts—and everything will
twinkle. But it won't remind you of anything, you see. It will all just
hang out there in the night like a colored balloon—like a big yellow
lantern on a pole."

Father Schwartz frowned as he suddenly thought of something.

"But don't get up close," he warned Rudolph, "because if you do | reality
you'll only feel the heat and the sweat and the life."

All this talking seemed particularly strange and awful to Rudolph,
because this man was a priest. He sat there, half terrified, his beautiful eyes open wide and staring at Father Schwartz. But underneath
his terror he felt that his own inner convictions were confirmed.
There was something ineffably gorgeous somewhere that had nothing
to do with God. He no longer thought that God was angry at him
about the original lie, because He must have understood that Rudolph
had done it to make things finer in the confessional, brightening up
the dinginess of his admissions by saying a thing radiant and proud.
At the moment when he had affirmed immaculate honor a silver pen-
non had flapped out into the breeze somewhere and there had been
the crunch of leather and the shine of silver spurs and a troop of
horsemen waiting for dawn on a low green hill. The sun had made
stars of light on their breastplates like the picture at home of the
German cuirassiers at Sedan. Franco-Prussian 1870

But now the priest was muttering inarticulate and heart-broken
words, and the boy became wildly afraid. Horror entered suddenly
in at the open window, and the atmosphere of the room changed.
Father Schwartz collapsed precipitously down on his knees, and let
his body settle back against a chair.

"Oh, my God!" he cried out, in a strange voice, and wilted to the
floor.

Then a human oppression rose from the priest's worn clothes, and
mingled with the faint smell of old food in the corners. Rudolph gave   sext
a sharp cry and ran in a panic from the house—while the collapsed
man lay there quite still, filling his room, filling it with voices and
faces until it was crowded with echolalia, and rang loud with a
steady, shrill note of laughter. *uncontrollable repeat of words spoken by another*

Outside the window the blue sirocco trembled over the wheat, and girls with yellow hair walked sensuously along roads that bounded the fields, calling innocent, exciting things to the young men who were working in the lines between the grain. Legs were shaped under starchless gingham, and rims of the necks of dresses were warm and damp. For five hours now hot fertile life had burned in the afternoon. It would be night in three hours, and all along the land there would be these blonde Northern girls and the tall young men from the farms lying out beside the wheat, under the moon.

1924   *All the Sad Young Men*

II

Glamor and Disillusionment

EDITOR'S NOTE

THIS second group consists of seven stories written between 1924, the year when Fitzgerald finished *The Great Gatsby,* and the time of Zelda's first breakdown in 1930. During those years he was devoting most of his energy to magazine stories and the stories continued to improve, after taking a leap forward at the time of *Gatsby;* but already the author was suffering from a form of neglect. The situation was in some ways preposterous. Here was one of our leading writers, doing some of his best work and having it featured in the most popular American magazines, and at the same time the critics were wondering what had become of him after his early success. The critics didn't read the *Saturday Evening Post* or expect to find serious fiction there, and Fitzgerald himself was so much affected by their attitude that he never reprinted some of his most effective stories.

There are three of the "junked and dismantled" stories in the present group. "Magnetism" (1928) was almost the only fruit of his first visit to Hollywood. He had gone there to write a script for Constance Talmadge and had worked hard on it, besides being the life of several wild parties, but the script was never produced. "Magnetism" is a serious study of the movie colony, even if it deals with the farcical dilemma of a good man and faithful husband who can't keep other women from falling in love with him. . . . "The Rough Crossing" (1929) was the souvenir of a stormy voyage to Genoa, during which Scott and Zelda had flirted with strangers and quarreled with each other. The first two paragraphs of the story went into Fitzgerald's notebook and were afterwards rewritten into Book II, Chapter XIX, of *Tender Is the Night.* . . . "The Bridal Party" (1930) was suggested by the famous wedding of Powell Fowler in the early summer of that same year. Better than anything else I have read it gives us the atmosphere of that brief period when the spirit of the Wall Street boom still flourished in the midst of the crash.

Two other stories in the present group were reprinted in *All the Sad Young Men*. "The Rich Boy" (1926) was the first serious work that Fitzgerald undertook after finishing *Gatsby*. Like the novel it reveals his complicated attitude toward the very rich, with its mixture of distrust, admiration and above all curiosity about how their minds work. Anson Hunter's central trait, in the story, is the sense of superiority that he feeds by captivating others. It makes him willing to help or destroy others, almost in the same gesture, but keeps him from surrendering anything of himself. In revealing this trait Fitzgerald shows how much he has learned about irony and understatement. . . . "The Baby Party" (1925) goes back to a somewhat earlier period. After spending a year in Great Neck, Long Island, and entertaining mobs of week-end guests, Fitzgerald was $5,000 in debt and had to stop work on *Gatsby*. He wrote himself out of debt by producing eleven stories, which he sold for more than $17,000. "I really worked hard as hell last winter," he said in a letter to Edmund Wilson—"but it was all trash and it nearly broke my heart as well as my iron constitution." Although it was written in a single all-night session, "The Baby Party" is far from being trash, and it is Fitzgerald's one expedition into the field of domestic comedy.

"The Last of the Belles" (1929) was reprinted in *Taps at Reveille*. Its portrait of Ailie Calhoun, with her charm and professional vanity, is filled out with incidents that Fitzgerald remembered from his courtship of Zelda. Like other stories written at the same period, "The Last of the Belles" is filled with regret for a vanished emotion, but the regret is seasoned with self-ridicule—as when the hero goes stumbling through the knee-deep underbrush that had covered the site of an army camp, "looking," as he said to himself, "for my youth in a clapboard or a strip of roofing or a rusty tomato can." . . . "Two Wrongs" (1930) was also reprinted in *Taps*. It dates from a period when Fitzgerald was recovering from a mild attack of tuberculosis—his second or third—and Zelda was studying hard to become a professional dancer. A great deal of his feeling about himself went into the story, together with his premonitions of disaster.

THE RICH BOY (1926) + Asym (1926)

I *the rich*

BEGIN WITH an individual, and before you know it you find that
you have created a type; begin with a type, and you find that you
have created—nothing. That is because we are all queer fish, queerer
behind our faces and voices than we want any one to know or than
we know ourselves. When I hear a man proclaiming himself an
"average, honest, open fellow," I feel pretty sure that he has some
definite and perhaps terrible abnormality which he has agreed to conceal—and his protestation of being average and honest and open is
his way of reminding himself of his misprision.

There are no types, no plurals. There is a rich boy, and this is his
and not his brothers' story. All my life I have lived among his
brothers but this one has been my friend. Besides, if I wrote about
his brothers I should have to begin by attacking all the lies that the
poor have told about the rich and the rich have told about themselves—such a wild structure they have erected that when we pick
up a book about the rich, some instinct prepares us for unreality.
Even the intelligent and impassioned reporters of life have made the
country of the rich as unreal as fairy-land.

Let me tell you about the very rich. They are different from you
and me. They possess and enjoy early, and it does something to them,
makes them soft where we are hard, and cynical where we are trust-
ful, in a way that, unless you were born rich, it is very difficult to
understand. They think, deep in their hearts, that they are better
than we are because we had to discover the compensations and
refuges of life for ourselves. Even when they enter deep into our
world or sink below us, they still think that they are better than we
are. They are different. The only way I can describe young Anson
Hunter is to approach him as if he were a foreigner and cling stubbornly to my point of view. If I accept his for a moment I am lost—
I have nothing to show but a preposterous movie.

II

Anson was the eldest of six children who would some day divide
a fortune of fifteen million dollars, and he reached the age of reason
—is it seven?—at the beginning of the century when daring young

women were already gliding along Fifth Avenue in electric "mobiles." In those days he and his brother had an English governess who spoke the language very clearly and crisply and well, so that the two boys grew to speak as she did—their words and sentences were all crisp and clear and not run together as ours are. They didn't talk exactly like English children but acquired an accent that is peculiar to fashionable people in the city of New York.

In the summer the six children were moved from the house on 71st Street to a big estate in northern Connecticut. It was not a fashionable locality—Anson's father wanted to delay as long as pos- sible his children's knowledge of that side of life. He was a man somewhat superior to his class, which composed New York society, and to his period, which was the snobbish and formalized vulgarity of the Gilded Age, and he wanted his sons to learn habits of con- centration and have sound constitutions and grow up into right-liv- ing and successful men. He and his wife kept an eye on them as well as they were able until the two older boys went away to school, but in huge establishments this is difficult—it was much simpler in the series of small and medium-sized houses in which my own youth was spent—I was never far out of the reach of my mother's voice, of the sense of her presence, her approval or disapproval.

Anson's first sense of his superiority came to him when he realized the half-grudging American deference that was paid to him in the Connecticut village. The parents of the boys he played with always inquired after his father and mother, and were vaguely excited when their own children were asked to the Hunters' house. He accepted this as the natural state of things, and a sort of impatience with all groups of which he was not the centre—in money, in position, in authority—remained with him for the rest of his life. He disdained to struggle with other boys for precedence—he expected it to be given him freely, and when it wasn't he withdrew into his family. His family was sufficient, for in the East money is still a somewhat feudal thing, a clan-forming thing. In the snobbish West, money sepa — rates families to form "sets."

At eighteen, when he went to New Haven, Anson was tall and thick-set, with a clear complexion and a healthy color from the ordered life he had led in school. His hair was yellow and grew in a funny way on his head, his nose was beaked—these two things kept him from being handsome—but he had a confident charm and a cer- tain brusque style, and the upper-class men who passed him on the street knew without being told that he was a rich boy and had gone to one of the best schools. Nevertheless, his very superiority kept him from being a success in college—the independence was mistaken for egotism, and the refusal to accept Yale standards with the proper

awe seemed to belittle all those who had. So, long before he gradu- (
ated, he began to shift the centre of his life to New York.

He was at home in New York—there was his own house with "the
kind of servants you can't get any more"—and his own family, of
which, because of his good humor and a certain ability to make
things go, he was rapidly becoming the centre, and the débutante *F matter*
parties, and the correct manly world of the men's clubs, and the occasional wild spree with the gallant girls whom New Haven only knew
from the fifth row. His aspirations were conventional enough—they
included even the irreproachable shadow he would some day marry,
but they differed from the aspirations of the majority of young men
in that there was no mist over them, none of that quality which is
variously known as "idealism" or "illusion." Anson accepted without reservation the world of high finance and high extravagance, of
divorce and dissipation, of snobbery and of privilege. Most of our
lives end as a compromise—it was as a compromise that his life
began.

He and I first met in the late summer of 1917 when he was just out
of Yale, and, like the rest of us, was swept up into the systematized
hysteria of the war. In the blue-green uniform of the naval aviation
he came down to Pensacola, where the hotel orchestras played "I'm
sorry, dear," and we young officers danced with the girls. Every one
liked him, and though he ran with the drinkers and wasn't an especially good pilot, even the instructors treated him with a certain
respect. He was always having long talks with them in his confident,
logical voice—talks which ended by his getting himself, or, more
frequently, another officer, out of some impending trouble. He was
convivial, bawdy, robustly avid for pleasure, and we were all surprised when he fell in love with a conservative and rather proper
girl.

Her name was Paula Legendre, a dark, serious beauty from somewhere in California. Her family kept a winter residence just outside
of town, and in spite of her primness she was enormously popular;
there is a large class of men whose egotism can't endure humor in a
woman. But Anson wasn't that sort, and I couldn't understand the
attraction of her "sincerity"—that was the thing to say about her—
for his keen and somewhat sardonic mind.

Nevertheless, they fell in love—and on her terms. He no longer
joined the twilight gathering at the De Soto bar, and whenever they
were seen together they were engaged in a long, serious dialogue,
which must have gone on several weeks. Long afterward he told me
that it was not about anything in particular but was composed on *expe*
both sides of immature and even meaningless statements—the emotional content that gradually came to fill it grew up not out of the

words but out of its enormous seriousness. It was a sort of hypnosis. Often it was interrupted, giving way to that emasculated humor we call fun; when they were alone it was resumed again, solemn, low-keyed, and pitched so as to give each other a sense of unity in feeling and thought. They came to resent any interruptions of it, to be unresponsive to facetiousness about life, even to the mild cynicism of their contemporaries. They were only happy when the dialogue was going on, and its seriousness bathed them like the amber glow of an open fire. Toward the end there came an interruption they did not resent—it began to be interrupted by passion.

Oddly enough, Anson was as engrossed in the dialogue as she was and as profoundly affected by it, yet at the same time aware that on his side much was insincere, and on hers much was merely simple. At first, too, he despised her emotional simplicity as well, but with his love her nature deepened and blossomed, and he could despise it no longer. He felt that if he could enter into Paula's warm safe life he would be happy. The long preparation of the dialogue removed any constraint—he taught her some of what he had learned from more adventurous women, and she responded with a rapt holy intensity. One evening after a dance they agreed to marry, and he wrote a long letter about her to his mother. The next day Paula told him that she was rich, that she had a personal fortune of nearly a million dollars.

III

It was exactly as if they could say "Neither of us has anything: we shall be poor together"—just as delightful that they should be rich instead. It gave them the same communion of adventure. Yet when Anson got leave in April, and Paula and her mother accompanied him North, she was impressed with the standing of his family in New York and with the scale on which they lived. Alone with Anson for the first time in the rooms where he had played as a boy, she was filled with a comfortable emotion, as though she were pre-eminently safe and taken care of. The pictures of Anson in a skull cap at his first school, of Anson on horseback with the sweetheart of a mysterious forgotten summer, of Anson in a gay group of ushers and bridesmaids at a wedding, made her jealous of his life apart from her in the past, and so completely did his authoritative person seem to sum up and typify these possessions of his that she was inspired with the idea of being married immediately and returning to Pensacola as his wife.

But an immediate marriage wasn't discussed—even the engagement was to be secret until after the war. When she realized that only two days of his leave remained, her dissatisfaction crystallized in the intention of making him as unwilling to wait as she was. They were driving to the country for dinner, and she determined to force the issue that night.

Now a cousin of Paula's was staying with them at the Ritz, a severe, bitter girl who loved Paula but was somewhat jealous of her impressive engagement, and as Paula was late in dressing, the cousin, who wasn't going to the party, received Anson in the parlor of the suite.

Anson had met friends at five o'clock and drunk freely and indiscreetly with them for an hour. He left the Yale Club at a proper time, and his mother's chauffeur drove him to the Ritz, but his usual capacity was not in evidence, and the impact of the steam-heated sitting-room made him suddenly dizzy. He knew it, and he was both amused and sorry.

Paula's cousin was twenty-five, but she was exceptionally naïve, and at first failed to realize what was up. She had never met Anson before, and she was surprised when he mumbled strange information and nearly fell off his chair, but until Paula appeared it didn't occur to her that what she had taken for the odor of a dry-cleaned uniform was really whiskey. But Paula understood as soon as she appeared; her only thought was to get Anson away before her mother saw him, and at the look in her eyes the cousin understood too.

When Paula and Anson descended to the limousine they found two men inside, both asleep; they were the men with whom he had been drinking at the Yale Club, and they were also going to the party. He had entirely forgotten their presence in the car. On the way to Hempstead they awoke and sang. Some of the songs were rough, and though Paula tried to reconcile herself to the fact that Anson had few verbal inhibitions, her lips tightened with shame and distaste.

Back at the hotel the cousin, confused and agitated, considered the incident, and then walked into Mrs. Legendre's bedroom, saying: "Isn't he funny?"

"Who is funny?"

"Why—Mr. Hunter. He seemed so funny."

Mrs. Legendre looked at her sharply.

"How is he funny?"

"Why, he said he was French. I didn't know he was French."

"That's absurd. You must have misunderstood." She smiled: "It was a joke."

The cousin shook her head stubbornly.

"No. He said he was brought up in France. He said he couldn't speak any English, and that's why he couldn't talk to me. And he couldn't!"

Mrs. Legendre looked away with impatience just as the cousin added thoughtfully, "Perhaps it was because he was so drunk," and walked out of the room.

This curious report was true. Anson, finding his voice thick and uncontrollable, had taken the unusual refuge of announcing that he spoke no English. Years afterwards he used to tell that part of the story, and he invariably communicated the uproarious laughter which the memory aroused in him.

Five times in the next hour Mrs. Legendre tried to get Hempstead on the phone. When she succeeded, there was a ten-minute delay before she heard Paula's voice on the wire.

"Cousin Jo told me Anson was intoxicated."

"Oh, no. . . ."

"Oh, yes. Cousin Jo says he was intoxicated. He told her he was French, and fell off his chair and behaved as if he was very intoxicated. I don't want you to come home with him."

"Mother, he's all right! Please don't worry about——"

"But I do worry. I think it's dreadful. I want you to promise me not to come home with him."

"I'll take care of it, mother. . . ."

"I don't want you to come home with him."

"All right, mother. Good-by."

"Be sure now, Paula. Ask some one to bring you."

Deliberately Paula took the receiver from her ear and hung it up. Her face was flushed with helpless annoyance. Anson was stretched out asleep in a bedroom up-stairs, while the dinner-party below was proceeding lamely toward conclusion.

The hour's drive had sobered him somewhat—his arrival was merely hilarious—and Paula hoped that the evening was not spoiled, after all, but two imprudent cocktails before dinner completed the disaster. He talked boisterously and somewhat offensively to the party at large for fifteen minutes, and then slid silently under the table; like a man in an old print—but, unlike an old print, it was rather horrible without being at all quaint. None of the young girls present remarked upon the incident—it seemed to merit only silence. His uncle and two other men carried him up-stairs, and it was just after this that Paula was called to the phone.

An hour later Anson awoke in a fog of nervous agony, through which he perceived after a moment the figure of his uncle Robert standing by the door.

". . . I said are you better?"

"What?"

"Do you feel better, old man?"

"Terrible," said Anson.

"I'm going to try you on another bromo-seltzer. If you can hold it down, it'll do you good to sleep."

With an effort Anson slid his legs from the bed and stood up.

"I'm all right," he said dully.

"Take it easy."

"I thin' if you gave me a glassbrandy I could go down-stairs."

"Oh, no——"

"Yes, that's the only thin'. I'm all right now. . . . I suppose I'm in Dutch dow' there."

"They know you're a little under the weather," said his uncle deprecatingly. "But don't worry about it. Schuyler didn't even get here. He passed away in the locker-room over at the Links."

Indifferent to any opinion, except Paula's, Anson was nevertheless determined to save the débris of the evening, but when after a cold bath he made his appearance most of the party had already left. Paula got up immediately to go home.

In the limousine the old serious dialogue began. She had known that he drank, she admitted, but she had never expected anything like this—it seemed to her that perhaps they were not suited to each other, after all. Their ideas about life were too different, and so forth. When she finished speaking, Anson spoke in turn, very soberly. Then Paula said she'd have to think it over; she wouldn't decide to-night; she was not angry but she was terribly sorry. Nor would she let him come into the hotel with her, but just before she got out of the car she leaned and kissed him unhappily on the cheek.

The next afternoon Anson had a long talk with Mrs. Legendre while Paula sat listening in silence. It was agreed that Paula was to brood over the incident for a proper period and then, if mother and daughter thought it best, they would follow Anson to Pensacola. On his part he apologized with sincerity and dignity—that was all; with every card in her hand Mrs. Legendre was unable to establish any advantage over him. He made no promises, showed no humility, only delivered a few serious comments on life which brought him off with rather a moral superiority at the end. When they came South three weeks later, neither Anson in his satisfaction nor Paula in her relief at the reunion realized that the psychological moment had passed forever.

expl

A returns for war + meets her in Palm Beach, but their moment had passed

IV *+ she marries Lowell Thayer*

He dominated and attracted her, and at the same time filled her with anxiety. Confused by his mixture of solidity and self-indulgence, of sentiment and cynicism—incongruities which her gentle mind was unable to resolve—Paula grew to think of him as two alternating personalities. When she saw him alone, or at a formal party, or with his casual inferiors, she felt a tremendous pride in his strong, attractive presence, the paternal, understanding stature of his mind. In other company she became uneasy when what had been a fine imperviousness to mere gentility showed its other face. The other face was gross, humorous, reckless of everything but pleasure. It startled her mind temporarily away from him, even led her into a short covert experiment with an old beau, but it was no use—after four months of Anson's enveloping vitality there was an anæmic pallor in all other men.

In July he was ordered abroad, and their tenderness and desire reached a crescendo. Paula considered a last-minute marriage—decided against it only because there were always cocktails on his breath now, but the parting itself made her physically ill with grief. After his departure she wrote him long letters of regret for the days of love they had missed by waiting. In August Anson's plane slipped down into the North Sea. He was pulled onto a destroyer after a night in the water and sent to hospital with pneumonia; the armistice was signed before he was finally sent home.

Then, with every opportunity given back to them, with no material obstacle to overcome, the secret weavings of their temperaments came between them, drying up their kisses and their tears, making their voices less loud to one another, muffling the intimate chatter of their hearts until the old communication was only possible by letters, from far away. One afternoon a society reporter waited for two hours in the Hunters' house for a confirmation of their engagement. Anson denied it; nevertheless an early issue carried the report as a leading paragraph—they were "constantly seen together at Southhampton, Hot Springs, and Tuxedo Park." But the serious dialogue had turned a corner into a long-sustained quarrel, and the affair was almost played out. Anson got drunk flagrantly and missed an engagement with her, whereupon Paula made certain behavioristic demands. His despair was helpless before his pride and his knowledge of himself: the engagement was definitely broken.

"Dearest," said their letters now, "Dearest, Dearest, when I wake up in the middle of the night and realize that after all it was not to be, I feel that I want to die. I can't go on living any more. Perhaps when we meet this summer we may talk things over and decide differently—we were so excited and sad that day, and I don't feel that I can live all my life without you. You speak of other people. Don't you know there are no other people for me, but only you. . . . ."

But as Paula drifted here and there around the East she would sometimes mention her gaieties to make him wonder. Anson was too acute to wonder. When he saw a man's name in her letters he felt

more sure of her and a little disdainful—he was always superior to
such things. But he still hoped that they would some day marry.

Meanwhile he plunged vigorously into all the movement and glitter
of post-bellum New York, entering a brokerage house, joining half
a dozen clubs, dancing late, and moving in three worlds—his own
world, the world of young Yale graduates, and that section of the
half-world which rests one end on Broadway. But there was always
a thorough and infractible eight hours devoted to his work in Wall
Street, where the combination of his influential family connection,
his sharp intelligence, and his abundance of sheer physical energy
brought him almost immediately forward. He had one of those in-
valuable minds with partitions in it; sometimes he appeared at his
office refreshed by less than an hour's sleep, but such occurrences
were rare. So early as 1920 his income in salary and commissions ex-
ceeded twelve thousand dollars.

As the Yale tradition slipped into the past he became more and
more of a popular figure among his classmates in New York, more
popular than he had ever been in college. He lived in a great house,
and had the means of introducing young men into other great houses.
Moreover, his life already seemed secure, while theirs, for the most
part, had arrived again at precarious beginnings. They commenced
to turn to him for amusement and escape, and Anson responded
readily, taking pleasure in helping people and arranging their affairs.

There were no men in Paula's letters now, but a note of tenderness
ran through them that had not been there before. From several
sources he heard that she had "a heavy beau," Lowell Thayer, a
Bostonian of wealth and position, and though he was sure she still
loved him, it made him uneasy to think that he might lose her, after
all. Save for one unsatisfactory day she had not been in New York
for almost five months, and as the rumors multiplied he became increasingly anxious to see her. In February he took his vacation and
went down to Florida.

Palm Beach sprawled plump and opulent between the sparkling
sapphire of Lake Worth, flawed here and there by house-boats at
anchor, and the great turquoise bar of the Atlantic Ocean. The huge
bulks of the Breakers and the Royal Poinciana rose as twin paunches
from the bright level of the sand, and around them clustered the
Dancing Glade, Bradley's House of Chance, and a dozen modistes
and milliners with goods at triple prices from New York. Upon the
trellised veranda of the Breakers two hundred women stepped right,
stepped left, wheeled, and slid in that then celebrated calisthenic
known as the double-shuffle, while in half-time to the music two
thousand bracelets clicked up and down on two hundred arms.

At the Everglades Club after dark Paula and Lowell Thayer and

Anson and a casual fourth played bridge with hot cards. It seemed to Anson that her kind, serious face was wan and tired—she had been around now for four, five, years. He had known her for three.

"Two spades."

"Cigarette? . . . Oh, I beg your pardon. By me."

"By."

"I'll double three spades."

There were a dozen tables of bridge in the room, which was filling up with smoke. Anson's eyes met Paula's, held them persistently even when Thayer's glance fell between them. . . .

"What was bid?" he asked abstractedly.

"Rose of Washington Square"

sang the young people in the corners:

> *"I'm withering there*
> *In basement air——"*

The smoke banked like fog, and the opening of a door filled the room with blown swirls of ectoplasm. Little Bright Eyes streaked past the tables seeking Mr. Conan Doyle among the Englishmen who were posing as Englishmen about the lobby.

"You could cut it with a knife."

". . . cut it with a knife."

". . . a knife."

At the end of the rubber Paula suddenly got up and spoke to Anson in a tense, low voice. With scarcely a glance at Lowell Thayer, they walked out the door and descended a long flight of stone steps—in a moment they were walking hand in hand along the moonlit beach.

"Darling, darling. . . ." They embraced recklessly, passionately, in a shadow. . . . Then Paula drew back her face to let his lips say what she wanted to hear—she could feel the words forming as they kissed again. . . . Again she broke away, listening, but as he pulled her close once more she realized that he had said nothing—only *"Darling! Darling!"* in that deep, sad whisper that always made her cry. Humbly, obediently, her emotions yielded to him and the tears streamed down her face, but her heart kept on crying: "Ask me—oh, Anson, dearest, ask me!"

"Paula. . . . *Paula!*"

The words wrung her heart like hands, and Anson, feeling her tremble, knew that emotion was enough. He need say no more, commit their destinies to no practical enigma. Why should he, when he might hold her so, biding his own time, for another year—forever? He was considering them both, her more than himself. For a moment, when she said suddenly that she must go back to her hotel, he hesi-

tated, thinking, first, "This is the moment, after all," and then: "No, | 1836
let it wait—she is mine. . . ."

He had forgotten that Paula too was worn away inside with the
strain of three years. Her mood passed forever in the night. |

He went back to New York next morning filled with a certain
restless dissatisfaction. Late in April, without warning, he received
a telegram from Bar Harbor in which Paula told him that she was |
engaged to Lowell Thayer, and that they would be married immedi- |
ately in Boston. What he never really believed could happen had
happened at last.

Anson filled himself with whiskey that morning, and going to the
office, carried on his work without a break—rather with a fear of
what would happen if he stopped. In the evening he went out as
usual, saying nothing of what had occurred; he was cordial, humorous, unabstracted. But one thing he could not help—for three days,
in any place, in any company, he would suddenly bend his head into
his hands and cry like a child.

*A meets & courts Dolly Karger. About to seduce her—twice! - he sees Paula's picture
on the wall & stops both times. Dolly also marries another.*

V

In 1922 when Anson went abroad with the junior partner to investigate some London loans, the journey intimated that he was to be
taken into the firm. He was twenty-seven now, a little heavy without
being definitely stout, and with a manner older than his years. Old
people and young people liked him and trusted him, and mothers felt
safe when their daughters were in his charge, for he had a way, when
he came into a room, of putting himself on a footing with the oldest |
and most conservative people there. "You and I," he seemed to say, |
"we're solid. We understand." *(F. always spoke [of the oldest woman in room])*

He had an instinctive and rather charitable knowledge of the weaknesses of men and women, and, like a priest, it made him the more
concerned for the maintenance of outward forms. It was typical of
him that every Sunday morning he taught in a fashionable Episcopal
Sunday-school—even though a cold shower and a quick change into
a cutaway coat were all that separated him from the wild night before.

After his father's death he was the practical head of his family,
and, in effect, guided the destinies of the younger children. Through
a complication his authority did not extend to his father's estate,
which was administrated by his Uncle Robert, who was the horsey
member of the family, a good-natured, hard-drinking member of that
set which centres about Wheatley Hills.

Uncle Robert and his wife, Edna, had been great friends of Anson's
youth, and the former was disappointed when his nephew's superior-

ity failed to take a horsey form. He backed him for a city club which was the most difficult in America to enter—one could only join if one's family had "helped to build up New York" (or, in other words, were rich before 1880)—and when Anson, after his election, neglected it for the Yale Club, Uncle Robert gave him a little talk on the subject. But when on top of that Anson declined to enter Robert Hunter's own conservative and somewhat neglected brokerage house, his manner grew cooler. Like a primary teacher who has taught all he knew, he slipped out of Anson's life.

There were so many friends in Anson's life—scarcely one for whom he had not done some unusual kindness and scarcely one whom he did not occasionally embarrass by his bursts of rough conversation or his habit of getting drunk whenever and however he liked. It annoyed him when any one else blundered in that regard—about his own lapses he was always humorous. Odd things happened to him and he told them with infectious laughter.

I was working in New York that spring, and I used to lunch with him at the Yale Club, which my university was sharing until the completion of our own. I had read of Paula's marriage, and one afternoon, when I asked him about her, something moved him to tell me the story. After that he frequently invited me to family dinners at his house and behaved as though there was a special relation between us, as though with his confidence a little of that consuming memory had passed into me.

I found that despite the trusting mothers, his attitude toward girls was not indiscriminately protective. It was up to the girl—if she showed an inclination toward looseness, she must take care of herself, even with him.

"Life," he would explain sometimes, "has made a cynic of me."

By life he meant Paula. Sometimes, especially when he was drinking, it became a little twisted in his mind, and he thought that she had callously thrown him over.

This "cynicism," or rather his realization that naturally fast girls were not worth sparing, led to his affair with Dolly Karger. It wasn't his only affair in those years, but it came nearest to touching him deeply, and it had a profound effect upon his attitude toward life.

Dolly was the daughter of a notorious "publicist" who had married into society. She herself grew up into the Junior League, came out at the Plaza, and went to the Assembly; and only a few old families like the Hunters could question whether or not she "belonged," for her picture was often in the papers, and she had more enviable attention than many girls who undoubtedly did. She was dark-haired, with carmine lips and a high, lovely color, which she concealed under pinkish-gray powder all through the first year out, because high color was unfashionable—Victorian-pale was the thing to be. She wore black, severe suits and stood with her hands in her pockets leaning a little forward, with a humorous restraint on her face. She danced exquisitely—better than anything she liked to dance—better than anything except making love. Since she was ten she had always been in love, and, usually, with some boy who didn't respond to her. Those who did—and there were many—bored her after a brief encounter, but for her failures she reserved the warmest spot in her heart. When she met them she would always try once more—sometimes she succeeded, more often she failed.

It never occurred to this gypsy of the unattainable that there was a certain resemblance in those who refused to love her—they shared a hard intuition that saw through to her weakness, not a weakness of emotion but a weakness of rudder. Anson perceived this when he first met her, less than a month after Paula's marriage. He was drinking rather heavily, and he pretended for a week that he was falling in love with her. Then he dropped her abruptly and forgot—immediately he took up the commanding position in her heart.

Like so many girls of that day Dolly was slackly and indiscreetly wild. The unconventionality of a slightly older generation had been simply one facet of a post-war movement to discredit obsolete manners—Dolly's was both older and shabbier, and she saw in Anson the two extremes which the emotionally shiftless woman seeks, an abandon to indulgence alternating with a protective strength. In his character she felt both the sybarite and the solid rock, and these two satisfied every need of her nature.

She felt that it was going to be difficult, but she mistook the reason —she thought that Anson and his family expected a more spectacular marriage, but she guessed immediately that her advantage lay in his tendency to drink.

They met at the large débutante dances, but as her infatuation increased they managed to be more and more together. Like most mothers, Mrs. Karger believed that Anson was exceptionally reliable, so she allowed Dolly to go with him to distant country clubs and suburban houses without inquiring closely into their activities or questioning her explanations when they came in late. At first these explanations might have been accurate, but Dolly's worldly ideas of capturing Anson were soon engulfed in the rising sweep of her emotion. Kisses in the back of taxis and motor-cars were no longer enough; they did a curious thing:

They dropped out of their world for a while and made another world just beneath it where Anson's tippling and Dolly's irregular hours would be less noticed and commented on. It was composed, this world, of varying elements—several of Anson's Yale friends and their wives, two or three young brokers and bond salesmen and a handful of unattached men, fresh from college, with money and a propensity to dissipation. What this world lacked in spaciousness and scale it made up for by allowing them a liberty that it scarcely permitted itself. Moreover, it centred around them and permitted Dolly the pleasure of a faint condescension—a pleasure which Anson, whose whole life was a condescension from the certitudes of his childhood, was unable to share.

He was not in love with her, and in the long feverish winter of their affair he frequently told her so. In the spring he was weary— he wanted to renew his life at some other source—moreover, he saw that either he must break with her now or accept the responsibility of a definite seduction. Her family's encouraging attitude precipitated his decision—one evening when Mr. Karger knocked discreetly at the library door to announce that he had left a bottle of old brandy in the dining-room, Anson felt that life was hemming him in. That night he wrote her a short letter in which he told her that he was going on his vacation, and that in view of all the circumstances they had better meet no more.

It was June. His family had closed up the house and gone to the country, so he was living temporarily at the Yale Club. I had heard about his affair with Dolly as it developed—accounts salted with humor, for he despised unstable women, and granted them no place in the social edifice in which he believed—and when he told me that night that he was definitely breaking with her I was glad. I had seen Dolly here and there, and each time with a feeling of pity at the hopelessness of her struggle, and of shame at knowing so much about her that I had no right to know. She was what is known as "a pretty little thing," but there was a certain recklessness which rather fascinated me. Her dedication to the goddess of waste would have been less obvious had she been less spirited—she would most certainly throw herself away, but I was glad when I heard that the sacrifice would not be consummated in my sight.

Anson was going to leave the letter of farewell at her house next morning. It was one of the few houses left open in the Fifth Avenue district, and he knew that the Kargers, acting upon erroneous information from Dolly, had foregone a trip abroad to give their daughter her chance. As he stepped out the door of the Yale Club into Madison Avenue the postman passed him, and he followed back inside. The first letter that caught his eye was in Dolly's hand.

He knew what it would be—a lonely and tragic monologue, full of the reproaches he knew, the invoked memories, the "I wonder if's"—all the immemorial intimacies that he had communicated to Paula Legendre in what seemed another age. Thumbing over some bills, he brought it on top again and opened it. To his surprise it was a short, somewhat formal note, which said that Dolly would be unable to go to the country with him for the week-end, because Perry Hull from Chicago had unexpectedly come to town. It added that Anson had brought this on himself: "— if I felt that you loved me as I love you I would go with you at any time, any place, but Perry is *so* nice, and he so much wants me to marry him——"

Anson smiled contemptuously—he had had experience with such decoy epistles. Moreover, he knew how Dolly had labored over this plan, probably sent for the faithful Perry and calculated the time of his arrival—even labored over the note so that it would make him jealous without driving him away. Like most compromises, it had neither force nor vitality but only a timorous despair.

Suddenly he was angry. He sat down in the lobby and read it again. Then he went to the phone, called Dolly and told her in his clear, compelling voice that he had received her note and would call for her at five o'clock as they had previously planned. Scarcely waiting for the pretended uncertainty of her "Perhaps I can see you for an hour," he hung up the receiver and went down to his office. On the way he tore his own letter into bits and dropped it in the street.

He was not jealous—she meant nothing to him—but at her pathetic ruse everything stubborn and self-indulgent in him came to the surface. It was a presumption from a mental inferior and it could not be overlooked. If she wanted to know to whom she belonged she would see.

He was on the door-step at quarter past five. Dolly was dressed for the street, and he listened in silence to the paragraph of "I can only see you for an hour," which she had begun on the phone.

"Put on your hat, Dolly," he said, "we'll take a walk."

They strolled up Madison Avenue and over to Fifth while Anson's shirt dampened upon his portly body in the deep heat. He talked little, scolding her, making no love to her, but before they had walked six blocks she was his again, apologizing for the note, offering not to see Perry at all as an atonement, offering anything. She thought that he had come because he was beginning to love her.

"I'm hot," he said when they reached 71st Street. "This is a winter suit. If I stop by the house and change, would you mind waiting for me down-stairs? I'll only be a minute."

She was happy; the intimacy of his being hot, of any physical fact about him, thrilled her. When they came to the iron-grated door and Anson took out his key she experienced a sort of delight.

Down-stairs it was dark, and after he ascended in the lift Dolly raised a curtain and looked out through opaque lace at the houses over the way. She heard the lift machinery stop, and with the notion of teasing him pressed the button that brought it down. Then on what was more than an impulse she got into it and sent it up to what she guessed was his floor.

"Anson," she called, laughing a little.

"Just a minute," he answered from his bedroom . . . then after a brief delay: "Now you can come in."

He had changed and was buttoning his vest.

"This is my room," he said lightly. "How do you like it?"

She caught sight of Paula's picture on the wall and stared at it in fascination, just as Paula had stared at the pictures of Anson's childish sweethearts five years before. She knew something about Paula —sometimes she tortured herself with fragments of the story.

Suddenly she came close to Anson, raising her arms. They embraced. Outside the area window a soft artificial twilight already hovered, though the sun was still bright on a back roof across the way. In half an hour the room would be quite dark. The uncalculated opportunity overwhelmed them, made them both breathless, and they clung more closely. It was imminent, inevitable. Still holding one another, they raised their heads—their eyes fell together upon Paula's picture, staring down at them from the wall.

Suddenly Anson dropped his arms, and sitting down at his desk tried the drawer with a bunch of keys.

"Like a drink?" he asked in a gruff voice.

"No, Anson."

He poured himself half a tumbler of whiskey, swallowed it, and then opened the door into the hall.

"Come on," he said.

Dolly hesitated.

"Anson—I'm going to the country with you tonight, after all. You understand that, don't you?"

"Of course," he answered brusquely.

In Dolly's car they rode on to Long Island, closer in their emotions than they had ever been before. They knew what would happen—not with Paula's face to remind them that something was lacking, but when they were alone in the still, hot Long Island night they did not care.

The estate in Port Washington where they were to spend the weekend belonged to a cousin of Anson's who had married a Montana copper operator. An interminable drive began at the lodge and twisted under imported poplar saplings toward a huge, pink Spanish house. Anson had often visited there before.

After dinner they danced at the Linx Club. About midnight Anson assured himself that his cousins would not leave before two—then he explained that Dolly was tired; he would take her home and return to the dance later. Trembling a little with excitement, they got into a borrowed car together and drove to Port Washington. As they reached the lodge he stopped and spoke to the night-watchman.

"When are you making a round, Carl?"

"Right away."

"Then you'll be here till everybody's in?"

"Yes, sir."

"All right. Listen: if any automobile, no matter whose it is, turns in at this gate, I want you to phone the house immediately." He put a five-dollar bill into Carl's hand. "Is that clear?"

"Yes, Mr. Anson." Being of the Old World, he neither winked nor smiled. Yet Dolly sat with her face turned slightly away.

Anson had a key. Once inside he poured a drink for both of them —Dolly left hers untouched—then he ascertained definitely the location of the phone, and found that it was within easy hearing distance of their rooms, both of which were on the first floor.

Five minutes later he knocked at the door of Dolly's room.

"Anson?" He went in, closing the door behind him. She was in bed, leaning up anxiously with elbows on the pillow; sitting beside her he took her in his arms.

"Anson, darling."

He didn't answer.

"Anson. . . . Anson! I love you. . . . Say you love me. Say it now—can't you say it now? Even if you don't mean it?"

He did not listen. Over her head he perceived that the picture of Paula was hanging here upon this wall.

He got up and went close to it. The frame gleamed faintly with thrice-reflected moonlight—within was a blurred shadow of a face that he saw he did not know. Almost sobbing, he turned around and stared with abomination at the little figure on the bed.

"This is all foolishness," he said thickly. "I don't know what I was thinking about. I don't love you and you'd better wait for somebody that loves you. I don't love you a bit, can't you understand?"

His voice broke, and he went hurriedly out. Back in the salon he was pouring himself a drink with uneasy fingers, when the front door opened suddenly, and his cousin came in.

"Why, Anson, I hear Dolly's sick," she began solicitously. "I hear she's sick. . . ."

"It was nothing," he interrupted, raising his voice so that it would carry into Dolly's room. "She was a little tired. She went to bed."

For a long time afterward Anson believed that a protective God sometimes interfered in human affairs. But Dolly Karger, lying awake and staring at the ceiling, never again believed in anything at all.

Anson stops married aunt's love affair, & her lover hangs him.

VI

When Dolly married during the following autumn, Anson was in
London on business. Like Paula's marriage, it was sudden, but it
affected him in a different way. At first he felt that it was funny,
and had an inclination to laugh when he thought of it. Later it depressed him—it made him feel old.

There was something repetitive about it—why, Paula and Dolly
had belonged to different generations. He had a foretaste of the sensation of a man of forty who hears that the daughter of an old
flame has married. He wired congratulations and, as was not the
case with Paula, they were sincere—he had never really hoped that
Paula would be happy.

When he returned to New York, he was made a partner in the
firm, and, as his responsibilities increased, he had less time on his
hands. The refusal of a life-insurance company to issue him a policy
made such an impression on him that he stopped drinking for a year,
and claimed that he felt better physically, though I think he missed
the convivial recounting of those Celliniesque adventures which, in
his early twenties, had played such a part in his life. But he never
abandoned the Yale Club. He was a figure there, a personality, and
the tendency of his class, who were now seven years out of college,
to drift away to more sober haunts was checked by his presence.

His day was never too full nor his mind too weary to give any sort
of aid to any one who asked it. What had been done at first through
pride and superiority had become a habit and a passion. And there
was always something—a younger brother in trouble at New Haven,
a quarrel to be patched up between a friend and his wife, a position
to be found for this man, an investment for that. But his specialty
was the solving of problems for young married people. Young married people fascinated him and their apartments were almost sacred
to him—he knew the story of their love-affair, advised them where
to live and how, and remembered their babies' names. Toward young
wives his attitude was circumspect: he never abused the trust which
their husbands—strangely enough in view of his unconcealed irregu-
larities—invariably reposed in him.

He came to take a vicarious pleasure in happy marriages, and to
be inspired to an almost equally pleasant melancholy by those that
went astray. Not a season passed that he did not witness the collapse
of an affair that perhaps he himself had fathered. When Paula was
divorced and almost immediately remarried to another Bostonian,
he talked about her to me all one afternoon. He would never love any
one as he had loved Paula, but he insisted that he no longer cared.

"I'll never marry," he came to say; "I've seen too much of it, and I know a happy marriage is a very rare thing. Besides, I'm too old."

But he did believe in marriage. Like all men who spring from a happy and successful marriage, he believed in it passionately—nothing he had seen would change his belief, his cynicism dissolved upon it like air. But he did really believe he was too old. At twenty-eight he began to accept with equanimity the prospect of marrying without romantic love; he resolutely chose a New York girl of his own class, pretty, intelligent, congenial, above reproach—and set about falling in love with her. The things he had said to Paula with sincerity, to other girls with grace, he could no longer say at all without smiling, or with the force necessary to convince.

"When I'm forty," he told his friends, "I'll be ripe. I'll fall for some chorus girl like the rest."

Nevertheless, he persisted in his attempt. His mother wanted to see him married, and he could now well afford it—he had a seat on the Stock Exchange, and his earned income came to twenty-five thousand a year. The idea was agreeable: when his friends—he spent most of his time with the set he and Dolly had evolved—closed themselves in behind domestic doors at night, he no longer rejoiced in his freedom. He even wondered if he should have married Dolly. Not even Paula had loved him more, and he was learning the rarity, in a single life, of encountering true emotion.

Just as this mood began to creep over him a disquieting story reached his ear. His Aunt Edna, a woman just this side of forty, was carrying on an open intrigue with a dissolute, hard-drinking young man named Cary Sloane. Every one knew of it except Anson's Uncle Robert, who for fifteen years had talked long in clubs and taken his wife for granted.

Anson heard the story again and again with increasing annoyance. Something of his old feeling for his uncle came back to him, a feeling that was more than personal, a reversion toward that family solidarity on which he had based his pride. His intuition singled out the essential point of the affair, which was that his uncle shouldn't be hurt. It was his first experiment in unsolicited meddling, but with his knowledge of Edna's character he felt that he could handle the matter better than a district judge or his uncle.

His uncle was in Hot Springs. Anson traced down the sources of the scandal so that there should be no possibility of mistake and then he called Edna and asked her to lunch with him at the Plaza next day. Something in his tone must have frightened her, for she was reluctant, but he insisted, putting off the date until she had no excuse for refusing.

She met him at the appointed time in the Plaza lobby, a lovely, faded, gray-eyed blonde in a coat of Russian sable. Five great rings, cold with diamonds and emeralds, sparkled on her slender hands. It occurred to Anson that it was his father's intelligence and not his uncle's that had earned the fur and the stones, the rich brilliance that buoyed up her passing beauty.

Though Edna scented his hostility, she was unprepared for the directness of his approach.

"Edna, I'm astonished at the way you've been acting," he said in a strong, frank voice. "At first I couldn't believe it."

"Believe what?" she demanded sharply.

"You needn't pretend with me, Edna. I'm talking about Cary Sloane. Aside from any other consideration, I didn't think you could treat Uncle Robert——"

"Now look here, Anson——" she began angrily, but his peremptory voice broke through hers:

"——and your children in such a way. You've been married eighteen years, and you're old enough to know better."

"You can't talk to me like that! You——"

"Yes, I can. Uncle Robert has always been my best friend." He was tremendously moved. He felt a real distress about his uncle, about his three young cousins.

Edna stood up, leaving her crab-flake cocktail untasted.

"This is the silliest thing——"

"Very well, if you won't listen to me I'll go to Uncle Robert and tell him the whole story—he's bound to hear it sooner or later. And afterward I'll go to old Moses Sloane."

Edna faltered back into her chair.

"Don't talk so loud," she begged him. Her eyes blurred with tears. "You have no idea how your voice carries. You might have chosen a less public place to make all these crazy accusations."

He didn't answer.

"Oh, you never liked me, I know," she went on. "You're just taking advantage of some silly gossip to try and break up the only interesting friendship I've ever had. What did I ever do to make you hate me so?"

Still Anson waited. There would be the appeal to his chivalry, then to his pity, finally to his superior sophistication—when he had shouldered his way through all these there would be admissions, and he could come to grips with her. By being silent, by being impervious, by returning constantly to his main weapon, which was his own true emotion, he bullied her into frantic despair as the luncheon hour slipped away. At two o'clock she took out a mirror and a handkerchief, shined away the marks of her tears and powdered the slight hollows where they had lain. She had agreed to meet him at her own house at five.

When he arrived she was stretched on a *chaise-longue* which was covered with cretonne for the summer, and the tears he had called up at luncheon seemed still to be standing in her eyes. Then he was aware of Cary Sloane's dark anxious presence upon the cold hearth.

"What's this idea of yours?" broke out Sloane immediately. "I understand you invited Edna to lunch and then threatened her on the basis of some cheap scandal."

Anson sat down.

"I have no reason to think it's only scandal."

"I hear you're going to take it to Robert Hunter, and to my father."

Anson nodded.

"Either you break it off—or I will," he said.

"What God damned business is it of yours, Hunter?"

"Don't lose your temper, Cary," said Edna nervously. "It's only a question of showing him how absurd——"

"For one thing, it's my name that's being handed around," interrupted Anson. "That's all that concerns you, Cary."

"Edna isn't a member of your family."

"She most certainly is!" His anger mounted. "Why—she owes this house and the rings on her fingers to my father's brains. When Uncle Robert married her she didn't have a penny."

They all looked at the rings as if they had a significant bearing on the situation. Edna made a gesture to take them from her hand.

"I guess they're not the only rings in the world," said Sloane.

"Oh, this is absurd," cried Edna. "Anson, will you listen to me? I've found out how the silly story started. It was a maid I discharged who went right to the Chilicheffs—all these Russians pump things out of their servants and then put a false meaning on them." She brought down her fist angrily on the table: "And after Robert lent them the limousine for a whole month when we were South last winter——"

"Do you see?" demanded Sloane eagerly. "This maid got hold of the wrong end of the thing. She knew that Edna and I were friends, and she carried it to the Chilicheffs. In Russia they assume that if a man and a woman——"

He enlarged the theme to a disquisition upon social relations in the Caucasus.

"If that's the case it better be explained to Uncle Robert," said Anson dryly, "so that when the rumors do reach him he'll know they're not true."

Adopting the method he had followed with Edna at luncheon he let them explain it all away. He knew that they were guilty and that presently they would cross the line from explanation into justification and convict themselves more definitely than he could ever do. By seven they had taken the desperate step of telling him the truth —Robert Hunter's neglect, Edna's empty life, the casual dalliance that had flamed up into passion—but like so many true stories it had the misfortune of being old, and its enfeebled body beat helplessly against the armor of Anson's will. The threat to go to Sloane's father sealed their helplessness, for the latter, a retired cotton broker out of Alabama, was a notorious fundamentalist who controlled his son by a rigid allowance and the promise that at his next vagary the allowance would stop forever.

They dined at a small French restaurant, and the discussion continued—at one time Sloane resorted to physical threats, a little later they were both imploring him to give them time. But Anson was obdurate. He saw that Edna was breaking up, and that her spirit must not be refreshed by any renewal of their passion.

At two o'clock in a small night-club on 53d Street, Edna's nerves suddenly collapsed, and she cried to go home. Sloane had been drinking heavily all evening, and he was faintly maudlin, leaning on the table and weeping a little with his face in his hands. Quickly Anson gave them his terms. Sloane was to leave town for six months, and he must be gone within forty-eight hours. When he returned there was to be no resumption of the affair, but at the end of a year Edna might, if she wished, tell Robert Hunter that she wanted a divorce and go about it in the usual way.

He paused, gaining confidence from their faces for his final word.

"Or there's another thing you can do," he said slowly, "if Edna wants to leave her children, there's nothing I can do to prevent your running off together."

"I want to go home!" cried Edna again. "Oh, haven't you done enough to us for one day?"

Outside it was dark, save for a blurred glow from Sixth Avenue down the street. In that light those two who had been lovers looked for the last time into each other's tragic faces, realizing that between them there was not enough youth and strength to avert their eternal parting. Sloane walked suddenly off down the street and Anson tapped a dozing taxi-driver on the arm.

It was almost four; there was a patient flow of cleaning water along the ghostly pavement of Fifth Avenue, and the shadows of two night women flitted over the dark façade of St. Thomas's church. Then the desolate shrubbery of Central Park where Anson had often played as a child, and the mounting numbers, significant as names, of the marching streets. This was his city, he thought, where his name had flourished through five generations. No change could alter the permanence of its place here, for change itself was the essential substratum by which he and those of his name identified themselves with the spirit of New York. Resourcefulness and a powerful will—for his threats in weaker hands would have been less than nothing—had beaten the gathering dust from his uncle's name, from the name of his family, from even this shivering figure that sat beside him in the car. *why prefer suicide to no money?*

Cary Sloane's body was found next morning on the lower shelf of a pillar of Queensboro Bridge. In the darkness and in his excitement he had thought that it was the water flowing black beneath him, but in less than a second it made no possible difference—unless he had planned to think one last thought of Edna, and call out her name as he struggled feebly in the water. *melodramatic & unconvincing*

As mother dies, increasing loneliness. VII *Meets Paula, now pregnant by 2nd husband.* *Spends night at their house & witnesses their domestic happiness.*

Anson never blamed himself for his part in this affair—the situation which brought it about had not been of his making. But the just suffer with the unjust, and he found that his oldest and somehow his most precious friendship was over. He never knew what distorted story Edna told, but he was welcome in his uncle's house no longer.

Just before Christmas Mrs. Hunter retired to a select Episcopal heaven, and Anson became the responsible head of his family. An unmarried aunt who had lived with them for years ran the house, and attempted with helpless inefficiency to chaperone the younger girls. All the children were less self-reliant than Anson, more conventional both in their virtues and in their shortcomings. Mrs. Hunter's death had postponed the début of one daughter and the wedding of another. Also it had taken something deeply material from all of them, for with her passing the quiet, expensive superiority of the Hunters came to an end.

For one thing, the estate, considerably diminished by two inheritance taxes and soon to be divided among six children, was not a notable fortune any more. Anson saw a tendency in his youngest sisters to speak rather respectfully of families that hadn't "existed" twenty years ago. His own feeling of precedence was not echoed in them—sometimes they were conventionally snobbish, that was all. For another thing, this was the last summer they would spend on the Connecticut estate; the clamor against it was too loud: "Who wants to waste the best months of the year shut up in that dead old town?" Reluctantly he yielded—the house would go into the market in the fall, and next summer they would rent a smaller place in

Westchester County. It was a step down from the expensive simplicity of his father's idea, and, while he sympathized with the
revolt, it also annoyed him; during his mother's lifetime he had
gone up there at least every other week-end—even in the gayest
summers.

Yet he himself was part of this change, and his strong instinct
for life had turned him in his twenties from the hollow obsequies
of that abortive leisure class. He did not see this clearly—he still
felt that there was a norm, a standard of society. But there was no
norm, it was doubtful if there ever had been a true norm in New
York. The few who still paid and fought to enter a particular set
succeeded only to find that as a society it scarcely functioned—or,
what was more alarming, that the Bohemia from which they fled sat
above them at table.

At twenty-nine Anson's chief concern was his own growing loneliness. He was sure now that he would never marry. The number of
weddings at which he had officiated as best man or usher was past
all counting—there was a drawer at home that bulged with the
official neckties of this or that wedding-party, neckties standing
for romances that had not endured a year, for couples who had passed
completely from his life. Scarf-pins, gold pencils, cuff-buttons, presents from a generation of grooms had passed through his jewel-box
and been lost—and with every ceremony he was less and less able
to imagine himself in the groom's place. Under his hearty good-will
toward all those marriages there was despair about his own.

And as he neared thirty he became not a little depressed at the
inroads that marriage, especially lately, had made upon his friend-
ships. Groups of people had a disconcerting tendency to dissolve
and disappear. The men from his own college—and it was upon
them he had expended the most time and affection—were the most
elusive of all. Most of them were drawn deep into domesticity, two
were dead, one lived abroad, one was in Hollywood writing con-
tinuities for pictures that Anson went faithfully to see.

Most of them, however, were permanent commuters with an
intricate family life centring around some suburban country
club, and it was from these that he felt his estrangement most
keenly.

In the early days of their married life they had all needed him;
he gave them advice about their slim finances, he exorcised their
doubts about the advisability of bringing a baby into two rooms
and a bath, especially he stood for the great world outside. But now
their financial troubles were in the past and the fearfully expected
child had evolved into an absorbing family. They were always glad
to see old Anson, but they dressed up for him and tried to impress

him with their present importance, and kept their troubles to themselves. They needed him no longer.

A few weeks before his thirtieth birthday the last of his early
and intimate friends was married. Anson acted in his usual rôle of
best man, gave his usual silver tea-service, and went down to the
usual *Homeric* to say good-by. It was a hot Friday afternoon in
May, and as he walked from the pier he realized that Saturday
closing had begun and he was free until Monday morning.

"Go where?" he asked himself.

The Yale Club, of course; bridge until dinner, then four or five
raw cocktails in somebody's room and a pleasant confused evening.
He regretted that this afternoon's groom wouldn't be along—they
had always been able to cram so much into such nights: they knew
how to attach women and how to get rid of them, how much consideration any girl deserved from their intelligent hedonism. A party
was an adjusted thing—you took certain girls to certain places and
spent just so much on their amusement; you drank a little, not
much, more than you ought to drink, and at a certain time in the
morning you stood up and said you were going home. You avoided
college boys, sponges, future engagements, fights, sentiment, and
indiscretions. That was the way it was done. All the rest was dissipation.

In the morning you were never violently sorry—you made no
resolutions, but if you had overdone it and your heart was slightly
out of order, you went on the wagon for a few days without saying
anything about it, and waited until an accumulation of nervous
boredom projected you into another party.

The lobby of the Yale Club was unpopulated. In the bar three
very young alumni looked up at him, momentarily and without
curiosity.

"Hello, there, Oscar," he said to the bartender. "Mr. Cahill been
around this afternoon?"

"Mr. Cahill's gone to New Haven."

"Oh . . . that so?"

"Gone to the ball game. Lot of men gone up."

Anson looked once again into the lobby, considered for a moment,
and then walked out and over to Fifth Avenue. From the broad window of one of his clubs—one that he had scarcely visited in five
years—a gray man with watery eyes stared down at him. Anson
looked quickly away—that figure sitting in vacant resignation, in
supercilious solitude, depressed him. He stopped and, retracing his
steps, started over 47th Street toward Teak Warden's apartment.
Teak and his wife had once been his most familiar friends—it was
a household where he and Dolly Karger had been used to go in

the days of their affair. But Teak had taken to drink, and his wife had remarked publicly that Anson was a bad influence on him. The remark reached Anson in an exaggerated form—when it was finally cleared up, the delicate spell of intimacy was broken, never to be renewed.

"Is Mr. Warden at home?" he inquired.

"They've gone to the country."

The fact unexpectedly cut at him. They were gone to the country and he hadn't known. Two years before he would have known the date, the hour, come up at the last moment for a final drink, and planned his first visit to them. Now they had gone without a word.

Anson looked at his watch and considered a week-end with his family, but the only train was a local that would jolt through the aggressive heat for three hours. And to-morrow in the country, and Sunday—he was in no mood for porch-bridge with polite undergraduates, and dancing after dinner at a rural roadhouse, a diminutive of gaiety which his father had estimated too well.

"Oh, no," he said to himself. . . . "No."

He was a dignified, impressive young man, rather stout now, but otherwise unmarked by dissipation. He could have been cast for a pillar of something—at times you were sure it was not society, at others nothing else—for the law, for the church. He stood for a few minutes motionless on the sidewalk in front of a 47th Street apartment-house; for almost the first time in his life he had nothing whatever to do.

Then he began to walk briskly up Fifth Avenue, as if he had just been reminded of an important engagement there. The necessity of dissimulation is one of the few characteristics that we share with dogs, and I think of Anson on that day as some well-bred specimen who had been disappointed at a familiar back door. He was going to see Nick, once a fashionable bartender in demand at all private dances, and now employed in cooling non-alcoholic champagne among the labyrinthine cellars of the Plaza Hotel.

"Nick," he said, "what's happened to everything?"

"Dead," Nick said.

"Make me a whiskey sour." Anson handed a pint bottle over the counter. "Nick, the girls are different; I had a little girl in Brooklyn and she got married last week without letting me know."

"That a fact? Ha-ha-ha," responded Nick diplomatically. "Slipped it over on you."

"Absolutely," said Anson. "And I was out with her the night before."

"Ha-ha-ha," said Nick, "ha-ha-ha!"

"Do you remember the wedding, Nick, in Hot Springs where I had the waiters and the musicians singing 'God save the King'?"

"Now where was that, Mr. Hunter?" Nick concentrated doubtfully. "Seems to me that was——"

"Next time they were back for more, and I began to wonder how much I'd paid them," continued Anson.

"—seems to me that was at Mr. Trenholm's wedding."

"Don't know him," said Anson decisively. He was offended that a strange name should intrude upon his reminiscences; Nick perceived this.

"Na—aw—" he admitted, "I ought to know that. It was one of your crowd—Brakins . . . Baker——"

"Bicker Baker," said Anson responsively. "They put me in a hearse after it was over and covered me up with flowers and drove me away."

"Ha-ha-ha," said Nick. "Ha-ha-ha."

Nick's simulation of the old family servant paled presently and Anson went up-stairs to the lobby. He looked around—his eyes met the glance of an unfamiliar clerk at the desk, then fell upon a flower from the morning's marriage hesitating in the mouth of a brass cuspidor. He went out and walked slowly toward the blood-red sun over Columbus Circle. Suddenly he turned around and, retracing his steps to the Plaza, immured himself in a telephone-booth.

Later he said that he tried to get me three times that afternoon, that he tried every one who might be in New York—men and girls he had not seen for years, an artist's model of his college days whose faded number was still in his address book—Central told him that even the exchange existed no longer. At length his quest roved into the country, and he held brief disappointing conversations with emphatic butlers and maids. So-and-so was out, riding, swimming, playing golf, sailed to Europe last week. Who shall I say phoned?

It was intolerable that he should pass the evening alone—the private reckonings which one plans for a moment of leisure lose every charm when the solitude is enforced. There were always women of a sort, but the ones he knew had temporarily vanished, and to pass a New York evening in the hired company of a stranger never occurred to him—he would have considered that that was something shameful and secret, the diversion of a travelling salesman in a strange town.

Anson paid the telephone bill—the girl tried unsuccessfully to joke with him about its size—and for the second time that afternoon started to leave the Plaza and go he knew not where. Near the revolving door the figure of a woman, obviously with child, stood sideways to the light—a sheer beige cape fluttered at her shoulders when the door turned and, each time, she looked impatiently toward it as if she were weary of waiting. At the first sight of her a strong nervous thrill of familiarity went over him, but not until he was within five feet of her did he realize that it was Paula.

"Why, Anson Hunter!"

His heart turned over.

"Why, Paula——"

"Why, this is wonderful. I can't believe it, *Anson*!"

She took both his hands, and he saw in the freedom of the gesture that the memory of him had lost poignancy to her. But not to him— he felt that old mood that she evoked in him stealing over his brain, that gentleness with which he had always met her optimism as if afraid to mar its surface.

"We're at Rye for the summer. Pete had to come East on business —you know of course I'm Mrs. Peter Hagerty now—so we brought the children and took a house. You've got to come out and see us."

"Can I?" he asked directly. "When?"

"When you like. Here's Pete." The revolving door functioned, giving up a fine tall man of thirty with a tanned face and a trim mustache. His immaculate fitness made a sharp contrast with Anson's increasing bulk, which was obvious under the faintly tight cut-away coat.

"You oughtn't to be standing," said Hagerty to his wife. "Let's sit down here." He indicated lobby chairs, but Paula hesitated.

"I've got to go right home," she said. "Anson, why don't you— why don't you come out and have dinner with us to-night? We're just getting settled, but if you can stand that——"

Hagerty confirmed the invitation cordially.

"Come out for the night."

Their car waited in front of the hotel, and Paula with a tired gesture sank back against silk cushions in the corner.

"There's so much I want to talk to you about," she said, "it seems hopeless."

"I want to hear about you."

"Well"—she smiled at Hagerty—"that would take a long time too. I have three children—by my first marriage. The oldest is five, then four, then three." She smiled again. "I didn't waste much time having them, did I?"

"Boys?"

"A boy and two girls. Then—oh, a lot of things happened, and I got a divorce in Paris a year ago and married Pete. That's all— except that I'm awfully happy."

In Rye they drove up to a large house near the Beach Club, from which there issued presently three dark, slim children who broke from an English governess and approached them with an esoteric cry. Abstractedly and with difficulty Paula took each one into her arms, a caress which they accepted stiffly, as they had evidently been told not to bump into Mummy. Even against their fresh faces Paula's skin showed scarcely any weariness—for all her physical languor she seemed younger than when he had last seen her at Palm Beach seven years ago.

At dinner she was preoccupied, and afterward, during the homage to the radio, she lay with closed eyes on the sofa, until Anson wondered if his presence at this time were not an intrusion. But at nine o'clock, when Hagerty rose and said pleasantly that he was going to leave them by themselves for a while, she began to talk slowly about herself and the past.

"My first baby," she said—"the one we call Darling, the biggest little girl—I wanted to die when I knew I was going to have her, because Lowell was like a stranger to me. It didn't seem as though she could be my own. I wrote you a letter and tore it up. Oh, you were *so* bad to me, Anson."

It was the dialogue again, rising and falling. Anson felt a sudden quickening of memory.

"Weren't you engaged once?" she asked—"a girl named Dolly something?"

"I wasn't ever engaged. I tried to be engaged, but I never loved anybody but you, Paula."

"Oh," she said. Then after a moment: "This baby is the first one I ever really wanted. You see, I'm in love now—at last."

He didn't answer, shocked at the treachery of her remembrance. She must have seen that the "at last" bruised him, for she continued:

"I was infatuated with you, Anson—you could make me do anything you liked. But we wouldn't have been happy. I'm not smart enough for you. I don't like things to be complicated like you do." She paused. "You'll never settle down," she said.

The phrase struck at him from behind—it was an accusation that of all accusations he had never merited.

"I could settle down if women were different," he said. "If I didn't understand so much about them, if women didn't spoil you for other women, if they had only a little pride. If I could go to sleep for a while and wake up into a home that was really mine—why, that's what I'm made for, Paula, that's what women have seen in me and liked in me. It's only that I can't get through the preliminaries any more."

Hagerty came in a little before eleven; after a whiskey Paula stood up and announced that she was going to bed. She went over and stood by her husband.

"Where did you go, dearest?" she demanded.

"I had a drink with Ed Saunders."

"I was worried. I thought maybe you'd run away."

She rested her head against his coat.

"He's sweet, isn't he, Anson?" she demanded.

"Absolutely," said Anson, laughing.

She raised her face to her husband.

"Well, I'm ready," she said. She turned to Anson: "Do you want to see our family gymnastic stunt?"

"Yes," he said in an interested voice.

"All right. Here we go!"

Hagerty picked her up easily in his arms.

"This is called the family acrobatic stunt," said Paula. "He carries me upstairs. Isn't it sweet of him?"

"Yes," said Anson.

Hagerty bent his head slightly until his face touched Paula's.

"And I love him," she said. "I've just been telling you, haven't I, Anson?"

"Yes," he said.

"He's the dearest thing that ever lived in this world; aren't you, darling? . . . Well, good night. Here we go. Isn't he strong?"

"Yes," Anson said.

"You'll find a pair of Pete's pajamas laid out for you. Sweet dreams—see you at breakfast."

"Yes," Anson said.

VIII

The older members of the firm insisted that Anson should go abroad for the summer. He had scarcely had a vacation in seven years, they said. He was stale and needed a change. Anson resisted.

"If I go," he declared, "I won't come back any more."

"That's absurd, old man. You'll be back in three months with all this depression gone. Fit as ever."

"No." He shook his head stubbornly. "If I stop, I won't go back to work. If I stop, that means I've given up—I'm through."

"We'll take a chance on that. Stay six months if you like—we're not afraid you'll leave us. Why, you'd be miserable if you didn't work."

They arranged his passage for him. They liked Anson—every one liked Anson—and the change that had been coming over him cast a sort of pall over the office. The enthusiasm that had invariably signalled up business, the consideration toward his equals and his inferiors, the lift of his vital presence—within the past four months

his intense nervousness had melted down these qualities into the
fussy pessimism of a man of forty. On every transaction in which
he was involved he acted as a drag and a strain.

"If I go I'll never come back," he said.

Three days before he sailed Paula Legendre Hagerty died in
childbirth. I was with him a great deal then, for we were crossing
together, but for the first time in our friendship he told me not a
word of how he felt, nor did I see the slightest sign of emotion. His
chief preoccupation was with the fact that he was thirty years old—
he would turn the conversation to the point where he could remind
you of it and then fall silent, as if he assumed that the statement
would start a chain of thought sufficient to itself. Like his partners,
I was amazed at the change in him, and I was glad when the *Paris*
moved off into the wet space between the worlds, leaving his princi-
pality behind.

"How about a drink?" he suggested.

We walked into the bar with that defiant feeling that characterizes
the day of departure and ordered four Martinis. After one cocktail
a change came over him—he suddenly reached across and slapped
my knee with the first joviality I had seen him exhibit for months.

"Did you see that girl in the red tam?" he demanded, "the one
with the high color who had the two police dogs down to bid
her good-by."

"She's pretty," I agreed.

"I looked her up in the purser's office and found out that she's
alone. I'm going down to see the steward in a few minutes. We'll
have dinner with her to-night."

After a while he left me, and within an hour he was walking up
and down the deck with her, talking to her in his strong, clear voice.
Her red tam was a bright spot of color against the steel-green sea,
and from time to time she looked up with a flashing bob of her head,
and smiled with amusement and interest, and anticipation. At dinner
we had champagne, and were very joyous—afterward Anson ran the
pool with infectious gusto, and several people who had seen me
with him asked me his name. He and the girl were talking and
laughing together on a lounge in the bar when I went to bed.

I saw less of him on the trip than I had hoped. He wanted to
arrange a foursome, but there was no one available, so I saw him only
at meals. Sometimes, though, he would have a cocktail in the bar,
and he told me about the girl in the red tam, and his adventures
with her, making them all bizarre and amusing, as he had a way of
doing, and I was glad that he was himself again, or at least the self
that I knew, and with which I felt at home. I don't think he was
ever happy unless some one was in love with him, responding to

The Rich Boy

him like filings to a magnet, helping him to explain himself, promising him something. What it was I do not know. Perhaps they promised that there would always be women in the world who would spend their brightest, freshest, rarest hours to nurse and protect that superiority he cherished in his heart.

1926   *All the Sad Young Men*

THE BABY PARTY

WHEN JOHN ANDROS felt old he found solace in the thought of life continuing through his child. The dark trumpets of oblivion were less loud at the patter of his child's feet or at the sound of his child's voice babbling mad non sequiturs to him over the telephone. The latter incident occurred every afternoon at three when his wife called the office from the country, and he came to look forward to it as one of the vivid minutes of his day.

He was not physically old, but his life had been a series of struggles up a series of rugged hills, and here at thirty-eight having won his battles against ill-health and poverty he cherished less than the usual number of illusions. Even his feeling about his little girl was qualified. She had interrupted his rather intense love-affair with his wife, and she was the reason for their living in a suburban town, where they paid for country air with endless servant troubles and the weary merry-go-round of the commuting train.

It was little Ede as a definite piece of youth that chiefly interested him. He liked to take her on his lap and examine minutely her fragrant, downy scalp and her eyes with their irises of morning blue. Having paid this homage John was content that the nurse should take her away. After ten minutes the very vitality of the child irritated him; he was inclined to lose his temper when things were broken, and one Sunday afternoon when she had disrupted a bridge game by permanently hiding up the ace of spades, he had made a scene that had reduced his wife to tears.

This was absurd and John was ashamed of himself. It was inevitable that such things would happen, and it was impossible that little Ede should spend all her indoor hours in the nursery up-stairs when she was becoming, as her mother said, more nearly a "real person" every day.

She was two and a half, and this afternoon, for instance, she was going to a baby party. Grown-up Edith, her mother, had telephoned the information to the office, and little Ede had confirmed the business by shouting "I yam going to a *pantry*!" into John's unsuspecting left ear.

"Drop in at the Markeys' when you get home, won't you, dear?"

resumed her mother. "It'll be funny. Ede's going to be all dressed up in her new pink dress——"

The conversation terminated abruptly with a squawk which indicated that the telephone had been pulled violently to the floor. John laughed and decided to get an early train out; the prospect of a baby party in some one else's house amused him.

"What a peach of a mess!" he thought humorously. "A dozen mothers, and each one looking at nothing but her own child. All the babies breaking things and grabbing at the cake, and each mama going home thinking about the subtle superiority of her own child to every other child there."

He was in a good humor to-day—all the things in his life were going better than they had ever gone before. When he got off the train at his station he shook his head at an importunate taxi man, and began to walk up the long hill toward his house through the crisp December twilight. It was only six o'clock but the moon was out, shining with proud brilliance on the thin sugary snow that lay over the lawns.

As he walked along drawing his lungs full of cold air his happiness increased, and the idea of a baby party appealed to him more and more. He began to wonder how Ede compared to other children of her own age, and if the pink dress she was to wear was something radical and mature. Increasing his gait he came in sight of his own house, where the lights of a defunct Christmas-tree still blossomed in the window, but he continued on past the walk. The party was at the Markeys' next door.

As he mounted the brick step and rang the bell he became aware of voices inside, and he was glad he was not too late. Then he raised his head and listened—the voices were not children's voices, but they were loud and pitched high with anger; there were at least three of them and one, which rose as he listened to a hysterical sob, he recognized immediately as his wife's.

"There's been some trouble," he thought quickly.

Trying the door, he found it unlocked and pushed it open.

The baby party began at half past four, but Edith Andros, calculating shrewdly that the new dress would stand out more sensationally against vestments already rumpled, planned the arrival of herself and little Ede for five. When they appeared it was already a flourishing affair. Four baby girls and nine baby boys, each one curled and washed and dressed with all the care of a proud and jealous heart, were dancing to the music of a phonograph. Never more than two or three were dancing at once, but as all were continually in motion running to and from their mothers for encouragement, the general effect was the same.

As Edith and her daughter entered, the music was temporarily drowned out by a sustained chorus, consisting largely of the word *cute* and directed toward little Ede, who stood looking timidly about and fingering the edges of her pink dress. She was not kissed—this is the sanitary age—but she was passed along a row of mamas each one of whom said "cu-u-ute" to her and held her pink little hand before passing her on to the next. After some encouragement and a few mild pushes she was absorbed into the dance, and became an active member of the party.

Edith stood near the door talking to Mrs. Markey, and keeping one eye on the tiny figure in the pink dress. She did not care for Mrs. Markey; she considered her both snippy and common, but John and Joe Markey were congenial and went in together on the commuting train every morning, so the two women kept up an elaborate pretense of warm amity. They were always reproaching each other for "not coming to see me," and they were always planning the kind of parties that began with "You'll have to come to dinner with us soon, and we'll go in to the theatre," but never matured further.

"Little Ede looks perfectly darling," said Mrs. Markey, smiling and moistening her lips in a way that Edith found particularly repulsive. "So *grown-up*—I can't *believe* it!"

Edith wondered if "little Ede" referred to the fact that Billy Markey, though several months younger, weighed almost five pounds more. Accepting a cup of tea she took a seat with two other ladies on a divan and launched into the real business of the afternoon, which of course lay in relating the recent accomplishments and insouciances of her child.

An hour passed. Dancing palled and the babies took to sterner sport. They ran into the dining-room, rounded the big table, and essayed the kitchen door, from which they were rescued by an expeditionary force of mothers. Having been rounded up they immediately broke loose, and rushing back to the dining-room tried the familiar swinging door again. The word "overheated" began to be used, and small white brows were dried with small white handkerchiefs. A general attempt to make the babies sit down began, but the babies squirmed off laps with peremptory cries of "Down! Down!" and the rush into the fascinating dining-room began anew.

This phase of the party came to an end with the arrival of refreshments, a large cake with two candles, and saucers of vanilla ice-cream. Billy Markey, a stout laughing baby with red hair and legs somewhat bowed, blew out the candles, and placed an experimental thumb on the white frosting. The refreshments were distributed, and the children ate, greedily but without confusion—they had behaved remarkably well all afternoon. They were modern babies who ate and slept at regular hours, so their dispositions were good, and their faces healthy and pink—such a peaceful party would not have been possible thirty years ago.

After the refreshments a gradual exodus began. Edith glanced anxiously at her watch—it was almost six, and John had not arrived. She wanted him to see Ede with the other children—to see how dignified and polite and intelligent she was, and how the only ice-cream spot on her dress was some that had dropped from her chin when she was joggled from behind.

"You're a darling," she whispered to her child, drawing her suddenly against her knee. "Do you know you're a darling? Do you *know* you're a darling?"

Ede laughed. "Bow-wow," she said suddenly.

"Bow-wow?" Edith looked around. "There isn't any bow-wow."

"Bow-wow," repeated Ede. "I want a bow-wow."

Edith followed the small pointing finger.

"That isn't a bow-wow, dearest, that's a teddy-bear."

"Bear?"

"Yes, that's a teddy-bear, and it belongs to Billy Markey. You don't want Billy Markey's teddy-bear, do you?"

Ede did want it.

She broke away from her mother and approached Billy Markey, who held the toy closely in his arms. Ede stood regarding him with inscrutable eyes, and Billy laughed.

Grown-up Edith looked at her watch again, this time impatiently.

The party had dwindled until, besides Ede and Billy, there were only two babies remaining—and one of the two remained only by virtue of having hidden himself under the dining-room table. It was selfish of John not to come. It showed so little pride in the child. Other fathers had come, half a dozen of them, to call for their wives, and they had stayed for a while and looked on.

There was a sudden wail. Ede had obtained Billy's teddy-bear by pulling it forcibly from his arms, and on Billy's attempt to recover it, she had pushed him casually to the floor.

"Why, Ede!" cried her mother, repressing an inclination to laugh.

Joe Markey, a handsome, broad-shouldered man of thirty-five, picked up his son and set him on his feet. "You're a fine fellow," he said jovially. "Let a girl knock you over! You're a fine fellow."

"Did he bump his head?" Mrs. Markey returned anxiously from bowing the next to last remaining mother out the door.

"No-o-o-o," exclaimed Markey. "He bumped something else, didn't you, Billy? He bumped something else."

Billy had so far forgotten the bump that he was already making an attempt to recover his property. He seized a leg of the bear which projected from Ede's enveloping arms and tugged at it but without success.

"No," said Ede emphatically.

Suddenly, encouraged by the success of her former half-accidental manœuvre, Ede dropped the teddy-bear, placed her hands on Billy's shoulders and pushed him backward off his feet.

This time he landed less harmlessly; his head hit the bare floor just off the rug with a dull hollow sound, whereupon he drew in his breath and delivered an agonized yell.

Immediately the room was in confusion. With an exclamation Markey hurried to his son, but his wife was first to reach the injured baby and catch him up into her arms.

"Oh, *Billy*," she cried, "what a terrible bump! She ought to be spanked."

Edith, who had rushed immediately to her daughter, heard this remark, and her lips came sharply together.

"Why, Ede," she whispered perfunctorily, "you bad girl!"

Ede put back her little head suddenly and laughed. It was a loud laugh, a triumphant laugh with victory in it and challenge and contempt. Unfortunately it was also an infectious laugh. Before her mother realized the delicacy of the situation, she too had laughed, an audible, distinct laugh not unlike the baby's, and partaking of the same overtones.

Then, as suddenly, she stopped.

Mrs. Markey's face had grown red with anger, and Markey, who had been feeling the back of the baby's head with one finger, looked at her, frowning.

"It's swollen already," he said with a note of reproof in his voice. "I'll get some witch-hazel."

But Mrs. Markey had lost her temper. "I don't see anything funny about a child being hurt!" she said in a trembling voice.

Little Ede meanwhile had been looking at her mother curiously. She noted that her own laugh had produced her mother's and she wondered if the same cause would always produce the same effect. So she chose this moment to throw back her head and laugh again.

To her mother the additional mirth added the final touch of hysteria to the situation. Pressing her handkerchief to her mouth she giggled irrepressibly. It was more than nervousness—she felt that in a peculiar way she was laughing with her child—they were laughing together.

It was in a way a defiance—those two against the world.

While Markey rushed up-stairs to the bathroom for ointment, his wife was walking up and down rocking the yelling boy in her arms.

"Please go home!" she broke out suddenly. "The child's badly hurt, and if you haven't the decency to be quiet, you'd better go home."

"Very well," said Edith, her own temper rising. "I've never seen any one make such a mountain out of——"

"Get out!" cried Mrs. Markey frantically. "There's the door, get out—I never want to see you in our house again. You or your brat either!"

Edith had taken her daughter's hand and was moving quickly toward the door, but at this remark she stopped and turned around, her face contracting with indignation.

"Don't you dare call her that!"

Mrs. Markey did not answer but continued walking up and down, muttering to herself and to Billy in an inaudible voice.

Edith began to cry.

"I will get out!" she sobbed, "I've never heard anybody so rude and c-common in my life. I'm glad your baby did get pushed down—he's nothing but a f-fat little fool anyhow."

Joe Markey reached the foot of the stairs just in time to hear this remark.

"Why, Mrs. Andros," he said sharply, "can't you see the child's hurt? You really ought to control yourself."

"Control m-myself!" exclaimed Edith brokenly. "You better ask her to c-control herself. I've never heard anybody so c-common in my life."

"She's insulting me!" Mrs. Markey was now livid with rage. "Did you hear what she said, Joe? I wish you'd put her out. If she won't go, just take her by the shoulders and put her out!"

"Don't you dare touch me!" cried Edith. "I'm going just as quick as I can find my c-coat!"

Blind with tears she took a step toward the hall. It was just at this moment that the door opened and John Andros walked anxiously in.

"John!" cried Edith, and fled to him wildly.

"What's the matter? Why, what's the matter?"

"They're—they're putting me out!" she wailed, collapsing against him. "He'd just started to take me by the shoulders and put me out. I want my coat!"

"That's not true," objected Markey hurriedly. "Nobody's going to put you out." He turned to John. "Nobody's going to put her out," he repeated. "She's——"

"What do you mean 'put her out'?" demanded John abruptly. "What's all this talk, anyhow?"

"Oh, let's go!" cried Edith. "I want to go. They're so *common*, John!"

"Look here!" Markey's face darkened. "You've said that about enough. You're acting sort of crazy."

"They called Ede a brat!"

For the second time that afternoon little Ede expressed emotion at an inopportune moment. Confused and frightened at the shouting voices, she began to cry, and her tears had the effect of conveying that she felt the insult in her heart.

"What's the idea of this?" broke out John. "Do you insult your guests in your own house?"

"It seems to me it's your wife that's done the insulting!" answered Markey crisply. "In fact, your baby there started all the trouble."

John gave a contemptuous snort. "Are you calling names at a little baby?" he inquired. "That's a fine manly business!"

"Don't talk to him, John," insisted Edith. "Find my coat!"

"You must be in a bad way," went on John angrily, "if you have to take out your temper on a helpless little baby."

"I never heard anything so damn twisted in my life," shouted Markey. "If that wife of yours would shut her mouth for a minute——"

"Wait a minute! You're not talking to a woman and child now——"

There was an incidental interruption. Edith had been fumbling on a chair for her coat, and Mrs. Markey had been watching her with hot, angry eyes. Suddenly she laid Billy down on the sofa, where he immediately stopped crying and pulled himself upright, and coming into the hall she quickly found Edith's coat and handed it to her without a word. Then she went back to the sofa, picked up Billy, and rocking him in her arms looked again at Edith with hot, angry eyes. The interruption had taken less than half a minute.

"Your wife comes in here and begins shouting around about how common we are!" burst out Markey violently. "Well, if we're so damn common, you'd better stay away! And, what's more, you'd better get out now!"

Again John gave a short, contemptuous laugh.

"You're not only common," he returned, "you're evidently an awful bully—when there's any helpless women and children around." He felt for the knob and swung the door open. "Come on, Edith.'

Taking up her daughter in her arms, his wife stepped outside and John, still looking contemptuously at Markey, started to follow.

"Wait a minute!" Markey took a step forward; he was trembling slightly, and two large veins on his temple were suddenly full of blood. "You don't think you can get away with that, do you? With me?"

Without a word John walked out the door, leaving it open.

Edith, still weeping, had started for home. After following her with his eyes until she reached her own walk, John turned back toward the lighted doorway where Markey was slowly coming down the slippery steps. He took off his overcoat and hat, tossed them off the path onto the snow. Then, sliding a little on the iced walk, he took a step forward.

At the first blow, they both slipped and fell heavily to the side-walk, half rising then, and again pulling each other to the ground. They found a better foothold in the thin snow to the side of the walk and rushed at each other, both swinging wildly and pressing out the snow into a pasty mud underfoot.

The street was deserted, and except for their short tired gasps and the padded sound as one or the other slipped down into the slushy mud, they fought in silence, clearly defined to each other by the full moonlight as well as by the amber glow that shone out of the open door. Several times they both slipped down together, and then for a while the conflict threshed about wildly on the lawn.

For ten, fifteen, twenty minutes they fought there senselessly in the moonlight. They had both taken off coats and vests at some silently agreed upon interval and now their shirts dripped from their backs in wet pulpy shreds. Both were torn and bleeding and so exhausted that they could stand only when by their position they mutually supported each other—the impact, the mere effort of a blow, would send them both to their hands and knees.

But it was not weariness that ended the business, and the very meaninglessness of the fight was a reason for not stopping. They stopped because once when they were straining at each other on the ground, they heard a man's footsteps coming along the sidewalk. They had rolled somehow into the shadow, and when they heard these footsteps they stopped fighting, stopped moving, stopped breathing, lay huddled together like two boys playing Indian until the footsteps had passed. Then, staggering to their feet, they looked at each other like two drunken men.

"I'll be damned if I'm going on with this thing any more," cried Markey thickly.

"I'm not going on any more either," said John Andros. "I've had enough of this thing."

Again they looked at each other, sulkily this time, as if each suspected the other of urging him to a renewal of the fight. Markey spat out a mouthful of blood from a cut lip; then he cursed softly, and picking up his coat and vest, shook off the snow from them in a surprised way, as if their comparative dampness was his only worry in the world.

"Want to come in and wash up?" he asked suddenly.

"No, thanks," said John. "I ought to be going home—my wife'll be worried."

He too picked up his coat and vest and then his overcoat and hat. Soaking wet and dripping with perspiration, it seemed absurd that less than half an hour ago he had been wearing all these clothes.

"Well—good night," he said hesitantly.

Suddenly they both walked toward each other and shook hands. It was no perfunctory hand-shake: John Andros's arm went around Markey's shoulder, and he patted him softly on the back for a little while.

"No harm done," he said brokenly.

"No—you?"

"No, no harm done."

"Well," said John Andros after a minute, "I guess I'll say good night."

Limping slightly and with his clothes over his arm, John Andros turned away. The moonlight was still bright as he left the dark patch of trampled ground and walked over the intervening lawn. Down at the station, half a mile away, he could hear the rumble of the seven o'clock train.

"But you must have been crazy," cried Edith brokenly. "I thought you were going to fix it all up there and shake hands. That's why I went away."

"Did you want us to fix it up?"

"Of course not, I never want to see them again. But I thought of course that was what you were going to do." She was touching the bruises on his neck and back with iodine as he sat placidly in a hot bath. "I'm going to get the doctor," she said insistently. "You may be hurt internally."

He shook his head. "Not a chance," he answered. "I don't want this to get all over town."

"I don't understand yet how it all happened."

"Neither do I." He smiled grimly. "I guess these baby parties are pretty rough affairs."

"Well, one thing—" suggested Edith hopefully, "I'm certainly glad we have beefsteak in the house for to-morrow's dinner."

"Why?"

"For your eye, of course. Do you know I came within an ace of ordering veal? Wasn't that the luckiest thing?"

Half an hour later, dressed except that his neck would accommodate no collar, John moved his limbs experimentally before the glass. "I believe I'll get myself in better shape," he said thoughtfully. "I must be getting old."

"You mean so that next time you can beat him?"

"I did beat him," he announced. "At least, I beat him as much as he beat me. And there isn't going to be any next time. Don't you go calling people common any more. If you get in any trouble, you just take your coat and go home. Understand?"

"Yes, dear," she said meekly. "I was very foolish and now I understand."

Out in the hall, he paused abruptly by the baby's door.

"Is she asleep?"

"Sound asleep. But you can go in and peek at her—just to say good night."

They tiptoed in and bent together over the bed. Little Ede, her cheeks flushed with health, her pink hands clasped tight together, was sleeping soundly in the cool, dark room. John reached over the railing of the bed and passed his hand lightly over the silken hair.

"She's asleep," he murmured in a puzzled way.

"Naturally, after such an afternoon."

"Miz Andros," the colored maid's stage whisper floated in from the hall, "Mr. and Miz Markey downstairs an' want to see you. Mr. Markey he's all cut up in pieces, mam'n. His face look like a roast beef. An' Miz Markey she 'pear mighty mad."

"Why, what incomparable nerve!" exclaimed Edith. "Just tell them we're not home. I wouldn't go down for anything in the world."

"You most certainly will." John's voice was hard and set.

"What?"

"You'll go down right now, and, what's more, whatever that other woman does, you'll apologize for what you said this afternoon. After that you don't ever have to see her again."

"Why—John, I can't."

"You've got to. And just remember that she probably hated to come over here just twice as much as you hate to go downstairs."

"Aren't you coming? Do I have to go alone?"

"I'll be down—in just a minute."

John Andros waited until she had closed the door behind her; then he reached over into the bed, and picking up his daughter, blankets and all, sat down in the rocking-chair holding her tightly in his arms. She moved a little, and he held his breath, but she was sleeping soundly, and in a moment she was resting quietly in the hollow of his elbow. Slowly he bent his head until his cheek was against her bright hair. "Dear little girl," he whispered. "Dear little girl, dear little girl."

John Andros knew at length what it was he had fought for so savagely that evening. He had it now, he possessed it forever, and for some time he sat there rocking very slowly to and fro in the darkness.

1925   *All the Sad Young Men*

MAGNETISM

THE PLEASANT, ostentatious boulevard was lined at prosperous intervals with New England Colonial houses—without ship models in the hall. When the inhabitants moved out here the ship models had at last been given to the children. The next street was a complete exhibit of the Spanish-bungalow phase of West Coast architecture; while two streets over, the cylindrical windows and round towers of 1897—melancholy antiques which sheltered swamis, yogis, fortune tellers, dressmakers, dancing teachers, art academies and chiropractors—looked down now upon brisk buses and trolley cars. A little walk around the block could, if you were feeling old that day, be a discouraging affair.

On the green flanks of the modern boulevard children, with their knees marked by the red stains of the mercurochrome era, played with toys with a purpose—beams that taught engineering, soldiers that taught manliness, and dolls that taught motherhood. When the dolls were so banged up that they stopped looking like real babies and began to look like dolls, the children developed affection for them. Everything in the vicinity—even the March sunlight—was new, fresh, hopeful and thin, as you would expect in a city that had tripled its population in fifteen years.

Among the very few domestics in sight that morning was a handsome young maid sweeping the steps of the biggest house on the street. She was a large, simple Mexican girl with the large, simple ambitions of the time and the locality, and she was already conscious of being a luxury—she received one hundred dollars a month in return for her personal liberty. Sweeping, Dolores kept an eye on the stairs inside, for Mr. Hannaford's car was waiting and he would soon be coming down to breakfast. The problem came first this morning, however—the problem as to whether it was a duty or a favor when she helped the English nurse down the steps with the perambulator. The English nurse always said "Please," and "Thanks very much," but Dolores hated her and would have liked, without any special excitement, to beat her insensible. Like most Latins under the stimulus of American life, she had irresistible impulses toward violence.

The nurse escaped, however. Her blue cape faded haughtily into the distance just as Mr. Hannaford, who had come quietly down-stairs, stepped into the space of the front door.

"Good morning." He smiled at Dolores; he was young and extraor-dinarily handsome. Dolores tripped on the broom and fell off the stoop. George Hannaford hurried down the steps, reached her as she was getting to her feet cursing volubly in Mexican, just touched her arm with a helpful gesture and said, "I hope you didn't hurt your-self."

"Oh, no."

"I'm afraid it was my fault; I'm afraid I startled you, coming out like that."

His voice had real regret in it; his brow was knit with solici-tude.

"Are you sure you're all right?"

"Aw, sure."

"Didn't turn your ankle?"

"Aw, no."

"I'm terribly sorry about it."

"Aw, it wasn't your fault."

He was still frowning as she went inside, and Dolores, who was not hurt and thought quickly, suddenly contemplated having a love affair with him. She looked at herself several times in the pantry mirror and stood close to him as she poured his coffee, but he read the paper and she saw that that was all for the morning.

Hannaford entered his car and drove to Jules Rennard's house. Jules was a French Canadian by birth, and George Hannaford's best friend; they were fond of each other and spent much time together. Both of them were simple and dignified in their tastes and in their way of thinking, instinctively gentle, and in a world of the volatile and the bizzare found in each other a certain quiet solidity.

He found Jules at breakfast.

"I want to fish for barracuda," said George abruptly. "When will you be free? I want to take the boat and go down to Lower Cali-fornia."

Jules had dark circles under his eyes. Yesterday he had closed out the greatest problem of his life by settling with his ex-wife for two hundred thousand dollars. He had married too young, and the former slavey from the Quebec slums had taken to drugs upon her failure to rise with him. Yesterday, in the presence of lawyers, her final gesture had been to smash his finger with the base of a telephone. He was tired of women for a while and welcomed the suggestion of a fishing trip.

"How's the baby?" he asked.

"The baby's fine."

"And Kay?"

"Kay's not herself, but I don't pay any attention. What did you do to your hand?"

"I'll tell you another time. What's the matter with Kay, George?"

"Jealous."

"Of who?"

"Helen Avery. It's nothing. She's not herself, that's all." He got up. "I'm late," he said. "Let me know as soon as you're free. Any time after Monday will suit me."

George left and drove out an interminable boulevard which narrowed into a long, winding concrete road and rose into the hilly country behind. Somewhere in the vast emptiness a group of buildings appeared, a barnlike structure, a row of offices, a large but quick restaurant and half a dozen small bungalows. The chauffeur dropped Hannaford at the main entrance. He went in and passed through various enclosures, each marked off by swinging gates and inhabited by a stenographer.

"Is anybody with Mr. Schroeder?" he asked, in front of a door lettered with that name.

"No, Mr. Hannaford."

Simultaneously his eye fell on a young lady who was writing at a desk aside, and he lingered a moment.

"Hello, Margaret," he said. "How are you, darling?"

A delicate, pale beauty looked up, frowning a little, still abstracted in her work. It was Miss Donovan, the script girl, a friend of many years.

"Hello. Oh, George, I didn't see you come in. Mr. Douglas wants to work on the book sequence this afternoon."

"All right."

"These are the changes we decided on Thursday night." She smiled up at him and George wondered for the thousandth time why she had never gone into pictures.

"All right," he said. "Will initials do?"

"Your initials look like George Harris'."

"Very well, darling."

As he finished, Pete Schroeder opened his door and beckoned him. "George, come here!" he said with an air of excitement. "I want you to listen to some one on the phone."

Hannaford went in.

"Pick up the phone and say 'Hello,'" directed Schroeder. "Don't say who you are."

"Hello," said Hannaford obediently.

"Who is this?" asked a girl's voice.

Hannaford put his hand over the mouthpiece. "What am I supposed to do?"

Schroeder snickered and Hannaford hesitated, smiling and suspicious.

"Who do you want to speak to?" he temporized into the phone.

"To George Hannaford, I want to speak to. Is this him?"

"Yes."

"Oh, George; it's me."

"Who?"

"Me—Gwen. I had an awful time finding you. They told me——"

"Gwen who?"

"Gwen—can't you hear? From San Francisco—last Thursday night."

"I'm sorry," objected George. "Must be some mistake."

"Is this George Hannaford?"

"Yes."

The voice grew slightly tart: "Well, this is Gwen Becker you spent last Thursday evening with in San Francisco. There's no use pretending you don't know who I am, because you do."

Schroeder took the apparatus from George and hung up the receiver.

"Somebody has been doubling for me up in Frisco," said Hannaford.

"So that's where you were Thursday night!"

"Those things aren't funny to me—not since that crazy Zeller girl. You can never convince them they've been sold because the man always looks something like you. What's new, Pete?"

"Let's go over to the stage and see."

Together they walked out a back entrance, along a muddy walk, and opening a little door in the big blank wall of the studio building entered into its half darkness.

Here and there figures spotted the dim twilight, figures that turned up white faces to George Hannaford, like souls in purgatory watching the passage of a half-god through. Here and there were whispers and soft voices and, apparently from afar, the gentle tremolo of a small organ. Turning the corner made by some flats, they came upon the white crackling glow of a stage with two people motionless upon it.

An actor in evening clothes, his shirt front, collar and cuffs tinted a brilliant pink, made as though to get chairs for them, but they shook their heads and stood watching. For a long while nothing happened on the stage—no one moved. A row of lights went off with a savage hiss, went on again. The plaintive tap of a hammer begged admission to nowhere in the distance; a blue face appeared among the blinding lights above and called something unintelligible into the upper blackness. Then the silence was broken by a low clear voice from the stage:

"If you want to know why I haven't got stockings on, look in my dressing room. I spoiled four pairs yesterday and two already this morning. . . . This dress weighs six pounds."

A man stepped out of the group of observers and regarded the girl's brown legs; their lack of covering was scarcely distinguishable, but, in any event, her expression implied that she would do nothing about it. The lady was annoyed, and so intense was her personality that it had taken only a fractional flexing of her eyes to indicate the fact. She was a dark, pretty girl with a figure that would be full-blown sooner than she wished. She was just eighteen.

Had this been the week before, George Hannaford's heart would have stood still. Their relationship had been in just that stage. He hadn't said a word to Helen Avery that Kay could have objected to, but something had begun between them on the second day of this picture that Kay had felt in the air. Perhaps it had begun even earlier, for he had determined, when he saw Helen Avery's first release, that she should play opposite him. Helen Avery's voice and the dropping of her eyes when she finished speaking, like a sort of exercise in control, fascinated him. He had felt that they both tolerated something, that each knew half of some secret about people and life, and that if they rushed toward each other there would be a romantic communion of almost unbelievable intensity. It was this element of promise and possibility that had haunted him for a fortnight and was now dying away.

Hannaford was thirty, and he was a moving-picture actor only through a series of accidents. After a year in a small technical college he had taken a summer job with an electric company, and his first appearance in a studio was in the rôle of repairing a bank of Klieg lights. In an emergency he played a small part and made good, but for fully a year after that he thought of it as a purely transitory episode in his life. At first much of it had offended him—the almost hysterical egotism and excitability hidden under an extremely thin veil of elaborate good-fellowship. It was only recently, with the advent of such men as Jules Rennard into pictures, that he began to see the possibilities of a decent and secure private life, much as his would have been as a successful engineer. At last his success felt solid beneath his feet.

He met Kay Tompkins at the old Griffith Studios at Mamaroneck and their marriage was a fresh, personal affair, removed from most stage marriages. Afterward they had possessed each other completely, had been pointed to: "Look, there's one couple in pictures who manage to stay together." It would have taken something out of many people's lives—people who enjoyed a vicarious security in the contemplation of their marriage—if they hadn't stayed together, and their love was fortified by a certain effort to live up to that.

He held women off by a polite simplicity that underneath was hard and watchful; when he felt a certain current being turned on he became emotionally stupid. Kay expected and took much more from men, but she. too, had a careful thermometer against her heart. Until the other night, when she reproached him for being interested in Helen Avery, there had been an absolute minimum of jealousy between them.

George Hannaford was still absorbed in the thought of Helen Avery as he left the studio and walked toward his bungalow over the way. There was in his mind, first, a horror that anyone should come between him and Kay, and second, a regret that he no longer carried that possibility in the forefront of his mind. It had given him a tremendous pleasure, like the things that had happened to him during his first big success, before he was so "made" that there was scarcely anything better ahead; it was something to take out and look at—a new and still mysterious joy. It hadn't been love, for he was critical of Helen Avery as he had never been critical of Kay. But his feeling of last week had been sharply significant and memorable, and he was restless, now that it had passed.

Working that afternoon, they were seldom together, but he was conscious of her and he knew that she was conscious of him.

She stood a long time with her back to him at one point, and when she turned at length, their eyes swept past each other's, brushing like bird wings. Simultaneously he saw they had gone far, in their way; it was well that he had drawn back. He was glad that someone came for her when the work was almost over.

Dressed, he returned to the office wing, stopping in for a moment to see Schroeder. No one answered his knock, and, turning the knob, he went in. Helen Avery was there alone.

Hannaford shut the door and they stared at each other. Her face was young, frightened. In a moment in which neither of them spoke, it was decided that they would have some of this out now. Almost thankfully he felt the warm sap of emotion flow out of his heart and course through his body.

"Helen!"

She murmured "What?" in an awed voice.

"I feel terribly about this." His voice was shaking.

Suddenly she began to cry; painful, audible sobs shook her. "Have you got a handkerchief?" she said.

He gave her a handkerchief. At that moment there were steps outside. George opened the door halfway just in time to keep Schroeder from entering on the spectacle of her tears.

"Nobody's in," he said facetiously. For a moment longer he kept his shoulder against the door. Then he let it open slowly.

Outside in his limousine, he wondered how soon Jules would be ready to go fishing.

II

From the age of twelve Kay Tompkins had worn men like rings on every finger. Her face was round, young, pretty and strong; a strength accentuated by the responsive play of brows and lashes around her clear, glossy, hazel eyes. She was the daughter of a senator from a Western state and she hunted unsuccessfully for glamour through a small Western city until she was seventeen, when she ran away from home and went on the stage. She was one of those people who are famous far beyond their actual achievement.

There was that excitement about her that seemed to reflect the excitement of the world. While she was playing small parts in Ziegfeld shows she attended proms at Yale, and during a temporary venture into pictures she met George Hannaford, already a star of the new "natural" type then just coming into vogue. In him she found what she had been seeking.

She was at present in what is known as a dangerous state. For six months she had been helpless and dependent entirely upon George, and now that her son was the property of a strict and possessive English nurse, Kay, free again, suddenly felt the need of proving herself attractive. She wanted things to be as they had been before the baby was thought of. Also she felt that lately George had taken her too much for granted; she had a strong instinct that he was interested in Helen Avery.

When George Hannaford came home that night he had minimized to himself their quarrel of the previous evening and was honestly surprised at her perfunctory greeting.

"What's the matter, Kay?" he asked after a minute. "Is this going to be another night like last night?"

"Do you know we're going out tonight?" she said, avoiding an answer.

"Where?"

"To Katherine Davis'. I didn't know whether you'd want to go——"

"I'd like to go."

"I didn't know whether you'd want to go. Arthur Busch said he'd stop for me."

They dined in silence. Without any secret thoughts to dip into like a child into a jam jar, George felt restless, and at the same time was aware that the atmosphere was full of jealousy, suspicion and anger. Until recently they had preserved between them something precious that made their house one of the pleasantest in Hollywood to enter. Now suddenly it might be any house; he felt common and he felt unstable. He had come near to making something bright and precious into something cheap and unkind. With a sudden surge of emotion, he crossed the room and was about to put his arm around her when the doorbell rang. A moment later Dolores announced Mr. Arthur Busch.

Busch was an ugly, popular little man, a continuity writer and lately a director. A few years ago they had been hero and heroine to him, and even now, when he was a person of some consequence in the picture world, he accepted with equanimity Kay's use of him for such purposes as tonight's. He had been in love with her for years, but, because his love seemed hopeless, it had never caused him much distress.

They went on to the party. It was a housewarming, with Hawaiian musicians in attendance, and the guests were largely of the old crowd. People who had been in the early Griffith pictures, even though they were scarcely thirty, were considered to be of the old crowd; they were different from those coming along now, and they were conscious of it. They had a dignity and straightforwardness about them from the fact that they had worked in pictures before pictures were bathed in a golden haze of success. They were still rather humble before their amazing triumph, and thus, unlike the new generation, who took it all for granted, they were constantly in touch with reality. Half a dozen or so of the women were especially aware of being unique. No one had come along to fill their places; here and there a pretty face had caught the public imagination for a year, but those of the old crowd were already legends, ageless and disembodied. With all this, they were still young enough to believe that they would go on forever.

George and Kay were greeted affectionately; people moved over and made place for them. The Hawaiians performed and the Duncan sisters sang at the piano. From the moment George saw who was here he guessed that Helen Avery would be here, too, and the fact annoyed him. It was not appropriate that she should be part of this gathering through which he and Kay had moved familiarly and tranquilly for years.

He saw her first when someone opened the swinging door to the kitchen, and when, a little later, she came out and their eyes met, he knew absolutely that he didn't love her. He went up to speak to her, and at her first words he saw something had happened to her, too, that had dissipated the mood of the afternoon. She had got a big part.

"And I'm in a daze!" she cried happily. "I didn't think there was a chance and I've thought of nothing else since I read the book a year ago."

"It's wonderful. I'm awfully glad."

He had the feeling, though, that he should look at her with a certain regret; one couldn't jump from such a scene as this afternoon to a plane of casual friendly interest. Suddenly she began to laugh.

"Oh, we're such actors, George—you and I."

"What do you mean?"

"You know what I mean."

"I don't."

"Oh, yes, you do. You did this afternoon. It was a pity we didn't have a camera."

Short of declaring then and there that he loved her, there was absolutely nothing more to say. He grinned acquiescently. A group formed around them and absorbed them, and George, feeling that the evening had settled something, began to think about going home. An excited and sentimental elderly lady—someone's mother—came up and began telling him how much she believed in him, and he was polite and charming to her, as only he could be, for half an hour. Then he went to Kay, who had been sitting with Arthur Busch all evening, and suggested that they go.

She looked up unwillingly. She had had several highballs and the fact was mildly apparent. She did not want to go, but she got up after a mild argument and George went upstairs for his coat. When he came down Katherine Davis told him that Kay had already gone out to the car.

The crowd had increased; to avoid a general good night he went out through the sun-parlor door to the lawn; less than twenty feet away from him he saw the figures of Kay and Arthur Busch against a bright street lamp; they were standing close together and staring into each other's eyes. He saw that they were holding hands.

After the first start of surprise George instinctively turned about, retraced his steps, hurried through the room he had just left, and came noisily out the front door. But Kay and Arthur Busch were still standing close together, and it was lingeringly and with abstracted eyes that they turned around finally and saw him. Then both of them seemed to make an effort; they drew apart as if it was a physical ordeal. George said good-by to Arthur Busch with special cordial-ity, and in a moment he and Kay were driving homeward through the clear California night.

He said nothing, Kay said nothing. He was incredulous. He suspected that Kay had kissed a man here and there, but he had never seen it happen or given it any thought. This was different; there had been an element of tenderness in it and there was something veiled and remote in Kay's eyes that he had never seen there before.

Without having spoken, they entered the house; Kay stopped by the library door and looked in.

"There's someone there," she said, and she added without interest: "I'm going upstairs. Good night."

As she ran up the stairs the person in the library stepped out into the hall.

"Mr. Hannaford——"

He was a pale and hard young man; his face was vaguely familiar, but George didn't remember where he had seen it before.

"Mr. Hannaford?" said the young man. "I recognize you from your pictures." He looked at George, obviously a little awed.

"What can I do for you?"

"Well, will you come in here?"

"What is it? I don't know who you are."

"My name is Donovan. I'm Margaret Donovan's brother." His face toughened a little.

"Is anything the matter?"

Donovan made a motion toward the door. "Come in here." His voice was confident now, almost threatening.

George hesitated, then he walked into the library. Donovan followed and stood across the table from him, his legs apart, his hands in his pockets.

"Hannaford," he said, in the tone of a man trying to whip himself up to anger, "Margaret wants fifty thousand dollars."

"What the devil are you talking about?" exclaimed George incredulously.

"Margaret wants fifty thousand dollars," repeated Donovan.

"You're Margaret Donovan's brother?"

"I am."

"I don't blieve it." But he saw the resemblance now. "Does Margaret know you're here?"

"She sent me here. She'll hand over those two letters for fifty thousand, and no questions asked."

"What letters?" George chuckled irresistibly. "This is some joke of Schroeder's, isn't it?"

"This ain't a joke, Hannaford. I mean the letters you signed your name to this afternoon."

III

An hour later George went upstairs in a daze. The clumsiness of the affair was at once outrageous and astounding. That a friend of seven years should suddenly request his signature on papers that were not what they were purported to be made all his surroundings seem diaphanous and insecure. Even now the design engrossed him more than a defense against it, and he tried to re-create the steps by which Margaret had arrived at this act of recklessness or despair.

She had served as script girl in various studios and for various directors for ten years; earning first twenty, now a hundred dollars a week. She was lovely-looking and she was intelligent; at any moment in those years she might have asked for a screen test, but some quality of initiative or ambition had been lacking. Not a few times had her opinion made or broken incipient careers. Still she waited at directors' elbows, increasingly aware that the years were slipping away.

That she had picked George as a victim amazed him most of all. Once, during the year before his marriage, there had been a momentary warmth; he had taken her to a Mayfair ball, and he remembered that he had kissed her going home that night in the car. The flirtation trailed along hesitatingly for a week. Before it could develop into anything serious he had gone East and met Kay.

Young Donovan had shown him a carbon of the letters he had signed. They were written on the typewriter that he kept in his bungalow at the studio, and they were carefully and convincingly worded. They purported to be love letters, asserting that he was Margaret Donovan's lover, that he wanted to marry her, and that for that reason he was about to arrange a divorce. It was incredible. Someone must have seen him sign them that morning; someone must have heard her say: "Your initials are like Mr. Harris'."

George was tired. He was training for a screen football game to be played next week, with the Southern California varsity as extras, and he was used to regular hours. In the middle of a confused and despairing sequence of thought about Margaret Donovan and Kay, he suddenly yawned. Mechanically he went upstairs, undressed and got into bed.

Just before dawn Kay came to him in the garden. There was a river that flowed past it now, and boats faintly lit with green and yellow lights moved slowly, remotely by. A gentle starlight fell like rain upon the dark, sleeping face of the world, upon the black mysterious bosoms of the trees, the tranquil gleaming water and the farther shore.

The grass was damp, and Kay came to him on hurried feet; her thin slippers were drenched with dew. She stood upon his shoes, nestling close to him, and held up her face as one shows a book open at a page.

"Think how you love me," she whispered. "I don't ask you to love me always like this, but I ask you to remember."

"You'll always be like this to me."

"Oh, no; but promise me you'll remember." Her tears were falling. "I'll be different, but somewhere lost inside of me there'll always be the person I am tonight."

The scene dissolved slowly and George struggled into consciousness. He sat up in bed; it was morning. In the yard outside he heard the nurse instructing his son in the niceties of behavior for two-month-old babies. From the yard next door a small boy shouted mysteriously: "Who let that barrier through on me?"

Still in his pajamas, George went to the phone and called his lawyers. Then he rang for his man, and while he was being shaved a certain order evolved from the chaos of the night before. First, he must deal with Margaret Donovan; second, he must keep the matter from Kay, who in her present state might believe anything; and, third, he must fix things up with Kay. The last seemed the most important of all.

As he finished dressing he heard the phone ring downstairs and, with an instinct of danger, picked up the receiver.

"Hello. . . . Oh, yes." Looking up, he saw that both his doors were closed. "Good morning, Helen. . . . It's all right, Dolores. I'm taking it up here." He waited till he heard the receiver click downstairs. "How are you this morning, Helen?"

"George, I called up about last night. I can't tell you how sorry I am."

"Sorry? Why are you sorry?"

"For treating you like that. I don't know what was in me, George. I didn't sleep all night thinking how terrible I'd been."

A new disorder established itself in George's already littered mind.

"Don't be silly," he said. To his despair he heard his own voice run on: "For a minute I didn't understand, Helen. Then I thought it was better so."

"Oh, George," came her voice after a moment, very low.

Another silence. He began to put in a cuff button.

"I had to call up," she said after a moment. "I couldn't leave things like that."

The cuff button dropped to the floor; he stooped to pick it up, and then said "Helen!" urgently into the mouthpiece to cover the fact that he had momentarily been away.

"What, George?"

At this moment the hall door opened and Kay, radiating a faint distaste, came into the room. She hesitated.

"Are you busy?"

"It's all right." He stared into the mouthpiece for a moment. "Well, good-by," he muttered abruptly and hung up the receiver. He turned to Kay: "Good morning."

"I didn't mean to disturb you," she said distantly.

"You didn't disturb me." He hesitated. "That was Helen Avery."

"It doesn't concern me who it was. I came to ask you if we're going to the Coconut Grove tonight."

"Sit down, Kay?"

"I don't want to talk."

"Sit down a minute," he said impatiently. She sat down. "How long are you going to keep this up?" he demanded.

"I'm not keeping up anything. We're simply through, George, and you know it as well as I do."

"That's absurd," he said. "Why, a week ago——"

"It doesn't matter. We've been getting nearer to this for months, and now it's over."

"You mean you don't love me?" He was not particularly alarmed. They had been through scenes like this before.

"I don't know. I suppose I'll always love you in a way." Suddenly she began to sob. "Oh, it's all so sad. He's cared for me so long."

George stared at her. Face to face with what was apparently a real emotion, he had no words of any kind. She was not angry, not threatening or pretending, not thinking about him at all, but concerned entirely with her emotions toward another man.

"What is it?" he cried. "Are you trying to tell me you're in love with this man?"

"I don't know," she said helplessly.

He took a step toward her, then went to the bed and lay down on it, staring in misery at the ceiling. After a while a maid knocked to say that Mr. Busch and Mr. Castle, George's lawyer, were below. The fact carried no meaning to him. Kay went into her room and he got up and followed her.

"Let's send word we're out," he said. "We can go away somewhere and talk this over."

"I don't want to go away."

She was already away, growing more mysterious and remote with every minute. The things on her dressing table were the property of a stranger.

He began to speak in a dry, hurried voice. "If you're still thinking about Helen Avery, it's nonsense. I've never given a damn for any-body but you."

They went downstairs and into the living room. It was nearly noon—another bright emotionless California day. George saw that Arthur Busch's ugly face in the sunshine was wan and white; he took a step toward George and then stopped, as if he were waiting for something—a challenge, a reproach, a blow.

In a flash the scene that would presently take place ran itself off in George's mind. He saw himself moving through the scene, saw his part, an infinite choice of parts, but in every one of them Kay would be against him and with Arthur Busch. And suddenly he rejected them all.

"I hope you'll excuse me," he said quickly to Mr. Castle. "I called you up because a script girl named Margaret Donovan wants fifty thousand dollars for some letters she claims I wrote her. Of course the whole thing is——" He broke off. It didn't matter. "I'll come to see you tomorrow." He walked up to Kay and Arthur, so that only they could hear.

"I don't know about you two—what you want to do. But leave me out of it; you haven't any right to inflict any of it on me, for after all it's not my fault. I'm not going to be mixed up in your emotions."

He turned and went out. His car was before the door and he said "Go to Santa Monica" because it was the first name that popped into his head. The car drove off into the everlasting hazeless sun-light.

He rode for three hours, past Santa Monica and then along toward Long Beach by another road. As if it were something he saw out of the corner of his eye and with but a fragment of his attention, he imagined Kay and Arthur Busch progressing through the afternoon. Kay would cry a great deal and the situation would seem harsh and unexpected to them at first, but the tender closing of the day would draw them together. They would turn inevitably toward each other and he would slip more and more into the position of the enemy out-side.

Kay had wanted him to get down in the dirt and dust of a scene and scramble for her. Not he; he hated scenes. Once he stooped to compete with Arthur Busch in pulling at Kay's heart, he would never be the same to himself. He would always be a little like Arthur Busch; they would always have that in common, like a shameful secret. There was little of the theater about George; the millions before whose eyes the moods and changes of his face had flickered during ten years had not been deceived about that. From the moment when, as a boy of twenty, his handsome eyes had gazed off into the imaginary distance of a Griffith Western, his audience had been really watching the progress of a straightforward, slow-thinking, romantic man through an accidentally glamorous life.

His fault was that he had felt safe too soon. He realized suddenly that the two Fairbankses, in sitting side by side at table, were not keeping up a pose. They were giving hostages to fate. This was perhaps the most bizarre community in the rich, wild, bored empire, and for a marriage to succeed here, you must expect nothing or you must be always together. For a moment his glance had wavered from Kay and he stumbled blindly into disaster.

As he was thinking this and wondering where he would go and what he should do, he passed an apartment house that jolted his memory. It was on the outskirts of town, a pink horror built to represent something, somewhere, so cheaply and sketchily that whatever it copied the architect must have long since forgotten. And suddenly George remembered that he had once called for Margaret Donovan here the night of a Mayfair dance.

"Stop at this apartment!" he called through the speaking tube.

He went in. The negro elevator boy stared open-mouthed at him as they rose in the cage. Margaret Donovan herself opened the door.

When she saw him she shrank away with a little cry. As he entered and closed the door she retreated before him into the front room. George followed.

It was twilight outside and the apartment was dusky and sad. The last light fell softly on the standardized furniture and the great gallery of signed photographs of moving-picture people that covered one wall. Her face was white, and as she stared at him she began nervously wringing her hands.

"What's this nonsense, Margaret?" George said, trying to keep any reproach out of his voice. "Do you need money that bad?"

She shook her head vaguely. Her eyes were still fixed on him with a sort of terror; George looked at the floor.

"I suppose this was your brother's idea. At least I can't believe you'd be so stupid." He looked up, trying to preserve the brusque masterly attitude of one talking to a naughty child, but at the sight of her face every emotion except pity left him. "I'm a little tired. Do you mind if I sit down?"

"No."

"I'm a little confused today," said George after a minute. "People seem to have it in for me today."

"Why, I thought"—her voice became ironic in midsentence—"I thought everybody loved you, George."

"They don't."

"Only me?"

"Yes," he said abstractedly.

"I wish it had been only me. But then, of course, you wouldn't have been you."

Suddenly he realized that she meant what she was saying.

"That's just nonsense."

"At least you're here," Margaret went on. "I suppose I ought to be glad of that. And I am. I most decidedly am. I've often thought of you sitting in that chair, just at this time when it was almost dark. I used to make up little one-act plays about what would happen then. Would you like to hear one of them? I'll have to begin by coming over and sitting on the floor at your feet."

Annoyed and yet spellbound, George kept trying desperately to seize upon a word or mood that would turn the subject.

"I've seen you sitting there so often that you don't look a bit more real than your ghost. Except that your hat has squashed your beautiful hair down on one side and you've got dark circles or dirt under your eyes. You look white, too, George. Probably you were on a party last night."

"I was. And I found your brother waiting for me when I got home."

"He's a good waiter, George. He's just out of San Quentin prison, where he's been waiting the last six years."

"Then it was his idea?"

"We cooked it up together. I was going to China on my share."

"Why was I the victim?"

"That seemed to make it realer. Once I thought you were going to fall in love with me five years ago."

The bravado suddenly melted out of her voice and it was still light enough to see that her mouth was quivering.

"I've loved you for years," she said—"since the first day you came West and walked into the old Realart Studio. You were so brave about people, George. Whoever it was, you walked right up to them and tore something aside as if it was in your way and began to know them. I tried to make love to you, just like the rest, but it was difficult. You drew people right up close to you and held them there, not able to move either way."

"This is all entirely imaginary," said George, frowning uncomfortably, "and I can't control——"

"No, I know. You can't control charm. It's simply got to be used. You've got to keep your hand in if you have it, and go through life attaching people to you that you don't want. I don't blame you. If you only hadn't kissed me the night of the Mayfair dance. I suppose it was the champagne."

George felt as if a band which had been playing for a long time in the distance had suddenly moved up and taken a station beneath his window. He had always been conscious that things like this were going on around him. Now that he thought of it, he had always been conscious that Margaret loved him, but the faint music of these emotions in his ear had seemed to bear no relation to actual life. They were phantoms that he had conjured up out of nothing; he had never imagined their actual incarnations. At his wish they should die inconsequently away.

"You can't imagine what it's been like," Margaret continued after a minute. "Things you've just said and forgotten, I've put myself asleep night after night remembering—trying to squeeze something more out of them. After that night you took me to the Mayfair other men didn't exist for me any more. And there were others, you know—lots of them. But I'd see you walking along somewhere about the lot, looking at the ground and smiling a little, as if something very amusing had just happened to you, the way you do. And I'd pass you and you'd look up and really smile: 'Hello, darling!' 'Hello, darling' and my heart would turn over. That would happen four times a day."

George stood up and she, too, jumped up quickly.

"Oh, I've bored you," she cried softly. "I might have known I'd bore you. You want to go home. Let's see—is there anything else? Oh, yes; you might as well have those letters."

Taking them out of a desk, she took them to a window and identified them by a rift of lamplight.

"They're really beautiful letters. They'd do you credit. I suppose it was pretty stupid, as you say, but it ought to teach you a lesson about—about signing things, or something." She tore the letters small and threw them in the wastebasket: "Now go on," she said.

"Why must I go now?"

For the third time in twenty-four hours sad and uncontrollable tears confronted him.

"Please go!" she cried angrily—"or stay if you like. I'm yours for the asking. You know it. You can have any woman you want in the world by just raising your hand. Would I amuse you?"

"Margaret——"

"Oh, go on then." She sat down and turned her face away. "After all, you'll begin to look silly in a minute. You wouldn't like that, would you? So get out."

George stood there helpless, trying to put himself in her place and say something that wouldn't be priggish, but nothing came.

He tried to force down his personal distress, his discomfort, his vague feeling of scorn, ignorant of the fact that she was watching him and understanding it all and loving the struggle in his face. Suddenly his own nerves gave way under the strain of the past twenty-four hours and he felt his eyes grow dim and his throat tighten. He shook his head helplessly. Then he turned away—still not knowing that she was watching him and loving him until she thought her heart would burst with it—and went out to the door.

IV

The car stopped before his house, dark save for small lights in the nursery and the lower hall. He heard the telephone ringing, but when he answered it, inside, there was no one on the line. For a few minutes he wandered about in the darkness, moving from chair to chair and going to the window to stare out into the opposite emptiness of the night.

It was strange to be alone, to feel alone. In his overwrought condition the fact was not unpleasant. As the trouble of last night had made Helen Avery infinitely remote, so his talk with Margaret had acted as a katharsis to his own personal misery. It would swing back upon him presently, he knew, but for a moment his mind was too tired to remember, to imagine or to care.

Half an hour passed. He saw Dolores issue from the kitchen, take the paper from the front steps and carry it back to the kitchen for a preliminary inspection. With a vague idea of packing his grip, he went upstairs. He opened the door of Kay's room and found her lying down.

For a moment he didn't speak, but moved around the bathroom between. Then he went into her room and switched on the lights.

"What's the matter?" he asked casually. "Aren't you feeling well?"

"I've been trying to get some sleep," she said. "George, do you think that girl's gone crazy?"

"What girl?"

"Margaret Donovan. I've never heard of anything so terrible in my life."

For a moment he thought that there had been some new development.

"Fifty thousand dollars!" she cried indignantly. "Why, I wouldn't give it to her even if it was true. She ought to be sent to jail."

"Oh, it's not so terrible as that," he said. "She has a brother who's a pretty bad egg and it was his idea."

"She's capable of anything," Kay said solemnly. "And you're just a fool if you don't see it. I've never liked her. She has dirty hair."

"Well, what of it?" he demanded impatiently, and added: "Where's Arthur Busch?"

"He went home right after lunch. Or rather I sent him home."

"You decided you were not in love with him?"

She looked up almost in surprise. "In love with him? Oh, you mean this morning. I was just mad at you; you ought to have known that. I was a little sorry for him last night, but I guess it was the highballs."

"Well, what did you mean when you——" He broke off. Wherever he turned he found a muddle, and he resolutely determined not to think.

"My heavens!" exclaimed Kay. "Fifty thousand dollars!"

"Oh, drop it. She tore up the letters—she wrote them herself—and everything's all right."

"George."

"Yes."

"Of course Douglas will fire her right away."

"Of course he won't. He won't know anything about it."

"You mean to say you're not going to let her go? After this?"

He jumped up. "Do you suppose she thought that?" he cried.

"Thought what?"

"That I'd have them let her go?"

"You certainly ought to."

He looked hastily through the phone book for her name.

"Oxford——" he called.

After an unusually long time the switchboard operator answered: "Bourbon Apartments."

"Miss Margaret Donovan, please."

"Why——" The operator's voice broke off. "If you'll just wait a minute, please." He held the line; the minute passed, then another. Then the operator's voice: "I couldn't talk to you then. Miss Donovan has had an accident. She's shot herself. When you called they were taking her through the lobby to St. Catherine's Hospital."

"Is she—is it serious?" George demanded frantically.

"They thought so at first, but now they think she'll be all right. They're going to probe for the bullet."

"Thank you."

He got up and turned to Kay.

"She's tried to kill herself," he said in a strained voice. "I'll have to go around to the hospital. I was pretty clumsy this afternoon and I think I'm partly responsible for this."

"George," said Kay suddenly.

"What?"

"Don't you think it's sort of unwise to get mixed up in this? People might say——"

"I don't give a damn what they say," he answered roughly.

He went to his room and automatically began to prepare for going out. Catching sight of his face in the mirror, he closed his eyes with a sudden exclamation of distaste, and abandoned the intention of brushing his hair.

"George," Kay called from the next room, "I love you."

"I love you too."

"Jules Rennard called up. Something about barracuda fishing. Don't you think it would be fun to get up a party? Men and girls both."

"Somehow the idea doesn't appeal to me. The whole idea of barracuda fishing——"

The phone rang below and he started. Dolores was answering it. It was a lady who had already called twice today.

"Is Mr. Hannaford in?"

"No," said Dolores promptly. She stuck out her tongue and hung up the phone just as George Hannaford came downstairs. She helped him into his coat, standing as close as she could to him, opened the door and followed a little way out on the porch.

"Meester Hannaford," she said suddenly, "that Miss Avery she call up five-six times today. I tell her you out and say nothing to missus."

"What?" He stared at her, wondering how much she knew about his affairs.

"She call up just now and I say you out."

"All right," he said absently.

"Meester Hannaford."

"Yes, Dolores."

"I deedn't hurt myself thees morning when I fell off the porch."

"That's fine. Good night, Dolores."

"Good night, Meester Hannaford."

George smiled at her, faintly, fleetingly, tearing a veil from between them, unconsciously promising her a possible admission to the thousand delights and wonders that only he knew and could command. Then he went to his waiting car and Dolores, sitting down on the stoop, rubbed her hands together in a gesture that might have expressed either ecstasy or strangulation, and watched the rising of the thin, pale California moon.

1928   *Previously Uncollected*

THE LAST OF THE BELLES

AFTER ATLANTA'S elaborate and theatrical rendition of Southern charm, we all underestimated Tarleton. It was a little hotter than anywhere we'd been—a dozen rookies collapsed the first day in that Georgia sun—and when you saw herds of cows drifting through the business streets, hi-yaed by colored drovers, a trance stole down over you out of the hot light: you wanted to move a hand or foot to be sure you were alive.

So I stayed out at camp and let Lieutenant Warren tell me about the girls. This was fifteen years ago, and I've forgotten how I felt, except that the days went along, one after another, better than they do now, and I was empty-hearted, because up North she whose legend I had loved for three years was getting married. I saw the clippings and newspaper photographs. It was "a romantic wartime wedding," all very rich and sad. I felt vividly the dark radiance of the sky under which it took place and, as a young snob, was more envious than sorry.

A day came when I went into Tarleton for a haircut and ran into a nice fellow named Bill Knowles, who was in my time at Harvard. He'd been in the National Guard division that preceded us in camp; at the last moment he had transferred to aviation and had been left behind.

"I'm glad I met you, Andy," he said with undue seriousness. "I'll hand you on all my information before I start for Texas. You see, there're really only three girls here—"

I was interested; there was something mystical about there being three girls.

"—and here's one of them now."

We were in front of a drug store and he marched me in and introduced me to a lady I promptly detested.

"The other two are Ailie Calhoun and Sally Carrol Happer."

I guessed from the way he pronounced her name that he was interested in Ailie Calhoun. It was on his mind what she would be doing while he was gone; he wanted her to have a quiet, uninteresting time.

At my age I don't even hesitate to confess that entirely unchivalrous images of Ailie Calhoun—that lovely name—rushed into my mind. At twenty-three there is no such thing as a preëmpted beauty; though, had Bill asked me, I would doubtless have sworn in all sincerity to care for her like a sister. He didn't; he was just fretting out loud at having to go. Three days later he telephoned me that he was leaving next morning and he'd take me to her house that night.

We met at the hotel and walked uptown through the flowery, hot twilight. The four white pillars of the Calhoun house faced the street, and behind them the veranda was dark as a cave with hanging, weaving, climbing vines.

When we came up the walk a girl in a white dress tumbled out of the front door, crying, "I'm so sorry I'm late!" and seeing us, added: "Why, I thought I heard you come ten minutes——"

She broke off as a chair creaked and another man, an aviator from Camp Harry Lee, emerged from the obscurity of the veranda.

"Why, Canby!" she cried. "How are you?"

He and Bill Knowles waited with the tenseness of open litigants.

"Canby, I want to whisper to you, honey," she said, after just a second. "You'll excuse us, Bill."

They went aside. Presently Lieutenant Canby, immensely displeased, said in a grim voice, "Then we'll make it Thursday, but that means sure." Scarcely nodding to us, he went down the walk, the spurs with which he presumably urged on his aeroplane gleaming in the lamplight.

"Come in—I don't just know your name——"

There she was—the Southern type in all its purity. I would have recognized Ailie Calhoun if I'd never heard Ruth Draper or read Marse Chan. She had the adroitness sugar-coated with sweet, voluble simplicity, the suggested background of devoted fathers, brothers and admirers stretching back into the South's heroic age, the unfailing coolness acquired in the endless struggle with the heat. There were notes in her voice that ordered slaves around, that withered up Yankee captains, and then soft, wheedling notes that mingled in unfamiliar loveliness with the night.

I could scarcely see her in the darkness, but when I rose to go—it was plain that I was not to linger—she stood in the orange light from the doorway. She was small and very blond; there was too much fever-colored rouge on her face, accentuated by a nose dabbed clownish white, but she shone through that like a star.

"After Bill goes I'll be sitting here all alone night after night. Maybe you'll take me to the country-club dances." The pathetic prophecy brought a laugh from Bill. "Wait a minute," Ailie murmured. "Your guns are all crooked."

She straightened my collar pin, looking up at me for a second with something more than curiosity. It was a seeking look, as if she asked, "Could it be you?" Like Lieutenant Canby, I marched off unwillingly into the suddenly insufficient night.

Two weeks later I sat with her on the same veranda, or rather she half lay in my arms and yet scarcely touched me—how she managed that I don't remember. I was trying unsuccessfully to kiss her, and had been trying for the best part of an hour. We had a sort of joke about my not being sincere. My theory was that if she'd let me kiss her I'd fall in love with her. Her argument was that I was obviously insincere.

In a lull between two of these struggles she told me about her brother who had died in his senior year at Yale. She showed me his picture—it was a handsome, earnest face with a Leyendecker forelock—and told me that when she met someone who measured up to him she'd marry. I found this family idealism discouraging; even my brash confidence couldn't compete with the dead.

The evening and other evenings passed like that, and ended with my going back to camp with the remembered smell of magnolia flowers and a mood of vague dissatisfaction. I never kissed her. We went to the vaudeville and to the country club on Saturday nights, where she seldom took ten consecutive steps with one man, and she took me to barbecues and rowdy watermelon parties, and never thought it was worth while to change what I felt for her into love. I see now that it wouldn't have been hard, but she was a wise nineteen and she must have seen that we were emotionally incompatible. So I became her confidant instead.

We talked about Bill Knowles. She was considering Bill; for, though she wouldn't admit it, a winter at school in New York and a prom at Yale had turned her eyes North. She said she didn't think she'd marry a Southern man. And by degrees I saw that she was consciously and voluntarily different from these other girls who sang nigger songs and shot craps in the country-club bar. That's why Bill and I and others were drawn to her. We recognized her.

June and July, while the rumors reached us faintly, ineffectually, of battle and terror overseas, Ailie's eyes roved here and there about the country-club floor, seeking for something among the tall young officers. She attached several, choosing them with unfailing perspicacity—save in the case of Lieutenant Canby, whom she claimed to despise, but, nevertheless, gave dates to "because he was so sincere" —and we apportioned her evenings among us all summer.

One day she broke all her dates—Bill Knowles had leave and was coming. We talked of the event with scientific impersonality— would he move her to a decision? Lieutenant Canby, on the contrary, wasn't impersonal at all; made a nuisance of himself. He told her

that if she married Knowles he was going to climb up six thousand
feet in his aeroplane, shut off the motor and let go. He frightened
her—I had to yield him my last date before Bill came.

On Saturday night she and Bill Knowles came to the country club.
They were very handsome together and once more I felt envious and
sad. As they danced out on the floor the three-piece orchestra was
playing *After You've Gone,* in a poignant incomplete way that I
can hear yet, as if each bar were trickling off a precious minute of
that time. I knew then that I had grown to love Tarleton, and I
glanced about half in panic to see if some face wouldn't come in for
me out of that warm, singing, outer darkness that yielded up couple
after couple in organdie and olive drab. It was a time of youth and
war, and there was never so much love around.

When I danced with Ailie she suddenly suggested that we go outside to a car. She wanted to know why didn't people cut in on her
tonight? Did they think she was already married?

"Are you going to be?"

"I don't know, Andy. Sometimes, when he treats me as if I were
sacred, it thrills me." Her voice was hushed and far away. "And
then——"

She laughed. Her body, so frail and tender, was touching mine,
her face was turned up to me, and there, suddenly, with Bill Knowles
ten yards off, I could have kissed her at last. Our lips just touched
experimentally; then an aviation officer turned a corner of the
veranda near us, peered into our darkness and hesitated.

"Ailie."

"Yes."

"You heard about this afternoon?"

"What?" She leaned forward, tenseness already in her voice.

"Horace Canby crashed. He was instantly killed."

She got up slowly and stepped out of the car.

"You mean he was killed?" she said.

"Yes. They don't know what the trouble was. His motor——"

"Oh-h-h!" Her rasping whisper came through the hands suddenly
covering her face. We watched her helplessly as she put her head on
the side of the car, gagging dry tears. After a minute I went for
Bill, who was standing in the stag line, searching anxiously about
for her, and told him she wanted to go home.

I sat on the steps outside. I had disliked Canby, but his terrible,
pointless death was more real to me then than the day's toll of
thousands in France. In a few minutes Ailie and Bill came out. Ailie
was whimpering a little, but when she saw me her eyes flexed and
she came over swiftly.

"Andy"—she spoke in a quick, low voice—"of course you must

never tell anybody what I told you about Canby yesterday. What he said, I mean."

"Of course not."

She looked at me a second longer as if to be quite sure. Finally she was sure. Then she sighed in such a quaint little way that I could hardly believe my ears, and her brow went up in what can only be described as mock despair.

"An-dy!"

I looked uncomfortably at the ground, aware that she was calling my attention to her involuntarily disastrous effect on men.

"Good night, Andy!" called Bill as they got into a taxi.

"Good night," I said, and almost added: "You poor fool."

II

Of course I should have made one of those fine moral decisions that people make in books, and despised her. On the contrary, I don't doubt that she could still have had me by raising her hand.

A few days later she made it all right by saying wistfully, "I know you think it was terrible of me to think of myself at a time like that, but it was such a shocking coincidence."

At twenty-three I was entirely unconvinced about anything, except that some people were strong and attractive and could do what they wanted, and others were caught and disgraced. I hoped I was of the former. I was sure Ailie was.

I had to revise other ideas about her. In the course of a long discussion with some girl about kissing—in those days people still talked about kissing more than they kissed—I mentioned the fact that Ailie had only kissed two or three men, and only when she thought she was in love. To my considerable disconcertion the girl figuratively just lay on the floor and howled.

"But it's true," I assured her, suddenly knowing it wasn't. "She told me herself."

"Ailie Calhoun! Oh, my heavens! Why, last year at the Tech spring house party——"

This was in September. We were going overseas any week now, and to bring us up to full strength a last batch of officers from the fourth training camp arrived. The fourth camp wasn't like the first three— the candidates were from the ranks; even from the drafted divisions. They had queer names without vowels in them, and save for a few young militiamen, you couldn't take it for granted that they came out of any background at all. The addition to our company was Lieutenant Earl Schoen from New Bedford, Massachusetts; as fine a physical specimen as I have ever seen. He was six-foot-three, with black hair, high color and glossy dark-brown eyes. He wasn't very smart and he was definitely illiterate, yet he was a good officer, high-tempered and commanding, and with that becoming touch of vanity that sits well on the military. I had an idea that New Bedford was a country town, and set down his bumptious qualities to that.

We were doubled up in living quarters and he came into my hut. Inside of a week there was a cabinet photograph of some Tarleton girl nailed brutally to the shack wall.

"She's no jane or anything like that. She's a society girl; goes with all the best people here."

The following Sunday afternoon I met the lady at a semi-private swimming pool in the country. When Ailie and I arrived, there was Schoen's muscular body rippling out of a bathing suit at the far end of the pool.

"Hey, lieutenant!"

When I waved back at him he grinned and winked, jerking his head toward the girl at his side. Then, digging her in the ribs, he jerked his head at me. It was a form of introduction.

"Who's that with Kitty Preston?" Ailie asked, and when I told her she said he looked like a street-car conductor, and pretended to look for her transfer.

A moment later he crawled powerfully and gracefully down the pool and pulled himself up at our side. I introduced him to Ailie.

"How do you like my girl, lieutenant?" he demanded. "I told you she was all right, didn't I?" He jerked his head toward Ailie; this time to indicate that his girl and Ailie moved in the same circles. "How about us all having dinner together down at the hotel some night?"

I left them in a moment, amused as I saw Ailie visibly making up her mind that here, anyhow, was not the ideal. But Lieutenant Earl Schoen was not to be dismissed so lightly. He ran his eyes cheerfully and inoffensively over her cute, slight figure, and decided that she would do even better than the other. Then minutes later I saw them in the water together, Ailie swimming away with a grim little stroke she had, and Schoen wallowing riotously around her and ahead of her, sometimes pausing and staring at her, fascinated, as a boy might look at a nautical doll.

While the afternoon passed he remained at her side. Finally Ailie came over to me and whispered, with a laugh: "He's a following me around. He thinks I haven't paid my carfare."

She turned quickly. Miss Kitty Preston, her face curiously flustered, stood facing us.

"Ailie Calhoun, I didn't think it of you to go out and delib'ately try to take a man away from another girl."—An expression of distress at the impending scene flitted over Ailie's face—"I thought you considered yourself above anything like that."

Miss Preston's voice was low, but it held that tensity that can be felt farther than it can be heard, and I saw Ailie's clear lovely eyes glance about in panic. Luckily, Earl himself was ambling cheerfully and innocently toward us.

"If you care for him you certainly oughtn't to belittle yourself in front of him," said Ailie in a flash, her head high.

It was her acquaintance with the traditional way of behaving against Kitty Preston's naive and fierce possessiveness, or if you prefer it, Ailie's "breeding" against the other's "commonness." She turned away.

"Wait a minute, kid!" cried Earl Schoen. "How about your address? Maybe I'd like to give you a ring on the phone."

She looked at him in a way that should have indicated to Kitty her entire lack of interest.

"I'm very busy at the Red Cross this month," she said, her voice as cool as her slicked-back blond hair. "Good-by."

On the way home she laughed. Her air of having been unwittingly involved in a contemptible business vanished.

"She'll never hold that young man," she said. "He wants somebody new."

"Apparently he wants Ailie Calhoun."

The idea amused her.

"He could give me his ticket punch to wear, like a fraternity pin. What fun! If mother ever saw anybody like that come in the house, she'd just lie down and die."

And to give Ailie credit, it was fully a fortnight before he did come to her house, although he rushed her until she pretended to be annoyed at the next country-club dance.

"He's the biggest tough, Andy," she whispered to me. "But he's so sincere."

She used the word "tough" without the conviction it would have carried had he been a Southern boy. She only knew it with her mind; her ear couldn't distinguish between one Yankee voice and another. And somehow Mrs. Calhoun didn't expire at his appearance on the threshold. The supposedly ineradicable prejudices of Ailie's parents were a convenient phenomenon that disappeared at her wish. It was her friends who were astonished. Ailie, always a little above Tarleton, whose beaus had been very carefully the "nicest" men of the camp —Ailie and Lieutenant Schoen! I grew tired of assuring people that she was merely distracting herself—and indeed every week or so there was someone new—an ensign from Pensacola, an old friend from New Orleans—but always, in between times, there was Earl Schoen.

Orders arrived for an advance party of officers and sergeants to proceed to the port of embarkation and take ship to France. My name was on the list. I had been on the range for a week and when I got back to camp, Earl Schoen buttonholed me immediately.

"We're giving a little farewell party in the mess. Just you and I and Captain Craker and three girls."

Earl and I were to call for the girls. We picked up Sally Carrol Happer and Nancy Lamar, and went on to Ailie's house; to be met at the door by the butler with the announcement that she wasn't home.

"Isn't home?" Earl repeated blankly. "Where is she?"

"Didn't leave no information about that; just said she wasn't home."

"But this is a darn funny thing!" he exclaimed. He walked around the familiar dusky veranda while the butler waited at the door. Something occurred to him. "Say," he informed me—"say, I think she's sore."

I waited. He said sternly to the butler, "You tell her I've got to speak to her a minute."

"How'm I goin' tell her that when she ain't home?"

Again Earl walked musingly around the porch. Then he nodded several times and said:

"She's sore at something that happened downtown."

In a few words he sketched out the matter to me.

"Look here; you wait in the car," I said. "Maybe I can fix this." And when he reluctantly retreated: "Oliver, you tell Miss Ailie I want to see her alone."

After some argument he bore this message and in a moment returned with a reply:

"Miss Ailie say she don't want to see that other gentleman about nothing never. She say come in if you like."

She was in the library. I had expected to see a picture of cool, outraged dignity, but her face was distraught, tumultuous, despairing. Her eyes were red-rimmed, as though she had been crying slowly and painfully, for hours.

"Oh, hello, Andy," she said brokenly. "I haven't seen you for so long. Has he gone?"

"Now, Ailie—"

"Now, Ailie!" she cried. "Now, Ailie! He spoke to me, you see. He lifted his hat. He stood there ten feet from me with that horrible—that horrible woman—holding her arm and talking to her, and then when he saw me he raised his hat. Andy, I didn't know what to do.

I had to go in the drug store and ask for a glass of water, and I was so afraid he'd follow in after me that I asked Mr. Rich to let me go out the back way. I never want to see him or hear of him again."

I talked. I said what one says in such cases. I said it for half an hour. I could not move her. Several times she answered by murmuring something about his not being "sincere," and for the fourth time I wondered what the word meant to her. Certainly not constancy; it was, I half suspected, some special way she wanted to be regarded.

I got up to go. And then, unbelievably, the automobile horn sounded three times impatiently outside. It was stupefying. It said as plainly as if Earl were in the room, "All right; go to the devil then! I'm not going to wait here all night."

Ailie looked at me aghast. And suddenly a peculiar look came into her face, spread, flickered, broke into a teary, hysterical smile.

"Isn't he awful?" she cried in helpless despair. "Isn't he terrible?"

"Hurry up," I said quickly. "Get your cape. This is our last night."

And I can still feel that last night vividly, the candlelight that flickered over the rough boards of the mess shack, over the frayed paper decorations left from the supply company's party, the sad mandolin down a company street that kept picking *My Indiana Home* out of the universal nostalgia of the departing summer. The three girls lost in this mysterious men's city felt something, too—a bewitched impermanence as though they were on a magic carpet that had lighted on the Southern countryside, and any moment the wind would lift it and waft it away. We toasted ourselves and the South. Then we left our napkins and empty glasses and a little of the past on the table, and hand in hand went out into the moonlight itself. Taps had been played; there was no sound but the far-away whinny of a horse, and a loud persistent snore at which we laughed, and the leathery snap of a sentry coming to port over by the guardhouse. Craker was on duty; we others got into a waiting car, motored into Tarleton and left Craker's girl.

Then Ailie and Earl, Sally and I, two and two in the wide back seat, each couple turned from the other, absorbed and whispering, drove away into the wide, flat darkness.

We drove through pine woods heavy with lichen and Spanish moss, and between the fallow cotton fields along a road white as the rim of the world. We parked under the broken shadow of a mill where there was the sound of running water and restive squawky birds and over everything a brightness that tried to filter in anywhere—into the lost nigger cabins, the automobile, the fastnesses of the heart. The South sang to us—I wonder if they remember. I remember—the cool pale faces, the somnolent amorous eyes and the voices:

"Are you comfortable?"

"Yes; are you?"

"Are you sure you are?"

"Yes."

Suddenly we knew it was late and there was nothing more. We turned home.

Our detachment started for Camp Mills next day, but I didn't go to France after all. We passed a cold month on Long Island, marched aboard a transport with steel helmets slung at our sides and then marched off again. There wasn't any more war. I had missed the war. When I came back to Tarleton I tried to get out of the Army, but I had a regular commission and it took most of the winter. But Earl Schoen was one of the first to be demobilized. He wanted to find a good job "while the picking was good." Ailie was noncommittal, but there was an understanding between them that he'd be back.

By January the camps, which for two years had dominated the little city, were already fading. There was only the persistent incinerator smell to remind one of all that activity and bustle. What life remained centred bitterly about divisional headquarters building with the disgruntled regular officers who had also missed the war.

And now the young men of Tarleton began drifting back from the ends of the earth—some with Canadian uniforms, some with crutches or empty sleeves. A returned battalion of the National Guard paraded through the streets with open ranks for their dead, and then stepped down out of romance forever and sold you things over the counters of local stores. Only a few uniforms mingled with the dinner coats at the country-club dance.

Just before Christmas, Bill Knowles arrived unexpectedly one day and left the next—either he gave Ailie an ultimatum or she had made up her mind at last. I saw her sometimes when she wasn't busy with returned heroes from Savannah and Augusta, but I felt like an outmoded survival—and I was. She was waiting for Earl Schoen with such a vast uncertainty that she didn't like to talk about it. Three days before I got my final discharge he came.

I first happened upon them walking down Market Street together, and I don't think I've ever been so sorry for a couple in my life; though I suppose the same situation was repeating itself in every city where there had been camps. Exteriorly Earl had about everything wrong with him that could be imagined. His hat was green, with a radical feather; his suit was slashed and braided in a grotesque fashion that national advertising and the movies have put an end to. Evidently he had been to his old barber, for his hair bloused neatly on his pink, shaved neck. It wasn't as though he had been shiny and poor, but the background of mill-town dance halls and outing clubs flamed out at you—or rather flamed out at Ailie. For she had never quite imagined the reality; in these clothes even the natural grace of that magnificent body had departed. At first he boasted of his fine job; it would get them along all right until he could "see some easy money." But from the moment he came back into her world on its own terms he must have known it was hopeless. I don't know what Ailie said or how much her grief weighed against her stupefaction. She acted quickly—three days after his arrival, Earl and I went North together on the train.

"Well, that's the end of that," he said moodily. "She's a wonderful girl, but too much of a highbrow for me. I guess she's got to marry some rich guy that'll give her a great social position. I can't see that stuck-up sort of thing." And then, later: "She said to come back and see her in a year, but I'll never go back. This aristocrat stuff is all right if you got the money for it, but——"

"But it wasn't real," he meant to finish. The provincial society in which he had moved with so much satisfaction for six months already appeared to him as affected, "dudish" and artificial.

"Say, did you see what I saw getting on the train?" he asked me after a while. "Two wonderful janes, all alone. What do you say we mosey into the next car and ask them to lunch? I'll take the one in blue." Halfway down the car he turned around suddenly. "Say, Andy," he demanded, frowning; "one thing—how do you suppose she knew I used to command a street car? I never told her that."

"Search me."

III

This narrative arrives now at one of the big gaps that stared me in the face when I began. For six years, while I finished at Harvard Law and built commercial aeroplanes and backed a pavement block that went gritty under trucks, Ailie Calhoun was scarcely more than a name on a Christmas card; something that blew a little in my mind on warm nights when I remembered the magnolia flowers. Occasionally an acquaintance of Army days would ask me, "What became of that blond girl who was so popular?" but I didn't know. I ran into Nancy Lamar at the Montmartre in New York one evening and learned that Ailie had become engaged to a man in Cincinnati, had gone North to visit his family and then broken it off. She was lovely as ever and there was always a heavy beau or two. But neither Bill Knowles nor Earl Schoen had ever come back.

And somewhere about that time I heard that Bill Knowles had

married a girl he met on a boat. There you are—not much of a patch to mend six years with.

Oddly enough, a girl seen at twilight in a small Indiana station started me thinking about going South. The girl, in stiff pink organdie, threw her arms about a man who got off our train and hurried him to a waiting car, and I felt a sort of pang. It seemed to me that she was bearing him off into the lost midsummer world of my early twenties, where time had stood still and charming girls, dimly seen like the past itself, still loitered along the dusky streets. I suppose that poetry is a Northern man's dream of the South. But it was months later that I sent off a wire to Ailie, and immediately followed it to Tarleton.

It was July. The Jefferson Hotel seemed strangely shabby and stuffy—a boosters' club burst into intermittent song in the dining room that my memory had long dedicated to officers and girls. I recognized the taxi driver who took me up to Ailie's house, but his "Sure, I do, lieutenant," was unconvincing. I was only one of twenty thousand.

It was a curious three days. I suppose some of Ailie's first young lustre must have gone the way of such mortal shining, but I can't bear witness to it. She was still so physically appealing that you wanted to touch the personality that trembled on her lips. No—the change was more profound than that.

At once I saw she had a different line. The modulations of pride, the vocal hints that she knew the secrets of a brighter, finer ante-bellum day, were gone from her voice; there was no time for them now as it rambled on in the half-laughing, half-desperate banter of the newer South. And everything was swept into this banter in order to make it go on and leave no time for thinking—the present, the future, herself, me. We went to a rowdy party at the house of some young married people, and she was the nervous, glowing centre of it. After all, she wasn't eighteen, and she was as attractive in her role of reckless clown as she had ever been in her life.

"Have you heard anything from Earl Schoen?" I asked her the second night, on our way to the country-club dance.

"No." She was serious for a moment. "I often think of him. He was the——" She hesitated.

"Go on."

"I was going to say the man I loved most, but that wouldn't be true. I never exactly loved him, or I'd have married him any old how, wouldn't I?" She looked at me questioningly. "At least I wouldn't have treated him like that."

"It was impossible."

"Of course," she agreed uncertainly. Her mood changed; she became flippant: "How the Yankees did deceive us poor little Southern girls. Ah, me!"

When we reached the country club she melted like a chameleon into the—to me—unfamiliar crowd. There was a new generation upon the floor, with less dignity than the ones I had known, but none of them were more a part of its lazy, feverish essence than Ailie. Possibly she had perceived that in her initial longing to escape from Tarleton's provincialism she had been walking alone, following a generation which was doomed to have no successors. Just where she lost the battle, waged behind the white pillars of her veranda, I don't know. But she had guessed wrong, missed out somewhere. Her wild animation, which even now called enough men around her to rival the entourage of the youngest and freshest, was an admission of defeat.

I left her house, as I had so often left it that vanished June, in a mood of vague dissatisfaction. It was hours later, tossing about my bed in the hotel, that I realized what was the matter, what had always been the matter—I was deeply and incurably in love with her. In spite of every incompatibility, she was still, she would always be to me, the most attractive girl I had ever known. I told her so next afternoon. It was one of those hot days I knew so well, and Ailie sat beside me on a couch in the darkened library.

"Oh, no, I couldn't marry you," she said, almost frightened; "I don't love you that way at all. . . . I never did. And you don't love me. I didn't mean to tell you now, but next month I'm going to marry another man. We're not even announcing it, because I've done that twice before." Suddenly it occurred to her that I might be hurt: "Andy, you just had a silly idea, didn't you? You know I couldn't ever marry a Northern man."

"Who is he?" I demanded.

"A man from Savannah."

"Are you in love with him?"

"Of course I am." We both smiled. "Of course I am! What are you trying to make me say?"

There were no doubts, as there had been with other men. She couldn't afford to let herself have doubts. I knew this because she had long ago stopped making any pretensions with me. This very naturalness, I realized, was because she didn't consider me as a suitor. Beneath her mask of an instinctive thoroughbred she had always been on to herself, and she couldn't believe that anyone not taken in to the point of uncritical worship could really love her. That was what she called being "sincere"; she felt most security with men like Canby and Earl Schoen, who were incapable of passing judgments on the ostensibly aristocratic heart.

"All right," I said, as if she had asked my permission to marry. "Now, would you do something for me?"

"Anything."

"Ride out to camp."

"But there's nothing left there, honey."

"I don't care."

We walked downtown. The taxi driver in front of the hotel repeated her objection: "Nothing there now, cap."

"Never mind. Go there anyhow."

Twenty minutes later he stopped on a wide unfamiliar plain powdered with new cotton fields and marked with isolated clumps of pine.

"Like to drive over yonder where you see the smoke?" asked the driver. "That's the new state prison."

"No. Just drive along this road. I want to find where I used to live."

An old race course, inconspicuous in the camp's day of glory, had reared its dilapidated grandstand in the desolation. I tried in vain to orient myself.

"Go along this road past that clump of trees, and then turn right—no, turn left."

He obeyed, with professional disgust.

"You won't find a single thing, darling," said Ailie. "The contractors took it all down."

We rode slowly along the margin of the fields. It might have been here——

"All right. I want to get out," I said suddenly.

I left Ailie sitting in the car, looking very beautiful with the warm breeze stirring her long, curly bob.

It might have been here. That would make the company streets down there and the mess shack, where we dined that night, just over the way.

The taxi driver regarded me indulgently while I stumbled here and there in the knee-deep underbrush, looking for my youth in a clapboard or a strip of roofing or a rusty tomato can. I tried to sight on a vaguely familiar clump of trees, but it was growing darker now and I couldn't be quite sure they were the right trees.

"They're going to fix up the old race course," Ailie called from the car. "Tarleton's getting quite doggy in its old age."

No. Upon consideration they didn't look like the right trees. All I could be sure of was this place that had once been so full of life and effort was gone, as if it had never existed, and that in another month Ailie would be gone, and the South would be empty for me forever.

THE ROUGH CROSSING

ONCE ON the long, covered piers, you have come into a ghostly country that is no longer Here and not yet There. Especially at night. There is a hazy yellow vault full of shouting, echoing voices. There is the rumble of trucks and the clump of trunks, the strident chatter of a crane and the first salt smell of the sea. You hurry through, even though there's time. The past, the continent, is behind you; the future is that glowing mouth in the side of the ship; this dim turbulent alley is too confusedly the present.

Up the gangplank, and the vision of the world adjusts itself, narrows. One is a citizen of a commonwealth smaller than Andorra. One is no longer so sure of anything. Curiously unmoved the men at the purser's desk, cell-like the cabin, disdainful the eyes of voyagers and their friends, solemn the officer who stands on the deserted promenade deck thinking something of his own as he stares at the crowd below. A last odd idea that one didn't really have to come, then the loud, mournful whistles, and the thing—certainly not a boat, but rather a human idea, a frame of mind—pushes forth into the big dark night.

Adrian Smith, one of the celebrities on board—not a very great celebrity, but important enough to be bathed in flash light by a photographer who had been given his name, but wasn't sure what his subject "did"—Adrian Smith and his blond wife, Eva, went up to the promenade deck, passed the melancholy ship's officer, and, finding a quiet aerie, put their elbows on the rail.

"We're going!" he cried presently, and they both laughed in ecstasy. "We've escaped. They can't get us now."

"Who?"

He waved his hand vaguely at the civic tiara.

"All those people out there. They'll come with their posses and their warrants and list of crimes we've committed, and ring the bell at our door on Park Avenue and ask for the Adrian Smiths, but what ho! the Adrian Smiths and their children and nurse are off for France."

"You make me think we really have committed crimes."

"They can't have you," he said, frowning. "That's one thing they're

254

after me about—they know I haven't got any right to a person like you, and they're furious. That's one reason I'm glad to get away."

"Darling," said Eva.

She was twenty-six—five years younger than he. She was something precious to everyone who knew her.

"I like this boat better than the *Majestic* or the *Aquitania*," she remarked, unfaithful to the ships that had served their honeymoon. "It's much smaller."

"But it's very slick and it has all those little shops along the corridors. And I think the staterooms are bigger."

"The people are very formal—did you notice?—as if they thought everyone else was a card sharp. And in about four days half of them will be calling the other half by their first names."

Four of the people came by now—a quartet of young girls abreast, making a circuit of the deck. Their eight eyes swept momentarily toward Adrian and Eva, and then swept automatically back, save for one pair which lingered for an instant with a little start. They belonged to one of the girls in the middle, who was, indeed, the only passenger of the four. She was not more than eighteen—a dark little beauty with the fine crystal gloss over her that, in brunettes, takes the place of a blonde's bright glow.

"Now, who's that?" wondered Adrian. "I've seen her before."

"She's pretty," said Eva.

"Yes." He kept wondering, and Eva deferred momentarily to his distraction; then, smiling up at him, she drew him back into their privacy.

"Tell me more," she said.

"About what?"

"About us—what a good time we'll have, and how we'll be much better and happier, and very close always."

"How could we be any closer?" His arm pulled her to him.

"But I mean never even quarrel any more about silly things. You know, I made up my mind when you gave me my birthday present last week"—her fingers caressed the fine seed pearls at her throat—"that I'd try never to say a mean thing to you again."

"You never have, my precious."

Yet even as he strained her against his side she knew that the moment of utter isolation had passed almost before it had begun. His antennæ were already out, feeling over this new world.

"Most of the people look rather awful," he said—"little and swarthy and ugly. Americans didn't use to look like that."

"They look dreary," she agreed. "Let's not get to know anybody, but just say together."

A gong was beating now, and stewards were shouting down the

decks, "Visitors ashore, please!" and voices rose to a strident chorus. For a while the gangplanks were thronged; then they were empty, and the jostling crowd behind the barrier waved and called unintelligible things, and kept up a grin of good will. As the stevedores began to work at the ropes a flat-faced, somewhat befuddled young man arrived in a great hurry and was assisted up the gangplank by a porter and a taxi driver. The ship having swallowed him as impassively as though he were a missionary for Beirut, a low, portentous vibration began. The pier with its faces commenced to slide by, and for a moment the boat was just a piece accidentally split off from it; then the faces became remote, voiceless, and the pier was one among many yellow blurs along the water front. Now the harbor flowed swiftly toward the sea.

On a northern parallel of latitude a hurricane was forming and moving south by southeast preceded by a strong west wind. On its course it was destined to swamp the Peter I. Eudim of Amsterdam, with a crew of sixty-six, to break a boom on the largest boat in the world, and to bring grief and want to the wives of several hundred seamen. This liner, leaving New York Sunday evening, would enter the zone of the storm Tuesday, and of the hurricane late Wednesday night.

II

Tuesday afternoon Adrian and Eva paid their first visit to the smoking room. This was not in accord with their intentions—they had "never wanted to see a cocktail again" after leaving America—but they had forgotten the staccato loneliness of ships, and all activity centered about the bar. So they went in for just a minute.

It was full. There were those who had been there since luncheon, and those who would be there until dinner, not to mention a faithful few who had been there since nine this morning. It was a prosperous assembly, taking its recreation at bridge, solitaire, detective stories, alcohol, argument and love. Up to this point you could have matched it in the club or casino life of any country, but over it all played a repressed nervous energy, a barely disguised impatience that extended to old and young alike. The cruise had begun, and they had enjoyed the beginning, but the show was not varied enough to last six days, and already they wanted it to be over.

At a table near them Adrian saw the pretty girl who had stared at him on the deck the first night. Again he was fascinated by her loveliness; there was no mist upon the brilliant gloss that gleamed through the smoky confusion of the room. He and Eva had decided from the passenger list that she was probably "Miss Elizabeth

D'Amido and maid," and he had heard her called Betsy as he walked
past a deck-tennis game. Among the young people with her was the
flat-nosed youth who had been "poured on board" the night of their
departure; yesterday he had walked the deck morosely, but he was
apparently reviving. Miss D'Amido whispered something to him, and
he looked over at the Smiths with curious eyes. Adrian was new
enough at being a celebrity to turn self-consciously away.

"There's a little roll. Do you feel it?" Eva demanded.

"Perhaps we'd better split a pint of champagne."

While he gave the order a short colloquy was taking place at the
other table; presently a young man rose and came over to them.

"Isn't this Mr. Adrian Smith?"

"Yes."

"We wondered if we couldn't put you down for the deck-tennis
tournament. We're going to have a deck-tennis tournament."

"Why——" Adrian hesitated.

"My name's Stacomb," burst out the young man. "We all know
your—your plays or whatever it is, and all that—and we wondered
if you wouldn't like to come over to our table."

Somewhat overwhelmed, Adrian laughed: Mr. Stacomb, glib, soft,
slouching, waited; evidently under the impression that he had delivered himself of a graceful compliment.

Adrian, understanding that, too, replied: "Thanks, but perhaps
you'd better come over here."

"We've got a bigger table."

"But we're older and more—more settled."

The young man laughed kindly, as if to say, "That's all right."

"Put me down," said Adrian. "How much do I owe you?"

"One buck. Call me Stac."

"Why?" asked Adrian, startled.

"It's shorter."

When he had gone they smiled broadly.

"Heavens," Eva gasped, "I believe they are coming over."

They were. With a great draining of glasses, calling of waiters,
shuffling of chairs, three boys and two girls moved to the Smiths'
table. If there was any diffidence, it was confined to the hosts; for
the new additions gathered around them eagerly, eying Adrian with
respect—too much respect—as if to say: "This was probably a mistake and won't be amusing, but maybe we'll get something out of it
to help us in our after life, like at school."

In a moment Miss D'Amido changed seats with one of the men
and placed her radiant self at Adrian's side, looking at him with
manifest admiration.

"I fell in love with you the minute I saw you," she said, audibly and without self-consciousness; "so I'll take all the blame for butting in. I've seen your play four times."

Adrian called a waiter to take their orders.

"You see," continued Miss D'Amido, "we're going into a storm, and you might be prostrated the rest of the trip, so I couldn't take any chances."

He saw that there was no undertone or innuendo in what she said, nor the need of any. The words themselves were enough, and the deference with which she neglected the young men and bent her politeness on him was somehow very touching. A little glow went over him; he was having rather more than a pleasant time.

Eva was less entertained; but the flat-nosed young man, whose name was Butterworth, knew people that she did, and that seemed to make the affair less careless and casual. She did not like meeting new people unless they had "something to contribute," and she was often bored by the great streams of them, of all types and conditions and classes, that passed through Adrian's life. She herself "had everything"—which is to say that she was well endowed with talents and with charm—and the mere novelty of people did not seem a sufficient reason for eternally offering everything up to them.

Half an hour later when she rose to go and see the children, she was content that the episode was over. It was colder on deck, with a damp that was almost rain, and there was a perceptible motion. Opening the door of her stateroom she was surprised to find the cabin steward sitting languidly on her bed, his head slumped upon the upright pillow. He looked at her listlessly as she came in, but made no move to get up.

"When you've finished your nap you can fetch me a new pillow-case," she said briskly.

Still the man didn't move. She perceived then that his face was green.

"You can't be seasick in here," she announced firmly. "You go and lie down in your own quarters."

"It's me side," he said faintly. He tried to rise, gave out a little rasping sound of pain and sank back again. Eva rang for the stewardess.

A steady pitch, toss, roll had begun in earnest and she felt no sympathy for the steward, but only wanted to get him out as quick as possible. It was outrageous for a member of the crew to be seasick. When the stewardess came in Eva tried to explain this, but now her own head was whirring, and throwing herself on the bed, she covered her eyes.

"It's his fault," she groaned when the man was assisted from the room. "I was all right and it made me sick to look at him. I wish he'd die."

In a few minutes Adrian came in.

"Oh, but I'm sick!" she cried.

"Why, you poor baby." He leaned over and took her in his arms. "Why didn't you tell me?"

"I was all right upstairs, but there was a steward—— Oh, I'm too sick to talk."

"You'd better have dinner in bed."

"Dinner! Oh, my heavens!"

He waited solicitously, but she wanted to hear his voice, to have it drown out the complaining sound of the beams.

"Where've you been?"

"Helping to sign up people for the tournament."

"Will they have it if it's like this? Because if they do I'll just lose for you."

He didn't answer; opening her eyes, she saw that he was frowning.

"I didn't know you were going in the doubles," he said.

"Why, that's the only fun."

"I told the D'Amido girl I'd play with her."

"Oh."

"I didn't think. You know I'd much rather play with you."

"Why didn't you, then?" she asked coolly.

"It never occurred to me."

She remembered that on their honeymoon they had been in the finals and won a prize. Years passed. But Adrian never frowned in this regretful way unless he felt a little guilty. He stumbled about, getting his dinner clothes out of the trunk, and she shut her eyes.

When a particular violent lurch startled her awake again he was dressed and tying his tie. He looked healthy and fresh, and his eyes were bright.

"Well, how about it?" he inquired. "Can you make it, or no?"

"No."

"Can I do anything for you before I go?"

"Where are you going?"

"Meeting those kids in the bar. Can I do anything for you?"

"No."

"Darling, I hate to leave you like this."

"Don't be silly. I just want to sleep."

That solicitous frown—when she knew he was crazy to be out and away from the close cabin. She was glad when the door closed. The thing to do was to sleep, sleep.

Up—down—sideways. Hey there, not so far! Pull her round the

corner there! Now roll her, right—left—— Crea-eak! Wrench! Swoop!

Some hours later Eva was dimly conscious of Adrian bending over her. She wanted him to put his arms around her and draw her up out of this dizzy lethargy, but by the time she was fully awake the cabin was empty. He had looked in and gone. When she awoke next the cabin was dark and he was in bed.

The morning was fresh and cool, and the sea was just enough calmer to make Eva think she could get up. They breakfasted in the cabin and with Adrian's help she accomplished an unsatisfactory makeshift toilet and they went up on the boat deck. The tennis tournament had already begun and was furnishing action for a dozen amateur movie cameras, but the majority of passengers were represented by lifeless bundles in deck chairs beside untasted trays.

Adrian and Miss D'Amido played their first match. She was deft and graceful; blatantly well. There was even more warmth behind her ivory skin than there had been the day before. The strolling first officer stopped and talked to her; half a dozen men whom she couldn't have known three days ago called her Betsy. She was already the pretty girl of the voyage, the cynosure of starved ship's eyes.

But after a while Eva preferred to watch the gulls in the wireless masts and the slow slide of the roll-top sky. Most of the passengers looked silly with their movie cameras that they had all rushed to get and now didn't know what to use for, but the sailors painting the lifeboat stanchions were quiet and beaten and sympathetic, and probably wished, as she did, that the voyage was over.

Butterworth sat down on the deck beside her chair.

"They're operating on one of the stewards this morning. Must be terrible in this sea."

"Operating? What for?" she asked listlessly.

"Appendicitis. They have to operate now because we're going into worse weather. That's why they're having the ship's party tonight."

"Oh, the poor man!" she cried, realizing it must be her steward.

Adrian was showing off now by being very courteous and thoughtful in the game.

"Sorry. Did you hurt yourself? . . . No, it was my fault. . . . You better put on your coat right away, pardner, or you'll catch cold."

The match was over and they had won. Flushed and hearty, he came up to Eva's chair.

"How do you feel?"

"Terrible."

"Winners are buying a drink in the bar," he said apologetically.

"I'm coming, too," Eva said, but an immediate dizziness made her sink back in her chair.

"You'd better stay here. I'll send you up something."

She felt that his public manner had hardened toward her slightly.

"You'll come back?"

"Oh, right away."

She was alone on the boat deck, save for a solitary ship's officer who slanted obliquely as he paced the bridge. When the cocktail arrived she forced herself to drink it, and felt better. Trying to distract her mind with pleasant things, she reached back to the sanguine talks that she and Adrian had had before sailing: There was the little villa in Brittany, the children learning French—that was all she could think of now—the little villa in Brittany, the children learning French—so she repeated the words over and over to herself until they became as meaningless as the wide white sky. The why of their being here had suddenly eluded her; she felt unmotivated, accidental, and she wanted Adrian to come back quick, all responsive and tender, to reassure her. It was in the hope that there was some secret of graceful living, some real compensation for the lost, careless confidence of twenty-one, that they were going to spend a year in France.

The day passed darkly, with fewer people around and a wet sky falling. Suddenly it was five o'clock, and they were all in the bar again, and Mr. Butterworth was telling her about his past. She took a good deal of champagne, but she was seasick dimly through it, as if the illness was her soul trying to struggle up through some thickening incrustation of abnormal life.

"You're my idea of a Greek goddess, physically," Butterworth was saying.

It was pleasant to be Mr. Butterworth's idea of a Greek goddess physically, but where was Adrian? He and Miss D'Amido had gone out on a forward deck to feel the spray. Eva heard herself promising to get out her colors and paint the Eiffel Tower on Butterworth's shirt front for the party tonight.

When Adrian and Betsy D'Amido, soaked with spray, opened the door with difficulty against the driving wind and came into the now-covered security of the promenade deck, they stopped and turned toward each other.

"Well?" she said. But he only stood with his back to the rail, looking at her, afraid to speak. She was silent, too, because she wanted him to be first; so for a moment nothing happened. Then she made a step toward him, and he took her in his arms and kissed her forehead.

"You're just sorry for me, that's all." She began to cry a little. "You're just being kind."

"I feel terribly about it." His voice was taut and trembling.

"Then kiss me."

The deck was empty. He bent over her swiftly.

"No, really kiss me."

He could not remember when anything had felt so young and fresh as her lips. The rain lay, like tears shed for him, upon the softly shining porcelain cheeks. She was all new and immaculate, and her eyes were wild.

"I love you," she whispered. "I can't help loving you, can I? When I first saw you—oh, not on the boat, but over a year ago—Grace Heally took me to a rehearsal and suddenly you jumped up in the second row and began telling them what to do. I wrote you a letter and tore it up."

"We've got to go."

She was weeping as they walked along the deck. Once more, imprudently, she held up her face to him at the door of her cabin. His blood was beating through him in wild tumult as he walked on to the bar.

He was thankful that Eva scarcely seemed to notice him or to know that he had been gone. After a moment he pretended an interest in what she was doing.

"What's that?"

"She's painting the Eiffel Tower on my shirt front for tonight," explained Butterworth.

"There," Eva laid away her brush and wiped her hands. "How's that?"

"A *chef-d'œuvre.*"

Her eyes swept around the watching group, lingered casually upon Adrian.

"You're wet. Go and change."

"You come too."

"I want another champagne cocktail."

"You've had enough. It's time to dress for the party."

Unwilling she closed her paints and preceded him.

"Stacomb's got a table for nine," he remarked as they walked along the corridor.

"The younger set," she said with unnecessary bitterness. "Oh, the younger set. And you just having the time of your life—with a child."

They had a long discussion in the cabin, unpleasant on her part and evasive on his, which ended when the ship gave a sudden gigantic heave, and Eva, the edge worn off her champagne, felt ill again.

There was nothing to do but to have a cocktail in the cabin, and after that they decided to go to the party—she believed him now, or she didn't care.

Adrian was ready first—he never wore fancy dress.

"I'll go on up. Don't be long."

"Wait for me, please; it's rocking so."

He sat down on a bed, concealing his impatience.

"You don't mind waiting, do you? I don't want to parade up there all alone."

She was taking a tuck in an oriental costume rented from the barber.

"Ships make people feel crazy," she said. "I think they're awful."

"Yes," he muttered absently.

"When it gets very bad I pretend I'm in the top of a tree, rocking to and fro. But finally I get pretending everything, and finally I have to pretend I'm sane when I know I'm not."

"If you get thinking that way you will go crazy."

"Look, Adrian." She held up the string of pearls before clasping them on. "Aren't they lovely?"

In Adrian's impatience she seemed to move around the cabin like a figure in a slow-motion picture. After a moment he demanded:

"Are you going to be long? It's stifling in here."

"You go on!" she fired up.

"I don't want——"

"Go on, please! You just make me nervous trying to hurry me."

With a show of reluctance he left her. After a moment's hesitation he went down a flight to a deck below and knocked at a door.

"Betsy."

"Just a minute."

She came out in the corridor attired in a red pea-jacket and trousers borrowed from the elevator boy.

"Do elevator boys have fleas?" she demanded. "I've got everything in the world on under this as a precaution."

"I had to see you," he said quickly.

"Careful," she whispered. "Mrs. Worden, who's supposed to be chaperoning me, is across the way. She's sick."

"I'm sick for you."

They kissed suddenly, clung close together in the narrow corridor, swaying to and fro with the motion of the ship.

"Don't go away," she murmured.

"I've got to. I've——"

Her youth seemed to flow into him, bearing him up into a delicate, romantic ecstasy that transcended passion. He couldn't relinquish it;

he had discovered something that he had thought was lost with his own youth forever. As he walked along the passage he knew that he had stopped thinking, no longer dared to think.

He met Eva going into the bar.

"Where've you been?" she asked with a strained smile.

"To see about the table."

She was lovely; her cool distinction conquered the trite costume and filled him with a resurgence of approval and pride. They sat down at a table.

The gale was rising hour by hour and the mere traversing of a passage had become a rough matter. In every stateroom trunks were lashed to the washstands, and the *Vestris* disaster was being reviewed in detail by nervous ladies, tossing, ill and wretched, upon their beds. In the smoking room a stout gentleman had been hurled backward and suffered a badly cut head; and now the lighter chairs and tables were stacked and roped against the wall.

The crowd who had donned fancy dress and were dining together had swollen to about sixteen. The only remaining qualification for membership was the ability to reach the smoking room. They ranged from a Groton-Harvard lawyer to an ungrammatical broker they had nicknamed Gyp the Blood, but distinctions had disappeared; for the moment they were samurai, chosen from several hundred for their triumphant resistance to the storm.

The gala dinner, overhung sardonically with lanterns and streamers, was interrupted by great communal slides across the room, precipitate retirements and spilled wine, while the ship roared and complained that under the panoply of a palace it was a ship after all. Upstairs afterward a dozen couples tried to dance, shuffling and galloping here and there in a crazy fandango, thrust around fantastically by a will alien to their own. In view of the condition of tortured hundreds below, there grew to be something indecent about it, like a revel in a house of mourning, and presently there was an egress of the ever-dwindling survivors toward the bar.

As the evening passed, Eva's feeling of unreality increased. Adrian had disappeared—presumably with Miss D'Amido—and her mind, distorted by illness and champagne, began to enlarge upon the fact; annoyance changed slowly to dark and brooding anger, grief to desperation. She had never tried to bind Adrian, never needed to—for they were serious people, with all sorts of mutual interests, and satisfied with each other—but this was a breach of the contract, this was cruel. How could he think that she didn't know?

It seemed several hours later that he leaned over her chair in the bar where she was giving some woman an impassioned lecture upon babies, and said:

"Eva, we'd better turn in."

Her lip curled. "So that you can leave me there and then come back to your eighteen-year——"

"Be quiet."

"I won't come to bed."

"Very well. Good night."

More time passed and the people at the table changed. The stewards wanted to close up the room, and thinking of Adrian—her Adrian—off somewhere saying tender things to someone fresh and lovely, Eva began to cry.

"But he's gone to bed," her last attendants assured her. "We saw him go."

She shook her head. She knew better. Adrian was lost. The long seven-year dream was broken. Probably she was punished for something she had done; as this thought occurred to her the shrieking timbers overhead began to mutter that she had guessed at last. This was for the selfishness to her mother, who hadn't wanted her to marry Adrian; for all the sins and omissions of her life. She stood up, saying she must go out and get some air.

The deck was dark and drenched with wind and rain. The ship pounded through valleys, fleeing from black mountains of water that roared toward it. Looking out at the night, Eva saw that there was no chance for them unless she could make atonement, propitiate the storm. It was Adrian's love that was demanded of her. Deliberately she unclasped her pearl necklace, lifted it to her lips—for she knew that with it went the freshest, fairest part of her life—and flung it out into the gale.

III

When Adrian awoke it was lunchtime, but he knew that some heavier sound than the bugle had called him up from his deep sleep. Then he realized that the trunk had broken loose from its lashings and was being thrown back and forth between a wardrobe and Eva's bed. With an exclamation he jumped up, but she was unharmed—still in costume and stretched out in deep sleep. When the steward had helped him secure the trunk, Eva opened a single eye.

"How are you?" he demanded, sitting on the side of her bed.

She closed the eye, opened it again.

"We're in a hurricane now," he told her. "The steward says it's the worst he's seen in twenty years."

"My head," she muttered. "Hold my head."

"How?"

"In front. My eyes are going out. I think I'm dying."

"Nonsense. Do you want the doctor?"

She gave a funny little gasp that frightened him; he rang and sent the steward for the doctor.

The young doctor was pale and tired. There was a stubble of beard upon his face. He bowed curtly as he came in and, turning to Adrian, said with scant ceremony:

"What's the matter?"

"My wife doesn't feel well."

"Well, what is it you want—a bromide?"

A little annoyed by his shortness, Adrian said: "You'd better examine her and see what she needs."

"She needs a bromide," said the doctor. "I've given orders that she is not to have any more to drink on this ship."

"Why not?" demanded Adrian in astonishment.

"Don't you know what happened last night?"

"Why, no, I was asleep."

"Mrs. Smith wandered around the boat for an hour, not knowing what she was doing. A sailor was set to follow her, and then the medical stewardess tried to get her to bed, and your wife insulted her."

"Oh, my heavens!" cried Eva faintly.

"The nurse and I had both been up all night with Steward Carton, who died this morning." He picked up his case. "I'll send down a bromide for Mrs. Smith. Good-by."

For a few minutes there was silence in the cabin. Then Adrian put his arm around her quickly.

"Never mind," he said. "We'll straighten it out."

"I remember now." Her voice was an awed whisper. "My pearls. I threw them overboard."

"Threw them overboard!"

"Then I began looking for you."

"But I was here in bed."

"I didn't believe it; I thought you were with that girl."

"She collapsed during dinner. I was taking a nap down here."

Frowning, he rang the bell and asked the steward for luncheon and a bottle of beer.

"Sorry, but we can't serve any beer to your cabin, sir."

When he went out Adrian exploded: "This is an outrage. You were simply crazy from that storm and they can't be so high-handed. I'll see the captain."

"Isn't that awful?" Eva murmured. "The poor man died."

She turned over and began to sob into her pillow. There was a knock at the door.

"Can I come in?"

The assiduous Mr. Butterworth, surprisingly healthy and immaculate, came into the crazily tipping cabin.

"Well, how's the mystic?" he demanded of Eva. "Do you remember praying to the elements in the bar last night?"

"I don't want to remember anything about last night."

They told him about the stewardess, and with the telling the situation lightened; they all laughed together.

"I'm going to get you some beer to have with your luncheon," Butterworth said. "You ought to get up on deck."

"Don't go," Eva said. "You look so cheerful and nice."

"Just for ten minutes."

When he had gone, Adrian rang for two baths.

"The thing is to put on our best clothes and walk proudly three times around the deck," he said.

"Yes." After a moment she added abstractedly: "I like that young man. He was awfully nice to me last night when you'd disappeared."

The bath steward appeared with the information that bathing was too dangerous today. They were in the midst of the wildest hurricane on the North Atlantic in ten years; there were two broken arms this morning from attempts to take baths. An elderly lady had been thrown down a staircase and was not expected to live. Furthermore, they had received the S O S signal from several boats this morning.

"Will we go to help them?"

"They're all behind us, sir, so we have to leave them to the *Mauretania*. If we tried to turn in this sea the portholes would be smashed."

This array of calamities minimized their own troubles. Having eaten a sort of luncheon and drunk the beer provided by Butterworth, they dressed and went on deck.

Despite the fact that it was only possible to progress step by step, holding on to rope or rail, more people were abroad than on the day before. Fear had driven them from their cabins, where the trunks bumped and the waves pounded the portholes and they awaited momentarily the call to the boats. Indeed, as Adrian and Eva stood on the transverse deck above the second class, there was a bugle call, followed by a gathering of stewards and stewardesses on the deck below. But the boat was sound; it had outlasted one of its cargo—Steward James Carton was being buried at sea.

It was very British and sad. There were the rows of stiff, disciplined men and women standing in the driving rain, and there was a shape covered by the flag of the Empire that lived by the sea. The chief purser read the service, a hymn was sung, the body slid off into the hurricane. With Eva's burst of wild weeping for this humble end, some last string snapped within her. Now she really didn't care. She responded eagerly when Butterworth suggested that he get some champagne to their cabin. Her mood worried Adrian; she wasn't used to so much drinking and he wondered what he ought to do. At his suggestion that they sleep instead, she merely laughed, and the bromide the doctor had sent stood untouched on the washstand. Pretending to listen to the insipidities of several Mr. Stacombs, he watched her; to his surprise and discomfort she seemed on intimate and even sentimental terms with Butterworth, and he wondered if this was a form of revenge for his attention to Betsy D'Amido.

The cabin was full of smoke, the voices went on incessantly, the suspension of activity, the waiting for the storm's end, was getting on his nerves. They had been at sea only four days; it was like a year.

The two Mr. Stacombs left finally, but Butterworth remained. Eva was urging him to go for another bottle of champagne.

"We've had enough," objected Adrian. "We ought to go to bed."

"I won't go to bed!" she burst out. "You must be crazy! You play around all you want, and then, when I find somebody I—I like, you want to put me to bed."

"You're hysterical."

"On the contrary, I've never been so sane."

"I think you'd better leave us, Butterworth," Adrian said. "Eva doesn't know what she's saying."

"He won't go. I won't let him go." She clasped Butterworth's hand passionately. "He's the only person that's been half decent to me."

"You'd better go, Butterworth," repeated Adrian.

The young man looked at him uncertainly.

"It seems to me you're being unjust to your wife," he ventured.

"My wife isn't herself."

"That's no reason for bullying her."

Adrian lost his temper. "You get out of here!" he cried.

The two men looked at each other for a moment in silence. Then Butterworth turned to Eva, said, "I'll be back later," and left the cabin.

"Eva, you've got to pull yourself together," said Adrian when the door closed.

She didn't answer, looked at him from sullen, half-closed eyes.

"I'll order dinner here for us both and then we'll try to get some sleep."

"I want to go up and send a wireless."

"Who to?"

"Some Paris lawyer. I want a divorce."

In spite of his annoyance, he laughed. "Don't be silly."

"Then I want to see the children."

"Well, go and see them. I'll order dinner."

He waited for her in the cabin twenty minutes. Then impatiently he opened the door across the corridor; the nurse told him that Mrs. Smith had not been there.

With a sudden prescience of disaster he ran upstairs, glanced in the bar, the salons, even knocked at Butterworth's door. Then a quick round of the decks, feeling his way through the black spray and rain. A sailor stopped him at a network of ropes.

"Orders are no one goes by, sir. A wave has gone over the wireless room."

"Have you seen a lady?"

"There was a young lady here——" He stopped and glanced around. "Hello, she's gone."

"She went up the stairs!" Adrian said anxiously. "Up to the wireless room!"

The sailor ran up to the boat deck; stumbling and slipping, Adrian followed. As he cleared the protected sides of the companionway, a tremendous body struck the boat a staggering blow and, as she keeled over to an angle of forty-five degrees, he was thrown in a helpless roll down the drenched deck, to bring up dizzy and bruised against a stanchion.

"Eva!" he called. His voice was soundless in the black storm. Against the faint light of the wireless-room window he saw the sailor making his way forward.

"Eva!"

The wind blew him like a sail up against a lifeboat. Then there was another shuddering crash, and high over his head, over the very boat, he saw a gigantic, glittering white wave, and in the split second that it balanced there he became conscious of Eva, standing beside a ventilator twenty feet away. Pushing out from the stanchion, he lunged desperately toward her, just as the wave broke with a smashing roar. For a moment the rushing water was five feet deep, sweeping with enormous force toward the side, and then a human body was washed against him, and frantically he clutched it and was swept with it back toward the rail. He felt his body bump against it, but desperately he held on to his burden; then, as the ship rocked slowly back, the two of them, still joined by his fierce grip, were rolled out exhausted on the wet planks. For a moment he knew no more.

IV

Two days later, as the boat train moved tranquilly south toward Paris, Adrian tried to persuade his children to look out the window at the Norman countryside.

"It's beautiful," he assured them. "All the little farms like toys. Why, in heaven's name, won't you look?"

"I like the boat better," said Estelle.

Her parents exchanged an infanticidal glance.

"The boat is still rocking for me," Eva said with a shiver. "Is it for you?"

"No. Somehow, it all seems a long way off. Even the passengers looked unfamiliar going through the customs."

"Most of them hadn't appeared above ground before."

He hesitated. "By the way, I cashed Butterworth's check for him."

"You're a fool. You'll never see the money again."

"He must have needed it pretty badly or he would not have come to me."

A pale and wan girl, passing along the corridor, recognized them and put her head through the doorway.

"How do you feel?"

"Awful."

"Me, too," agreed Miss D'Amido. "I'm vainly hoping my fiancé will recognize me at the Gare du Nord. Do you know two waves went over the wireless room?"

"So we heard," Adrian answered dryly.

She passed gracefully along the corridor and out of their life.

"The real truth is that none of it happened," said Adrian after a moment. "It was a nightmare—an incredibly awful nightmare."

"Then, where are my pearls?"

"Darling, there are better pearls in Paris. I'll take the responsibility for those pearls. My real belief is that you saved the boat."

"Adrian, let's never get to know anyone else, but just stay together always—just we two."

He tucked her arm under his and they sat close. "Who do you suppose those Adrian Smiths on the boat were?" he demanded. "It certainly wasn't me."

"Nor me."

"It was two other people," he said, nodding to himself. "There are so many Smiths in this world."

1929   *Previously Uncollected*

THE BRIDAL PARTY

THERE WAS the usual insincere little note saying: "I wanted you to be the first to know." It was a double shock to Michael, announcing, as it did, both the engagement and the imminent marriage; which, moreover, was to be held, not in New York, decently and far away, but here in Paris under his very nose, if that could be said to extend over the Protestant Episcopal Church of the Holy Trinity, Avenue George-Cinq. The date was two weeks off, early in June.

At first Michael was afraid and his stomach felt hollow. When he left the hotel that morning, the *femme de chambre*, who was in love with his fine, sharp profile and his pleasant buoyancy, scented the hard abstraction that had settled over him. He walked in a daze to his bank, he bought a detective story at Smith's on the Rue de Rivoli, he sympathetically stared for a while at a faded panorama of the battlefields in a tourist-office window and cursed a Greek tout who followed him with a half-displayed packet of innocuous post cards warranted to be very dirty indeed.

But the fear stayed with him, and after a while he recognized it as the fear that now he would never be happy. He had met Caroline Dandy when she was seventeen, possessed her young heart all through her first season in New York, and then lost her, slowly, tragically, uselessly, because he had no money and could make no money; because, with all the energy and good will in the world, he could not find himself; because, loving him still, Caroline had lost faith and begun to see him as something pathetic, futile and shabby, outside the great, shining stream of life toward which she was inevitably drawn.

Since his only support was that she loved him, he leaned weakly on that; the support broke, but still he held on to it and was carried out to sea and washed up on the French coast with its broken pieces still in his hands. He carried them around with him in the form of photographs and packets of correspondence and a liking for a maudlin popular song called *Among My Souvenirs*. He kept clear of other girls, as if Caroline would somehow know it and reciprocate with a faithful heart. Her note informed him that he had lost her forever.

It was a fine morning. In front of the shops in the Rue de Castiglione, proprietors and patrons were on the sidewalk gazing upward, for the Graf Zeppelin, shining and glorious, symbol of escape and destruction—of escape, if necessary, through destruction—glided in the Paris sky. He heard a woman say in French that it would not her astonish if that commenced to let fall the bombs. Then he heard another voice, full of husky laughter, and the void in his stomach froze. Jerking about, he was face to face with Caroline Dandy and her fiancé.

"Why, Michael! Why, we were wondering where you were. I asked at the Guaranty Trust, and Morgan and Company, and finally sent a note to the National City——"

Why didn't they back away? Why didn't they back right up, walking backward down the Rue de Castiglione, across the Rue de Rivoli, through the Tuileries Gardens, still walking backward as fast as they could till they grew vague and faded out across the river?

"This is Hamilton Rutherford, my fiancé."

"We've met before."

"At Pat's, wasn't it?"

"And last spring in the Ritz Bar."

"Michael, where have you been keeping yourself?"

"Around here." This agony. Previews of Hamilton Rutherford flashed before his eyes—a quick series of pictures, sentences. He remembered hearing that he had bought a seat in 1920 for a hundred and twenty-five thousand of borrowed money, and just before the break sold it for more than half a million. Not handsome like Michael, but vitally attractive, confident, authoritative, just the right height over Caroline there—Michael had always been too short for Caroline when they danced.

Rutherford was saying: "No, I'd like it very much if you'd come to the bachelor dinner. I'm taking the Ritz Bar from nine o'clock on. Then right after the wedding there'll be a reception and breakfast at the Hotel George-Cinq."

"And, Michael, George Packman is giving a party day after tomorrow at Chez Victor, and I want you to be sure and come. And also to tea Friday at Jebby West's; she'd want to have you if she knew where you were. What's your hotel, so we can send you an invitation? You see, the reason we decided to have it over here is because mother has been sick in a nursing home here and the whole clan is in Paris. Then Hamilton's mother's being here too——"

The entire clan; they had always hated him, except her mother; always discouraged his courtship. What a little counter he was in this game of families and money! Under his hat his brow sweated with the humiliation of the fact that for all his misery he was worth just exactly so many invitations. Frantically he began to mumble something about going away.

Then it happened—Caroline saw deep into him, and Michael knew that she saw. She saw through to his profound woundedness, and something quivered inside her, died out along the curve of her mouth and in her eyes. He had moved her. All the unforgettable impulses of first love had surged up once more; their hearts had in some way touched across two feet of Paris sunlight. She took her fiancé's arm suddenly, as if to steady herself with the feel of it.

They parted. Michael walked quickly for a minute; then he stopped, pretending to look in a window, and saw them farther up the street, walking fast into the Place Vendôme, people with much to do.

He had things to do also—he had to get his laundry.

"Nothing will ever be the same again," he said to himself. "She will never be happy in her marriage and I will never be happy at all any more."

The two vivid years of his love for Caroline moved back around him like years in Einstein's physics. Intolerable memories arose—of rides in the Long Island moonlight; of a happy time at Lake Placid with her cheeks so cold there, but warm just underneath the surface; of a despairing afternoon in a little café on Forty-eighth Street in the last sad months when their marriage had come to seem impossible.

"Come in," he said aloud.

The concierge with a telegram; brusque because Mr. Curly's clothes were a little shabby. Mr. Curly gave few tips; Mr. Curly was obviously a *petit client.*

Michael read the telegram.

"An answer?" the concierge asked.

"No," said Michael, and then, on an impulse: "Look."

"Too bad—too bad," said the concierge. "Your grandfather is dead."

"Not too bad," said Michael. "It means that I come into a quarter of a million dollars."

Too late by a single month; after the first flush of the news his misery was deeper than ever. Lying awake in bed that night, he listened endlessly to the long caravan of a circus moving through the street from one Paris fair to another.

When the last van had rumbled out of hearing and the corners of the furniture were pastel blue with the dawn, he was still thinking of the look in Caroline's eyes that morning—the look that seemed to say: "Oh, why couldn't you have done something about it? Why couldn't you have been stronger, made me marry you? Don't you see how sad I am?"

Michael's fists clenched.

"Well, I won't give up till the last moment," he whispered. "I've had all the bad luck so far, and maybe it's turned at last. One takes what one can get, up to the limit of one's strength, and if I can't have her, at least she'll go into this marriage with some of me in her heart."

II

Accordingly he went to the party at Chez Victor two days later, upstairs and into the little salon off the bar where the party was to assemble for cocktails. He was early; the only other occupant was a tall lean man of fifty. They spoke.

"You waiting for George Packman's party?"

"Yes. My name's Michael Curly."

"My name's——"

Michael failed to catch the name. They ordered a drink, and Michael supposed that the bride and groom were having a gay time.

"Too much so," the other agreed, frowning. "I don't see how they stand it. We all crossed on the boat together; five days of that crazy life and then two weeks of Paris. You"—he hesitated, smiling faintly —"you'll excuse me for saying that your generation drinks too much."

"Not Caroline."

"No, not Caroline. She seems to take only a cocktail and a glass of champagne, and then she's had enough, thank God. But Hamilton drinks too much and all this crowd of young people drink too much. Do you live in Paris?"

"For the moment," said Michael.

"I don't like Paris. My wife—that is to say, my ex-wife, Hamilton's mother—lives in Paris."

"You're Hamilton Rutherford's father?"

"I have that honor. And I'm not denying that I'm proud of what he's done; it was just a general comment."

"Of course."

Michael glanced up nervously as four people came in. He felt suddenly that his dinner coat was old and shiny; he had ordered a new one that morning. The people who had come in were rich and at home in their richness with one another—a dark, lovely girl with a hysterical little laugh whom he had met before; two confident men whose jokes referred invariably to last night's scandal and tonight's potentialities, as if they had important rôles in a play that extended indefinitely into the past and the future. When Caroline arrived, Michael had scarcely a moment of her, but it was enough to note that, like all the others, she was strained and tired. She was pale beneath her rouge; there were shadows under her eyes. With a mixture of relief and wounded vanity, he found himself placed far from her and at another table; he needed a moment to adjust himself to his surroundings. This was not like the immature set in which he and Caroline had moved; the men were more than thirty and had an air of sharing the best of this world's good. Next to him was Jebby West, whom he knew; and, on the other side, a jovial man who immediately began to talk to Michael about a stunt for the bachelor dinner: They were going to hire a French girl to appear with an actual baby in her arms, crying: "Hamilton, you can't desert me now!" The idea seemed stale and unamusing to Michael, but its originator shook with anticipatory laughter.

Farther up the table there was talk of the market—another drop today, the most appreciable since the crash; people were kidding Rutherford about it: "Too bad, old man. You better not get married, after all."

Michael asked the man on his left, "Has he lost a lot?"

"Nobody knows. He's heavily involved, but he's one of the smartest young men in Wall Street. Anyhow, nobody ever tells you the truth."

It was a champagne dinner from the start, and toward the end it reached a pleasant level of conviviality, but Michael saw that all these people were too weary to be exhilarated by any ordinary stimulant; for weeks they had drunk cocktails before meals like Americans, wines and brandies like Frenchmen, beer like Germans, whisky-and-soda like the English, and as they were no longer in the twenties, this preposterous *mélange*, that was like some gigantic cocktail in a nightmare, served only to make them temporarily less conscious of the mistakes of the night before. Which is to say that it was not really a gay party; what gayety existed was displayed in the few who drank nothing at all.

But Michael was not tired, and the champagne stimulated him and made his misery less acute. He had been away from New York for more than eight months and most of the dance music was unfamiliar to him, but at the first bars of the "Painted Doll", to which he and Caroline had moved through so much happiness and despair the previous summer, he crossed to Caroline's table and asked her to dance.

She was lovely in a dress of thin ethereal blue, and the proximity of her crackly yellow hair, of her cool and tender gray eyes, turned his body clumsy and rigid; he stumbled with their first step on the floor. For a moment it seemed that there was nothing to say; he wanted to tell her about his inheritance, but the idea seemed abrupt, unprepared for.

"Michael, it's so nice to be dancing with you again."

He smiled grimly.

"I'm so happy you came," she continued. "I was afraid maybe you'd be silly and stay away. Now we can be just good friends and natural together. Michael, I want you and Hamilton to like each other."

The engagement was making her stupid; he had never heard her make such a series of obvious remarks before.

"I could kill him without a qualm," he said pleasantly, "but he looks like a good man. He's fine. What I want to know is, what happens to people like me who aren't able to forget?"

As he said this he could not prevent his mouth from drooping suddenly, and glancing up, Caroline saw, and her heart quivered violently, as it had the other morning.

"Do you mind so much, Michael?"

"Yes."

For a second as he said this, in a voice that seemed to have come up from his shoes, they were not dancing; they were simply clinging together. Then she leaned away from him and twisted her mouth into a lovely smile.

"I didn't know what to do at first, Michael. I told Hamilton about you—that I'd cared for you an awful lot—but it didn't worry him, and he was right. Because I'm over you now—yes, I am. And you'll wake up some sunny morning and be over me just like that."

He shook his head stubbornly.

"Oh, yes. We weren't for each other. I'm pretty flighty, and I need somebody like Hamilton to decide things. It was that more than the question of—of——"

"Of money." Again he was on the point of telling her what had happened, but again something told him it was not the time.

"Then how do you account for what happened when we met the other day," he demanded helplessly—"what happened just now? When we just pour toward each other like we used to—as if we were one person, as if the same blood was flowing through both of us?"

"Oh, don't," she begged him. "You mustn't talk like that; everything's decided now. I love Hamilton with all my heart. It's just that I remember certain things in the past and I feel sorry for you—for us—for the way we were."

Over her shoulder, Michael saw a man come toward them to cut in. In a panic he danced her away, but inevitably the man came on.

"I've got to see you alone, if only for a minute," Michael said quickly. "When can I?"

"I'll be at Jebby West's tea tomorrow," she whispered as a hand fell politely upon Michael's shoulder.

But he did not talk to her at Jebby West's tea. Rutherford stood next to her, and each brought the other into all conversations. They left early. The next morning the wedding cards arrived in the first mail.

Then Michael, grown desperate with pacing up and down his room, determined on a bold stroke; he wrote to Hamilton Rutherford, asking him for a rendezvous the following afternoon. In a short telephone communication Rutherford agreed, but for a day later than Michael had asked. And the wedding was only six days away.

They were to meet in the bar of the Hotel Jena. Michael knew what he would say: "See here, Rutherford, do you realize the responsibility you're taking in going through with this marriage? Do you realize the harvest of trouble and regret you're sowing in persuading a girl into something contrary to the instincts of her heart?" He would explain that the barrier between Caroline and himself had been an artificial one and was now removed, and demand that the matter be put up to Caroline frankly before it was too late.

Rutherford would be angry, conceivably there would be a scene, but Michael felt that he was fighting for his life now.

He found Rutherford in conversation with an older man, whom Michael had met at several of the wedding parties.

"I saw what happened to most of my friends," Rutherford was saying, "and I decided it wasn't going to happen to me. It isn't so difficult; if you take a girl with common sense, and tell her what's what, and do your stuff damn well, and play decently square with her, it's a marriage. If you stand for any nonsense at the beginning, it's one of these arrangements—within five years the man gets out, or else the girl gobbles him up and you have the usual mess."

"Right!" agreed his companion enthusiastically. "Hamilton, boy, you're right."

Michael's blood boiled slowly.

"Doesn't it strike you," he inquired coldly, "that your attitude went out of fashion about a hundred years ago?"

"No, it didn't," said Rutherford pleasantly, but impatiently. "I'm as modern as anybody. I'd get married in an aeroplane next Saturday if it'd please my girl."

"I don't mean that way of being modern. You can't take a sensitive woman——"

"Sensitive? Women aren't so darn sensitive. It's fellows like you who are sensitive; it's fellows like you they exploit—all your devotion and kindness and all that. They read a couple of books and see a few pictures because they haven't got anything else to do, and then they say they're finer in grain than you are, and to prove it they take the bit in their teeth and tear off for a fare-you-well—just about as sensitive as a fire horse."

"Caroline happens to be sensitive," said Michael in a clipped voice.

At this point the other man got up to go; when the dispute about the check had been settled and they were alone, Rutherford leaned back to Michael as if a question had been asked him.

"Caroline's more than sensitive," he said. "She's got sense."

His combative eyes, meeting Michael's, flickered with a gray light. "This all sounds pretty crude to you, Mr. Curly, but it seems to me that the average man nowadays just asks to be made a monkey of by some woman who doesn't even get any fun out of reducing him to that level. There are darn few men who possess their wives any more, but I am going to be one of them."

To Michael it seemed time to bring the talk back to the actual situation: "Do you realize the responsibility you're taking?"

"I certainly do," interrupted Rutherford. "I'm not afraid of responsibility. I'll make the decisions—fairly, I hope, but anyhow they'll be final."

"What if you didn't start right?" said Michael impetuously. "What if your marriage isn't founded on mutual love?"

"I think I see what you mean," Rutherford said, still pleasant. "And since you've brought it up, let me say that if you and Caroline had married, it wouldn't have lasted three years. Do you know what your affair was founded on? On sorrow. You got sorry for each other. Sorrow's a lot of fun for most women and for some men, but it seems to me that a marriage ought to be based on hope." He looked at his watch and stood up.

"I've got to meet Caroline. Remember, you're coming to the bachelor dinner day after tomorrow."

Michael felt the moment slipping away. "Then Caroline's personal feelings don't count with you?" he demanded fiercely.

"Caroline's tired and upset. But she has what she wants, and that's the main thing."

"Are you referring to yourself?" demanded Michael incredulously.

"Yes."

"May I ask how long she's wanted you?"

"About two years." Before Michael could answer, he was gone.

During the next two days Michael floated in an abyss of helplessness. The idea haunted him that he had left something undone that would sever this knot drawn tighter under his eyes. He phoned Caroline, but she insisted that it was physically impossible for her to see him until the day before the wedding, for which day she granted him a tentative rendezvous. Then he went to the bachelor dinner, partly in fear of an evening alone at his hotel, partly from a feeling that by his presence at that function he was somehow nearer to Caroline, keeping her in sight.

The Ritz Bar had been prepared for the occasion by French and American banners and by a great canvas covering one wall, against which the guests were invited to concentrate their proclivities in breaking glasses.

At the first cocktail, taken at the bar, there were many slight spillings from many trembling hands, but later, with the champagne, there was a rising tide of laughter and occasional bursts of song.

Michael was surprised to find what a difference his new dinner coat, his new silk hat, his new, proud linen made in his estimate of himself; he felt less resentment toward all these people for being so rich and assured. For the first time since he had left college he felt rich and assured himself; he felt that he was part of all this, and even entered into the scheme of Johnson, the practical joker, for the appearance of the woman betrayed, now waiting tranquilly in the room across the hall.

"We don't want to go too heavy," Johnson said, "because I imagine Ham's had a pretty anxious day already. Did you see Fullman Oil's sixteen points off this morning?"

"Will that matter to him?" Michael asked, trying to keep the interest out of his voice.

"Naturally. He's in heavily; he's always in everything heavily. So far he's had luck; anyhow, up to a month ago."

The glasses were filled and emptied faster now, and men were shouting at one another across the narrow table. Against the bar a group of ushers was being photographed, and the flash light surged through the room in a stifling cloud.

"Now's the time," Johnson said. "You're to stand by the door, remember, and we're both to try and keep her from coming in—just till we get everybody's attention."

He went on out into the corridor, and Michael waited obediently by the door. Several minutes passed. Then Johnson reappeared with a curious expression on his face.

"There's something funny about this."

"Isn't the girl there?"

"She's there all right, but there's another woman there, too; and it's nobody we engaged either. She wants to see Hamilton Rutherford, and she looks as if she had something on her mind."

They went out into the hall. Planted firmly in a chair near the door sat an American girl a little the worse for liquor, but with a determined expression on her face. She looked up at them with a jerk of her head.

"Well, j'tell him?" she demanded. "The name is Marjorie Collins, and he'll know it. I've come a long way, and I want to see him now and quick, or there's going to be more trouble than you ever saw." She rose unsteadily to her feet.

"You go in and tell Ham," whispered Johnson to Michael. "Maybe he'd better get out. I'll keep her here."

Back at the table, Michael leaned close to Rutherford's ear and, with a certain grimness, whispered:

"A girl outside named Marjorie Collins says she wants to see you. She looks as if she wanted to make trouble."

Hamilton Rutherford blinked and his mouth fell ajar; then slowly the lips came together in a straight line and he said in a crisp voice:

"Please keep her there. And send the head barman to me right away."

Michael spoke to the barman, and then, without returning to the table, asked quietly for his coat and hat. Out in the hall again, he passed Johnson and the girl without speaking and went out into the Rue Cambon. Calling a cab, he gave the address of Caroline's hotel.

His place was beside her now. Not to bring bad news, but simply to be with her when her house of cards came falling around her head. Rutherford had implied that he was soft—well, he was hard enough not to give up the girl he loved without taking advantage of every chance within the pale of honor. Should she turn away from Rutherford, she would find him there.

She was in; she was surprised when he called, but she was still dressed and would be down immediately. Presently she appeared in a dinner gown, holding two blue telegrams in her hand. They sat down in armchairs in the deserted lobby.

"But, Michael, is the dinner over?"

"I wanted to see you, so I came away."

"I'm glad." Her voice was friendly, but matter-of-fact. "Because I'd just phoned your hotel that I had fittings and rehearsals all day tomorrow. Now we can have our talk after all."

"You're tired," he guessed. "Perhaps I shouldn't have come."

"No. I was waiting up for Hamilton. Telegrams that may be important. He said he might go on somewhere, and that may mean any hour, so I'm glad I have someone to talk to."

Michael winced at the impersonality in the last phrase.

"Don't you care when he gets home?"

"Naturally," she said, laughing, "but I haven't got much say about it, have I?"

"Why not?"

"I couldn't start by telling him what he could and couldn't do."

"Why not?"

"He wouldn't stand for it."

"He seems to want merely a housekeeper," said Michael ironically.

"Tell me about your plans, Michael," she asked quickly.

"My plans? I can't see any future after the day after tomorrow. The only real plan I ever had was to love you."

Their eyes brushed past each other's, and the look he knew so well was staring out at him from hers. Words flowed quickly from his heart:

"Let me tell you just once more how well I've loved you, never wavering for a moment, never thinking of another girl. And now when I think of all the years ahead without you, without any hope, I don't want to live, Caroline darling. I used to dream about our home, our children, about holding you in my arms and touching your face and hands and hair that used to belong to me, and now I just can't wake up."

Caroline was crying softly. "Poor Michael—poor Michael." Her hand reached out and her fingers brushed the lapel of his dinner coat. "I was so sorry for you the other night. You looked so thin, and as if you needed a new suit and somebody to take care of you." She sniffled and looked more closely at his coat. "Why, you've got a new suit! And a new silk hat! Why, Michael, how swell!" She laughed, suddenly cheerful through her tears. "You must have come into money, Michael; I never saw you so well turned out."

For a moment, at her reaction, he hated his new clothes.

"I have come into money," he said. "My grandfather left me about a quarter of a million dollars."

"Why, Michael," she cried, "how perfectly swell! I can't tell you how glad I am. I've always thought you were the sort of person who ought to have money."

"Yes, just too late to make a difference."

The revolving door from the street groaned around and Hamilton Rutherford came into the lobby. His face was flushed, his eyes were restless and impatient.

"Hello, darling; hello, Mr. Curly." He bent and kissed Caroline. "I broke away for a minute to find out if I had any telegrams. I see you've got them there." Taking them from her, he remarked to Curly, "That was an odd business there in the bar, wasn't it? Especially as I understand some of you had a joke fixed up in the same line." He opened one of the telegrams, closed it and turned to Caroline with the divided expression of a man carrying two things in his head at once.

"A girl I haven't seen for two years turned up," he said. "It seemed to be some clumsy form of blackmail, for I haven't and never have had any sort of obligation toward her whatever."

"What happened?"

"The head barman had a Sûreté Générale man there in ten minutes and it was settled in the hall. The French blackmail laws make ours look like a sweet wish, and I gather they threw a scare into her that she'll remember. But it seems wiser to tell you."

"Are you implying that I mentioned the matter?" said Michael stiffly.

"No," Rutherford said slowly. "No, you were just going to be on hand. And since you're here, I'll tell you some news that will interest you even more."

He handed Michael one telegram and opened the other.

"This is in code," Michael said.

"So is this. But I've got to know all the words pretty well this last week. The two of them together mean that I'm due to start life all over."

Michael saw Caroline's face grow a shade paler, but she sat quiet as a mouse.

"It was a mistake and I stuck to it too long," continued Rutherford. "So you see I don't have all the luck, Mr. Curly. By the way, they tell me you've come into money."

"Yes," said Michael.

"There we are, then." Rutherford turned to Caroline. "You understand, darling, that I'm not joking or exaggerating. I've lost almost every cent I had and I'm starting life over."

Two pairs of eyes were regarding her—Rutherford's noncommittal and unrequiring, Michael's hungry, tragic, pleading. In a minute she had raised herself from the chair and with a little cry thrown herself into Hamilton Rutherford's arms.

"Oh, darling," she cried, "what does it matter! It's better; I like it better, honestly I do! I want to start that way; I want to! Oh, please don't worry or be sad even for a minute!"

"All right, baby," said Rutherford. His hand stroked her hair gently for a moment; then he took his arm from around her.

"I promised to join the party for an hour," he said. "So I'll say good night, and I want you to go to bed soon and get a good sleep. Good night, Mr. Curly. I'm sorry to have let you in for all these financial matters."

But Michael had already picked up his hat and cane. "I'll go along with you," he said.

III

It was such a fine morning. Michael's cutaway hadn't been delivered, so he felt rather uncomfortable passing before the cameras and moving-picture machines in front of the little church on the Avenue George-Cinq.

It was such a clean, new church that it seemed unforgivable not to be dressed properly, and Michael, white and shaky after a sleepless night, decided to stand in the rear. From there he looked at the back of Hamilton Rutherford, and the lacy, filmy back of Caroline, and the fat back of George Packman, which looked unsteady, as if it wanted to lean against the bride and groom.

The ceremony went on for a long time under the gay flags and pennons overhead, under the thick beams of June sunlight slanting down through the tall windows upon the well-dressed people.

As the procession, headed by the bride and groom, started down the aisle, Michael realized with alarm he was just where everyone would dispense with their parade stiffness, become informal and speak to him.

So it turned out. Rutherford and Caroline spoke first to him; Rutherford grim with the strain of being married, and Caroline lovelier than he had ever seen her, floating all softly down through the friends and relatives of her youth, down through the past and forward to the future by the sunlit door.

Michael managed to murmur, "Beautiful, simply beautiful," and then other people passed and spoke to him—old Mrs. Dandy, straight from her sickbed and looking remarkably well, or carrying it off like the very fine old lady she was; and Rutherford's father and mother, ten years divorced, but walking side by side and looking made for each other and proud. Then all Caroline's sisters and their husbands and her little nephews in Eton suits, and then a long parade, all speaking to Michael because he was still standing paralyzed just at that point where the procession broke.

He wondered what would happen now. Cards had been issued for a reception at the George-Cinq; an expensive enough place, heaven knew. Would Rutherford try to go through with that on top of those disastrous telegrams? Evidently, for the procession outside was streaming up there through the June morning, three by three and four by four. On the corner the long dresses of girls, five abreast, fluttered many-colored in the wind. Girls had become gossamer again, perambulatory flora; such lovely fluttering dresses in the bright noon wind.

Michael needed a drink; he couldn't face that reception line without a drink. Diving into a side doorway of the hotel, he asked for the bar, whither a *chasseur* led him through half a kilometer of new American-looking passages.

But—how did it happen?—the bar was full. There were ten—fifteen men and two—four girls, all from the wedding, all needing a drink. There were cocktails and champagne in the bar; Rutherford's cocktails and champagne, as it turned out, for he had engaged the whole bar and the ballroom and the two great reception rooms and all the stairways leading up and down, and windows looking out over the whole square block of Paris. By and by Michael went and joined the long, slow drift of the receiving line. Through a flowery mist of "Such a lovely wedding," "My dear, you were simply lovely," "You're a lucky man, Rutherford" he passed down the line. When Michael came to Caroline, she took a single step forward and kissed him on the lips, but he felt no contact in the kiss; it was unreal and he floated on away from it. Old Mrs. Dandy, who had always liked him, held his hand for a minute and thanked him for the flowers he had sent when he heard she was ill.

"I'm so sorry not to have written; you know, we old ladies are grateful for——" The flowers, the fact that she had not written, the wedding—Michael saw that they all had the same relative importance to her now; she had married off five other children and seen two of the marriages go to pieces, and this scene, so poignant, so confusing to Michael, appeared to her simply a familiar charade in which she had played her part before.

A buffet luncheon with champagne was already being served at small tables and there was an orchestra playing in the empty ballroom. Michael sat down with Jebby West; he was still a little embarrassed at not wearing a morning coat, but he perceived now that he was not alone in the omission and felt better. "Wasn't Caroline divine?" Jebby West said. "So entirely self-possessed. I asked her this morning if she wasn't a little nervous at stepping off like this. And she said, 'Why should I be? I've been after him for two years, and now I'm just happy, that's all.'"

"It must be true," said Michael gloomily.

"What?"

"What you just said."

He had been stabbed, but, rather to his distress, he did not feel the wound.

He asked Jebby to dance. Out on the floor, Rutherford's father and mother were dancing together.

"It makes me a little sad, that," she said. "Those two hadn't met for years; both of them were married again and she divorced again. She went to the station to meet him when he came over for Caroline's wedding, and invited him to stay at her house in the Avenue du Bois with a whole lot of other people, perfectly proper, but he was afraid his wife would hear about it and not like it, so he went to a hotel. Don't you think that's sort of sad?"

An hour or so later Michael realized suddenly that it was afternoon. In one corner of the ballroom an arrangement of screens like a moving-picture stage had been set up and photographers were taking official pictures of the bridal party. The bridal party, still as death and pale as wax under the bright lights, appeared, to the dancers circling the modulated semidarkness of the ballroom, like those jovial or sinister groups that one comes upon in The Old Mill at an amusement park.

After the bridal party had been photographed, there was a group of the ushers; then the bridesmaids, the families, the children. Later, Caroline, active and excited, having long since abandoned the repose implicit in her flowing dress and great bouquet, came and plucked Michael off the floor.

"Now we'll have them take one of just old friends." Her voice implied that this was best, most intimate of all. "Come here, Jebby, George—not you, Hamilton; this is just my friends—Sally——"

A little after that, what remained of formality disappeared and the hours flowed easily down the profuse stream of champagne. In the modern fashion, Hamilton Rutherford sat at the table with his arm about an old girl of his and assured his guests, which included not a few bewildered but enthusiastic Europeans, that the party was not nearly at an end; it was to reassemble at Zelli's after midnight. Michael saw Mrs. Dandy, not quite over her illness, rise to go and become caught in polite group after group, and he spoke of it to one of her daughters, who thereupon forcibly abducted her mother and called her car. Michael felt very considerate and proud of himself after having done this, and drank much more champagne.

"It's amazing," George Packman was telling him enthusiastically. "This show will cost Ham about five thousand dollars, and I understand they'll be just about his last. But did he countermand a bottle of champagne or a flower? Not he! He happens to have it—that young man. Do you know that T. G. Vance offered him a salary of fifty thousand dollars a year ten minutes before the wedding this morning? In another year he'll be back with the millionaires."

The conversation was interrupted by a plan to carry Rutherford out on communal shoulders—a plan which six of them put into effect, and then stood in the four-o'clock sunshine waving good-by to the bride and groom. But there must have been a mistake somewhere, for five minutes later Michael saw both bride and groom descending the stairway to the reception, each with a glass of champagne held defiantly on high.

"This is our way of doing things," he thought. "Generous and fresh and free; a sort of Virgina-plantation hospitality, but at a different pace now, nervous as a ticker tape."

Standing unself-consciously in the middle of the room to see which was the American ambassador, he realized with a start that he hadn't really thought of Caroline for hours. He looked about him with a sort of alarm, and then he saw her across the room, very bright and young, and radiantly happy. He saw Rutherford near her, looking at her as if he could never look long enough, and as Michael watched them they seemed to recede as he had wished them to do that day in the Rue de Castiglione—recede and fade off into joys and griefs of their own, into the years that would take the toll of Rutherford's fine pride and Caroline's young, moving beauty; fade far away, so that now he could scarcely see them, as if they were shrouded in something as misty as her white, billowing dress.

Michael was cured. The ceremonial function, with its pomp and its revelry, had stood for a sort of initiation into a life where even his regret could not follow them. All the bitterness melted out of him suddenly and the world reconstituted itself out of the youth and happiness that was all around him, profligate as the spring sunshine. He was trying to remember which one of the bridesmaids he had made a date to dine with tonight as he walked forward to bid Hamilton and Caroline Rutherford good-by.

1930   *Previously Uncollected*

TWO WRONGS

I

"LOOK AT those shoes," said Bill—"twenty-eight dollars."

Mr. Brancusi looked. "Purty."

"Made to order."

"I knew you were a great swell. You didn't get me up here to show me those shoes, did you?"

"I am not a great swell. Who said I was a great swell?" demanded Bill. "Just because I've got more education than most people in show business."

"And then, you know, you're a handsome young fellow," said Brancusi dryly.

"Sure I am—compared to you anyhow. The girls think I must be an actor, till they find out. . . . Got a cigarette? What's more, I look like a man—which is more than most of these pretty boys round Times Square do."

"Good-looking. Gentleman. Good shoes. Shot with luck."

"You're wrong there," objected Bill. "Brains. Three years—nine shows—four big hits—only one flop. Where do you see any luck in that?"

A little bored, Brancusi just gazed. What he would have seen—had he not made his eyes opaque and taken to thinking about something else—was a fresh-faced young Irishman exuding aggressiveness and self-confidence until the air of his office was thick with it. Presently, Brancusi knew, Bill would hear the sound of his own voice and be ashamed and retire into his other humor—the quietly superior, sensitive one, the patron of the arts, modelled on the intellectuals of the Theatre Guild. Bill McChesney had not quite decided between the two, such blends are seldom complete before thirty.

"Take Ames, take Hopkins, take Harris—take any of them," Bill insisted. "What have they got on me? What's the matter? Do you want a drink?"—seeing Brancusi's glance wander toward the cabinet on the opposite wall.

"I never drink in the morning. I just wondered who was it keeps on knocking. You ought to make it stop it. I get a nervous fidgets, kind of half crazy, with that kind of thing."

Bill went quickly to the door and threw it open.

"Nobody," he said. . . . "Hello! What do you want?"

"Oh, I'm so sorry," a voice answered; "I'm terribly sorry. I got so excited and I didn't realize I had this pencil in my hand."

"What is it you want?"

"I want to see you, and the clerk said you were busy. I have a letter for you from Alan Rogers, the playwright—and I wanted to give it to you personally."

"I'm busy," said Bill. "See Mr. Cadorna."

"I did, but he wasn't very encouraging, and Mr. Rogers said—"

Brancusi, edging over restlessly, took a quick look at her. She was very young, with beautiful red hair, and more character in her face than her chatter would indicate; it did not occur to Mr. Brancusi that this was due to her origin in Delaney, South Carolina.

"What shall I do?" she inquired, quietly laying her future in Bill's hands. "I had a letter to Mr. Rogers, and he just gave me this one to you."

"Well, what do you want me to do—marry you?" exploded Bill.

"I'd like to get a part in one of your plays."

"Then sit down and wait. I'm busy. . . . Where's Miss Cohalan?" He rang a bell, looked once more, crossly, at the girl and closed the door of his office. But during the interruption his other mood had come over him, and he resumed his conversation with Brancusi in the key of one who was hand in glove with Reinhardt for the artistic future of the theatre.

By 12:30 he had forgotten everything except that he was going to be the greatest producer in the world and that he had an engagement to tell Sol Lincoln about it at lunch. Emerging from his office, he looked expectantly at Miss Cohalan.

"Mr. Lincoln won't be able to meet you," she said. "He jus' 'is minute called."

"Just this minute," repeated Bill, shocked. "All right. Just cross him off that list for Thursday night."

Miss Cohalan drew a line on a sheet of paper before her.

"Mr. McChesney, now you haven't forgotten me, have you?

He turned to the red-headed girl.

"No," he said vaguely, and then to Miss Cohalan: "That's all right: ask him for Thursday anyhow. To hell with him."

He did not want to lunch alone. He did not like to do anything alone now, because contacts were too much fun when one had prominence and power.

"If you would just let me talk to you two minutes—" she began.

"Afraid I can't now." Suddenly he realized that she was the most beautiful person he had ever seen in his life.

He stared at her.

"Mr. Rogers told me—"

"Come and have a spot of lunch with me," he said, and then, with an air of great hurry, he gave Miss Cohalan some quick and contradictory instructions and held open the door.

They stood on Forty-second Street and he breathed his pre-empted air—there is only enough air there for a few people at a time. It was November and the first exhilarating rush of the season was over, but he could look east and see the electric sign of one of his plays, and west and see another. Around the corner was the one he had put on with Brancusi—the last time he would produce anything except alone.

They went to the Bedford, where there was a to-do of waiters and captains as he came in.

"This is ver' tractive restaurant," she said, impressed and on company behavior.

"This is hams' paradise." He nodded to several people. "Hello, Jimmy—Bill. . . . Hello there, Jack. . . . That's Jack Dempsey. . . . I don't eat here much. I usually eat up at the Harvard Club."

"Oh, did you go to Harvard? I used to know—"

"Yes." He hesitated; there were two versions about Harvard, and he decided suddenly on the true one. "Yes, and they had me down for a hick there, but not any more. About a week ago I was out on Long Island at the Gouverneer Haights—very fashionable people— and a couple of Gold Coast boys that never knew I was alive up in Cambridge began pulling this 'Hello, Bill, old boy' on me."

He hesitated and suddenly decided to leave the story there.

"What do you want—a job?" he demanded. He remembered suddenly that she had holes in her stockings. Holes in stockings always moved him, softened him.

"Yes, or else I've got to go home," she said. "I want to be a dancer—you know, Russian Ballet. But the lessons cost so much. so I've got to get a job. I thought it'd give me stage presence anyhow."

"Hoofer, eh?"

"Oh, no, serious."

"Well, Pavlova's a hoofer, isn't she?"

"Oh, no." She was shocked at this profanity, but after a moment she continued: "I took with Miss Campbell—Georgia Berriman Campbell—back home—maybe you know her. She took from Ned Wayburn, and she's really wonderful. She—"

"Yeah?" he said abstractedly. "Well, it's a tough business—cast-

ing agencies bursting with people that can all do anything, till I
give them a try. How old are you?"

"Eighteen."

"I'm twenty-six. Came here four years ago without a cent."

"My!"

"I could quit now and be comfortable the rest of my life."

"My!"

"Going to take a year off next year—get married. . . . Ever
hear of Irene Rikker?"

"I should say! She's about my favorite of all."

"We're engaged."

"My!"

When they went out into Times Square after a while he said carelessly, "What are you doing now?"

"Why, I'm trying to get a job.

"I mean right this minute."

"Why, nothing."

"Do you want to come up to my apartment on Forty-sixth Street
and have some coffee?"

Their eyes met, and Emmy Pinkard made up her mind she could
take care of herself.

It was a great bright studio apartment with a ten-foot divan, and
after she had coffee and he a highball, his arm dropped round her
shoulder.

"Why should I kiss you?" she demanded. "I hardly know you,
and besides, you're engaged to somebody else."

"Oh, that! She doesn't care."

"No, really!"

"You're a good girl."

"Well, I'm certainly not an idiot."

"All right, go on being a good girl."

She stood up, but lingered a minute, very fresh and cool, and not
upset at all.

"I suppose this means you won't give me a job?" she asked pleasantly.

He was already thinking about something else—about an interview and a rehearsal—but now he looked at her again and saw that
she still had holes in her stockings. He telephoned:

"Joe, this is the Fresh Boy. . . . You didn't think I knew you
called me that, did you? . . . It's all right. . . . Say, have you got
those three girls for the party scene? Well, listen; save one for a
Southern kid I'm sending around today."

He looked at her jauntily, conscious of being such a good
fellow.

"Well, I don't know how to thank you. And Mr. Rogers," she added audaciously. "Good-by, Mr. McChesney."

He disdained to answer.

II

During rehearsal he used to come around a great deal and stand watching with a wise expression, as if he knew everything in people's minds; but actually he was in a haze about his own good fortune and didn't see much and didn't for the moment care. He spent most of his week-ends on Long Island with the fashionable people who had "taken him up." When Brancusi referred to him as the "big social butterfly," he would answer, "Well, what about it? Didn't I go to Harvard? You think they found me in a Grand Street apple cart, like you?" He was well liked among his new friends for his good looks and good nature, as well as his success.

His engagement to Irene Rikker was the most unsatisfactory thing in his life; they were tired of each other but unwilling to put an end to it. Just as, often, the two richest young people in a town are drawn together by the fact, so Bill McChesney and Irene Rikker, borne side by side on waves of triumph, could not spare each other's nice appreciation of what was due such success. Nevertheless, they indulged in fiercer and more frequent quarrels, and the end was approaching. It was embodied in one Frank Llewellen, a big, fine-looking actor playing opposite Irene. Seeing the situation at once, Bill became bitterly humorous about it; from the second week of rehearsals there was tension in the air.

Meanwhile Emmy Pinkard, with enough money for crackers and milk, and a friend who took her out to dinner, was being happy. Her friend, Easton Hughes from Delaney, was studying at Columbia to be a dentist. He sometimes brought along other lonesome young men studying to be dentists, and at the price, if it can be called that, of a few casual kisses in taxicabs, Emmy dined when hungry. One afternoon she introduced Easton to Bill McChesney at the stage door, and afterward Bill made his facetious jealousy the basis of their relationship.

"I see that dental number has been slipping it over on me again. Well, don't let him give you any laughing gas is my advice."

Though their encounters were few, they always looked at each other. When Bill looked at her he stared for an instant as if he had not seen her before, and then remembered suddenly that she was to be teased. When she looked at him she saw many things—a bright day outside, with great crowds of people hurrying through the streets; a very good new limousine that waited at the curb for

two people with very good new clothes, who got in and went somewhere that was just like New York, only away, and more fun there.
Many times she had wished she had kissed him, but just as many
times she was glad she hadn't; since, as the weeks passed he grew
less romantic, tied up, like the rest of them, to the play's laborious
evolution.

They were opening in Atlantic City. A sudden moodiness, apparent to everyone, came over Bill. He was short with the director and
sarcastic with the actors. This, it was rumored, was because Irene
Rikker had come down with Frank Llewellen on a different train.
Sitting beside the author on the night of the dress rehearsal, he was
an almost sinister figure in the twilight of the auditorium; but he
said nothing until the end of the second act, when, with Llewellen
and Irene Rikker on the stage alone, he suddenly called:

"We'll go over that again—and cut out the mush!"

Llewellen came down to the footlights.

"What do you mean—cut out the mush?" he inquired. "Those
are the lines, aren't they?"

"You know what I mean—stick to business."

"I don't know what you mean."

Bill stood up. "I mean all that damn whispering."

"There wasn't any whispering. I simply asked—"

"That'll do—take it over."

Llewellen turned away furiously and was about to proceed, when
Bill added audibly: "Even a ham has got to do his stuff."

Llewellen whipped about. "I don't have to stand that kind of talk,
Mr. McChesney."

"Why not? You're a ham, aren't you? When did you get ashamed
of being a ham? I'm putting on this play and I want you to stick
to your stuff." Bill got up and walked down the aisle. "And when
you don't do it, I'm going to call you just like anybody else."

"Well, you watch out for your tone of voice—"

"What'll you do about it?"

Llewellen jumped down into the orchestra pit.

"I'm not taking anything from you!" he shouted.

Irene Rikker called to them from the stage, "For heaven's sake,
are you two crazy?" And then Llewellen swung at him, one short,
mighty blow. Bill pitched back across a row of seats, fell through
one, splintering it, and lay wedged there. There was a moment's
wild confusion, then people holding Llewellen, then the author, with
a white face, pulling Bill up, and the stage manager crying: "Shall
I kill him, chief? Shall I break his fat face?" and Llewellen panting
and Irene Rikker frightened.

"Get back there!" Bill cried, holding a handkerchief to his face and teetering in the author's supporting arms. "Everybody get back! Take that scene again, and no talk! Get back, Llewellen!"

Before they realized it they were all back on the stage, Irene pulling Llewellen's arm and talking to him fast. Someone put on the auditorium lights full and then dimmed them again hurriedly. When Emmy came out presently for her scene, she saw in a quick glance that Bill was sitting with a whole mask of handkerchiefs over his bleeding face. She hated Llewellen and was afraid that presently they would break up and go back to New York. But Bill had saved the show from his own folly, since for Llewellen to take the further initiative of quitting would hurt his professional standing. The act ended and the next one began without an interval. When it was over, Bill was gone.

Next night, during the performance, he sat on a chair in the wings in view of everyone coming on or off. His face was swollen and bruised, but he neglected to seem conscious of the fact and there were no comments. Once he went around in front, and when he returned, word leaked out that two of the New York agencies were making big buys. He had a hit—they all had a hit.

At the sight of him to whom Emmy felt they all owed so much, a great wave of gratitude swept over her. She went up and thanked him.

"I'm a good picker, red-head," he agreed grimly.

"Thank you for picking me."

And suddenly Emmy was moved to a rash remark.

"You've hurt your face so badly!" she exclaimed. "Oh, I think it was so brave of you not to let everything go to pieces last night."

He looked at her hard for a moment and then an ironic smile tried unsuccessfully to settle on his swollen face.

"Do you admire me, baby?"

"Yes."

"Even when I fell in the seats, did you admire me?"

"You got control of everything so quick."

"That's loyalty for you. You found something to admire in that fool mess."

And her happiness bubbled up into, "Anyhow, you behaved just wonderfully." She looked so fresh and young that Bill, who had had a wretched day, wanted to rest his swollen cheek against her cheek.

He took both the bruise and the desire with him to New York next morning; the bruise faded, but the desire remained. And when they opened in the city, no sooner did he see other men begin to crowd around her beauty than she became this play for him, this success, the thing that he came to see when he came to the theatre. After a good run it closed just as he was drinking too much and needed someone on the gray days of reaction. They were married suddenly in Connecticut, early in June.

III

Two men sat in the Savoy Grill in London, waiting for the Fourth of July. It was already late in May.

"Is he a nice guy?" asked Hubbel.

"Very nice," answered Brancusi; "very nice, very handsome, very popular." After a moment, he added: "I want to get him to come home."

"That's what I don't get about him," said Hubbel. "Show business over here is nothing compared to home. What does he want to stay here for?"

"He goes around with a lot of dukes and ladies."

"Oh?"

"Last week when I met him he was with three ladies—Lady this, Lady that, Lady the other thing."

"I thought he was married."

"Married three years," said Brancusi, "got a fine child, going to have another."

He broke off as McChesney came in, his very American face staring about boldly over the collar of a box-shouldered topcoat.

"Hello, Mac; meet my friend Mr. Hubbel."

"J'doo," said Bill. He sat down, continuing to stare around the bar to see who was present. After a few minutes Hubbel left, and Bill asked:

"Who's that bird?"

"He's only been here a month. He ain't got a title yet. You been here six months, remember."

Bill grinned.

"You think I'm high-hat, don't you? Well, I'm not kidding myself anyhow. I like it; it gets me. I'd like to be the Marquis of McChesney."

"Maybe you can drink yourself into it," suggested Brancusi.

"Shut your trap. Who said I was drinking? Is that what they say now? Look here; if you can tell me any American manager in the history of the theatre who's had the success that I've had in London in less than eight months, I'll go back to America with you tomorrow. If you'll just tell me—"

"It was with your old shows. You had two flops in New York."

Bill stood up, his face hardening.

"Who do you think you are?" he demanded. "Did you come over here to talk to me like that?"

"Don't get sore now, Bill. I just want you to come back. I'd say anything for that. Put over three seasons like you had in '22 and '23, and you're fixed for life."

"New York makes me sick," said Bill moodily. "One minute you're a king; then you have two flops, they go around saying you're on the toboggan."

Brancusi shook his head.

"That wasn't why they said it. It was because you had that quarrel with Aronstael, your best friend."

"Friend hell!"

"Your best friend in business anyhow. Then—"

"I don't want to talk about it." He looked at his watch. "Look here; Emmy's feeling bad so I'm afraid I can't have dinner with you tonight. Come around to the office before you sail."

Five minutes later, standing by the cigar counter, Brancusi saw Bill enter the Savoy again and descend the steps that led to the tea room.

"Grown to be a great diplomat," thought Brancusi; "he used to just say when he had a date. Going with these dukes and ladies is polishing him up even more."

Perhaps he was a little hurt, though it was not typical of him to be hurt. At any rate he made a decision, then and there, that McChesney was on the down grade; it was quite typical of him that at that point he erased him from his mind forever.

There was no outward indication that Bill was on the down grade; a hit at the New Strand, a hit at the Prince of Wales, and the weekly grosses pouring in almost as well as they had two or three years before in New York. Certainly a man of action was justified in changing his base. And the man who, an hour later, turned into his Hyde Park house for dinner had all the vitality of the late twenties. Emmy, very tired and clumsy, lay on a couch in the upstairs sitting room. He held her for a moment in his arms.

"Almost over now," he said. "You're beautiful."

"Don't be ridiculous."

"It's true. You're always beautiful. I don't know why. Perhaps because you've got character, and that's always in your face, even when you're like this."

She was pleased; she ran her hand through his hair.

"Character is the greatest thing in the world," he declared, "and you've got more than anybody I know."

"Did you see Brancusi?"

"I did, the little louse! I decided not to bring him home to dinner."

"What was the matter?"

"Oh, just snooty—talking about my row with Aronstael, as if it was my fault."

She hesitated, closed her mouth tight and then said quietly, "You got into that fight with Aronstael because you were drinking."

He rose impatiently.

"Are you going to start—"

"No, Bill, but you're drinking too much now. You know you are."

Aware that she was right, he evaded the matter and they went in to dinner. On the glow of a bottle of claret he decided he would go on the wagon tomorrow till after the baby was born.

"I always stop when I want, don't I? I always do what I say. You never saw me quit yet."

"Never yet."

They had coffee together, and afterward he got up.

"Come back early," said Emmy.

"Oh, sure. . . . What's the matter, baby?"

"I'm just crying. Don't mind me. Oh, go on; don't just stand there like a big idiot."

"But I'm worried, naturally. I don't like to see you cry."

"Oh, I don't know where you go in the evenings; I don't know who you're with. And that Lady Sybil Combrinck who kept phoning. It's all right, I suppose, but I wake up in the night and I feel so alone, Bill. Because we've always been together, haven't we, until recently?"

"But we're together still . . . What's happened to you, Emmy?"

"I know—I'm just crazy. We'd never let each other down, would we? We never have—"

"Of course not."

"Come back early, or when you can."

He looked in for a minute at the Prince of Wales Theatre; then he went into the hotel next door and called a number.

"I'd like to speak to her Ladyship. Mr. McChesney calling."

It was some time before Lady Sybil answered:

"This is rather a surprise. It's been several weeks since I've been lucky enough to hear from you."

Her voice was flip as a whip and cold as automatic refrigeration, in the mode grown familiar since British ladies took to piecing themselves together out of literature. It had fascinated Bill for a while, but just for a while. He had kept his head.

"I haven't had a minute," he explained easily. "You're not sore, are you?"

"I should scarcely say 'sore'."

"I was afraid you might be; you didn't send me an invitation to you party tonight. My idea was that after we talked it all over we agreed—"

"You talked a great deal," she said; "possibly a little too much." Suddenly, to Bill's astonishment, she hung up.

"Going British on me," he thought. "A little skit entitled The Daughter of a Thousand Earls."

The snub roused him, the indifference revived his waning interest. Usually women forgave his changes of heart because of his obvious devotion to Emmy, and he was remembered by various ladies with a not unpleasant sigh. But he had detected no such sigh upon the phone.

"I'd like to clear up this mess," he thought. Had he been wearing evening clothes, he might have dropped in at the dance and talked it over with her, still he didn't want to go home. Upon consideration it seemed important that the misunderstanding should be fixed up at once, and presently he began to entertain the idea of going as he was; Americans were excused unconventionalities of dress. In any case, it was not nearly time, and, in the company of several highballs, he considered the matter for an hour.

At midnight he walked up the steps of her Mayfair house. The coat-room attendants scrutinized his tweeds disapprovingly and a footman peered in vain for his name on the list of guests. Fortunately his friend Sir Humphrey Dunn arrived at the same time and convinced the footman it must be a mistake.

Inside, Bill immediately looked about for his hostess.

She was a very tall young woman, half American and all the more intensely English. In a sense, she had discovered Bill McChesney, vouched for his savage charms; his retirement was one of her most humiliating experiences since she had begun being bad.

She stood with her husband at the head of the receiving line—Bill had never seen them together before. He decided to choose a less formal moment for presenting himself.

As the receiving went on interminably, he became increasingly uncomfortable. He saw a few people he knew, but not many, and he was conscious that his clothes were attracting a certain attention; he was aware also that Lady Sybil saw him and could have relieved his embarrassment with a wave of her hand, but she made no sign. He was sorry he had come, but to withdraw now would be absurd, and going to a buffet table, he took a glass of champagne.

When he turned around she was alone at last, and he was about to approach her when the butler spoke to him:

"Pardon me, sir. Have you a card?"

"I'm a friend of Lady Sybil's," said Bill impatiently. He turned away, but the butler followed.

"I'm sorry, sir, but I'll have to ask you to step aside with me and straighten this up."

"There's no need. I'm just about to speak to Lady Sybil now."

"My orders are different, sir," said the butler firmly.

Then, before Bill realized what was happening, his arms were pressed quietly to his sides and he was propelled into a little ante-room back of the buffet.

There he faced a man in a pince-nez in whom he recognized the Combrincks' private secretary.

The secretary nodded to the butler, saying, "This is the man"; whereupon Bill was released.

"Mr. McChesney," said the secretary, "you have seen fit to force your way here without a card, and His Lordship requests that you leave his house at once. Will you kindly give me the check for your coat?"

Then Bill understood, and the single word that he found applicable to Lady Sybil sprang to his lips; whereupon the secretary gave a sign to two footmen, and in a furious struggle Bill was carried through a pantry where busy bus boys stared at the scene, down a long hall, and pushed out a door into the night. The door closed; a moment later it was opened again to let his coat billow forth and his cane clatter down the steps.

As he stood there, overwhelmed, stricken aghast, a taxicab stopped beside him and the driver called:

"Feeling ill, gov'nor?"

"What?"

"I know where you can get a good pick-me-up, gov'nor. Never too late." The door of the taxi opened on a nightmare. There was a cabaret that broke the closing hours; there was being with strangers he had picked up somewhere; then there were arguments, and trying to cash a check, and suddenly proclaiming over and over that he was William McChesney, the producer, and convincing no one of the fact, not even himself. It seemed important to see Lady Sybil right away and call her to account; but presently nothing was important at all. He was in a taxicab whose driver had just shaken him awake in front of his own home.

The telephone was ringing as he went in, but he walked stonily past the maid and only heard her voice when his foot was on the stair.

"Mr. McChesney, it's the hospital calling again. Mrs. McChesney's there and they've been phoning every hour."

Still in a daze, he held the receiver up to his ear.

"We're calling from the Midland Hospital, for your wife. She was delivered of a still-born child at nine this morning."

"Wait a minute." His voice was dry and cracking. "I don't understand."

After a while he understood that Emmy's child was dead and
she wanted him. His knees sagged groggily as he walked down the
street, looking for a taxi.

The room was dark; Emmy looked up and saw him from a rumpled bed.

"It's you!" she cried. "I thought you were dead! Where did
you go?"

He threw himself down on his knees beside the bed, but she
turned away.

"Oh, you smell awful," she said. "It makes me sick."

But she kept her hand in his hair, and he knelt there motionless
for a long time.

"I'm done with you," she muttered, "but it was awful when I
thought you were dead. Everybody's dead. I wish I was dead."

A curtain parted with the wind, and as he rose to arrange it, she
saw him in the full morning light, pale and terrible, with rumpled
clothes and bruises on his face. This time she hated him instead of
those who had hurt him. She could feel him slipping out of her
heart, feel the space he left, and all at once he was gone, and she
could even forgive him and be sorry for him. All this in a minute.

She had fallen down at the door of the hospital, trying to get out
of the taxicab alone.

IV

When Emmy was well, physically and mentally, her incessant idea
was to learn to dance; the old dream inculcated by Miss Georgia
Berriman Campbell of South Carolina persisted as a bright avenue
leading back to first youth and days of hope in New York. To her,
dancing meant that elaborate blend of tortuous attitudes and formal
pirouettes that evolved out of Italy several hundred years ago and
reached its apogee in Russia at the beginning of this century. She
wanted to use herself on something she could believe in, and it
seemed to her that the dance was woman's interpretation of music;
instead of strong fingers, one had limbs with which to render.
Tschaikowsky and Stravinski; and feet could be as eloquent in
Chopiniana as voices in "The Ring." At the bottom, it was something sandwiched in between the acrobats and the trained seals; at
the top it was Pavlova and art.

Once they were settled in an apartment back in New York, she
plunged into her work like a girl of sixteen—four hours a day at
bar exercises, attitudes, sauts, arabesques and pirouettes. It became

the realest part of her life, and her only worry was whether or not she was too old. At twenty-six she had ten years to make up, but she was a natural dancer with a fine body—and that lovely face.

Bill encouraged it; when she was ready he was going to build the first real American ballet around her. There were even times when he envied her her absorption; for affairs in his own line were more difficult since they had come home. For one thing, he had made enemies in those early days of self-confidence; there were exaggerated stories of his drinking and of his being hard on actors and difficult to work with.

It was against him that he had always been unable to save money and must beg a backing for each play. Then, too, in a curious way, he was intelligent, as he was brave enough to prove in several uncommercial ventures, but he had no Theatre Guild behind him, and what money he lost was charged against him.

There were successes, too, but he worked harder for them, or it seemed so, for he had begun to pay a price for his irregular life. He always intended to take a rest or give up his incessant cigarettes, but there was so much competition now—new men coming up, with new reputations for infallibility—and besides, he wasn't used to regularity. He liked to do his work in those great spurts, inspired by black coffee, that seem so inevitable in show business, but which took so much out of a man after thirty. He had come to lean, in a way, on Emmy's fine health and vitality. They were always together, and if he felt a vague dissatisfaction that he had grown to need her more than she needed him, there was always the hope that things would break better for him next month, next season.

Coming home from ballet school one November evening, Emmy swung her little gray bag, pulled her hat far down over her still damp hair, and gave herself up to pleasant speculation. For a month she had been aware of people who had come to the studio especially to watch her—she was ready to dance. Once she had worked just as hard and for as long a time on something else—her relations with Bill—only to reach a climax and misery and despair, but here there was nothing to fail her except herself. Yet even now she felt a little rash in thinking: "Now it's come. I'm going to be happy."

She hurried, for something had come up today that she must talk over with Bill.

Finding him in the living room, she called him to come back while she dressed. She began to talk without looking around:

"Listen what happened!" Her voice was loud, to compete with the water running in the tub. "Paul Makova wants me to dance with him at the Metropolitan this season; only it's not sure, so it's a secret—even I'm not supposed to know."

"That's great."

"The only thing is whether it wouldn't be better for me to make a début abroad? Anyhow Donilof says I'm ready to appear. What do you think?"

"I don't know."

"You don't sound very enthusiastic."

"I've got something on my mind. I'll tell you about it later. Go on."

"That's all, dear. If you still feel like going to Germany for a month, like you said, Donilof would arrange a début for me in Berlin, but I'd rather open here and dance with Paul Makova. Just imagine—" She broke off, feeling suddenly through the thick skin of her elation how abstracted he was. "Tell me what you've got on your mind."

"I went to Doctor Kearns this afternoon."

"What did he say?" Her mind was still singing with her own happiness. Bill's intermittent attacks of hypochondria had long ceased to worry her.

"I told him about that blood this morning, and he said what he said last year—it was probably a little broken vein in my throat. But since I'd been coughing and was worried, perhaps it was safer to take an X-ray and clear the matter up. Well, we cleared it up all right. My left lung is practically gone."

"Bill!"

"Luckily there are no spots on the other."

She waited, horribly afraid.

"It's come at a bad time for me," he went on steadily, "but it's got to be faced. He thinks I ought to go to the Adirondacks or to Denver for the winter, and his idea is Denver. That way it'll probably clear up in five or six months."

"Of course we'll have to—" she stopped suddenly.

"I wouldn't expect you to go—especially if you have this opportunity."

"Of course I'll go," she said quickly. "Your health comes first. We've always gone everywhere together."

"Oh, no."

"Why, of course." She made her voice strong and decisive. "We've always been together. I couldn't stay here without you. When do you have to go?"

"As soon as possible. I went in to see Brancusi to find out if he wanted to take over the Richmond piece, but he didn't seem enthusiastic." His face hardened. "Of course there won't be anything else for the present, but I'll have enough, with what's owing—"

"Oh, if I was only making some money!" Emmy cried. "You work so hard and here I've been spending two hundred dollars a week for just my dancing lessons alone—more than I'll be able to earn for years."

"Of course in six months I'll be as well as ever—he says."

"Sure, dearest; we'll get you well. We'll start as soon as we can."

She put an arm around him and kissed his cheek.

"I'm just an old parasite," she said. "I should have known my darling wasn't well."

He reached automatically for a cigarette, and then stopped.

"I forgot—I've got to start cutting down smoking." He rose to the occasion suddenly: "No, baby, I've decided to go alone. You'd go crazy with boredom out there, and I'd just be thinking I was keeping you away from your dancing."

"Don't think about that. The thing is to get you well."

They discussed the matter hour after hour for the next week, each of them saying everything except the truth—that he wanted her to go with him and that she wanted passionately to stay in New York. She talked it over guardedly with Donilof, her ballet master, and found that he thought any postponement would be a terrible mistake. Seeing other girls in the ballet school making plans for the winter, she wanted to die rather than go, and Bill saw all the involuntary indications of her misery. For a while they talked of compromising on the Adirondacks, whither she would commute by aeroplane for the week-ends, but he was running a little fever now and he was definitely ordered West.

Bill settled it all one gloomy Sunday night, with that rough, generous justice that had first made her admire him, that made him rather tragic in his adversity, as he had always been bearable in his overweening success:

"It's just up to me, baby. I got into this mess because I didn't have any self-control—you seem to have all of that in this family—and now it's only me that can get me out. You've worked hard at your stuff for three years and you deserve your chance—and if you came out there now you'd have it on me the rest of my life." He grinned. "And I couldn't stand that. Besides, it wouldn't be good for the kid."

Eventually she gave in, ashamed of herself, miserable—and glad. For the world of her work, where she existed without Bill, was bigger to her now than the world in which they existed together. There was more room to be glad in one than to be sorry in the other.

Two days later, with his ticket bought for that afternoon at five, they passed the last hours together, talking of everything hopeful. She protested still, and sincerely; had he weakened for a moment she would have gone. But the shock had done something to him, and he showed more character under it than he had for years. Perhaps it would be good for him to work it out alone.

"In the spring!" they said.

Then in the station with little Billy, and Bill saying: "I hate these grave-side partings. You leave me here. I've got to make a phone call from the train before it goes."

They had never spent more than a night apart in six years, save when Emmy was in the hospital; save for the time in England they had a good record of faithfulness and of tenderness toward each other, even though she had been alarmed and often unhappy at this insecure bravado from the first. After he went through the gate alone, Emmy was glad he had a phone call to make and tried to picture him making it.

She was a good woman; she had loved him with all her heart. When she went out into Thirty-third Street, it was just as dead as dead for a while, and the apartment he paid for would be empty of him, and she was here, about to do something that would make her happy.

She stopped after a few blocks, thinking: "Why, this is terrible—what I'm doing! I'm letting him down like the worst person I ever heard of. I'm leaving him flat and going off to dinner with Donilof and Paul Makova, whom I like for being beautiful and for having the same color eyes and hair. Bill's on the train alone."

She swung little Billy around suddenly as if to go back to the station. She could see him sitting in the train, with his face so pale and tired, and no Emmy.

"I can't let him down," she cried to herself as wave after wave of sentiment washed over her. But only sentiment—hadn't he let her down—hadn't he done what he wanted in London?

"Oh, poor Bill!"

She stood irresolute, realizing for one last honest moment how quickly she would forget this and find excuses for what she was doing. She had to think hard of London, and her conscience cleared. But with Bill all alone in the train it seemed terrible to think that way. Even now she could turn and go back to the station and tell him that she was coming, but still she waited, with life very strong in her, fighting for her. The sidewalk was narrow where she stood; presently a great wave of people, pouring out of the theatre, came flooding along it, and she and little Billy were swept along with the crowd.

In the train, Bill telephoned up to the last minute, postponed going back to his stateroom, because he knew it was almost certain that he would not find her there. After the train started he went back and, of course, there was nothing but his bags in the rack and some magazines on the seat.

He knew then that he had lost her. He saw the set-up without any illusions—this Paul Makova, and months of proximity, and loneliness—afterward nothing would ever be the same. When he had thought about it all a long time, reading *Variety* and *Zit's* in between, it began to seem, each time he came back to it, as if Emmy somehow were dead.

"She was a fine girl—one of the best. She had character." He realized perfectly that he had brought all this on himself and that there was some law of compensation involved. He saw, too, that by going away he had again become as good as she was; it was all evened up at last.

He felt beyond everything, even beyond his grief, an almost comfortable sensation of being in the hands of something bigger than himself; and grown a little tired and unconfident—two qualities he could never for a moment tolerate—it did not seem so terrible if he were going West for a definite finish. He was sure that Emmy would come at the end, no matter what she was doing or how good an engagement she had.

1930   *Taps at Reveille*

III

Retrospective: Basil and Josephine

EDITOR'S NOTE

WHEN I said in the Introduction that Fitzgerald's stories, taken together, formed a sort of autobiography, I did not mean to suggest that they could be followed as a guide to the events of his life. They changed or disguised the events, as stories always do, but the best of them served as a faithful record of his emotions. In the end it was his life, as lived, that became the most impressive of his fictional creations. If we have some knowledge of the life it gives a new dimension to the stories, and these in turn help us to understand the life by telling us how Fitzgerald felt in each new situation.

That is the rule, but the Basil stories are an exception. Written in 1928, they tell us nothing about Fitzgerald's emotions at the time, except that he was unhappy about himself and in a mood for retrospection. He relived his boyhood in the stories and made little effort to disguise the fact that he was writing autobiography. Almost every incident happened in life and almost every character can be identified. Basil Duke Lee was of course Fitzgerald himself; his friends Riply Buckner, Bill Kempf and Hubert Blair were, in life and respectively, Cecil Reid, Paul Ballion and Reuben Warner. The Scandal Detectives of the story really existed and their Book of Scandal has been preserved, in the shape of a "Thoughtbook" that Fitzgerald kept when he was fourteen; most of his thoughts were about girls. St. Regis School, where Basil was "The Freshest Boy," was of course the Newman School; during his first year at Newman, Fitzgerald was just as miserable as his hero. "The Captured Shadow" was the name of a play that he wrote and directed for the Elizabethan Club in St. Paul before his sixteenth birthday. It was a success, as in the story.

There were nine Basil stories in all; one has never been published and the other eight appeared in the *Saturday Evening Post*. Maxwell Perkins wanted to publish them as a book, but Fitzgerald hesitated—partly because he feared they were too much like the

Penrod stories that Booth Tarkington had written as he emerged
from a period of heavy drinking. Actually the Penrod stories were
of another generation and they were observed, not felt from within,
but that didn't comfort Fitzgerald. He said in his notebook: "Tarkington. I have a horror of going into a personal debauch and coming
out of it devitalized with no interest except an acute observation of
the behavior of colored people, children and dogs." At last Perkins
persuaded him to revise five of the stories (not including Perkins'
favorite, "A Night at the Fair") for republication in *Taps at Reveille*.
I have included three of the revised stories in the present group. "The
Captured Shadow" is by far the best, for its self-portrait of a writer
at the begining of his career, but "The Freshest Boy" is a minor
classic of prep-school life and "The Scandal Detectives" contains a
fine picture of the children gathering in the Whartons' yard "for that
soft and romantic time before supper."

The Josephine stories—five of them, published in 1930 and 1931—
were also retrospective, but in a different fashion, since Fitzgerald
was trying to think his way back into the mind of a girl with whom
he was desperately in love during his years at Princeton. She was also
Isabelle, in *This Side of Paradise*, and suggested the heroine of
"Winter Dreams." Long afterwards she said of the stories, in a letter
to Arthur Mizener, "I was too thoughtless in those days and too much
in love with love to think of consequences. These things he has em-
phasized—and overemphasized in the Josephine stories, but it is
only fair to say that I asked for some of them." When she paid a
short visit to Hollywood in 1937 Fitzgerald had lunch with her and
was almost ready to fall in love all over again.

At one time he considered making a book out of the stories, called
My Girl Josephine, but most of them were too loosely constructed to
be his best work. Three were reprinted in *Taps at Reveille*. "A
Woman with a Past," included here, is better than the others for its
insights into the dreams of a boarding-school girl and its picture of
her first big dance at New Haven.

THE SCANDAL DETECTIVES

I

IT WAS a hot afternoon in May and Mrs. Buckner thought that a pitcher of fruit lemonade might prevent the boys from filling up on ice cream at the drug store. She belonged to that generation, since retired, upon whom the great revolution in American family life was to be visited; but at that time she believed that her children's relation to her was much as hers had been to her parents, for this was more than twenty years ago.

Some generations are close to those that succeed them; between others the gap is infinite and unbridgeable. Mrs. Buckner—a woman of character, a member of Society in a large Middle-Western city—carrying a pitcher of fruit lemonade through her own spacious back yard, was progressing across a hundred years. Her own thoughts would have been comprehensible to her great-grandmother; what was happening in a room above the stable would have been entirely unintelligible to them both. In what had once served as the coachman's sleeping apartment, her son and a friend were not behaving in a normal manner, but were, so to speak, experimenting in a void. They were making the first tentative combinations of the ideas and materials they found ready at their hand—ideas destined to become, in future years, first articulate, then startling and finally commonplace. At the moment when she called up to them they were sitting with disarming quiet upon the still unhatched eggs of the mid-twentieth century.

Riply Buckner descended the ladder and took the lemonade. Basil Duke Lee looked abstractedly down at the transaction and said, "Thank you very much, Mrs. Buckner."

"Are you sure it isn't too hot up there?"

"No, Mrs. Buckner. It's fine."

It was stifling; but they were scarcely conscious of the heat, and they drank two tall glasses each of the lemonade without knowing that they were thirsty. Concealed beneath a sawed-out trapdoor from which they presently took it was a composition book bound in imitation red leather which currently absorbed much of their attention. On its first page was inscribed, if you penetrated the secret of the lemon-juice ink: "THE BOOK OF SCANDAL, written by Riply Buckner, Jr., and Basil D. Lee, Scandal Detectives."

In this book they had set down such deviations from rectitude on the part of their fellow citizens as had reached their ears. Some of these false steps were those of grizzled men, stories that had become traditions in the city and were embalmed in the composition book by virtue of indiscreet exhumations at family dinner tables. Others were the more exciting sins, confirmed or merely rumored, of boys and girls their own age. Some of the entries would have been read by adults with bewilderment, others might have inspired wrath, and there were three or four contemporary reports that would have prostrated the parents of the involved children with horror and despair.

One of the mildest items, a matter they had hesitated about setting down, though it had shocked them only last year, was: "Elwood Leaming has been to the Burlesque Show three or four times at the Star."

Another, and perhaps their favorite, because of its uniqueness, set forth that "H. P. Cramner committed some theft in the East he could be imprisoned for and had to come here"—H. P. Cramner being now one of the oldest and "most substantial" citizens of the city.

The single defect in the book was that it could only be enjoyed with the aid of the imagination, for the invisible ink must keep its secrets until that day when, the pages being held close to the fire, the items would appear. Close inspection was necessary to determine which pages had been used—already a rather grave charge against a certain couple had been superimposed upon the dismal facts that Mrs. R. B. Cary had consumption and that her son, Walter Cary, had been expelled from Pawling School. The purpose of the work as a whole was not blackmail. It was treasured against the time when its protagonists should "do something" to Basil and Riply. Its possession gave them a sense of power. Basil, for instance, had never seen Mr. H. P. Cramner make a single threatening gesture in Basil's direction, but let him even hint that he was going to do something to Basil and there preserved against him was the record of his past.

It is only fair to say that at this point the book passes entirely out of this story. Years later a janitor discovered it beneath the trap-door, and finding it apparently blank, gave it to his little girl; so the misdeeds of Elwood Leaming and H. P. Cramner were definitely entombed at last beneath a fair copy of Lincoln's Gettysburg Address.

The book was Basil's idea. He was more the imaginative and in most ways the stronger of the two. He was a shining-eyed, brown-

haired boy of fourteen, rather small as yet, and bright and lazy at
school. His favorite character in fiction was Arsène Lupin, the gentleman burglar, a romantic phenomenon lately imported from Europe
and much admired in the first bored decades of the century.

Riply Buckner, also in short pants, contributed to the partnership
a breathless practicality. His mind waited upon Basil's imagination
like a hair trigger and no scheme was too fantastic for his immediate
"Let's do it!" Since the school's third baseball team, on which they
had been pitcher and catcher, decomposed after an unfortunate April
season, they had spent their afternoons struggling to evolve a way
of life which should measure up to the mysterious energies ferment-
ing inside them. In the cache beneath the trapdoor were some
"slouch" hats and bandanna handkerchiefs, some loaded dice, half of
a pair of handcuffs, a rope ladder of a tenuous crochet persuasion for
rear-window escapes into the alley, and a make-up box containing
two old theatrical wigs and crêpe hair of various colors—all to be
used when they decided what illegal enterprises to undertake.

Their lemonades finished, they lit Home Runs and held a desultory
conversation which touched on crime, professional baseball, sex and
the local stock company. This broke off at the sound of footsteps and
familiar voices in the adjoining alley.

From the window, they investigated. The voices belonged to Margaret Torrence, Imogene Bissel and Connie Davies, who were cutting
through the alley from Imogene's back yard to Connie's at the end
of the block. The young ladies were thirteen, twelve and thirteen
years old respectively, and they considered themselves alone, for in
time to their march they were rendering a mildly daring parody in
a sort of whispering giggle and coming out strongly on the finale:
"Oh, my dar-ling Clemen-tine."

Basil and Riply leaned together from the window, then remembering their undershirts sank down behind the sill.

"We heard you!" they cried together.

The girls stopped and laughed. Margaret Torrence chewed exag-
geratedly to indicate gum, and gum with a purpose. Basil immediately understood.

"Whereabouts?" he demanded.

"Over at Imogene's house."

They had been at Mrs. Bissel's cigarettes. The implied recklessness
of their mood interested and excited the two boys and they prolonged the conversation. Connie Davies had been Riply's girl during
dancing-school term; Margaret Torrence had played a part in Basil's
recent past; Imogene Bissel was just back from a year in Europe.
During the last month neither Basil nor Riply had thought about
girls, and, thus refreshed, they became conscious that the centre of

the world had shifted suddenly from the secret room to the little group outside.

"Come on up," they suggested.

"Come on out. Come on down to the Whartons' yard."

"All right."

Barely remembering to put away the Scandal Book and the box of disguises, the two boys hurried out, mounted their bicycles and rode up the alley.

The Whartons' own children had long grown up, but their yard was still one of those predestined places where young people gather in the afternoon. It had many advantages. It was large, open to other yards on both sides, and it could be entered upon skates or bicycles from the street. It contained an old seesaw, a swing and a pair of flying rings; but it had been a rendezvous before these were put up, for it had a child's quality—the thing that makes young people huddle inextricably on uncomfortable steps and desert the houses of their friends to herd on the obscure premises of "people nobody knows." The Whartons' yard had long been a happy compromise; there were deep shadows there all day long and ever something vague in bloom, and patient dogs around, and brown spots worn bare by countless circling wheels and dragging feet. In sordid poverty, below the bluff two hundred feet away, lived the "micks"—they had merely inherited the name, for they were now largely of Scandinavian descent—and when other amusements palled, a few cries were enough to bring a gang of them swarming up the hill, to be faced if numbers promised well, to be fled from into convenient houses if things went the other way.

It was five o'clock and there was a small crowd gathered there for that soft and romantic time before supper—a time surpassed only by the interim of summer dusk thereafter. Basil and Riply rode their bicycles around abstractedly, in and out of trees, resting now and then with a hand on someone's shoulder, shading their eyes from the glow of the late sun that, like youth itself, is too strong to face directly, but must be kept down to an undertone until it dies away.

Basil rode over to Imogene Bissel and balanced idly on his wheel before her. Something in his face then must have attracted her, for she looked up at him, looked at him really, and slowly smiled. She was to be a beauty and belle of many proms in a few years. Now her large brown eyes and large beautifully shaped mouth and the high flush over her thin cheek bones made her face gnome-like and offended those who wanted a child to look like a child. For a moment Basil was granted an insight into the future; the spell of her vitality crept over him suddenly. For the first time in his life he realized a girl completely as something opposite and complementary to him, and he was subject to a warm chill of mingled pleasure and pain. It was a definite experience and he was immediately conscious of it. The summer afternoon became lost in her suddenly—the soft air, the shadowy hedges and banks of flowers, the orange sunlight, the laughter and voices, the tinkle of a piano over the way—the odor left all these things and went into Imogene's face as she sat there looking up at him with a smile.

For a moment it was too much for him. He let it go, incapable of exploiting it until he had digested it alone. He rode around fast in a circle on his bicycle, passing near Imogene without looking at her. When he came back after a while and asked if he could walk home with her, she had forgotten the moment, if it had ever existed for her, and was almost surprised. With Basil wheeling his bicycle beside her, they started down the street.

"Can you come out tonight?" he asked eagerly. "There'll probably be a bunch in the Whartons' yard."

"I'll ask mother."

"I'll telephone you. I don't want to go unless you'll be there."

"Why?" She smiled at him again, encouraging him.

"Because I don't want to."

"But why don't you want to?"

"Listen," he said quickly. "What boys do you like better than me?"

"Nobody. I like you and Hubert Blair best."

Basil felt no jealousy at the coupling of this name with his. There was nothing to do about Hubert Blair but accept him philosophically, as other boys did when dissecting the hearts of other girls.

"I like you better than anybody," he said deliriously.

The weight of the pink dappled sky above him was not endurable. He was plunging along through air of ineffable loveliness while warm freshets sprang up in his blood and he turned them, and with them his whole life, like a stream toward this girl.

They reached the carriage door at the side of her house.

"Can't you come in, Basil?"

"No." He saw immediately that that was a mistake, but it was said now. The intangible present had eluded him. Still he lingered. "Do you want my school ring?"

"Yes, if you want to give it to me."

"I'll give it to you tonight." His voice shook slightly as he added, "That is, I'll trade."

"What for?"

"Something."

"What?" Her color spread; she knew.

"You know. Will you trade?"

Imogene looked around uneasily. In the honey-sweet silence that had gathered around the porch, Basil held his breath.

"You're awful," she whispered. "Maybe. . . . Good-by."

II

It was the best hour of the day now and Basil was terribly happy. This summer he and his mother and sister were going to the lakes and next fall he was starting away to school. Then he would go to Yale and be a great athlete, and after that—if his two dreams had fitted onto each other chronologically instead of existing independently side by side—he was due to become a gentleman burglar. Everything was fine. He had so many alluring things to think about that it was hard to fall asleep at night.

That he was now crazy about Imogene Bissel was not a distraction, but another good thing. It had as yet no poignancy, only a brilliant and dynamic excitement that was bearing him along toward the Wharton yard through the May twilight.

He wore his favorite clothes—white duck knickerbockers, pepper-and-salt Norfolk jacket, a Belmont collar and a gray knitted tie. With his brown hair wet and shining, he made a handsome little figure as he turned in upon the familiar but not reënchanted lawn and joined the voices in the gathering darkness. Three or four girls who lived in neighboring houses were present, and almost twice as many boys; and a slightly older group adorning the side veranda made a warm, remote nucleus against the lamps of the house and contributed occasional mysterious ripples of laughter to the already overburdened night.

Moving from shadowy group to group, Basil ascertained that Imogene was not yet here. Finding Margaret Torrence, he spoke to her aside, lightly.

"Have you still got that old ring of mine?"

Margaret had been his girl all year at dancing school, signified by the fact that he had taken her to the cotillion which closed the season. The affair had languished toward the end; none the less, his question was undiplomatic.

"I've got it somewhere," Margaret replied carelessly. "Why? Do you want it back?"

"Sort of."

"All right. I never did want it. It was you that made me take it, Basil. I'll give it back to you tomorrow."

"You couldn't give it to me tonight, could you?" His heart leaped as he saw a small figure come in at the rear gate. "I sort of want to get it tonight."

"Oh, all right, Basil."

She ran across the street to her house and Basil followed. Mr. and Mrs. Torrence were on the porch, and while Margaret went upstairs for the ring he overcame his excitement and impatience and answered those questions as to the health of his parents which are so meaningless to the young. Then a sudden stiffening came over him, his voice faded off and his glazed eyes fixed upon a scene that was materializing over the way.

From the shadows far up the street, a swift, almost flying figure emerged and floated into the patch of lamplight in front of the Whartons' house. The figure wove here and there in a series of geometric patterns, now off with a flash of sparks at the impact of skates and pavement, now gliding miraculously backward, describing a fantastic curve, with one foot lifted gracefully in the air, until the young people moved forward in groups out of the darkness and crowded to the pavement to watch. Basil gave a quiet little groan as he realized that of all possible nights, Hubert Blair had chosen this one to arrive.

"You say you're going to the lakes this summer, Basil. Have you taken a cottage?"

Basil became aware after a moment that Mr. Torrence was making this remark for the third time.

"Oh, yes, sir," he answered—"I mean, no. We're staying at the club."

"Won't that be lovely?" said Mrs. Torrence.

Across the street, he saw Imogene standing under the lamp-post and in front of her Hubert Blair, his jaunty cap on the side of his head, maneuvering in a small circle. Basil winced as he heard his chuckling laugh. He did not perceive Margaret until she was beside him, pressing his ring into his hand like a bad penny. He muttered a strained hollow good-by to her parents, and, weak with apprehension, followed her back across the street.

Hanging back in a shadow, he fixed his eyes not on Imogene but on Hubert Blair. There was undoubtedly something rare about Hubert. In the eyes of children less than fifteen, the shape of the nose is the distinguishing mark of beauty. Parents may call attention to lovely eyes, shining hair or gorgeous coloring, but the nose and its juxtaposition on the face is what the adolescent sees. Upon the lithe, stylish, athletic torso of Hubert Blair was set a conventional chubby face, and upon this face was chiseled the piquant, retroussé nose of a Harrison Fisher girl.

He was confident; he had personality, uninhibited by doubts or moods. He did not go to dancing school—his parents had moved to the city only a year ago—but already he was a legend. Though most of the boys disliked him, they did homage to his virtuosic athletic ability, and for the girls his every movement, his pleasantries, his very indifference, had a simply immeasurable fascination. Upon several previous occasions Basil had discovered this; now the discouraging comedy began to unfold once more.

Hubert took off his skates, rolled one down his arm and caught it by the strap before it reached the pavement; he snatched the ribbon from Imogene's hair and made off with it, dodging from under her arms as she pursued him, laughing and fascinated, around the yard. He cocked one foot behind the other and pretended to lean an elbow against a tree, missed the tree on purpose and gracefully saved himself from falling. The boys watched him noncommittally at first. Then they, too, broke out into activity, doing stunts and tricks as fast as they could think of them until those on the porch craned their necks at the sudden surge of activity in the garden. But Hubert coolly turned his back on his own success. He took Imogene's hat and began setting it in various quaint ways upon his head. Imogene and the other girls were filled with delight.

Unable any longer to endure the nauseous spectacle, Basil went up to the group and said, "Why, hello, Hube," in as negligent a tone as he could command.

Hubert answered: "Why, hello, old—old Basil the Boozle," and set the hat a different way on his head, until Basil himself couldn't resist an unwilling chortle of laughter.

"Basil the Boozle! Hello, Basil the Boozle!" The cry circled the garden. Reproachfully he distinguished Riply's voice among the others.

"Hube the Boob!" Basil countered quickly; but his ill humor detracted from the effect though several boys repeated it appreciatively.

Gloom settled upon Basil, and through the heavy dusk the figure of Imogene began to take on a new, unattainable charm. He was a romantic boy and already he had endowed her heavily from his fancy. Now he hated her for her indifference, but he must perversely linger near in the vain hope of recovering the penny of ecstasy so wantonly expended this afternoon.

He tried to talk to Margaret with decoy animataion, but Margaret was not responsive. Already a voice had gone up in the darkness calling in a child. Panic seized upon him; the blessed hour of summer evening was almost over. At a spreading of the group to let pedestrians through, he maneuvered Imogene unwillingly aside.

"I've got it," he whispered. "Here it is. Can I take you home?"

She looked at him distractedly. Her hand closed automatically on the ring.

"What? Oh, I promised Hubert he could take me home." At the

sight of his face she pulled herself from her trance and forced a note of indignation. "I saw you going off with Margaret Torrence just as soon as I came into the yard."

"I didn't. I just went to get the ring."

"Yes, you did! I saw you!"

Her eyes moved back to Hubert Blair. He had replaced his roller skates and was making little rhythmic jumps and twirls on his toes, like a witch doctor throwing a slow hypnosis over an African tribe. Basil's voice, explaining and arguing, went on, but Imogene moved away. Helplessly he followed. There were other voices calling in the darkness now and unwilling responses on all sides.

"All right, mother!"

"I'll be there in a second, mother."

"Mother, can't I please stay out five minutes more?"

"I've got to go," Imogene cried. "It's almost nine."

Waving her hand and smiling absently at Basil, she started off down the street. Hubert pranced and stunted at her side, circled around her and made entrancing little figures ahead.

Only after a minute did Basil realize that another young lady was addressing him.

"What?" he demanded absently.

"Hubert Blair is the nicest boy in town and you're the most conceited," repeated Margaret Torrence with deep conviction.

He stared at her in pained surprise. Margaret wrinkled her nose at him and yielded up her person to the now-insistent demands coming from across the street. As Basil gazed stupidly after her and then watched the forms of Imogene and Hubert disappear around the corner, there was a low mutter of thunder along the sultry sky and a moment later a solitary drop plunged through the lamplit leaves overhead and splattered on the sidewalk at his feet. The day was to close in rain.

III

It came quickly and he was drenched and running before he reached his house eight blocks away. But the change of weather had swept over his heart and he leaped up every few steps, swallowing the rain and crying "Yo-o-o!" aloud, as if he himself were a part of the fresh, violent disturbance of the night. Imogene was gone, washed out like the day's dust on the sidewalk. Her beauty would come back into his mind in brighter weather, but here in the storm he was alone with himself. A sense of extraordinary power welled up in him, until to leave the ground permanently with one of his wild leaps would not have surprised him. He was a lone wolf, secret and untamed; a night prowler, demoniac and free. Only when he reached his own house did his emotion begin to turn, speculatively and almost without passion, against Hubert Blair.

He changed his clothes, and putting on pajamas and dressing-gown descended to the kitchen, where he happened upon a new chocolate cake. He ate a fourth of it and drank most of a bottle of milk. His elation somewhat diminished, he called up Riply Buckner on the phone.

"I've got a scheme," he said.

"What about?"

"How to do something to H. B. with the S. D."

Riply understood immediately what he meant. Hubert had been so indiscreet as to fascinate other girls besides Miss Bissell that evening.

"We'll have to take in Bill Kampf," Basil said.

"All right."

"See you at recess tomorrow. . . . Good night!"

IV

Four days later, when Mr. and Mrs. George P. Blair were finishing dinner, Hubert was called to the telephone. Mrs. Blair took advantage of his absence to speak to her husband of what had been on her mind all day.

"George, those boys, or whatever they are, came again last night."

He frowned.

"Did you see them?"

"Hilda did. She almost caught one of them. You see, I told her about the note they left last Tuesday, the one that said, 'First warning, S.D.,' so she was ready for them. They rang the back-door bell this time and she answered it straight from the dishes. If her hands hadn't been soapy she could have caught one, because she grabbed him when he handed her a note, but her hands were soapy so he slipped away."

"What did he look like?"

"She said he might have been a very little man, but she thought he was a boy in a false face. He dodged like a boy, she said, and she thought he had short pants on. The note was like the other. It said 'Second warning, S.D.' "

"If you've got it, I'd like to see it after dinner."

Hubert came back from the phone. "It was Imogene Bissell," he said. "She wants me to come over to her house. A bunch are going over there tonight."

"Hubert," asked his father, "do you know any boy with the initials S.D.?"

"No, sir."

"Have you thought?"

"Yeah, I thought. I knew a boy named Sam Davis, but I haven't seen him for a year."

"Who was he?"

"Oh, a sort of tough. He was at Number 44 School when I went there."

"Did he have it in for you?"

"I don't think so."

"Who do you think could be doing this? Has anybody got it in for you that you know about?

"I don't know, papa; I don't think so."

"I don't like the looks of this thing," said Mr. Blair thoughtfully. "Of course it may be only some boys, but it may be—"

He was silent. Later, he studied the note. It was in red ink and there was a skull and crossbones in the corner, but being printed, it told him nothing at all.

Meanwhile Hubert kissed his mother, set his cap jauntily on the side of his head, and passing through the kitchen stepped out on the back stoop, intending to take the usual short cut along the alley. It was a bright moonlit night and he paused for a moment on the stoop to tie his shoe. If he had but known that the telephone call just received had been a decoy, that it had not come from Imogene Bissel's house, had not indeed been a girl's voice at all, and that shadowy and grotesque forms were skulking in the alley just outside the gate, he would not have sprung so gracefully and lithely down the steps with his hands in his pockets or whistled the first bar of the Grizzly Bear into the apparently friendly night.

His whistle aroused varying emotions in the alley. Basil had given his daring and successful falsetto imitation over the telephone a little too soon, and though the Scandal Detectives had hurried, their preparations were not quite in order. They had become separated. Basil, got up like a Southern planter of the old persuasion, just outside the Blairs' gate; Bill Kampf, with a long Balkan mustache attached by a wire to the lower cartilage of his nose, was approaching in the shadow of the fence; but Riply Buckner, in a full rabbinical beard, was impeded by a length of rope he was trying to coil and was still a hundred feet away. The rope was an essential part of their plan; for, after much cogitation, they had decided what they were going to do to Hubert Blair. They were going to tie him up, gag him and put him in his own garbage can.

The idea at first horrified them—it would ruin his suit, it was awfully dirty and he might smother. In fact the garbage can, symbol of all that was repulsive, won the day only because it made every other idea seem tame. They disposed of the objections—his suit could be cleaned, it was where he ought to be anyhow, and if they left the lid off he couldn't smother. To be sure of this they had paid a visit of inspection to the Buckners' garbage can and stared into it, fascinated, envisaging Hubert among the rinds and eggshells. Then two of them, at least, resolutely put that part out of their minds and concentrated upon the luring of him into the alley and the overwhelming of him there.

Hubert's cheerful whistle caught them off guard and each of the three stood stock-still, unable to communicate with the others. It flashed through Basil's mind that if he grabbed Hubert without Riply at hand to apply the gag as had been arranged, Hubert's cries might alarm that gigantic cook in the kitchen who had almost taken him the night before. The thought threw him into a state of indecision. At that precise moment Hubert opened the gate and came out into the alley.

The two stood five feet apart, staring at each other, and all at once Basil made a startling discovery. He discovered he liked Hubert Blair—liked him as well as any boy he knew. He had absolutely no wish to lay hands on Hubert Blair and stuff him into a garbage can, jaunty cap and all. He would have fought to prevent that contingency. As his mind, unstrung by his situation, gave pasture to this inconvenient thought, he turned and dashed out of the alley and up the street.

For a moment the apparition had startled Hubert, but when it turned and made off he was heartened and gave chase. Out-distanced, he decided after fifty yards to let well enough alone; and returning to the alley, started rather precipitously down toward the other end —and came face to face with another small and hairy stranger.

Bill Kampf, being more simply organized than Basil, had no scruples of any kind. It had been decided to put Hubert into a garbage can, and though he had nothing at all against Hubert, the idea had made a pattern on his brain which he intended to follow. He was a natural man—that is to say, a hunter—and once a creature took on the aspect of a quarry, he would pursue it without qualms until it stopped struggling.

But he had been witness to Basil's inexplicable flight, and supposing that Hubert's father had appeared and was now directly behind him, he, too, faced about and made off down the alley. Presently he met Riply Buckner, who, without waiting to inquire the cause of his flight, enthusiastically joined him. Again Hubert was surprised into pursuing a little way. Then, deciding once and for all to let well enough alone, he returned on a dead run to his house.

Meanwhile Basil had discovered that he was not pursued, and keeping in the shadows, made his way back to the alley. He was not frightened—he had simply been incapable of action. The alley was empty; neither Bill nor Riply was in sight. He saw Mr. Blair come to the back gate, open it, look up and down and go back into the house. He came closer. There was a great chatter in the kitchen—Hubert's voice, loud and boastful, and Mrs. Blair's frightened, and the two Swedish domestics contributing bursts of hilarious laughter. Then through an open window he heard Mr. Blair's voice at the telephone:

"I want to speak to the chief of police. . . . Chief, this is George P. Blair. . . . Chief, there's a gang of toughs around here who—"

Basil was off like a flash, tearing at his Confederate whiskers as he ran.

V

Imogene Bissel, having just turned thirteen, was not accustomed to having callers at night. She was spending a bored and solitary evening inspecting the months' bills which were scattered over her mother's desk, when she heard Hubert Blair and his father admitted into the front hall.

"I just thought I'd bring him over myself," Mr. Blair was saying to her mother. "There seems to be a gang of toughs hanging around our alley tonight."

Mrs. Bissel had not called upon Mrs. Blair and she was considerably taken aback by this unexpected visit. She even entertained the uncharitable thought that this was a crude overture, undertaken by Mr. Blair on behalf of his wife.

"Really!" she exclaimed. "Imogene will be delighted to see Hubert, I'm sure. . . . Imogene!"

"These toughs were evidently lying in wait for Hubert," continued Mr. Blair. "But he's a pretty spunky boy and he managed to drive them away. However, I didn't want him to come down here alone."

"Of course not," she agreed. But she was unable to imagine why Hubert should have come at all. He was a nice enough boy, but surely Imogene had seen enough of him the last three afternoons. In fact, Mrs. Bissel was annoyed, and there was a minimum of warmth in her voice when she asked Mr. Blair to come in.

They were still in the hall, and Mr. Blair was just beginning to perceive that all was not as it should be, when there was another ring at the bell. Upon the door being opened, Basil Lee, red-faced and breathless, stood on the threshold.

"How do you do, Mrs. Bissel? Hello, Imogene!" he cried in an unnecessarily hearty voice. "Where's the party?"

The salutation might have sounded to a dispassionate observer somewhat harsh and unnatural, but it fell upon the ears of an already disconcerted group.

"There isn't any party," said Imogene wonderingly.

"What?" Basil's mouth dropped open in exaggerated horror, his voice trembled slightly. "You mean to say you didn't call me up and tell me to come over here to a party?"

"Why, of course not, Basil!"

Imogene was excited by Hubert's unexpected arrival and it occurred to her that Basil had invented this excuse to spoil it. Alone of those present, she was close to the truth; but she underestimated the urgency of Basil's motive, which was not jealousy but mortal fear.

"You called *me* up, didn't you, Imogene?" demanded Hubert confidently.

"Why, no, Hubert! I didn't call up anybody."

Amid a chorus of bewildered protestations, there was another ring at the doorbell and the pregnant night yielded up Riply Buckner, Jr., and William S. Kampf. Like Basil, they were somewhat rumpled and breathless, and they no less rudely and peremptorily demanded the whereabouts of the party, insisting with curious vehemence that Imogene had just now invited them over the phone.

Hubert laughed, the others began to laugh and the tensity relaxed. Imogene, because she believed Hubert, now began to believe them all. Unable to restrain himself any longer in the presence of this unhoped-for audience, Hubert burst out with his amazing adventure.

"I guess there's a gang laying for us all!" he exclaimed. "There were some guys laying for me in our alley when I went out. There was a big fellow with gray whiskers, but when he saw me he ran away. Then I went along the alley and there was a bunch more, sort of foreigners or something, and I started after'm and they ran. I tried to catchem, but I guess they were good and scared, because they ran too fast for *me*."

So interested were Hubert and his father in the story that they failed to perceive that three of his listeners were growing purple in the face or to mark the uproarious laughter that greeted Mrs. Bissel's polite proposal that they have a party, after all.

"Tell about the warnings, Hubert," prompted Mr. Blair. "You see, Hubert had received these warnings. Did you boys get any warnings?"

"I did," said Basil suddenly. "I got a sort of warning on a piece of paper about a week ago."

For a moment, as Mr. Blair's worried eye fell upon Basil, a strong sense not precisely of suspicion but rather of obscure misgiving passed over him. Possibly that odd aspect of Basil's eyebrows, where wisps of crêpe hair still lingered, connected itself in his subconscious mind with what was bizarre in the events of the evening. He shook his head somewhat puzzled. Then his thoughts glided back restfully to Hubert's courage and presence of mind.

Hubert, meanwhile, having exhausted his facts, was making tentative leaps into the realms of imagination.

"I said, 'So, you're the guy that's been sending these warnings,' and he swung his left at me, and I dodged and swung my right back at him. I guess I must have landed, because he gave a yell and ran. Gosh, he could run! You'd ought to of seen him, Bill—he could run as fast as you."

"Was he big?" asked Basil, blowing his nose noisily.

"Sure! About as big as father."

"Were the other ones big too?"

"Sure! They were pretty big. I didn't wait to see. I just yelled, 'You get out of here, you bunch of toughs, or I'll show you!' They started to sort of fight, but I swung my right at one of them and they didn't wait for any more."

"Hubert says he thinks they were Italians," interrupted Mr. Blair. "Didn't you, Hubert?"

"They were sort of funny-looking," Hubert said. "One fellow looked like an Italian."

Mrs. Bissel led the way to the dining room, where she had caused a cake and grape juice supper to be spread. Imogene took a chair by Hubert's side.

"Now tell me all about it, Hubert," she said, attentively folding her hands.

Hubert ran over the adventure once more. A knife now made its appearance in the belt of one conspirator; Hubert's parleys with them lengthened and grew in volume and virulence. He had told them just what they might expect if they fooled with him. They had started to draw knives, but had thought better of it and taken to flight.

In the middle of this recital there was a curious snorting sound from across the table, but when Imogene looked over, Basil was spreading jelly on a piece of coffee cake and his eyes were brightly innocent. A minute later, however, the sound was repeated, and this time she intercepted a specifically malicious expression upon his face.

"I wonder what you'd have done, Basil," she said cuttingly. "I'll bet you'd be running yet!"

Basil put the piece of coffee cake in his mouth and immediately choked on it—an accident which Bill Kampf and Riply Buckner found hilariously amusing. Their amusement at various casual incidents at table seemed to increase as Hubert's story continued. The alley now swarmed with malefactors, and as Hubert struggled on against overwhelming odds, Imogene found herself growing restless —without in the least realizing that the tale was boring her. On the contrary, each time Hubert recollected new incidents and began again, she looked spitefully over at Basil, and her dislike for him grew.

When they moved into the library, Imogene went to the piano, where she sat alone while the boys gathered around Hubert on the couch. To her chagrin, they seemed quite content to listen indefinitely. Odd little noises squeaked out of them from time to time, but whenever the narrative slackened they would beg for more.

"Go on, Hubert. Which one did you say could run as fast as Bill Kampf?"

She was glad when, after half an hour, they all got up to go.

"It's a strange affair from beginning to end," Mr. Blair was saying. "I don't like it. I'm going to have a detective look into the matter tomorrow. What did they want of Hubert? What were they going to do to him?"

No one offered a suggestion. Even Hubert was silent, contemplating his possible fate with certain respectful awe. During breaks in his narration the talk had turned to such collateral matters as murders and ghosts, and all the boys had talked themselves into a state of considerable panic. In fact each had come to believe, in varying degrees, that a band of kidnappers infested the vicinity.

"I don't like it," repeated Mr. Blair. "In fact I'm going to see all of you boys to your own homes."

Basil greeted this offer with relief. The evening had been a mad success, but furies once aroused sometimes get out of hand. He did not feel like walking the streets alone tonight.

In the hall, Imogene, taking advantage of her mother's somewhat fatigued farewell to Mr. Blair, beckoned Hubert back into the library. Instantly attuned to adversity, Basil listened. There was a whisper and a short scuffle, followed by an indiscreet but unmistakable sound. With the corners of his mouth falling, Basil went out the door. He had stacked the cards dexterously, but Life had played a trump from its sleeve at the last.

A moment later they all started off, clinging together in a group, turning corners with cautious glances behind and ahead. What Basil

and Riply and Bill expected to see as they peered warily into the
sinister mouths of alleys and around great dark trees and behind
concealing fences they did not know—in all probability the same
hairy and grotesque desperadoes who had lain in wait for Hubert
Blair that night.

VI

A week later Basil and Riply heard that Hubert and his mother
had gone to the seashore for the summer. Basil was sorry. He had
wanted to learn from Hubert some of the graceful mannerisms that
his contemporaries found so dazzling and that might come in so
handy next fall when he went away to school. In tribute to Hubert's
passing, he practised leaning against a tree and missing it and rolling
a skate down his arm, and he wore his cap in Hubert's manner, set
jauntily on the side of his head.

This was only for a while. He perceived eventually that though
boys and girls would always listen to him while he talked, their
mouths literally moving in response to his, they would never look at
him as they had looked at Hubert. So he abandoned the loud
chuckle that so annoyed his mother and set his cap straight upon his
head once more.

But the change in him went deeper than that. He was no longer
sure that he wanted to be a gentleman burglar, though he still read
of their exploits with breathless admiration. Outside of Hubert's
gate, he had for a moment felt morally alone; and he realized that
whatever combinations he might make of the materials of life would
have to be safely within the law. And after another week he found
that he no longer grieved over losing Imogene. Meeting her, he saw
only the familiar little girl he had always known. The ecstatic
moment of that afternoon had been a premature birth, an emotion
left over from an already fleeting spring.

He did not know that he had frightened Mrs. Blair out of town
and that because of him a special policeman walked a placid beat
for many a night. All he knew was the vague and restless yearn-
ings of three long spring months were somehow satisfied. They
reached combustion in that last week—flared up, exploded and
burned out. His face was turned without regret toward the bound-
less possibilities of summer.

1928   *Taps at Reveille*

THE FRESHEST BOY

IT WAS a hidden Broadway restaurant in the dead of the night, and a brilliant and mysterious group of society people, diplomats and members of the underworld were there. A few minutes ago the sparkling wine had been flowing and a girl had been dancing gaily upon a table, but now the whole crowd were hushed and breathless. All eyes were fixed upon the masked but well-groomed man in the dress suit and opera hat who stood nonchalantly in the door.

"Don't move, please," he said, in a well-bred, cultivated voice that had, nevertheless, a ring of steel in it. "This thing in my hand might —go off."

His glance roved from table to table—fell upon the malignant man higher up with his pale saturnine face, upon Heatherly, the suave secret agent from a foreign power, then rested a little longer, a little more softly perhaps, upon the table where the girl with dark hair and dark tragic eyes sat alone.

"Now that my purpose is accomplished, it might interest you to know who I am." There was a gleam of expectation in every eye. The breast of the dark-eyed girl heaved faintly and a tiny burst of subtle French perfume rose into the air. "I am none other than that elusive gentleman, Basil Lee, better known as the Shadow."

Taking off his well-fitting opera hat, he bowed ironically from the waist. Then, like a flash, he turned and was gone into the night.

"You get up to New York only once a month," Lewis Crum was saying, "and then you have to take a master along."

Slowly, Basil Lee's glazed eyes returned from the barns and billboards of the Indiana countryside to the interior of the Broadway Limited. The hypnosis of the swift telegraph poles faded and Lewis Crum's stolid face took shape against the white slip-cover of the opposite bench.

"I'd just duck the master when I got to New York," said Basil.

"Yes, you would!"

"I bet I would."

"You try it and you'll see."

"What do you mean saying I'll see, all the time, Lewis? What'll I see?"

His very bright dark-blue eyes were at this moment fixed upon his companion with boredom and impatience. The two had nothing in common except their age, which was fifteen, and the lifelong friendship of their fathers—which is less than nothing. Also they were bound from the same Middle-Western city for Basil's first and Lewis' second year at the same Eastern school.

But, contrary to all the best traditions, Lewis the veteran was miserable and Basil the neophyte was happy. Lewis hated school. He had grown entirely dependent on the stimulus of a hearty vital mother, and as he felt her slipping farther and farther away from him, he plunged deeper into misery and homesickness. Basil, on the other hand, had lived with such intensity on so many stories of boarding-school life that, far from being homesick, he had a glad feeling of recognition and familiarity. Indeed, it was with some sense of doing the appropriate thing, having the traditional rough-house, that he had thrown Lewis' comb off the train at Milwaukee last night for no reason at all.

To Lewis, Basil's ignorant enthusiasm was distasteful—his instinctive attempt to dampen it had contributed to the mutual irritation.

"I'll tell you what you'll see," he said ominously. "They'll catch you smoking and put you on bounds."

"No, they won't, because I won't be smoking. I'll be in training for football."

"Football! Yeah! Football!"

"Honestly, Lewis, you don't like anything, do you?"

"I don't like football. I don't like to go out and get a crack in the eye." Lewis spoke aggressively, for his mother had canonized all his timidities as common sense. Basil's answer, made with what he considered kindly intent, was the sort of remark that creates lifelong enmities.

"You'd probably be a lot more popular in school if you played football," he suggested patronizingly.

Lewis did not consider himself unpopular. He did not think of it in that way at all. He was astounded.

"You wait!" he cried furiously. "They'll take all that freshness out of you."

"Clam yourself," said Basil, coolly plucking at the creases of his first long trousers. "Just clam yourself."

"I guess everybody knows you were the freshest boy at the Country Day!"

"Clam yourself," repeated Basil, but with less assurance. "Kindly clam yourself."

"I guess I know what they had in the school paper about you—" Basil's own coolness was no longer perceptible.

"If you don't clam yourself," he said darkly, "I'm going to throw your brushes off the train too."

The enormity of this threat was effective. Lewis sank back in his seat, snorting and muttering, but undoubtedly calmer. His reference had been to one of the most shameful passages in his companion's life. In a periodical issued by the boys of Basil's late school there had appeared, under the heading Personals:

"If someone will please poison young Basil, or find some other means to stop his mouth, the school at large and myself will be much obliged."

The two boys sat there fuming wordlessly at each other. Then, resolutely, Basil tried to re-inter this unfortunate souvenir of the past. All that was behind him now. Perhaps he had been a little fresh, but he was making a new start. After a moment, the memory passed and with it the train and Lewis' dismal presence—the breath of the East came sweeping over him again with a vast nostalgia. A voice called him out of the fabled world; a man stood beside him with a hand on his sweater-clad shoulder.

"Lee!"

"Yes, sir."

"It all depends on you now. Understand?"

"Yes, sir."

"All right," the coach said, "go in and win."

Basil tore the sweater from his stripling form and dashed out on the field. There were two minutes to play and the score was 3 to 0 for the enemy, but at the sight of young Lee, kept out of the game all year by a malicious plan of Dan Haskins, the school bully, and Weasel Weems, his toady, a thrill of hope went over the St. Regis stand.

"33-12-16-22!" barked Midget Brown, the diminutive little quarterback.

It was his signal——

"Oh, gosh!" Basil spoke aloud, forgetting the late unpleasantness. "I wish we'd get there before tomorrow."

II

ST. REGIS SCHOOL, EASTCHESTER,
November 18, 19——

"DEAR MOTHER: There is not much to say today, but I thought I would write you about my allowance. All the boys have a bigger allowance than me, because there are a lot of little things I have to get, such as shoe laces, etc. School is still very nice and am having a fine time, but football is over and there is not much to do. I am going to New York this week to see a show. I do not know yet what it will be, but probably the Quacker Girl or little boy Blue as they are both very good. Dr. Bacon is very nice and there's a good phycission in the village. No more now as I have to study Algebra.

"Your Affectionate Son,
"BASIL D. LEE."

As he put the letter in its envelope, a wizened little boy came into the deserted study hall where he sat and stood staring at him.

"Hello," said Basil, frowning.

"I been looking for you," said the little boy, slowly and judicially. "I looked all over—up in your room and out in the gym, and they said you probably might of sneaked off in here."

"What do you want?" Basil demanded.

"Hold your horses, Bossy."

Basil jumped to his feet. The little boy retreated a step.

"Go on, hit me!" he chirped nervously. "Go on, hit me, cause I'm just half your size—Bossy."

Basil winced. "You call me that again and I'll spank you."

"No, you won't spank me. Brick Wales said if you ever touched any of us—"

"But I never did touch any of you."

"Didn't you chase a lot of us one day and didn't Brick Wales—"

"Oh, what do you want?" Basil cried in desperation.

"Doctor Bacon wants you. They sent me after you and somebody said maybe you sneaked in here."

Basil dropped his letter in his pocket and walked out—the little boy and his invective following him through the door. He traversed a long corridor, muggy with that odor best described as the smell of stale caramels that is so peculiar to boys' schools, ascended a stairs and knocked at an unexceptional but formidable door.

Doctor Bacon was at his desk. He was a handsome, redheaded Episcopal clergyman of fifty whose original real interest in boys was now tempered by the flustered cynicism which is the fate of all headmasters and settles on them like green mould. There were certain preliminaries before Basil was asked to sit down—gold-rimmed glasses had to be hoisted up from nowhere by a black cord and fixed on Basil to be sure that he was not an impostor; great masses of paper on the desk had to be shuffled through, not in search of anything but as a man nervously shuffles a pack of cards.

"I had a letter from your mother this morning—ah—Basil." The use of his first name had come to startle Basil. No one else in school had yet called him anything but Bossy or Lee. "She feels that your marks have been poor. I believe you have been sent here at a certain amount of—ah—sacrifice and she expects—"

Basil's spirit writhed with shame, not at his poor marks but that his financial inadequacy should be so bluntly stated. He knew that he was one of the poorest boys in a rich boys' school.

Perhaps some dormant sensibility in Doctor Bacon became aware of his discomfort; he shuffled through the papers once more and began on a new note.

"However, that was not what I sent for you about this afternoon. You applied last week for permission to go to New York on Saturday, to a matinée. Mr. Davis tells me that for almost the first time since school opened you will be off bounds tomorrow."

"Yes, sir."

"That is not a good record. However, I would allow you to go to New York if it could be arranged. Unfortunately, no masters are available this Saturday."

Basil's mouth dropped ajar. "Why, I—why, Doctor Bacon, I know two parties that are going. Couldn't I go with one of them?"

Doctor Bacon ran through all his papers very quickly. "Unfortunately, one is composed of slightly older boys and the other group made arrangements some weeks ago."

"How about the party that's going to the *Quaker Girl* with Mr. Dunn?"

"It's that party I speak of. They feel that their arrangements are complete and they have purchased seats together."

Suddenly Basil understood. At the look in his eye Doctor Bacon went on hurriedly:

"There's perhaps one thing I can do. Of course there must be several boys in the party so that the expenses of the master can be divided up among all. If you can find two other boys who would like to make up a party, and let me have their names by five o'clock, I'll send Mr. Rooney with you."

"Thank you," Basil said.

Doctor Bacon hesitated. Beneath the cynical incrustations of many years an instinct stirred to look into the unusual case of this boy and find out what made him the most detested boy in school. Among boys and masters there seemed to exist an extraordinary hostility toward him, and though Doctor Bacon had dealt with many sorts of schoolboy crimes, he had neither by himself nor with the aid of trusted sixth-formers been able to lay his hands on its underlying cause. It was probably no single thing, but a combination of things; it was most probably one of those intangible questions of personality. Yet he remembered that when he first saw Basil he had considered him unusually prepossessing.

He sighed. Sometimes these things worked themselves out. He wasn't one to rush in clumsily. "Let us have a better report to send home next month, Basil."

"Yes, sir."

Basil ran quickly downstairs to the recreation room. It was Wednesday and most of the boys had already gone into the village of Eastchester, whither Basil, who was still on bounds, was forbidden to follow. When he looked at those still scattered about the pool tables and piano, he saw that it was going to be difficult to get anyone to go with him at all. For Basil was quite conscious that he was the most unpopular boy at school.

It had begun almost immediately. One day, less than a fortnight after he came, a crowd of the smaller boys, perhaps urged on to it, gathered suddenly around him and began calling him Bossy. Within the next week he had two fights, and both times the crowd was vehemently and eloquently with the other boy. Soon after, when he was merely shoving indiscriminately, like every one else, to get into the dining room, Carver, the captain of the football team, turned about and, seizing him by the back of the neck, held him and dressed him down savagely. He joined a group innocently at the piano and was told, "Go on away. We don't want you around."

After a month he began to realize the full extent of his unpopularity. It shocked him. One day after a particularly bitter humiliation he went up to his room and cried. He tried to keep out of the way for a while, but it didn't help. He was accused of sneaking off here and there, as if bent on a series of nefarious errands. Puzzled and wretched, he looked at his face in the glass, trying to discover there the secret of their dislike—in the expression of his eyes, his smile.

He saw now that in certain ways he had erred at the outset—he had boasted, he had been considered yellow at football, he had pointed out people's mistakes to them, he had shown off his rather extraordinary fund of general information in class. But he had tried to do better and couldn't understand his failure to atone. It must be too late. He was queered forever.

He had, indeed, become the scapegoat, the immediate villain, the sponge which absorbed all malice and irritability abroad—just as the most frightened person in a party seems to absorb all the others' fear, seems to be afraid for them all. His situation was not helped by the fact, obvious to all, that the supreme self-confidence with which he had come to St. Regis in September was thoroughly broken. Boys taunted him with impunity who would not have dared raise their voices to him several months before.

This trip to New York had come to mean everything to him—surcease from the misery of his daily life as well as a glimpse into the long-awaited heaven of romance. Its postponement for week after week due to his sins—he was constantly caught reading after lights, for example, driven by his wretchedness into such vicarious escapes from reality—had deepened his longing until it was a burning hunger. It was unbearable that he should not go, and he told over the short list of those whom he might get to accompany him. The possibilities were Fat Gaspar, Treadway, and Bugs Brown. A quick journey to their rooms showed that they had all availed themselves of the Wednesday permission to go into Eastchester for the afternoon.

Basil did not hesitate. He had until five o'clock and his only chance was to go after them. It was not the first time he had broken bounds, though the last attempt had ended in disaster and an extension of his confinement. In his room, he put on a heavy sweater—an overcoat was a betrayal of intent—replaced his jacket over it and hid a cap in his back pocket. Then he went downstairs and with an elaborately careless whistle struck out across the lawn for the gymnasium. Once there, he stood for a while as if looking in the windows, first the one close to the walk, then one near the corner of the building. From here he moved quickly, but not too quickly, into a grove of lilacs. Then he dashed around the corner, down a long stretch of lawn that was blind from all windows and, parting the strands of a wire fence, crawled through and stood upon the grounds of a neighboring estate. For the moment he was free. He put on his cap against the chilly November wind, and set out along the half-mile road to town.

Eastchester was a suburban farming community, with a small shoe factory. The institutions which pandered to the factory workers were the ones patronized by the boys—a movie house, a quick-lunch wagon on wheels known as the Dog and the Bostonian Candy Kitchen. Basil tried the Dog first and happened immediately upon a prospect.

This was Bugs Brown, a hysterical boy, subject to fits and strenuously avoided. Years later he became a brilliant lawyer, but at that time he was considered by the boys of St. Regis to be a typical lunatic because of his peculiar series of sounds with which he assuaged his nervousness all day long.

He consorted with boys younger than himself, who were without the prejudices of their elders, and was in the company of several when Basil came in.

"Who-ee!" he cried. "Ee-ee-ee!" He put his hand over his mouth and bounced it quickly, making a wah-wah-wah sound. "It's Bossy Lee! It's Bossy Lee! It's Boss-Boss-Boss-Boss-Bossy Lee!"

"Wait a minute, Bugs," said Basil anxiously, half afraid that Bugs would go finally crazy before he could persuade him to come to town. "Say, Bugs, listen. Don't, Bugs—wait a minute. Can you come up to New York Saturday afternoon?"

"Whe-ee-ee!" cried Bugs to Basil's distress. "Whee-ee-ee!"

"Honestly, Bugs, tell me, can you? We could go up together if you could go."

"I've got to see a doctor," said Bugs, suddenly calm. "He wants to see how crazy I am."

"Can't you have him see about it some other day?" said Basil without humor.

"Whee-ee-ee!" cried Bugs.

"All right then," said Basil hastily. "Have you seen Fat Gaspar in town?"

Bugs was lost in shrill noise, but someone had seen Fat: Basil was directed to the Bostonian Candy Kitchen.

This was a gaudy paradise of cheap sugar. Its odor, heavy and sickly and calculated to bring out a sticky sweat upon an adult's palms, hung suffocatingly over the whole vicinity and met one like a strong moral dissuasion at the door. Inside, beneath a pattern of flies, material as black point lace, a line of boys sat eating heavy dinners of banana splits, maple nut, and chocolate marshmallow nut sundaes. Basil found Fat Gaspar at a table on the side.

Fat Gaspar was at once Basil's most unlikely and most ambitious quest. He was considered a nice fellow—in fact he was so pleasant that he had been courteous to Basil and had spoken to him politely all fall. Basil realized that he was like that to everyone, yet it was just possible that Fat liked him, as people used to in the past, and he was driven desperately to take a chance. But it was undoubtedly a presumption, and as he approached the table and saw the stiffened faces which the other two boys turned toward him, Basil's hope diminished.

"Say, Fat—" he said, and hesitated. Then he burst forth suddenly. "I'm on bounds, but I ran off because I had to see you. Doctor Bacon told me I could go to New York Saturday if I could get two other boys to go. I asked Bugs Brown and he couldn't go, and I thought I'd ask you."

He broke off, furiously embarrassed, and waited. Suddenly the two boys with Fat burst into a shout of laughter.

"Bugs wasn't crazy enough!"

Fat Gaspar hesitated. He couldn't go to New York Saturday and ordinarily he would have refused without offending. He had nothing against Basil; nor, indeed, against anybody; but boys have only a certain resistance to public opinion and he was influenced by the contemptuous laughter of the others.

"I don't want to go," he said indifferently. "Why do you want to ask *me*?"

Then, half in shame, he gave a deprecatory little laugh and bent over his ice cream.

"I just thought I'd ask you," said Basil.

Turning quickly away, he went to the counter and in a hollow and unfamiliar voice ordered a strawberry sundae. He ate it mechanically, hearing occasional whispers and snickers from the table behind. Still in a daze, he started to walk out without paying his check, but the clerk called him back and he was conscious of more derisive laughter.

For a moment he hesitated whether to go back to the table and hit one of those boys in the face, but he saw nothing to be gained. They would say the truth—that he had done it because he couldn't get anybody to go to New York. Clenching his fists with impotent rage, he walked from the store.

He came immediately upon his third prospect, Treadway. Treadway had entered St. Regis late in the year and had been put in to room with Basil the week before. The fact that Treadway hadn't witnessed his humiliations of the autumn encouraged Basil to behave naturally toward him, and their relations had been, if not intimate, at least tranquil.

"Hey, Treadway," he cried, still excited from the affair in the Bostonian, "can you come up to New York to a show Saturday afternoon?"

He stopped, realizing that Treadway was in the company of Brick Wales, a boy he had had a fight with and one of his bitterest enemies. Looking from one to the other, Basil saw a look of impatience in Treadway's face and a faraway expression in Brick Wales', and he realized what must have been happening. Treadway, making his way into the life of the school, had just been enlightened as to the status of his roommate. Like Fat Gaspar, rather than acknowledge himself eligible to such an intimate request, he preferred to cut their friendly relations short.

"Not on your life," he said briefly. "So long." The two walked past him into the candy kitchen.

Had these slights, so much the bitterer for their lack of passion, been visited upon Basil in September, they would have been unbearable. But since then he had developed a shell of hardness which, while it did not add to his attractiveness, spared him certain delicacies of torture. In misery enough, and despair and self-pity, he went the other way along the street for a little distance until he could control the violent contortions of his face. Then, taking a roundabout route, he started back to school.

He reached the adjoining estate, intending to go back the way he had come. Half-way through a hedge, he heard footsteps approaching along the sidewalk and stood motionless, fearing the proximity of masters. Their voices grew nearer and louder; before he knew it he was listening with horrified fascination:

"—so, after he tried Bugs Brown, the poor nut asked Fat Gaspar to go with him and Fat said, 'What do you ask me for?' It serves him right if he couldn't get anybody at all."

It was the dismal but triumphant voice of Lewis Crum.

III

Up in his room, Basil found a package lying on his bed. He knew its contents and for a long time he had been eagerly expecting it, but such was his depression that he opened it listlessly. It was a series of eight color reproductions of Harrison Fisher girls "on glossy paper, without printing or advertising matter and suitable for framing."

The pictures were named Dora, Marguerite, Babette, Lucille, Gretchen, Rose, Katherine and Mina. Two of them—Marguerite and Rose—Basil looked at, slowly tore up and dropped in the wastebasket, as one who disposes of the inferior pups from a litter. The other six he pinned at intervals around the room. Then he lay down on his bed and regarded them.

Dora, Lucille and Katherine were blonde; Gretchen was medium; Babette and Mina were dark. After a few minutes, he found that he was looking oftenest at Dora and Babette and, to a lesser extent, at Gretchen, though the latter's Dutch cap seemed unromantic and precluded the element of mystery. Babette, a dark little violet-eyed beauty in a tight-fitting hat, attracted him most; his eyes came to rest on her at last.

"Babette," he whispered to himself—"beautiful Babette."

The sound of the word, so melancholy and suggestive, like "Vilia" or "I'm happy at Maxim's" on the phonograph, softened him and, turning over on his face, he sobbed into the pillow. He took hold of the bed rails over his head and, sobbing and straining, began to talk to himself brokenly—how he hated them and whom he hated—he listed a dozen—and what he would do to them when he was great and powerful. In previous moments like these he had always rewarded Fat Gaspar for his kindness, but now he was like the rest. Basil set upon him, pummeling him unmercifully, or laughed sneeringly when he passed him blind and begging on the street.

He controlled himself as he heard Treadway come in, but did not move or speak. He listened as the other moved about the room, and after a while became conscious that there was an unusual opening of closets and bureau drawers. Basil turned over, his arm concealing his tear-stained face. Treadway had an armful of shirts in his hand.

"What are you doing?" Basil demanded.

His roommate looked at him stonily. "I'm moving in with Wales," he said.

"Oh!"

Treadway went on with his packing. He carried out a suitcase full, then another, took down some pennants and dragged his trunk into the hall. Basil watched him bundle his toilet things into a towel and take one last survey about the room's new barrenness to see if there was anything forgotten.

"Good-by," he said to Basil, without a ripple of expression on his face.

"Good-by."

Treadway went out. Basil turned over once more and choked into the pillow.

"Oh, poor Babette!" he cried huskily. "Poor little Babette! Poor little Babette!"

Babette, svelte and piquant, looked down at him coquettishly from the wall.

IV

Doctor Bacon, sensing Basil's predicament and perhaps the extremity of his misery, arranged it that he should go into New York, after all. He went in the company of Mr. Rooney, the football coach and history teacher. At twenty Mr. Rooney had hesitated for some time between joining the police force and having his way paid through a small New England college; in fact he was a hard specimen and Doctor Bacon was planning to get rid of him at Christmas. Mr. Rooney's contempt for Basil was founded on the latter's ambiguous and unreliable conduct on the football field during the past season—he had consented to take him to New York for reasons of his own.

Basil sat meekly beside him on the train, glancing past Mr. Rooney's bulky body at the Sound and the fallow fields of Westchester County. Mr. Rooney finished his newspaper, folded it up and sank into a moody silence. He had eaten a large breakfast and the exigencies of time had not allowed him to work it off with exercise. He remembered that Basil was a fresh boy, and it was time he did something fresh and could be called to account. This reproachless silence annoyed him.

"Lee," he said suddenly, with a thinly assumed air of friendly interest, "why don't you get wise to yourself?"

"What sir?" Basil was startled from his excited trance of this morning.

"I said why don't you get wise to yourself?" said Mr. Rooney in a somewhat violent tone. "Do you want to be the butt of the school all your time here?"

"No, I don't," Basil was chilled. Couldn't all this be left behind for just one day?

"You oughtn't to get so fresh all the time. A couple of times in history class I could just about have broken your neck." Basil could think of no appropriate answer. "Then out playing football," continued Mr. Rooney "—you didn't have any nerve. You could play better than a lot of 'em when you wanted, like that day against the Pomfret seconds, but you lost your nerve."

"I shouldn't have tried for the second team," said Basil. "I was too light. I should have stayed on the third."

"You were yellow, that was all the trouble. You ought to get wise to yourself. In class, you're always thinking of something else. If you don't study, you'll never get to college."

"I'm the youngest boy in the fifth form," Basil said rashly.

"You think you're pretty bright, don't you?" He eyed Basil ferociously. Then something seemed to occur to him that changed his attitude and they rode for a while in silence. When the train began to run through the thickly clustered communities near New York, he spoke again in a milder voice and with an air of having considered the matter for a long time:

"Lee, I'm going to trust you."

"Yes, sir."

"You go and get some lunch and then go on to your show. I've got some business of my own I got to attend to, and when I've finished I'll try to get to the show. If I can't, I'll anyhow meet you outside." Basil's heart leaped up. "Yes, sir."

"I don't want you to open your mouth about this at school—I mean, about me doing some business of my own."

"No, sir."

"We'll see if you can keep your mouth shut for once," he said, making it fun. Then he added, on a note of moral sternness, "And no drinks, you understand that?"

"Oh, no, sir!" The idea shocked Basil. He had never tasted a drink, nor even contemplated the possibility, save the intangible and nonalcoholic champagne of his café dreams.

On the advice of Mr. Rooney he went for luncheon to the Manhattan Hotel, near the station, where he ordered a club sandwich, French fried potatoes and a chocolate parfait. Out of the corner of his eye he watched the nonchalant, debonair, blasé New Yorkers at neighboring tables, investing them with a romance by which these possible fellow citizens of his from the Middle West lost nothing. School had fallen from him like a burden; it was no more than an unheeded clamor, faint and far away. He even delayed opening the letter from the morning's mail which he found in his pocket, because it was addressed to him at school.

He wanted another chocolate parfait, but being reluctant to bother the busy waiter any more, he opened the letter and spread it before him instead. It was from his mother:

"Dear Basil: This is written in great haste, as I didn't want to frighten you by telegraphing. Grandfather is going abroad to take the waters and he wants you and me to come too. The idea is that you'll go to school at Grenoble or Montreux for the rest of the year and learn the languages and we'll be close by. That is, if you want to. I know how you like St. Regis and playing football and baseball, and of course there would be none of that; but on the other hand, it would be a nice change, even if it postponed your entering Yale by an extra year. So, as usual, I want you to do just as you like. We will be leaving home almost as soon as you get this and will come to the Waldorf in New York, where you can come in and see us for a few days, even if you decide to stay. Think it over, dear.

"With love to my dearest boy,
"Mother."

Basil got up from his chair with a dim idea of walking over to the Waldorf and having himself locked up safely until his mother came. Then, impelled to some gesture, he raised his voice and in one of his first basso notes called boomingly and without reticence for the waiter. No more St. Regis! No more St. Regis! He was almost strangling with happiness.

"Oh, gosh!" he cried to himself. "Oh, golly! Oh, gosh! Oh, gosh!" No more Doctor Bacon and Mr. Rooney and Brick Wales and Fat Gaspar. No more Bugs Brown and on bounds and being called Bossy. He need no longer hate them, for they were impotent shadows in the stationary world that he was sliding away from, sliding past, waving his hand. "Good-by!" he pitied them. "Good-by!"

It required the din of Forty-second Street to sober his maudlin joy. With his hand on his purse to guard against the omnipresent pickpocket, he moved cautiously toward Broadway. What a day! He would tell Mr. Rooney—Why, he needn't ever go back! Or perhaps it would be better to go back and let them know what he was going to do, while they went on and on in the dismal, dreary round of school.

He found the theater and entered the lobby with its powdery feminine atmosphere of a matinée. As he took out his ticket, his gaze was caught and held by a sculptured profile a few feet away. It was that of a well-built blond young man of about twenty with a strong chin and direct gray eyes. Basil's brain spun wildly for a moment and then came to rest upon a name—more than a name—upon a legend, a sign in the sky. What a day! He had never seen the young man before, but from a thousand pictures he knew beyond the possibility of a doubt that it was Ted Fay; the Yale football captain, who had almost single-handed beaten Harvard and Princeton last fall. Basil felt a sort of exquisite pain. The profile turned away; the crowd revolved; the hero disappeared. But Basil would know all through the next hours that Ted Fay was here too.

In the rustling, whispering, sweet-smelling darkness of the theater he read the program. It was the show of all shows that he wanted to see, and until the curtain actually rose the program itself had a curious sacredness—a prototype of the thing itself. But when the curtain rose it became waste paper to be dropped carelessly to the floor.

ACT. I. *The Village Green of a Small Town near New York.*

It was too bright and blinding to comprehend all at once, and it went so fast that from the very first Basil felt he had missed things; he would make his mother take him again when she came—next week—tomorrow.

An hour passed. It was very sad at this point—a sort of gay sadness, but sad. The girl—the man. What kept them apart even now? Oh, those tragic errors and misconceptions. So sad. Couldn't they look into each other's eyes and *see*?

In a blaze of light and sound, of resolution, anticipation and imminent trouble, the act was over.

He went out. He looked for Ted Fay and thought he saw him leaning rather moodily on the plush wall at the rear of the theater, but he could not be sure. He bought cigarettes and lit one, but fancying at the first puff that he heard a blare of music he rushed back inside.

Act II. *The Foyer of the Hotel Astor.*

Yes, she was, indeed, like that song—a Beautiful Rose of the Night. The waltz buoyed her up, brought her with it to a point of aching beauty and then let her slide back to life across its last bars as a leaf slants to earth across the air. The high life of New York! Who could blame her if she was carried away by the glitter of it all, vanishing into the bright morning of the amber window borders or into distant and entrancing music as the door opened and closed that led to the ballroom? The toast of the shining town.

Half an hour passed. Her true love brought her roses like herself and she threw them scornfully at his feet. She laughed and turned to the other, and danced—danced madly, wildly. Wait! That delicate treble among the thin horns, the low curving note from the great strings. There it was again, poignant and aching, sweeping like a great gust of emotion across the stage, catching her again like a leaf helpless in the wind:

"Rose—Rose—Rose of the night,
When the spring moon is bright you'll be fair—"

A few minutes later, feeling oddly shaken and exalted, Basil drifted outside with the crowd. The first thing upon which his eyes fell was the almost forgotten and now curiously metamorphosed specter of Mr. Rooney.

Mr. Rooney had, in fact, gone a little to pieces. He was, to begin with, wearing a different and much smaller hat than when he left Basil at noon. Secondly, his face had lost its somewhat gross aspect and turned a pure and even delicate white, and he was wearing his necktie and even portions of his shirt on the outside of his unaccountably wringing-wet overcoat. How, in the short space of four hours, Mr. Rooney had got himself in such shape is explicable only by the pressure of confinement in a boys' school upon a fiery outdoor spirit. Mr. Rooney was born to toil under the clear light of heaven and, perhaps half consciously, he was headed toward his inevitable destiny.

"Lee," he said dimly, "you ought to get wise to y'self. I'm going to put you wise y'self."

To avoid the ominous possibility of being put wise to himself in the lobby, Basil uneasily changed the subject.

"Aren't you coming to the show?" he asked, flattering Mr. Rooney by implying that he was in any condition to come to the show. "It's a wonderful show."

Mr. Rooney took off his hat, displaying wringing-wet matted hair. A picture of reality momentarily struggled for development in the back of his brain.

"We got to get back to school," he said in a somber and unconvinced voice.

"But there's another act," protested Basil in horror. "I've got to stay for the last act."

Swaying, Mr. Rooney looked at Basil, dimly realizing that he had put himself in the hollow of this boy's hand.

"All righ'," he admitted. "I'm going to get somethin' to eat. I'll wait for you next door."

He turned abruptly, reeled a dozen steps and curved dizzily into a bar adjoining the theater. Considerably shaken, Basil went back inside.

ACT III. *The Roof Garden of Mr. Van Astor's House. Night.*

Half an hour passed. Everything was going to be all right, after all. The comedian was at his best now, with the glad appropriateness of laughter after tears, and there was a promise of felicity in the bright tropical sky. One lovely plaintive duet, and then abruptly the long moment of incomparable beauty was over.

Basil went into the lobby and stood in thought while the crowd passed out. His mother's letter and the show had cleared his mind of bitterness and vindictiveness—he was his old self and he wanted to do the right thing. He wondered if it was the right thing to get Mr. Rooney back to school. He walked toward the saloon, slowed up as he came to it and, gingerly opening the swinging door, took a quick peer inside. He saw only that Mr. Rooney was not one of those drinking at the bar. He walked down the street a little way, came back and tried again. It was as if he thought the doors were teeth to bite him, for he had the old-fashioned Middle-Western boy's horror of the saloon. The third time he was successful. Mr. Rooney was sound asleep at a table in the back of the room.

Outside again Basil walked up and down, considering. He would give Mr. Rooney half an hour. If, at the end of that time, he had not come out, he would go back to school. After all, Mr. Rooney had laid for him ever since football season—Basil was simply washing his hands of the whole affair, as in a day or so he would wash his hands of school.

He had made several turns up and down, when, glancing up an

alley that ran beside the theater his eye was caught by the sign, Stage
Entrance. He could watch the actors come forth.

He waited. Women streamed by him, but those were the days
before Glorification and he took these drab people for wardrobe
women or something. Then suddenly a girl came out and with her
a man, and Basil turned and ran a few steps up the street as if
afraid they would recognize him—and ran back, breathing as if with
a heart attack—for the girl, a radiant little beauty of nineteen, was
Her and the young man by her side was Ted Fay.

Arm in arm, they walked past him, and irresistibly Basil followed.
As they walked, she leaned toward Ted Fay in a way that gave them
a fascinating air of intimacy. They crossed Broadway and turned
into the Knickerbocker Hotel, and twenty feet behind them Basil
followed, in time to see them go into a long room set for afternoon
tea. They sat at a table for two, spoke vaguely to a waiter, and then,
alone at last, bent eagerly toward each other. Basil saw that Ted
Fay was holding her gloved hand.

The tea room was separated only by a hedge of potted firs from
the main corridor. Basil went along this to a lounge which was almost
up against their table and sat down.

Her voice was low and faltering, less certain than it had been in
the play, and very sad: "Of course I do, Ted." For a long time, as
their conversation continued, she repeated "Of course I do" or "But
I do, Ted." Ted Fay's remarks were too low for Basil to hear.

"—— says next month, and he won't be put off any more. . . .
I do in a way, Ted. It's hard to explain, but he's done everything for
mother and me. . . . There's no use kidding myself. It was a fool-
proof part and any girl he gave it to was made right then and
there. . . . He's been awfully thoughtful. He's done everything for
me."

Basil's ears were sharpened by the intensity of his emotion; now
he could hear Ted Fay's voice too:

"And you say you love me."

"But don't you see I promised to marry him more than a year ago."

"Tell him the truth—that you love me. Ask him to let you off."

"This isn't musical comedy, Ted."

"That was a mean one," he said bitterly.

"I'm sorry, dear, Ted darling, but you're driving me crazy going
on this way. You're making it so hard for me."

"I'm going to leave New Haven, anyhow."

"No, you're not. You're going to stay and play baseball this spring.
Why, you're an ideal to all those boys! Why, if you——"

He laughed shortly. "You're a fine one to talk about ideals."

"Why not? I'm living up to my responsibility to Beltzman; you've got to make up your mind just like I have—that we can't have each other."

"Jerry! Think what you're doing! All my life, whenever I hear that waltz——"

Basil got to his feet and hurried down the corridor, through the lobby and out of the hotel. He was in a state of wild emotional confusion. He did not understand all he had heard, but from his clandestine glimpse into the privacy of these two, with all the world that his short experience could conceive of at their feet, he had gathered that life for everybody was a struggle, sometimes magnificent from a distance, but always difficult and surprisingly simple and a little sad.

They would go on. Ted Fay would go back to Yale, put her picture in his bureau drawer and knock out home runs with the bases full this spring—at 8:30 the curtain would go up and She would miss something warm and young out of her life, something she had had this afternoon.

It was dark outside and Broadway was a blazing forest fire as Basil walked slowly along toward the point of brightest light. He looked up at the great intersecting planes of radiance with a vague sense of approval and possession. He would see it a lot now, lay his restless heart upon this greater restlessness of a nation—he would come whenever he could get off from school.

But that was all changed—he was going to Europe. Suddenly Basil realized that he wasn't going to Europe. He could not forego the molding of his own destiny just to alleviate a few months of pain. The conquest of the successive worlds of school, college and New York—why, that was his true dream that he had carried from boyhood into adolescence, and because of the jeers of a few boys he had been about to abandon it and run ignominiously up a back alley! He shivered violently, like a dog coming out of the water, and simultaneously he was reminded of Mr. Rooney.

A few minutes later he walked into the bar, past the quizzical eyes of the bartender and up to the table where Mr. Rooney still sat asleep. Basil shook him gently, then firmly. Mr. Rooney stirred and perceived Basil.

"G'wise to yourself," he muttered drowsily. "G'wise to yourself an' let me alone."

"I am wise to myself," said Basil. "Honest, I am wise to myself, Mr. Rooney. You got to come with me into the washroom and get cleaned up, and then you can sleep on the train again, Mr. Rooney. Come on, Mr. Rooney, please——"

V

It was a long hard time. Basil got on bounds again in December and wasn't free again until March. An indulgent mother had given him no habits of work and this was almost beyond the power of anything but life itself to remedy, but he made numberless new starts and failed and tried again.

He made friends with a new boy named Maplewood after Christmas, but they had a silly quarrel; and through the winter term, when a boys' school is shut in with itself and only partly assuaged from its natural savagery by indoor sports, Basil was snubbed and slighted a good deal for his real and imaginary sins, and he was much alone. But on the other hand, there was Ted Fay, and Rose of the Night on the phonograph—"All my life whenever I hear that waltz"—and the remembered lights of New York, and the thought of what he was going to do in football next autumn and the glamorous mirage of Yale and the hope of spring in the air.

Fat Gaspar and a few others were nice to him now. Once when he and Fat walked home together by accident from downtown they had a long talk about actresses—a talk that Basil was wise enough not to presume upon afterward. The smaller boys suddenly decided that they approved of him, and a master who had hitherto disliked him put his hand on his shoulder walking to a class one day. They would all forget eventually—maybe during the summer. There would be new fresh boys in September; he would have a clean start next year.

One afternoon in February, playing basketball, a great thing happened. He and Brick Wales were at forward on the second team and in the fury of the scrimmage the gymnasium echoed with sharp slapping contacts and shrill cries.

"Here yar!"

"Bill! Bill!"

Basil had dribbled the ball down the court and Brick Wales, free, was crying for it.

"Here yar! Lee! Hey! Lee-y!"

Lee-y!

Basil flushed and made a poor pass. He had been called by a nickname. It was a poor makeshift, but it was something more than the stark bareness of his surname or a term of derision. Brick Wales went on playing, unconscious that he had done anything in particular or that he had contributed to the events by which another boy was saved from the army of the bitter, the selfish, the neurasthenic and the unhappy. It isn't given to us to know those rare moments when people are wide open and the lightest touch can wither or heal. A moment too late and we can never reach them any more in this world. They will not be cured by our most efficacious drugs or slain with our sharpest swords.

Lee-y! It could scarcely be pronounced. But Basil took it to bed with him that night, and thinking of it, holding it to him happily to the last, fell easily to sleep.

1928   *Taps at Reveille*

THE CAPTURED SHADOW

BASIL DUKE LEE shut the front door behind him and turned on the dining-room light. His mother's voice drifted sleepily downstairs:

"Basil, is that you?"

"No, mother, it's a burglar."

"It seems to me twelve o'clock is pretty late for a fifteen-year-old boy."

"We went to Smith's and had a soda."

Whenever a new responsibility devolved upon Basil he was "a boy almost sixteen," but when a privilege was in question, he was "a fifteen-year-old boy."

There were footsteps above, and Mrs. Lee, in kimono, descended to the first landing.

"Did you and Riply enjoy the play?"

"Yes, very much."

"What was it about?"

"Oh, it was just about this man. Just an ordinary play."

"Didn't it have a name?"

" 'Are You a Mason?' "

"Oh." She hesitated, covetously watching his alert and eager face, holding him there. "Aren't you coming to bed?"

"I'm going to get something to eat."

"Something more?"

For a moment he didn't answer. He stood in front of a glassed-in bookcase in the living room, examining its contents with an equally glazed eye.

"We're going to get up a play," he said suddenly. "I'm going to write it."

"Well—that'll be very nice. Please come to bed soon. You were up late last night, too, and you've got dark circles under your eyes."

From the bookcase Basil presently extracted "Van Bibber and Others," from which he read while he ate a large plate of straw softened with a half pint of cream. Back in the living room he sat for a few minutes at the piano, digesting, and meanwhile staring at the colored cover of a song from "The Midnight Sons." It showed

346

three men in evening clothes and opera hats sauntering jovially along Broadway against the blazing background of Times Square.

Basil would have denied incredulously the suggestion that that was currently his favorite work of art. But it was.

He went upstairs. From a drawer of his desk he took out a composition book and opened it.

BASIL DUKE LEE

St. Regis School
Eastchester, Conn.
Fifth Form French

and on the next page, under Irregular Verbs:

PRESENT

je connais   *nous con*
tu connais
il connaît

He turned over another page.

MR. WASHINGTON SQUARE
A Musical Comedy by
Basil Duke Lee
Music by Victor Herbert

ACT I

*[The porch of the Millionaires' Club, near New York.
Opening Chorus*, Leilia *and* Debutantes:

> *We sing not soft, we sing not loud*
> *For no one ever heard an opening chorus.*
> *We are a very merry crowd*
> *But no one ever heard an opening chorus.*
> *We're just a crowd of debutantes*
> *As merry as can be*
> *And nothing that there is could ever bore us*
> *We're the wittiest ones, the prettiest ones,*
> *In all society*
> *But no one ever heard an opening chorus.*

Leilia (*stepping forward*): Well, girls, has Mr. Washington Square been around here today?

Basil turned over a page. There was no answer to Leilia's question. Instead in capitals was a brand-new heading:

HIC! HIC! HIC!

A Hilarious Farce in One Act
by

Basil Duke Lee

SCENE

[*A fashionable apartment near Broadway, New York City. It is almost midnight. As the curtain goes up there is a knocking at the door and a few minutes later it opens to admit a handsome man in a full evening dress and a companion. He has evidently been imbibing, for his words are thick, his nose is red, and he can hardly stand up. He turns up the light and comes down centre.*]

Stuyvesant: Hic! Hic! Hic!
O'Hara (*his companion*): Begorra, you been sayin' nothing else all this evening.

Basil turned over a page and then another, reading hurriedly, but not without interest.

Professor Pumpkin: Now, if you are an educated man, as you claim, perhaps you can tell me the Latin word for "this."
Stuyvesant: Hic! Hic! Hic!
Professor Pumpkin: Correct. Very good indeed. I——

At this point Hic! Hic! Hic! came to an end in midsentence. On the following page, in just as determined a hand as if the last two works had not faltered by the way, was the heavily underlined beginning of another:

THE CAPTURED SHADOW

A Melodramatic Farce in Three Acts
by Basil Duke Lee

SCENE

[*All three acts take place in the library of the* van bakers' *house in New York. It is well furnished with a red lamp on one side and some crossed spears and helmets and so on and a divan and a general air of an oriental den.*
When the curtain rises Miss Saunders, Leilia Van Baker *and*]

ESTELLA CARRAGE *are sitting at a table.* MISS SAUNDERS *is an old maid about forty very kittenish.* LEILIA *is pretty with dark hair.* ESTELLA *has light hair. They are a striking combination.*

"The Captured Shadow" filled the rest of the book and ran over into several loose sheets at the end. When it broke off Basil sat for a while in thought. This had been a season of "crook comedies" in New York, and the feel, the swing, the exact and vivid image of the two he had seen, were in the foreground of his mind. At the time they had been enormously suggestive, opening out into a world much larger and more brilliant than themselves that existed outside their windows and beyond their doors, and it was this suggested world rather than any conscious desire to imitate "Officer 666" that had inspired the effort before him. Presently he printed ACT II at the head of a new tablet and began to write.

An hour passed. Several times he had recourse to a collection of joke books and to an old Treasury of Wit and Humor which embalmed the faded Victorian cracks of Bishop Wilberforce and Sydney Smith. At the moment when, in his story, a door moved slowly open, he heard a heavy creak upon the stairs. He jumped to his feet, aghast and trembling, but nothing stirred; only a white moth bounced against the screen, a clock struck the half-hour far across the city, a bird whacked its wings in a tree outside.

Voyaging to the bathroom at half-past four, he saw with a shock that morning was already blue at the window. He had stayed up all night. He remembered that people who stayed up all night went crazy and, transfixed in the hall, he tried agonizingly to listen to himself, to feel whether or not he was going crazy. The things around him seemed prenaturally unreal, and rushing frantically back into his bedroom, he began tearing off his clothes, racing after the vanishing night. Undressed, he threw a final regretful glance at his pile of manuscript—he had the whole next scene in his head. As a compromise with incipient madness he got into bed and wrote for an hour more.

Late next morning he was startled awake by one of the ruthless Scandinavian sisters who, in theory, were the Lees' servants. "Eleven o'clock!" she shouted. "Five after!"

"Let me alone," Basil mumbled. "What do you come and wake me up for?"

"Somebody downstairs." He opened his eyes. "You ate all the cream last night," Hilda continued. "Your mother didn't have any for her coffee."

"All the cream!" he cried. "Why, I saw some more."

"It was sour."

"That's terrible," he exclaimed, sitting up. "Terrible!"

For a moment she enjoyed his dismay. Then she said, "Riply Buckner's downstairs," and went out, closing the door.

"Send him up!" he called after her. "Hilda, why don't you ever listen for a minute? Did I get any mail?"

There was no answer. A moment later Riply came in.

"My gosh, are you still in bed?"

"I wrote on the play all night. I almost finished Act Two." He pointed to his desk.

"That's what I want to talk to you about," said Riply. "Mother thinks we ought to get Miss Halliburton."

"What for?"

"Just to sort of be there."

Though Miss Halliburton was a pleasant person who combined the occupations of French teacher and bridge teacher, unofficial chaperon and children's friend, Basil felt that her superintendence would give the project an unprofessional ring.

"She wouldn't interfere," went on Riply, obviously quoting his mother. "I'll be the business manager and you'll direct the play, just like we said, but it would be good to have her there for prompter and to keep order at rehearsals. The girls' mothers'll like it."

"All right," Basil agreed reluctantly. "Now look, let's see who we'll have in the cast. First, there's the leading man—this gentleman burglar that's called The Shadow. Only it turns out at the end that he's really a young man about town doing it on a bet, and not really a burglar at all."

"That's you."

"No, that's you."

"Come on! You're the best actor," protested Riply.

"No, I'm going to take a smaller part, so I can coach."

"Well, haven't I got to be business manager?"

Selecting the actresses, presumably all eager, proved to be a difficult matter. They settled finally on Imogene Bissel for leading lady; Margaret Torrence for her friend, and Connie Davies for "Miss Saunders, an old maid very kittenish."

On Riply's suggestion that several other girls wouldn't be pleased at being left out, Basil introduced a maid and a cook, "who could just sort of look in from the kitchen." He rejected firmly Riply's further proposal that there should be two or three maids, "a sort of sewing woman," and a trained nurse. In a house so clogged with femininity even the most umbrageous of gentleman burglars would have difficulty in moving about.

"I'll tell you two people we won't have," Basil said meditatively— "that's Joe Gorman and Hubert Blair."

"I wouldn't be in it if we had Hubert Blair," asserted Riply.

"Neither would I."

Hubert Blair's almost miraculous successes with girls had caused Basil and Riply much jealous pain.

They began calling up the prospective cast and immediately the enterprise received its first blow. Imogene Bissel was going to Rochester, Minnesota, to have her appendix removed, and wouldn't be back for three weeks.

They considered.

"How about Margaret Torrence?"

Basil shook his head. He had vision of Leilia Van Baker as someone rarer and more spirited than Margaret Torrence. Not that Leilia had much being, even to Basil—less than the Harrison Fisher girls pinned around his wall at school. But she was not Margaret Torrence. She was no one you could inevitably see by calling up half an hour before on the phone.

He discarded candidate after candidate. Finally a face began to flash before his eyes, as if in another connection, but so insistently that at length he spoke the name.

"Evelyn Beebe."

"Who?"

Though Evelyn Beebe was only sixteen, her precocious charms had elevated her to an older crowd and to Basil she seemed of the very generation of his heroine, Leilia Van Baker. It was a little like asking Sarah Bernhardt for her services, but once her name had occurred to him, other possibilities seemed pale.

At noon they rang the Beebe's door-bell, stricken by a paralysis of embarrassment when Evelyn opened the door herself and, with politeness that concealed a certain surprise, asked them in.

Suddenly, through the portiere of the living room, Basil saw and recognized a young man in golf knickerbockers.

"I guess we better not come in," he said quickly.

"We'll come some other time," Riply added.

Together they started precipitately for the door, but she barred their way.

"Don't be silly," she insisted. "It's just Andy Lockheart."

Just Andy Lockheart—winner of the Western Golf Championship at eighteen, captain of his freshman baseball team, handsome, successful at everything he tried, a living symbol of the splendid, glamorous world of Yale. For a year Basil had walked like him and tried unsuccessfully to play the piano by ear as Andy Lockheart was able to do.

Through sheer ineptitude at escaping, they were edged into the room. Their plan suddenly seemed presumptuous and absurd.

Perceiving their condition Evelyn tried to soothe them with pleasant banter.

"Well, it's about time you came to see me," she told Basil. "Here I've been sitting home every night waiting for you—ever since the Davies dance. Why haven't you been here before?"

He stared at her blankly, unable even to smile, and muttered: "Yes, you have."

"I have though. Sit down and tell me why you've been neglecting me! I suppose you've both been rushing the beautiful Imogene Bissel."

"Why, I understand—" said Basil. "Why, I heard from somewhere that she's gone up to have some kind of an appendicitis—that is—" He ran down to a pitch of inaudibility as Andy Lockheart at the piano began playing a succession of thoughtful chords, which resolved itself into the maxixe, an eccentric stepchild of the tango. Kicking back a rug and lifting her skirts a little, Evelyn fluently tapped out a circle with her heels around the floor.

They sat inanimate as cushions on the sofa watching her. She was almost beautiful, with rather large features and bright fresh color, behind which her heart seemed to be trembling a little with laughter. Her voice and her lithe body were always mimicking, ceaselessly caricaturing every sound and movement near by, until even those who disliked her admitted that "Evelyn could always make you laugh." She finished her dance now with a false stumble and an awed expression as she clutched at the piano, and Basil and Riply chuckled. Seeing their embarrassment lighten, she came and sat down beside them, and they laughed again when she said: "Excuse my lack of self-control."

"Do you want to be the leading lady in a play we're going to give?" demanded Basil with sudden desperation. "We're going to have it at the Martindale School, for the benefit of the Baby Welfare."

"Basil, this is so sudden."

Andy Lockheart turned around from the piano.

"What're you going to give—a minstrel show?"

"No, it's a crook play named "The Captured Shadow." Miss Halliburton is going to coach it." He suddenly realized the convenience of that name to shelter himself behind.

"Why don't you give something like "The Private Secretary"?" interrupted Andy. "There's a good play for you. We gave it my last year at school."

"Oh, no, it's all settled," said Basil quickly. "We're going to put on this play that I wrote."

"You wrote it yourself?" exclaimed Evelyn.

"Yes."

"My-y gosh!" said Andy. He began to play again.

"Look, Evelyn," said Basil. "It's only for three weeks, and you'd be the leading lady."

She laughed. "Oh, no. I couldn't. Why don't you get Imogene?"

"She's sick, I tell you. Listen——"

"Or Margaret Torrence?"

"I don't want anybody but you."

The directness of this appeal touched her and momentarily she hesitated. But the hero of the Western Golf Championship turned around from the piano with a teasing smile and she shook her head.

"I can't do it, Basil. I may have to go East with the family."

Reluctantly Basil and Riply got up.

"Gosh, I wish you'd be in it, Evelyn."

"I wish I could."

Basil lingered, thinking fast, wanting her more than ever; indeed, without her, it scarcely seemed worth while to go on with the play. Suddenly a desperate expedient took shape on his lips:

"You certainly would be wonderful. You see, the leading man is going to be Hubert Blair."

Breathlessly he watched her, saw her hesitate.

"Good-by," he said.

She came with them to the door and then out on the veranda, frowning a little.

"How long did you say the rehearsals would take?" she asked thoughtfully.

II

On an August evening three days later Basil read the play to the cast on Miss Halliburton's porch. He was nervous and at first there were interruptions of "Louder" and "Not so fast." Just as his audience was beginning to be amused by the repartee of the two comic crooks—repartee that had seen service with Weber and Fields—he was interrupted by the late arrival of Hubert Blair.

Hubert was fifteen, a somewhat shallow boy save for two or three felicities which he possessed to an extraordinary degree. But one excellence suggests the presence of others, and young ladies never failed to respond to his most casual fancy, enduring his fickleness of heart and never convinced that his fundamental indifference might not be overcome. They were dazzled by his flashing self-confidence, by his cherubic ingenuousness, which concealed a shrewd talent for getting around people, and by his extraordinary physical grace. Long-legged, beautifully proportioned, he had that tumbler's balance usually characteristic only of men "built near the ground." He was

in constant motion that was a delight to watch, and Evelyn Beebe
was not the only older girl who had found in him a mysterious promise and watched him for a long time with something more than
curiosity.

He stood in the doorway now with an expression of bogus rever
ence on his round pert face.

"Excuse me," he said. "Is this the First Methodist Episcopal
Church?" Everybody laughed—even Basil. "I didn't know. I thought
maybe I was in the right church, but in the wrong pew."

They laughed again, somewhat discouraged. Basil waited until
Hubert had seated himself beside Evelyn Beebe. Then he began to
read once more, while the others, fascinated, watched Hubert's efforts
to balance a chair on its hind legs. This squeaky experiment continued as an undertone to the reading. Not until Basil's desperate
"Now, here's where you come in, Hube," did attention swing back
to the play.

Basil read for more than an hour. When, at the end, he closed the
composition book and looked up shyly, there was a burst of spon-
taneous applause. He had followed his models closely, and for all its
grotesqueries, the result was actually interesting—it was a play.
Afterward he lingered, talking to Miss Halliburton, and he walked
home glowing with excitement and rehearsing a little by himself
into the August night.

The first week of rehearsal was a matter of Basil climbing back
and forth from auditorium to stage, crying, "No! Look here, Connie;
you come in more like this." Then things began to happen. Mrs. Van
Schellinger came to rehearsal one day and, lingering afterward, announced that she couldn't let Gladys be in "a play about crimi-
nals." Her theory was that this element could be removed; for
instance, the two comic crooks could be changed to "two funny
farmers."

Basil listened with horror. When she had gone he assured Miss
Halliburton that he would change nothing. Luckily Gladys played
the cook, an interpolated part that could be summarily struck out,
but her absence was felt in another way. She was tranquil and tractable, "the most carefully brought-up girl in town," and at her withdrawal rowdiness appeared during rehearsals. Those who had only
such lines as "I'll ask Mrs. Van Baker, sir," in Act I and "No,
ma'am," in Act III showed a certain tendency to grow restless in between. So now it was:

"Please keep that dog quiet or else send him home!" or:
"Where's that maid? Wake up, Margaret, for heaven's sake!" or:
"What is there to laugh at that's so darn funny?"

More and more the chief problem was the tactful management of

Hubert Blair. Apart from his unwillingness to learn his lines, he was a satisfactory hero, but off the stage he became a nuisance. He gave an endless private performance for Evelyn Beebe, which took such forms as chasing her amorously around the hall or flipping peanuts over his shoulder to land mysteriously on the stage. Called to order, he would mutter, "Aw, shut up yourself," just loud enough for Basil to guess, but not to hear.

But Evelyn Beebe was all that Basil had expected. Once on the stage she compelled a breathless attention, and Basil recognized this by adding to her part. He envied the half-sentimental fun that she and Hubert derived from their scenes together and he felt a vague, impersonal jealousy that almost every night after rehearsal they drove around together in Hubert's car.

One afternoon when matters had progressed a fortnight, Hubert came in an hour late, loafed through the first act and then informed Miss Halliburton that he was going home.

"What for?" Basil demanded.

"I've got some things I got to do."

"Are they important?"

"What business is that of yours?"

"Of course it's my business," said Basil heatedly, whereupon Miss Halliburton interfered.

"There's no use of anybody getting angry. What Basil means, Hubert, is that if it's just some small thing—why, we're all giving up our pleasure to make this play a success."

Hubert listened with obvious boredom.

"I've got to drive downtown and get father."

He looked coolly at Basil, as if challenging him to deny the adequacy of this explanation.

"They why did you come an hour late?" demanded Basil.

"Because I had to do something for mother."

A group had gathered and he glanced around triumphantly. It was one of those sacred excuses, and only Basil saw that it was disingenuous.

"Oh, tripe!" he said.

"Maybe you think so—Bossy."

Basil took a step toward him, his eyes blazing.

"What'd you say?"

"I said 'Bossy.' Isn't that what they call you at school?"

It was true. It had followed him home. Even as he went white with rage a vast impotence surged over him at the realization that the past was always lurking near. The faces of school were around him, sneering and watching. Hubert laughed.

"Get out!" said Basil in a strained voice. "Go on! Get right out!"

Hubert laughed again, but as Basil took a step toward him he retreated.

"I don't want to be in your play anyhow. I never did."

"Then go on out of this hall."

"Now, Basil!" Miss Halliburton hovered breathlessly beside them. Hubert laughed again and looked about for his cap.

"I wouldn't be in your crazy old show," he said. He turned slowly and jauntily, and sauntered out the door.

Riply Buckner read Hubert's part that afternoon, but there was a cloud upon the rehearsal. Miss Beebe's performance lacked its customary verve and the others clustered and whispered, falling silent when Basil came near. After the rehearsal, Miss Halliburton, Riply and Basil held a conference. Upon Basil flatly refusing to take the leading part, it was decided to enlist a certain Mayall De Bec, known slightly to Riply, who had made a name for himself in theatricals at the Central High School.

But next day a blow fell that was irreparable. Evelyn, flushed and uncomfortable, told Basil and Miss Halliburton that her family's plans had changed—they were going East next week and she couldn't be in the play after all. Basil understood. Only Hubert had held her this long.

"Good-by," he said gloomily.

His manifest despair shamed her and she tried to justify herself. "Really, I can't help it. Oh, Basil, I'm so sorry!"

"Coudn't you stay over a week with me after your family goes?" Miss Halliburton asked innocently.

"Not possibly. Father wants us all to go together. That's the only reason. If it wasn't for that I'd stay."

"All right," Basil said. "Good-by."

"Basil, you're not mad, are you?" A gust of repentance swept over her. "I'll do anything to help. I'll come to rehearsals this week until you get someone else, and then I'll try to help her all I can. But father says we've got to go."

In vain Riply tried to raise Basil's morale after the rehearsal that afternoon, making suggestions which he waved contemptuously away. Margaret Torrence? Connie Davies? They could hardly play the parts they had. It seemed to Basil as if the undertaking was falling to pieces before his eyes.

It was still early when he got home. He sat dispiritedly by his bedroom window, watching the little Barnfield boy playing a lonesome game by himself in the yard next door.

His mother came in at five, and immediately sensed his depression.

"Teddy Barnfield has the mumps," she said, in an effort to distract him. "That's why he's playing there all alone."

"Has he?" he responded listlessly.

"It isn't at all dangerous, but it's very contagious. You had it when you were seven."

"H'm."

She hesitated.

"Are you worrying about your play? Has anything gone wrong?"

"No, mother. I just want to be alone."

After a while he got up and started after a malted milk at the soda fountain around the corner. It was half in his mind to see Mr. Beebe and ask him if he couldn't postpone his trip East. If he could only be sure that that was Evelyn's real reason.

The sight of Evelyn's nine-year-old brother coming along the street broke in on his thoughts.

"Hello, Ham. I hear you're going away."

Ham nodded.

"Going next week. To the seashore."

Basil looked at him speculatively, as if, through his proximity to Evelyn, he held the key to the power of moving her.

"Where are you going now?" he asked.

"I'm going to play with Teddy Barnfield."

"What!" Basil exclaimed. "Why, didn't you know—" He stopped. A wild, criminal idea broke over him; his mother's words floated through his mind: "It isn't at all dangerous, but it's very contagious." If little Ham Beebe got the mumps, and Evelyn *couldn't* go away—

He came to a decision quickly and coolly.

"Teddy's playing in his back yard," he said. "If you want to see him without going through his house, why don't you go down this street and turn up the alley?"

"All right. Thanks," said Ham trustingly.

Basil stood for a minute looking after him until he turned the corner into the alley, fully aware that it was the worst thing he had ever done in his life.

III

A week later Mrs. Lee had an early supper—all Basil's favorite things: chipped beef, French-fried potatoes, sliced peaches and cream, and devil's food.

Every few minutes Basil said, "Gosh! I wonder what time it is," and went out in the hall to look at the clock. "Does that clock work right?" he demanded with sudden suspicion. It was the first time the matter had ever interested him.

"Perfectly all right. If you eat so fast you'll have indigestion and then you won't be able to act well."

"What do you think of the program?" he asked for the third time. "Riply Buckner, Jr., presents Basil Duke Lee's comedy, 'The Captured Shadow.'"

"I think it's very nice."

"He doesn't really present it."

"It sounds very well though."

"I wonder what time it is?" he inquired.

"You just said it was ten minutes after six."

"Well, I guess I better be starting."

"Eat your peaches, Basil. If you don't eat you won't be able to act."

"I don't have to act," he said patiently. "All I am is a small part, and it wouldn't matter—" It was too much trouble to explain.

"Please don't smile at me when I come on, mother," he requested. "Just act as if I was anybody else."

"Can't I even say how-do-you-do?"

"What?" Humor was lost on him. He said good-by. Trying very hard to digest not his food but his heart, which had somehow slipped down into his stomach, he started off for the Martindale School.

As its yellow windows loomed out of the night his excitement became insupportable; it bore no resemblance to the building he had been entering so casually for three weeks. His footsteps echoed symbolically and portentously in its deserted hall; upstairs there was only the janitor setting out the chairs in rows, and Basil wondered about the vacant stage until someone came in.

It was Mayall De Bec, the tall, clever, not very likeable youth they had imported from Lower Crest Avenue to be the leading man. Mayall, far from being nervous, tried to engage Basil in casual conversation. He wanted to know if Basil thought Evelyn Beebe would mind if he went to see her sometime when the show was over. Basil supposed not. Mayall said he had a friend whose father owned a brewery who owned a twelve-cylinder car.

Basil said, "Gee!"

At quarter to seven the participants arrived in groups—Riply Buckner with the six boys he had gathered to serve as ticket takers and ushers; Miss Halliburton, trying to seem very calm and reliable; Evelyn Beebe, who came in as if she were yielding herself up to something and whose glance at Basil seemed to say: "Well, it looks as if I'm really going through with it after all."

Mayall De Bec was to make up the boys and Miss Halliburton the girls. Basil soon came to the conclusion that Miss Halliburton knew nothing about make-up, but he judged it diplomatic, in that lady's overwrought condition, to say nothing, but to take each girl to Mayall for corrections when Miss Halliburton had done.

An exclamation from Bill Kampf, standing at a crack in the curtain, brought Basil to his side. A tall bald-headed man in spectacles had come in and was shown to a seat in the middle of the house, where he examined the program. He was the public. Behind those waiting eyes, suddenly so mysterious and incalculable, was the secret of the play's failure or success. He finished the program, took off his glasses and looked around. Two old ladies and two little boys came in, followed immediately by a dozen more.

"Hey, Riply," Basil called softly. "Tell them to put the children down in front."

Riply, struggling into his policeman's uniform, looked up, and the long black mustache on his upper lip quivered indignantly.

"I thought of that long ago."

That hall, filling rapidly, was now alive with the buzz of conversation. The children in front were jumping up and down in their seats, and everyone was talking and calling back and forth save the several dozen cooks and housemaids who sat in stiff and quiet pairs about the room.

Then, suddenly, everything was ready. It was incredible. "Stop! Stop!" Basil wanted to say. "It can't be ready. There must be something—there always has been something," but the darkened auditorium and the piano and violin from Geyer's Orchestra playing *Meet Me in the Shadows* belied his words. Miss Saunders, Leilia Van Baker and Leilia's friend, Estella Carrage, were already seated on the stage, and Miss Halliburton stood in the wings with the prompt book. Suddenly the music ended and the chatter in front died away.

"Oh, gosh!" Basil thought. "Oh, my gosh!"

The curtain rose. A clear voice floated up from somewhere. Could it be from that unfamiliar group on the stage?

I will, Miss Saunders. I tell you I will!

But, Miss Leilia, I don't consider the newspapers proper for young ladies nowadays.

I don't care. I want to read about this wonderful gentleman burglar they call The Shadow.

It was actually going on. Almost before he realized it, a ripple of laughter passed over the audience as Evelyn gave her imitation of Miss Saunders behind her back.

"Get ready, Basil," breathed Miss Halliburton.

Basil and Bill Kampf, the crooks, each took an elbow of Victor Van Baker, the dissolute son of the house, and made ready to aid him through the front door.

It was strangely natural to be out on the stage with all those eyes looking up encouragingly. His mother's face floated past him, other faces that he recognized and remembered.

Bill Kampf stumbled on a line and Basil picked him up quickly and went on.

MISS SAUNDERS: So you are alderman from the Sixth Ward?
RABBIT SIMMONS: Yes, ma'am.
MISS SAUNDERS (*shaking her head kittenishly*): Just what is an alderman?
CHINAMAN RUDD: An alderman is halfway between a politician and a pirate.

This was one of Basil's lines that he was particularly proud of—but there was not a sound from the audience, not a smile. A moment later Bill Kampf absent-mindedly wiped his forehead with his handkerchief and then stared at it, startled by the red stains of make-up on it—and the audience roared. The theatre was like that.

MISS SAUNDERS: Then you believe in spirits, Mr. Rudd.
CHINAMAN RUDD: Yes, ma'am, I certainly do believe in spirits. Have you got any?

The first big scene came. On the darkened stage a window rose slowly and Mayall De Bec, "in a full evening dress," climbed over the sill. He was tiptoeing cautiously from one side of the stage to the other, when Leilia Van Baker came in. For a moment she was frightened, but he assured her that he was a friend of her brother Victor. They talked. She told him naïvely yet feelingly of her admiration for The Shadow, of whose exploits she had read. She hoped, though, that The Shadow would not come here tonight, as the family jewels were all in that safe at the right.

The stranger was hungry. He had been late for his dinner and so had not been able to get any that night. Would he have some crackers and milk? That would be fine. Scarcely had she left the room when he was on his knees by the safe, fumbling at the catch, undeterred by the unpromising word "Cake" stencilled on the safe's front. It swung open, but he heard footsteps outside and closed it just as Leilia came back with the crackers and milk.

They lingered, obviously attracted to each other. Miss Saunders came in, very kittenish, and was introduced. Again Evelyn mimicked her behind her back and the audience roared. Other members of the household appeared and were introduced to the stranger.

What's this? A banging at the door, and Mulligan, a policeman, rushes in.

We have just received word from the Central Office that the notorious Shadow has been seen climbing in the window! No one can leave this house tonight!

The curtain fell. The first rows of the audience—the younger brothers and sisters of the cast—were extravagant in their enthusiasm. The actors took a bow.

A moment later Basil found himself alone with Evelyn Beebe on the stage. A weary doll in her make-up she was leaning against a table.

"Heigh-ho, Basil," she said.

She had not quite forgiven him for holding her to her promise after her little brother's mumps had postponed their trip East, and Basil had tactfully avoided her, but now they met in the genial glow of excitement and success.

"You were wonderful," he said—"Wonderful!"

He lingered a moment. He could never please her, for she wanted someone like herself, someone who could reach her through her senses, like Hubert Blair. Her intuition told her that Basil was of a certain vague consequence; beyond that his incessant attempts to make people think and feel, bothered and wearied her. But suddenly, in the glow of the evening, they leaned forward and kissed peacefully, and from that moment, because they had no common ground even to quarrel on, they were friends for life.

When the curtain rose upon the second act Basil slipped down a flight of stairs and up another to the back of the hall, where he stood watching in the darkness. He laughed silently when the audience laughed, enjoying it as if it were a play he had never seen before.

There was a second and a third act scene that were very similar. In each of them The Shadow, alone on the stage, was interrupted by Miss Saunders. Mayall De Bec, having had but ten days of rehearsal, was inclined to confuse the two, but Basil was totally unprepared for what happened. Upon Connie's entrance Mayall spoke his third-act line and involuntarily Connie answered in kind.

Others coming on the stage were swept up in the nervousness and confusion, and suddenly they were playing the third act in the middle of the second. It happened so quickly that for a moment Basil had only a vague sense that something was wrong. Then he dashed down one stairs and up another and into the wings, crying:

"Let down the curtain! Let down the curtain!"

The boys who stood there aghast sprang to the rope. In a minute Basil, breathless, was facing the audience.

"Ladies and gentlemen," he said, "there's been changes in the cast and what just happened was a mistake. If you'll excuse us we'd like to do that scene over."

He stepped back in the wings to a flutter of laughter and applause. "All right, Mayall!" he called excitedly. "On the stage alone. Your line is: 'I just want to see that the jewels are all right,' and Connie's is: 'Go ahead, don't mind me.' All right! Curtain up!"

In a moment things righted themselves. Someone brought water for Miss Halliburton, who was in a state of collapse, and as the act ended they all took a curtain call once more. Twenty minutes later it was over. The hero clasped Leilia Van Baker to his breast, confessing that he was The Shadow, "and a captured Shadow at that"; the curtain went up and down, up and down; Miss Halliburton was dragged unwillingly on the stage and the ushers came up the aisles laden with flowers. Then everything became informal and the actors mingled happily with the audience, laughing and important, congratulated from all sides. An old man whom Basil didn't know came up to him and shook his hand, saying, "You're a young man that's going to be heard from some day," and a reporter from the paper asked him if he was really only fifteen. It might all have been very bad and demoralizing for Basil, but it was already behind him. Even as the crowd melted away and the last few people spoke to him and went out, he felt a great vacancy come into his heart. It was over, it was done and gone—all that work, and interest and absorption. It was a hollowness like fear.

"Good night, Miss Halliburton. Good night, Evelyn."

"Good night, Basil. Congratulations, Basil. Good night."

"Where's my coat? Good night, Basil."

"Leave your costumes on the stage, please. They've got to go back tomorrow."

He was almost the last to leave, mounting to the stage for a moment and looking around the deserted hall. His mother was waiting and they strolled home together through the first cool night of the year.

"Well, I thought it went very well indeed. Were you satisfied?" He didn't answer for a moment. "Weren't you satisfied with the way it went?"

"Yes." He turned his head away.

"What's the matter?"

"Nothing," and then, "Nobody really cares, do they?"

"About what?"

"About anything."

"Everybody cares about different things. I care about you, for instance."

Instinctively he ducked away from a hand extended caressingly
toward him: "Oh, don't. I don't mean like that."

"You're just overwrought, dear."

"I am not overwrought. I just feel sort of sad."

"You shouldn't feel sad. Why, people told me after the play—"

"Oh, that's all over. Don't talk about that—don't ever talk to me
about that any more."

"Then what are you sad about?"

"Oh, about a little boy."

"What little boy?"

"Oh, little Ham—you wouldn't understand."

"When we get home I want you to take a real hot bath and quiet
your nerves."

"All right."

But when he got home he fell immediately into deep sleep on the
sofa. She hesitated. Then covering him with a blanket and a comforter, she pushed a pillow under his protesting head and went
upstairs.

She knelt for a long time beside her bed.

"God, help him! help him," she prayed, "because he needs help
that I can't give him any more."

1928   *Taps at Reveille*

A WOMAN WITH A PAST

I

DRIVING SLOWLY through New Haven, two of the young girls became alert. Josephine and Lillian darted soft frank glances into strolling groups of three or four undergraduates, into larger groups on corners, which swung about as one man to stare at their receding heads. Believing that they recognized an acquaintance in a solitary loiterer, they waved wildly, whereupon the youth's mouth fell open, and as they turned the next corner he made a dazed dilatory gesture with his hand. They laughed. "We'll send him a post card when we get back to school tonight, to see if it really was him."

Adele Craw, sitting on one of the little seats, kept on talking to Miss Chambers, the chaperone. Glancing sideways at her, Lillian winked at Josephine without batting an eye, but Josephine had gone into a reverie.

This was New Haven—city of her adolescent dreams, of glittering proms where she would move on air among men as intangible as the tunes they danced to. City sacred as Mecca, shining as Paris, hidden as Timbuktu. Twice a year the life-blood of Chicago, her home, flowed into it, and twice a year flowed back, bringing Christmas or bringing summer. Bingo, bingo, bingo, that's the lingo; love of mine, I pine for one of your glances; the darling boy on the left there; underneath the stars I wait.

Seeing it for the first time, she found herself surprisingly unmoved—the men they passed seemed young and rather bored with the possibilities of the day, glad of anything to stare at; seemed undynamic and purposeless against the background of bare elms, lakes of dirty snow and buildings crowded together under the February sky. A wisp of hope, a well-turned-out derby-crowned man, hurrying with stick and suitcase toward the station, caught her attention, but his reciprocal glance was too startled, too ingenuous. Josephine wondered at the extent of her own disillusionment.

She was exactly seventeen and she was blasé. Already she had been a sensation and a scandal; she had driven mature men to a state of disequilibrium; she had, it was said, killed her grandfather, but as he was over eighty at the time perhaps he just died. Here and there in the Middle West were discouraged little spots which upon inspection turned out to be the youths who had once looked full into her green and wistful eyes. But her love affair of last summer had ruined her faith in the all-sufficiency of men. She had grown bored with the waning September days—and it seemed as though it had happened once too often. Christmas with its provocative shortness, its travelling glee clubs, had brought no one new. There remained to her only a persistent, a physical hope; hope in her stomach that there was someone whom she would love more than he loved her.

They stopped at a sporting-goods store and Adele Craw, a pretty girl with clear honorable eyes and piano legs, purchased the sporting equipment which was the reason for their trip—they were the spring hockey committee for the school. Adele was in addition the president of the senior class and the school's ideal girl. She had lately seen a change for the better in Josephine Perry—rather as an honest citizen might guilelessly approve a peculator retired on his profits. On the other hand, Adele was simply incomprehensible to Josephine—admirable, without doubt, but a member of another species. Yet with the charming adaptability that she had hitherto reserved for men, Josephine was trying hard not to disillusion her, trying to be honestly interested in the small, neat, organized politics of the school.

Two men who had stood with their backs to them at another counter turned to leave the store, when they caught sight of Miss Chambers and Adele. Immediately they came forward. The one who spoke to Miss Chambers was thin and rigid of face. Josephine recognized him as Miss Brereton's nephew, a student at New Haven, who had spent several week-ends with his aunt at the school. The other man Josephine had never seen before. He was tall and broad, with blond curly hair and an open expression in which strength of purpose and a nice consideration were pleasantly mingled. It was not the sort of face that generally appealed to Josephine. The eyes were obviously without a secret, without a sidewise gambol, without a desperate flicker to show that they had a life of their own apart from the mouth's speech. The mouth itself was large and masculine; its smile was an act of kindness and control. It was rather with curiosity as to the sort of man who would be attentive to Adele Craw that Josephine continued to look at him, for his voice that obviously couldn't lie greeted Adele as if this meeting was the pleasant surprise of his day.

In a moment Josephine and Lillian were called over and introduced

"This is Mr. Waterbury"—that was Miss Brereton's nephew—
"and Mr. Dudley Knowleton."

Glancing at Adele, Josephine saw on her face an expression of
tranquil pride, even of possession. Mr. Knowleton spoke politely,
but it was obvious that though he looked at the younger girls he did
not quite see them. But since they were friends of Adele's he made
suitable remarks, eliciting the fact that they were both coming down
to New Haven to their first prom the following week. Who were their
hosts? Sophomores; he knew them slightly. Josephine thought that
was unnecessarily superior. Why, they were the charter members of
the Loving Brothers' Association—Ridgeway Saunders and George
Davey—and on the glee-club trip the girls they picked out to rush
in each city considered themselves a sort of elite, second only to the
girls they asked to New Haven.

"And oh, I've got some bad news for you," Knowleton said to
Adele. "You may be leading the prom. Jack Coe went to the infirmary
with appendicitis, and against my better judgment I'm the provisional chairman." He looked apologetic. "Being one of these stone-
age dancers, the two-step king, I don't see how I ever got on the
committee at all."

When the car was on its way back to Miss Brereton's school,
Josephine and Lillian bombarded Adele with questions.

"He's an old friend from Cincinnati," she explained demurely.
"He's captain of the baseball team and he was last man for Skull
and Bones."

"You're going to the prom with him?"

"Yes. You see, I've known him all my life."

Was there a faint implication in this remark that only those who
had known Adele all her life knew her at her true worth?

"Are you engaged?" Lillian demanded.

Adele laughed. "Mercy, I don't think of such matters. It doesn't
seem to be time for that sort of thing yet, does it?" ("Yes," interpolated Josephine silently.) "We're just good friends. I think there
can be a perfectly healthy friendship between a man and a girl without a lot of—"

"Mush," supplied Lillian helpfully.

"Well, yes, but I don't like that word. I was going to say without
a lot of sentimental romantic things that ought to come later."

"Bravo, Adele!" said Miss Chambers somewhat perfunctorily.

But Josephine's curiosity was unappeased.

"Doesn't he say he's in love with you, and all that sort of thing?"

"Mercy, no! Dud doesn't believe in such stuff any more than I
do. He's got enough to do at New Haven, serving on the committees
and the team."

"Oh!" said Josephine.

She was oddly interested. That two people who were attracted to each other should never even say anything about it but be content to "not believe in such stuff," was something new in her experience. She had known girls who had no beaus, others who seemed to have no emotions, and still others who lied about what they thought and did; but here was a girl who spoke of the attentions of the last man tapped for Skull and Bones as if they were two of the limestone gargoyles that Miss Chambers had pointed out on the just completed Harkness Hall. Yet Adele seemed happy—happier than Josephine, who had always believed that boys and girls were made for nothing but each other, and as soon as possible.

In the light of his popularity and achievements, Knowleton seemed more attractive. Josephine wondered if he would remember her and dance with her at the prom, or if that depended on how well he knew her escort, Ridgeway Saunders. She tried to remember whether she had smiled at him when he was looking at her. If she had really smiled he would remember her and dance with her. She was still trying to be sure of that over her two French irregular verbs and her ten stanzas of the Ancient Mariner that night; but she was still uncertain when she fell asleep.

II

Three gay young sophomores, the founders of the Loving Brothers' Associaton, took a house together for Josephine, Lillian and a girl from Farmington and their three mothers. For the girls it was a first prom, and they arrived at New Haven with all the nervousness of the condemned; but a Sheffield fraternity tea in the afternoon yielded up such a plethora of boys from home, and boys who had visited there and friends of those boys, and new boys with unknown possibilities but obvious eagerness, that they were glowing with self-confidence as they poured into the glittering crowd that thronged the armory at ten.

It was impressive; for the first time Josephine was at a function run by men upon men's standards—an outward projection of the New Haven world from which women were excluded and which went on mysteriously behind the scenes. She perceived that their three escorts, who had once seemed the very embodiments of worldliness, were modest fry in this relentless microcosm of accomplishment and success. A man's world! Looking around her at the glee-club concert, Josephine had felt a grudging admiration for the good fellowship, the good feeling. She envied Adele Craw, barely glimpsed in the dressing-room, for the position she automatically occupied by being Dudley Knowleton's girl tonight. She envied her more stepping off under the draped bunting through a gateway of hydrangeas at the head of the grand march, very demure and faintly unpowdered in a plain white dress. She was temporarily the centre of all attention, and at the sight something that had long lain dormant in Josephine awakened—her sense of a problem, a scarcely defined possibility.

"Josephine," Ridgeway Saunders began, "you can't realize how happy I am now that it's come true. I've looked forward to this so long, and dreamed about it—"

She smiled up at him automatically, but her mind was elsewhere, and as the dance progressed the idea continued to obsess her. She was rushed from the beginning; to the men from the tea were added a dozen new faces, a dozen confident or timid voices, until, like all the more popular girls, she had her own queue trailing her about the room. Yet all this had happened to her before, and there was something missing. One might have ten men to Adele's two, but Josephine was abruptly aware that here a girl took on the importance of the man who had brought her.

She was discomforted by the unfairness of it. A girl earned her popularity by being beautiful and charming. The more beautiful and charming she was, the more she could afford to disregard public opinion. It seemed absurd that simply because Adele had managed to attach a baseball captain, who mightn't know anything about girls at all, or be able to judge their attractions, she should be thus elevated in spite of her thick ankles, her rather too pinkish face.

Josephine was dancing with Ed Bement from Chicago. He was her earliest beau, a flame of pigtail days in dancing school when one wore white cotton stockings, lace drawers with a waist attached and ruffled dresses with the inevitable sash.

"What's the matter with me?" she asked Ed, thinking aloud. "For months I've felt as if I were a hundred years old, and I'm just seventeen and that party was only seven years ago."

"You've been in love a lot since then," Ed said.

"I haven't," she protested indignantly. "I've had a lot of silly stories started about me, without any foundation, usually by girls who were jealous."

"Jealous of what?"

"Don't get fresh," she said tartly. "Dance me near Lillian."

Dudley Knowleton had just cut in on Lillian. Josephine spoke to her friend; then waiting until their turns would bring them face to face over a space of seconds, she smiled at Knowleton. This time she made sure that smile intersected as well as met glance, that he passed beside the circumference of her fragrant charm. If this had been named like French perfume of a later day it might have been called

"Please." He bowed and smiled back; a minute later he cut in on her.

It was in an eddy in a corner of the room and she danced slower so that he adapted himself, and for a moment they went around in a slow circle.

"You looked so sweet leading the march with Adele," she told him. "You seemed so serious and kind, as if the others were a lot of children. Adele looked sweet, too." And she added on an inspiration, "At school I've taken her for a model."

"You have!" She saw him conceal his sharp surprise as he said, "I'll have to tell her that."

He was handsomer than she had thought, and behind his cordial good manners there was a sort of authority. Though he was correctly attentive to her, she saw his eyes search the room quickly to see if all went well; he spoke quietly, in passing, to the orchestra leader, who came down deferentially to the edge of his dais. Last man for Bones. Josephine knew what that meant—her father had been Bones. Ridgeway Saunders and the rest of the Loving Brothers' Association would certainly not be Bones. She wondered, if there had been a Bones for girls, whether she would be tapped—or Adele Craw with her ankles, symbol of solidity.

> Come on o-ver here,
> Want to have you near;
> Come on join the part-y,
> Get a wel-come heart-y.

"I wonder how many boys here have taken you for a model," she said. "If I were a boy you'd be exactly what I'd like to be. Except I'd be terribly bothered having girls falling in love with me all the time."

"They don't," he said simply. "They never have."

"Oh, yes—but they hide it because they're so impressed with you, and they're afraid of Adele."

"Adele wouldn't object." And he added hastily, "—if it ever happened. Adele doesn't believe in being serious about such things."

"Are you engaged to her?"

He stiffened a little. "I don't believe in being engaged till the right time comes."

"Neither do I," agreed Josephine readily. "I'd rather have one good friend than a hundred people hanging around being mushy all the time."

"Is that what that crowd does that keeps following you around tonight?"

"What crowd?" she asked innocently.

"The fifty per cent of the sophomore class that's rushing you."

"A lot of parlor snakes," she said ungratefully.

Josephine was radiantly happy now as she turned beautifully 'through the newly enchanted hall in the arms of the chairman of the prom committee. Even this extra time with him she owed to the awe which he inspired in her entourage; but a man cut in eventually and there was a sharp fall in her elation. The man was impressed that Dudley Knowleton had danced with her; he was more respectful, and his modulated admiration bored her. In a little while, she hoped, Dudley Knowleton would cut back, but as midnight passed, dragging on another hour with it, she wondered if after all it had only been a courtesy to a girl from Adele's school. Since then Adele had probably painted him a neat little landscape of Josephine's past. When finally he approached her she grew tense and watchful, a state which made her exteriorly pliant and tender and quiet. But instead of dancing he drew her into the edge of a row of boxes.

"Adele had an accident on the cloakroom steps. She turned her ankle a little and tore her stocking on a nail. She'd like to borrow a pair from you because you're staying near here and we're way out at the Lawn Club."

"Of course."

"I'll run over with you—I have a car outside."

"But you're busy, you mustn't bother."

"Of course I'll go with you."

There was thaw in the air; a hint of thin and lucid spring hovered delicately around the elms and cornices of buildings whose bareness and coldness had so depressed her the week before. The night had a quality of asceticism, as if the essence of masculine struggle were seeping everywhere through the little city where men of three centuries had brought their energies and aspirations for winnowing. And Dudley Knowleton sitting beside her, dynamic and capable, was symbolic of it all. It seemed that she had never met a man before.

"Come in, please," she said as he went up the steps of the house with her. "They've made it very comfortable."

There was an open fire burning in the dark parlor. When she came downstairs with the stockings she went in and stood beside him, very still for a moment, watching it with him. Then she looked up, still silent, looked down, looked at him again.

"Did you get the stockings?" he asked, moving a little.

"Yes," she said breathlessly. "Kiss me for being so quick."

He laughed as if she said something witty and moved toward the door. She was smiling and her disappointment was deeply hidden as they got into the car.

"It's been wonderful meeting you," she told him. "I can't tell you how many ideas I've gotten from what you said."

"But I haven't any ideas."

"You have. All that about not getting engaged till the proper time comes. I haven't had much opportunity to talk to a man like you. Otherwise my ideas would be different, I guess. I've just realized that I've been wrong about a lot of things. I used to want to be exciting. Now I want to help people."

"Yes," he agreed, "that's very nice."

He seemed about to say more when they arrived at the armory. In their absence supper had begun; and crossing the great floor by his side, conscious of many eyes regarding them, Josephine wondered if people thought that they had been up to something.

"We're late," said Knowleton when Adele went off to put on the stockings. "The man you're with has probably given you up long ago. You'd better let me get you something here."

"That would be too divine."

Afterward, back on the floor again, she moved in a sweet aura of abstraction. The followers of several departed belles merged with hers until now no girl on the floor was cut in on with such frequency. Even Miss Brereton's nephew, Ernest Waterbury, danced with her in stiff approval. Danced? With a tentative change of pace she simply swung from man to man in a sort of hands-right-and-left around the floor. She felt a sudden need to relax, and as if in answer to her mood a new man was presented, a tall, sleek Southerner with a persuasive note:

"You lovely creacha. I been strainin my eyes watchin your cameo face floatin round. You stand out above all these othuz like an Amehken Beauty Rose over a lot of field daisies."

Dancing with him a second time, Josephine hearkened to his pleadings.

"All right. Let's go outside."

"It wasn't outdaws I was considerin," he explained as they left the floor. "I happen to have a mortgage on a nook right hee in the building."

"All right."

Book Chaffee, of Alabama, led the way through the cloakroom, through a passage to an inconspicuous door.

"This is the private apartment of my friend Sergeant Boone, instructa of the battery. He wanted to be particularly sure it'd be used as a nook tonight and not a readin room or anything like that."

Opening the door he turned on a dim light; she came in and he shut it behind her, and they faced each other.

"Mighty sweet," he murmured. His tall face came down, his long arms wrapped around her tenderly, and very slowly so that their eyes met for quite a long time, he drew her up to him. Josephine kept thinking that she had never kissed a Southern boy before.

They started apart at the sudden sound of a key turning in the lock outside. Then there was a muffled snicker followed by retreating footsteps, and Book sprang for the door and wrenched at the handle, just as Josephine noticed that this was not only Sergeant Boone's parlor; it was his bedroom as well.

"Who was it?" she demanded. "Why did they lock us in?"

"Some funny boy. I'd like to get my hands on him."

"Will he come back?"

Book sat down on the bed to think. "I couldn't say. Don't even know who it was. But if somebody on the committee came along it wouldn't look too good, would it?"

Seeing her expression change, he came over and put his arm around her. "Don't you worry, honey. We'll fix it."

She returned his kiss, briefly but without distraction. Then she broke away and went into the next apartment, which was hung with boots, uniform coats and various military equipment.

"There's a window up here," she said. It was high in the wall and had not been opened for a long time. Book mounted on a chair and forced it ajar.

"About ten feet down," he reported, after a moment, "but there's a big pile of snow just underneath. You might get a nasty fall and you'll sure soak your shoes and stockin's."

"We've got to get out," Josephine said sharply.

"We'd better wait and give this funny man a chance——"

"I won't wait. I want to get out. Look—throw out all the blankets from the bed and I'll jump on that: or you jump first and spread them over the pile of snow."

After that it was merely exciting. Carefully Book Chaffee wiped the dust from the window to protect her dress; then they were struck silent by a footstep that approached—and passed the outer door. Book jumped, and she heard him kicking profanely as he waded out of the soft drift below. He spread the blankets. At the moment when Josephine swung her legs out the window, there was the sound of voices outside the door and the key turned again in the lock. She landed softly, reaching for his hand, and convulsed with laughter they ran and skidded down the half block toward the corner, and reaching the entrance to the armory, they stood panting for a moment, breathing in the fresh night. Book was reluctant to go inside.

"Why don't you let me conduct you where you're stayin? We can sit around and sort of recuperate."

She hesitated, drawn toward him by the community of their late predicament; but something was calling her inside, as if the fulfillment of her elation awaited her there.

"No," she decided.

As they went in she collided with a man in a great hurry, and looked up to recognize Dudley Knowleton.

"So sorry," he said. "Oh hello—"

"Won't you dance me over to my box?" she begged him impulsively. "I've torn my dress."

As they started off he said abstractedly: "The fact is, a little mischief has come up and the buck has been passed to me. I was going along to see about it."

Her heart raced wildly and she felt the need of being another sort of person immediately.

"I can't tell you how much it's meant meeting you. It would be wonderful to have one friend I could be serious with without being all mushy and sentimental. Would you mind if I wrote you a letter— I mean, would Adele mind?"

"Lord, no." His smile had become utterly unfathomable to her. As they reached the box she thought of one more thing:

"Is it true that the baseball team is training at Hot Springs during Easter?"

"Yes. You going there?"

"Yes. Good night, Mr. Knowleton."

But she was destined to see him once more. It was outside the men's coat room, where she waited among a crowd of other pale survivors and their paler mothers, whose wrinkles had doubled and tripled with the passing night. He was explaining something to Adele, and Josephine heard the phrase, "The door was locked, and the window open—"

Suddenly it occurred to Josephine that, meeting her coming in damp and breathless, he must have guessed at the truth—and Adele would doubtless confirm his suspicion. Once again the spectre of her old enemy, the plain and jealous girl, arose before her. Shutting her mouth tight together she turned away.

But they had seen her, and Adele called to her in her cheerful ringing voice:

"Come say good night. You were so sweet about the stockings. Here's a girl you won't find doing shoddy, silly things, Dudley." Impulsively she leaned and kissed Josephine on the cheek. "You'll see I'm right, Dudley—next year she'll be the most respected girl in school."

III

As things go in the interminable days of early March, what happened next happened quickly. The annual senior dance at Miss Brereton's school came on a night soaked through with spring, and all the junior girls lay awake listening to the sighing tunes from the gymnasium. Between the numbers, when boys up from New Haven and Princeton wandered about the grounds, cloistered glances looked down from dark open windows upon the vague figures.

Not Josephine, though she lay awake like the others. Such vicarious diversions had no place in the sober patterns she was spinning now from day to day; yet she might as well have been in the forefront of those who called down to the men and threw notes and entered into conversations, for destiny had suddenly turned against her and was spinning a dark web of its own.

> Lit-tle lady, don't be depressed and blue,
> After all, we're both in the same can-noo—

Dudley Knowleton was over in the gymnasium fifty yards away, but proxmity to a man did not thrill her as it would have done a year ago—not, at least, in the same way. Life, she saw now, was a serious matter, and in the modest darkness a line of a novel ceaselessly recurred to her: "He is a man fit to be the father of my children." What were the seductive graces, the fast lines of a hundred parlor snakes compared to such realities. One couldn't go on forever kissing comparative strangers behind half-closed doors.

Under her pillow now were two letters, answers to her letters. They spoke in a bold round hand of the beginning of baseball practice; they were glad Josephine felt as she did about things; and the writer certainly looked forward to seeing her at Easter. Of all the letters she had ever received they were the most difficult from which to squeeze a single drop of heart's blood—one couldn't even read the "Yours" of the subscription as "Your"—but Josephine knew them by heart. They were precious because he had taken the time to write them; they were eloquent in the very postage stamp because he used so few.

She was restless in her bed—the music had begun again in the gymnasium:

> Oh, my love, I've waited so long for you,
> Oh, my love, I'm singing this song for you—
> Oh-h-h—

From the next room there was light laughter, and then from below a male voice, and a long interchange of comic whispers. Josephine recognized Lillian's laugh and the voices of two other girls. She could imagine them as they lay across the window in their nightgowns, their heads just showing from the open window. "Come right down," one boy kept saying. "Don't be formal—come just as you are."

There was a sudden silence, then a quick crunching of footsteps on gravel, a suppressed snicker and a scurry, and the sharp, protesting groan of several beds in the next room and the banging of a door down the hall. Trouble for somebody, maybe. A few minutes later Josephine's door half opened, she caught a glimpse of Miss Kwain against the dim corridor light, and then the door closed.

The next afternoon Josephine and four other girls, all of whom denied having breathed so much as a word into the night, were placed on probation. There was absolutely nothing to do about it. Miss Kwain had recognized their faces in the window and they were all from two rooms. It was an injustice, but it was nothing compared to what happened next. One week before Easter vacation the school motored off on a one-day trip to inspect a milk farm—all save the ones on probation. Miss Chambers, who sympathized with Josephine's misfortune, enlisted her services in entertaining Mr. Ernest Waterbury, who was spending a week-end with his aunt. This was only vaguely better than nothing, for Mr. Waterbury was a very dull, very priggish young man. He was so dull and so priggish that the following morning Josephine was expelled from school.

It had happened like this: They had strolled in the grounds, they had sat down at a garden table and had tea. Ernest Waterbury had expressed a desire to see something in the chapel, just a few minutes before his aunt's car rolled up the drive. The chapel was reached by descending winding mock-medieval stairs; and, her shoes still wet from the garden, Josephine had slipped on the top step and fallen five feet directly into Mr. Waterbury's unwilling arms, where she lay helpless, convulsed with irrestible laughter. It was in this position that Miss Brereton and the visiting trustee had found them.

"But I had nothing to do with it!" declared the ungallant Mr. Waterbury. Flustered and outraged, he was packed back to New Haven, and Miss Brereton, connecting this with last week's sin, proceeded to lose her head. Josephine, humiliated and furious, lost hers, and Mr. Perry, who happened to be in New York, arrived at the school the same night. At his passionate indignation, Miss Brereton collapsed and retracted, but the damage was done, and Josephine

packed her trunk. Unexpectedly, monstrously, just as it had begun
to mean something, her school life was over.

For the moment all her feelings were directed against Miss Brereton, and the only tears she shed at leaving were of anger and resentment. Riding with her father up to New York, she saw that while at
first he had instinctively and whole-heartedly taken her part, he felt
also a certain annoyance with her misfortune.

"We'll all survive," he said. "Unfortunately, even that old idiot
Miss Brereton will survive. She ought to be running a reform school."
He brooded for a moment. "Anyhow, your mother arrives tomorrow
and you and she can go down to Hot Springs as you planned."

"Hot Springs!" Josephine cried, in a choked voice. "Oh, no!"

"Why not?" he demanded in surprise. "It seems the best thing to
do. Give it a chance to blow over before you go back to Chicago."

"I'd rather go to Chicago," said Josephine breathlessly. "Daddy,
I'd much rather go to Chicago."

"That's absurd. Your mother's started East and the arrangements
are all made. At Hot Springs you can get out and ride and play golf
and forget that old she-devil—"

"Isn't there another place in the East we could go? There's people
I know going to Hot Springs who'll know all about this, people that
I don't want to meet—girls from school."

"Now, Jo, you keep your chin up—this is one of those times.
Sorry I said that about letting it blow over in Chicago; if we hadn't
made other plans we'd go back and face every old shrew and gossip
in town right away. When anybody slinks off in a corner they think
you've been up to something bad. If anybody says anything to you,
you tell them the truth—what I said to Miss Brereton. You tell
them she said you could come back and I damn well wouldn't let
you go back."

"They won't believe it."

There would be, at all events, four days of respite at Hot Springs
before the vacations of the schools. Josephine passed this time taking golf lessons from a professional so newly arrived from Scotland
that he surely knew nothing of her misadventure; she even went
riding with a young man one afternoon, feeling almost at home with
him after his admission that he had flunked out of Princeton in
February—a confidence, however, which she did not reciprocate in
kind. But in the evenings, despite the young man's importunity, she
stayed with her mother, feeling nearer to her than she ever had
before.

But one afternoon in the lobby Josephine saw by the desk two
dozen good-looking young men waiting by a stack of bat cases and
bags, and knew that what she dreaded was at hand. She ran upstairs

and with an invented headache dined there that night, but after dinner she walked restlessly around their apartment. She was ashamed not only of her situation but of her reaction to it. She had never felt any pity for the unpopular girls who skulked in dressing-rooms because they could attract no partners on the floor, or for girls who were outsiders at Lake Forest, and now she was like them—hiding miserably out of life. Alarmed lest already the change was written in her face, she paused in front of the mirror, fascinated as ever by what she found there.

"The darn fools," she said aloud. And as she said it her chin went up and the faint cloud about her eyes lifted. The phrases of the myriad love letters she had received passed before her eyes; behind her, after all, was the reassurance of a hundred lost and pleading faces, of innumerable tender and pleading voices. Her pride flooded back into her till she could see the warm blood rushing up into her cheeks.

There was a knock at the door—it was the Princeton boy.

"How about slipping downstairs?" he proposed. "There's a dance. It's full of E-lies, the whole Yale baseball team. I'll pick up one of them and introduce you and you'll have a big time. How about it?"

"All right, but I don't want to meet anybody. You'll just have to dance with me all evening."

"You know that suits me."

She hurried into a new spring evening dress of the frailest fairy blue. In the excitement of seeing herself in it, it seemed as if she had shed the old skin of winter and emerged a shining chrysalis with no stain; and going downstairs her feet fell softly just off the beat of the music from below. It was a tune from a play she had seen a week ago in New York, a tune with a future—ready for gayeties as yet unthought of, lovers not yet met. Dancing off, she was certain that life had innumerable beginnings. She had hardly gone ten steps when she was cut in upon by Dudley Knowleton.

"Why, Josephine!" He had never used her first name before—he stood holding her hand. "Why, I'm so glad to see you. I've been hoping and hoping you'd be here."

She soared skyward on a rocket of surprise and delight. He was actually glad to see her—the expression on his face was obviously sincere. Could it be possible that he hadn't heard?

"Adele wrote me you might be here. She wasn't sure."

—Then he knew and didn't care; he liked her anyhow.

"I'm in sackcloth and ashes," she said.

"Well, they're very becoming to you."

"You know what happened—" she ventured.

"I do. I wasn't going to say anything, but it's generally agreed that

Waterbury behaved like a fool—and it's not going to be much help to him in the elections next month. Look—I want you to dance with some men who are just starving for a touch of beauty."

Presently she was dancing with, it seemed to her, the entire team at once. Intermittently Dudley Knowleton cut back in, as well as the Princeton man, who was somewhat indignant at this unexpected competition. There were many girls from many schools in the room, but with an admirable team spirit the Yale men displayed a sharp prejudice in Josephine's favor; already she was pointed out from the chairs along the wall.

But interiorly she was waiting for what was coming, for the moment when she would walk with Dudley Knowleton into the warm, Southern night. It came naturally, just at the end of a number, and they strolled along an avenue of early-blooming lilacs and turned a corner and another corner. . . .

"You were glad to see me, weren't you?" Josephine said.

"Of course."

"I was afraid at first. I was sorriest about what happened at school because of you. I'd been trying so hard to be different—because of you."

"You mustn't think of that school business any more. Everybody that matters knows you got a bad deal. Forget it and start over.'

"Yes," she agreed tranquilly. She was happy. The breeze and the scent of lilacs—that was she, lovely and intangible; the rustic bench where they sat and the trees—that was he, rugged and strong beside her, protecting her.

"I'd thought so much of meeting you here," she said after a minute. "You'd been so good for me, that I thought maybe in a different way I could be good for you—I mean I know ways of having a good time that you don't know. For instance, we've certainly got to go horseback riding by moonlight some night. That'll be fun."

He didn't answer.

"I can really be very nice when I like somebody—that's really not often," she interpolated hastily, "not seriously. But I mean when I do feel seriously that a boy and I are really friends I don't believe in having a whole mob of other boys hanging around taking up time. I like to be with him all the time, all day and all evening, don't you?"

He stirred a little on the bench; he leaned forward with his elbows on his knees, looking at his strong hands. Her gently modulated voice sank a note lower.

"When I like anyone I don't even like dancing. It's sweeter to be alone."

Silence for a moment.

"Well, you know"—he hesitated, frowning—"as a matter of fact, I'm mixed up in a lot of engagements made some time ago with some people." He floundered about unhappily. "In fact, I won't even be at the hotel after tomorrow. I'll be at the house of some people down the valley—a sort of house party. As a matter of fact, Adele's getting here tomorrow."

Absorbed in her own thoughts, she hardly heard him at first, but at the name she caught her breath sharply.

"We're both to be at this house party while we're here, and I imagine it's more or less arranged what we're going to do. Of course, in the daytime I'll be here for baseball practice."

"I see." Her lips were quivering. "You won't be—you'll be with Adele."

"I think that—more or less—I will. She'll—want to see you, of course."

Another silence while he twisted his big fingers and she helplessly imitated the gesture.

"You were just sorry for me," she said. "You like Adele—much better."

"Adele and I understand each other. She's been more or less my ideal since we were children together."

"And I'm not your kind of girl." Josephine's voice trembled with a sort of fright. "I suppose because I've kissed a lot of boys and got a reputation for a speed and raised the deuce."

"It isn't that."

"Yes, it is," she declared passionately. "I'm just paying for things." She stood up. "You'd better take me back inside so I can dance with the kind of boys that like me."

She walked quickly down the path, tears of misery streaming from her eyes. He overtook her by the steps, but she only shook her head and said, "Excuse me for being so fresh. I'll grow up—I got what was coming to me—it's all right."

A little later when she looked around the floor for him he had gone —and Josephine realized with a shock that for the first time in her life, she had tried for a man and failed. But, save in the very young, only love begets love, and from the moment Josephine had perceived that his interest in her was merely kindness she realized the wound was not in her heart but in her pride. She would forget him quickly, but she would never forget what she had learned from him. There were two kinds of men, those you played with and those you might marry. And as this passed through her mind, her restless eyes wandered casually over the group of stags, resting very lightly on Mr. Gordon Tinsley, the current catch of Chicago, reputedly the richest young man in the Middle West. He had never paid any attention to

young Josephine until tonight. Ten minutes ago he had asked her to
go driving with him tomorrow.

But he did not attract her—and she decided to refuse. One mustn't
run through people, and, for the sake of a romantic half-hour, trade
a possibility that might develop—quite seriously—later, at the
proper time. She did not know that this was the first mature thought
that she had ever had in her life, but it was.

The orchestra were packing their instruments and the Princeton
man was still at her ear, still imploring her to walk out with him
into the night. Josephine knew without cogitation which sort of man
he was—and the moon was bright even on the windows. So with a
certain sense of relaxation she took his arm and they strolled out to
the pleasant bower she had so lately quitted, and their faces turned
toward each other, like little moons under the great white one which
hovered high over the Blue Ridge; his arm dropped softly about her
yielding shoulder.

"Well?" he whispered.

"Well?"

1930   *Taps at Reveille*

IV

Last Act and Epilogue

THERE had been intimations of disaster—"faintly signaled, like a nervous beating of the feet"—in some of the stories Fitzgerald wrote from 1928 to 1930. By the end of 1930 the disaster was upon him; Zelda was a patient in a Swiss sanitarium, where the doctors were unable to promise that she would recover, and Fitzgerald was beginning to think of himself as an alcoholic. One result of the new situation was a new type of story, more complicated emotionally, with less regret for the past and more dignity in the face of real sorrow.

"Babylon Revisited" (1931) is the first of the later stories and one of the best he ever wrote. It shows that an age has ended in the year since "The Bridal Party." Charles Wales, who might have figured in the crowded background of the earlier story, is now a lonely survivor wandering through Paris like a bewildered mastodon. "I lost everything I wanted in the boom," he says to the head barman at the Ritz; and then he adds to himself, "The snow of twenty-nine wasn't real snow. If you didn't want it to be snow, you just paid some money." . . . "Crazy Sunday" was the fruit of a second trip to Hollywood, in the winter of 1931–32. It reveals the author's admiration for Irving Thalberg, who served as model not only for the director in the story but also for the hero of *The Last Tycoon*. More than that, Fitzgerald had learned how to deal with the illogic of extremely complicated emotions. . . . "Family in the Wind" (1932) is the study of an alcoholic doctor, but in some ways it is also a defense of the author's career.

In 1933 Fitzgerald was too busy with the manuscript of *Tender Is the Night* to do much writing for the magazines, and after the novel was published he was distracted with worries about Zelda's third breakdown and what he called his "lesion of vitality"; he began to fear that he was losing his talent. "I can never write anything completely bad," he said belligerently; and the boast was true to the extent that even the trivial stories he sold to *Liberty* and *Collier's* after the *Post* stopped printing his work had something good in each of them, if only a scene or an incidental remark that gave dignity to his characters; but the plots were beginning to be carelessly put together and the subjects were far from his own experience.

In Hollywood the type of energy that he had formerly devoted to writing long magazine stories went into moving-picture scripts, but he was also writing shorter pieces for *Esquire* and some of these—not all, but ten or twelve of the best—proved to be another development for Fitzgerald. "At last I am mature," he said in his ruin, and these are really mature stories—without the glitter and high spirits of his early work, without boasting or self-pity or nostalgia, and even without the strong rhythms and incantatory words he had once used to intensify the emotions of his characters. The emotions in these stories have no need of being intensified. The best of them are so close to his personal tragedy that the emotion is in the events themselves, which have merely to be stated in the barest language.

In the present group there are seven short stories from Fitzgerald's last years. "An Alcoholic Case" suggests his own dilemma, unforgettably, and "The Long Way Out" suggests Zelda's. "Financing Finnegan" is a comedy, if a painful one, about the debts he owed to his agent Harold Ober and his editor Maxwell Perkins. It is a relief to learn that the debts were paid almost in full before Finnegan died. The two Pat Hobby sketches are selected from a group of seventeen that were written for *Esquire* in 1939–40. Pat wasn't the author himself, but in his comic degradation he was what the author sometimes feared that he might become. "Three Hours between Planes" is simply a good and honestly told story, but "The Lost Decade" is more than that. Written in the summer of 1939, when Fitzgerald was recovering from the long after-effects of his worst spree, it is his memorial to the years when he "was taken drunk . . . every-which-way drunk." It is also his promise that the rest of his life, however short, would be different—as indeed it was.

BABYLON REVISITED

"AND WHERE'S Mr. Campbell?" Charlie asked.

"Gone to Switzerland. Mr. Campbell's a pretty sick man, Mr. Wales." =Wales=

"I'm sorry to hear that. And George Hardt?" Charlie inquired.

"Back in America, gone to work."

"And where is the Snow Bird?" *Anaw w cocaine addict*

"He was in here last week. Anyway, his friend, Mr. Schaeffer, is in Paris." SHEFHEFR

Two familiar names from the long list of a year and a half ago. Charlie scribbled an address in his notebook and tore out the page.

"If you see Mr. Schaeffer, give him this," he said. "It's my brother-in-law's address. I haven't settled on a hotel yet." *foob*

He was not really disappointed to find Paris was so empty. But the stillness in the Ritz bar was strange and portentous. It was not an American bar any more—he felt polite in it, and not as if he owned it. It had gone back into France. He felt the stillness from the moment he got out of the taxi and saw the doorman, usually in a frenzy of activity at this hour, gossiping with a *chasseur* by the servants' PORTER entrance.

Passing through the corridor, he heard only a single, bored voice in the once-clamorous women's room. When he turned into the bar he traveled the twenty feet of green carpet with his eyes fixed straight ahead by old habit; and then, with his foot firmly on the rail, he turned and surveyed the room, encountering only a single pair of eyes that fluttered up from a newspaper in the corner. Charlie asked for the head barman, Paul, who in the latter days of the bull market had come to work in his own custom-built car—disembarking, however, with due nicety at the nearest corner. But Paul was at his country house today and Alix giving him information.

"No, no more," Charlie said, "I'm going slow these days."

Alix congratulated him: "You were going pretty strong a couple of years ago."

"I'll stick to it all right," Charlie assured him. "I've stuck to it for over a year and a half now."

"How do you find conditions in America?"

385

"I haven't been to America for months. I'm in business in Prague, representing a couple of concerns there. They don't know about me down there."

Alix smiled.

"Remember the night of George Hardt's bachelor dinner here?" said Charlie. "By the way, what's become of Claude Fessenden?"

Alix lowered his voice confidentially: "He's in Paris, but he doesn't come here any more. Paul doesn't allow it. He ran up a bill of thirty thousand francs, charging all his drinks and his lunches, and usually his dinner, for more than a year. And when Paul finally told him he had to pay, he gave him a bad check."

Alix shook his head sadly.

"I don't understand it, such a dandy fellow. Now he's all bloated up—" He made a plump apple of his hands.

Charlie watched a group of strident queens installing themselves in a corner.

"Nothing affects them," he thought. "Stocks rise and fall, people loaf or work, but they go on forever." The place oppressed him. He called for the dice and shook with Alix for the drink.

"Here for long, Mr. Wales?"

"I'm here for four or five days to see my little girl."

"Oh-h! You have a little girl?"

Outside, the fire-red, gas-blue, ghost-green signs shone smokily through the tranquil rain. It was late afternoon and the streets were in movement; the *bistros* gleamed. At the corner of the Boulevard des Capucines he took a taxi. The Place de la Concorde moved by in pink majesty; they crossed the logical Seine, and Charlie felt the sudden provincial quality of the left bank.

Charlie directed his taxi to the Avenue de l'Opera, which was out of his way. But he wanted to see the blue hour spread over the magnificent façade, and imagine that the cab horns, playing endlessly the first few bars of *Le Plus que Lent*, were the trumpets of the Second Empire. They were closing the iron grill in front of Brentano's Book-store, and people were already at dinner behind the trim little bourgeois hedge of Duval's. He had never eaten at a really cheap restaurant in Paris. Five-course dinner, four francs fifty, eighteen cents, wine included. For some odd reason he wished that he had.

As they rolled on to the Left Bank and he felt its sudden provincialism, he thought, "I spoiled this city for myself. I didn't realize it, but the days came along one after another, and then two years were gone, and everything was gone, and I was gone."

He was thirty-five, and good to look at. The Irish mobility of his face was sobered by a deep wrinkle between his eyes. As he rang his brother-in-law's bell in the Rue Palatine, the wrinkle deepened till it pulled down his brows; he felt a cramping sensation in his belly. From behind the maid who opened the door darted a lovely little girl of nine who shrieked "Daddy!" and flew up, struggling like a fish, into his arms. She pulled his head around by one ear and set her cheek against his.

"My old pie," he said.

"Oh, daddy, daddy, daddy, daddy, dads, dads, dads!"

She drew him into the salon, where the family waited, a boy and a girl his daughter's age, his sister-in-law and her husband. He greeted Marion with his voice pitched carefully to avoid either feigned enthusiasm or dislike, but her response was more frankly tepid, though she minimized her expression of unalterable distrust by directing her regard toward his child. The two men clasped hands in a friendly way and Lincoln Peters rested his for a moment on Charlie's shoulder.

The room was warm and comfortably American. The three children moved intimately about, playing through the yellow oblongs that led to other rooms; the cheer of six o'clock spoke in the eager smacks of the fire and the sounds of French activity in the kitchen. But Charlie did not relax; his heart sat up rigidly in his body and he drew confidence from his daughter, who from time to time came close to him, holding in her arms the doll he had brought.

"Really extremely well," he declared in answer to Lincoln's question. "There's a lot of business there that isn't moving at all, but we're doing even better than ever. In fact, damn well. I'm bringing my sister over from America next month to keep house for me. My income last year was bigger than it was when I had money. You see, the Czechs——"

His boasting was for a specific purpose; but after a moment, seeing a faint restiveness in Lincoln's eye, he changed the subject:

"Those are fine children of yours, well brought up, good manners."

"We think Honoria's a great little girl too."

Marion Peters came back from the kitchen. She was a tall woman with worried eyes, who had once possessed a fresh American loveliness. Charlie had never been sensitive to it and was always surprised when people spoke of how pretty she had been. From the first there had been an instinctive antipathy between them.

"Well, how do you find Honoria?" she asked.

"Wonderful. I was astonished how much she's grown in ten months. All the children are looking well."

"We haven't had a doctor for a year. How do you like being back in Paris?"

"It seems very funny to see so few Americans around."

"I'm delighted," Marion said vehemently. "Now at least you can *post-Depression*

go into a store without their assuming you're a millionaire. We've suffered like everybody, but on the whole it's a good deal pleasanter."

"But it was nice while it lasted," Charlie said. "We were a sort of royalty, almost infallible, with a sort of magic around us. In the bar this afternoon"—he stumbled, seeing his mistake—"there wasn't a man I knew."

She looked at him keenly. "I should think you'd have had enough, of bars."

"I only stayed a minute. I take one drink every afternoon, and no more."

"Don't you want a cocktail before dinner?" Lincoln asked.

"I take only one drink every afternoon, and I've had that."

"I hope you keep to it," said Marion.

Her dislike was evident in the coldness with which she spoke, but Charlie only smiled; he had larger plans. Her very aggressiveness gave him an advantage, and he knew enough to wait. He wanted them to initiate the discussion of what they knew had brought him to Paris.

At dinner he couldn't decide whether Honoria was most like him or her mother. Fortunate if she didn't combine the traits of both that had brought them to disaster. A great wave of protectiveness went over him. He thought he knew what to do for her. He believed in character; he wanted to jump back a whole generation and trust in character again as the eternally valuable element. Everything else wore out.

He left soon after dinner, but not to go home. He was curious to see Paris by night with clearer and more judicious eyes than those of other days. He bought a *strapontin* for the Casino and watched Josephine Baker go through her chocolate arabesques.

folding seat

old places

After an hour he left and strolled toward Montmartre, up the Rue Pigalle into the Place Blanche. The rain had stopped and there were a few people in evening clothes disembarking from taxis in front of cabarets, and *cocottes* prowling singly or in pairs, and many Negroes. He passed a lighted door from which issued music, and stopped with the sense of familiarity; it was Bricktop's, where he had parted with so many hours and so much money. A few doors farther on he found another ancient rendezvous and incautiously put his head inside. Immediately an eager orchestra burst into sound, a pair of professional dancers leaped to their feet and a maître d'hôtel swooped toward him, crying, "Crowd just arriving, sir!" But he withdrew quickly.

nightclubs

"You have to be damn drunk," he thought.

Zelli's was closed, the bleak and sinister cheap hotels surrounding it were dark; up in the Rue Blanche there was more light and a local, colloquial French crowd. The Poet's Cave had disappeared, but the two great mouths of the Café of Heaven and the Café of Hell still yawned—even devoured, as he watched, the meager contents of a tourist bus—a German, a Japanese, and an American couple who glanced at him with frightened eyes.

So much for the effort and ingenuity of Montmartre. All the catering to vice and waste was on an utterly childish scale, and he suddenly realized the meaning of the word "dissipate"—to dissipate into thin air; to make nothing out of something. In the little hours of the night every move from place to place was an enormous human jump, an increase of paying for the privilege of slower and slower motion.

He remembered thousand-franc notes given to an orchestra for playing a single number, hundred-franc notes tossed to a doorman for calling a cab.

But it hadn't been given for nothing.

It had been given, even the most wildly squandered sum, as an offering to destiny that he might not remember the things most worth remembering, the things that now he would always remember—his child taken from his control, his wife escaped to a grave in Vermont.

In the glare of a *brasserie* a woman spoke to him. He bought her some eggs and coffee, and then, eluding her encouraging stare, gave her a twenty-franc note and took a taxi to his hotel.

II

He woke upon a fine fall day—football weather. The depression of yesterday was gone and he liked the people on the streets. At noon he sat opposite Honoria at Le Grand Vatel, the only restaurant he could think of not reminiscent of champagne dinners and long luncheons that began at two and ended in a blurred and vague twilight.

"Now, how about vegetables? Oughtn't you to have some vegetables?"

"Well, yes."

"Here's *épinards* and *chou-fleur* and carrots and *haricots*."

"I'd like *chou-fleur*."

"Wouldn't you like to have two vegetables?"

"I usually only have one at lunch."

The waiter was pretending to be inordinately fond of children. *"Qu'elle est mignonne la petite! Elle parle exactement comme une Française."*

"How about dessert? Shall we wait and see?"

The waiter disappeared. Honoria looked at her father expectantly.

"What are we going to do?"

"First, we're going to that toy store in the Rue Saint-Honoré and buy you anything you like. And then we're going to the vaudeville at the Empire."

She hesitated. "I like it about the vaudeville, but not the toy store."

"Why not?"

"Well, you brought me this doll." She had it with her. "And I've got lots of things. And we're not rich any more, are we?"

"We never were. But today you are to have anything you want."

"All right," she agreed resignedly.

When there had been her mother and a French nurse he had been inclined to be strict; now he extended himself, reached out for a new tolerance; he must be both parents to her and not shut any of her out of communication.

"I want to get to know you," he said gravely. "First let me introduce myself. My name is Charles J. Wales, of Prague."

"Oh, daddy!" her voice cracked with laughter.

"And who are you, please?" he persisted, and she accepted a rôle immediately: "Honoria Wales, Rue Palatine, Paris."

"Married or single?"

"No, not married. Single."

He indicated the doll. "But I see you have a child, madame."

Unwilling to disinherit it, she took it to her heart and thought quickly: "Yes, I've been married, but I'm not married now. My husband is dead."

He went on quickly, "And the child's name?"

"Simone. That's after my best friend at school."

"I'm very pleased that you're doing so well at school."

"I'm third this month," she boasted. "Elsie"—that was her cousin —"is only about eighteenth, and Richard is about at the bottom."

"You like Richard and Elsie, don't you?"

"Oh, yes. I like Richard quite well and I like her all right."

Cautiously and casually he asked: "And Aunt Marion and Uncle Lincoln—which do you like best?"

"Oh, Uncle Lincoln, I guess."

He was increasingly aware of her presence. As they came in, a murmur of ". . . adorable" followed them, and now the people at the next table bent all their silences upon her, staring as if she were something no more conscious than a flower.

"Why don't I live with you?" she asked suddenly. "Because mamma's dead?"

"You must stay here and learn more French. It would have been hard for daddy to take care of you so well."

"I don't really need much taking care of any more. I do everything for myself."

Going out of the restaurant, a man and a woman unexpectedly hailed him.

"Well, the old Wales!"

"Hello there, Lorraine. . . . Dunc."   = *quarrels*

Sudden ghosts out of the past: Duncan Schaeffer, a friend from college. Lorraine Quarrles, a lovely, pale blonde of thirty; one of a crowd who had helped them make months into days in the lavish times of three years ago.

"My husband couldn't come this year," she said, in answer to his question. "We're poor as hell. So he gave me two hundred a month and told me I could do my worst on that. . . . This your little girl?"

"What about coming back and sitting down?" Duncan asked.

"Can't do it." He was glad for an excuse. As always, he felt Lorraine's passionate, provocative attraction, but his own rhythm was different now.

"Well, how about dinner?" she asked.

"I'm not free. Give me your address and let me call you."

"Charlie, I believe you're sober," she said judicially. "I honestly believe he's sober, Dunc. Pinch him and see if he's sober."

Charlie indicated Honoria with his head. They both laughed.

"What's your address?" said Duncan skeptically.

He hesitated, unwilling to give the name of his hotel.

"I'm not settled yet. I'd better call you. We're going to see the vaudeville at the Empire."

"There! That's what I want to do," Lorraine said. "I want to see some clowns and acrobats and jugglers. That's just what we'll do, Dunc."

"We've got to do an errand first," said Charlie. "Perhaps we'll see you there."

"All right, you snob. . . . Good-by, beautiful little girl."

"Good-by."

Honoria bobbed politely.   *even more so t 2nd time*

Somehow, an unwelcome encounter. They liked him because he   *wire drek over*
was functioning, because he was serious; they wanted to see him, because he was stronger than they were now, because they wanted to draw a certain sustenance from his strength.

At the Empire, Honoria proudly refused to sit upon her father's folded coat. She was already an individual with a code of her own, and Charlie was more and more absorbed by the desire of putting a little of himself into her before she crystallized utterly. It was hopeless to try to know her in so short a time.

Between the acts they came upon Duncan and Lorraine in the lobby where the band was playing.

"Have a drink?"

"All right, but not up at the bar. We'll take a table."

"The perfect father."

Listening abstractedly to Lorraine, Charlie watched Honoria's eyes leave their table, and he followed them wistfully about the room, wondering what they saw. He met her glance and she smiled.

"I liked that lemonade," she said.

What had she said? What had he expected? Going home in a taxi afterward, he pulled her over until her head rested against his chest.

"Darling, do you ever think about your mother?"

"Yes, sometimes," she answered vaguely.

"I don't want you to forget her. Have you got a picture of her?"

"Yes, I think so. Anyhow, Aunt Marion has.Why don't you want me to forget her?"

"She loved you very much."

"I loved her too."

They were silent for a moment.

"Daddy, I want to come and live with you," she said suddenly.

His heart leaped; he had wanted it to come like this.

"Aren't you perfectly happy?"

"Yes, but I love you better than anybody. And you love me better than anybody, don't you, now that mummy's dead?"

"Of course I do. But you won't always like me best, honey. You'll grow up and meet somebody your own age and go marry him and forget you ever had a daddy."

"Yes, that's true," she agreed tranquilly.

He didn't go in. He was coming back at nine o'clock and he wanted to keep himself fresh and new for the thing he must say then.

"When you're safe inside, just show yourself in that window."

"All right. Good-by, dads, dads, dads, dads."

He waited in the dark street until she appeared, all warm and glowing, in the window above and kissed her fingers out into the night.

III

They were waiting. Marion sat behind the coffee service in a dignified black dinner dress that just faintly suggested mourning. Lincoln was walking up and down with the animation of one who had already been talking. They were as anxious as he was to get into the question. He opened it almost immediately:

[handwritten annotations at top: "with last lunch w Hon + interview w Peters / diff last lunch + Marion's attitude"]

[handwritten margin note: "Marion assure 39K —"]

"I suppose you know what I want to see you about—why I really came to Paris."

Marion played with the black stars on her necklace and frowned.

"I'm awfully anxious to have a home," he continued. "And I'm awfully anxious to have Honoria in it. I appreciate your taking in Honoria for her mother's sake, but things have changed now"—he hesitated and then continued more forcibly—"changed radically with me, and I want to ask you to reconsider the matter. It would be silly for me to deny that about three years ago I was acting badly——"

Marion looked up at him with hard eyes.

"—but all that's over. As I told you, I haven't had more than a drink a day for over a year, and I take that drink deliberately, so that the idea of alcohol won't get too big in my imagination. You see the idea?"

"No," said Marion succinctly.

"It's a sort of stunt I set myself. It keeps the matter in proportion."

"I get you," said Lincoln. "You don't want to admit it's got any attraction for you."

"Something like that. Sometimes I forget and don't take it. But I try to take it. Anyhow, I couldn't afford to drink in my position. The people I represent are more than satisfied with what I've done, and I'm bringing my sister over from Burlington to keep house for me, and I want awfully to have Honoria too. You know that even when her mother and I weren't getting along well we never let anything that happened touch Honoria. I know she's fond of me and I know I'm able to take care of her and—well, there you are. How do you feel about it?"

He knew that now he would have to take a beating. It would last an hour or two hours, and it would be difficult, but if he modulated his inevitable resentment to the chastened attitude of the reformed sinner, he might win his point in the end. *[handwritten margin note: "prodigal son theme"]*

Keep your temper, he told himself. You don't want to be justified. You want Honoria.

Lincoln spoke first: "We've been talking it over ever since we got your letter last month. We're happy to have Honoria here. She's a dear little thing, and we're glad to be able to help her, but of course that isn't the question——"

Marion interrupted suddenly. "How long are you going to stay sober, Charlie?" she asked.

"Permanently, I hope."

"How can anybody count on that?"

"You know I never did drink heavily until I gave up business and came over here with nothing to do. Then Helen and I began to run around with——"

"Please leave Helen out of it. I can't bear to hear you talk about her like that."

He stared at her grimly; he had never been certain how fond of each other the sisters were in life.

"My drinking only lasted about a year and a half—from the time we came over until I—collapsed."

"It was time enough."

"It was time enough," he agreed.

"My duty is entirely to Helen," she said. "I try to think what she would have wanted me to do. Frankly, from the night you did that terrible thing you haven't really existed for me. I can't help that. She was my sister."

"Yes."

"When she was dying she asked me to look out for Honoria. If you hadn't been in a sanitarium then, it might have helped matters."

He had no answer.

"I'll never in my life be able to forget the morning when Helen knocked at my door, soaked to the skin and shivering, and said you'd locked her out."

Charlie gripped the sides of the chair. This was more difficult than he expected; he wanted to launch out into a long expostulation and explanation, but he only said: "The night I locked her out——" and she interrupted, "I don't feel up to going over that again."

After a moment's silence Lincoln said: "We're getting off the subject. You want Marion to set aside her legal guardianship and give you Honoria. I think the main point for her is whether she has confidence in you or not."

"I don't blame Marion," Charlie said slowly, "but I think she can have entire confidence in me. I had a good record up to three years ago. Of course, it's within human possibilities I might go wrong any time. But if we wait much longer I'll lose Honoria's childhood and my chance for a home." He shook his head, "I'll simply lose her, don't you see?"

"Yes, I see," said Lincoln.

"Why didn't you think of all this before?" Marion asked.

"I suppose I did, from time to time, but Helen and I were getting along badly. When I consented to the guardianship, I was flat on my back in a sanitarium and the market had cleaned me out. I knew I'd acted badly, and I thought if it would bring any peace to Helen, I'd agree to anything. But now it's different. I'm functioning, I'm behaving damn well, so far as——"

"Please don't swear at me," Marion said.

He looked at her, startled. With each remark the force of her dislike became more and more apparent. She had built up all her fear of life into one wall and faced it toward him. This trivial reproof was possibly the result of some trouble with the cook several hours before. Charlie became increasingly alarmed at leaving Honoria in this atmosphere of hostility against himself; sooner or later it would come out, in a word here, a shake of the head there, and some of that distrust would be irrevocably implanted in Honoria. But he pulled his temper down out of his face and shut it up inside him; he had won a point, for Lincoln realized the absurdity of Marion's remark and asked her lightly since when she had objected to the word "damn."

"Another thing," Charlie said: "I'm able to give her certain advantages now. I'm going to take a French governess to Prague with me. I've got a lease on a new apartment——"

He stopped, realizing that he was blundering. They couldn't be expected to accept with equanimity the fact that his income was again twice as large as their own.

"I suppose you can give her more luxuries than we can," said Marion. "When you were throwing away money we were living along watching every ten francs. . . . I suppose you'll start doing it again."

"Oh, no," he said. "I've learned. I worked hard for ten years, you know—until I got lucky in the market, like so many people. Terribly lucky. It didn't seem any use working any more, so I quit."

There was a long silence. All of them felt their nerves straining, and for the first time in a year Charlie wanted a drink. He was sure now that Lincoln Peters wanted him to have his child.

Marion shuddered suddenly; part of her saw that Charlie's feet were planted on the earth now, and her own maternal feeling recognized the naturalness of his desire; but she had lived for a long time with a prejudice—a prejudice founded on a curious disbelief in her sister's happiness, and which, in the shock of one terrible night, had turned to hatred for him. It had all happened at a point in her life where the discouragement of ill health and adverse circumstances made it necessary for her to believe in tangible villainy and a tangible villain.

"I can't help what I think!" she cried out suddenly. "How much you were responsible for Helen's death, I don't know. It's something you'll have to square with your own conscience."

An electric current of agony surged through him; for a moment he was almost on his feet, an unuttered sound echoing in his throat. He hung on to himself for a moment, another moment.

"Hold on there," said Lincoln uncomfortably. "I never thought you were responsible for that."

"Helen died of heart trouble," Charlie said dully.

"Yes, heart trouble." Marion spoke as if the phrase had another meaning for her.

Then, in the flatness that followed her outburst, she saw him plainly and she knew he had somehow arrived at control over the situation. Glancing at her husband, she found no help from him, and as abruptly as if it were a matter of no importance, she threw up the sponge.

"Do what you like!" she cried, springing up from her chair. "She's your child. I'm not the person to stand in your way. I think if it were my child I'd rather see her—" She managed to check herself. "You two decide it. I can't stand this. I'm sick. I'm going to bed."

She hurried from the room; after a moment Lincoln said:

"This has been a hard day for her. You know how strongly she feels—" His voice was almost apologetic: "When a woman gets an idea in her head."

"Of course."

"It's going to be all right. I think she sees now that you—can provide for the child, and so we can't very well stand in your way or Honoria's way."

"Thank you, Lincoln."

"I'd better go along and see how she is."

"I'm going."

He was still trembling when he reached the street, but a walk down the Rue Bonaparte to the *quais* set him up, and as he crossed the Seine, fresh and new by the *quai* lamps, he felt exultant. But back in his room he couldn't sleep. The image of Helen haunted him. Helen whom he had loved so until they had senselessly begun to abuse each other's love, tear it into shreds. On that terrible February night that Marion remembered so vividly, a slow quarrel had gone on for hours. There was a scene at the Florida, and then he attempted to take her home, and then she kissed young Webb at a table; after that there was what she had hysterically said. When he arrived home alone he turned the key in the lock in wild anger. How could he know she would arrive an hour later alone, that there would be a snowstorm in which she wandered about in slippers, too confused to find a taxi? Then the aftermath, her escaping pneumonia by a miracle, and all the attendant horror. They were "reconciled," but that was the beginning of the end, and Marion, who had seen with her own eyes and who imagined it to be one of many scenes from her sister's martyrdom, never forgot.

Going over it again brought Helen nearer, and in the white, soft light that steals upon half sleep near morning he found himself talking to her again. She said that he was perfectly right about Honoria and that she wanted Honoria to be with him. She said she was glad he was being good and doing better. She said a lot of other things— very friendly things—but she was in a swing in a white dress, and swinging faster and faster all the time, so that at the end he could not hear clearly all that she said.

IV

He woke up feeling happy. The door of the world was open again. He made plans, vistas, futures for Honoria and himself, but suddenly he grew sad, remembering all the plans he and Helen had made. She had not planned to die. The present was the thing—work to do and someone to love. But not to love too much, for he knew the injury that a father can do to a daughter or a mother to a son by attaching them too closely: afterward, out in the world, the child would seek in the marriage partner the same blind tenderness and, failing probably to find it, turn against love and life.

It was another bright, crisp day. He called Lincoln Peters at the bank where he worked and asked if he could count on taking Honoria when he left for Prague. Lincoln agreed that there was no reason for delay. One thing—the legal guardianship. Marion wanted to retain that a while longer. She was upset by the whole matter, and it would oil things if she felt that the situation was still in her control for another year. Charlie agreed, wanting only the tangible, visible child.

Then the question of a governess. Charles sat in a gloomy agency and talked to a cross Béarnaise and to a buxom Breton peasant, neither of whom he could have endured. There were others whom he would see tomorrow.

He lunched with Lincoln Peters at Griffons, trying to keep down his exultation.

"There's nothing quite like your own child," Lincoln said. "But you understand how Marion feels too."

"She's forgotten how hard I worked for seven years there," Charlie said. "She just remembers one night."

"There's another thing." Lincoln hesitated. "While you and Helen were tearing around Europe throwing money away, we were just getting along. I didn't touch any of the prosperity because I never got ahead enough to carry anything but my insurance. I think Marion felt there was some kind of injustice in it—you not even working toward the end, and getting richer and richer."

"It went just as quick as it came," said Charlie.

"Yes, a lot of it stayed in the hands of *chasseurs* and saxophone players and maîtres d'hôtel—well, the big party's over now. I just said that to explain Marion's feeling about those crazy years. If you drop in about six o'clock tonight before Marion's too tired, we'll settle the details on the spot."

Back at his hotel, Charlie found a *pneumatique* that had been redirected from the Ritz bar where Charlie had left his address for the purpose of finding a certain man.

"DEAR CHARLIE: You were so strange when we saw you the other day that I wondered if I did something to offend you. If so, I'm not conscious of it. In fact, I have thought about you too much for the last year, and it's always been in the back of my mind that I might see you if I came over here. We *did* have such good times that crazy spring, like the night you and I stole the butcher's tricycle, and the time we tried to call on the president and you had the old derby rim and the wire cane. Everybody seems so old lately, but I don't feel old a bit. Couldn't we get together some time today for old time's sake? I've got a vile hang-over for the moment, but will be feeling better this afternoon and will look for you about five in the sweatshop at the Ritz.

"Always devotedly,

"LORRAINE."

His first feeling was one of awe that he had actually, in his mature years, stolen a tricycle and pedaled Lorraine all over the Étoile between the small hours and dawn. In retrospect it was a nightmare. Locking out Helen didn't fit in with any other act of his life, but the tricycle incident did—it was one of many. How many weeks or months of dissipation to arrive at that condition of utter irresponsibility?

He tried to picture how Lorraine had appeared to him then—very attractive; Helen was unhappy about it, though she said nothing. Yesterday, in the restaurant, Lorraine had seemed trite, blurred, worn away. He emphatically did not want to see her, and he was glad Alix had not given away his hotel address. It was a relief to think, instead, of Honoria, to think of Sundays spent with her and of saying good morning to her and of knowing she was there in his house at night, drawing her breath in the darkness.

At five he took a taxi and bought presents for all the Peters—a piquant cloth doll, a box of Roman soldiers, flowers for Marion, big linen handkerchiefs for Lincoln.

He saw, when he arrived in the apartment, that Marion had accepted the inevitable. She greeted him now as though he were a recalcitrant member of the family, rather than a menacing outsider. Honoria had been told she was going; Charlie was glad to see that her tact made her conceal her excessive happiness. Only on his lap did she whisper her delight and the question "When?" before she slipped away with the other children.

He and Marion were alone for a minute in the room, and on an impulse he spoke out boldly:

"Family quarrels are bitter things. They don't go according to any rules. They're not like aches or wounds; they're more like splits in the skin that won't heal because there's not enough material. I wish you and I could be on better terms."

"Some things are hard to forget," she answered. "It's a question of confidence." There was no answer to this and presently she asked, "When do you propose to take her?"

"As soon as I can get a governess. I hoped the day after to-morrow."

"That's impossible. I've got to get her things in shape. Not before Saturday."

He yielded. Coming back into the room, Lincoln offered him a drink.

"I'll take my daily whisky," he said.

It was warm here, it was a home, people together by a fire. The children felt very safe and important; the mother and father were serious, watchful. They had things to do for the children more important than his visit here. A spoonful of medicine was, after all, more important than the strained relations between Marion and himself. They were not dull people, but they were very much in the grip of life and circumstances. He wondered if he couldn't do something to get Lincoln out of his rut at the bank.

A long peal at the door-bell; the *bonne à tout faire* passed through and went down the corridor. The door opened upon another long ring, and then voices, and the three in the salon looked up expectantly; Richard moved to bring the corridor within his range of vision, and Marion rose. Then the maid came back along the corridor, closely followed by the voices, which developed under the light into Duncan Schaeffer and Lorraine Quarrles.

They were gay, they were hilarious, they were roaring with laughter. For a moment Charlie was astounded; unable to understand how they ferreted out the Peters' address.

"Ah-h-h!" Duncan wagged his finger roguishly at Charlie. "Ah-h-h!"

They both slid down another cascade of laughter. Anxious and at a loss, Charlie shook hands with them quickly and presented them to Lincoln and Marion. Marion nodded, scarcely speaking. She had drawn back a step toward the fire; her little girl stood beside her, and Marion put an arm about her shoulder.

With growing annoyance at the intrusion, Charlie waited for them to explain themselves. After some concentration Duncan said:

"We came to invite you out to dinner. Lorraine and I insist that all this chi-chi, cagy business 'bout your address got to stop."

Charlie came closer to them, as if to force them backward down the corridor.

"Sorry, but I can't. Tell me where you'll be and I'll phone you in half an hour."

This made no impression. Lorraine sat down suddenly on the side of a chair, and focusing her eyes on Richard, cried, "Oh, what a nice little boy! Come here, little boy." Richard glanced at his mother, but did not move. With a perceptible shrug of her shoulders, Lorraine turned back to Charlie:

"Come and dine. Sure your cousins won' mine. See you so sel'om. Or solemn."

"I can't," said Charlie sharply. "You two have dinner and I'll phone you."

Her voice became suddenly unpleasant. "All right, we'll go. But I remember once when you hammered on my door at four A.M. I was enough of a good sport to give you a drink. Come on, Dunc."

Still in slow motion, with blurred, angry faces, with uncertain feet, they retired along the corridor.

threat of all life

"Good night," Charlie said.

"Good night!" responded Lorraine emphatically.

When he went back into the salon Marion had not moved, only now her son was standing in the circle of her other arm. Lincoln was still swinging Honoria back and forth like a pendulum from side to side.

"What an outrage!" Charlie broke out. "What an absolute outrage!"

Neither of them answered. Charlie dropped into an armchair, picked up his drink, set it down again and said:

"People I haven't seen for two years having the colossal nerve——"

He broke off. Marion had made the sound "Oh!" in one swift, furious breath, turned her body from him with a jerk and left the room.

Lincoln set down Honoria carefully.

"You children go in and start your soup," he said, and when they obeyed, he said to Charlie:

"Marion's not well and she can't stand shocks. That kind of people make her really physically sick."

wrong 385m

"I didn't tell them to come here. They wormed your name out of somebody. They deliberately——"

"Well, it's too bad. It doesn't help matters. Excuse me a minute."

Left alone, Charlie sat tense in his chair. In the next room he could hear the children eating, talking in monosyllables, already oblivious to the scene between their elders. He heard a murmur of conversation from a farther room and then the ticking bell of a telephone receiver picked up, and in a panic he moved to the other side of the room and out of earshot.

In a minute Lincoln came back. "Look here, Charlie. I think we'd better call off dinner for tonight. Marion's in bad shape."

"Is she angry with me?"

"Sort of," he said, almost roughly. "She's not strong and——"

"You mean she's changed her mind about Honoria?"

"She's pretty bitter right now. I don't know. You phone me at the bank tomorrow."

"I wish you'd explain to her I never dreamed these people would come here. I'm just as sore as you are."

"I couldn't explain anything to her now."

Charlie got up. He took his coat and hat and started down the corridor. Then he opened the door of the dining room and said in a strange voice, "Good night, children."

Honoria rose and ran around the table to hug him.

"Good night, sweetheart," he said vaguely, and then trying to make his voice more tender, trying to conciliate something, "Good night, dear children."

V

ends same place as it starts 385

Charlie went directly to the Ritz bar with the furious idea of finding Lorraine and Duncan, but they were not there, and he realized that in any case there was nothing he could do. He had not touched his drink at the Peters', and now he ordered a whisky-and-soda. Paul came over to say hello.

"It's a great change," he said sadly. "We do about half the business we did. So many fellows I hear about back in the States lost everything, maybe not in the first crash, but then in the second. Your friend George Hardt lost every cent, I hear. Are you back in the States?"

"No, I'm in business in Prague."

"I heard that you lost a lot in the crash."

"I did," and he added grimly, "but I lost everything I wanted in the boom."

"Selling short."

"Something like that."

Again the memory of those days swept over him like a nightmare —the people they had met travelling; then people who couldn't add a row of figures or speak a coherent sentence. The little man Helen had consented to dance with at the ship's party, who had insulted her ten feet from the table; the women and girls carried screaming with drink or drugs out of public places——

——The men who locked their wives out in the snow, because the snow of twenty-nine wasn't real snow. If you didn't want it to be snow, you just paid some money.

He went to the phone and called the Peters' apartment; Lincoln answered.

"I called up because this thing is on my mind. Has Marion said anything definite?"

"Marion's sick," Lincoln answered shortly. "I know this thing isn't altogether your fault, but I can't have her go to pieces about it. I'm afraid we'll have to let it slide for six months; I can't take the chance of working her up to this state again."

"I see."

"I'm sorry, Charlie."

He went back to his table. His whisky glass was empty, but he shook his head when Alix looked at it questioningly. There wasn't much he could do now except send Honoria some things; he would send her a lot of things tomorrow. He thought rather angrily that this was just money—he had given so many people money. . . .

"No, no more," he said to another waiter. "What do I owe you?"

He would come back some day; they couldn't make him pay forever. But he wanted his child, and nothing was much good now, beside that fact. He wasn't young any more, with a lot of nice thoughts and dreams to have by himself. He was absolutely sure Helen wouldn't have wanted him to be so alone.

1931   *Taps at Reveille*

CRAZY SUNDAY

I

IT WAS Sunday—not a day, but rather a gap between two other days. Behind, for all of them, lay sets and sequences, the long waits under the crane that swung the microphone, the hundred miles a day by automobiles to and fro across a county, the struggles of rival ingenuities in the conference rooms, the ceaseless compromise, the clash and strain of many personalities fighting for their lives. And now Sunday, with individual life starting up again, with a glow kindling in eyes that had been glazed with monotony the afternoon before. Slowly as the hours waned they came awake like "Puppenfeen" in a toy shop: an intense colloquy in a corner, lovers disappearing to neck in a hall. And the feeling of "Hurry, it's not too late, but for God's sake hurry before the blessed forty hours of leisure are over."

Joel Coles was writing continuity. He was twenty-eight and not yet broken by Hollywood. He had had what were considered nice assignments since his arrival six months before and he submitted his scenes and sequences with enthusiasm. He referred to himself modestly as a hack but really did not think of it that way. His mother had been a successful actress; Joel had spent his childhood between London and New York trying to separate the real from the unreal, or at least to keep one guess ahead. He was a handsome man with the pleasant cow-brown eyes that in 1913 had gazed out at Broadway audiences from his mother's face.

When the invitation came it made him sure that he was getting somewhere. Ordinarily he did not go out on Sundays but stayed sober and took work home with him. Recently they had given him a Eugene O'Neill play destined for a very important lady indeed. Everything he had done so far had pleased Miles Calman, and Miles Calman was the only director on the lot who did not work under a supervisor and was responsible to the money men alone. Everything was clicking into place in Joel's career. ("This is Mr. Calman's secretary. Will you come to tea from four to six Sunday—he lives in Beverly Hills, number——.")

Joel was flattered. It would be a party out of the top-drawer. It was a tribute to himself as a young man of promise. The Marion Davies crowd, the high-hats, the big currency numbers, perhaps even Dietrich and Garbo and the Marquise, people who were not seen everywhere, would probably be at Calman's.

"I won't take anything to drink," he assured himself. Calman was audibly tired of rummies, and thought it was a pity the industry could not get along without them.

Joel agreed that writers drank too much—he did himself, but he wouldn't this afternoon. He wished Miles would be within hearing when the cocktails were passed to hear his succinct, unobtrusive, "No, thank you."

Miles Calman's house was built for great emotional moments—there was an air of listening, as if the far silences of its vistas hid an audience, but this afternoon it was thronged, as though people had been bidden rather than asked. Joel noted with pride that only two other writers from the studio were in the crowd, an ennobled limey and, somewhat to his surprise, Nat Keogh, who had evoked Calman's impatient comment on drunks.

Stella Calman (Stella Walker, of course) did not move on to her other guests after she spoke to Joel. She lingered—she looked at him with the sort of beautiful look that demands some sort of acknowledgment and Joel drew quickly on the dramatic adequacy inherited from his mother:

"Well, you look about sixteen! Where's your kiddy car?"

She was visibly pleased; she lingered. He felt that he should say something more, something confident and easy—he had first met her when she was struggling for bits in New York. At the moment a tray slid up and Stella put a cocktail glass into his hand.

"Everybody's afraid, aren't they?" he said, looking at it absently. "Everybody watches for everybody else's blunders, or tries to make sure they're with people that'll do them credit. Of course that's not true in your house," he covered himself hastily. "I just meant generally in Hollywood."

Stella agreed. She presented several people to Joel as if he were very important. Reassuring himself that Miles was at the other side of the room, Joel drank the cocktail.

"So you have a baby?" he said. "That's the time to look out. After a pretty woman has had her first child, she's very vulnerable, because she wants to be reassured about her own charm. She's got to have some new man's unqualified devotion to prove to herself she hasn't lost anything."

"I never get anybody's unqualified devotion," Stella said rather resentfully.

"They're afraid of your husband."

"You think that's it?" She wrinkled her brow over the idea; then the conversation was interrupted at the exact moment Joel would have chosen.

Her attentions had given him confidence. Not for him to, join safe groups, to slink to refuge under the wings of such acquaintances as he saw about the room. He walked to the window and looked out toward the Pacific, colorless under its sluggish sunset. It was good here—the American Riviera and all that, if there were ever time to enjoy it. The handsome, well-dressed people in the room, the lovely girls, and the—well, the lovely girls. You couldn't have everything.

He saw Stella's fresh boyish face, with the tired eyelid that always drooped a little over one eye, moving about among her guests and he wanted to sit with her and talk a long time as if she were a girl instead of a name; he followed her to see if she paid anyone as much attention as she had paid him. He took another cocktail—not because he needed confidence but because she had given him so much of it. Then he sat down beside the director's mother.

"Your son's gotten to be a legend, Mrs. Calman—Oracle and a Man of Destiny and all that. Personally, I'm against him but I'm in a minority. What do you think of him? Are you impressed? Are you surprised how far he's gone?"

"No, I'm not surprised," she said calmly. "We always expected a lot from Miles."

"Well now, that's unusual," remarked Joel. "I always think all mothers are like Napoleon's mother. My mother didn't want me to have anything to do with the entertainment business. She wanted me to go to West Point and be safe."

"We always had every confidence in Miles." . . .

He stood by the built-in bar of the dining room with the good-humored, heavy-drinking, highly paid Nat Keogh.

"—I made a hundred grand during the year and lost forty grand gambling, so now I've hired a manager."

"You mean an agent," suggested Joel.

"No, I've got that too. I mean a manager. I make over everything to my wife and then he and my wife get together and hand me out the money. I pay him five thousand a year to hand me out my money."

"You mean your agent."

"No, I mean my manager, and I'm not the only one—a lot of other irresponsible people have him."

"Well, if you're irresponsible why are you responsible enough to hire a manager?"

"I'm just irresponsible about gambling. Look here——"

A singer performed; Joel and Nat went forward with the others to listen.

II

The singing reached Joel vaguely; he felt happy and friendly toward all the people gathered there, people of bravery and industry, superior to a bourgeoisie that outdid them in ignorance and loose living, risen to a position of the highest prominence in a nation that for a decade had wanted only to be entertained. He liked them—he loved them. Great waves of good feeling flowed through him.

As the singer finished his number and there was a drift toward the hostess to say good-by, Joel had an idea. He would give them "Building It Up," his own composition. It was his only parlor trick, it had amused several parties and it might please Stella Walker. Possessed by the hunch, his blood throbbing with the scarlet corpuscles of exhibitionism, he sought her.

"Of course," she cried. "Please! Do you need anything?"

"Someone has to be the secretary that I'm supposed to be dictating to."

"I'll be her."

As the word spread, the guests in the hall, already putting on their coats to leave, drifted back and Joel faced the eyes of many strangers. He had a dim foreboding, realizing that the man who had just performed was a famous radio entertainer. Then someone said "Sh!" and he was alone with Stella, the center of a sinister Indian-like half-circle. Stella smiled up at him expectantly—he began.

His burlesque was based upon the cultural limitations of Mr. Dave Silverstein, an independent producer; Silverstein was presumed to be dictating a letter outlining a treatment of a story he had bought.

"—a story of divorce, the younger generators and the Foreign Legion," he heard his voice saying, with the intonations of Mr. Silverstein. "But we got to build it up, see?"

A sharp pang of doubt struck through him. The faces surrounding him in the gently molded light were intent and curious, but there was no ghost of a smile anywhere; directly in front the Great Lover of the screen glared at him with an eye as keen as the eye of a potato. Only Stella Walker looked up at him with a radiant, never faltering smile.

"If we make him a Menjou type, then we get a sort of Michael Arlen only with a Honolulu atmosphere."

Still not a ripple in front, but in the rear a rustling, a perceptible shift toward the left, toward the front door.

"—then she says she feels this sex appil for him and he burns out and says 'Oh, go on destroy yourself——' "

At some point he heard Nat Keogh snicker and here and there were a few encouraging faces, but as he finished he had the sickening realization that he had made a fool of himself in view of an important section of the picture world, upon whose favor depended his career.

For a moment he existed in the midst of a confused silence, broken by a general trek for the door. He felt the undercurrent of derision that rolled through the gossip; then—all this was in the space of ten seconds—the Great Lover, his eye hard and empty as the eye of a *Jack Gilbert* needle, shouted "Boo! Boo!" voicing in an overtone what he felt was the mood of the crowd. It was the resentment of the professional toward the amateur, of the community toward the stranger, the thumbs-down of the clan.

Only Stella Walker was still standing near and thanking him as if he had been an unparalleled success, as if it hadn't occurred to her that anyone hadn't liked it. As Nat Keogh helped him into his overcoat, a great wave of self-disgust swept over him and he clung desperately to his rule of never betraying an inferior emotion until he no longer felt it.

"I was a flop," he said lightly, to Stella. "Never mind, it's a good number when appreciated. Thanks for your coöperation."

The smile did not leave her face—he bowed rather drunkenly and Nat drew him toward the door. . . .

The arrival of his breakfast awakened him into a broken and ruined world. Yesterday he was himself, a point of fire against an industry, today he felt that he was pitted under an enormous disadvantage, against those faces, against individual contempt and collective sneer. Worse than that, to Miles Calman he was become one of those rummies, stripped of dignity, whom Calman regretted he was compelled to use. To Stella Walker on whom he had forced a martyrdom to preserve the courtesy of her house—her opinion he did not dare to guess. His gastric juices ceased to flow and he set his poached eggs back on the telephone table. He wrote:

"DEAR MILES: You can imagine my profound self-disgust. I confess to a taint of exhibitionism, but at six o'clock in the afternoon, in broad daylight! Good God! My apologies to your wife.
"Yours ever,
"JOEL COLES."

Joel emerged from his office on the lot only to slink like a malefactor to the tobacco store. So suspicious was his manner that one of the studio police asked to see his admission card. He had decided

to eat lunch outside when Nat Keogh, confident and cheerful, overtook him.

"What do you mean you're in permanent retirement? What if
that Three-Piece Suit did boo you?

"Why, listen," he continued, drawing Joel into the studio restaurant. "The night of one of his premières at Grauman's, Joe Squires
kicked his tail while he was bowing to the crowd. The ham said
Joe'd hear from him later but when Joe called him up at eight o'clock
next day and said, 'I thought I was going to hear from you,' he hung
up the phone." *MGM was making a film called Freaks*

The preposterous story cheered Joel, and he found a gloomy con-
solation in staring at the group at the next table, the sad, lovely
Siamese twins, the mean dwarfs, the proud giant from the circus picture. But looking beyond at the yellow-stained faces of pretty
women, their eyes all melancholy and startling with mascara, their
ball gowns garish in full day, he saw a group who had been at Calman's and winced.

"Never again," he exclaimed aloud, "absolutely my last social
appearance in Hollywood!"

The following morning a telegram was waiting for him at his
office:

2nd invitation — Norma Thalberg sent this to F

"You were one of the most agreeable people at our party. Expect
you at my sister June's buffet supper next Sunday. ＼

"STELLA WALKER CALMAN."

Norma Shearer Thalberg

The blood rushed fast through his veins for a feverish minute.
Incredulously he read the telegram over.

"Well, that's the sweetest thing I ever heard of in my life!"

III

Crazy Sunday again. Joel slept until eleven, then he read a newspaper to catch up with the past week. He lunched in his room on
trout, avocado salad and a pint of California wine. Dressing for the
tea, he selected a pin-check suit, a blue shirt, a burnt orange tie.
There were dark circles of fatigue under his eyes. In his second-hand
car he drove to the Riviera apartments. As he was introducing himself to Stella's sister, Miles and Stella arrived in riding clothes—
they had been quarreling fiercely most of the afternoon on all the
dirt roads back of Beverly Hills.   *Miles Robt Montgomery at Th's party*

Miles Calman, tall, nervous, with a desperate humor and the un-
happiest eyes Joel ever saw, was an artist from the top of his curi-

ously shaped head to his niggerish feet. Upon these last he stood firmly—he had never made a cheap picture though he had sometimes paid heavily for the luxury of making experimental flops. In spite of his excellent company, one could not be with him long without realizing that he was not a well man.

From the moment of their entrance Joel's day bound itself up inextricably with theirs. As he joined the group around them Stella turned away from it with an impatient little tongue click—and Miles Calman said to the man who happened to be next to him:

"Go easy on Eva Goebel. There's hell to pay about her at home." Miles turned to Joel, "I'm sorry I missed you at the office yesterday. I spent the afternoon at the analyst's."

"You being psychoanalyzed?"

"I have been for months. First I went for claustrophobia, now I'm trying to get my whole life cleared up. They say it'll take over a year."

"There's nothing the matter with your life," Joel assured him.

"Oh, no? Well, Stella seems to think so. Ask anybody—they can all tell you about it," he said bitterly.

A girl perched herself on the arm of Miles' chair; Joel crossed to Stella, who stood disconsolately by the fire.

"Thank you for your telegram," he said. "It was darn sweet. I can't imagine anybody as good-looking as you are being so good-humored."

She was a little lovelier than he had ever seen her and perhaps the unstinted admiration in his eyes prompted her to unload on him—it did not take long, for she was obviously at the emotional bursting point.

"—and Miles has been carrying on this thing for two years, and I never knew. Why, she was one of my best friends, always in the house. Finally when people began to come to me, Miles had to admit it."

She sat down vehemently on the arm of Joel's chair. Her riding breeches were the color of the chair and Joel saw that the mass of her hair was made up of some strands of red gold and some of pale gold, so that it could not be dyed, and that she had on no make-up. She was that good-looking——

Still quivering with the shock of her discovery, Stella found unbearable the spectacle of a new girl hovering over Miles; she led Joel into a bedroom, and seated at either end of a big bed they went on talking. People on their way to the washroom glanced in and made wisecracks, but Stella, emptying out her story, paid no attention. After a while Miles stuck his head in the door and said, "There's

no use trying to explain something to Joel in half an hour that I
don't understand myself and the psychoanalyst says will take a
whole year to understand."

She talked on as if Miles were not there. She loved Miles, she
said—under considerable difficulties she had always been faithful
to him.

"The psychoanalyst told Miles that he had a mother complex. In
his first marriage he transferred his mother complex to his wife, you
see—and then his sex turned to me. But when we married the thing
repeated itself—he transferred his mother complex to me and all his
libido turned toward this other woman."

Joel knew that this probably wasn't gibberish—yet it sounded like
gibberish. He knew Eva Goebel; she was a motherly person, older
and probably wiser than Stella, who was a golden child.

Miles now suggested impatiently that Joel come back with them
since Stella had so much to say, so they drove out to the mansion in
Beverly Hills. Under the high ceilings the situation seemed more
dignified and tragic. It was an eerie bright night with the dark very
clear outside of all the windows and Stella all rose-gold raging and
crying around the room. Joel did not quite believe in picture
actresses' grief. They have other preoccupations—they are beautiful
rose-gold figures blown full of life by writers and directors, and after
hours they sit around and talk in whispers and giggle innuendoes,
and the ends of many adventures flow through them.

Sometimes he pretended to listen and instead thought how well
she was got up—sleek breeches with a matched set of legs in them,
an Italian-colored sweater with a little high neck, and a short brown
chamois coat. He couldn't decide whether she was an imitation of an
English lady or an English lady was an imitation of her. She hovered
somewhere between the realest of realities and the most blatant of
impersonations.

"Miles is so jealous of me that he questions everything I do," she
cried scornfully. "When I was in New York I wrote him that I'd
been to the theater with Eddie Baker. Miles was so jealous he
phoned me ten times in one day."

"I was wild," Miles snuffled sharply, a habit he had in times of
stress. "The analyst couldn't get any results for a week."

Stella shook her head despairingly. "Did you expect me just to sit
in the hotel for three weeks?"

"I don't expect anything. I admit that I'm jealous. I try not to be.
I worked on that with Dr. Bridgebane, but it didn't do any good. I
was jealous of Joel this afternoon when you sat on the arm of his
chair."

"You were?" She started up. "You were! Wasn't there somebody

on the arm of your chair? And did you speak to me for two
hours?"

"You were telling your troubles to Joel in the bedroom."

"When I think that that woman"—she seemed to believe that to
omit Eva Goebel's name would be to lessen her reality—"used to
come here——"

"All right—all right," said Miles wearily. "I've admitted everything and I feel as bad about it as you do." Turning to Joel he began
talking about pictures, while Stella moved restlessly along the far
walls, her hands in her breeches pockets.

"They've treated Miles terribly," she said, coming suddenly back
into the conversation as if they'd never discussed her personal
affairs. "Dear, tell him about old Beltzer trying to change your
picture."

As she stood hovering protectively over Miles, her eyes flashing
with indignation in his behalf, Joel realized that he was in love with
her. Stifled with excitement he got up to say good night.

With Monday the week resumed its workaday rhythm, in sharp
contrast to the theoretical discussions, the gossip and scandal of
Sunday; there was the endless detail of script revision—"Instead of
a lousy dissolve, we can leave her voice on the sound track and cut
to a medium shot of the taxi from Bell's angle or we can simply pull
the camera back to include the station, hold it a minute and then
pan to the row of taxis"—by Monday afternoon Joel had again forgotten that people whose business was to provide entertainment were
ever privileged to be entertained. In the evening he phoned Miles'
house. He asked for Miles but Stella came to the phone.

"Do things seem better?"

"Not particularly. What are you doing next Saturday evening?"

"Nothing."

"The Perrys are giving a dinner and theater party and Miles
won't be here—he's flying to South Bend to see the Notre Dame-
California game. I thought you might go with me in his place."

After a long moment Joel said, "Why—surely. If there's a conference I can't make dinner but I can get to the theater."

"Then I'll say we can come."

Joel walked his office. In view of the strained relations of the Cal-
mans, would Miles be pleased, or did she intend that Miles shouldn't
know of it? That would be out of the question—if Miles didn't
mention it Joel would. But it was an hour or more before he could
get down to work again.

Wednesday there was a four-hour wrangle in a conference room
crowded with planets and nebulæ of cigarette smoke. Three men and
a woman paced the carpet in turn, suggesting or condemning, speak-

ing sharply or persuasively, confidently or despairingly. At the end
Joel lingered to talk to Miles.

The man was tired—not with the exaltation of fatigue but life-
tired, with his lids sagging and his beard prominent over the blue
shadows near his mouth.

"I hear you're flying to the Notre Dame game."

Miles looked beyond him and shook his head.

"I've given up the idea."

"Why?"

"On account of you." Still he did not look at Joel.

"What the hell, Miles?"

"That's why I've given it up." He broke into a perfunctory laugh
at himself. "I can't tell what Stella might do just out of spite—
she's invited you to take her to the Perrys', hasn't she? I wouldn't
enjoy the game."

The fine instinct that moved swiftly and confidently on the set,
muddled so weakly and helplessly through his personal life.

"Look, Miles," Joel said frowning. "I've never made any passes
whatsoever at Stella. If you're really seriously canceling your trip
on account of me, I won't go to the Perrys' with her. I won't see her.
You can trust me absolutely."

Miles looked at him, carefully now.

"Maybe." He shrugged his shoulders. "Anyhow there'd just be
somebody else. I wouldn't have any fun."

"You don't seem to have much confidence in Stella. She told me
she'd always been true to you."

"Maybe she has." In the last few minutes several more muscles
had sagged around Miles' mouth. "But how can I ask anything of
her after what's happened? How can I expect her—" He broke off
and his face grew harder as he said, "I'll tell you one thing, right or
wrong and no matter what I've done, if I ever had anything on her
I'd divorce her. I can't have my pride hurt—that would be the last
straw."

His tone annoyed Joel, but he said:

"Hasn't she calmed down about the Eva Goebel thing?"

"No." Miles snuffled pessimistically. "I can't get over it either."

"I thought it was finished."

"I'm trying not to see Eva again, but you know it isn't easy just
to drop something like that—it isn't some girl I kissed last night in
a taxi. The psychoanalyst says——"

"I know," Joel interrupted. "Stella told me." This was depressing.
"Well, as far as I'm concerned if you go to the game I won't see
Stella. And I'm sure Stella has nothing on her conscience about any
body."

"Maybe not," Miles repeated listlessly. "Anyhow I'll stay and take her to the party. Say," he said suddenly, "I wish you'd come too. I've got to have somebody sympathetic to talk to. That's the trouble —I've influenced Stella in everything. Especially I've influenced her so that she likes all the men I like—it's very difficult."

"It must be," Joel agreed.

IV

Joel could not get to the dinner. Self-conscious in his silk hat against the unemployment, he waited for the others in front of the Hollywood Theater and watched the evening parade: obscure replicas of bright, particular picture stars, spavined men in polo coats, a stomping dervish with the beard and staff of an apostle, a pair of chic Filipinos in collegiate clothes, reminder that this corner of the Republic opened to the seven seas, a long fantastic carnival of young shouts which proved to be a fraternity initiation. The line split to pass two smart limousines that stopped at the curb.

There she was, in a dress like ice-water, made in a thousand pale-blue pieces, with icicles trickling at the throat. He started forward.

"So you like my dress?"

"Where's Miles?"

"He flew to the game after all. He left yesterday morning—at least I think—" She broke off. "I just got a telegram from South Bend saying that he's starting back. I forgot—you know all these people?"

The party of eight moved into the theater.

Miles had gone after all and Joel wondered if he should have come. But during the performance, with Stella a profile under the pure grain of light hair, he thought no more about Miles. Once he turned and looked at her and she looked back at him, smiling and meeting his eyes for as long as he wanted. Between the acts they smoked in the lobby and she whispered:

"They're all going to the opening of Jack Johnson's night club— I don't want to go, do you?"

"Do we have to?"

"I suppose not." She hesitated. "I'd like to talk to you. I suppose we could go to our house—if I were only sure——"

Again she hesitated and Joel asked:

"Sure of what?"

"Sure that—oh, I'm haywire I know, but how can I be sure Miles went to the game?"

"You mean you think he's with Eva Goebel?"

"No, not so much that—but supposing he was here watching everything I do. You know Miles does odd things sometimes. Once he father?

wanted a man with a long beard to drink tea with him and he sent down to the casting agency for one, and drank tea with him all afternoon."

"That's different. He sent you a wire from South Bend—that proves he's at the game."

After the play they said good night to the others at the curb and were answered by looks of amusement. They slid off along the golden garish thoroughfare through the crowd that had gathered around Stella.

"You see he could arrange the telegrams," Stella said, "very easily."

That was true. And with the idea that perhaps her uneasiness was justified, Joel grew angry: if Miles had trained a camera on them he felt no obligations toward Miles. Aloud he said:

"That's nonsense."

There were Christmas trees already in the shop windows and the full moon over the boulevard was only a prop, as scenic as the giant boudoir lamps of the corners. On into the dark foliage of Beverly Hills that flamed as eucalyptus by day, Joel saw only the flash of a white face under his own, the arc of her shoulder. She pulled away suddenly and looked up at him.

"Your eyes are like your mother's," she said. "I used to have a scrap book full of pictures of her."

"Your eyes are like your own and not a bit like any other eyes," he answered.

Something made Joel look out into the grounds as they went into the house, as if Miles were lurking in the shrubbery. A telegram waited on the hall table. She read aloud:

"CHICAGO.

"Home tomorrow night. Thinking of you. Love.

"MILES."

"You see," she said, throwing the slip back on the table, "he could easily have faked that." She asked the butler for drinks and sandwiches and ran upstairs, while Joel walked into the empty reception rooms. Strolling about he wandered to the piano where he had stood in disgrace two Sundays before.

"Then we could put over," he said aloud, "a story of divorce, the younger generation and the Foreign Legion."

His thoughts jumped to another telegram.

"You were one of the most agreeable people at our party——"

An idea occurred to him. If Stella's telegram had been purely a gesture of courtesy then it was likely that Miles had inspired it, for it was Miles who had invited him. Probably Miles had said:

"Send him a wire—he's miserable—he thinks he's queered himself."

It fitted in with "I've influenced Stella in everything. Especially I've influenced her so that she likes all the men I like." A woman would do a thing like that because she felt sympathetic—only a man would do it because he felt responsible.

When Stella came back into the room he took both her hands.

"I have a strange feeling that I'm a sort of pawn in a spite game you're playing against Miles," he said.

"Help yourself to a drink."

"And the odd thing is that I'm in love with you anyhow." —Joel   Miles

The telephone rang and she freed herself to answer it.

"Another wire from Miles," she announced. "He dropped it, or it says he dropped it, from the airplane at Kansas City."

"I suppose he asked to be remembered to me."

"No, he just said he loved me. I believe he does. He's so very weak."

"Come sit beside me," Joel urged her.

It was early. And it was still a few minutes short of midnight a half-hour later, when Joel walked to the cold hearth, and said tersely:

"Meaning that you haven't any curiosity about me?"

"Not at all. You attract me a lot and you know it. The point is that I suppose I really do love Miles."

"Obviously."

"And tonight I feel uneasy about everything."

He wasn't angry—he was even faintly relieved that a possible entanglement was avoided. Still as he looked at her, the warmth and softness of her body thawing her cold blue costume, he knew she was one of the things he would always regret.

"I've got to go," he said. "I'll phone a taxi."

"Nonsense—there's a chauffeur on duty."

He winced at her readiness to have him go, and seeing this she kissed him lightly and said, "You're sweet, Joel." Then suddenly three things happened: he took down his drink at a gulp, the phone rang loud through the house and a clock in the hall struck in trumpet notes.

Nine—ten—eleven—twelve——

Joel sleeps
+ Stella
↓

V

after midnight

It was Sunday again. Joel realized that he had come to the theater this evening with the work of the week still hanging about him like cerements. He had made love to Stella as he might attack some matter to be cleaned up hurriedly before the day's end. But this was

3rd Sun

↑

Sunday—the lovely, lazy perspective of the next twenty-four hours
unrolled before him—every minute was something to be approached
with lulling indirection, every moment held the germ of innumerable
possibilities. Nothing was impossible—everything was just beginning. He poured himself another drink.

With a sharp moan, Stella slipped forward inertly by the telephone. Joel picked her up and laid her on the sofa. He squirted soda-
water on a handkerchief and slapped it over her face. The telephone
mouthpiece was still grinding and he put it to his ear.

"—the plane fell just this side of Kansas City. The body of Miles
Calman has been identified and——" *like Stahr in planned end of LT*

He hung up the receiver.

"Lie still," he said, stalling, as Stella opened her eyes.

"Oh, what's happened?" she whispered. "Call them back. Oh,
what's happened?"

"I'll call them right away. What's your doctor's name?"

"Did they say Miles was dead?"

"Lie quiet—is there a servant still up?"

"Hold me—I'm frightened."

He put his arm around her.

"I want the name of your doctor," he said sternly. "It may be a
mistake but I want someone here."

"It's Doctor—Oh, God, is Miles dead?"

Joel ran upstairs and searched through strange medicine cabinets
for spirits of ammonia. When he came down Stella cried:

"He isn't dead—I know he isn't. This is part of his scheme. He's
torturing me. I know he's alive. I can feel he's alive."

"I want to get hold of some close friend of yours, Stella. You
can't stay here alone tonight."

"Oh, no," she cried. "I can't see anybody. You stay. I haven't got
any friend." She got up, tears streaming down her face. "Oh, Miles
is my only friend. He's not dead—he can't be dead. I'm going there
right away and see. Get a train. You'll have to come with me."

"You can't. There's nothing to do tonight. I want you to tell me
the name of some woman I can call: Lois? Joan? Carmel? Isn't
there somebody?"   *Moran*   *Myerns*

Stella stared at him blindly.

"Eva Goebel was my best friend," she said.

Joel thought of Miles, his sad and desperate face in the office two
days before. In the awful silence of his death all was clear about
him. He was the only American-born director with both an interesting temperament and an artistic conscience. Meshed in an industry,
he had paid with his ruined nerves for having no resilience, no
healthy cynicism, no refuge—only a pitiful and precarious escape.

There was a sound at the outer door—it opened suddenly, and there were footsteps in the hall.

"Miles!" Stella screamed. "Is it you, Miles? Oh, it's Miles."

A telegraph boy appeared in the doorway.

"I couldn't find the bell. I heard you talking inside."

The telegram was a duplicate of the one that had been phoned. While Stella read it over and over, as though it were a black lie, Joel telephoned. It was still early and he had difficulty getting anyone; when finally he succeeded in finding some friends he made Stella take a stiff drink.

"You'll stay here, Joel," she whispered, as though she were half-asleep. "You won't go away. Miles liked you—he said you—" She shivered violently, "Oh, my God, you don't know how alone I feel." Her eyes closed, "Put your arms around me. Miles had a suit like that." She started bolt upright. "Think of what he must have felt. He was afraid of almost everything, anyhow."

She shook her head dazedly. Suddenly she seized Joel's face and held it close to hers.

"You won't go. You like me—you love me, don't you? Don't call up anybody. Tomorrow's time enough. You stay here with me tonight."

He stared at her, at first incredulously, and then with shocked understanding. In her dark groping Stella was trying to keep Miles alive by sustaining a situation in which he had figured—as if Miles' mind could not die so long as the possibilities that had worried him still existed. It was a distraught and tortured effort to stave off the realization that he was dead.

Resolutely Joel went to the phone and called a doctor.

"Don't, oh, don't call anybody!" Stella cried. "Come back here and put your arms around me."

"Is Doctor Bales in?"

"Joel," Stella cried. "I thought I could count on you. Miles liked you. He was jealous of you—Joel, come here."

Ah then—if he betrayed Miles she would be keeping him alive—for if he were really dead how could he be betrayed?

"—has just had a very severe shock. Can you come at once, and get hold of a nurse?"

"Joel!"

Now the door-bell and the telephone began to ring intermittently, and automobiles were stopping in front of the door.

"But you're not going," Stella begged him. "You're going to stay, aren't you?"

"No," he answered. "But I'll be back, if you need me."

Standing on the steps of the house which now hummed and palpitated with the life that flutters around death like protective leaves, he began to sob a little in his throat.

"Everything he touched he did something magical to," he thought. "He even brought that little gamin alive and made her a sort of masterpiece."

And then:

"What a hell of a hole he leaves in this damn wilderness— already!"

And then with a certain bitterness, "Oh, yes, I'll be back—I'll be back!"

1932　　　　　　　　　　　　　　　　　　　*Taps at Reveille*

FAMILY IN THE WIND

THE TWO men drove up the hill toward the blood-red sun. The cotton fields bordering the road were thin and withered, and no breeze stirred in the pines.

"When I am totally sober," the doctor was saying—"I mean when I am totally sober—I don't see the same world that you do. I'm like a friend of mine who had one good eye and got glasses made to correct his bad eye; the result was that he kept seeing elliptical suns and falling off tilted curbs, until he had to throw the glasses away. Granted that I am thoroughly anaesthetized the greater part of the day—well, I only undertake work that I know I can do when I am in that condition."

"Yeah," agreed his brother Gene uncomfortably. The doctor was a little tight at the moment and Gene could find no opening for what he had to say. Like so many Southerners of the humbler classes, he had a deep-seated courtesy, characteristic of all violent and passionate lands—he could not change the subject until there was a moment's silence, and Forrest would not shut up.

"I'm very happy," he continued, "or very miserable. I chuckle or I weep alcoholically and, as I continue to slow up, life accommodatingly goes faster, so that the less there is of myself inside, the more diverting becomes the moving picture without. I have cut myself off from the respect of my fellow man, but I am aware of a compensatory cirrhosis of the emotions. And because my sensitivity, my pity, no longer has direction, but fixes itself on whatever is at hand, I have become an exceptionally good fellow—much more so than when I was a good doctor."

As the road straightened after the next bend and Gene saw his house in the distance, he remembered his wife's face as she had made him promise, and he could wait no longer: "Forrest, I got a thing——"

But at that moment the doctor brought his car to a sudden stop in front of a small house just beyond a grove of pines. On the front steps a girl of eight was playing with a gray cat.

"This is the sweetest little kid I ever saw," the doctor said to

Gene, and then to the child, in a grave voice: "Helen, do you need any pills for kitty?

The little girl laughed.

"Well, I don't know," she said doubtfully. She was playing another game with the cat now and this came as rather an interruption.

"Because kitty telephoned me this morning," the doctor continued, "and said her mother was neglecting her and couldn't I get her a trained nurse from Montgomery."

"She did not." The little girl grabbed the cat close indignantly; the doctor took a nickel from his pocket and tossed it to the steps.

"I recommend a good dose of milk," he said as he put the car into gear. "Good night, Helen."

"Good night, doctor."

As they drove off, Gene tried again: "Listen; stop," he said. "Stop here a little way down . . . Here."

The doctor stopped the car and the brothers faced each other. They were alike as to robustness of figure and a certain asceticism of feature and they were both in their middle forties; they were unlike in that the doctor's glasses failed to conceal the veined, weeping eyes of a soak, and that he wore corrugated city wrinkles; Gene's wrinkles bounded fields, followed the lines of rooftrees, of poles propping up sheds. His eyes were a fine, furry blue. But the sharpest contrast lay in the fact that Gene Janney was a country man while Dr. Forrest Janney was obviously a man of education.

"Well?" the doctor asked.

"You know Pinky's at home," Gene said, looking down the road.

"So I hear," the doctor answered noncommittally.

"He got in a row in Birmingham and somebody shot him in the head." Gene hesitated. "We got Doc Behrer because we thought maybe you wouldn't—maybe you wouldn't——"

"I wouldn't," agreed Doctor Janney blandly.

"But look, Forrest; here's the thing," Gene insisted. "You know how it is—you often say Doc Behrer doesn't know nothing. Shucks, I never thought he was much either. He says the bullet's pressing on the—pressing on the brain, and he can't take it out without causin' a hemmering, and he says he doesn't know whether we could get him to Birmingham or Montgomery, or not, he's so low. Doc wasn't no help. What we want——"

"No," said his brother, shaking his head. "No."

"I just want you to look at him and tell us what to do," Gene begged. "He's unconscious, Forrest. He wouldn't know you; you'd hardly know him. Thing is his mother's about crazy."

"She's in the grip of a purely animal instinct." The doctor took from his hip a flask containing half water and half Alabama corn, and drank. "You and I know that boy ought to been drowned the day he was born."

Gene flinched. "He's bad," he admitted, "but I don't know—You see him lying there——"

As the liquor spread over the doctor's insides he felt an instinct to do something, not to violate his prejudices but simply to make some gesture, to assert his own moribund but still struggling will to power.

"All right, I'll see him," he said. "I'll do nothing myself to help him, because he ought to be dead. And even his death wouldn't make up for what he did to Mary Decker."

Gene Janney pursed his lips. "Forrest, you sure about that?"

"Sure about it!" exclaimed the doctor. "Of course I'm sure. She died of starvation; she hadn't had more than a couple cups of coffee in a week. And if you looked at her shoes, you could see she'd walked for miles."

"Doc Behrer says——"

"What does he know? I performed the autopsy the day they found her on the Birmingham Highway. There was nothing the matter with her but starvation. That—that"—his voice shook with feeling— "that Pinky got tired of her and turned her out, and she was trying to get home. It suits me fine that he was invalided home himself a couple of weeks later."

As he talked, the doctor had plunged the car savagely into gear and let the clutch out with a jump; in a moment they drew up before Gene Janney's home.

It was a square frame house with a brick foundation and a well-kept lawn blocked off from the farm, a house rather superior to the buildings that composed the town of Bending and the surrounding agricultural area, yet not essentially different in type or in its interior economy. The last of the plantation houses in this section of Alabama had long disappeared, the proud pillars yielding to poverty, rot and rain.

Gene's wife, Rose, got up from her rocking-chair on the porch.

"Hello, doc." She greeted him a little nervously and without meeting his eyes. "You been a stranger here lately."

The doctor met her eyes for several seconds. "How do you do, Rose," he said. "Hi, Edith . . . Hi, Eugene"—this to the little boy and girl who stood beside their mother; and then: "Hi, Butch!" to the stocky youth of nineteen who came around the corner of the house hugging a round stone.

"Goin to have a sort of low wall along the front here—kind of neater," Gene explained.

All of them had a lingering respect for the doctor. They felt reproachful toward him because they could no longer refer to him as their celebrated relative—"one of the bess surgeons up in Montgomery, yes, suh"—but there was his learning and the position he had fessional suicide by taking to cynicism and drink. He had come home to Bending and bought a half interest in the local drug store two years ago, keeping up his license, but practising only when sorely needed.

"Rose," said Gene, "doc says he'll take a look at Pinky."

Pinky Janney, his lips curved mean and white under a new beard, lay in bed in a darkened room. When the doctor removed the bandage from his head, his breath blew into a low groan, but his paunchy body did not move. After a few minutes, the doctor replaced the bandage and, with Gene and Rose, returned to the porch.

"Behrer wouldn't operate?" he asked.

"No."

"Why didn't they operate in Birmingham?"

"I don't know."

"H'm." The doctor put on his hat. "That bullet ought to come out, and soon. It's pressing against the carotid sheath. That's the—anyhow, you can't get him to Montgomery with that pulse."

"What'll we do?" Gene's question carried a little tail of silence as he sucked his breath back.

"Get Behrer to think it over. Or else get somebody in Montgomery. There's about a 25 per cent chance that the operation would save him; without the operation he hasn't any chance at all."

"Who'll we get in Montgomery?" asked Gene.

"Any good surgeon would do it. Even Behrer could do it if he had any nerve."

Suddenly Rose Janney came close to him, her eyes straining and burning with an animal maternalism. She seized his coat where it hung open.

"Doc, you do it! You can do it. You know you were as good a surgeon as any of em once. Please, doc, you go on do it."

He stepped back a little so that her hands fell from his coat, and held out his own hands in front of him.

"See how they tremble?" he said with elaborate irony. "Look close and you'll see. I wouldn't dare operate."

"You could do it all right," said Gene hastily, "with a drink to stiffen you up."

The doctor shook his head and said, looking at Rose: "No. You see, my decisions are not reliable, and if anything went wrong, it would seem to be my fault." He was acting a little now—he chose his words carefully. "I hear that when I found that Mary Decker died of starvation, my opinion was questioned on the ground that I was a drunkard."

"I didn't say that," lied Rose breathlessly.

"Certainly not. I just mention it to show how careful I've got to be." He moved down the steps. "Well, my advice is to see Behrer again, or, failing that, get somebody from the city. Good night."

But before he had reached the gate, Rose came tearing after him, her eyes white with fury.

"I did say you were a drunkard!" she cried. "When you said Mary Decker died of starvation, you made it out as if it was Pinky's fault—you, swilling yourself full of corn all day! How can anybody tell whether you know what you're doing or not? Why did you think so much about Mary Decker, anyhow—a girl half your age? Everybody saw how she used to come in your drug store and talk to you——"

Gene, who had followed, seized her arms. "Shut up now, Rose . . . Drive along, Forrest."

Forrest drove along, stopping at the next bend to drink from his flask. Across the fallow cotton fields he could see the house where Mary Decker had lived, and had it been six months before, he might have detoured to ask her why she hadn't come into the store that day for her free soda, or to delight her with a sample cosmetic left by a salesman that morning. He had not told Mary Decker how he felt about her; never intended to—she was seventeen, he was forty-five, and he no longer dealt in futures—but only after she ran away to Birmingham with Pinky Janney, did he realize how much his love for her had counted in his lonely life.

His thoughts went back to his brother's house.

"Now, if I were a gentleman," he thought, "I wouldn't have done like that. And another person might have been sacrificed to that dirty dog, because if he died afterward Rose would say I killed him."

Yet he felt pretty bad as he put his car away; not that he could have acted differently, but just that it was all so ugly.

He had been home scarcely ten minutes when a car creaked to rest outside and Butch Janney came in. His mouth was set tight and his eyes were narrowed as though to permit of no escape to the temper that possessed him until it should be unleashed upon its proper objective.

"Hi, Butch."

"I want to tell you, Uncle Forrest, you can't talk to my mother thataway. I'll kill you, you talk to my mother like that!"

"Now shut up, Butch, and sit down," said the doctor sharply.

"She's already bout sick on account of Pinky, and you come over and talk to her like that."

"Your mother did all the insulting that was done, Butch. I just took it."

"She doesn't know what she's saying and you ought to understand that."

The doctor thought a minute. "Butch, what do you think of Pinky?"

Butch hesitated uncomfortably. "Well, I can't say I ever thought so much of him"—his tone changed defiantly—"but after all, he's my own brother——"

"Wait a minute, Butch. What do you think of the way he treated Mary Decker?"

But Butch had shaken himself free, and now he let go the artillery of his rage:

"That ain't the point; the point is anybody that doesn't do right to my mother has me to answer to. It's only fair when you got all the education——"

"I got my education myself, Butch."

"I don't care. We're going to try again to get Doc Behrer to operate or get us some fellow from the city. But if we can't I'm coming and get you, and you're going to take that bullet out if I have to hold a gun to you while you do it." He nodded, panting a little; then he turned and went out and drove away.

"Something tells me," said the doctor to himself, "that there's no more peace for me in Chilton County." He called to his colored boy to put supper on the table. Then he rolled himself a cigarette and went out on the back stoop.

The weather had changed. The sky was now overcast and the grass stirred restlessly and there was a sudden flurry of drops without a sequel. A minute ago it had been warm, but now the moisture on his forehead was suddenly cool, and he wiped it away with his handkerchief. There was a buzzing in his ears and he swallowed and shook his head. For a moment he thought he must be sick; then suddenly the buzzing detached itself from him, grew into a swelling sound, louder and ever nearer, that might have been the roar of an approaching train.

II

Butch Janney was halfway home when he saw it—a huge, black, approaching cloud whose lower edge bumped the ground. Even as he stared at it vaguely, it seemed to spread until it included the whole southern sky, and he saw pale electric fire in it and heard an increasing roar. He was in a strong wind now; blown debris, bits of broken branches, splinters, larger objects unidentifiable in the growing darkness, flew by him. Instinctively he got out of his car and, by now hardly able to stand against the wind, ran for a bank, or rather found himself thrown and pinned against a bank. Then for a minute, two minutes, he was in the black centre of pandemonium.

First there was the sound, and he was part of the sound, so engulfed in it and possessed by it that he had no existence apart from it. It was not a collection of sounds, it was just Sound itself; a great screeching bow drawn across the chords of the universe. The sound and force were inseparable. The sound as well as the force held him to what he felt was the bank like a man crucified. Somewhere in this first moment his face, pinned sideways, saw his automobile make a little jump, spin halfway around and then go bobbing off over a field in a series of great helpless leaps. Then began the bombardment, the sound dividing its sustained cannon note into the cracks of a gigantic machine gun. He was only half-conscious as he felt himself become part of one of those cracks, felt himself lifted away from the bank to tear through space, through a blinding, lacerating mass of twigs and branches, and then, for an incalculable time, he knew nothing at all.

His body hurt him. He was lying between two branches in the top of a tree; the air was full of dust and rain, and he could hear nothing; it was a long time before he realized that the tree he was in had been blown down and that his involuntary perch among the pine needles was only five feet from the ground.

"Say, man!" he cried, aloud, outraged. "Say, man! Say, what a wind! Say, man!"

Made acute by pain and fear, he guessed that he had been standing on the tree's root and had been catapulted by the terrific wrench as the big pine was torn from the earth. Feeling over himself, he found that his left ear was caked full of dirt, as if someone had wanted to take an impression of the inside. His clothes were in rags, his coat had torn on the back seam, and he could feel where, as some stray gust tried to undress him, it had cut into him under the arms.

Reaching the ground, he set off in the direction of his father's house, but it was a new and unfamiliar landscape he traversed. The Thing—he did not know it was a tornado—had cut a path a quarter of a mile wide, and he was confused, as the dust slowly settled, by vistas he had never seen before. It was unreal that Bending church tower should be visible from here; there had been groves of trees between.

But where was here? For he should be close to the Baldwin house;

only as he tripped over great piles of boards, like a carelessly kept
lumberyard, did Butch realize that there was no more Baldwin house,
and then, looking around wildly, that there was no Necrawney house
on the hill, no Peltzer house below it. There was not a light, not a
sound, save the rain falling on the fallen trees.

He broke into a run. When he saw the bulk of his father's house
in the distance, he gave a "Hey!" of relief, but coming closer, he
realized that something was missing. There were no outhouses and
the built-on wing that held Pinky's room had been sheared completely away.

"Mother!" he called. "Dad!" There was no answer; a dog bounded
out of the yard and licked his hand. . . .

. . . It was full dark twenty minutes later when Doc Janney
stopped his car in front of his own drug store in Bending. The electric lights had gone out, but there were men with lanterns in the
street, and in a minute a small crowd had collected around him. He
unlocked the door hurriedly.

"Somebody break open the old Wiggins Hospital." He pointed
across the street. "I've got six badly injured in my car. I want some
fellows to carry em in. Is Doc Behrer here?"

"Here he is," offered eager voices out of the darkness as the
doctor, case in hand, came through the crowd. The two men stood
face to face by lantern light, forgetting that they disliked each
other.

"God knows how many more there's going to be," said Doc Janney.
"I'm getting dressing and disinfectant. There'll be a lot of fractures—" He raised his voice, "Somebody bring me a barrel!"

"I'll get started over there," said Doc Behrer. "There's about half
a dozen more crawled in."

"What's been done?" demanded Doc Janney of the men who followed him into the drug store. "Have they called Birmingham and
Montgomery?"

"The telephone wires are down, but the telegraph got through."

"Well, somebody get Doctor Cohen from Wettala, and tell any
people who have automobiles to go up the Willard Pike and cut
across toward Corsica and all through those roads there. There's not
a house left at the crossroads by the nigger store. I passed a lot of
folks walking in, all of them hurt, but I didn't have room for anybody else." As he talked he was throwing bandages, disinfectant and
'drugs into a blanket. "I thought I had a lot more stuff than this in
stock! And wait!" he called. "Somebody drive out and look down in
that hollow where the Wooleys live. Drive right across the fields—
the road's blocked. . . . Now, you with the cap—Ed Jenks, ain't it?"

"Yes, doc."

"You see what I got here? You collect everything in the store that looks like this and bring it across the way, understand?"

"Yes, doc."

As the doctor went out into the street, the victims were streaming into town—a woman on foot with a badly injured child, a buckboard full of groaning Negroes, frantic men gasping terrible stories. Everywhere confusion and hysteria mounted in the dimly illumined darkness. A mud-covered reporter from Birmingham drove up in a sidecar, the wheels crossing the fallen wires and brushwood that clogged the street, and there was the siren of a police car from Cooper, thirty miles away.

Already a crowd pressed around the doors of the hospital, closed these three months for lack of patients. The doctor squeezed past the mêleé of white faces and established himself in the nearest ward, grateful for the waiting row of old iron beds. Doctor Behrer was already at work across the hall.

"Get me half a dozen lanterns," he ordered.

"Doctor Behrer wants iodine and adhesive."

"All right, there it is. . . . Here, you, Shinkey, stand by the door and keep everybody out except cases that can't walk. Somebody run over and see if there ain't some candles in the grocery store."

The street outside was full of sound now—the cries of women, the contrary directions of volunteer gangs trying to clear the highway, the tense staccato of people rising to an emergency. A little before midnight arrived the first unit of the Red Cross. But the three doctors, presently joined by two others from near-by villages, had lost track of time long before that. The dead began to be brought in by ten o'clock; there were twenty, twenty-five, thirty, forty—the list grew. Having no more needs, these waited, as became simple husbandmen, in a garage behind, while the stream of injured—hundreds of them—flowed through the old hospital built to house only a score The storm had dealt out fractures of the leg, collar bone, ribs and hip, lacerations of the back, elbows, ears, eyelids, nose; there were wounds from flying planks, and odd splinters in odd places, and a scalped man, who would recover to grow a new head of hair. Living or dead, Doc Janney knew every face, almost every name.

"Don't you fret now. Billy's all right. Hold still and let me tie this. People are drifting in every minute, but it's so consarned dark they can't find 'em—All right, Mrs. Oakey. That's nothing. Ev here'll touch it with iodine . . . Now let's see this man."

Two o'clock. The old doctor from Wettala gave out, but now there were fresh men from Montgomery to take his place. Upon the air of the room, heavy with disinfectant, floated the ceaseless babble of human speech reaching the doctor dimly through the layer after layer of increasing fatigue:

". . . Over and over—just rolled me over and over. Got hold of a bush and the bush came along too."

"Jeff! Where's Jeff?"

". . . I bet that pig sailed a hundred yards——"

"—just stopped the train in time. All the passengers got out and helped pull the poles——"

"Where's Jeff?"

"He says, 'Let's get down cellar,' and I says, 'We ain't got no cellar'——"

"—If there's no more stretchers, find some light doors."

". . . Five seconds? Say, it was more like five minutes!"

At some time he heard that Gene and Rose had been seen with their two youngest children. He had passed their house on the way in and, seeing it standing, hurried on. The Janney family had been lucky; the doctor's own house was outside the sweep of the storm.

Only as he saw the electric lights go on suddenly in the streets and glimpsed the crowd waiting for hot coffee in front of the Red Cross did the doctor realize how tired he was.

"You better go rest," a young man was saying. "I'll take this side of the room. I've got two nurses with me."

"All right—all right. I'll finish this row."

The injured were being evacuated to the cities by train as fast as their wounds were dressed, and their places taken by others. He had only two beds to go—in the first one he found Pinky Janney.

He put his stethoscope to the heart. It was beating feebly. That he, so weak, so nearly gone, had survived this storm at all was remarkable. How he had got there, who had found him and carried him, was a mystery in itself. The doctor went over the body; there were small contusions and lacerations, two broken fingers, the dirt-filled ears that marked every case—nothing else. For a moment the doctor hesitated, but even when he closed his eyes, the image of Mary Decker seemed to have receded, eluding him. Something purely professional that had nothing to do with human sensibilities had been set in motion inside him, and he was powerless to head it off. He held out his hands before him; they were trembling slightly.

"Hell's bells!" he muttered.

He went out of the room and around the corner of the hall, where he drew from his pocket the flask containing the last of the corn and water he had had in the afternoon. He emptied it. Returning to the ward, he disinfected two instruments and applied a local anaesthetic to a square section at the base of Pinky's skull where the wound had healed over the bullet. He called a nurse to his side and then, scalpel in hand, knelt on one knee beside his nephew's bed.

III

Two days later the doctor drove slowly around the mournful countryside. He had withdrawn from the emergency work after the first desperate night, feeling that his status as a pharmacist might embarrass his collaborators. But there was much to be done in bringing the damage to outlying sections under the aegis of the Red Cross, and he devoted himself to that.

The path of the demon was easy to follow. It had pursued an irregular course on its seven-league boots, cutting cross country, through woods, or even urbanely keeping to roads until they curved, when it went off on its own again. Sometimes the trail could be traced by cotton fields, apparently in full bloom, but this cotton came from the insides of hundreds of quilts and mattresses redistributed in the fields by the storm.

At a lumber pile that had lately been a Negro cabin, he stopped a moment to listen to a dialogue between two reporters and two shy pickaninnies. The old grandmother, her head bandaged, sat among the ruins, gnawing some vague meat and moving her rocker ceaselessly.

"But where is the river you were blown across?" one of the reporters demanded.

"There."

"Where?"

The pickaninnies looked to their grandmother for aid.

"Right there behind you-all," spoke up the old woman.

The newspapermen looked disgustedly at a muddy stream four yards wide.

"That's no river."

"That's a Menada River, we always calls it ever since I was a gull. Yes, suh, that's a Menada River. An' them two boys was blowed right across it an set down on the othah side just as pretty, 'thout any hurt at all. Chimney fell on me," she concluded, feeling her head.

"Do you mean to say that's all it was?" demanded the younger reporter indignantly. "That's the river they were blown across! And one hundred and twenty million people have been led to believe——"

"That's all right, boys," interrupted Doc Janney. "That's a right good river for these parts. And it'll get bigger as those little fellahs get older."

He tossed a quarter to the old woman and drove on.

Passing a country church, he stopped and counted the new brown mounds that marred the graveyard. He was nearing the centre of the holocaust now. There was the Howden house where three had been killed; there remained a gaunt chimney, a rubbish heap and a scarecrow surviving ironically in the kitchen garden. In the ruins of the house across the way a rooster strutted on top of a piano, reigning vociferously over an estate of trunks, boots, cans, books, calendars, rugs, chairs and window frames, a twisted radio and a legless sewing machine. Everywhere there was bedding—blankets, mattresses, bent springs, shredded padding—he had not realized how much of people's lives was spent in bed. Here and there, cows and horses, often stained with disinfectant, were grazing again in the fields. At intervals there were Red Cross tents, and sitting by one of these, with the gray cat in her arms, the doctor came upon little Helen Kilrain. The usual lumber pile, like a child's building game knocked down in a fit of temper, told the story.

"Hello, dear," he greeted her, his heart sinking. "How did kitty like the tornado?"

"She didn't."

"What did she do?"

"She meowed."

"Oh."

"She wanted to get away, but I hanged on to her and she scratched me—see?"

He glanced at the Red Cross tent.

"Who's taking care of you?"

"The lady from the Red Cross and Mrs. Wells," she answered. "My father got hurt. He stood over me so it wouldn't fall on me, and I stood over kitty. He's in the hospital in Birmingham. When he comes back, I guess he'll build our house again."

The doctor winced. He knew that her father would build no more houses; he had died that morning. She was alone, and she did not know she was alone. Around her stretched the dark universe, impersonal, inconscient. Her lovely little face looked up at him confidently as he asked: "You got any kin anywhere, Helen?"

"I don't know."

"You've got kitty, anyhow, haven't you?"

"It's just a cat," she admitted calmly, but anguished by her own betrayal of her love, she hugged it closer.

"Taking care of a cat must be pretty hard."

"Oh, no," she said hurriedly. "It isn't any trouble at all. It doesn't eat hardly anything."

He put his hand in his pocket, and then changed his mind suddenly.

"Dear, I'm coming back and see you later—later today. You take take good care of kitty now, won't you?"

"Oh, yes," she answered lightly.

The doctor drove on. He stopped next at a house that had escaped damage. Walt Cupps, the owner, was cleaning a shotgun on his front porch.

"What's that, Walt? Going to shoot up the next tornado?"

"Ain't going to be a next tornado."

"You can't tell. Just take a look at that sky now. It's getting mighty dark."

Walt laughed and slapped his gun. "Not for a hundred years, anyhow. This here is for looters. There's a lot of 'em around, and not all black either. Wish when you go to town that you'd tell 'em to scatter some militia out here."

"I'll tell em now. You come out all right?"

"I did, thank God. With six of us in the house. It took off one hen, and probably it's still carrying it around somewhere."

The doctor drove on toward town, overcome by a feeling of uneasiness he could not define.

"It's the weather," he thought. "It's the same kind of feel in the air there was last Saturday."

For a month the doctor had felt an urge to go away permanently. Once this countryside had seemed to promise peace. When the impetus that had lifted him temporarily out of tired old stock was exhausted, he had come back here to rest, to watch the earth put forth, and live on simple, pleasant terms with his neighbors. Peace! He knew that the present family quarrel would never heal, nothing would ever be the same; it would all be bitter forever. And he had seen the placid countryside turned into a land of mourning. There was no peace here. Move on!

On the road he overtook Butch Janney walking to town.

"I was coming to see you," said Butch, frowning. "You operated on Pinky after all, didn't you?"

"Jump in. . . . Yes, I did. How did you know?"

"Doc Behrer told us." He shot a quick look at the doctor, who did not miss the quality of suspicion in it. "They don't think he'll last out the day."

"I'm sorry for your mother."

Butch laughed unpleasantly. "Yes, you are."

"I said I'm sorry for your mother," said the doctor sharply.

"I heard you."

They drove for a moment in silence.

"Did you find your automobile?"

"Did I?" Butch laughed ruefully. "I found something—I don't know whether you'd call it a car any more. And, you know, I could of had tornado insurance for twenty-five cents." His voice trembled indignantly: "Twenty-five cents—but who would ever of thought of getting tornado insurance?"

It was growing darker; there was a thin crackle of thunder far to the southward.

"Well, all I hope," said Butch with narrowed glance, "is that you hadn't been drinking anything when you operated on Pinky."

"You know, Butch," the doctor said slowly, "that was a pretty dirty trick of mine to bring that tornado here."

He had not expected the sarcasm to hit home, but he expected a retort—when suddenly he caught sight of Butch's face. It was fish-white, the mouth was open, the eyes fixed and staring, and from the throat came a mewling sound. Limply he raised one hand before him, and then the doctor saw.

Less than a mile away, an enormous, top-shaped black cloud filled the sky and bore toward them, dipping and swirling, and in front of it sailed already a heavy, singing wind.

"It's come back!" the doctor yelled.

Fifty yards ahead of them was the old iron bridge spanning Bilby Creek. He stepped hard on the accelerator and drove for it. The fields were full of running figures headed in the same direction. Reaching the bridge, he jumped out and yanked Butch's arm.

"Get out, you fool! Get out!"

A nerveless mass stumbled from the car; in a moment they were in a group of half a dozen, huddled in the triangular space that the bridge made with the shore.

"Is it coming here?"

"No, it's turning!"

"We had to leave grampa!"

"Oh, save me, save me! Jesus save me! Help me!"

"Jesus save my soul!"

There was a quick rush of wind outside, sending little tentacles under the bridge with a curious tension in them that made the doctor's skin crawl. Then immediately there was a vacuum, with no more wind, but a sudden thresh of rain. The doctor crawled to the edge of the bridge and put his head up cautiously.

"It's passed," he said. "We only felt the edge; the centre went way to the right of us."

He could see it plainly; for a second he could even distinguish objects in it—shrubbery and small trees, planks and loose earth. Crawling farther out, he produced his watch and tried to time it, but the thick curtain of rain blotted it from sight.

Soaked to the skin, he crawled back underneath. Butch lay shivering in the farthest corner, and the doctor shook him.

"It went in the direction of your house!" the doctor cried. "Pull yourself together! Who's there?"

"No one," Butch groaned. "They're all down with Pinky."

The rain had changed to hail now; first small pellets, then larger ones, and larger, until the sound of the fall upon the iron bridge was an ear-splitting tattoo.

The spared wretches under the bridge were slowly recovering, and in the relief there were titters of hysterical laughter. After a certain point of strain, the nervous system makes its transitions without dignity or reason. Even the doctor felt the contagion.

"This is worse than a calamity," he said dryly. "It's getting to be a nuisance."

IV

There were to be no more tornadoes in Alabama that spring. The second one—it was popularly thought to be the first one come back; for to the people of Chilton County it had become a personified force, definite as a pagan god—took a dozen houses, Gene Janney's among them, and injured about thirty people. But this time—perhaps because everyone had developed some scheme of self-protection —there were no fatalities. It made its last dramatic bow by sailing down the main street of Bending, prostrating the telephone poles and crushing in the fronts of three shops, including Doc Janney's drug store.

At the end of a week, houses were going up again, made of the old boards; and before the end of the long, lush Alabama summer the grass would be green again on all the graves. But it would be years before the people of the country ceased to reckon events as happening "before the tornado" or "after the tornado,"—and for many families things would never be the same.

Doctor Janney decided that this was as good a time to leave as any. He sold the remains of his drug store, gutted alike by charity and catastrophe, and turned over his house to his brother until Gene could rebuild his own. He was going up to the city by train, for his car had been rammed against a tree and couldn't be counted on for much more than the trip to the station.

Several times on the way in he stopped by the roadside to say good-by—once it was to Walter Cupps.

"So it hit you, after all," he said, looking at the melancholy back house which alone marked the site.

"It's pretty bad," Walter answered. "But just think; they was six of us in or about the house and not one was injured. I'm content to give thanks to God for that."

"You were lucky there, Walt," the doctor agreed. "Do you happen to have heard whether the Red Cross took little Helen Kilrain to Montgomery or to Birmingham?"

"To Montgomery. Say, I was there when she came into town with that cat, tryin' to get somebody to bandage up its paw. She must of walked miles through that rain and hail, but all that mattered to her was her kitty. Bad as I felt, I couldn't help laughin' at how spunky she was."

The doctor was silent for a moment. "Do you happen to recollect if she has any people left?"

"I don't, suh," Walter replied, "but I think as not."

At his brother's place, the doctor made his last stop. They were all there, even the youngest, working among the ruins; already Butch had a shed erected to house the salvage of their goods. Save for this the most orderly thing surviving was the pattern of round white stone which was to have inclosed the garden.

The doctor took a hundred dollars in bills from his pocket and handed it to Gene.

"You can pay it back, sometime, but don't strain yourself," he said. "It's money I got from the store." He cut off Gene's thanks: "Pack up my books carefully when I send for 'em."

"You reckon to practice medicine up there, Forrest?"

"I'll maybe try it."

The brothers held on to each other's hands for a moment; the two youngest children came up to say good-by. Rose stood in the background in an old blue dress—she had no money to wear black for her eldest son.

"Good-by, Rose," said the doctor.

"Good-by," she responded, and then added in a dead voice, "Good luck to you, Forrest."

For a moment he was tempted to say something conciliatory, but he saw it was no use. He was up against the maternal instinct, the same force that had sent little Helen through the storm with her injured cat.

At the station he bought a one-way ticket to Montgomery. The village was drab under the sky of a retarded spring, and as the train pulled out, it was odd to think that six months ago it had seemed to him as good a place as any other.

He was alone in the white section of the day coach; presently he felt for a bottle on his hip and drew it forth. "After all, a man of forty-five is entitled to more artificial courage when he starts over again." He began thinking of Helen. "She hasn't got any kin. I guess she's my little girl now."

He patted the bottle, then looked down at it as if in surprise.

"Well, we'll have to put you aside for a while, old friend. Any cat that's worth all that trouble and care is going to need a lot of grade-B milk."

He settled down in his seat, looking out the window. In his memory of the terrible week the winds still sailed about him, came in as draughts through the corridor of the car—winds of the world— cyclones, hurricanes, tornadoes—gray and black, expected or unforeseen, some from the sky, some from the caves of hell.

But he would not let them touch Helen again—if he could help it.

He dozed momentarily, but a haunting dream woke him: *"Daddy stood over me and I stood over kitty."*

"All right, Helen," he said aloud, for he often talked to himself, "I guess the old brig can keep afloat a little longer—in any wind."

1932   *Taps at Reveille*

AN ALCOHOLIC CASE

"LET—GO—that—oh-h-h! Please, now, will you? *Don't* start drinking again! Come on—give me the bottle. I told you I'd stay awake givin it to you. Come on. If you do like that a-way—then what are you going to be like when you go home. Come on—leave it with me —I'll leave half in the bottle. Pul-lease. You know what Dr. Carter says—I'll stay awake and give it to you, or else fix some of it in the bottle—come on—like I told you, I'm too tired to be fightin you all night. . . . All right, drink your fool self to death."

"Would you like some beer?" he asked.

"No, I don't want any beer. Oh, to think that I have to look at you drunk again. My God!"

"Then I'll drink the Coca-Cola."

The girl sat down panting on the bed.

"Don't you believe in anything?" she demanded.

"Nothing you believe in—please—it'll spill."

She had no business there, she thought, no business trying to help him. Again they struggled, but after this time he sat with his head in his hands awhile, before he turned around once more.

"Once more you try to get it I'll throw it down," she said quickly. "I will—on the tiles in the bathroom."

"Then I'll step on the broken glass—or you'll step on it."

"Then let go—oh you promised——"

Suddenly she dropped it like a torpedo, sliding underneath her hand and slithering with a flash of red and black and the words: Sir Galahad, Distilled Louisville Gin. He took it by the neck and tossed it through the open door to the bathroom.

It was on the floor in pieces and everything was silent for awhile and she read *Gone With the Wind* about things so lovely that had happened long ago. She began to worry that he would have to go into the bathroom and might cut his feet, and looked up from time to time to see if he would go in. She was very sleepy—the last time she looked up he was crying and he looked like an old Jewish man she had nursed once in California; he had had to go to the bathroom many times. On this case she was unhappy all the time but she thought:

An Alcoholic Case 437

"I guess if I hadn't liked him I wouldn't have stayed on the case."

With a sudden resurgence of conscience she got up and put a chair in front of the bathroom door. She had wanted to sleep because he had got her up early that morning to get a paper with the story of the Yale-Dartmouth game in it and she hadn't been home all day. That afternoon a relative of his had come to see him and she had waited outside in the hall where there was a draft with no sweater to put over her uniform.

As well as she could she arranged him for sleeping, put a robe over his shoulders as he sat slumped over his writing table, and one on his knees. She sat down in the rocker but she was no longer sleepy; there was plenty to enter on the chart and treading lightly about she found a pencil and put it down:

Pulse 120
Respiration 25
Temp. 98—98.4—98.2
Remarks—
—She could make so many:
Tried to get bottle of gin. Threw it away and broke it.
She corrected it to read:
In the struggle it dropped and was broken. Patient was generally difficult.

She started to add as part of her report: *I never want to go on an alcoholic case again,* but that wasn't in the picture. She knew she could wake herself at seven and clean up everything before his niece awakened. It was all part of the game. But when she sat down in the chair she looked at his face, white and exhausted, and counted his breathing again, wondering why it had all happened. He had been so nice today, drawn her a whole strip of his cartoon just for fun and given it to her. She was going to have it framed and hang it in her room. She felt again his thin wrists wrestling against her wrist and remembered the awful things he had said, and she thought too of what the doctor had said to him yesterday:

"You're too good a man to do this to yourself."

She was tired and didn't want to clean up the glass on the bathroom floor, because as soon as he breathed evenly she wanted to get him over to the bed. But she decided finally to clean up the glass first; on her knees, searching a last piece of it, she thought:

—This isn't what I ought to be doing. And this isn't what *he* ought to be doing.

Resentfully she stood up and regarded him. Through the thin delicate profile of his nose came a light snore, sighing, remote, inconsolable. The doctor had shaken his head in a certain way, and she knew that really it was a case that was beyond her. Besides, on her card at the agency was written, on the advice of her elders, "No Alcoholics."

She had done her whole duty, but all she could think of was that when she was struggling about the room with him with that gin bottle there had been a pause when he asked her if she had hurt her elbow against a door and that she had answered: "You don't know how people talk about you, no matter how you think of yourself—" when she knew he had a long time ceased to care about such things.

The glass was all collected—as she got out a broom to make sure, she realized that the glass, in its fragments, was less than a window through which they had seen each other for a moment. He did not know about her sisters, and Bill Markoe whom she had almost married, and she did not know what had brought him to this pitch, when there was a picture on his bureau of his young wife and his two sons and him, all trim and handsome as he must have been five years ago. It was so utterly senseless—as she put a bandage on her finger where she had cut it while picking up the glass she made up her mind she would never take an alcoholic case again.

II

It was early the next evening. Some Halloween jokester had split the side windows of the bus and she shifted back to the Negro section in the rear for fear the glass might fall out. She had her patient's check but no way to cash it at this hour; there was a quarter and a penny in her purse.

Two nurses she knew were waiting in the hall of Mrs. Hixson's Agency.

"What kind of case have you been on?"

"Alcoholic," she said.

"Oh yes—Gretta Hawks told me about it—you were on with that cartoonist who lives at the Forest Park Inn."

"Yes, I was."

"I hear he's pretty fresh."

"He's never done anything to bother me," she lied. "You can't treat them as if they were committed——"

"Oh, don't get bothered—I just heard that around town—oh, you know—they want you to play around with them——"

"Oh, be quiet," she said, surprised at her own rising resentment.

In a moment Mrs. Hixson came out and, asking the other two to wait, signaled her into the office.

"I don't like to put young girls on such cases," she began. "I got your call from the hotel."

"Oh, it wasn't bad, Mrs. Hixson. He didn't know what he was

doing and he didn't hurt me in any way. I was thinking much more of my reputation with you. He was really nice all day yesterday. He drew me——"

"I didn't want to send you on that case." Mrs. Hixson thumbed through the registration cards. "You take T.B. cases, don't you? Yes, I see you do. Now here's one——"

The phone rang in a continuous chime. The nurse listened as Mrs. Hixson's voice said precisely:

"I will do what I can—that is simply up to the doctor. . . . That is beyond my jurisdiction. . . . Oh, hello, Hattie, no, I can't now. Look, have you got any nurse that's good with alcoholics? There's somebody up at the Forest Park Inn who needs somebody. Call back will you?"

She put down the receiver. "Suppose you wait outside. What sort of man is this, anyhow? Did he act indecently?"

"He held my hand away," she said, "so I couldn't give him an injection."

"Oh, an invalid he-man," Mrs. Hixson grumbled. "They belong in sanitaria. I've got a case coming along in two minutes that you can get a little rest on. It's an old woman——"

The phone rang again. "Oh, hello, Hattie. . . . Well, how about that big Svensen girl? She ought to be able to take care of any alcoholic. . . . How about Josephine Markham? Doesn't she live in your apartment house? . . . Get her to the phone." Then after a moment, "Joe, would you care to take the case of a well-known cartoonist, or artist, whatever they call themselves, at Forest Park Inn? . . . No, I don't know, but Dr. Carter is in charge and will be around about ten o'clock."

There was a long pause; from time to time Mrs. Hixson spoke:

"I see. . . . Of course, I understand your point of view. Yes, but this isn't supposed to be dangerous—just a little difficult. I never like to send girls to a hotel because I know what riff-raff you're liable to run into. . . . No, I'll find somebody. Even at this hour. Never mind and thanks. Tell Hattie I hope the hat matches the negligee. . . ."

Mrs. Hixson hung up the receiver and made notations on the pad before her. She was a very efficient woman. She had been a nurse and had gone through the worst of it, had been a proud, idealistic, overworked probationer, suffered the abuse of smart internes and the insolence of her first patients, who thought that she was something to be taken into camp immediately for premature commitment to the service of old age. She swung around suddenly from the desk.

"What kind of cases do you want? I told you I have a nice old woman——"

The nurse's brown eyes were alight with a mixture of thoughts —the movie she had just seen about Pasteur and the book they had all read about Florence Nightingale when they were student nurses. And their pride, swinging across the streets in the cold weather at Philadelphia General, as proud of their new capes as debutantes in their furs going in to balls at the hotels.

"I—I think I would like to try the case again," she said amid a cacophony of telephone bells. "I'd just as soon go back if you can't find anybody else."

"But one minute you say you'll never go on an alcoholic case again and the next minute you say you want to go back to one."

"I think I overestimated how difficult it was. Really, I think I could help him."

"That's up to you. But if he tried to grab your wrists."

"But he couldn't," the nurse said. "Look at my wrists: I played basketball at Waynesboro High for two years. I'm quite able to take care of him."

Mrs. Hixson looked at her for a long minute. "Well, all right," she said. "But just remember that nothing they say when they're drunk is what they mean when they're sober—I've been all through that; arrange with one of the servants that you can call on him, because you never can tell—some alcoholics are pleasant and some of them are not, but all of them can be rotten."

"I'll remember," the nurse said.

It was an oddly clear night when she went out, with slanting particles of thin sleet making white of a blue-black sky. The bus was the same that had taken her into town, but there seemed to be more windows broken now and the bus driver was irritated and talked about what terrible things he would do if he caught any kids. She knew he was just talking about the annoyance in general, just as she had been thinking about the annoyance of an alcoholic. When she came up to the suite and found him all helpless and distraught she would despise him and be sorry for him.

Getting off the bus, she went down the long steps to the hotel, feeling a little exalted by the chill in the air. She was going to take care of him because nobody else would, and because the best people of her profession had been interested in taking care of the cases that nobody else wanted.

She knocked at his study door, knowing just what she was going to say.

He answered it himself. He was in dinner clothes even to a derby hat—but minus his studs and tie.

"Oh, hello," he said casually. "Glad you're back. I woke up a while ago and decided I'd go out. Did you get a night nurse?"

"I'm the night nurse too," she said. "I decided to stay on twenty-four hour duty."

He broke into a genial, indifferent smile.

"I saw you were gone, but something told me you'd come back. Please find my studs. They ought to be either in a little tortoise shell box or——"

He shook himself a little more into his clothes, and hoisted the cuffs up inside his coat sleeves.

"I thought you had quit me," he said casually.

"I thought I had, too."

"If you look on that table," he said, "you'll find a whole strip of cartoons that I drew you."

"Who are you going to see?" she asked.

"It's the President's secretary," he said. "I had an awful time trying to get ready. I was about to give up when you came in. Will you order me some sherry?"

"One glass," she agreed wearily.

From the bathroom he called presently:

"Oh, nurse, nurse, Light of my Life, where is another stud?"

"I'll put it in."

In the bathroom she saw the pallor and the fever on his face and smelled the mixed peppermint and gin on his breath.

"You'll come up soon?" she asked. "Dr. Carter's coming at ten."

"What nonsense! You're coming down with me."

"Me?" she exclaimed. "In a sweater and skirt? Imagine!"

"Then I won't go."

"All right then, go to bed. That's where you belong anyhow. Can't you see these people tomorrow?"

"No, of course not."

"Of course not!"

She went behind him and reaching over his shoulder tied his tie—his shirt was already thumbed out of press where he had put in the studs, and she suggested:

"Won't you put on another one, if you've got to meet some people you like?"

"All right, but I want to do it myself."

"Why can't you let me help you?" she demanded in exasperation. "Why can't you let me help you with your clothes? What's a nurse for—what good am I doing?"

He sat down suddenly on the toilet seat.

"All right—go on."

"Now don't grab my wrist," she said, and then, "Excuse me."

"Don't worry. It didn't hurt. You'll see in a minute."

She had the coat, vest and stiff shirt off him but before she could pull his undershirt over his head he dragged at his cigarette, delaying her.

"Now watch this," he said. "One—two—three."

She pulled up the undershirt; simultaneously he thrust the crimson-gray point of the cigarette like a dagger against his heart. It crushed out against a copper plate on his left rib about the size of a silver dollar, and he said "ouch!" as a stray spark fluttered down against his stomach.

Now was the time to be hardboiled, she thought. She knew there were three medals from the war in his jewel box, but she had risked many things herself: tuberculosis among them and one time something worse, though she had not known it and had never quite forgiven the doctor for not telling her.

"You've had a hard time with that, I guess," she said lightly as she sponged him. "Won't it ever heal?"

"Never. That's a copper plate."

"Well, it's no excuse for what you're doing to yourself."

He bent his great brown eyes on her, shrewd—aloof, confused. He signaled to her, in one second, his Will to Die, and for all her training and experience she knew she could never do anything constructive with him. He stood up, steadying himself on the washbasin and fixing his eye on some place just ahead.

"Now, if I'm going to stay here you're not going to get at that liquor," she said.

Suddenly she knew he wasn't looking for that. He was looking at the corner where he had thrown the bottle the night before. She stared at his handsome face, weak and defiant—afraid to turn even halfway because she knew that death was in that corner where he was looking. She knew death—she had heard it, smelt its unmistakable odor, but she had never seen it before it entered into anyone, and she knew this man saw it in the corner of his bathroom; that it was standing there looking at him while he spit from a feeble cough and rubbed the result into the braid of his trousers. It shone there . . . crackling for a moment as evidence of the last gesture he ever made.

She tried to express it next day to Mrs. Hixson:

"It's not like anything you can beat—no matter how hard you try. This one could have twisted my wrists until he strained them and that wouldn't matter so much to me. It's just that you can't really help them and it's so discouraging—it's all for nothing."

1937   *Previously uncollected*

THE LONG WAY OUT

WE WERE talking about some of the older castles in Touraine and we touched upon the iron cage in which Louis XI imprisoned Cardinal Balue for six years, then upon oubliettes and such horrors. I had seen several of the latter, simply dry wells thirty or forty feet deep where a man was thrown to wait for nothing; since I have such a tendency to claustrophobia that a Pullman berth is a certain nightmare, they had made a lasting impression. So it was rather a relief when a doctor told this story—that is, it was a relief when he began it, for it seemed to have nothing to do with the tortures long ago.

There was a young woman named Mrs. King who was very happy with her husband. They were well-to-do and deeply in love, but at the birth of her second child she went into a long coma and emerged with a clear case of schizophrenia or "split personality." Her delusion, which had something to do with the Declaration of Independence, had little bearing on the case and as she regained her health it began to disappear. At the end of ten months she was a convalescent patient scarcely marked by what had happened to her and very eager to go back into the world.

She was only twenty-one, rather girlish in an appealing way and a favorite with the staff of the sanitarium. When she became well enough so that she could take an experimental trip with her husband there was a general interest in the venture. One nurse had gone into Philadelphia with her to get a dress, another knew the story of her rather romantic courtship in Mexico and everyone had seen her two babies on visits to the hospital. The trip was to Virginia Beach for five days.

It was a joy to watch her make ready, dressing and packing meticulously and living in the gay trivialities of hair waves and such things. She was ready half an hour before the time of departure and she paid some visits on the floor in her powder-blue gown and her hat that looked like one minute after an April shower. Her frail lovely face, with just that touch of startled sadness that often lingers after an illness, was alight with anticipation.

"We'll just do nothing," she said. "That's my ambition. To get up when I want to for three straight mornings and stay up late for three straight nights. To buy a bathing suit by myself and order a meal."

When the time approached Mrs. King decided to wait downstairs instead of in her room and as she passed along the corridors, with an orderly carrying her suitcase, she waved to the other patients, sorry that they too were not going on a gorgeous holiday. The superintendent wished her well, two nurses found excuses to linger and share her infectious joy.

"What a beautiful tan you'll get, Mrs. King."

"Be sure and send a postcard."

About the time she left her room her husband's car was hit by a truck on his way from the city—he was hurt internally and was not expected to live more than a few hours. The information was received at the hospital in a glassed-in office adjoining the hall where Mrs. King waited. The operator, seeing Mrs. King and knowing that the glass was not sound proof, asked the head nurse to come immediately. The head nurse hurried aghast to a doctor and he decided what to do. So long as the husband was still alive it was best to tell her nothing, but of course she must know that he was not coming today.

Mrs. King was greatly disappointed.

"I suppose it's silly to feel that way," she said. "After all these months what's one more day? He said he'd come tomorrow, didn't he?"

The nurse was having a difficult time but she managed to pass it off until the patient was back in her room. Then they assigned a very experienced and phlegmatic nurse to keep Mrs. King away from other patients and from newspapers. By the next day the matter would be decided one way or another.

But her husband lingered on and they continued to prevaricate. A little before noon next day one of the nurses was passing along the corridor when she met Mrs. King, dressed as she had been the day before but this time carrying her own suitcase.

"I'm going to meet my husband," she explained. "He couldn't come yesterday but he's coming today at the same time."

The nurse walked along with her. Mrs. King had the freedom of the building and it was difficult to simply steer her back to her room, and the nurse did not want to tell a story that would contradict what the authorities were telling her. When they reached the front hall she signaled to the operator, who fortunately understood. Mrs. King gave herself a last inspection in the mirror and said:

"I'd like to have a dozen hats just like this to remind me to be this happy always."

When the head nurse came in frowning a minute later she demanded:

"Don't tell me George is delayed?"

"I'm afraid he is. There is nothing much to do but be patient."

Mrs. King laughed ruefully. "I wanted him to see my costume when it was absolutely new."

"Why, there isn't a wrinkle in it."

"I guess it'll last till tomorrow. I oughtn't to be blue about waiting one more day when I'm so utterly happy."

"Certainly not."

That night her husband died and at a conference of doctors next morning there was some discussion about what to do—it was a risk to tell her and a risk to keep it from her. It was decided finally to say that Mr. King had been called away and thus destroy her hope of an immediate meeting; when she was reconciled to this they could tell her the truth.

As the doctors came out of the conference one of them stopped and pointed. Down the corridor toward the outer hall walked Mrs. King carrying her suitcase.

Dr. Pirie, who had been in special charge of Mrs. King, caught his breath.

"This is awful," he said. "I think perhaps I'd better tell her now. There's no use saying he's away when she usually hears from him twice a week, and if we say he's sick she'll want to go to him. Anybody else like the job?"

II

One of the doctors in the conference went on a fortnight's vacation that afternoon. On the day of his return in the same corridor at the same hour, he stopped at the sight of a little procession coming toward him—an orderly carrying a suitcase, a nurse and Mrs. King dressed in the powder-blue suit and wearing the spring hat.

"Good morning, Doctor," she said. "I'm going to meet my husband and we're going to Virginia Beach. I'm going to the hall because I don't want to keep him waiting."

He looked into her face, clear and happy as a child's. The nurse signaled to him that it was as ordered, so he merely bowed and spoke of the pleasant weather.

"It's a beautiful day," said Mrs. King, "but of course even if it was raining it would be a beautiful day for me."

The doctor looked after her, puzzled and annoyed—why are they letting this go on, he thought. What possible good can it do?

Meeting Dr. Pirie, he put the question to him.

"We tried to tell her," Dr. Pirie said. "She laughed and said we were trying to see whether she's still sick. You could use the word unthinkable in an exact sense here—his death is unthinkable to her."

"But you can't just go on like this."

"Theoretically no," said Dr. Pirie. "A few days ago when she packed up as usual the nurse tried to keep her from going. From out in the hall I could see her face, see her begin to go to pieces—for the first time, mind you. Her muscles were tense and her eyes glazed and her voice was thick and shrill when she very politely called the nurse a liar. It was touch and go there for a minute whether we had a tractable patient or a restraint case—and I stepped in and told the nurse to take her down to the reception room."

He broke off as the procession that had just passed appeared again, headed back to the ward. Mrs. King stopped and spoke to Dr. Pirie.

"My husband's been delayed," she said. "Of course I'm disappointed but they tell me he's coming tomorrow and after waiting so long one more day doesn't seem to matter. Don't you agree with me, Doctor?"

"I certainly do, Mrs. King."

She took off her hat.

"I've got to put aside these clothes—I want them to be as fresh tomorrow as they are today." She looked closely at the hat. "There's a speck of dust on it, but I think I can get it off. Perhaps he won't notice."

"I'm sure he won't."

"Really I don't mind waiting another day. It'll be this time tomorrow before I know it, won't it?"

When she had gone along the younger doctor said:

"There are still the two children."

"I don't think the children are going to matter. When she 'went under,' she tied up this trip with the idea of getting well. If we took it away she'd have to go to the bottom and start over."

"Could she?"

"There's no prognosis," said Dr. Pirie. "I was simply explaining why she was allowed to go to the hall this morning."

"But there's tomorrow morning and the next morning."

"There's always the chance," said Dr. Pirie, "that some day he will be there."

The doctor ended his story here, rather abruptly. When we pressed him to tell what happened he protested that the rest was anticlimax —that all sympathy eventually wears out and that finally the staff of the sanitarium had simply accepted the fact.

"But does she still go to meet her husband?"

"Oh yes, it's always the same—but the other patients, except new ones, hardly look up when she passes along the hall. The nurses manage to substitute a new hat every year or so but she still wears the same suit. She's always a little disappointed but she makes the best of it, very sweetly too. It's not an unhappy life as far as we know, and in some funny way it seems to set an example of tranquillity to the other patients. For God's sake let's talk about something else—let's go back to oubliettes."

1937   *Previously uncollected*

FINANCING FINNEGAN

FINNEGAN and I have the same literary agent to sell our writings for us, but though I'd often been in Mr. Cannon's office just before and just after Finnegan's visits, I had never met him. Likewise we had the same publisher and often when I arrived there Finnegan had just departed. I gathered from a thoughtful sighing way in which they spoke of him—

"Ah—Finnegan—"

"Oh yes, Finnegan was here."

—that the distinguished author's visit had been not uneventful. Certain remarks implied that he had taken something with him when he went—manuscripts, I supposed, one of those great successful novels of his. He had taken "it" off for a final revision, a last draft, of which he was rumored to make ten in order to achieve that facile flow, that ready wit, which distinguished his work. I discovered only gradually that most of Finnegan's visits had to do with money.

"I'm sorry you're leaving," Mr. Cannon would tell me, "Finnegan will be here tomorrow." Then after a thoughtful pause "I'll probably have to spend some time with him."

I don't know what note in his voice reminded me of a talk with a nervous bank president when Dillinger was reported in the vicinity. His eyes looked out into the distance and he spoke as to himself.

"Of course he may be bringing a manuscript. He has a novel he's working on, you know. And a play too." He spoke as though he were talking about some interesting but remote events of the cinquecento; but his eyes became more hopeful as he added: "Or maybe a short story."

"He's very versatile, isn't he?" I said.

"Oh yes," Mr. Cannon perked up. "He can do anything—anything when he puts his mind to it. There's never been such a talent."

"I haven't seen much of his work lately."

"Oh, but he's working hard. Some of the magazines have stories of his that they're holding."

"Holding for what?"

"Oh, for a more appropriate time—an upswing. They like to think they have something of Finnegan's."

His was indeed a name with ingots in it. His career had started brilliantly and if it had not kept up to its first exalted level, at least it started brilliantly all over again every few years. He was the perennial man of promise in American letters—what he could actually do with words was astounding, they glowed and coruscated —he wrote sentences, paragraphs, chapters that were masterpieces of fine weaving and spinning. It was only when I met some poor devil of a screen writer who had been trying to make a logical story out of one of his books that I realized he had his enemies.

"It's all beautiful when you read it," this man said disgustedly, "but when you write it down plain it's like a week in the nut-house."

From Mr. Cannon's office I went over to my publishers on Fifth Avenue and there too I learned in no time that Finnegan was expected tomorrow. Indeed he had thrown such a long shadow before him that the luncheon where I expected to discuss my own work was largely devoted to Finnegan. Again I had the feeling that my host, Mr. George Jaggers, was talking not to me but to himself.

"Finnegan's a great writer," he said.

"Undoubtedly."

"And he's really quite all right, you know."

As I hadn't questioned the fact I inquired whether there was any doubt about it.

"Oh no," he said hurriedly. "It's just that he's had such a run of hard luck lately——"

I shook my head sympathetically. "I know. That diving into a half-empty pool was a tough break."

"Oh, it wasn't half-empty. It was full of water. Full to the brim. You ought to hear Finnegan on the subject—he makes a side-splitting story of it. It seems he was in a run-down condition and just diving from the side of the pool, you know—" Mr. Jaggers pointed his knife and fork at the table, "and he saw some young girls diving from the fifteen-foot board. He says he thought of his lost youth and went up to do the same and made a beautiful swan dive—but his shoulder broke while he was still in the air." He looked at me rather anxiously. "Haven't you heard of cases like that—a ball player throwing his arm out of joint?"

I couldn't think of any orthopedic parallels at the moment.

"And then," he continued dreamily, "Finnegan had to write on the ceiling."

"On the ceiling?"

"Practically. He didn't give up writing—he has plenty of guts, that fellow, though you may not believe it. He had some sort of arrangement built that was suspended from the ceiling and he lay on his back and wrote in the air."

I had to grant that it was a courageous arrangement.

"Did it affect his work?" I inquired. "Did you have to read his stories backward—like Chinese?"

"They were rather confused for a while," he admitted, "but he's all right now. I got several letters from him that sounded more like the old Finnegan—full of life and hope and plans for the future——"

The faraway look came into his face and I turned the discussion to affairs closer to my heart. Only when we were back in his office did the subject recur—and I blush as I write this because it includes confessing something I seldom do—reading another man's telegram. It happened because Mr. Jaggers was intercepted in the hall and when I went into his office and sat down it was stretched out open before me:

With fifty I could at least pay typist and get haircut and pencils life has become impossible and I exist on dream of good news desperately Finnegan

I couldn't believe my eyes—fifty dollars, and I happened to know that Finnegan's price for short stories was somewhere around three thousand. George Jaggers found me still staring dazedly at the telegram. After he read it he stared at me with stricken eyes.

"I don't see how I can conscientiously do it," he said.

I started and glanced around to make sure I was in the prosperous publishing office in New York. Then I understood—I had misread the telegram. Finnegan was asking for fifty thousand as an advance —a demand that would have staggered any publisher no matter who the writer was.

"Only last week," said Mr. Jaggers disconsolately, "I sent him a hundred dollars. It puts my department in the red every season, so I don't dare tell my partners any more. I take it out of my own pocket—give up a suit and a pair of shoes."

"You mean Finnegan's broke?"

"Broke!" He looked at me and laughed soundlessly—in fact I didn't exactly like the way that he laughed. My brother had a nervous—but that is afield from this story. After a minute he pulled himself together. "You won't say anything about this, will you? The truth is Finnegan's been in a slump, he's had blow after blow in the past few years, but now he's snapping out of it and I know we'll get back every cent we've——" He tried to think of a word but "given him" slipped out. This time it was he who was eager to change the subject.

Don't let me give the impression that Finnegan's affairs absorbed
me during a whole week in New York—it was inevitable, though,
that being much in the offices of my agent and my publisher, I happened in on a lot. For instance, two days later, using the telephone
in Mr. Cannon's office, I was accidentally switched in on a conversation he was having with George Jaggers. It was only partly eavesdropping, you see, because I could only hear one end of the conversation and that isn't as bad as hearing it all.

"But I got the impression he was in good health . . . he did say
something about his heart a few months ago but I understood it
got well . . . yes, and he talked about some operation he wanted
to have—I think he said it was cancer. . . . Well, I felt like telling
him I had a little operation up my sleeve too, that I'd have had by
now if I could afford it. . . . No, I didn't say it. He seemed in such
good spirits that it would have been a shame to bring him down. He's
starting a story today, he read me some of it on the phone . . .

". . . I did give him twenty-five because he didn't have a cent
in his pocket . . . oh, yes—I'm sure he'll be all right now. He
sounds as if he means business."

I understood it all now. The two men had entered into a silent
conspiracy to cheer each other up about Finnegan. Their investment
in him, in his future, had reached a sum so considerable that Finnegan belonged to them. They could not bear to hear a word against
him—even from themselves.

II

I spoke my mind to Mr. Cannon.

"If this Finnegan is a four-flusher you can't go on indefinitely
giving him money. If he's through he's through and there's nothing
to be done about it. It's absurd that you should put off an operation
when Finnegan's out somewhere diving into half-empty swimming
pools."

"It was full," said Mr. Cannon patiently—"full to the brim."

"Well, full or empty the man sounds like a nuisance to me."

"Look here," said Cannon, "I've got a call from Hollywood due
on the wire. Meanwhile you might glance over that." He threw a
manuscript into my lap. "Maybe it'll help you understand. He
brought it in yesterday."

It was a short story. I began it in a mood of disgust but before
I'd read five minutes I was completely immersed in it, utterly
charmed, utterly convinced and wishing to God I could write like
that. When Cannon finished his phone call I kept him waiting while
I finished it and when I did there were tears in these hard old pro-

fessional eyes. Any magazine in the country would have run it first in any issue.

But then nobody had ever denied that Finnegan could write.

III

Months passed before I went again to New York, and then, so far as the offices of my agent and my publisher were concerned, I descended upon a quieter, more stable world. There was at last time to talk about my own conscientious if uninspired literary pursuits, to visit Mr. Cannon in the country and to kill summer evenings with George Jaggers where the vertical New York starlight falls like lingering lightning into restaurant gardens. Finnegan might have been at the North Pole—and as a matter of fact he was. He had quite a group with him, including three Bryn Mawr anthropologists, and it sounded as if he might collect a lot of material there. They were going to stay several months, and if the thing had somehow the ring of a promising little houseparty about it, that was probably due to my jealous, cynical disposition.

"We're all just delighted," said Cannon. "It's a God-send for him. He was fed up and he needed just this—this—"

"Ice and snow," I supplied.

"Yes, ice and snow. The last thing he said was characteristic of him. Whatever he writes is going to be pure white—it's going to have a blinding glare about it."

"I can imagine it will. But tell me—who's financing it? Last time I was here I gathered the man was insolvent."

"Oh, he was really very decent about that. He owed me some money and I believe he owed George Jaggers a little too." He "believed," the old hypocrite. He knew damn well. "So before he left he made most of his life insurance over to us. That's in case he doesn't come back—those trips are dangerous of course."

"I should think so," I said, "especially with three anthropologists."

"So Jaggers and I are absolutely covered in case anything happens —it's as simple as that."

"Did the life-insurance company finance the trip?"

He fidgeted perceptibly.

"Oh, no. In fact when they learned the reason for the assignments they were a little upset. George Jaggers and I felt that when he had a specific plan like this with a specific book at the end of it, we were justified in backing him a little further."

"I don't see it," I said flatly.

"You don't?" The old harassed look came back into his eyes

"Well, I'll admit we hesitated. In principle I know it's wrong. I used to advance authors small sums from time to time, but lately I've made a rule against it—and kept it. It's only been waived once in the last two years and that was for a woman who was having a bad struggle—Margaret Trahill, do you know her? She was an old girl of Finnegan's, by the way."

"Remember I don't even know Finnegan."

"That's right. You must meet him when he comes back—if he does come back. You'd like him—he's utterly charming."

Again I departed from New York, to imaginative North Poles of my own, while the year rolled through summer and fall. When the first snap of November was in the air, I thought of the Finnegan expedition with a sort of shiver and any envy of the man departed. He was probably earning any loot, literary or anthropological, he might bring back. Then, when I hadn't been back in New York three days, I read in the paper that he and some other members of his party had walked off into a snowstorm when the food supply gave out, and the Arctic had claimed another sacrifice.

I was sorry for him, but practical enough to be glad that Cannon and Jaggers were well protected. Of course, with Finnegan scarcely cold—if such a simile is not too harrowing—they did not talk about it but I gathered that the insurance companies had waived *habeas corpus* or whatever it is in their lingo, and it seemed quite sure that they would collect.

His son, a fine looking young fellow, came into George Jaggers' office while I was there and from him I could guess at Finnegan's charm—a shy frankness together with an impression of a very quiet, brave battle going on inside of him that he couldn't quite bring himself to talk about—but that showed as heat lightning in his work.

"The boy writes well too," said George after he had gone. "He's brought in some remarkable poems. He's not ready to step into his father's shoes, but there's a definite promise."

"Can I see one of his things?"

"Certainly—here's one he left just as he went out."

George took a paper from his desk, opened it and cleared his throat. Then he squinted and bent over a little in his chair.

"*Dear Mr. Jaggers,*" he began, "*I didn't like to ask you this in person—*" Jaggers stopped, his eyes reading ahead rapidly.

"How much does he want?" I inquired.

He sighed.

"He gave me the impression that this was some of his work," he said in a pained voice.

"But it is," I consoled him. "Of course he isn't quite ready to step into his father's shoes."

I was sorry afterwards to have said this, for after all Finnegan had paid his debts, and it was nice to be alive now that better times were back and books were no longer rated as unnecessary luxuries. Many authors I knew who had skimped along during the depression were now making long-deferred trips or paying off mortgages or turning out the more finished kind of work that can only be done with a certain leisure and security. I had just got a thousand dollars advance for a venture in Hollywood and was going to fly out with all the verve of the old days when there was chicken feed in every pot. Going in to say good-by to Cannon and collect the money, it was nice to find he too was profiting—wanted me to go along and see a motor boat he was buying.

But some last-minute stuff came up to delay him and I grew impatient and decided to skip it. Getting no response to a knock on the door of his sanctum, I opened it anyhow.

The inner office seemed in some confusion. Mr. Cannon was on several telephones at once and dictating something about an insurance company to a stenographer. One secretary was getting hurriedly into her hat and coat as upon an errand and another was counting bills from her purse upon a table.

"It'll be only a minute," said Cannon, "it's just a little office riot —you never saw us like this."

"Is it Finnegan's insurance?" I couldn't help asking. "Isn't it any good?"

"His insurance—oh, perfectly all right, perfectly. This is just a matter of trying to raise a few hundred in a hurry. The banks are closed and we're all contributing."

"I've got that money you just gave me," I said. "I don't need all of it to get to the coast." I peeled off a couple of hundred. "Will this be enough?"

"That'll be fine—it just saves us. Never mind, Miss Carlsen. Mrs. Mapes, you needn't go now."

"I think I'll be running along," I said.

"Just wait two minutes," he urged. "I've only got to take care of this wire. It's really splendid news. Bucks you up."

It was a cablegram from Oslo, Norway—before I began to read I was full of a premonition.

Am miraculously safe here but detained by authorities please wire passage money for four people and two hundred extra I am bringing back plenty greetings from the dead.
                                                                Finnegan

"Yes, that's splendid," I agreed. "He'll have a story to tell now."

"Won't he though," said Cannon. "Miss Carlsen, will you wire the parents of those girls—and you'd better inform Mr. Jaggers."

As we walked along the street a few minutes later, I saw that Mr. Cannon, as if stunned by the wonder of this news, had fallen into a brown study, and I did not disturb him, for after all I did not know Finnegan and could not whole-heartedly share his joy. His mood of silence continued until we arrived at the door of the motor boat show. Just under the sign he stopped and stared upward, as if aware for the first time where we were going.

"Oh, my," he said, stepping back. "There's no use going in here now. I thought we were going to get a drink."

We did. Mr. Cannon was still a little vague, a little under the spell of the vast surprise—he fumbled so long for the money to pay his round that I insisted it was on me.

I think he was in a daze during that whole time because, though he is a man of the most punctilious accuracy, the two hundred I handed him in his office has never shown to my credit in the statements he has sent me. I imagine, though, that some day I will surely get it because some day Finnegan will click again and I know that people will clamor to read what he writes. Recently I've taken it upon myself to investigate some of the stories about him and I've found that they're mostly as false as the half-empty pool. That pool was full to the brim.

So far there's only been a short story about the polar expedition, a love story. Perhaps it wasn't as big a subject as he expected. But the movies are interested in him—if they can get a good long look at him first and I have every reason to think that he will come through. He'd better.

1938   *Previously uncollected*

PAT HOBBY HIMSELF

A PATRIOTIC SHORT

PAT HOBBY, the writer and the Man, had his great success in
Hollywood during what Irvin Cobb refers to as "the mosaic swim-
ming-pool age—just before the era when they had to have a shin-
bone of St. Sebastian for a clutch lever."

Mr. Cobb no doubt exaggerates, for when Pat had his pool in
those fat days of silent pictures, it was entirely cement, unless you
should count the cracks where the water stubbornly sought its own
level through the mud.

"But it *was* a pool," he assured himself one afternoon more than
a decade later. Though he was now more than grateful for this small
chore he had assigned him by producer Berners—one week at two-
fifty—all the insolence of office could not take that memory away.

He had been called in to the studio to work upon a humble short.
It was based on the career of General Fitzhugh Lee, who fought for
the Confederacy and later for the U.S.A. against Spain—so it would
offend neither North nor South. And in the recent conference Pat
had tried to co-operate.

"I was thinking—" he suggested to Jack Berners, "—that it
might be a good thing if we could give it a Jewish touch."

"What do you mean?" demanded Jack Berners quickly.

"Well I thought—the way things are and all, it would be a sort
of good thing to show that there were a number of Jews in it too."

"In what?"

"In the Civil War." Quickly he reviewed his meager history.
"They were, weren't they?"

"Naturally," said Berners, with some impatience. "I suppose
everybody was except the Quakers."

"Well, my idea was that we could have this Fitzhugh Lee in love
with a Jewish girl. He's going to be shot at curfew so she grabs
a church bell——"

Jack Berners leaned forward earnestly.

"Say, Pat, you want this job, don't you? Well, I told you the
story. You got the first script. If you thought up this tripe to please
me you're losing your grip."

456

Was that a way to treat a man who had once owned a pool which had been talked about by—

That was how he happened to be thinking about his long-lost swimming pool as he entered the shorts department. He was remembering a certain day over a decade ago in all its details, how he had arrived at the studio in his car driven by a Filipino in uniform; the deferential bow of the guard at the gate which had admitted car and all to the lot, his ascent to that long-lost office which had a room for the secretary and was really a director's office . . .

His reverie was broken off by the voice of Ben Brown, head of the shorts department, who walked him into his own chambers.

"Jack Berners just phoned me," he said. "We don't want any new angles, Pat. We've got a good story. Fitzhugh Lee was a dashing cavalry commander. He was a nephew of Robert E. Lee and we want to show him at Appomattox, pretty bitter and all that. And then show how he became reconciled—we'll have to be careful because Virginia is swarming with Lees—and how he finally accepts a U.S. commission from President McKinley——"

Pat's mind darted back again into the past. The President—that was the magic word that had gone around that morning many years ago. The President of the United States was going to make a visit to the lot. Everyone had been agog about it—it seemed to mark a new era in pictures, because a President of the United States had never visited a studio before. The executives of the company were all dressed up—from a window of his long-lost Beverly Hills house Pat had seen Mr. Maranda, whose mansion was next door to him, bustle down his walk in a cutaway coat at nine o'clock, and had known that something was up. He thought maybe it was clergy, but when he reached the lot he had found it was the President of the United States himself who was coming . . .

"Clean up the stuff about Spain," Ben Brown was saying. "The guy that wrote it was a red and he's got all the Spanish officers with ants in their pants. Fix up that."

In the office assigned him Pat looked at the script of *True to Two Flags*. The first scene showed General Fitzhugh Lee at the head of his cavalry receiving word that Petersburg had been evacuated. In the script Lee took the blow in pantomime, but Pat was getting two-fifty a week—so, casually and without effort, he wrote in one of his favorite lines:

LEE: (*to his officers*)
Well, what are you standing here gawking for? DO *something!*

6. *Medium Shot. Officers pepping up, slapping each other on back, etc.*

Dissolve to:

To what? Pat's mind dissolved once more into the glamorous past. On that happy day in the twenties his phone had rung at about noon. It had been Mr. Maranda.

"Pat, the President is lunching in the private dining room. Doug Fairbanks can't come so there's a place empty and anyhow we think there ought to be one writer there."

His memory of the luncheon was palpitant with glamor. The Great Man had asked some questions about pictures and had told a joke and Pat had laughed and laughed with the others—all of them solid men together—rich, happy and successful.

Afterwards the President was to go on some sets and see some scenes taken and still later he was going to Mr. Maranda's house to meet some of the women stars at tea. Pat was not invited to that party but he went home early anyhow and from his veranda saw the cortège drive up, with Mr. Maranda beside the President in the back seat. Ah he was proud of pictures then—of his position in them— of the President of the happy country where he was born . . .

Returning to reality Pat looked down at the script of *True to Two Flags* and wrote slowly and thoughtfully: *Insert: A calendar—with the years plainly marked and the sheets blowing off in a cold wind, to show Fitzhugh Lee growing older and older.*

His labors had made him thirsty—not for water, but he knew better than to take anything else his first day on the job. He got up and went out into the hall and along the corridor to the water-cooler.

As he walked he slipped back into his reverie.

That had been a lovely California afternoon, so Mr. Maranda had taken his exalted guest and the coterie of stars into his garden, which adjoined Pat's garden. Pat had gone out his back door and followed a low privet hedge keeping out of sight—and then acci-dentally had come face to face with the Presidential party.

The President had smiled and nodded. Mr. Maranda smiled and nodded.

"You met Mr. Hobby at lunch," Mr. Maranda said to the President. "He's one of our writers."

"Oh, yes," said the President. "You write the pictures."

"Yes, I do," said Pat.

The President glanced over into Pat's property.

"I suppose," he said, "that you get lots of inspiration sitting by the side of that fine pool."

"Yes," said Pat. "Yes, I do."

. . . Pat filled his cup at the cooler. Down the hall there was a group approaching—Jack Berners, Ben Brown and several other executives and with them a girl to whom they were very attentive and deferential. He recognized her face—she was the girl of the year, the It Girl, the Oomph Girl, the Glamor Girl, the girl for whose services every studio was in violent competition.

Pat lingered over his drink. He had seen many phonies break in and break out again, but this girl was the real thing, someone to stir every pulse in the nation. He felt his own heart beat faster. Finally, as the procession drew near, he put down the cup, dabbed at his hair with his hand and took a step out into the corridor.

The girl looked at him—he looked at the girl. Then she took one arm of Jack Berners' and one of Ben Brown's and suddenly the party seemed to walk right through him—so that he had to take a step back against the wall.

An instant later Jack Berners turned around and said back to him, "Hello, Pat." And then some of the others threw half glances around but no one else spoke, so interested were they in the girl.

In his office, Pat looked at the scene, where President McKinley offers a United States commission to Fitzhugh Lee. Suddenly he gritted his teeth and bore down on his pencil as he wrote:

LEE

Mr. President, you can take your commission and go straight to hell.

Then he bent down over his desk, his shoulders shaking as he thought of that happy day when he had had a swimming pool.

TWO OLD-TIMERS

PHIL MACEDON, once the Star of Stars, and Pat Hobby, script writer, had collided out on Sunset near the Beverly Hills Hotel. It was five in the morning and there was liquor in the air as they argued and Sergeant Gaspar took them around to the station house. Pat Hobby, a man of forty-nine, showed fight, apparently because Phil Macedon failed to acknowledge that they were old acquaintances.

He accidentally bumped Sergeant Gaspar, who was so provoked

that he put him in a little barred room while they waited for the
captain to arrive.

Chronologically Phil Macedon belonged between Eugene O'Brien
and Robert Taylor. He was still a handsome man in his early fifties
and he had saved enough from his great days for a hacienda in the
San Fernando Valley; there he rested as full of honors, as rollick-
some and with the same purposes in life as Man o' War.

With Pat Hobby life had dealt otherwise. After twenty-one years
in the industry, script and publicity, the accident found him driving
a 1935 car which had lately become the property of the Acme Loan
Co. And once, back in 1928, he had reached the point of having a
private swimming pool.

He glowered from his confinement, still resenting Macedon's
failure to acknowledge that they had ever met before.

"I suppose you don't remember Colman," he said sarcastically.
"Or Connie Talmadge or Bill Corker or Allan Dwan."

Macedon lit a cigarette with the sort of timing in which the
silent screen has never been surpassed, and offered one to Sergeant
Gaspar.

"Couldn't I come in tomorrow?" he asked. "I have a horse to
exercise——"

"I'm sorry, Mr. Macedon," said the cop—sincerely, for the actor
was an old favorite of his. "The captain is due here any minute.
After that we won't be holding *you.*"

"It's just a formality," said Pat, from his cell.

"Yeah, it's just a—" Sergeant Gaspar glared at Pat. "It may not
be any formality for *you.* Did you ever hear of the sobriety test?"

Macedon flicked his cigarette out the door and lit another.

"Suppose I come back in a couple of hours," he suggested.

"No," regretted Sergeant Gaspar. "And since I have to detain
you, Mr. Macedon, I want to take the opportunity to tell you what
you meant to me once. It was that picture you made, *The Final
Push,* it meant a lot to every man who was in the war."

"Oh, yes," said Macedon, smiling.

"I used to try to tell my wife about the war—how it was, with
the shells and the machine guns—I was in there seven months with
the 26th New England—but she never understood. She'd point her
finger at me and say 'Boom! you're dead,' and so I'd laugh and stop
trying to make her understand."

"Hey, can I get out of here?" demanded Pat.

"You shut up!" said Gaspar fiercely. "You probably wasn't in the
war."

"I was in the Motion Picture Home Guard," said Pat. "I had bad
eyes."

"Listen to him," said Gaspar disgustedly. "That's what all them slackers say. Well, the war was *some*thing. And after my wife saw that picture of yours I never had to explain to her. She knew. She always spoke different about it after that—never just pointed her finger at me and said 'Boom!' I'll never forget the part where you was in that shell hole. That was so real it made my hands sweat."

"Thanks," said Macedon graciously. He lit another cigarette. "You see, I was in the war myself and I knew how it was. I knew how it felt."

"Yes, sir," said Gaspar appreciatively. "Well, I'm glad of the opportunity to tell you what you did for me. You—you explained the war to my wife."

"What are you talking about?" demanded Pat Hobby suddenly. "That war picture Bill Corker did in 1925?"

"There he goes again," said Gaspar. "Sure—*The Birth of a Nation*. Now you pipe down till the captain comes."

"Phil Macedon knew me then all right," said Pat resentfully. "I even watched him work on it one day."

"I just don't happen to remember you, old man," said Macedon politely. "I can't help that."

"You remember the day Bill Corker shot that shell-hole sequence, don't you? Your first day on the picture?"

There was a moment's silence.

"When will the captain be here?" Macedon asked.

"Any minute now, Mr. Macedon."

"Well, I remember," said Pat, "because I was there when he had that shell hole dug. He was out there on the back lot at nine o'clock in the morning with a gang of hunkies to dig the hole and four cameras. He called you up from a field telephone and told you to go to the costumer and get into a soldier suit. Now you remember?"

"I don't load my mind with details, old man."

"You called up that they didn't have one to fit you and Corker told you to shut up and get into one anyhow. When you got out to the back lot you were sore as hell because your suit didn't fit."

Macedon smiled charmingly.

"You have a most remarkable memory. Are you sure you have the right picture—and the right actor?" he asked.

"Am I!" said Pat grimly. "I can see you right now. Only you didn't have much time to complain about the uniform because that wasn't Corker's plan. He always thought you were the toughest ham in Hollywood to get anything natural out of—and he had a scheme. He was going to get the heart of the picture shot by noon—before you even knew you were acting. He turned you around and shoved you down into that shell hole on your fanny, and yelled 'Camera.'"

"That's a lie," said Phil Macedon. "I *got* down."

"Then why did you start yelling?" demanded Pat. "I can still hear you: 'Hey, what's the idea! Is this some God damn gag? You get me out of here or I'll walk out on you!'

"And all the time you were trying to claw your way up the side of that pit, so damn mad you couldn't see. You'd almost get up and then you'd slide back and lie there with your face working—till finally you began to bawl and all this time Bill had four cameras on you. After about twenty minutes you gave up and just lay there, heaving. Bill took a hundred feet of that and then he had a couple of prop men pull you out."

The police captain had arrived in the squad car. He stood in the doorway against the first gray of dawn.

"What you got here, Sergeant? A drunk?"

Sergeant Gaspar walked over to the cell, unlocked it and beckoned Pat to come out. Pat blinked a moment—then his eyes fell on Phil Macedon and he shook his finger at him.

"So you see I *do* know you," he said. "Bill Corker cut that piece of film and titled it so you were supposed to be a doughboy whose pal had just been killed. You wanted to climb out and get at the Germans in revenge, but the shells bursting all around and the concussions kept knocking you back in."

"What's it about?" demanded the captain.

"I want to prove I know this guy," said Pat. "Bill said the best moment in the picture was when Phil was yelling, 'I've already broken my first finger nail!' Bill titled it, 'Ten Huns will go to hell to shine your shoes!'"

"You've got here 'collision with alcohol,'" said the captain looking at the blotter. "Let's take these guys down to the hospital and give them the test."

"Look here now," said the actor, with his flashing smile, "my name's Phil Macedon."

The captain was a political appointee and very young. He remembered the name and the face, but he was not especially impressed because Hollywood was full of has-beens.

They all got into the squad car at the door.

After the test Macedon was held at the station house until friends could arrange bail. Pat Hobby was discharged, but his car would not run, so Sergeant Gaspar offered to drive him home.

"Where do you live?" he asked as they started off.

"I don't live anywhere tonight," said Pat. "That's why I was driving around. When a friend of mine wakes up I'll touch him for a couple of bucks and go to a hotel."

"Well now," said Sergeant Gaspar, "I got a couple of bucks that ain't working."

The great mansions of Beverly Hills slid by and Pat waved his hand at them in salute.

"In the good old days," he said, "I used to be able to drop into some of those houses day or night. And Sunday mornings——"

"Is that all true you said in the station," Gaspar asked, "—about how they put him in the hole?"

"Sure, it is," said Pat. "That guy needn't have been so upstage. He's just an old-timer like me."

1940   *Previously uncollected*

THREE HOURS BETWEEN PLANES

IT WAS a wild chance but Donald was in the mood, healthy and bored, with a sense of tiresome duty done. He was now rewarding himself. Maybe.

When the plane landed he stepped out into a midwestern summer night and headed for the isolated pueblo airport, conventionalized as an old red "railway depot." He did not know whether she was alive, or living in this town, or what was her present name. With mounting excitement he looked through the phone book for her father who might be dead too, somewhere in these twenty years.

No. Judge Harmon Holmes—Hillside 3194.

A woman's amused voice answered his inquiry for Miss Nancy Holmes.

"Nancy is Mrs. Walter Gifford now. Who is this?"

But Donald hung up without answering. He had found out what he wanted to know and had only three hours. He did not remember any Walter Gifford and there was another suspended moment while he scanned the phone book. She might have married out of town.

No. Walter Gifford—Hillside 1191. Blood flowed back into his fingertips.

"Hello?"

"Hello. Is Mrs. Gifford there—this is an old friend of hers."

"This is Mrs. Gifford."

He remembered, or thought he remembered, the funny magic in the voice.

"This is Donald Plant. I haven't seen you since I was twelve years old."

"Oh-h-h!" The note was utterly surprised, very polite, but he could distinguish in it neither joy nor certain recognition.

"—Donald!" added the voice. This time there was something more in it than struggling memory.

". . . when did you come back to town?" Then cordially, "Where are you?"

"I'm out at the airport—for just a few hours."

"Well, come up and see me."

"Sure you're not just going to bed."

"Heavens, no!" she exclaimed. "I was sitting here—having a highball by myself. Just tell your taxi man . . ."

On his way Donald analyzed the conversation. His words "at the airport" established that he had retained his position in the upper bourgeoisie. Nancy's aloneness might indicate that she had matured into an unattractive woman without friends. Her husband might be either away or in bed. And—because she was always ten years old in his dreams—the highball shocked him. But he adjusted himself with a smile—she was very close to thirty.

At the end of a curved drive he saw a dark-haired little beauty standing against the lighted door, a glass in her hand. Startled by her final materialization, Donald got out of the cab, saying:

"Mrs. Gifford?"

She turned on the porch light and stared at him, wide-eyed and tentative. A smile broke through the puzzled expression.

"Donald—it *is* you—we all change so. Oh, this is re*mark*able!"

As they walked inside, their voices jingled the words "all these years," and Donald felt a sinking in his stomach. This derived in part from a vision of their last meeting—when she rode past him on a bicycle, cutting him dead—and in part from fear lest they have nothing to say. It was like a college reunion—but there the failure to find the past was disguised by the hurried boisterous occasion. Aghast, he realized that this might be a long and empty hour. He plunged in desperately.

"You always were a lovely person. But I'm a little shocked to find you as beautiful as you are."

It worked. The immediate recognition of their changed state, the bold compliment, made them interesting strangers instead of fumbling childhood friends.

"Have a highball?" she asked. "No? Please don't think I've become a secret drinker, but this was a blue night. I expected my husband but he wired he'd be two days longer. He's very nice, Donald, and very attractive. Rather your type and coloring." She hesitated, "—and I think he's interested in someone in New York—and I don't know."

"After seeing you it sounds impossible," he assured her. "I was married for six years, and there was a time I tortured myself that way. Then one day I just put jealousy out of my life forever. After my wife died I was very glad of that. It left a very rich memory—nothing marred or spoiled or hard to think over."

She looked at him attentively, then sympathetically as he spoke.

"I'm very sorry," she said. And after a proper moment, "You've changed a lot. Turn your head. I remember father saying, 'That boy has a brain.' "

"You probably argued against it."

"I was impressed. Up to then I thought everybody had a brain. That's why it sticks in my mind."

"What else sticks in your mind?" he asked smiling.

Suddenly Nancy got up and walked quickly a little away.

"Ah, now," she reproached him. "That isn't fair! I suppose I was a naughty girl."

"You were not," he said stoutly. "And I *will* have a drink now."

As she poured it, her face still turned from him, he continued: "Do you think you were the only little girl who was ever kissed?"

"Do you like the subject?" she demanded. Her momentary irritation melted and she said: "What the hell! We *did* have fun. Like in the song."

"On the sleigh ride."

"Yes—and somebody's picnic—Trudy James'. And at Frontenac that—those summers."

It was the sleigh ride he remembered most and kissing her cool cheeks in the straw in one corner while she laughed up at the cold white stars. The couple next to them had their backs turned and he kissed her little neck and her ears and never her lips.

"And the Macks' party where they played post office and I couldn't go because I had the mumps," he said.

"I don't remember that."

"Oh, you were there. And you were kissed and I was crazy with jealousy like I never have been since."

"Funny I don't remember. Maybe I wanted to forget."

"But why?" he asked in amusement. "We were two perfectly innocent kids. Nancy, whenever I talked to my wife about the past, I told her you were the girl I loved *al*most as much as I loved her. But I think I really loved you just as much. When we moved out of town I carried you like a cannon ball in my insides."

"Were you *that* much—stirred up?"

"My God, yes! I—" He suddenly realized that they were standing just two feet from each other, that he was talking as if he loved her in the present, that she was looking up at him with her lips half-parted and a clouded look in her eyes.

"Go on," she said, "I'm ashamed to say—I like it. I didn't know you were so upset *then*. I thought it was *me* who was upset."

"You!" he exclaimed. "Don't you remember throwing me over at the drugstore." He laughed. "You stuck out your tongue at me."

"I don't remember at all. It seemed to me *you* did the throwing over." Her hand fell lightly, almost consolingly on his arm. "I've got a photograph book upstairs I haven't looked at for years. I'll dig it out."

Donald sat for five minutes with two thoughts—first the hopeless impossibility of reconciling what different people remembered about the same event—and secondly that in a frightening way Nancy moved him as a woman as she had moved him as a child. Half an hour had developed an emotion that he had not known since the death of his wife—that he had never hoped to know again.

Side by side on a couch they opened the book between them. Nancy looked at him, smiling and very happy.

"Oh, this is *such* fun," she said. "Such fun that you're so nice, that you remember me so—beautifully. Let me tell you—I wish I'd known it then! After you'd gone I hated you."

"What a pity," he said gently.

"But not now," she reassured him, and then impulsively, "Kiss and make up—

". . . that isn't being a good wife," she said after a minute. "I really don't think I've kissed two men since I was married."

He was excited—but most of all confused. Had he kissed Nancy? or a memory? or this lovely trembly stranger who looked away from him quickly and turned a page of the book?

"Wait!" he said. "I don't think I could *see* a picture for a few seconds."

"We won't do it again. I don't feel so very calm myself."

Donald said one of those trival things that cover so much ground. "Wouldn't it be awful if we fell in love again."

"Stop it!" She laughed, but very breathlessly. "It's all over. It was a moment. A moment I'll have to forget."

"Don't tell your husband."

"Why not? Usually I tell him everything."

"It'll hurt him. Don't ever tell a man such things."

"All right I won't."

"Kiss me once more," he said inconsistently, but Nancy had turned a page and was pointing eagerly at a picture.

"Here's you," she cried. "Right away!"

He looked. It was a little boy in shorts standing on a pier with a sailboat in the background.

"I remember—" she laughed triumphantly, "—the very day it was taken. Kitty took it and I stole it from her."

For a moment Donald failed to recognize himself in the photo—then, bending closer—he failed utterly to recognize himself.

"That's not me," he said.

"Oh yes. It was at Frontenac—the summer we—we used to go to the cave."

"What cave? I was only three days in Frontenac." Again he strained his eyes at the slightly yellowed picture. "And that isn't me. That's Donald *Bowers*. We did look rather alike."

Now she was staring at him—leaning back, seeming to lift away from him.

"But you're Donald Bowers!" she exclaimed; her voice rose a little. "No, you're not. You're Donald *Plant*."

"I told you on the phone."

She was on her feet—her face faintly horrified.

"Plant! Bowers! I must be crazy. Or it was that drink? I was mixed up a little when I first saw you. Look here! What have I told you?"

He tried for a monkish calm as he turned a page of the book.

"Nothing at all," he said. Pictures that did not include him formed and re-formed before his eyes—Frontenac—a cave—Donald Bowers —"You threw *me* over!"

Nancy spoke from the other side of the room.

"You'll never tell this story," she said. "Stories have a way of getting around."

"There isn't any story," he hesitated. But he thought: So she *was* a bad little girl.

And now suddenly he was filled with wild raging jealousy of little Donald Bowers—he who had banished jealousy from his life forever. In the five steps he took across the room he crushed out twenty years and the existence of Walter Gifford with his stride.

"Kiss me again, Nancy," he said, sinking to one knee beside her chair, putting his hand upon her shoulder. But Nancy strained away.

"You said you had to catch a plane."

"It's nothing. I can miss it. It's of no importance."

"Please go," she said in a cool voice. "And please try to imagine how I feel."

"But you act as if you don't remember me," he cried, "—as if you don't remember Donald *Plant!*"

"I do. I remember you too . . . But it was all so long ago." Her voice grew hard again. "The taxi number is Crestwood 8484."

On his way to the airport Donald shook his head from side to side. He was completely himself now but he could not digest the experience. Only as the plane roared up into the dark sky and its passengers became a different entity from the corporate world below did he draw a parallel from the fact of its flight. For five blinding minutes he had lived like a madman in two worlds at once. He had been a boy of twelve and a man of thirty-two, indissolubly and help-lessly commingled.

Donald had lost a good deal, too, in those hours between the planes —but since the second half of life is a long process of getting rid of things, that part of the experience probably didn't matter.

1941 *Previously uncollected*

THE LOST DECADE

ALL SORTS of people came into the offices of the news-weekly and Orrison Brown had all sorts of relations with them. Outside of office hours he was "one of the editors"—during work time he was simply a curly-haired man who a year before had edited the Dartmouth *Jack-O-Lantern* and was now only too glad to take the undesirable assignments around the office, from straightening out illegible copy to playing call boy without the title.

He had seen this visitor go into the editor's office—a pale, tall man of forty with blond statuesque hair and a manner that was neither shy nor timid, nor otherworldly like a monk, but something of all three. The name on his card, Louis Trimble, evoked some vague memory, but having nothing to start on, Orrison did not puzzle over it—until a buzzer sounded on his desk, and previous experience warned him that Mr. Trimble was to be his first course at lunch.

"Mr. Trimble—Mr. Brown," said the Source of all luncheon money. "Orrison—Mr. Trimble's been away a long time. Or he *feels* it's a long time—almost twelve years. Some people would consider themselves lucky to've missed the last decade."

"That's so," said Orrison.

"I can't lunch today," continued his chief. "Take him to Voisin or 21 or anywhere he'd like. Mr. Trimble feels there're lots of things he hasn't seen."

Trimble demurred politely.

"Oh, I can get around."

"I know it, old boy. Nobody knew this place like you did once—and if Brown tries to explain the horseless carriage just send him back here to me. And you'll be back yourself by four, won't you?"

Orrison got his hat.

"You've been away ten years?" he asked while they went down in the elevator.

"They'd begun the Empire State Building," said Trimble. "What does that add up to?"

"About 1928. But as the chief said, you've been lucky to miss a lot." As a feeler he added, "Probably had more interesting things to look at."

"Can't say I have."

They reached the street and the way Trimble's face tightened at the roar of traffic made Orrison take one more guess.

"You've been out of civilization?"

"In a sense." The words were spoken in such a measured way that Orrison concluded this man wouldn't talk unless he wanted to—and simultaneously wondered if he could have possibly spent the thirties in a prison or an insane asylum.

"This is the famous 21," he said. "Do you think you'd rather eat somewhere else?"

Trimble paused, looking carefully at the brownstone house.

"I can remember when the name 21 got to be famous," he said, "about the same year as Moriarity's." Then he continued almost apologetically, "I thought we might walk up Fifth Avenue about five minutes and eat wherever we happened to be. Some place with young people to look at."

Orrison gave him a quick glance and once again thought of bars and gray walls and bars; he wondered if his duties included introducing Mr. Trimble to complaisant girls. But Mr. Trimble didn't look as if that was in his mind—the dominant expression was of absolute and deep-seated curiosity and Orrison attempted to connect the name with Admiral Byrd's hideout at the South Pole or flyers lost in Brazilian jungles. He was, or he had been, quite a fellow—that was obvious. But the only definite clue to his environment—and to Orrison the clue that led nowhere—was his countryman's obedience to the traffic lights and his predilection for walking on the side next to the shops and not the street. Once he stopped and gazed into a haberdasher's window.

"Crêpe ties," he said. "I haven't seen one since I left college."

"Where'd you go?"

"Massachusetts Tech."

"Great place."

"I'm going to take a look at it next week. Let's eat somewhere along here—" They were in the upper Fifties "—you choose."

There was a good restaurant with a little awning just around the corner.

"What do you want to see most?" Orrison asked, as they sat down.

Trimble considered.

"Well—the back of people's heads," he suggested. "Their necks—how their heads are joined to their bodies. I'd like to hear what those two little girls are saying to their father. Not exactly what they're

saying but whether the words float or submerge, how their mouths
shut when they've finished speaking. Just a matter of rhythm—Cole
Porter came back to the States in 1928 because he felt that there
were new rhythms around."

Orrison was sure he had his clue now, and with nice delicacy did
not pursue it by a millimeter—even suppressing a sudden desire to
say there was a fine concert in Carnegie Hall tonight.

"The weight of spoons," said Trimble, "so light. A little bowl with
a stick attached. The cast in that waiter's eye. I knew him once but
he wouldn't remember me."

But as they left the restaurant the same waiter looked at Trimble
rather puzzled as if he almost knew him. When they were outside
Orrison laughed:

"After ten years people will forget."

"Oh, I had dinner there last May—" He broke off in an abrupt
manner.

It was all kind of nutsy, Orrison decided—and changed himself
suddenly into a guide.

"From here you get a good candid focus on Rockefeller Center,"
he pointed out with spirit "—and the Chrysler Building and the
Armistead Building, the daddy of all the new ones."

"The Armistead Building," Trimble rubber-necked obediently.
"Yes—I designed it."

Orrison shook his head cheerfully—he was used to going out with
all kinds of people. But that stuff about having been in the restaurant last May . . .

He paused by the brass entablature in the cornerstone of the building. "Erected 1928," it said.

Trimble nodded.

"But I was taken drunk that year—every-which-way drunk. So I
never saw it before now."

"Oh." Orrison hesitated. "Like to go in now?"

"I've been in it—lots of times. But I've never seen it. And now it
isn't what I want to see. I wouldn't ever be able to see it now. I
simply want to see how people walk and what their clothes and
shoes and hats are made of. And their eyes and hands. Would you
mind shaking hands with me?"

"Not at all, sir."

"Thanks. Thanks. That's very kind. I suppose it looks strange—
but people will think we're saying good-bye. I'm going to walk up
the avenue for awhile, so we *will* say good-bye. Tell your office I'll
be in at four."

Orrison looked after him when he started out, half expecting him to turn into a bar. But there was nothing about him that suggested or ever had suggested drink.

"Jesus," he said to himself. "Drunk for ten years."

He felt suddenly of the texture of his own coat and then he reached out and pressed his thumb against the granite of the building by his side.

1939 *Previously uncollected*

